A
Garland Series

VICTORIAN FICTION

NOVELS OF FAITH AND DOUBT

*A collection of 121 novels
in 92 volumes, selected by
Professor Robert Lee Wolff,
Harvard University,
with a separate introductory volume
written by him
especially for this series.*

WORKERS IN THE DAWN

George Gissing

Three volumes in one

Garland Publishing, Inc., New York & London

1976

Bibliographical note:

this facsimile has been made from a copy in the
Beinecke Library of Yale University
(Ip.G447.880)

Library of Congress Cataloging in Publication Data

Gissing, George Robert, 1887-1903.
    Workers in the dawn.

    (Victorian fiction : Novels of faith and doubt ; 75)
    Reprint of the 1880 ed. published by Remington,
London.
    I. Title. II. Series.
PZ3.G45Wo10   [PR4716]   823'.8   75-1527
ISBN 0-8240-1599-1

WORKERS IN THE DAWN.

A Novel.

IN THREE VOLUMES.

BY

GEORGE R. GISSING.

VOL. I.

London :

REMINGTON AND CO.,

5, ARUNDEL STREET, STRAND, W.C.

1880.

CONTENTS.

WORKERS IN THE DAWN.

CHAPTER I.

MARKET-NIGHT.

WALK with me, reader, into Whitecross Street. It is Saturday night, the market-night of the poor; also the one evening in the week which the weary toilers of our great city can devote to ease and recreation in the sweet assurance of a morrow unenslaved. Let us see how they spend this " Truce of God;" our opportunities will be of the best in the district we are entering.

As we suddenly turn northwards out of the dim and quiet regions of Barbican, we are at first confused by the glare of lights and the hubbub of cries. Pressing through an ever-moving crowd, we find ourselves in a long and narrow street, forming, from end to end, one busy market. Besides the ordinary shops, amongst which the conspicuous fronts of the butchers' and the grocers' predominate, the street is lined along either pavement with rows of stalls and booths, each illuminated

with flaring naphtha-lamps, the flames of which
shoot up fiercely at each stronger gust of
wind, filling the air around with a sickly
odour, and throwing a weird light upon the
multitudinous faces.   Behind the lights stand
men, women and children, each hallooing in
every variety of intense key—from the shrillest
conceivable piping to a thunderous roar,
which well-nigh deafens one—the prices and
the merits of their wares.   The fronts of the
houses, as we glance up towards the deep
blackness overhead, have a decayed, filthy,
often an evil, look ; and here and there, on
either side, is a low, yawning archway, or a
passage some four feet wide, leading presum-
ably to human habitations.   Let us press
through the throng to the mouth of one of
these and look in, as long as the reeking
odour will permit us. Straining the eyes into
horrible darkness, we behold a blind alley,
the unspeakable abominations of which are
dimly suggested by a gas-lamp flickering at
the further end.   Here and there through a
window glimmers a reddish light, forcing one
to believe that people actually do live here ;
otherwise the alley is deserted, and the footstep echoes as we tread cautiously up the
narrow slum.   If we look up, we perceive
that strong beams are fixed across between
the fronts of the houses—sure sign of the
rottenness which everywhere prevails. Listen !
That was the shrill screaming of an infant

which came from one of the nearest dens. Yes, children are born here, and men and women die. Let us devoutly hope that the deaths exceed the births.

Now back into the street, for already we have become the observed of a little group of evil-looking fellows gathered round the entrance. Let us press once more through the noisy crowd, and inspect the shops and stalls. Here is exposed for sale an astounding variety of goods. Loudest in their cries, and not the least successful in attracting customers, are the butchers, who, with knife and chopper in hand, stand bellowing in stentorian tones the virtues of their meat; now inviting purchasers with their—" Lovely, love-ly, l-ove-ly ! Buy ! buy buy buy—buy !" now turning to abuse each other with a foul-mouthed virulence surpassing description. See how the foolish artisan's wife, whose face bears the evident signs of want and whose limbs shiver under her insufficient rags, lays down a little heap of shillings in return for a lump, half gristle, half bone, of question-able meat—ignorant that with half the money she might buy four times the quantity of far more healthy and sustaining food.

But now we come to luxuries. Here is a stall where lie oysters and whelks, ready stripped of their shells, offering an irresistible temptation to the miserable-looking wretches who stand around, sucking in the vinegared

and peppered dainties till their stomachs are
appeased, or their pockets empty. Next is a
larger booth, where all manner of old linen,
torn muslin, stained and faded ribbons,
draggled trimming, and the like, is exposed
for sale, piled up in foul and clammy heaps,
which, as the slippery-tongued rogue, with a
yard in his hand turns and tumbles it for the
benefit of a circle of squalid and shivering
women, sends forth a reek stronger than that
from the basket of rotten cabbage on the
next stall. How the poor wretches ogle the
paltry rags, feverishly turn their money in
their hands, discuss with each other in greedy
whispers the cheapness or otherwise of the
wares! Then we have an immense pile of
old iron, which to most would appear wholly
useless; but see how now and then a grimy-
handed workman stops to rummage among it,
and maybe finds something of use to him in
his labour.

Here again, elevated on a cart, stands a
vender of second-hand umbrellas, who, as he
holds up the various articles of his stock and
bangs them open under the street-lamps that
purchasers may bear witness to their solidity,
yells out a stream of talk amazing in its
mixture of rude wit, coarse humour, and
voluble impudence. " Here's a humbereller ! "
he cries, " Look at this 'ere ; now do ! Fit
for the Jewk o' York, the Jewk of Cork, or
any other member of the no—bility. A s fo

my own grace, I hassure yer, I never uses
any other! Come, who says 'alf-a-crownd for
this?—No?—Why, then, two bob—one an'-
a-tanner—a bob! Gone, and damned cheap
too!" This man makes noise enough; but
here, close behind him, is an open shop-front
with a mingled array of household utensils
defying description, the price chalked in large
figures on each, and on a stool stands a little
lad, clashing incessantly with an enormous
hammer upon a tray as tall as himself, and
with his piercing young voice doing his
utmost to attract hearers. Next we have a
stall covered with cheap and trashy ornaments, chipped glass vases of a hundred
patterns, picture-frames, lamps, watch-chains,
rings; things such as may tempt a few of the
hard-earned coppers out of a young wife's
pocket, or induce the working lad to spend a
shilling for the delight of some consumptive
girl, with the result, perhaps, of leading her
to seek in the brothel a relief from the slow
death of the factory or the work-room. As
we push along we find ourselves clung to
by something or other, and, looking down,
see a little girl, perhaps four years old, the
very image of naked wretchedness, holding
up, with shrill, pitiful appeals, a large piece of
salt, for which she wants one halfpenny—no
more, she assures us, than one half-penny.
She clings persistently and will not be shaken
off. Poor little thing; most likely failure to

sell her salt will involve a brutal beating when she returns to the foul nest which she calls home. We cannot carry the salt, but we give her a copper and she runs off, delighted. Follow her, and we see with some surprise that she runs to a near eating-house, one of many we have observed. Behind the long counter stands a man and a woman, the former busy in frying flat fish over a huge fire, the latter engaged in dipping a ladle into a large vessel which steams profusely ; and in front of the counter stands a row of hungry-looking people, devouring eagerly the flakes of fish and the greasy potatoes as fast as they come from the pan, whilst others are served by the woman to little basins of stewed eels from the steaming tureen. But the good people of Whitecross Street are thirsty as well as hungry, and there is no lack of gin-palaces to supply their needs. Open the door and look into one of these. Here a group are wrangling over a disputed toss or bet, here two are coming to blows, there are half-a-dozen young men and women, all half drunk, mauling each other with vile caresses ; and all the time, from the lips of the youngest and the oldest, foams forth such a torrent of inanity, abomination, and horrible blasphemy which bespeaks the very depth of human— aye, or of bestial—degradation. And notice how, between these centres and the alleys into which we have peered, shoeless children,

slipshod and bareheaded women, tottering old men, are constantly coming and going with cans or jugs in their hands. Well, is it not Saturday night? And how can the week's wages be better spent than in procuring a few hours' unconsciousness of the returning Monday.

The crowd that constantly throngs from one end of the street to the other is very miscellaneous, comprehending alike the almost naked wretch who creeps along in the hope of being able to steal a mouthful of garbage, and the respectably clad artisan and his wife, seeing how best they can lay out their money for the ensuing week. The majority are women, some carrying children in their arms, some laden with a basket full of purchases, most with no covering on their heads but the corner of a shawl.

But look at the faces! Here is a young mother with a child sucking at her bare breast, as she chaffers with a man over a pound of potatoes. Suddenly she turns away with reddened cheeks, shrinking before a vile jest which creates bursts of laughter in the by-standers. Pooh! She is evidently new in this quarter, perhaps come up of late from the country. Wait a year, and you will see her joining in the laugh at her own expense, with as much gusto as that young woman behind her, whose features, under more favourable circumstances, might have had something of beauty, but starvation and dirt and exposure have coarsened the grain and made her teeth grin woefully between her thin lips.

Or look at the woman on the other side, who is laughing till she cries. Does not every line of her face bespeak the baseness of her nature? Cannot one even guess at the vile trade by which she keeps her limbs covered with those layers of gross fat, whilst those around her are so pinched and thin? Her cheeks hang flabbily, and her eyes twinkle with a vicious light. A deep scar marks her forehead, a memento of some recent drunken brawl. When she has laughed her fill, she turns to look after a child which is being dragged through the mud by her skirts, being scarcely yet able to walk, and, bidding it with a cuff and a curse not to leave loose of her, pushes on stoutly through the crowd.

One could find matter for hour-long observation in the infinite variety of vice and misery depicted in the faces around. It must be confessed that the majority do not seem unhappy; they jest with each other amid their squalor; they have an evident pleasure in buying and selling; they would be surprised if they knew you pitied them. And the very fact that they are unconscious of their degradation afflicts one with all the keener pity. We suffer them to become brutes in our midst, and inhabit dens which clean animals would shun, to derive their joys from sources from which a cultivated mind shrinks as from a pestilential vapour. And can we console ourselves with the reflection that they do not feel their misery?

Well, this is the Whitecross Street of to-day; but it is in this street rather more than twenty years ago that my story opens. There is not much difference between now and then, except that the appearance of the shops is perhaps improved, and the sanitary condition of the neighbourhood a trifle more attended to; the description, on the whole, may remain unaltered.

It was about half-past ten on a Saturday night, towards the close of November. All day long it had been snowing, but the snow had melted as it reached the ground, forming endless puddles of mire, into which the unceasing tramp of the crowd had trodden all manner of refuse from the market-stalls, till the whole street reeked with foul odours. Amid the throng, about half-way up the street, we notice a figure presenting a striking contrast to its surroundings. It is that of a gentleman, apparently some five and thirty years old, wearing the habit of a clergyman, and who, judging from the glances he casts on either side as he with difficulty makes his way through the noisome crowd, is very far from at home amid such sights and sounds. His face, which was smooth-shaven, of very delicate complexion, and handsome almost to effeminacy, was crossed one moment by a look of the profoundest commiseration, the next gave expression of profound disgust and horror, as his eye fell on the objects and persons nearest him; and not unfrequently he moved considerably out of his direct course in order to avoid some spectacle especially repulsive. As he proceeded along the street, he kept glancing at the alleys and narrow lanes branching off on either hand, apparently in search of some particular locality.

At length, having entered a small shop to make inquiries, he crossed the road, and after some hesitation, was turning into a narrow, loathsome alley, which the light of a street lamp showed, bore the name of Adam and Eve Court, when a little girl, suddenly rushing out of the darkness, bumped unawares against him and fell to the ground, breaking to pieces a jug which she held in her hands. She did not begin to cry, but, instantly springing to her feet, proceeded to assail the cause of her accident with a stream of the foulest abuse, which would have been dreadful enough on the lips of a grown-up man, but appeared unutterably so as coming from a child.

" You've broke the jug, you have ! " screamed the little creature at last, having exhausted her epithets; " you've broke the jug, you have ; and you'll 'ave to pay for it, you will. Come now, pay for the jug, will you, mister ?"

" Good God !" exclaimed the gentleman, half to himself, " what a hell I have got into !"

Then, taking a shilling from his pocket, he gave it to the child.

" Will that be enough ?"

" Maybe it will."

" Stop ! Can you tell me which is No. 9 in this yard ?"

" And what d'yer want with No. 9, eh ?" asked the child, biting the coin as she spoke ; " I lives there."

" Then you can show me the house, I suppose ?"

" Can if I chooses. What d'yer want with No. 9, eh ? "

" Is there anyone named Golding living there ?"

The child surveyed her questioner for a few moments with precociously evil eyes, then suddenly exclaimed—

" Last house but two. You'll have to knock twice." After which she rushed out into the street and was lost in the crowd.

The inquirer followed the direction indicated, and, picking his steps through the filth as carefully as the darkness allowed, with many an uneasy glance on either side and up at the houses, came at length in front of No. 9. He found the door standing open, but his eyes were unable to pierce a single foot into the dense blackness within. With a shudder, he groped for the knocker, and knocked loudly twice.

He repeated the summons several times before any notice was taken. At length, however, a window was thrown open above, and a shrill woman's voice cried out—

" What are you wantin' of ? Who is it ?

" Is there a Mr. Golding living here ?" asked the visitor, stepping back and endeavouring to catch sight of the speaker.

" There's one o' that name dyin' here, I'm thinkin'," returned a gruff voice, in a tone meant to be humorous. " What do you want with him, mister ? Does he owe yer money ? 'Cos if he do, I'm thinkin' ye'll have to look out sharp after it."

" Would you be so good as to show me to his room ?" cried the visitor. " I particularly wish to see him."

" Third floor back," screamed the female voice. " I s'pose yer don't want showin' the way up-stairs, do yer ?"

The stranger entered the coal-black portal of the house, and, groping with his hands, made his way up-stairs till a door suddenly opened and a woman with a candle in her hand appeared. She seemed half undressed, her face, which was naturally hideous, was grimy with untold layers of dirt, and her whole appearance, lighted by the gleam from the tallow dip, was anything but reassuring. She started slightly when she perceived the elegant figure of the clergyman, and her manner at once became more respectful.

" Mr. Golding's room's on the next floor, sir. I doubt you'll find him in a bad way."

" Is he seriously ill ? "

" Well, sir, my 'usband thinks him so bad as he's sent off our Jinny to the parish doctor ; but she ain't come back yet. We've done what we could for him, I'm sure sir ; but, you see, being that he was so fond of liquor like, and being that he owes us near on a month's rent a'ready, sir, you see it warn't to be expected as we could do as much as we might a' done if he'd been a better lodger, you see, sir. If anythink 'appens to him, sir (which, and I'm sure, I 'ope as it won't), d'ye think, sir, he 'as any friends as wouldn't like to see poor people suffer by him, and as 'ud pay his back rent, and—"

It was impossible to say how long the woman would have gone on in this manner, for the appearance of the stranger seemed to work strongly upon her, and the fire of greed flashed from her green eyes ; but the latter cut her short in the midst of her speech and, with a hurried word or two, stepped quickly up to the next story.

The door stood slightly ajar, and feeble rays of light made their way on to the landing. As his knock met with no reply, the clergyman walked quietly in without invitation. The scene which met his eyes was one of indescribable squalor and misery. The room, which was some ten feet square and about six in height, contained absolutely no furniture save a rude three-legged table. The floor was rugged and sloped from one side down towards the other, as if the foundations of the house were gradually sinking; the walls and ceiling in places showed great spots of moisture, and the small window, in which several panes had been broken and were replaced by brown paper, was sheltered by no blind or curtain, and gave admittance to a draught which swept round the room almost as keenly as the wind in the open air. On the table burned a candle thrust into the broken neck of a bottle, and by its light the visitor was enabled dimly to discern the living occupants of the garret. In one corner, as far removed out of the draught of the window as possible, a few ragged clothes had been spread upon the floor, and on these lay the figure of a man in his trowsers and shirt only, his face hidden in the bundled-up coat which formed his pillow. By his side, his head resting on the man's arm, lay a little boy, apparently some eight years old. Both were sleeping; the boy with the deep motionless sleep of utter weariness, the man with occasional groans and tosses, and now and then a rattle in his throat, and struggling for breath, which, however, did not awake him.

The clergyman took the candle in his hand and held it down so as to illumine the faces of the sleepers. That of the child was pale, meagre, sickly-looking, but withal pleasant in its natural outlines, particularly the mouth, which seemed to indicate a sweetness of disposition seldom found in these nurslings of misery. His hair, though thick and somewhat matted through neglect, was very fair, and fell naturally in rough curls about the forehead. It was necessary to move the man's head slightly in order to examine his face, and, as his eyes fell upon the features, the visitor drew back suddenly with a low exclamation of mingled surprise, pity, and disgust. The face itself was not ill-formed, bearing in its lineaments an unmistakable resemblance to the child; but want, sickness and vice had wrought such effects upon it as almost entirely to destroy the agreeable character which the physiognomy must once have possessed. It was the face of a comparatively young man; certainly he could not be more than thirty. The cheeks were sunk in ghastly hollows, the nostrils were unnaturally distended by his hard breathing, the teeth were strongly clenched so that no breath could pass through the lips, the whole face was livid in hue. Death seemed to be even then overcoming him in his sleep.

The visitor set down the candle hastily, and, uttering a low exclamation of horror, moved as if to call assistance. But at once he appeared to alter his purpose, and, returning to the side of the sleeper, shook him by the shoulder, calling, as he did so—

"Golding! Golding!"

The man showed no sign of returning to consciousness, but the disturbance awoke the child, who moved slowly to a sitting position, rubbed his eyes, and at length began to sob quietly, paying no attention whatever to the stranger. The latter persevered for a few minutes in his endeavours to arouse the sick man, but, finding his efforts vain, was on the point of hurrying from the room, when the door opened, and the woman who had accosted him on the stairs came in, holding in her hand a glass of something which smoked.

"The doctor's a dre'ful long while a comin', sir," she said, in a wheedling sort of tone. "I thought as 'ow a drop of somethink warm 'ud, may be, do the poor gentleman good. Never mind the hexpense, sir; we likes to do what little good we can in our small way, yer know."

"He is unconscious," replied the clergyman, whose name we may at once say was Norman. "I cannot awake him. Are you sure the messenger saw the doctor?"

"Oh, quite sure, sir. Yer know the

parish doctor ain't over pertikler in comin' just when he's wanted. But he won't be long now. Maybe you'd take a drop yerself, sir? No! Well, it don't suit everybody's stomach, certainly. So 'ere's yer very good 'ealth, sir, an' th' 'ealth of the poor gentleman too."

As she ceased she poured the warm liquor down her scraggy throat, leered hideously at the clergyman, and left the room.

Mr. Norman began to pace backwards and forwards in the utmost impatience, rubbing his hands together, intertwisting his fingers, and showing every sign of extreme nervousness. In some ten minutes eleven o'clock sounded from the church hard by, and as the tones ceased a slight commotion was evident upon the stairs. At once footsteps began to ascend rapidly, and Mr. Norman, with a sigh of relief, hurried to the door just in time to meet upon the threshold a young, earnest-looking man, whom the clergyman greeted with instinctive confidence. The doctor examined Golding for a few minutes in silence, then turned away from him with a slight shrug of the shoulders.

" Too late," he said, looking at the clergyman, " much too late. He won't last an hour."

" I feared it."

" Drink, sir, drink, and a dozen other ailments induced by it. I should only be wasting my time here at present, but I will look in about ten to-morrow."

" You can't prescribe anything?"

" Quite useless," replied the doctor, decisively. " You take a special interest in him?"

"He was an old college friend of mine, poor fellow. It is more than eight years since I saw him, but I could not have believed such a change possible."

The doctor made a few sympathetic remarks, bowed, and ran down stairs as quickly as he had come up. Mr. Norman tried once more to awaken the dying man to consciousness, but with no immediate result. So he turned his attention to the child, who still sat in the same place sobbing quietly.

" Is that your father?" he asked the boy, scanning the haggard features of his face with nervous glances.

The child sobbed out an affirmative reply, but no more. At this moment the sick man stirred slightly, and Mr. Norman saw his eyes slowly open.

" Golding!" he exclaimed, kneeling down by his side. "Do you see me? Do you know me?"

For some minutes no sign of consciousness manifested itself; but then the man made obvious efforts to speak. His face was dreadfully distorted in the struggle for breath, but no sound escaped him save a hollow rattle in his throat. The clergyman bent nearer to him in the hope of hearing a word, and, as he did so, Golding suddenly grasped him by the arm, and with his head and eyes made convulsive motions in the direction of the child. For a moment the grasp of his hands on Mr. Norman's arm was fearful in its violence, then it all at once relaxed, the perpetual rattle ceased, the eyes became fixed in a steady stare at the ceiling.

The candle had burnt to the socket, and the smoke rising from it in a narrow white column filled the room with its smell. The room was quite dark save for a faint gleam which came from a bedroom window on the opposite side of the court. In the house was absolute silence. The street was too far off for any sound from such buyers and sellers as might still linger there to be heard in the recesses of Adam and Eve Court. As the clergyman stood for a few moments, irresolute in the dark, he heard the voice of a woman screaming from a window opposite, and the laugh of a drunken man reeling into a house hard by. At length he rose to his feet and left the room.

On the first landing the woman again met him with a candle in her hand.

" Has anythink 'appened, sir ? " she asked.

"He is dead," replied Mr. Norman.

" Eh! poor fellow! You don't 'appen to know, sir, if he's got any friends besides yerself, sir? Maybe there's somebody, sir, as mightn't like him to die in this way sir, an' him owin'—"

" I will myself see to all that," interrupted the clergyman, turning away from the harpy's hideous face in loathing. " I wanted to tell you that I am going to take away his child with me. I will return in the morning."

" Oh, very well, sir. I'm sure it's good of you to take thought of the child. I've took a great deal o' care of him, sir, an' he's been a good bit of expense to me one way an' another. You see the gen'leman *would* drink, an'—"

The clergyman cut short the old hag's protestations by once more ascending to the garret, having just taken the candle from her hand. He bent down to the boy, and said, in a low voice—

" Come with me, my poor child. Come quietly. You mustn't wake your father, for he is very poorly."

The child shook off the speaker's hands, and took hold of the arm of the corpse as if to prevent himself from being removed by force.

" Why should I go with you ?" exclaimed the child, impulsively. " I'm going to stay with father, I am. I'll wait till he wakes. I don't know you at all, do I ?"

Mr. Norman reflected for a moment, then spoke in a kind, low voice—

" Your father is dead, my poor child. He will never wake."

The boy stared with terror in the speaker's face, then sprang to the dead man's side, and grasped the face in his hands. He seemed to understand that the stranger had told him the truth. He fell upon his face on the floor, sobbing as if his heart would break, and between his sobs, crying—

" Father, father ! "

It was vain to endeavour to take him away, and Mr. Norman was ultimately obliged to leave him alone in the garret with the corpse. Making his way down the pitch-black, creaking staircase, he passed into the open air. It was with a sigh of relief that he looked upwards, and in the narrow space, between the tops of the houses, saw a few stars shining, for it had now ceased snowing and the frost had began to dry the ground. There were still people moving about Whitecross-street when he entered it, but the noise of the market had ceased, and all the lights were extinguished. Not without apprehensive glances at some of the figures which slouched by him in the darkness, Mr. Norman hurried along over the half-formed ice, and the still reeking remnants from the stalls, till at length he reached a more open neighbourhood. Here he soon found an opportunity of taking a cab, and before long reached his hotel in Oxford-street.

CHAPTER II.

EDWARD NORMAN had the good fortune, at a comparatively early age, to find himself comfortably established as incumbent of the parish of Bloomford, which comprised some five hundred inhabitants in all, and was delightfully situated in one of the pleasantest of the southern counties. The duties resulting from his position were, as may be imagined, not very arduous, and the compensation, from a purely sordid point of view—that treasure upon earth which the clergy doubtless prize merely as a type of the heavenly treasure which will one day be theirs—was far from doing discredit to those " pious ancestors " of the village, whose liberality, as in all such cases, it was pleasantly understood to represent. It would, however, have been a heart steeped to the very root in the poison of Democracy, Communism, and kindred evils which could have grudged Edward Norman his charming little rectory and the thousand a year which enabled him to keep it in repair, for, in very truth, it would have been difficult to find a clergyman of a sweeter disposition, a kindlier heart, a sunnier intellect than his.

His very appearance enforced one to conceive towards him a mingled sentiment of affection and compassion ; for though his eye was ever bright, his lofty forehead unwrinkled, his cheek ever answering with a warm flush to the affectionate impulses of his heart, yet the first glance showed you that the man was an invalid, that his days were in all probability numbered. His malady was consumption ; it had made its first decided appearance when he came of age, and now that he was almost thirty-five he could entertain no hope of its relaxing the hold it had gained upon his constitution.

The rectory of Bloomford was situated on a gently sloping hill-side, about a quarter of a mile above the church. It was a picturesque old building, with a roof of red tiles and a multiplicity of chimneys and gables, with small latticed windows in the upper story, broad eaves beneath which endless birds made their nests, and, over all, a forest of ivy, so old that the stems were like the trunks of trees. Before the house lay a carefully-tended flower garden, behind it a kitchen garden and an orchard, all around which ran a crumbling brick wall, some six feet high, on the outside thickly overgrown with the abounding ivy, within kept clear for the training of peach and plum trees. Even now, at the end of November, it was by no means a dreary place, for its smallness always

gave it a compact and comfortable air; while
in the autumn evenings all the front windows
would glow with the warm reflection of the
setting sun, and the smoke from the high
chimnies curl up in many-hued shapes which
seemed to bespeak the home-like comfort
within.   As you viewed the house from the
front, there was, indeed, an object which
gave it an air of individuality as distinguished
from any other pleasantly situated country
house; this was a somewhat newly-built
tower, mainly of glass, which constituted a
modest observatory, containing a large tele-
scope, which was one of the chief delights of
the clergyman's existence.   This tower he
had had built immediately after his entering
upon the living, not without considerable
scandal in the neighbourhood, where Mr.
Norman was in consequence at first regarded
as a species of Dr. Faustus, with whom it
might possibly be dangerous, notwithstanding
the apparent soundness of his doctrine, to
hold much connection.   It had indeed been
formally decided at a meeting of the Bloomford Ladies' Sewing Club: " That this club
considers the study of astronomy to be a
sinful *prying* into the mysteries of the
Almighty, and consequently a wilful tempting
of His displeasure; that this club is surprised
and grieved that a *clergyman* of the Church
of England should set such an example to
the *weaklings* of his flock; and that this club

do, in consequence, prepare a *memorial* on this subject, to be duly presented to the Rev. Mr. Norman on the *earliest* fitting opportunity." This resolution was written out, with the due emphasis, by the secretary of the club, but the memorial was never presented, owing, I believe, to the fact that the personal amiability of the reverend gentleman in a very short time succeeded in utterly disarming the suspicions of the fair inquisitors. At that time a large majority of the club were unmarried ladies, and it may not unreasonably be concluded that the fact of Mr. Norman being then a bachelor of twenty-four had an appreciable influence in weakening their zeal for the preservation of the Creator's privacy. This had been some ten years since, and at present the only memorial of those early prejudices existed in the person of a poor old woman of the village, who, having gone harmlessly crazy just at the time when the rector's presumption had been the great topic of conversation, still never failed to pass him without asking, with a respectful curtesy—

" What's the latest news from heaven, my lord ?"

The respectable subscribers to our circulating libraries would not owe me much thanks were I to describe in detail the oft-treated history of a clergyman's search among his fair parishioners for a suitable partner of his cares, or, perhaps I should say, the hot competition among the latter for the possession of the dearly-coveted honour, the position of a parson's wife. Without unnecessary amplitude of description, therefore, I shall content myself with saying that, before Edward Norman had been a year in his cure, the lot had been drawn, and the happy maid had received her prize; nor could the most envious assert that in choosing Helen Burton for his bride, the clergyman had laid himself open to imputations on his taste or his generosity. Helen had long been, undisputedly, the village beauty, but so humble was her social position that not one of the damsels who boasted of their place in the aristocracy of the district had for a moment dreamed of her as a rival. She was nothing more than the daughter of the principal tailor in Bloomford, but her father was a man of the strictest integrity, even of some intellectual pretensions, and universally respected by all who were so unfortunate as to be tainted with the modern heresy that money does *not* make the man. Helen had, thanks to this worthy man's care, received an education which would compare very favourably indeed even with that possessed by the daughters of Sir Bedford Lamb, one of the members for the county, whose seat was only some two miles distant from Bloomford. It was indeed then to the astonishment of all,

but to the scandalisation—and that affected
—of only the few, that Helen Burton had
become Mrs. Norman.

Edward Norman loved his wife devotedly,
passionately. Upon her he lavished all the
treasures of his dreamy, sentimental, poetical
temperament. From his first sight of her
she had become the goddess of his thought,
the centre of every hope and longing which
shed its fragrance upon his calm, contempla-
tive life; and when at length these aspirations were fulfilled, and she had become the
goddess of his hearth, the man felt as if life
had nothing more to give him. But from the
very exuberance of its bounty towards him
did life become more than ever dear, and this
in face of the fact that it was gradually,
hopelessly slipping away from him. But
sometimes again this very hopelessness bred
within him a refinement of delight to which
a healthier man could scarcely have attained.
As, during the early months of their marriage, he often sat through the long summer
evenings in the quietness of his study, holding Helen's hand within his own, and both
together gazing westwards on the melting
glories of the sunset, he felt that to gradually sink into his grave cared for at every
moment by this angel whom Fate had sent to
bless him, and drink in the ever-deepening
fervour of her love as she felt him passing
from her side, to hold, when all was over,

for ever a sacred place in so pure a mind—at times he felt that these were delights **far** superior to the possession of the most **robust** health and hopes of the longest life. To be sure there was a tinge of refined **selfishness** in this; but that was a part of his nature. And what purest affection is without it?

But in these hopes he had deceived himself. Before his bliss had lasted for **a year** it seemed about to be crowned by the birth of a child. The child—a girl—was indeed born, but at the expense of its mother's life.

Edward Norman's grief was sacred **even** to the impertinence of village gossip. When, a few weeks after, a beer-muddled rustic happened to stray late at night in the neighbourhood of the churchyard, and next morning spread the report among his fellow-yokels that he had seen a ghost by the **new** grave stretching up its arms in the moonlight, his story did not attract much comment, for the hearts of the humblest, which, **after** all, are human, whispered that the agony of a husband over a young wife's tomb was not a subject for trivial chatter.

But when the period of more or **less** lachrymose sympathy had waned with the rector's first year of bereavement, other thoughts began once more to spring in the young female mind of Bloomford. If **Mr.** Norman had been interesting before, **how** infinitely more so had he now become. The movement for a fresh attack upon his sensibilities took first of all the ominous form of sympathy for his child, poor little Helen. What a shocking thing it was that the little darling—such an absolute little angel—had no mother to care for it. How was it possible that it should be sufficiently tended by the hired nurse-girl, even though overseered by the rector's housekeeper, Mrs. Cope, a worthy old lady who had watched Edward Norman's own cradle, and, shortly after his wife's death, had gladly complied with his written request that she would undertake the guidance of his household? Of course, such a state of affairs was absolutely contrary to the nature of things—it might even be said to the divine law; for it should be noted that these ladies, who had once been shocked at the clergyman's astronomical studies, were anything but backward in interpreting the thoughts and the wishes of Providence when it suited them to do so. But then arose the question among the more serious as to whether a clergyman could, consistently with his sacred office, take unto himself a second fleshly comforter. The younger maidens firmly maintained that there was nothing shocking in such a course, and to such an extent did their views preponderate that when, by chance, an inoffensive damsel of sixty summers, whose turn it was

to read aloud for an evening to the Bloomford Ladies' Mutual Improvement Society
(a recent development of the Sewing-Club be-
fore-mentioned) came, in the "Vicar of Wake-
field," to those unfortunate sentiments of Dr.
Primrose on the very question at issue, she
was forthwith stopped by a chorus of dis-
sentients, and the book was no more read
aloud in the Society; it being whispered by
one or two members, that, after all, Goldsmith did not display that delicacy of conception necessary in one whose works are to be
fitted for mutual improvement.

Whether Mr. Norman was aware of this
and the like matters it would not be easy to
say; in all probability not. His life became
every day more solitary and secluded; to such
an extent, indeed, as to give rise to the remonstrances of his more sensible friends. As
his wont was, he listened with amiability to
all who found an opportunity of addressing
him, but without the slightest effect upon his
conduct.

By nature little disposed to social life, he
now lived more and more in the company of
his books and his thoughts. His grief had,
of course, calmed as time wore on; had
become, indeed, somewhat of a quiet pleasure, finding its expression in long hours of
reverie wherein his thoughts were busiest
with multiplying idealisations of his dead
wife, and of the bliss he had enjoyed with

her; or, at other times, in looking forward to the day when little Helen would revive her mother's loveliness in the full blush of womanhood, and wondering whether he would live to see it.

Under such circumstances, he was rather glad to avail himself of the popular sympathy in order to provide a pretext for his much-loved retirement. His health was another, and a real cause for abstinence from too active exertions. His malady progressed, very slowly but perceptibly, and, some five years after his wife's death, a special illness rendered it absolutely necessary that he should have the benefit of a change of air. He accordingly obtained leave of absence from his duties, and passed rather more than a month in the south of France. It was immediately after his return to Bloomford that a letter from Golding came to his hand, resulting in his sudden visit to London, the circumstances of which have been detailed in the last chapter.

Three days after this, Edward Norman was sitting at breakfast in the little morning-room which looked northwards, upon what was in summer the pleasantest part of the garden—a fair lawn, bordered with flower-beds, and enclosed with thick growths of laburnum. The room itself was light and cheerful, the choice and arrangement of its ornaments remaining still a sacred memorial of the taste of its former mistress. Every-thing bespoke the utmost elegance and refinement in him who now alone used the room, impressing the beholder with ideas fully borne out by the appearance of the clergyman himself.

He was sitting in an arm-chair by the fire-side, a small low table bearing the tray which held his simple breakfast. He wore a hand-some dressing-gown closely folded around him, from beneath the bottom of which ap-peared a pair of spotless woollen slippers. A newspaper lay on the table, which had apparently not yet been opened, but an ex-quisite little copy of Horace formed his com-panion at breakfast instead, which he perused with a languid pleasure through his gold-rimmed eye-glasses.

It did not, however, seem to engross his attention, for his eyes frequently wandered to the windows and looked out upon the rays of faint sunlight which, struggling through ominous clouds, fell athwart the lawn and upon the leafless laburnums. At one of these glances his face suddenly assumed a look of keener interest. This was caused by the sight of two children, a little girl, perhaps eight years old, with a face of delicate pretti-ness, and dressed in a handsome little winter costume which became her wonderfully, and by her side a boy, in appearance much older, though in reality about the same age. The clothing had undergone a reformation; but the handsome, pale, attenuated features, and the curling yellow hair were evidently those of poor Golding's child. He seemed to follow his graceful little companion with reluctance, scarcely ever raising his eyes to look at the objects around him, but keeping them bent upon the grass.

The expression on his face was sorrowful in the extreme; tears seemed momentarily about to start from his eyes. The remarks which the little girl addressed to him he seemed not to understand; at all events, he scarcely attempted to answer them. The two were not quite alone, but were followed at the distance of a few yards by a cheerful-looking middle-aged woman, who knitted as she walked, casting each moment curious glances at the children in front of her. This was Mrs. Cope, the rector's worthy housekeeper. In her cheeks still lived much of the bloom which had made her not a little admired, when, as a country maiden of sixteen, she had been called to act as handmaid of Edward Norman himself, then aged one year.

Mrs. Cope was now a widow, and among the most active of the plotters against Mr. Norman's peace in Bloomford there were not a few who looked with a jealous eye upon this lady. If the rector had begun by marrying a tailor's daughter, who could guarantee that

he would not once more bid defiance to the
world by taking to wife his housekeeper?
The more prudish even whispered that it
really was not very delicate in Mr. Norman
to permit the residence in his ladyless house
of a "female" of Mrs. Cope's years and
appearance.

The rector's eyes were still fixed upon the
figures on the lawn, when a sudden ring at
the door-bell announced the arrival of a
visitor. A moment after a servant tapped at
the door, and proclaimed—

"Mr. Whiffle."

This gentleman was no other than the
curate of the parish. His appearance and
character appear to me to merit a few lines of
description. In stature he stood some five
feet, no more, and his head looked very much
too large for this diminutive body. Probably
this effect was increased by the peculiarities
of his hair, which stood almost on end in
large, coarse, reddish clusters over the top of
his head; the pressure of a hat seemed to
have not the slightest effect upon its stubborn
elasticity. He wore extremely stiff whiskers,
also red in hue, but no moustache. The
habitual expression of his face was irresistibly
comic; the eyes being very large and constantly moving in the drollest manner, whilst
his nose, slightly celestial in tendency, and
the peculiar conformation of his mouth and
chin gave his countenance something of a

Hibernian cast, though the man was true-born English. His constant attitude was very upright, as if to make the most of his inches, with the fore-finger of either hand inserted in his waistcoat pockets, and with his toes, upon which he regularly rose as he spoke, decidedly turned in towards each other. Such was the outward and visible appearance of Mr. Orlando Whiffle. Of his character I shall not say much at present, leaving it for the divination of the acute reader. I may, however, remark that the man was a living satire upon the Church of which he was a servant, an admirable caricature, far excelling anything that a professed ridiculer of ecclesiasticism could possibly have conceived. His age was about forty, and he had officiated as curate in Bloomford since the arrival of Mr. Norman. At that time, some ten years ago, he already rejoiced in a family of three sons and two daughters, and the circle of his *patria potestas* had since been widened by the arrival of three more daughters. And yet Mr. Whiffle was a light-hearted man.

He advanced into the room with his usual bow, which, like everything he did, was very much exaggerated and extremely ridiculous, then stepped briskly up to a low arm-chair over against that occupied by the rector, and dropped into it with quite a startling suddenness.

" Good-morning, Mr. Whiffle," said the rector, not taking the trouble to rise. " Quite a pleasant morning."

" Remarkably so, sir. The singing of the sparrows quite charmed me as I came along."

" Of the sparrows, Mr. Whiffle ? "

" Possibly they may have been another species of bird, sir. I have never given much attention to natural history. The Church does not encourage it."

He spoke in a sprightly, jerky manner, twirling his soft, clerical hat in his hand, and constantly shuffling uneasily on his chair.

" Did you come across the lawn ? " asked the rector, smiling slightly.

" I did, sir. And I observed there a young gentleman of whose existence here I was not previously aware. May I ask who ? "

" He is the child of an old friend of mine —a man in a humble position in life—who has just died and left, as far as he was aware of, no relatives. I have undertaken to take care of the boy."

" Ah ! Interesting, very interesting ! You will send him to school, I presume ? He is hardly old enough for a boarding-school yet."

" Nor advanced enough. The poor child has received absolutely no education of any kind."

" Ah ! Interesting beyond expression. Absolutely virgin soil for the ploughshare of instruction ; absolutely unturned ground for the seed of fundamental ideas ! I think I have already hinted to you, sir, that I am preparing a pamphlet on the subject of 'Fundamental Ideas,' in which I prove that there are three such ideas, and three only, which should never fail to be first of all instilled into the youthful mind. The first of these is the Inviolability of the Church as by Law Established; the second is the Immutability of the Poor Laws; the third is the Condemnability of Dissent. These I am wont, in my facetious way, to term my three 'Abilities,'—ha, ha, ha! I fancy I shall prove to the satisfaction of all readers that an education grounded upon the basework of these three ideas would be the very ideal of what education should be."

"I am hardly at one with you as to your second," said Mr. Norman, "and I imagine that if you had accompanied me in a walk I took the other day in London, you would have replaced it by some more fitting one—say the Immutability of Human Wretchedness. Did you ever happen to walk through Whitecross Street when you lived in London, Mr. Whiffle?"

"Whitecross Street, my dear sir? I had the happiness of officiating for a brief period in the very parish which includes it."

"Indeed? Then I need not describe it to you. Good God! I shall be haunted to my dying day with the scenes I beheld there last Saturday night."

"Very bad locality, sir; remarkably bad. Indeed, I may say it surpasses my limited comprehension that such localities should be permitted to exist in a land enjoying the inestimable blessing of a Holy Catholic and Apostolic Church. Upon my word, sir, that is one of the things that one should preach a crusade against! Yes, if I had the happiness of holding a living in London, I would commence to preach a crusade against Whitecross Street to-morrow—I mean next Sunday."

Mr. Whiffle, according to his habit, rose to his feet in the excitement of speaking, crushed his hat emphatically upon the table, thrust his fingers deep into his waistcoat pockets, and swayed backwards and forwards on his toes. As he concluded, he plumped down again into his easy chair.

"But I imagine, Mr. Whiffle, that the first step towards abolishing such horrors would consist of a judicious alteration in those Poor Laws which you pledge yourself to maintain."

Mr. Norman had scarcely a serious air when conversing with his curate. You could see that he took a pleasure in bringing out the man's eccentricities and internally making merry over them.

"No such thing, sir!" exclaimed Mr. Whiffle, "that is, I mean, if you permit me to urge my opinion against that of my rector. I assure you, sir, I have given thought to the subject. It is not the Poor Laws at fault;

it is inherent impracticability in the nature of the lower classes which renders these Laws comparatively inoperative. Depend upon it, sir, the spread of Dissent among these off-scourings of the earth, if I may so express myself, is the origin and root of the evil. They lack respect for the Established Church, sir."

"Possibly there may be something in what you say, Mr. Whiffle."

"I have in my head, sir, the details of a pamphlet on the subject of Dissent. I will venture to submit it to you in a short time. If there is one thing against which the Church should at once preach a crusade, it is that canker in the blossom of contemporary society, if I may so express myself—Dissent!"

"It was horrible, horrible!" said the rector, speaking more to himself than to Mr. Whiffle. "The thought oftenest in my mind whilst in that hideous scene was: How can we wonder that men doubt the existence of God?"

"Precisely the same thought has often occurred to myself. Really, one ought to carry about with one small selected volumes of religious evidences, especially for such occasions."

There was silence for some minutes, during which Mr. Whiffle whistled a *Te Deum* in a very low tone. Mr. Norman then suddenly seemed to rouse himself.

"But I have been wandering," he said. "My real reason for begging you to look in this morning was that I might consult you on the subject of Arthur's education. The child's name is Arthur Golding. Do you think your leisure would permit of your giving the child two or three hours' teaching a day?"

"My dear sir!" exclaimed Mr. Whiffle, starting to his feet, "I should be overjoyed to be entrusted with such a duty! It would be the proudest day for me since that ever-memorable one upon which I entered the Church!"

"I am glad it so entirely chimes with your inclinations. As I said, the poor lad is terribly backward. He is, moreover, quite unusually sensitive for a child. I fancy that in any case we must wait some little time before attempting to do anything with him. I never saw a child suffer so as he has done in consequence of his father's death. Suppose I walk over to you this evening, if it continues fine, and bring Arthur with me? The sight of your children might cheer him."

"Precisely, precisely!" exclaimed Orlando, who grew more cheery than ever when reminded of his family—for did not a tutorship imply a stipend? "Let us say seven o'clock, my dear sir. At that hour we shall all be gathered round the hearth in domestic peace, I hope."

"So be it."

Very shortly after this Mr. Whiffle rose and took his leave. He was, it should be noticed, a man by no means devoid of information, which, when he kept clear of clerical matters, he could make tolerable use of. He was a fair classical scholar, but especially an excellent arithmetician, so that Edward Norman had not acted with such indiscretion as might at first sight appear in proposing to entrust to him such an important matter as a child's education.

The rector had not seen fit, however, to make Mr. Whiffle his confidant in the exact story of Arthur Golding's antecedents. Nothing would be gained by doing so; on the contrary Orlando's active tongue would scarcely fail to circulate among the parishioners stories which were far better kept secret. But that afternoon Mr. Norman, in writing a letter to the only intimate friend he possessed, by name Gilbert Gresham, an artist who was just then travelling in Italy, gave a full account of the evening he had passed in Whitecross Street.

It was only in these letters to his friend that Edward Norman gave utterance to his real feelings. In miscellaneous company he was always under obvious restraints ; with such men as his curate and sundry of the neighbouring clergy who occasionally visited him he was at ease, often gravely satirical, but still not himself. Thus it came about that various estimates of his character were in circulation among his acquaintances. Possibly he did not himself possess much more real insight into his own nature than did these superficial observers.

" And whom do you think," the letter went on, after describing vividly the horrors of Whitecross Street, " whom do you think I discovered in one of the foulest recesses of this Pandemonium ? No other than my once dear friend, Arthur Golding. Of course you remember him quite well, though I recollect he was not an intimate acquaintance of yours ; he did not belong to your set at Balliol. He was a schoolfellow of mine to begin with, and we never lost sight of each other for more than a few weeks at a time during half a dozen years or so. Little did I imagine then that I should one day find him at the last gasp in a London garret. He had written to me, poor fellow, begging that I would come and see him, as he feared he was drawing to his end ; but, by a piece of stupidity on the part of my housekeeper, the letter was not forwarded to me. I found him unconscious. After I had watched by his side for some time his senses appeared partially to return to him. Though he was unable to speak, he pointed to his child, a boy of some eight years, who lay by his side, and I console myself with the idea that rendered his last moments easier by showing that I understood his wish.

"Poor Golding! At his best he was, in appearance, the handsomest youth I ever knew; his beauty, indeed, was almost feminine, and, I suspect, indicated rather plainly the weak parts of his character. I had entirely lost sight of him for many years. Even when I last parted from him in those brighter days he was all but an habitual drunkard; I remember warning him with all the severity I was capable of—Heaven knows that is not saying much!—of the terrible path upon which he was entering. But I could little foresee the horrors through which his brief life would struggle to that pitiful end.

"I found in his pocket, after his death, a long letter, written in an almost illegible hand, and intended for myself; perhaps he meant me to receive it after his death, for it was ready addressed and stamped, though written more than a week before. In this he revealed to me a secret I could never have suspected. It seems that, shortly after the birth of the child, he fell into severe difficulties, in consequence of which he was ultimately compelled to obtain a clerkship of some kind. His salary, however, proved insufficient to his needs, and, in a fatal moment, he yielded to a terrible temptation, and robbed his employers. He was found out, and suffered the punishment for his crime. This was the blow that hopelessly shattered what little of energy and purpose his life had hitherto retained.

" You will wonder how it was that he **never** applied to me for some kind of assistance before his ruin had become irretrievable, **for,** with my means and connections, I might well have been expected to help him.   Ah ! that awakens sore memories, and necessitates the narrative of a part of my own history, which as yet I have never poured into even your friendly ears.   You must have wondered who the wretched woman was who, as Golding's wife, bore a share in this life-tragedy, **and** had vanished before the close of it.

" Do you remember ' Laura,' the laughing-eyed angel of whom I used to prate to you from morning to night; whom I told you I **had** loved from a child, for whose sake I learned by heart one of Petrarch's sonnets every **day** of my life ?   It makes me miserable to think of her, and I must tell what I have to tell in very few words.   Well, at the end of the last term we spent together at the University, Golding came to spend a few weeks with **me** amid the delights of my Warwickshire home. At that time, as I have said, he was a charming fellow, and a few days sufficed to **make** him as much at his ease with all my **friends** and acquaintances as I was myself.   He **saw** Laura, could not but fall madly in love **with** her ; in an evil hour persuaded her to reciprocate his passion, and—to cut the story **short** —eloped with her.   At first I raved **against** him like a madman, feeling sure he had merely carried off the girl to ruin her. With all my energy I hunted him down, and, to my amazement, found that the two were married. Of course we quarrelled violently, and there you have the explanation of our broken intimacy.

" Now you will not wonder at my determining to adopt his child, whose name is also Arthur, for is he not *her* child, the child of that Laura who was once—alas! alas!—more than the world to me? Oh, God! what she must have gone through! In his letter Golding did not mention her name; but I have had the courage to ask the boy what he knew of his mother, and he tells me she died in the hospital a long time ago. It was a relief to hear it.

" And so I shall bring the boy up as my own, to be a brother to Helen. Will he grow up imbued with his father's vices, and make me wish that I had left him to struggle for his bitter existence in the seething sewer out of which I have plucked him? Who knows? He seems rather a strange lad; I half think I shall like him, for it is certain he has something of his mother's face, though most of his father's. He is as gentle as a girl, and, I should imagine, of very tolerable natural abilities. Well, I must do all I can for his education, but of course his future lies in the lap of the gods. I will not fail to acquaint you with his progress—or the reverse."

CHAPTER III.

Mr. Norman, who was but a slight eater, adhered to the country rule, and took a midday dinner. This meal was always shared by little Helen, who at other times ate in her nursery with Mrs. Cope. The present day beheld the unusual spectacle of two children at the table, one on each side of the rector, who glanced at them alternately : at the one with a look of pride and affection, at the other with interest, not devoid of pain.

Truly, the contrast was decided enough. On the right hand was the little girl, whose young life had known no trouble more severe than the cutting of teeth and the whooping-cough, with bright, chubby face, which smiled even during sleep, a head covered with ringlets of the purest gold, beneath her chin a spotless pinafore, sitting severely upright on her high, cane-bottomed chair, as if in conscious dignity of her dominion, past, present and to come; handling her spoon with a natural grace, and, at the same time, somewhat of an "old-fashioned" air, such as would have made a stranger smile ; her figure lit up by a ray of sunlight, which streamed full upon her through the window; as a rule, silent and thoughtful, but when spoken to, replying with a considerate gravity or a quiet mirth, alike in advance of her years.

Opposite to her sat the boy, the neglected waif of Whitecross Street, whose eight years had scarcely known a joy; in all that regards the higher nature of man far more ignorant than the little girl; in all that is base and ugly and fearful all but matured in experience.

In his outer appearance there was nothing now incongruous or repulsive; his agreeable features looked far better in the neat suit of clothes in which he was now attired than with the rags in which Mr. Norman had first seen him. But for all that it was painful to regard him. He evidently felt so completely estranged at this elegant table—he who had been accustomed to make his meals off a crust, gnawed whilst sitting on a door-step, or wandering about the streets. He did not know what to do with his knife and fork, his plate would not remain steady whilst he endeavoured to cut his meat; he kept slipping fowards on the chair, which was much too large for him; in short, he was utterly miserable. The only thing he could really succeed in eating was bread, and of that he ate as much as possible to satisfy the keen hunger he felt.

And, in addition to these temporary

troubles, that look of deep sadness still rested on his face, bespeaking the one great sorrow which oppressed him. In answer to the remarks which the rector now and then addressed to him, he replied with a monosyllable, hanging his head, and seeming frightened at the sound of his own voice. He kept looking on each side of him, nervously apprehensive lest anyone should be watching him. Out of absolute pity, Mr. Norman cut the dinner as short as possible.

When released from table, Arthur, being told he might dispose of himself as he would, wandered out into the orchard behind the house, and finding a bench placed in an out-of-the-way corner, sat down and gave himself up to his thoughts, whatever they were.

Meantime little Helen, as usual after dinner, had drawn a footstool close to her father's arm-chair and sat gazing upon the fire reflectively, waiting for the usual conversation to be opened. Her father did not appear likely to open his lips first, so the little girl broke silence.

"Father, you said Arthur's father was dead?"

"Yes, dear."

"And why doesn't Arthur wear black?"

The rector paused for a moment, then replied by asking another question.

"Do you think it right to wear black when a relative dies, Helen?"

" Everybody does so, father."

" And why do they ?"

" I suppose to show that they are sorry."

" More often to make a show of sorrow they do not feel, Helen. If one is really sorry what is gained by letting all the world know it ?"

" Then you do not think it right to wear black, father ?"

" It is a custom; but I think a rather foolish one."

There was a long pause, during which Helen reflected on this point.

" Father," she said, at length, " are not a great many customs very foolish ?"

" Very many, dear."

" Then if they are foolish, and people know it, as of course they must do, why ever do not people cease doing such things ?"

Helen had now come to one of those knotty points which she had not unfrequently arrived at in her mental excursions. As she spoke her fine eyes sparkled and her voice trembled with a species of irritation.

Shaking back her curls with a pretty little movement which was habitual to her, she sat looking up into her father's face, awaiting an answer.

" Custom, Helen," replied Mr. Norman with a smile, as he ran his fingers through the golden ringlets which hid the child's ears, " is a mighty god which, more or less, all the world worships, and to which it offers the most precious sacrifices—often that which it holds dearest. It does not matter whether they are willing or not to make the sacrifice. They have all their lives worshipped the god Custom with their eyes open, and whatever it be that he claims from them they are bound to lay it upon his altar and there burn it. Sometimes it is with bursting hearts that they see their dearest hopes perishing in the flame; but it avails nothing. The god Custom is without pity."

"I understand you, father," replied the child, nodding her head gravely. And again there was silence for some time. Helen was the first to break it.

"Father, I read to you the other morning about the religion of the Greeks. The book said that we are better than the Greeks, for they had a great many false gods, whilst we have only one, the true one. Don't you think we also have a great many false gods? Is not the god Custom one of them?"

The rector looked with some surprise at the speaker; but he evidently had a keen delight in her precocious wisdom.

"You are very right, Helen," he replied. "The only difference is that we do not openly confess our gods, or make images of them. The gods of the Greeks were beautiful, and their images still form the noblest creations of art which the world has seen. Were we

to make images of our false gods, they would
be so terribly hideous that men would run
away from them."

"But is it possible, father, to worship
these many false gods and the one true God
at the same time?"

"There are very few indeed worship the
true God," replied the rector, gravely. "Even
many of those who think they do so have
really no idea what God is."

"I am glad you think so, father. There
is Mrs. Simpson, who teaches in the Sunday
school, and who is always asking us such
nasty questions about the Devil; don't you
think she is one of those people, father?"

Mr. Norman merely smiled.

Helen was too wise to press for a more explicit reply. After reflecting for a moment,
she laid her hand on her father's knee, and,
looking up into his face with that expression
of pure simplicity blended with curious intelligence, which gave such an unutterable
charm to her young face, asked—

"Father, what *is* God?"

Edward Norman started, and for a moment averted his face; but he quickly
recovered himself, and, fondling the child's
hands in both his own, spoke gravely.

"That is a more difficult question than
you think, my dear little girl. It is *the* most
difficult question that we can ask ourselves
in this world. Do you ever feel that you have

it in your power to choose between two things you would like to do, and when you come to think them over, see clearly that one is good and the other bad?"

"Oh, often, father!"

"And which do you feel you ought to do, the good thing or the bad thing?"

"The good thing."

"Very well. Did you ever compare two objects together and say to yourself that one is beautiful and one is ugly?"

"Often."

"And which of these would you keep if you had the choice?"

"The beautiful thing, of course."

"You are right. Then you have learned that there is something in your mind which gives you the power of distinguishing between a good and a bad action, a beautiful and an ugly thing, and also bids you choose the good and the beautiful rather than the bad or the ugly. And this *something* is God."

Helen made no reply, and very shortly after she rose, kissed her father, as usual, and ran to look for Arthur.

Edward Norman passed the rest of his afternoon in writing letters.

Shortly after tea, in accordance with the arrangement made with Mr. Whiffle, the rector set out in Arthur's company for the curate's residence. This was situated some quarter of an hour's walk off, and the way

thither led across bare fields. Mr. Norman
took the boy's hand, and questioned him as
they walked, endeavouring to destroy the
painful diffidence which marked Arthur's
conduct in his company. Between the questions and replies, Arthur looked up once or
twice as if about to speak, but always dropped
his head when his eye met Mr. Norman's.

" Is there something you wish to say,
Arthur?" asked the latter, at length.

" Where—where have they buried father,
sir?" was the question spoken in trembling
tones.

" I will take you to see some day," replied
the rector.

" You will?" asked Arthur, with eagerness.

" Yes, but not just yet. Do you think
you can be happy with us here, Arthur?"

" I'll try to be, sir," replied the boy.

Then the rector began to describe the
delights of the country in summer time, the
beauty of the fields when they had cast off
their winter garments, and clad themselves
with grass and flowers and sunlight, to greet
the coming of spring; he did his best to
interest the boy in scenes and occupations
which the latter's fancy, through inexperience
of the beautiful, was quite unable to realise.
He did not seem heedless to these prospects,
for once or twice he looked up at the speaker
with an expression of surprise, but then

ensued a sigh as the old look of melancholy took possession of his features.

"I am taking you, Arthur," said the rector, at last, "to see a gentleman who will do his best to teach you, and make a clever man of you. You say you never went to school?"

"No, sir. Father began to teach me to read, but he hadn't time, and soon left off. He always said the school cost too much."

"Do you think you shall like to learn?"

"I think so, sir."

"That's right. A man is very little use in the world if he has not a good deal of knowledge, so I know you will do your best to learn all Mr. Whiffle wishes to teach you."

"Father knew a great deal."

"Did he? Who told you so, Arthur?"

"I remember mother saying so, a long time ago. But she said that learning was no good, and didn't bring in any money."

"That is not the only use of learning, my boy. But here we are; we will talk about it again as we go home."

It was now quite dark, and the wind, which grew colder and stronger, was howling over the long hill-side, and sweeping hither and thither clouds of rustling skeleton leaves. The house they stood before had a particularly desolate appearance. In front of it was what should have been a garden, a space some six yards long by four deep, in the

middle of which grew a hideous abortion of
a tree. Whether it was that the æsthetic
sentiments of the Whiffle family possessed
but little prominence, or that the lack of
space necessitated the preference of the useful
to the agreeable, this space was converted
into a yard for drying clothes, the abortive
tree serving as a centre, whence a number of
clothes-lines radiated, being affixed to poles
planted against the low wall encircling the
space. At present these lines were thickly
hung with linen, which, thanks to the efforts
of the night wind, was careering about the
lines in a frantic manner, producing a decidedly peculiar effect when seen through the
dark. Glimmering behind these self-con-
stituted streamers appeared a few feeble
lights, apparently coming from the windows
of the house. A wicket in the wall gave
admission to the sacred precincts, and Mr.
Norman entered with his companion. As
they drew near the door, above all the dismal
howling of the wind, the cracking and flapping
of the wet clothes, and the shrill rustling of
dead leaves, such a chorus of infantine screams
and squalls, mingled with such a shouting of
maturer voices, the whole being accompanied
by what appeared to be a beating upon drums,
an occasional blowing of a horn, and the not
unfrequent crash as of falling crockery, met
the astonished ear, that Mr. Norman might
well be excused when he knocked hastily and

loudly, in fear lest some sudden misfortune had befallen the dwelling of his worthy curate. The knock remained unanswered, and it appearing to the rector that the urgency of the case warranted a slight disregard of ceremony, he turned the handle and entered the house.

In front appeared a flight of stairs, upon which a small oil lamp stood, faintly illumining the entrance. On either hand was a door, that on the right being, as Mr. Norman was aware, the door of the curate's so-called study, that to the left leading into the room where the family mostly lived. The latter stood slightly ajar, and from the other side of it proceeded the hubbub, which was as yet far from diminishing. On pushing open the door, an extraordinary scene disclosed itself. In a room tolerably well furnished as dining and sitting-room combined, appeared to be collected the whole of the Whiffle family; Mr. Orlando Whiffle, Mrs. Whiffle, and the eight children. Half the table was covered with a white cloth, and laid with tea things, the other half was covered with a heap of newly-washed clothes, which Mrs. Whiffle had evidently been in the process of ironing when the present *fracas* commenced. The following was the tableau : in the centre of the room stood Mr. Whiffle, his coat thrown off, his hair more stubbornly self-assertive than ever, in the act of administering corporal

punishment to his first-born, Master Augustus
Whiffle. With one arm he had secured the
lithe youngster in that position which is
technically known as " chancery," while the
other hand, armed with a schoolmaster's cane,
descended with alarming rapidity upon the
most sensitive portion of the captive's frame.
From every pore of Mr. Whiffle's body the
perspiration streamed profusely, and, not
content with the violence of his muscular
exertion, he was engaged in the hopeless task
of endeavouring to drown with his own voice
the yells of his struggling victim. Poor Mrs.
Whiffle, a very little, inoffensive-looking
woman, from whose eyes the tears were
streaming at the sight of young Augustus'
sufferings, was doing her best with cries and
entreaties to mitigate her husband's wrath,
whilst at the same time it was all she could
do to exercise surveillance over the other
seven children. Three of these, two girls
and a very little boy, had crept under the
table in terror, where, notwithstanding, they
were doing their best simultaneously to empty
a small pot of jam, one moment squalling in
fright and sympathy, the next licking their
lips in satisfaction after a delicious mouthful.
Another little boy, evidently hard-hearted
and callous to his brother's sufferings, had
taken advantage of his mother's back being
turned, to mount a lofty chair and grasp at
a sugar basin which stood on the top shelf

of an open cupboard, and now stood balancing
himself in a position which was not a little
dangerous. The sixth, a little girl, Mrs.
Whiffle had inadvertently knocked over into
the fire-place, and was now endeavouring,
by the way, as it were, to solace, but only
with the result of increasing its howling.
And, finally, the seventh and eighth, who
were twins, and were now lying together in
a cradle close by the table, not content with
vying in the exercise of their shrill pipes,
were taking a still more effective method
of attracting attention by lugging one corner
of the table cloth, which they had succeeded
in catching hold of, till one by one the tea
things began to roll on to the floor, some
breaking, some spilling their contents, all
adding their individual cracks and bumps
to the total of domestic discord.

The appearance of the rector at the door
was instantaneous in its effect, one moment
din insufferable, the next, absolute silence,
save for the suppressed moaning of the twins,
the sobs of the rest of the children and their
mother, and the pantings of Mr. Whiffle,
whose appearance, as he stood with one arm
still raised over the body of his prostrate
son, made a very excellent caricature of a
victorious gladiator appealing to the verdict
of thumbs. Silence was broken by the rector's
mild and good-natured tones.

"I fear I have come at an inopportune

moment," he said, bowing courteously to the distracted lady of the house, who was hurriedly doing her best to put things in order.

"Not at all, my dear sir, not at all," panted Mr. Whiffle, in his usual sprightly manner, wiping his forehead the while with an immense yellow silk handkerchief. "You beheld me in the act of visiting with condign chastisement a refractory young son of the Church, that is all, I assure you."

Then, turning to his wife, he added—

"My dear, I quite neglected to tell you that Mr. Norman was so good as to promise to look in this evening. My dear sir, this incorrigible young Israelite, whom I should have called Benoni rather than Augustus, for he verily seems destined to be the son of my sorrow, was, just before you entered, caught in the very act—*in flagrante delicto*—of emptying the milk pot over a sermon which I have been at more than usual pains to compose. Do you not agree with me in thinking that even now the offence exceeds the punishment?"

Mr. Norman replied by a few humorous remarks, and then proceeded by means of a little kindly attention to each of the children, as his manner was, to restore what order he could into this house of perpetual discord. By accepting Mrs. Whiffle's offer of a cup of tea, he caused a smile once more to rise to the face of that much suffering woman, who was indeed so accustomed to episodes such as that just concluded that it very soon passed out of her mind.

The cup of tea finished as soon as possible, he left Arthur to the attention of Mrs. Whiffle and her brood, and gladly accepted the curate's invitation to cross the passage and enter the study. Here the disorder was little inferior to that exhibited in the other room, but as it was only books that were strewn about in every corner, in every stage of delapidation, and mostly covered with the thickest conceivable layer of dust, the rector bore it with more equanimity. Mr. Whiffle enlivened a small fire which was struggling in the grate, and invited his visitor to be seated.

" You must be very fond of children, Mr. Whiffle," began the rector, whilst the other was putting on a very ragged old coat which he took from behind the door.

" Yes, sir, yes—that is, moderately fond of them. Not that I should care to have a large family, though. Large families, in my opinion, are the source of much evil. Indeed, that is one of the tendencies of the present age against which the Church ought really to exert the plenitude of its powers. Yes; one should preach a crusade against large families. I have, in fact, a pamphlet in hand on that very subject. I hope to finish it in a week, and then I shall be so bold as to request the

favour of your perusal and judgment, my
dear sir."

Mr. Norman did not smile, or indeed
express any especial interest in the matter;
he was too well accustomed to his curate's
humours. Orlando Whiffle never seemed to
entertain the slightest suspicion that some
might be tempted to consider his own family
as already deserving of the epithet—large.
Of this he was perfectly unconscious. And
when he announced the speedy completion of
a pamphlet on the subject he was equally
unconscious of exposing another of his peculiarities which might well have excited a sense
of the ridiculous. It was—or was supposed
to be—the constant occupation of his leisure
to engage in the composition of pamphlets on
an infinity of subjects, with the curious circumstance that he had never been known to
publish, or indeed to complete, one of them.
At least three times a week he announced to
the rector his intention immediately to submit to his criticism a brief *brochure* on some
burning question of the day; but Mr. Norman's critical powers must have languished
from inaction had they found no other field
than Mr. Whiffle's literary productions. But
to the curate himself there was nothing
ridiculous in all this; he simply was not
aware of his own inconsistencies.

Having turned aside the literary topic,
with a suitable remark, Edward Norman then

proceeded to the more immediate object of his visit, and stated briefly the plan he thought it would be advisable to pursue in Arthur's preliminary instruction.

"Have you thought at all, sir," asked Mr. Whiffle, "what his career in life shall be?"

"Not precisely. It is hardly a momentous question yet."

"Train him up to the service of the Temple!" cried Mr. Whiffle, with enthusiasm. "Make of him a pillar of the Establishment! I have thought over the matter the whole day, my dear sir, and the more I reflect upon that boy's features the more convinced I am that he was born to be a bishop. I once entered upon an exhaustive study of comparative physiognomy, my dear sir, and even went so far as to pen a pamphlet on what I purposed making one division of a great work: the 'Ecclesiastical Physiognomy.' I will hunt it up and let you see it. Close study of the countenances of our prelates, sir, has given me fundamental ideas on the subject. I pronounce it: Arthur Golding will one day rule a diocese, and to Orlando Whiffle will be due the credit of having instilled into his mind the fundamental principles of the great Establishment he is to adorn!"

"We shall see," responded the rector, coolly, "whether he shows a turn for the Church."

"A turn, my dear sir! In a child of his age there *is* no—no turn! We can make what we like of him! That is the very point I always insist upon as firmly in my arguments on the subject of education. If only The Church is permitted an opportunity of conducting the education of children from their earliest years, she will have no difficulty in imbuing one and all with sound Church principles. It is the decreasing influence of The Church in this sphere of youthful education to which is due the prevalence of false doctrine, heresy and schism, and to which will ere long be attributed the downfall of this nation's prosperity!"

It will be observed that I always print "The Church" in Mr. Whiffle's speeches, for, indeed, the capitals are my only possible method of indicating the tone in which he pronounced these words. All the arrogance of priestly tyranny, all the bombast of clerical professions, all the fatuity of ecclesiastical self-esteem arose before the mind like a picture at the sound of "The Church" as pronounced by Mr. Whiffle. The man gloried in the words; he rolled them on his tongue as an exquisite delicacy. And yet it would have been difficult to account for his enthusiasm, for as yet the Church had given him nothing save various curacies, the incomes of which scarcely sufficed to maintain his ever-increasing family. In all probability it was his fundamentally vulgar nature sympathising with the arrogant pretentions and abortive performances of the institution he belonged to. Pre-eminence in the Church was for Mr. Whiffle the goal of all earthly wishes, and it was very characteristic of the man's nature that down in the depths of his heart, unspoken midst all his inconsequential chatter, rested and grew a firm expectation that one day, though it might be long in coming, that Church would recognise the abilities of its faithful servant, and Orlando Whiffle would, even in this life, find his reward.

It was the favourite employment of his reveries to trace his own hypothetical course up the scale of clerical dignities till, in sweet fancy, he saw himself pocketing the first year's income of a bishop's see. For in his devotion to the Establishment he was by no means free from worldly views, though it would be inaccurate to represent these as his only motive. Whenever conversation touched on the subject of ecclesiastical salaries, as it not unfrequently would when a few curates of the country-side met together, Orlando Whiffle felt himself in his element. He possessed an amount of knowledge on the subject to which few could pretend. On this, indeed, he might have been capable of writing a pamphlet, and a remarkably interesting pamphlet it would have been. He was great on the topic of simony, spoke of it with a kind of predilection, and a calm ignoring of moral objections such as only an ecclesiastic can pretend to. Clerical agencies he was well acquainted with, and could tell you their respective advantages or disadvantages better than the agents themselves. But most delightful was it to hear him speak of a clerical scandal, any disgraceful case that might for the moment be attracting attention in the papers. What breathless interest he took in such revelations. Shame ! he exhibited not a grain of it. He gloried in the foulest details. You would have thought, to hear him, that no one but a clergyman had a right to disgrace the name of humanity.

But to return to our narration. The interview did not last long, for the terms, which were no unimportant item in the business, were speedily and satisfactorily arranged. When the two returned to the parlour they found Arthur sitting on a stool by the fireside, quite surrounded by a swarm of young Whiffles, who were assailing him with all manner of questions, and had evidently succeeded in making him perfectly uncomfortable.

" Well, my dear boy," exclaimed the curate, laying his hands upon his head, " tomorrow we take our first trip on the flowery paths of culture. Have you learnt your Catechism, my boy ?"

Arthur looked up in bewilderment, then turned away from the faces gazing at him, and shook his head.

" Cheer up, Arthur !" put in Mr. Norman, encouragingly. " We'll soon remedy all that, won't we ?"

It was not many minutes before they took their departure, and the boy was evidently glad to exchange the warm but noisy room for the dark, windy fields. As the rector passed out of the door, Mr. Whiffle took the opportunity of whispering to him—

" A bishop, my dear sir ; a bishop, or I'll never prophesy again !"

CHAPTER IV.

Two or three days passed, and Mr. Whiffle had seen no reason to alter his preconceived opinion. The boy, though, as might have been expected, very ignorant, was far from stupid, and his extreme docility rendered the task of teaching him decidedly agreeable. When Arthur was able to read all the letters of the alphabet readily and correctly, Mr. Whiffle grew elate; his sanguine temperament made him already look forward to the day when he should commence the Greek Testament with his pupil. Already he saw him grown into a promising young prig, carping at interpretations of the Sacrament, and dogmatizing on the Holy Ghost. Unhappily, Mr. Whiffle's anticipations were not destined to fulfilment.

When with his tutor, or in the company of any of the family, Arthur preserved a quiet, sad demeanour, doing his best to answer with a smile when spoken to, but at other times showing little, if any, interest in what went on around him. It was clear to every one that on the third day of his presence at the Rectory he was not a whit more at home than he had been on the first. Edward Norman took him occasionally for a short walk, spoke to him comfortingly and encouragingly, and did his best to win the boy's confidence; but the rector was hardly of that nature which disposes itself readily to enter into the joys and the sorrows of children; when he spoke to Arthur it was as he would have spoken to a grown-up person. He was quite unable to understand the state of that young mind, darkened with ignorance and all the dreary memories of the past, or of the over-sensitive heart, wrung with unutterable grief at the loss of a father. Mrs. Cope was more successful in understanding his sorrows; once or twice a few kind, motherly words from her brought the hot tears rushing from the child's eyes, and so gave him relief for the moment. But even she rapidly became aware that it was not an ordinary nature with which they had to deal, and foresaw that the process of reconciling him to his new life would be long and painful. To little Helen, Arthur was evidently a profound mystery. She would frequently take a book to a stool at a little distance from him, and then, under the pretence of reading, in reality sit watching him for a long time. On one such occasion Mr. Norman had withdrawn from the room, and the children were left alone together. Arthur was sitting on a low chair, his hands clasped over his knees, his head drooping down on his breast, and in the stillness of the room, only broken by the crackling of a bright fire, Helen could hear him sighing from time to time. After watching him for many minutes with a curiously reflective look, she suddenly rose and went to his side.

"Arthur," she said, "why do you sit so?"

"I am thinking of my father," replied Arthur, who was under less restraint with Helen than with the others.

"Was he a good father?" asked the little girl. "Was he like mine?"

"He was very good; but he wasn't as rich as your father."

"If he was good, Arthur," resumed Helen, after a moment's reflection, "why didn't he teach you to read, like my father does me? You are older than I am, you know."

"He used to tell me it was better to know nothing. He said I should be better off if I couldn't read or write."

Helen opened her eyes very wide.

"Then I'm sure he wasn't good if he said that," she pronounced decidedly. "My father tells me that a man is no good in the world if he can't read and write, and I'm sure father knows."

The boy had again sunk his head, and made no reply.

"And my father says," pursued Helen, "that the more you know, the more good you are able to do to people. That's why I'm learning as much as I can. I mean to do a great deal of good some day, Arthur; don't you?"

"I don't know how," replied the boy, looking curiously up into Helen's face.

"Oh, but I do! When I'm a little older I'm going to teach a school in Bloomford, and I shall only take those children that are poor and can't afford to pay anything; father says I may. And when I'm old enough to have money of my own, I shall go and see the poor people in Bloomford—and there are a great many, you know—and I shall give them a shilling at a time—father says it isn't wise to give too much—to buy what they want with. Don't you think you'd like to do that, Arthur?"

"Perhaps so," replied the boy.

"Arthur," resumed Helen, "what are you going to be when you're a man?"

"Don't know."

"I know what I should be."

"What?"

"I should write books, books like those in father's study. I don't mean silly tale books, but books that would do people good. Father says there's nothing like a good book, and I'm sure he's right."

She waited for a reply, but none came. It was evident that Arthur's thoughts were far away; he did not seem to have heard her last sentence at all. With a little sigh of impatience she rose from her seat, shaking the golden ringlets from her face.

"Arthur!" she exclaimed, after looking round the room thoughtfully.

"What."

"Do you like looking at pictures?"

"I—I think so," he replied, with hesitation.

Helen took off a side table a large volume of engravings which it was all she could do to carry. Placing it on the floor in front of her companion she opened it gravely and invited Arthur to inspect it with her. Little by little the boy's interest increased; he listened more attentively to Helen's explanations, and began himself to make comments. Here at length was something attractive enough to hold his attention and liberate his mind from perpetual brooding over his sorrows. For nearly an hour the two were deeply engaged—Helen explaining at length in her precocious manner, here and there pointing a moral, and always referring to what her father had said with regard to any unusually knotty point; Arthur listening attentively, occasionally asking questions which displayed considerably more intelligence than would have been expected, and even at times laughing, though this very rarely. Whilst they were in the middle of the volume Mr. Norman opened the door. He was not observed, and, after gazing with some astonishment at the unusual sight, he withdrew quietly, without disturbing them.

But the relief proved only momentary. When next Helen desired to amuse her companion in the same manner, it soon appeared that the novelty had passed away; she could not succeed in arousing in him more than a languid interest. His desire of loneliness increased. Whenever an opportunity presented itself he would steal out of sight to that remote corner of the orchard, which he had discovered, and there would sit for hours, hidden from the windows at the back of the house by a thick holly-tree, insensible to the cold, which began to be severe, and even to rain and snow. Mr. Whiffle began to entertain less sanguine hopes with regard to his pupil. His progress by no means kept pace with the expectations which the first few days had excited. The boy seemed to dread the recurring lesson-hours, and at times was even stubborn when Mr. Whiffle essayed the influence of a little severity. It was very clear that Arthur Golding would never be taught by force.

" A frightful example, my dear sir," exclaimed the curate to Mr. Norman, after a more than usually hopeless hour, " a frightful example of early years passed without the salutary influence of clerical admonition! I do not say positively that I renounce my hopes with regard to his future—but I fear, I fear."

It was now drawing on to Christmas, and the approach of that season brought accession of life to the rather monotonous routine of the Rectory. A distant cousin of Mr. Norman, who had no blood relations living, had recently been married, and now, in accordance with an invitation, brought his wife to pass the Christmas at Bloomford. This young lady, who was of a remarkably mercurial disposition, soon succeeded in effecting what she styled a reformation in the domestic arrangements of her reverend cousin. She immediately interested herself in all the leading families of the neighbourhood, threw herself with enthusiasm into the multifarious schemes for Christmas festivities in connection with the Church, which hitherto had been left entirely to the care of Mr. Whiffle, subscribed for Christmas trees, gave her co-operation towards a Christmas bazaar, and made herself, in a very few days, a conspicuous feature in the frivolous life of Bloomford. The consequence was that the Rectory was invaded by a host of visitors. Mr. Norman shrugged his shoulders and began devoutly to wish that he had never invited the disturber of his dearly-loved quietude. But it could not be said that his cousin gave him any trouble beyond, indeed, taking possession of all the best rooms in his house. She installed herself as mistress, herself gave instructions with regard to the meals, herself invited whom she pleased to tea, paying no attention whatever to the civil hints of Mrs. Cope, who was nothing less than scandalised at this unwonted *bouleversement* of her time-honoured supremacy. All the young ladies of Bloomford seized upon the opportunity with joy. Once more did Mr. Norman become a subject of active interest, once more was his persistent bachelorhood cried shame upon by all eligible ladies, once more did the attacks upon his susceptibilities commence, and this time in his own house. The vote and interest of the mercurial cousin was solicited far and near, and she promised her best exertions on behalf of some dozen confidential old ladies who had daughters they were extremely desirous of getting off their hands. Mr. Norman was dragged perforce from the retirement of his study; he was made to take part personally in the ornamenting of the church with evergreens; he was beguiled by his lively cousin into visits to all sorts of people at all possible or impossible hours, and was always received with a degree of attention quite alarming, and which he could not in the least understand; he was made the recipient of more invitations than he could possibly respond to. Everybody was all at once dreadfully solicitous with regard to his health. Though no one knew his precise ailment it was obvious that he had drooped during the last few years, and how sad a thing it was for so delightful a man to sink into a premature grave unsoothed by the tender cares of wifely affection. Many old ladies adopted the motherly tone towards him, and told him plainly that he ought to marry. Edward Norman merely smiled, and gave his promise that he would think the matter over. And as often as he succeeded in shaking off the hounds and bestowing himself safely in the cool recesses of his study, he vowed internally that when once these visitors had taken their departure he would never again open his house to them or any one else.

The position of the children in the house during all this ferment was not a pleasant one. The *bruyante* cousin could not be expected to entertain any liking for such " troublesome little chits," as she termed them, and, on the part of Helen at least, this distaste was cordially reciprocated.

The little lady was, to begin with, mortally jealous. What right had this stranger to come and monopolise the society of her father—*her* father, in whom her being was centred ? Since the strangers had been in the house her regular lesson hours had been hopelessly disturbed. Instead of going to her father's study and reading to him on a stool by his knee for certain hours during the day, as she had always been accustomed to do, she was now obliged to do her lessons with Mrs. Cope, and, after her father, Helen

considered that to look up to Mrs. Cope as a
teacher was decidedly *infra dig.* The way in
which the little woman revenged herself was
characteristic. Instead of reading from her
book like a docile pupil, waiting for Mrs.
Cope's corrections and comments, and consulting her with regard to difficulties, she
constituted herself the teacher, and made her
book a kind of text, upon which she proceeded to discourse to the old lady in a highly
improving manner, never failing to refer to
" her father " as the ultimate source of appeal
in any case where her dictum and that of Mrs.
Cope found themselves at hopeless variance.

But this state of affairs, though occasionally flattering to Helen's vanity, was, she
felt, very far from satisfactory; and she not
unfrequently delivered her sentiments anent
the prolonged visit of the cousins in no unmistakable terms.

As for Arthur, the poor boy was depressed
almost to illness. Mrs. Cope had discovered
his seat in the orchard, and took every opportunity of disturbing him when he retired
thither, fancying that he only required to be
kept in the presence of the family to throw
aside his mopish habits. The result was,
that he found another place, in a field, still
further away from the house, and often sat
there beneath a hedge, on the damp ground,
till he was all but insensible from cold and
hunger.

On his return from such prolonged absences Mrs. Cope would sometimes scold him severely; but this had the effect of hardening his mind against her. Once when she had been unusually severe, he suddenly turned upon her with eyes that flashed with anger, his cheeks pale as death, and his little hands clenched together; and when she shrank back, quite frightened at his look, he burst into a violent fit of weeping, and threw himself passionately all his length upon the floor.

The same afternoon he asked a servant, who had often spoken kindly to him, the way to London; and she, without thinking much of his reasons for asking such a question, told him in reply the names of several villages through which the road lay. He said nothing, but walked away thoughtfully.

Mr. Whiffle had given him up as a bad job, though he still continued to give him his lessons *pro forma*. Once Arthur fairly played truant at lesson hour, and the rector sent him that evening to the curate's house to ask pardon by way of penance. Mr. Whiffle improved the occasion.

"Did he not know by this time that obedience to pastors and masters was enjoined by the Catechism of the Church of England as by law established? Did he not know, moreover, that to play truant was, from a mere worldly point of view, a piece of

gross disrespect towards the teacher, and
that, in a case where that teacher was an
ordained minister of the Church this disrespect amounted to irreligion? Had he no
hankering after the sweets of a liberal education? Did it not cut him to the heart to
visit the church on Sunday and, from absolute inability to read the Prayer-book, be
obliged to keep staring about him to see
when the congregation stood, when they sat,
and when they knelt?" &c., &c., &c.

But all this wrought no impression upon
the poor lad. In the depths of his heart was
a firmly-rooted suffering which Mr. Whiffle
was quite incapable of comprehending, and
which Edward Norman divined, indeed, but
knew not how to remedy.

Arthur felt away from home; Bloomford
could never be anything to him but a foreign
land. Throughout the whole of his young life
he had never known but one true friend, and
that friend his father. Despite all the miserable excesses by which he hastened his death
—despite the fearful valley of suffering
through which he had dragged his poor
child, Golding had truly loved the boy, and
Arthur had passionately reciprocated his
affection. Though throughout the last two
years of his life Golding had passed through
all the stages of brutalisation which it is
possible for such a nature as his, originally
far from bad, to undergo, he had never once

shown active cruelty to his child, had never
once struck him, and had never used harsh
language to him without the next moment
bitterly repenting and doing his best to atone.
True, he had half-starved the boy, had
brought him up in foul haunts of poverty,
wretchedness and crime, where it was a
miracle his young nature retained anything
of nobility, had utterly neglected to teach
him, had even cynically said that he would
get through his life better if he remained
rude and untaught. Yet all this was the
result of impaired faculties rather than of an
ill-disposed heart.

More than half his days he had been mad
with the poison of drink. Often and often
he reproached himself with the fierce energy
of a ruined soul for all the wrongs he was
guilty of towards his offspring; many an oath
he took to amend his vile life if only for the
sake of Arthur; but when the hour of temptation came again he was as powerless to
resist as the pebble dragged back into the
depths of the ocean by the cliff-rending
breaker.

And for all that the child loved him with
all the strength of an intensely affectionate
nature, clung to him as the sole object upon
which to expend the riches of his overflowing
heart, impossible to depict the agony which
in a moment clouded his life when he knew
that his father was dead. And ever since he

had been at Bloomford this agony had gnawed
at the springs of youthful energy and hope,
had made his life, in the midst of these un-
sympathising strangers, a very torment to
him. He had become possessed of an ever-
growing, irrepressible desire to return to
London.

He knew that he should no more find his
father there, that he had not a friend to whom
he could appeal for assistance; but still there
was the dumb, strong desire to find himself
once more in the scenes where he had lived
with his father; he felt that he should then
be more at home. He would visit his father's
grave; the people of the house he had lived
in would tell him where that was. He felt,
in his instinctive, unreflecting way, that it
would be a happiness to fall down upon it
and die, so unutterably wretched was he.
The feeling actuating him was as the longing
of a child for the mother's breast, the ardent,
soul-quelling desire of a lover to gain the side
of an absent mistress; the yearning of the
mariner on a desert island for the home he
will never see again. As I have said, he did
not reflect upon his longing; he would not
then have been a child of eight years. It was
instinct, and all the more invincible.

When the Rectory was full of visitors he
shrank into his bedroom, and there remained in cold and darkness till Mrs. Cope
came to search for him and send him to bed.

Yet, even in these depths of misery there were chords in his nature which could be touched, and excite a momentary diversion from his brooding over the past. One night there was a lady visiting at the house who played skilfully on the piano. As Arthur sat in his dark hiding-place, the drawing-room door happened to be opened whilst this lady was playing. The sweet notes fell upon his ear with an effect that nothing else could have produced. A fine spark of heavenly fire, which lay beneath all the rude externals of his being, throbbed momentarily into brighter life at the voice of the keys. The next moment the door was shut again, and the music became indistinguishable. But he could not resist the impulse to hear more. Stealing out of the bedroom, he crept down stairs on tip-toe. The hall was vacant. He approached the drawing-room door and stood with his ear against it, drinking in the melody in brief forgetfulness of his troubles. In a few moments he fancied he heard a step descending the upper stairs. Dreading to be found here, he rushed to the house-door, and out into the night. The ground was frozen hard, and light snow was just beginning to fall. Guided still by his ear, he made his way over some barren flower-beds to beneath the drawing-room windows. The night was so perfectly still that he heard the music here almost as well as within the house. Crouching on the fresh-fallen snow, he listened, all unconscious of the cold, till the music ceased.

Perhaps it might commence again. In hope of this he waited, waited till the snow had quite covered him with white flakes, till his teeth chattered and his hands and feet were numb. Then he re-entered the house and crept silently up-stairs.

He had opened the bedroom door before he observed that there was a light within, and on entering he found himself face to face with Mrs. Cope. The good lady was horrified; she scolded severely, she even threatened corporal punishment. Arthur said not a word, but allowed himself to be hurried into bed. Then, when Mrs. Cope had gone and he was alone in the dark, he burst into passionate weeping, and so at length sobbed himself to sleep.

Early on the following morning, just after the servants had risen and had opened the door, a little, shivering form crept silently down stairs, paused a moment in the hall to see that no one was about, then ran quickly into the garden. Thence it passed into a field, and, crossing this, entered the high road.

It was Arthur. Possibly he had come out for a walk before breakfast; his constant desire of solitude would account for his stealing from the house so quietly. But why had he forgotten to put on his little overcoat? It had ceased snowing some time during the night, and frost had since made the surface hard; but the sky looked leaden and lowering in the early daylight; it would snow again ere long. The cold was piercing, and the wind, which ever and again swept the fields, froze everything that it touched. Surely it was a strange morning to take an early walk, without an overcoat too.

A country fellow happened to be coming along the road just as Arthur emerged into it. The boy stopped him and inquired his way to a certain village distant about two miles. Having received the direction he set off running. Had he been given a commission from the rector that he showed such eagerness to reach the place? Mr. Norman had occasionally sent him on little errands in the hope of affording him distraction. But this was too great a distance, and before breakfast.

In something more than an hour he reached the village, and, choosing a retired spot, sat down to rest for a few moments. He was very tired, and, despite the severity of the morning, the perspiration stood on his forehead, he had run so quickly.

In a short time he rose again, and again inquired of a passer-by the way to another village, still farther off. The man looked at his questioner in some surprise, but gave him the desired information. Once away from the houses the boy began again to run, looking from time to time behind him, as if afraid of pursuers. For nearly three hours he toiled along, wearied at length beyond running, and indeed scarcely able to walk. He began to feel very hungry, too. Why did he not turn back towards Bloomford, where food and shelter and friendly faces awaited him? He seemed to have no such thought.

Before one or two cottages, which he passed, he made a pause. His hunger had grown so severe that he was on the point of knocking at the door and begging for a little food, but each time his courage failed him, and he passed on. He felt dreadfully thirsty, too, and, to relieve himself, broke off lumps of hard snow from the ground, and let them melt in his mouth. So great was his weariness now that he could scarcely trail his limbs along. He was, be it remembered, only eight years old, and weak besides, and he must have travelled nearly eight miles. Again and again he sat down to rest, now on the snow-covered bank at the roadside, now on a stile which led off the road into fields, and each time he rose it was with a feeling that he could go no further. He did not give way to despair and cry; but his eyes were bloodshot from the cutting wind, his

cheeks were pale and haggard-looking, his
limbs trembled wtih cold and fatigue. For
he was no longer able to walk quick enough
to keep himself warm. He felt as though
sensation was quitting all his limbs.

The noon was past, and not a ray of sunshine had yet illumined the dreary tracts of
snow-clad country. Neither had it as yet
snowed; but now every moment the welkin
grew more leaden, and the wind whistled
along the scraggy hedge-rows with an ominous note. At length a few white specks
began to appear against the gathering gloom
of the sky, then Arthur felt something blow
velvety soft against his face, and before long
it began to snow in earnest. No house was
now within sight, and as he felt his feet sink
and clog in the fast deepening drifts, the
piercing wind seemed to the child to freeze
his very heart; cold despair had bound the
very source of tears, but, though he could
not cry, for a moment he wished that he were
back at the Rectory. Unable to toil a yard
further he staggered to the road-side, and
sunk down to rest.

He felt sleepy; not even the falling snow
was able to keep him awake; and he knew
that by degrees he fell into a reclining
posture. He did not do so purposely, it
seemed that he could not help it. And he
felt far from uncomfortable. The sensation
of deadening cold had departed, and a

pleasant warmth wrapped his limbs. In a few moments he seemed to dream. A dark object bent over him, and raised his cap from his face, and then it seemed as if he were raised to a great height by a force which he could not resist; but still his sensation of comfort was not disturbed. Then he seemed to be moving through the air, still over-shadowed by the dark object. Then, for a time, he ceased to dream, and dark weariness bound all his senses. But this passed as the dream renewed itself. Again the delightful enjoyment of warmth, but this time there seemed to be light as well, and a low sound, as of voices, grew upon his ear. The light grew more intense; he once more felt the ability to stir, and, rousing himself with an effort, found that it had not been all a dream. He was sitting in a large easy-chair, before him cracked and blazed an immense fire, and around him stood a group of people. One, an elderly woman, was chafing his hands, and behind her stood a man with a glass of something in his hand that steamed and smelt deliciously. The rest were children, staring at him in silence.

The woman spoke to him in a kindly voice, asking if he felt better, and, on his replying in the affirmative, began to question him as to the reason of his wandering alone on such a stormy evening. It appeared that her husband, coming home along the high road, had seen Arthur half asleep, half fainting, in the snow, had picked him up in his arms, and carried him to his house, which was not a quarter of a mile off.

In answer to their inquiries Arthur had but one reply : He was going to London. Had he friends in London? He said, yes. He made no attempt to explain his journey, maintaining stolid silence in answer to all other questions regarding it. And how did he intend getting to London? He didn't know; he was going to walk; but just now he felt so hungry.

They set some food before him, and by degrees he satisfied his hunger. Then, when he had eaten and drank enough, the woman, after a brief discussion apart with her husband, bade him follow her upstairs. Here he was helped to take his clothes off, and was put to bed.

He slept all night without a dream. When he awoke there were two children dressing in the room by the dim light which came through the small casement. Arthur could see that it was still snowing. Without speaking a word he jumped out of bed and commenced putting on his clothes, the other children all the time eyeing him curiously.

He descended the stairs, and found the husband and wife seated at breakfast before a large fire. The room was a large kitchen, the floor beautifully clean, the walls garnished with pewter and crockery, everything betokening order and comfort.

"Eh! Here's this poor child up already!" exclaimed the woman in surprise. "How do you feel this morning?"

Arthur replied that he felt hungry.

"Why, that's right!" exclaimed the man, in a hearty tone, laughing as he spoke. "There ain't so much amiss with a lad when he says he's hungry. Come and warm yourself, boy."

Arthur complied gladly, and in a few minutes was partaking of a hearty breakfast. When he had finished, the woman looked curiously at him for some minutes, and then said—

"And so you want to get to London, do you? You're a young un to be travelling about by yourself in weather like this, and I can't quite make you out. But if you've got friends in London and nowhere else, why to London you must go, that's the long and short of it. Do you know how far it is, lad?"

Arthur shook his head.

"Well, hard upon forty miles. Do you think you can walk that to-day?"

"I can try," replied the boy, simply.

The man and woman burst out laughing.

"Well, I can't make it out at all," said the former, once more. "But I hope there's nothing wrong. Now look—I'm going to

take you up to the railway station here, and
get you a ticket for London. If you once
get there, do you think you can find your
friends?"

The boy replied that he was sure he could.

"Very good. Then as soon as you're
ready we'll be off, for I haven't much time to
spare."

In the meantime the woman had cut
several mightily substantial sandwiches,
which she now wrapped in a piece of paper
and put into Arthur's hand, bidding him eat
them during the journey. The man having
encased himself in a huge overcoat, then took
Arthur by the hand and led him out of the
house. The boy had already been provided
by the kindly dame with a thick muffler
which belonged to one of her own children,
and thus he suffered less when he met the
morning wind. The woman and children
stood at the door watching him till he had
turned a corner and was out of sight.

The man was as good as his word. He
purchased a third-class ticket, which he bade
Arthur be careful not to lose; and, having
seen him safely seated in the train, which
steamed into the station thickly draped with
snow, he gave him a few coppers and hearty
wishes, and waved his hand to him as the
train moved quickly away. Truly he had
been a good Samaritan.

In a couple of hours Arthur once more

stood in London—confused by the rapid
events of the morning, hustled by the thick
crowd upon the platform, not knowing
where to turn or what to do. He made his
way into the open street. Here it was not
snowing, but evidently had been a very short
time ago, and the pavement was thick with
slush. The child's heart sank within him as
he stood close up to the wall to be out of the
way of the hurrying crowds, grasping in one
hand the remnant of his sandwiches, in the
other the few coppers that he had received as
a parting gift from his kindly host. Whither
should he now turn his steps ?

The hesitation and the fear were only for a
few moments. After all, he was in London, in
the midst of all the rush and roar with which
he was so familiar, which had gone on around
him ever since he could recollect. Compared
with the monotonous quiet of Bloomford this
was indeed home, and as the words rose to
his lips a flush of hope warmed his veins ; he
began to walk quickly along the sloppy
streets.

Once or twice he inquired his way—the
way to Whitecross Street; for it was to the
house where he had last of all lived that he
bent his steps—to the house and the room
where he had seen his father last. Of friends
to whom he could go and beg shelter he had
literally none. The landlady of his latest
abode was his only acquaintance.

About noon he reached Whitecross Street. Very foul did its hideous face peep forth from the covering of slush and grime and all unutterable abominations; but to Arthur it meant home, and he hailed its appearance. He reached the entrance of the court, he ran quickly to the house-door. There stood the landlady, in her hands a jug of beer, which she had just fetched for her dinner. She opened her eyes in astonishment.

"Eh, I'm damn'd if that 'ere kid ain't come back again! S'elp me God!"

"How do you do, Mrs. Blatherwick?" said Arthur, smiling.

"How do I do, young un? Why, what are *you* a doin' 'ere, I'd like to know?"

Arthur scarcely knew what to say. The coarse, unfriendly tone of the woman had checked the words he was about to utter, and he stood looking down in silence.

"Is our old room let yet, Mrs. Blatherwick?" he at length plucked up courage to ask.

"And what d'yer want to know for, eh?" replied the woman.

"Because, if it isn't," stammered the boy, "I wish you'd let me sleep there to-night. I haven't anywhere else to go to."

"Ain't got nowhere else to go to?" echoed Mrs. Blatherwick in surprise. "Why, I thought as you'd gone to live with the parson?"

"I—I've left him," said Arthur, timidly.

"Oh, you've left him, 'ev yer? Then yer may jist go an' get a lodgin' of them as'll give it yer."

She was on the point of turning away into the house when a sudden thought appeared to strike her, and she stopped.

"How much money have yer got in yer pockets, eh?" she asked, her vicious-looking eyes sparkling the while.

"I've got fourpence," replied Arthur, showing the coppers. "Will you let me have a night's lodging for fourpence, Mrs. Blatherwick?"

The landlady reflected a moment, and the result seemed favourable.

"Come in with yer," she said. "Yer don't expect to 'ave no dinner, do yer?"

"I've got all I want," replied Arthur, showing his sandwiches.

"Come along, then," snarled the woman. "Don't keep me standin' 'ere all day."

And she preceded him into the house, taking a draught out of the jug as she went.

CHAPTER V.

ARTHUR followed Mrs. Blatherwick down dark and damp stairs into a cellar-kitchen, where the principal light was that emitted by a large fire. On the fire was a frying-pan, in which was at that moment hissing and spluttering a goodly beef-steak, the odour of which filled the kitchen and made poor Arthur's mouth water. Otherwise it was a vile place, reeking with moisture, foul with indescribable filth, the ceiling black with the smoke of hundreds of fires, the floor marked here and there with the corpse of a crushed black-beetle. On a wooden table, drawn up to the fire, stood the preparations for the good lady's mid-day meal, and to that, having discovered that the steak was just done, Mrs. Blatherwick accordingly addressed herself. Arthur sat on a broken chair, meanwhile, eyeing the woman with hungry eyes, and doing his best to satisfy his own stomach with the scraps of dry bread and meat which remained to him.

Whilst she was in the midst of her meal a step was heard descending the stairs, a heavy, reeling, uncertain step. A moment after a man entered. He looked about twenty-two or twenty-three. His face was that of a hopeless sot, a flabby, meaningless, bestial face, which only on occasions was enlivened by a twinkle of evil in one of the dull, fishy eyes. He was very tall, and his body seemed to be insecurely jointed; when he staggered across the kitchen and dropped himself into a chair, it seemed as though the shock would dislocate his limbs. Arthur knew this individual; it was Mrs. Blatherwick's eldest son, by name Bill.

Bill was not at present more drunk than usual, though a casual observer would certainly have concluded that he had been indulging past his wont. He had so soaked himself with brutalising liquors ever since he had been able to raise a can to his mouth, that the present state of bodily laxity and mental obfuscation was normal to him. As he sat gazing with half-opened eyes at Arthur, apparently not quite able to recall his identity, his mother commenced to abuse him on the score of his idleness and drunkenness.

A conversation ensued which I shall not endeavour to repeat, under fear of being stigmatised as a "realist" by the critical world.

Arthur took no special heed of it. Alas! his ears were but too well accustomed to sounds such as these. He was, moreover, so weary with his journey that, under the influence of the fire, he sank to sleep in his chair.

When he awoke daylight had long since passed away. The fire blazed more cheerfully than ever, and, with the assistance of a tallow dip standing on the table, effectually lighted up the room. Bill Blatherwick had disappeared, most probably had long since assumed his wonted corner in the " Rose and Crown ; " but his mother was at present busy in preparing a cup of tea.

" Are y' 'ungry ?" she snarled at Arthur, as soon as his moving proclaimed him awake.

He replied in the affirmative, and received a hunch of very stale bread.

" If ye're thirsty, there's the tap," added the woman, pointing to a foul corner of the kitchen, where at intervals spots of water dripped from a tap on to a stone slab.

Arthur walked to it, held his hands cup-like, to receive the water, and quenched his thirst.

In the meantime Mrs. Blatherwick poured out for herself a cup of strong tea, and assumed a seat in the full glow of the fire.

" Well, young un," she began sharply, after a few minutes' thought, " what are you come back 'ere for, eh ?"

The suddenness and fierce tone of the question seemed all at once to bring, for the first time, the full sense of his position before the child's mind. Casting a glance of helpless pleading, first at the woman, then round the bare walls of the cellar, he suddenly burst into tears.

"Where have they buried my father?" he sobbed out, after giving full vent for a minute to the distress which overmastered him. "Will you please to tell me, Mrs. Blatherwick?"

"How the devil should I know?" replied the woman, with a croaking laugh. "Is that all ye're 'ere for—to arst questens like that?"

There was silence for a moment; then Mrs. Blatherwick resumed.

"Where 'ev yer been livin'?"

"I—I don't know," sobbed Arthur.

"Well, how did yer get back 'ere? Yer know that, I s'pose?"

The boy recounted his adventures between Bloomford and London. As he concluded, Mrs. Blatherwick shrugged her shoulders.

"Well," she said, "if ye stay 'ere to-night yer'll 'ev to pay, as I s'pose yer know."

Arthur thrust his hand eagerly into his pocket and drew out the few coppers his unknown friend had given him.

Mrs. Blatherwick appropriated them without hesitation.

"An' what are yer goin' to do for a livin', eh?" she then asked.

"I'm sure I don't know," replied Arthur, still sobbing. "Could you help me to find something, Mrs. Blatherwick?"

"Maybe I could," said the woman. "I've got somethink i' my 'ead, but I doubt it's too good for yer."

"Do you think so, Mrs. Blatherwick? What is it?"

"No, no; it's too good for yer."

"Please tell me what it is, Mrs. Blatherwick. I'd try my best."

"Yer would, eh?"

"I'm sure I would."

"What d'yer say, then, to go round singin' with Bill? Now didn't I say as it was too good for yer? Yer couldn't sing well enough, could yer, now?"

"I—I'd try my best, Mrs. Blatherwick," stammered Arthur. "I think I could if someone told me how."

"Yer do, eh?"

"Yes, Mrs. Blatherwick. Might I live here if I did that?"

"I don't know but yer might, if ye did well."

"In father's room, Mrs. Blatherwick?" asked the boy, eagerly.

"P'r'aps."

"Oh, I'm sure I could do it, if only some-one would show me how," cried Arthur, drawing his chair nearer to the woman.

"Then I'll learn yer," replied Mrs. Blatherwick, taking a draught of her tea. "I'll say the words first, an' then you say

'em arfter; an' when yer know the words,
I'll learn yer the tune."

The lesson began. It was a somewhat
singular picture, that of the old hag on one
side of the fire, her repulsive features lit up
by its blaze, her hand beating time upon her
knee, as she recited the words in a sing-song
tone which showed clearly that she had no
understanding of their meaning; opposite to
her the handsome-faced boy, neatly dressed,
with his light hair waving over his temples
and shining like gold in the blaze from the
grate, his lips parted in his eagerness to learn
the words of the song—or, as it seemed,
hymn—and his blue eyes still glistening with
the moisture of recent tears. The words
recited were these :—

> Behold the lilies of the field,
>   They toil not, neither spin,
> But yet our Father gives to them
>   The raiment they stand in.
>
> Behold the little birds in air,
>   They care not for the morrow,
> And yet our Heavenly Father sees
>   They have no need to borrow.
>
> So we will trust to God above,
>   For we are better far
> Than lilies and than sparrows both;
>   For His children we are.

Arthur's quick memory had soon caught
up the rhythm of these beautiful lines,
greatly to Mrs. Blatherwick's astonishment;
whereupon the latter proceeded to chant them
to their appropriate melody, bidding Arthur

pay good heed and learn the air. The air was lugubrious in the extreme, just fitted for being sung by a sturdy mendicant of the streets, and it lost nothing in effect when rendered by the now croaking, now whining, now snarling falsetto of Mrs. Blatherwick. So she began:—

> Be—'old—thee—lee—lees—hof—thee—field,
> They—tile—not—nei—ther—spin;

and at the end of each verse Arthur took up the strain and did his best to imitate the whining nasality which his instructress exhibited in such perfection. It was not to be expected that he should all at once reach the summits of his new art, but he did so far well as to earn Mrs. Blatherwick's approbation. By about nine o'clock he had thoroughly learnt both words and air. Accordingly his landlady gave him leave to ascend to the garret in which he had formerly lived with his father, and there to remain for the rest of the night.

This room had not been occupied since poor Golding had left it in his coffin, and now contained neither more nor less furniture than on the night of his death. Somehow or other the pieces of brown paper supplying the places of the broken panes of glass had got torn off, and the wind blew into the room with chilling breath. Despite all this discomfort, poor Arthur heaved a sigh of relief

as he entered the door. Having done his best
to make it fast behind him, by drawing with
difficulty a very rusty bolt, he ran with a low
cry to the corner in which his father had
lain when last he saw him, and flinging himself on the spot, wept aloud in the bitterness
of his heart. Outside it was raining hard,
and each fierce gust of wind swept large drops
through the gaps in the windows, making the
floor quite wet. The room would have been
perfectly dark, save for a slight gleam which
shone from a window directly opposite, where
there was no blind to conceal the bright fire
and the oil lamp by which two women were
sitting at their needles. The child did not
notice the darkness; it was nothing to him,
for the terrible gloom within his heart would
have made the lightest chamber seem black
as midnight. For half an hour he lay upon
the floor, a prey to anguish such as few grown
men are capable of experiencing.

He was roused from a species of lethargy
at length by the sound of ten o'clock pealing
from a church hard by. Feeling tired, he
took off his coat, rolled it up to form a pillow,
and lay down with the intention of sleeping.
But it was long before he succeeded in attaining that happy oblivion. The noises outside
attracted his attention irresistibly; he endeavoured to separate the different elements
out of the mingled sounds which made themselves heard amid the wind and rain.

Presently the latter ceased, and surprised by a ray of strange light which suddenly streamed through the window and made a large white square upon the floor, he looked up and saw that the full moon was struggling for life amid surging billows of clouds. Shortly ensued noises in the room below his; there were angry voices, followed by blows and the smashing of crockery. It was nothing new, he was aware of the quarrelsome habits of the people underneath. Then the court grew suddenly lively with a gathering of children, who had eagerly escaped from the houses on the cessation of the rain. No matter that it was drawing on towards midnight, there were the voices of children four or five years old, screaming and calling as if it were noonday; for the wholesome division of time made for the children of the rich is all unknown to these nurselings of Whitecross Street. They seemed at length to be joining in a game, which consisted partly in going round and round in a circle, chanting a song the while. Arthur knew the game and the song well enough; the latter began with the words :—

There is a happy land, far, far away;

and as he listened to the shrill chorus of young voices he found himself unconsciously joining with them. And so at length, blending the words of this song with those of the

hymn which Mrs. Blatherwick had just
taught him, he was overcome with weariness
and fell asleep.

It wanted three days to Christmas; accordingly no time was to be lost in making
the most of that spasmodic spirit of charity
which appears to possess certain people at
this period of the year. Mrs. Blatherwick
roused Arthur from his slumbers about seven
the next morning, and bade him get up
quickly. He was not, however, to continue
to wear the clothes in which Mr. Norman
had clad him; instead of these the landlady
made him assume a pair of trousers and a
coat so ragged and filthy that they would
scarcely hold together, and were absolutely
no protection against the cold. The other
clothes Mrs. Blatherwick took away with
her; doubtless she had an object in so doing.

Though roused so early it was not till
shortly after nine o'clock that Bill Blatherwick issued forth upon his day's work, accompanied by the shivering and wretched
child. Bill's scene of action lay for the most
part in the wealthier neighbourhood of the
West End, and the charitable persons who
ministered to his support were not in the
habit of rising with the lark. Arthur had
never as yet seen Bill in professional costume,
and the appearance of the latter slightly
surprised him. The mendicant wore his
ordinary garments, for it would have been

impossible to find worse, but over each eye he had tied a large green shade, the pair being not unlike the blinkers of horses, which signified that he had sustained the irreparable misfortune of loss of eyesight. He had, moreover, all at once become one-armed, the left being so skilfully disposed that nothing but a close examination could have shown that it was not in reality amputated. On his head was a chimney-pot hat, terribly battered, around which was wrapped a piece of white cardboard, bearing these words, half in written, half in printed, characters :—

"CHRISTIEN FRENDS!
Pray concider a widood Father
The victim of a Explogion
And may God bless you."

In his right hand he held a stick, and he directed Arthur to guide him by the empty sleeve on the other side. In this manner they issued out of Whitecross Street and proceeded westwards.

The morning was dry and cold, and before long large flakes of snow began to fall. Bill was rather glad of this than otherwise; it enhanced the pathos of the situation, and abundant were the coppers thrown down from windows for the relief of the blind widower and his motherless boy. Truly it was not without cause that the mendicant whined out his trust that in proportion as he

excelled in moral worth the lilies of the field
and the birds of the air, a kindly Providence
would take thought for his future sustenance.
It was a bad street indeed which did not
produce three pennies, and when it is taken
into consideration that Bill *did*, as a rule,
thirty streets a day, there will no longer be
wonder as to how he procured the means
of spending such pleasant evenings at the
" Rose and Crown." The severity of the
weather was nothing to him, for underneath
his miserable outward clothing he always
took care to have good warm shirts where-
with to ward off the onslaughts of the north-
east wind. But poor Arthur possessed no
such means of comfort, and the suffering he
underwent was indeed cruel. For all the
protection that his rags afforded him he
might as well have been naked, every blast
which swept along the white-lined streets
sent a shower of snow-flakes through the
interstices of his garments on to his very skin.
The first hour of his torture sufficed to render
his hands and feet numb beyond perception
of pain, which was perhaps a blessing ; but
the other parts of his body were kept in
constant suffering from other sources than
the cold. For Bill, who was as rank a bully
and coward as ever sang hymns to procure
the wherewithal for a glass of gin, found a
constant source of amusement in secretly
torturing the poor boy. One moment he

would unexpectedly pinch his arm till his nails almost met in the flesh; or, when he thought himself secure from observation, he would deal him a severe blow with the stick he held in his hand, hissing terrific threats in his ear when a cry of pain burst from the sufferer's lips; or he would purposely tread with his heavy-soled boots upon the boy's almost bare feet; in short he was inexhaustible in the discovery of exquisite tortures, grinning with delight as he saw them take effect to the full extent of his wishes. When at noon he retreated into a miserable den in the regions of Holborn, where he was well known, and there partook of a very substantial meal, he took a fierce delight in eyeing from beneath his raised blinkers the hungry glances of the boy, who, with pinched lips and hollow cheeks, sat gazing with wolfish eagerness at the fare which he was forbidden to touch. When Bill had finished his meal, Arthur received a dry crust, which he seized upon thankfully, and gnawed as they once more took their way through the driving snow. He felt as though it would have relieved him to have cried, but the very source of tears seemed frozen within him.

With the falling night they turned their steps homewards, and another piece of dry bread, together with a steaming cup of what it pleased Mrs. Blatherwick to style coffee, formed Arthur's supper, after which he was bidden to betake himself once more to the garret, where he found a mattress and one or two old blankets—signs of his landlady's growing consideration. In the morning once more began his sufferings.

At length it was Christmas Eve,—an occasion celebrated in Whitecross Street just as much as in the homes of wealth and refinement. With dusk the revels began, and, till the hour of closing, the public-houses swarmed with men, women, and children doing their best to welcome with due rejoicing the birthday of Christianity. Far be it from me to emulate the skill of those numberless holy men who have exhausted their inventions in describing those regions which are to be the future home of no inconsiderable portion of the human race; but, had I a tithe of their descriptive power, O, what a hell could I depict in the Whitecross Street of this Christmas Eve! Out of the very depths of human depravity bubbled up the foulest miasmata which the rottenness of the human heart can breed, usurping the dominion of the pure air of heaven, stifling a whole city with their infernal reek.

The very curs that had followed their masters into the gin-palaces shrank out into the street again, affrighted by the brutal din. Here was a dense, surging crowd around the doors of such a house, surrounding two men who had been flung bodily forth by half a dozen policemen, and who now wallowed in the filth of the gutter, rending each other with tooth and nail, till one of them was carried off insensible or dead. Here rushed along the street a band of women, raving mad with drink and the passions it had aroused, rendering the gift of speech a hideous curse by the language they yelled aloud. Here were children, all but naked, wrangling and fighting for the possession of a jug of liquor which they had somehow procured. And, amid all, the shops and booths, ablaze with light, were doing the briskest trade of any day of the year. Here was poverty cheating poverty of its last pence ; here was garbage sold for meat and poison for bread ; from every hole and corner of the street and its foul allies peered vice and crime. Nay, as the newspapers will shortly tell us, even murder was not absent from this Christmas Eve. Walk here with me hand-in-hand, O cynic, thou who holdest that the roots of humanity spring from the seed of evil, walk here with me, and, if thou wilt, declare thy belief confirmed.

Christmas Eve! There are midnight services to-night in London churches, and voices are lifted up in hymn and praise, glorification of God that he has sent His Son to proclaim peace on earth and goodwill to men, to be the herald of a time when universal love shall rule the earth. In the great houses of the

West End—those from which rained the coppers which Bill Blatherwick was at present spending at the "Rose and Crown," the very heart of the hell I have described—in these houses there are Christmas trees tonight, and gaily-dressed children sport beneath the flash of the magnificent chandeliers, half mad with the enjoyment of the merriest night of the year. What if Bill Blatherwick himself, bestially drunk as he now is, were to be transported bodily into one of these mansions and then thrown down upon the carpet—a novel excitement for these Christmas guests! Would it strike any of them, with the terrific force of a God-sent revelation, that to them individually was due a share of the evil which has bred such an utterable abomination? Alas! Whitecross Street is very far off in that shocking East End which it is quite improper to think of, let alone visit, and there is but little possibility that its reek, powerful as it is, would pierce these stone walls and make itself felt above the perfumes which fill the dazzling chambers.

And in all this Arthur Golding bore his part. Mrs. Blatherwick, having got completely drunk long before dark, was quite extravagant in her benevolence to him. She even gave him the pot out of which she was drinking "four-half" from the nearest public-house, and bade him, with a curse, drink as much as he would. He did so, and, shortly after, finding himself unnoticed by the people who streamed in and out of the house, wandered into the streets and looked about him. He had no playmates here, and was perforce alone, for the boisterousness of the children terrified him, and an instinctive delicacy made him shrink from their rude games.

Intent upon the varied scenes surrounding him he wandered out of Whitecross Street into the larger streets beyond, pausing at each large shop he passed, and doing his best to imagine that the lights warmed him. The grocers' shops particularly attracted his attention, laid out in all the magnificence of Christmas provisions, and his eyes gloated over what seemed to him the priceless delicacies which flashed and glistened in the light of the gas-jets.

Before one shop in particular he stood a long while, gazing at a vast array of crystallised fruits which filled the window. He could imagine, though he had never tasted, the delicious sweetness of these fruits, and, all insensible to the fierce blasts which were cutting him to the very bone, he enjoyed in fancy such feasts as only the Prophet's faithful in Paradise would be capable of realising. Tearing himself from these delights he came to an eating-house, and here, instead of a sweet, enjoyed in fancy a savoury repast. The window was filled with large beef-steak pies, placed on perforated tin, from beneath which issued clouds of steam and kept the pies warm.   Now and again a brawny arm, bared to the elbow, would appear through the steam, and with a great knife, would pierce into one of these succulent delicacies, causing such streams of gravy to flow, and exposing to the view such luscious gobbets of fat, that a cry of envious pleasure broke from the child's hungry lips.

Not Schecabac at the Barmecide's table, not Sancho Panza, when Dr. Rizio seemed to bid fair to starve him in his island, ever suffered so from the tortures of stimulated but unsatisfied appetite as did poor little Arthur in front of these shops.   And when shortly after he came to one where a whole roast pig was exposed to view, dressed in such a manner as to suggest delights which only Charles Lamb could fitly celebrate, the ravenous boy felt he could have pounced upon it like a beast of prey and torn it limb from limb in the ferocity of his hunger.

He had strayed as far as the corner of Old Street and City Road, when his eye was caught by the glow of a little fire which marked the spot where a baked-potato man had his stand.   The man was doing a brisk trade just now, and Arthur was tempted to join the small group which stood around him and timidly held out his hands towards the warmth of the fire. This was grateful to his half-frozen limbs, but even more so was the delightful odour which exhaled as often as the man opened the little iron door and took out a potato to hand to a customer.

Oh, could he but afford a baked potato! He well knew the price of them was one half-penny, and yet they were as much out of his reach as if they had cost a pound. With greedy eyes he followed the man's every movement, saw him, as each customer advanced, draw out a brown-jacket, open it, and sprinkle on the inside salt and pepper. Then he watched the purchaser taking the first bite as he walked away, and was half persuaded to spring upon him like a young tiger and rend the food from his grasp.

Again and again he walked away, and as often returned. The potato-man had not been unobservant of his comings and goings; once or twice he had been on the point of bidding him be off, but he was not a hasty-tempered man, and something in the boy's face forbade harshness. At length, when no customer was by, and Arthur had been standing for several minutes warming him-self, the man suddenly inquired—

"What for you, my man?"

Arthur started and turned to hurry away, but the man called him back.

"Here, young un, don't look so scared.

Give us your 'arfpenny, an' 'ere's a big un for you."

Arthur stammered that he had not a half-penny.

"Ain't got a 'arfpenny? D'yer mean to say you've spent all your earnins' already?"

"They never give me anything to spend," replied the boy.

"Yer look 'ungry," said the man, after looking at him for a moment.

"I'm very hungry," was all that Arthur could reply.

"Hum! I thought as much. Maybe you could eat a tater?"

"That I could," said the hungry boy.

The man took out a large flowery potato and broke it open.

"D'yer like pepper, young un?"

"Yes, please."

"And salt?—of course you does. 'Ere goes. Now let's see if yer know how to eat."

Arthur seized the potato with almost savage eagerness, and devoured it, steaming hot as it was. He was then going off, after thanking his friend, but the latter put another potato in his hands and bade him eat it on his way home. He seemed to have a certain pleasure in the boy's look of gratitude.

"Well, well, it's Christmas Eve," he muttered to himself as he watched Arthur walk away;

"and a penny ain't so much arter all. Poor little devil!"

And if every man in London had been as judiciously charitable that night as was the baked-potato man, the Christmas Day which followed would have been rich with a blossoming of unwonted happiness.

CHAPTER VI.

FAIN would Arthur have visited the friendly corner again on the following night, but delicacy withheld him—that fine element of his nature which differentiated him from the ordinary street Arab. It being Christmas Day, Mrs. Blatherwick had exerted herself to induce her hopeful son to make the most of the propitious season; but she soon became aware that the jovialities of the previous evening had rendered Bill absolutely incapable of standing upright, to say nothing of melodiously declaring his trust in Providence in the wonted manner. So she very reluctantly allowed him to remain all day in his comatose condition, and revenged herself by setting Arthur to perform, for several hours, some of the hardest and most menial labour her ingenuity could suggest.

But at night the boy became once more free, and again wandered about the streets. About nine o'clock he watched, from afar off, the baked-potato man wheel up his oven and settle down at the wonted corner, but he approached no nearer.

During the next few days Bill Blatherwick

once more resumed his professional duties, and from morning to night Arthur guided his blind and maimed parent along the snowbound streets, suffering the extremes of cold and hunger, as well as all the tortures which the brutal ingenuity of his master could conceive, and singing a hundred times a day the hymn about the lilies of the field and the birds of the air.

Very frequently a passer-by would turn to look at his pale and wan features, admiring the beauty of their outlines, and the thick golden hair which fell almost to his shoulders and was apparent through the rents of his cap.

Bill soon learned the value of the boy's personal appearance; he had gained twice as much money daily since Arthur had been with him than he had previously been accustomed to. Yet he seemed every day to grow more malicious towards him, taking a keener delight in making him endure hunger and thirst, at times almost laming him with savage kicks or blows, and always threatening the most terrific penalties if ever he should complain of the treatment he received.

Arthur's nature was long-suffering, but not unconscious of resentment, and at length Bill perpetrated on him a piece of cruelty which roused all the indignation lurking in his child's heart, and for the moment revealed an intensity of passion in his character which had never before made itself known.

Bill was partaking of a glass of his favourite beverage in a public-house one noon and had left Arthur standing outside. The boy was tortured with a terrible thirst, of which he had not dared to complain to Bill; but now that the latter's back was turned he seized the opportunity, and bent to drink the puddly water of a horse-trough which stood at the edge of the pavement. He was in the midst of a long draught when a hand suddenly descended on the back of his neck, and, before he was aware, plunged him overhead in the trough. The street was a small one, and Bill had taken advantage of its loneliness to indulge himself in a congenial amusement.

But he had driven his jocosity too far. Starting to his feet, the boy turned and sprang like a young leopard upon his persecutor; sprang at his head, clutched him round the neck, and fixed with his teeth fiercely in the bully's cheek, whilst with his feet he belaboured the mendicant's lower extremities.

Bill roared like a bull, thus drawing forth several men from the public-house, who laughed heartily, and began to make bets on the event of the struggle. It was, of course, too uneven for the result to be long doubtful. For a moment Arthur's madness gave him an energy which repelled all the man's efforts to free himself; he ground his teeth deep into the flesh with the ferocity of a wild beast.

But in a few minutes Bill shook him off with a desperate effort, dashed him on the ground, trod upon him with his heavy clogs, and began to beat him about the head with his stick, when the men from the public-house interfered and stayed his hand. It was then found that the boy had fainted. He was carried into the house, and Bill followed him.

Whilst Arthur was being attended to by a compassionate barmaid, the mendicant bound up the wound in his cheek as well as he could, sticking-plaster having been forthcoming (for a due consideration) from the landlord. It did not appear very serious; Bill was in the habit of receiving far worse damage than this in his nightly brawls. But the exhaustion of the affair had naturally resulted in thirst, and Bill was easily persuaded by the other men present to resume his previous seat and call for a copious joram of the " same as before."

Arthur, on recovering, was accommodated with a seat between his master and the wall, where he sat with his eyes closed and his face deadly pale, the constant object of Bill's ominous observation.

So productive of amusing conversation was the little episode that the shades of the De-

cember night had already begun to darken
upon the City before Bill could prevail upon
himself to leave his place and bid Arthur
precede him into the street. The mendicant's
walk was not quite so steady as it might have
been, and there was a curious look in his
bloodshot eyes when he regarded his little
companion, which suggested the possibility of
drink having made his usually malicious
nature absolutely dangerous.

It was against Bill's ordinary habits to
partake of liquor in the daytime; the practice
was, to say the least of it, destructive to the
interests of his profession. When he once
began to drink it was extremely difficult for
him to abstain till he had reached the state
of insensibility, and such proved the case on
the present occasion.

On leaving the public-house he had promised himself that he would avoid entering
another till he had reached home and taken
measures for the suitable punishment of his
assailant. But he had already taken too
much to allow of his adhering to a resolution.

They were threading the neighbourhood of
Saffron Hill on their way citywards (Bill
always preferred these backways to the more
open thoroughfares), when he was hailed by
a "pal" from the doorway of a dram-shop,
and, wholly unable to resist the temptation,
he dragged Arthur along after him (when he
reached these localities he always threw

aside the various items of his disguse) and entered.

More than an hour was spent here, and before he departed Bill was completely drunk. He told the story of the attack made upon him, and amused himself and his companions by occasionally administering severe blows to Arthur either with his stick or his fist.

The boy's blood boiled within him, but he remained silent and motionless. When at length they once more issued into the street Bill staggered along in the darkness, supporting himself on the boy's shoulder, shouting out curses with what voice he had left, and perpetually slipping over the ice and snow, which the bitter frost-wind bound harder every moment on the narrow paths. They lost their way, for Arthur was totally strange in the neighbourhood, and Bill was quite incapable of guiding himself.

When at length they turned into an alley darker than any yet, the passion brooding in Arthur's breast rose lightning-like to his brain in the form of a fierce thought. Glancing around, he saw at once that not a soul was near. It needed but a slight push—a weaker hand than Arthur's would have sufficed—and the sot reeled and fell heavily to the ground.

Acting in pursuance of instinct rather than upon deliberate reflection, the boy groped for the leather bag which held the day's harvest

of coppers, wrenched it in a moment off the
drunkard's neck, and bounded away through
the darkness.

Not for a moment did he look back, but
pursued his breathless course along streets
he had no knowledge of, turning out of one
into another from a blind impulse which bade
him thus avoid pursuit. He fancied he could
hear Bill's voice yelling after him; once or
twice he seemed to hear rapid footsteps close
upon his heels; but he never turned to look
round. He did not stop in his headlong course
till, slipping on the ice, he fell violently, and
lay almost senseless on the pavement.

After a few moments he crept into a doorway, and there lay panting. With this one
great effort of escaping his strength seemed
to have deserted him; he felt unable to
rise to his feet. He was not cold now, he
did not feel hungry; all his body seemed
consumed with a terrific thirst. On looking
round him he saw the flaring front of a
public-house at a few yards' distance, and a
longing for drink—drink warm and sweet,
like that they had given him when he recovered from his fainting fit—came irresistibly upon him.

With trembling hands he hid the wallet as
well as he could under his rags, having first
taken out a few coppers, which he held
clenched in his fist. After one or two efforts
he succeeded in staggering to his feet, crossed

the road, and, hesitating but for a moment, pushed open the door of the public-house and entered the bar. Pressing through a crowd of drinkers, he succeeded in giving an order which he had often heard Bill give, and was quickly supplied with a smoking tumbler.

The men around him looked at the slight, childish form, and began to laugh and joke. One of them, who seemed good-tempered in his cups, lifted the boy on to his knee and played with his fine hair, whilst another proposed to "stand" him another glass. Arthur wished for nothing better. His tongue was now loosened, and his native timidity had given place to a boldness which shrank from nothing. He drank the second glass, and after that a third, then offered to pay for glasses round to the group of men who were amusing themselves with him. This nearly exhausted his stock of coppers. Then he sang, he danced, he shouted; and at length, though quite unconscious of how or why it came about, he felt a heavy grasp on his shoulder, and the next moment found himself lying on the pavement in the open air.

For a moment the recollection of Bill Blatherwick flashed upon his mind, and, starting to his feet, he endeavoured to run. Again and again he fell his whole length, the last time he did so, feeling something warm on his face, which he tried to wipe off with his hand, and became half conscious that it was blood.

Then a long period seemed to pass, in which he was conscious of nothing; and after that he suddenly found himself standing by a small fire, with someone speaking to him. There was a pleasant smell in the air, too, and at length he recognised his friend the baked-potato man.

"An' what a' you been a doin' of, eh ?" asked the man, eyeing Arthur suspiciously. "Come, you get orff 'ome, d'ye 'ear ?"

The child endeavoured to reply in a long, stammering account of his sufferings, of the cruelties he had received at the hands of the Blatherwicks, of many other things that were nothing at all to the purpose, talking all the time as if in a dream, and once on the point of falling into the red-hot grate, had not the man held him up. Then again he became quite unconscious of everything, and so he remained for many hours.

When he once more came to his senses it was about nine o'clock on New Year's morning. He was lying on a straw mattress, well covered up with warm clothes, in a little room directly under the rafters of the house.

It was a fine morning, and the sun, though with but little warmth in its beams, threw a cheerful light on a prospect of chimneys and slated roofs. Arthur looked around him in surprise and fright, for the room was quite strange to him. He rose with difficulty to his feet, and, as the sunlight met his eyes, staggered back as if suddenly smitten on the head. His senses reeled; his mouth and throat were so parched that he could scarcely fetch his breath; he felt so utterly, miserably ill that, falling back upon his bed again, he began to moan and cry in the extremity of his suffering.

There was another bed in the room which had evidently been occupied during the night, but beyond this there was no furniture. Outside the window, however, were hung two or three bird-cages containing canaries, which so far enjoyed the sunshine as to be doing their best to sing a little, despite the sharp morning air which ruffled their yellow plumage and made them keep continually hopping about for the sake of warmth. A stronger *roulade* than usual from one of them had succeeded at length in attracting his attention, when the door suddenly opened, and a man entered, whom he at once recognised as his friend of the baked-potatoes.

"Well, young un, how goes it?" shouted the man in a cheerful voice.

"I feel very bad," groaned Arthur, in reply. "Where have I got to, sir? This isn't Mrs. Blatherwick's, is it?"

The other having reassured him on this point, Arthur was persuaded to dress, an operation which, as may be imagined, did not, in his case, require any great length of time. His friend then conducted him out of the room, and down several flights of dark and creaking stairs, till he found himself in a small parlour, very comfortably furnished, where a bright fire was burning, and the table was covered with preparations for breakfast. Two or three little children were running in and out of the room, all dressed in that humble sort of finery which even the poorest can procure at the cost of a few pence expended in various coloured ribbons, and all evidently in a delighted state of mind highly befitting the morning of a New Year.

At the table sat the father of the family, waited upon by a very young and sickly-looking woman, whom it was hard to believe to be the mother of the boisterous children, though such was the fact. He was a short but broad-shouldered man, with an extremely red face, which would have borne a highly comic expression, had not the absence of one eye given it a touch of repulsiveness. As it was, his countenance was decidedly grotesque, and, as he ate, which he did voraciously, he twisted it into such a variety of extraordinary shapes that, had it not been for the absence of spectators, one would have believed he was doing it to excite amusement. We may as well state at once that his name was Michael Rumball.

The nature of Mr. Rumball's business was pretty clearly indicated by the objects surrounding him. All round the parlour walls were suspended bird-cages, mostly occupied; some large and evidently used for the purposes of breeding, others only containing a single singing-bird. The room had two doors, one that by which Arthur and his guide had entered, the other looking into the shop, which a glance showed to be filled with all manner of live-stock, not birds alone, but rabbits, hares, guinea-pigs and many other species dear to amateur naturalists. For the locality was Little St. Andrew Street, and Mr. Rumball's shop was one of many similar for which the neighbourhood is noted. The situation of the parlour, just in the rear of such a miscellaneous collection, certainly had its disadvantages, among them the constant impregnation of the atmosphere with a most potent and peculiar odour; but probably in this matter, as in all others, habit became a second nature, and nobody seemed at all offended by the scents.

"Well, Mike," exclaimed the baked-potato man, as he drew the boy in by the shoulders and thrust him, with a rough sort of kindness, into a chair, "'ere's the young shaver as I carried 'ome last night. And pretty down in the mouth he do look! Cheer up, young 'un!"

The baked-potato man, who rejoiced in the

name of Ned Quirk, spoke in a hearty and jovial voice, though the tones were terribly husky. The huskiness was not, as is so often the case, the result of drink, for Ned was a strictly temperate man, but was simply the result of his trade; for, whilst turning an honest penny by his potatoes at night, he exercised during the day the business of a costermonger, hawking vegetables and the like about the streets and thundering out the qualities and prices of his wares in tones which had but few rivals, even among the coster fraternity. To the same cause was due a peculiar twist in his mouth, which gave to his face a curious expression. This slight deformity is no uncommon thing amongst men of his trade, and results from the habit of constant shouting.

" Can you eat a bit?" continued Ned, eyeing the boy with kindly compassion.

" I'm not hungry," replied Arthur, turning away from the food. " My head's so bad."

"Ah!" interposed Mike Rumball, in a cracked voice, with one of his drollest facial twists, " you've been a departin' from the ways of right'ousness, an' a sittin' in the seat of the scornful, young un. Come now, hain't you?"

" Now don't go on with the boy, Mike, there's a good fellow," said Mrs. Rumball, whose maternal heart was touched with pity at Arthur's sad plight. " I always will say as Ned Quirk is a good-'arted fellow, an' it was like him to bring the boy along with him. What's yer name, my poor boy?"

"Arthur Golding," replied the boy, continuing to stare in the utmost surprise at all around him.

"Well now, Arthur, you'll drink a cup o' tea, and may be you'll feel better for it. There now."

Arthur drank the grateful fluid, and after a few minutes certainly did begin to feel better. In the meanwhile the three children had gathered round him, and were watching him curiously as he swallowed the last drop out of the half-pint mug.

"Run out into the street, all o' you!" cried Mrs. Rumball. "Play there till Mr. Quirk's ready for you. He won't be so long I dare say."

"Not two minutes, young 'uns," cried Ned Quirk. "An' now," he added, turning to Arthur, "dy yer think as you can find yer way 'ome, my lad?"

"I—I have no real home, sir," stammered Arthur, terrified at the idea of being taken back to Mrs. Blatherwick's.

"How's that?" broke in Mike. "Foxes has 'oles, an' the birds o' the air has nests, yer know—leastwise most on 'em—an' I can't b'lieve as you're a hexception to the rule."

Then Arthur took courage and repeated in more connected language what he had already

told Ned Quirk half unconsciously on the
preceding night, relating all the sufferings he
had undergone at the hands of the Blatherwicks, but carefully abstaining from giving
precise information as to those amiable
persons' whereabouts, and remaining equally
silent on the subject of his brief stay with
Mr. Norman.

"It's a 'ard case," said Ned Quirk, reflectively, and he drew on a very big overcoat. "What can we do with the lad,
Mike?"

"Well, yer know, Ned, charity covers a
multitude o' sins. Maybe we could find him
a job. How old are you, young un?"

"Nearly nine, sir."

"Hum! Old enough to be gettin' yer
livin', my lad."

"I tell you what, Mike," said Ned Quirk,
"I mustn't keep these 'ere young uns o'
yourn waitin'; they'll tear me to pieces else.
You keep Arthur 'ere till I come back, an'
that's about four this arternoon, if the
weather 'olds up. Then we'll talk the matter
over. Don't be afear'd to give him somethin' to eat; I'll stand to that, old boy."

The explanation of Ned Quirk's hurry was
this. In his quality of itinerary tradesman
he was possessed of a small cart and a
smaller donkey, both of which he was in the
habit of utilising on special occasions for the
purpose of small pleasure-trips, being most

frequently accompanied in the same by the three children of his friend, Michael Rumball. Now, to-day, being at one and the same time Sunday and New Year's Day, and the weather being unusually propitious for the time of year, an excursion extraordinary had been planned to no less a distance than Hampstead Heath, with the purpose, as we have heard, of lasting the whole day. The diminutive but well-fed and sprightly-looking donkey had already been standing harnessed at the door for nearly a quarter of an hour, and was evidently growing impatient to show his holiday mettle. So as soon as Ned had wrapped himself in his great coat—which, bye-the-by, had been so often and so variously patched as almost to resemble the coat of many colours worn by Joseph of old—he was dragged to the door by the noisy youngsters, and followed thither at a more leisurely pace by Mr. and Mrs. Rumball. In a minute the children had climbed into the two-wheeled vehicle, ensconcing themselves in the receptacles appropriated on week-days to potatoes, herrings, &c., and now sat hallooing their delight to a whole crowd of dirty-faced little ragamuffins who stood around with envious looks, though the eldest of them did not hesitate to make sarcastic remarks on the general appearance of the turn-out. Ned Quirk was not behindhand, but sprang to his wonted seat in front, rested his legs wide apart on the shafts, grasped the rope-reins, twitched the donkey's ears with a stick of holly, and away they went at a sharp pace, pursued to the end of the street by a swarm of yelling tatterdemalions.

Michael Rumball (who, bye-the-by, had been in his youth a shining light among the Ranter fraternity, and had often uplifted his voice at the street corners, or amid the sanctified enthusiasm of camp-meetings,) reflected much during the day, taking counsel at times with his wife. The result of it all he expressed the same evening, when, Ned Quirk having returned and the children having been sent to bed, the two friends sat over their pipes, with Arthur between them.

" You see, young un," began Mr. Rumball, " we don't want for to turn you out o' doors, 'specially in winter time when the nights is cold; but you see we ain't great nobs as 'as got their ten thousand a year, so no more we can't be expected to keep you in lux'ry, you see. An' then I'm not by any means sewer as it 'ud be a good thing for you if we could; I myself believe in workin' for one's livin', it comes sweeter like. You remember the hymn:

> How doth the little busy bee,
> Improve each shinin' hower ?

Well, that's always been my motto, you see, young un; at least sin' I left off certain practices, as Mrs. Rumball wouldn't thank me for referrin' tew. Then there's that other passage, as no doubt you knows very well, about what I did when I was a child, and 'ow I come to alter my ways when I grow'd to be a man ; and as you're growin' to be a man, you see, it's time you bore that passage in mind. Well, the long an' short of it all is, that Ned Quirk and me, we thinks we see our way to put you into the line of a honest livin' ; and as you seem to a' been 'itherto in rayther queerish 'ands, maybe you won't be sorry to hear it. Now, if we do this for you, I've one thing to ask. Will you hengage to give my missus there all you earn every night, or every Saturday night, as may be, an' trust to us to find you bed an' board ? Is it a fair bargain ? "

" Yes, sir, thank you," replied Arthur, overjoyed in his heart to think he had found such good friends.

" Well, then, we won't say any more about it—but shake hands. There, Ned Quirk, I hain't made so long a speech not sin' I called upon the Almighty in public prayer for two hours and a half, by Aldgate Pump, some two-an'-twenty years gone by."

Ned nodded approval, and the counsel shortly broke up. Arthur went to the truckle bed he had occupied on the previous night with a lighter heart than he had perhaps ever known. But before he went to sleep his thoughts wandered, as was their wont, to that garret in Whitecross Street and the face he had seen there for the last time, still and cold, and he sobbed himself into forgetfulness.

On the morrow begun the work-a-day New Year, and with it Arthur's first real entrance upon the business of life. Two doors off Mike Rumball's shop was a small greengrocer's, where not only vegetables and coals were sold, but also cat's meat, the sale of the latter generally constituting so important a business as alone to suffice for the energies of one tradesman. But the energies of Mrs. Hannah Clinkscales were not to be gauged by the ordinary standards.

She was a notable woman who had, like Dogberry, "had losses," and to whom the sole result of three marriages remained in the shape of her little daughter, Lizzie; to this child her mother was devoted heart and soul. No toil was too severe to undertake, no pinching too much to suffer, no meanness too low to practise, inasmuch as the one end of them all, that which hallowed the means, was the future happiness of Lizzie.

Mrs. Clinkscales happened to be in want of a lad, to assist her in the shop. The daughter, Lizzie, though nearly eleven years old, was never allowed to do anything resembling menial work. She kept the books, and did it, too, in a very beautiful little hand which was her mother's envy and delight, but below this she could not be allowed to descend. When Mike Rumball first offered

Arthur's services Mrs. Clinkscales was doubtful. The lad was incapable of carrying half
a hundred of coals, that was clear, and he had
no experience whatever in weighing out
goods or cutting up cat's-meat; but after a
little persuasive conversation on Mike's part,
an arrangement was somehow come to and
Arthur was to be engaged. His duties were
numerous. In the morning he went round a
large circle of customers carrying a cat's-
meat basket on his arm, and, that accomplished, he weighed out coals, occasionally
made a sale, kept the shop clean, chopped up
old wood to sell by the pound, and perpetually ran errands; so that the day was
amply filled up, and his weekly remuneration
was, to begin with, five shillings—payment
which Mrs. Clinkscales always spoke of on
Saturday night as "extravagant to a degree."

In those days there were no school-
boards, and impertinencies, such as the arts
of reading and writing, the uselessness, nay,
the deleteriousness, of which cannot but be
patent to all admirers of the good old times,
including all those individuals who—not without reason—dread the growth of democratic
principles among the poor; these arts were
far from interfering with Arthur's honest
diligence. He had not remained long enough
under the tutorship of Mr. Orlando Whiffle to
greatly benefit thereby, and, though he had
at first made promising progress with his

letters, the reading of words of one syllable and the designing of very questionable pothooks had been the most that it had been his privilege to attain. And now in a very short time the pressure of new occupations had driven even that little out of his head. But the few weeks of his abode at Bloomford Rectory had not been unimportant in the boy's life. The recollection of those days long continued to linger in his memory, as a sweet scent will sometimes cling to a handkerchief which has grown old and been made to serve ignoble uses. So short had been the period, and so severe the sufferings which had suddenly succeeded upon it, that the memory was little more to him than that of a vision seen in sleep, but nevertheless, it was a delight. He had not enjoyed it at the time, for that he had been too distressed in mind ; he had not felt at home among those novel scenes; but now, when they at times recurred to him, they brought with them a sense of beauty and peace, of the joys belonging to a higher existence, something which he could never have conceived of but for that experience, but which mingled a secret discontent, a half-felt longing, with the menial toil of his present every-day life. He thought of Mr. Norman and his kind grave tone, and felt an emotion of gratitude well in his heart; he thought of little Helen Norman, and wished he could again walk hand-in-hand with her along the spacious lawn.

CHAPTER VII.

ASPIRATIONS.

BUT the intellect of a boy cannot feed on dreams, and Arthur Golding, though he continued extremely quiet and retiring in his habits, soon began to fill an appreciable place in the family groups to which he had been introduced. As he had to get up each day at half-past six, and very seldom got to bed before eleven o'clock, he did not see very much of the Rumball's, except at meals, and yet he continued to excite that kindly feeling in the members of the household which had first of all been aroused by his sad condition and interesting looks.

Ned Quirk regarded him indeed with almost paternal feelings, never failing to choose a stray moment of leisure to impart to him excellent advice, and from the first day holding himself responsible for the maintenance of his *protégé* in the item of wearing apparel. As Ned possessed, to use his own words, "neither chick nor child," this burden fell light upon him. He took a species of pride in seeing Arthur well dressed on Sunday, and indeed the boy looked remarkably well on such occasions, his handsome features and beautiful hair imparting a certain elegance to his appearance in spite of the humble character of his garments. Ned Quirk never made any remarks about him, at all events not in Arthur's hearing, but none the less it was plain that he watched his growth with great interest. Who could tell but the boy might one day attain to the dignity of a donkey-cart of his own, and cry out greens in a manner which even Ned might approve of?

Sunday indeed was a blissful day to Arthur, bringing him rest from toil and freedom to indulge in those curious day-dreams which he preferred much to other society, but which were very little compatible, at least in Mrs. Clinkscales' eyes, with the formation of sound business habits. On Sunday afternoon, when the children were playing in the street, and Mrs. Rumball had sat down for a nap, and Mike and Ned were dozing over their Sunday papers by the fire, Arthur took a delight in sitting alone in the darkened shop, watching by the light which streamed through the round holes in the shutters the movements of the birds in their cages, and the rabbits in their hutches.

There was a strange fascination for him in the voices and all the habits of these poor prisoners. At times he would whistle airs in a very low tone, enticing the birds to break out into song. There were one or two old parrots, which remained in the shop some time, with which he stood on extremely intimate terms ; they allowed him to scratch their heads, to put his finger in their beak unhurt, to stroke their feathers, and would learn a variety of peculiar sounds from his lips. And when one of them particularly pleased him by its cleverness he would laugh underneath his breath, for fear of attracting the attention of others, who would have spoilt his pleasure.

But before long he had a human friend in whose company he grew to take even greater delight than in that of the birds. This was Lizzie Clinkscales. Lizzie was strictly forbidden by her mother to enter the shop except with very good reason, and consequently it was nearly a month before Arthur had obtained more than a passing glimpse of the little girl, who once or twice walked out through the shop in all the dignity of her blue frock and velvet hat with a partridge's feather in it, to make some purchases for her mother, though it was her regular habit to adopt the more retired exit by the house-door in the alley just on the right hand of the shop. Lizzie grew by degrees accustomed to the sight of Arthur, and even appeared to take an interest in him. Every day she went to school somewhere in the neighbourhood of Leicester Square, and before long Arthur got into the habit of watching for her as she came back at twelve. Lizzie was a very pretty little girl, and the sight of her pleased Arthur ; once or twice he said to himself that she looked like Helen Norman, though in reality she was very different. As he stood in the doorway of the shop he could see her coming ever so far at the end of the street, for her blue dress made her conspicuous. Often she would be holding her slate up in one hand, making out a sum as she walked ; or else she would have her slate and her bag slung over one arm and be reading a lesson-book ; for Lizzie was pre-eminently indus-trious and made excellent use of the oppor-tunities her hard-working mother gave her. If Arthur happened to be away on an errand at such times he would fret and feel annoyed, often running back at a breakneck speed to be in time for the child's return.

One evening Mrs. Clinkscales had gone out and had left Arthur in sole charge of the business. The boy was sitting in the back of the shop, as far away from the noise and lights of the street as possible, indulging in one of his favourite reveries, when he was aroused by a light step behind him, and, jumping to his feet for fear of being caught thus by his mistress, found that it was Lizzie who had stolen upon him. She had her slate in her hand and came up holding it out to Arthur, who stood in abashed wonder.

" Can you do Rule of Three ? " she asked,

speaking in a frank, pretty voice, not unmingled, however, with something which expressed her sense of the condescension she was showing in addressing the boy in the shop.

Arthur looked at her in astonishment. He could not understand her, and, even had he done so, his natural shyness would have rendered him incapable of replying.

"Rule of Three, you know," said Lizzie, drawing herself up slightly. "Those sums with the three terms."

Arthur shook his head, but still did not speak.

"You can't? What a pity! I wanted to ask you to show me how to work out this horrid sum. Do just read it over and see."

The boy took the book passively as it was offered to him. Something like tears were rising to his eyes.

"You can read, can't you?" said Lizzie, in a slightly offended tone.

"No, miss, I can't," stammered poor Arthur, terribly ashamed of himself.

"Can't read!" echoed Lizzie, in astonishment. "How dreadful! But don't you mean to learn?"

"I've no chance, miss," replied Arthur, humbly, with his head cast down.

"Would you like to?" asked the child, in a tone of pitying interest.

"Yes, indeed I should," he replied.

"Well, I tell you what I'll do," said Lizzie. "You're a nice quiet boy, and not so ugly as those we had before, and I don't seem to hate you like I did them. So I'll ask ma if she'll let me teach you to read. Now, shall I?" cried the child, her face glowing with pleasure.

Arthur had to stammer some answer, but could not succeed in uttering any words. Just at that moment a customer came into the shop, and Lizzie darted away into the house.

Arthur was left in a state of bewildered delight, not, however, unmixed with fear, at the prospect of what Lizzie was about to undertake for him. Nor was his apprehension groundless. In about half an hour Mrs. Clinkscales returned and entered the house to change her somewhat noticeable walking apparel for those more serviceable garments in which she was wont to wait in the shop. Arthur waited for her reappearance with trembling; he felt sure that Lizzie would lose no time in putting her request. When Mrs. Hannah again appeared in the shop it was with a ruffled brow and flushed cheeks. Her temper was evidently upset, and, when such was the case, the good lady had the art of making herself very disagreeable indeed. All the rest of the evening she seemed to be doing her best to render Arthur uncomfortable. She set him work to do which was beyond his strength, and abused him in no measured terms because he did not do it; she raked up by-gone subjects of complaint, and then rated him for them as if they had only just occurred; once indeed she did what she had never done before, gave him a sound box on the ears, wholly without cause. Arthur bore all, in his usual manner, uncomplainingly. Child as he was he had no difficulty in judging it all to be the result of Lizzie's ill-advised suggestion; and since he knew that Lizzie would be grieved at losing her request, he felt it to be his own duty to bear the mother's wrath submissively. That was his due share.

Arthur had already several times given indications of what in a child of higher birth we might, perhaps, be allowed to call chivalrous feeling; as it is, I suppose we must content ourselves with allowing the poor lad a negative commendation, and say that he was in some degree distinguished from other boys of his position by a certain want of brutality, an absence of vulgar selfishness. Already he displayed a consideration towards the female sex which the vast majority of youngsters brought up in his circumstances have no suspicion of. He liked the society of females, and with them was far more open and unreserved than with men or boys. To Mrs. Rumball he had always behaved with unfailing respect, occasionally with even a timid display of affection; which indeed that good woman was scarcely capable of nicely comprehending, but which nevertheless she felt, and rewarded by affection in return. Even to Mrs. Clinkscales, who certainly possessed very few of the distinctive qualities of the gentler sex, Arthur displayed his innate chivalry—for such indeed it was. But to Lizzie, who was not quite two years older than himself, and whom he had such few chances of observing, he had already erected in his young heart a temple for far-off worship —worship as pure as that of the vestals who guarded the undying flame. We have read of poets who declared themselves to be in love at precarious ages, and it was the kind of love to which they refer, a virgin adoration uninfused with the least breath of passion, that Arthur cherished towards Lizzie. Possibly, he too, was going to grow up a poet; who could tell?

On the following morning he was on the watch to see her starting for school, and when he saw her blue frock appear from the alley and pass into the streets his heart throbbed. She did not look round, but went on in her usual way, reading her book. Arthur experienced an overpowering feeling of gratitude as he gazed after her, gratitude to her for having wished to benefit him. Then a sudden thought flashed into his head. What was to prevent him beginning to learn to read by himself, relying upon the assistance from time to time of Mrs. Rumball or Ned Quirk? He thought he still remembered his letters, at all events he could get them from the first piece of newspaper that came into his hands. And if indeed he *did* learn to read, what a triumph it would be to steal a moment some day, in defiance of Mrs. Clinkscales' *surveillance,* and whisper into Lizzie's ear the glorious fact of his acquisition! His breast throbbed with something of heroic fire as these thoughts welled in his mind. Taking up an old piece of a paper that lay underneath his feet, he sought eagerly to renew his acquaintance with the letters printed in the largest type. Alas! it was now nearly half a year since he had abruptly quitted the tuition of Mr. Whiffle, he had all but totally forgotten the alphabet. "Never mind," he said to himself, "I will get Mrs. Rumball to teach me." And he set to work at his task of chopping up old wood.

The same evening Mrs. Clinkscales was again out, but only for a very short time. It sufficed however for the execution of a purpose which a sharp little brain hidden beneath a mass of rich curls had contrived during the day. Scarcely was Arthur left alone when once more the blue frock stole like a gleam of light into the shop. The child held out a little old, much-worn book in her hand.

"Ma's a cross old thing!" she exclaimed,

laughing, and speaking with that mixture of pride and sweetness which was characteristic of her in a peculiar degree. " You mustn't mind her, you know. She said she wouldn't let me teach you for the world; and perhaps she's right, for she's very particular about the acquaintances I make. But I've brought you an old spelling book of mine. The letters are all very large there. You must try and get someone to help you, you know; for it's very disgraceful not to be able to read, I'm sure. Don't let ma see it for the world; put it underneath your coat somewhere. Now do your best, won't you?"

Though doubtless all unconscious of the importance of her acts, Lizzie was in reality exercising a vast influence on Arthur Golding, determining perhaps the whole current of his future life. Who can tell what importance is to be attributed to each apparently insignificant event which directs our course in childhood? When Arthur took the little old spelling-book from the child's hand and hid it hastily under his coat, giving in return a stammered word of thanks and a look which spoke an eloquence of gratitude, he received an impulse the result of which would not cease till his dying day. The following day happened to be Sunday, and Arthur took the earliest opportunity to draw Mrs. Rumball aside, and tell her of his earnest desire to learn to read. Mrs. Rumball was somewhat surprised. As a matter of course, she and her husband had had their own children taught the recondite art, though she certainly could not have satisfactorily informed you why they had gone to the expense; but that any child should of itself conceive a wish to be able to read, nay, be even willing to undergo considerable labour and trouble to this end, that indeed was something which surpassed her limited capacity to understand. The same afternoon, she having acquainted Mike with the astonishing news, a counsel was held round the fire, at which Arthur was cited to appear and to give a good and sufficient reason for the peculiar request he had ventured to prefer. The boy could only urge, in a timid voice, his great desire to know somewhat more than he did, and his hope that some day he might, with the assistance of this advanced learning, aspire to a position in life more exalted than his present one.

"The lad shows a good bit o' 'cuteness, arter all, Mike," urged Ned Quirk, who had from the first listened not unfavourably. "I'm not sewer as there's so much harm in learnin' to read an' write, an' maybe there's some little good in it. What d'ye say, Mike?"

"Well, I dunno, Ned. There's somethink to be said on both sides. I used to sing a hymn as began:

> Where Providence has fix'd your station,
> It is your duty *to* remain,
> Content to bear with each vexation,
> And 'ope as heaven 'll reward your pain ;

or at least somethin' like that. There *is* such a thing, you know, Ned, as settin' oneself above one's nat'ral claims, and bein' led astray by the pride of hintellect."

" You're right, Mike ; but for all that I, for my part, can't see no harm in readin' an' writin'. I tell you what it is, Mike. Don't you bother yer 'ead about the matter. I 'appen to know of a night school in Grafton-street here, where I've a notion they don't pay so very much for their larnin'. Now if I'll pay for the lad to go there, will you tackle Hannah Clinkscales, and make her let him horff his work two or three nights a week for a hour or so ?"

Ultimately this plan was agreed upon. After much sore argument—in which Mrs. Clinkscales began by stoutly asserting that she would turn Arthur away and procure another lad if he thought of so far forgetting his position as to learn to read and write—she consented very reluctantly, upon the persistence in their request of Mr. and Mrs. Rumball and Ned Quirk united, to let Arthur be free from nine to ten on three nights in the week, deducting, however, sixpence from his wages on this account. Truly the gate of the realms of learning did not open to Arthur Golding at the first blast of the summoning trumpet and let him in to walk henceforth on flowery paths.

It was now the middle of summer, and Arthur had to be up very early each morning. In spite of this it was seldom he did not contrive to snatch a quarter of an hour at his spelling-book before he left his bedroom. Ned Quirk, as we know, occupied the same room, and, in order not to wake him, Arthur would dress with the greatest quietness, take his book from under the pillow—where he always put it before going to bed, in consequence of Ned having once said in joke that learning would work its way into his head as he slept—then throw up the window gently and sit down in the fresh morning breeze.

Whilst Ned's prodigious snores well-nigh shook the ceiling within, sweeter sounds greeted the boy from without. Just outside his window hung a number of bird-cages, containing several larks, one or two thrushes, a blackbird, and a linnet. The window faced full to the east, and as soon as the earliest rays of the rising sun smote across the wide expanse of tiled roofs and fell upon the encaged birds, they woke one after another from their short slumbers, and each in his own language poured forth his song of greeting to the day. The larks especially sang with an almost frantic rapture, each striving to outdo the other in the elevation of his note and the prolonged energy of his strain, till the whole neighbourhood far around rang with the melodious contest.   And when at length they paused, rather from powerlessness to express their wild joy than from weariness at their exertions, the thrushes or the blackbird would intervene with notes deep, rich, and full, piping as if buried in their native groves amidst the rustle of young leaves and the flash of dew-drops trembling in the first gleam of morning.

Weary as Arthur often was, and hard as he often found it to tear himself from his bed, he always had his reward in this concert, whilst the air of heaven, gently playing with his fair hair, quickly drove away the pain of weariness and breathed the energy of renovated life throughout his young being.   It was well for Arthur that Nature had gifted him with a perception of her beauties ; man as yet had done little to raise him from that slough of lower earth in which all but a minute minority of the poor toil and fret and curse away their little lives.

Mike Rumball was not himself possessed to any great extent with the love of sweetness and light, nor was he a likely man to stretch a hand to a generous boy struggling blindly upwards. From the first he had given only a very qualified approval to the nightschool scheme, thinking far more of the weekly sixpence which Arthur would lose from his wages than of the intellectual re-

compense he would acquire, and very shortly
one or two little circumstances occurred
which appeared to him to confirm his never
quite lulled apprehensions and to demonstrate
most incontestably that Arthur " was not
the lad he 'ad been sin' the day as he took to
cultivatin' the pride of hintellect." It chanced
that Mike had let a bedroom in his house to
an individual named Tuck, who, during the
summer months at least, got his living in a
peculiar manner. He was, in short, one of
those men you may see any fine morning in
Piccadilly designing all manner of figures on
the pavement in coloured chalks, and inti-
mating, by a scroll written above the same,
that the work was not performed solely out
of love for art or a desire of affording pleasure to the public in general, but rather with
the ulterior object of acquiring the means of
life. Besides his drawings on the flags, he
executed at home, or in the streets, similar
drawings on pieces of wood and cardboard,
some representing fishes, others ships on a
stormy sea, others a group of flowers.

By some chance Arthur Golding made the
acquaintance of this man, and many an odd
moment did he steal to visit him and examine
his work. The artist was an idle, drunken,
good-for-nothing fellow enough, but now and
then he had a few ideas somewhat above the
level of his surroundings, and Arthur found
unceasing pleasure in his conversation. The

result of this connection was that the boy
began to possess himself of odd bits of chalk,
sometimes begging coloured pieces from his
friend, and to make a display of his artistic
powers on the walls and floor of his bedroom
or on the pavement of the alley that ran by
the corner of the shop. He had not to go
far for subjects; those birds and animals in
the shop, in which he took such an interest,
naturally occurred to his mind as models to
copy. Accordingly he exhausted his inven-
tion in depicting every kind of feathered
creature he could conceive, most of them, it
must be confessed, bearing but a distant resemblance to those which it falls within the lot
of ordinary mortals to behold. Possibly they
might have exhibited some likeness to those
ideas of the animal world in the existence of
which Plato and his disciples put their faith.

By dint of much practice—for in every
leisure moment he ran to some quiet spot
where he could exercise his chalk unobserved,
even his reading suffering severely from this
alienation of attention—he would no doubt
have soon effected great improvements in the
character of his designs, but he was not destined to follow the bent of his genius in
unconstrained freedom.

Ned Quirk had first of all observed this
strange tendency, but, like a reflective man,
he had held his peace and merely observed,
probably concluding that there were more

things in heaven and earth than his philosophy e'er dreamt of, and that possibly this might be one of those, which therefore it behoved a wise man to consider before delivering a judgment upon. But when before long the chalked floors and walls came to the notice of Mike Rumball, that gentleman was by no means backward in expressing an immediate opinion.

"I told you 'ow it 'ud be, Ned Quirk," he observed, in confidence. "Afore this 'ere lad o' yourn took to hankerin' arter schoolin' and such-like things, he was a good enough lad in his way; but when that kind o' humbug began I know'd as it was all up with him. It was no good o' me liftin' up my voice, like the Prophet Jonah, an' a de-claimin' agin sich folly, as you know I did. I was like a voice a cryin' in the wilderness, an' you paid no 'eed to me. I tell you what it is, that 'ere lad is goin' to the bad, Ned, and you can see it as well as I can. When a lad takes to chalkin' nastiness on walls an' floors, I knows what it means; it shows a depraved mind. An' what's more, I won't 'ave it in *my* 'ouse! We shall 'ave him thievin' next, mark my word, an' then who'll be to blame? Why we, of course, as let him go on in his evil ways without a warnin' of him. If I see a chalk-mark arter this blessed day, young Arthur Golding takes his 'ook out of the 'ouse of Mike Rumball!"

There was no good in disputing such an energetic declaration of opinion as this, and Ned Quirk accordingly warned his *protégé* quietly of the wrath he had aroused. The result was that the drawing on walls ceased, but by no means the drawing altogether. It had already become a passion with Arthur; he could not throw away his chalks entirely, however severe the penalties with which he was threatened. So he got into the habit of collecting from all possible quarters scraps of paper either white or printed upon, and on these he continued to draw when no eyes observed him, afterwards tearing up and throwing away those drawings which did not please him, whilst those which appeared better done he stowed away carefully on the top of a cupboard in the bedroom, well knowing that no one ever went near to disturb them. About this time, too, Ned Quirk bought him a slate, as he needed it for his sums at school, and this Arthur turned to the service of his talent for designing, only it grieved him terribly whenever he had drawn a bird or animal rather better than usual that he was obliged to rub it out immediately, thus committing what already appeared to his young mind as the worst sin he knew of—the destruction of something that was beautiful in his eyes.

Mike's resentment did not end with his stern forbiddance of future " chalking," but, on his divining the source of Arthur's disease, aimed at a radical cure. In short, he gave to Mr. Tuck an abrupt notice to quit, which the artist, at the end of a week's time, perforce obeyed.

This was a cruel blow to Arthur, and he felt it severely. After peeping into Tuck's room once, in the hope of seeing the drawings which were his wonted delight, and on perceiving it bare, swept and garnished for a new tenant, he could not restrain his feelings, and, turning away, wept bitterly. Unfortunately, Mike Rumball had watched him, and, when he saw his distress break out in tears, the man's short temper was exhausted. In his irritation he gave the boy a sound cuff on the ears, and with angry words sent him off to his work.

Ned Quirk heard of this the same night from Mrs. Rumball, and he was grieved at it. When he retired to bed he found Arthur already in his, and, as he at first thought, asleep. But he soon heard stifled sobs proceeding from beneath the counterpane, and, rough fellow as he was, his heart conceived true sympathy for the boy, though certainly unable to estimate the cause of his suffering. He called to him, and on Arthur at length replying in a broken voice, he took a seat by his bedside and spoke words of comfort.

" Come, come, Arthur lad," he said, " there's no call to take on i' this way, as I

knows on. What is it as troubles you, my
boy? Mike don't mean no 'arm, though
maybe he was rayther rough this mornin'.
He'd been bothered in his mind, you see,
about some money as he's lost. Come, cheer
up."

Arthur still held his head down, and his
body trembled from time to time, though the
sobs had stopped.

"I know it's 'ard on yer," pursued honest
Ned, "to stop horff yer little 'musements
like, but, you see, Mike don't like to 'ev his
rooms sp'iled. An' then he thinks as 'ow you
ain't quite goin' on as you should, wastin' yer
time, an' sich like. It's all for yer own good,
Arthur, I'm sewer. For myself, I don't give
no 'pinion about this 'ere chalkin' an'
scratchin', 'cos I don't understand it, yer see,
but pr'aps yer won't be sorry in a few years
as you was early broke of the 'abit. An'
now tell me, lad, 'ow ye're gettin' on with yer
schoolin'?"

"Pretty well, I think, thank you, Mr.
Quirk," replied Arthur, somewhat sorrowfully
though.

"Why that's right! An' can you read
them 'ere words o' three syllabums yet, as
you was talkin' on?"

"Very nearly. I think I shall in a week
or two."

"Why, better still. 'Ere's a sixpence for
you, Arthur. I'd a unus'al good night to-

night wi' th' 'taters, an' so I can afford it. An' don't mind what Mike says, you 'ear? He's a good chap, but he 'as his fancies, like all on us. An' get on wi' yer readin', writin', an' 'rithumtic, lad; stick to 'em. Depend on it, *they'll* do you good, some day or other. But leave the chalkin' an' scratchin' till ye've got more time to waste, that's a good lad."

Verily Ned Quirk had sound notions in his way, and his advice, when his lights were considered, was far from discreditable. But what advice, however excellent, was ever acted upon in this world? Arthur, indeed, persevered with his three R's, but as to giving up the drawing, as I have already said, it was impossible for him. He had, indeed, an end in view in connection with it, and one far too important to admit of neglect. It was no other than a burning desire, kept close, like so many other hopes and wishes, in the recesses of his own breast, to complete a drawing which he could account worthy of being presented to Lizzie Clinkscales. This was a terribly daring idea, that he well knew; but the thought was so unutterably attractive to him that it was impossible of renunciation.

This was the inward energy which made him persevere in his efforts, spite of all discouragement. He felt that a word of praise from Lizzie would compensate him a thousand times for all the misapprehension of others.

And at length he flattered himself that he had accomplished his task. With the greatest difficulty he had begged from Mrs. Rumball a fair sheet of white paper, only a little crumpled, in which she had brought home something from the grocer's, and, after straightening this out, and cutting it square to the best of his ability, he had drawn upon it, in coloured chalks, purchased with the sixpence Ned Quirk had given him, the likeness of an old parrot, a particular favourite of his, failing not to give his picture the advantage of all that brilliancy of plumage of which relentless Time had in a great measure deprived the original. For rather more than a week Arthur had employed every leisure moment in completing this picture, first of all studying his model with a careful eye, then stealing upstairs to his bedroom and enriching his drawing with the results of his observation.

Then, after many desperate attempts, when at length he had almost despaired of finding an opportunity to make the offering of his completed work to her for whom it was intended, one day he found himself in the shop alone when Lizzie happened to come through. With fear and trembling he drew out the paper, which he had kept neatly folded in four in the inside pocket of his coat for more than a fortnight, and, totally unable of uttering those appropriate words which he had so long dwelt upon in his mind, he held it out with a timid hand to the girl. Lizzie took it with a look of good-natured surprise, and, on opening it out, burst into an exclamation of pleasure.

"Where did you find it?" she asked, examining the gaudy plumage, the shrewd-looking eyes, the portentious beak of the bird with keen delight.

"I did it myself, miss," replied Arthur, his eyes moist with pleasure at seeing his work thus appreciated.

"*You* did it!" exclaimed Lizzie, a trifle contemptuously.

"Yes, indeed I did, Miss Lizzie," urged the boy, with eagerness. "I drew it myself, and, if you please, I—I did it for you."

"For me! But did you really do it yourself, and for me?"

"*Really*, miss. Upon my word I did, and to give to you. I—I should so like you to take it."

Lizzie laughed that clear, joyous laugh of hers, and, after still viewing the picture for some minutes, folded it up again carefully and put it in a little bag she was carrying.

"There," she said; "I promise you to keep it. I couldn't believe you did it at first, you know. I like it very much. And—and —I think I ought to shake hands with you; for after all, you know, it was kind of you to do it for me. There!"

She held out one of her delicate, fairy hands, and Arthur, in trembling wonder, pressed it in his rather dirty palm.   Then with a nod and another cheerful, ringing laugh, Lizzie tripped away. Many years after she still kept the picture of the parrot, and looked at it when, perhaps, Arthur himself had forgotten the circumstance entirely.

CHAPTER VIII.

PROGRESS.

ARTHUR'S progress at the night school was
very rapid, and his teacher, a poor book-
binder's assistant, who, for the most moderate
of compensations, took upon his shoulders
the duty of the State, and devoted his
evenings to the instruction of half-a-dozen
ragged lads and as many grown-up men, soon
regarded him as his favourite pupil. Being
an observant man he was not long before he
discovered the boy's turn for drawing, having
now and then perceived sketches on the backs
of his copy-books or on his slate, which, rude
as they were, appeared to him to display
something of unusual talent in so young a
hand. He encouraged Arthur to bring and
show him some of the drawings which, as he
soon learned, he was in the habit of making
at home. On seeing these his teacher was
still more surprised and pleased. From that
day he added his influence to those many
hankerings after a change of occupation
which Arthur had himself began to feel, and
promised that, if he came to hear of any place
that he thought would suit his pupil, he would
do his best to secure it. In the meantime he

urged the boy to work hard at his reading and writing, and to such effect that, when Arthur had been attending the classes for a little more than a year, he was already able to read with very fair facility and to write a hand which, if not a striking example of caligraphy, was at all events tolerably legible. He was now approaching the termination of his eleventh year.

One day he had been on an errand for Mrs. Clinkscales into Tottenham Court Road, and had, moreover, as had become rather his habit of late, wandered somewhat out of his direct road, walking dreamily along with his eyes fixed on the pavement, feeding his mind with the dim outlines of a thousand strange or beautiful fancies. He had turned out of Tottenham Court Road into Goodge Street, and thence again into a narrow passage, known as Charlotte Place, and here he stopped, as he always did instinctively, before a shop where newspapers and books were exposed for sale in the windows. It was a very small shop, over the door of which was painted the inscription: "Samuel Tollady, Printer." As Arthur looked over the illustrated papers which lay open in the window, his eye fell on a card suspended at the back, upon which were the words: "A Boy Wanted." His heart leaped in his breast as he carefully read these words. Why should he not go in and offer his services? But a sensitive timidity for a time withheld him. Suppose he were to apply, and suppose he were to be so successful as to obtain the place, what would Mrs. Clinkscales say, what would Mike Rumball and Ned Quirk say? His mind drawn hither and thither by questionings and doubts he passed slowly on; he paused; he turned back; again he read the notice. At length, with much apprehension, he resolved upon tempting his fortune, and walked into the shop.

Behind the counter, with a book open on his lap, was sitting an oldish gentleman— gentleman was written upon every line of his face, notwithstanding his circumstances—in spectacles, with head all but bald, and a bold, massive forehead which might have been the envy of a Greek sage. His lips, though firmly knit, had yet a sweetness of expression irresistibly attractive, and his eyes spoke a gentle kindliness which, as they met those of Arthur, at once emboldened him. His dress was marked by a fastidious neatness, though much worn; his waistcoat buttoned close up to his neck, around which he wore an old-fashioned neckerchief, which gave him, at first sight, something of a clerical appearance. As he spoke to Arthur he kept tapping with his fingers on the open pages of his book, evidently a habit with him.

" If you please, sir, do you want a boy?" asked Arthur.

" I do," replied Mr. Tollady, for he it was, speaking in a grave but musical voice. " Have you come to apply for the place?"

" Yes, if you please, sir."

The printer surveyed the applicant for a few moments with care, and the results of his examination did not, to judge from the expression of his face, appear unfavourable. Nor indeed was there anything in Arthur's appearance which should have made it otherwise. During the last two years he had grown considerably, and was now rather tall for his age, but slender and of a strikingly graceful form. His hair had somewhat moderated in its luxuriance of growth, but was still extremely fair, and still fell on each side of his forehead in pleasing ripples. In his features there was nothing vulgar; he was, in reality, a striking resemblance of what his ill-fated father had been at the same age. His eyes were of light blue, his nose of a Grecian type, his lips and chin moulded in form expressive of extreme sensibility and gentleness of disposition, showing traces, moreover, though as yet in but a slight degree, of an instability in moral character which was hereditary. The latter feature was not, however, so predominant that it might not very possibly give way beneath a judicious training. But where was that training to come from?

" What is your age, my boy?" asked Mr. Tollady.

" Nearly eleven, sir."

" Indeed ! I took you for more than twelve. You can read and write ? "

" Yes, sir," replied Arthur, though with more hesitation, dropping his eyes as he spoke.

The old gentleman observed this, and, in a quiet manner which had nothing alarming in it, he proceeded to examine Arthur in these particulars. He appeared satisfied with the result. Then he questioned him about his present position, and at length, after a conversation lasting nearly a quarter of an hour, he dismissed him with the promise that he would himself walk down into Little St. Andrew Street in the course of the day, and see Mr. Rumball.

He kept his word—in his life he had never failed to do so—and had that afternoon a rather lengthy colloquy with Michael, from whom he ultimately learnt as much about Arthur Golding's antecedents as the latter himself knew.

" You will, I am sure, sir," said Mr. Tollady, " pardon me the trouble I am giving you. I like this boy's appearance very much, and should like, if possible, to employ him. But as I do not want a mere errand boy, but one who would live in the house with me and be entrusted with many little things of some importance to me, I should wish to be well assured of the character of the one I engaged."

Mike listened with bent brows, his hands

thrust deep into his trousers pockets. The
fact of the matter was, he was not altogether
pleased with this "new departure" of his
young lodger. To begin with it appeared to
him that, before Arthur had taken any such
step as applying for a new situation, he,
Michael Rumball, ought certainly to have
been consulted; his sense of importance was
a trifle hurt. Secondly, there was to be considered the fact that, in the event of Arthur
taking the new place, the weekly wages which
the boy had hitherto always given into Mrs.
Rumball's hands with scrupulous fidelity each
Saturday night would henceforth cease to
form an item in the household income. This
was serious, and required consideration.

"The boy having come to you under rather
peculiar circumstances," pursued Mr. Tollady,
interpreting, with a generosity characteristic
of him, Mike's hesitation in a very much more
favourable sense than was its due, "gives you
naturally an interest in him, and you must be
assured that he will really be making a change
for the better in coming to me. Now I think
there can be no doubt of it. As I shall provide him with everything, I shall not be able
to pay him high wages, but I shall undertake
to teach him by degrees my own business,
that of a printer, and so put into his hands
the means of earning a very good living
whenever he leaves me. Does that meet with
your approval?"

Mike still hesitated. The voice of selfishness was loud within him at this moment, and all but stifled the still, small voice of conscience which Mike, as years went on, became, it is to be feared, less and less in the habit of heeding.

"I tell you how it is, Mister," he said at length. "I've got a partner like in this 'ere business, an' that's Ned Quirk, the man as brought the lad 'ome that night I was tellin' yer of. Now I think, yer see, as I ought to talk it over with Ned afore I come to a decision. Suppose we say I talk it over to-night, an' you comes an' sees me agin to-morrow; will that suit?"

Mr. Tollady perforce adopted this decision, and took his leave. The same night Michael Rumball communicated the visit to Ned Quirk. In all probability he would not have done so at all, and would have contented himself with returning an unfavourable answer to his visitor on the morrow, but for the reflection that Arthur would doubtless himself acquaint Ned with what he had done, and thus render the artifice useless. Ned, to do him justice, was made of firmer clay than Mike, and, when he heard the opportunity which lay before his *protégé*, even though it was made to appear as untempting as possible by Mike's perverse description, he had not two opinions on the matter, but immediately affirmed that the place must be secured. A long and some-

what heated discussion followed, during which
Mike inveighed, with something of that
eloquence which had formerly been at the
service of the Ranter persuasion, against that
deplorable pride of intellect which Ned had
always, he said, done his best to instil into
the lad and which would one day, mark that!
be his ruin. He hadn't much opinion, for
his own part, of reading and writing for boys,
for they were clearly a direct temptation to
forgery ; but for a boy to become a printer
was still worse, inasmuch as it inevitably led
to the fabrication of spurious bank-notes,
whereupon would follow exportation and all
its concomitant evils. Ned Quirk laughed
these remarks to scorn and was strong in his
support of the gospel of "getting on," which
is no bad gospel after all, if read in its true
sense, but which, like some other gospels that
could be mentioned, is not unfrequently sadly
misinterpreted. Ned had a respect for learning, while Mike certainly had not, and in a
matter such as this, where he was truly interested, would yield to no man. For the
first time since their acquaintance a serious
breach seemed likely to take place between
these two worthies ; but, just at the critical
stage, Mrs. Rumball came in with a woman's
tact and was successful in allaying the storm.
She had always entertained a great respect
for Ned Quirk's opinions, and now she placed
herself on his side in the argument. The

result could not be doubtful; Mike yielded, though, after all, with but an ill grace, and it was decided that Arthur should go to Mr. Tollady's.

Of course a week's notice had to be given to Mrs. Clinkscales, which that lady received with a slight toss of the head, and a wish that the boy might find better treatment elsewhere than he had received from her, expressed in a tone which clearly indicated that she had no expectation of the wish being realised. Arthur had only one real sorrow in leaving the scene of his earliest servitude, and that was that he should no more be able to watch each day the coming and going of the blue frock and hat with the partridge feather, around which had woven themselves the brightest of his boyish dreams and fancies. Yes, even his hopes had, in a measure, connected themselves with Lizzie. Speculating, as children do, on the course of his future life, he had often determined in his own mind that he would work hard till he became "rich," not rich only as Mrs. Clinkscales would have understood the word, but superlatively wealthy. And when that time came, when he had made his money, had bought a large house in one of those magnificent quarters of the town which he seldom visited, had servants without end and all manner of luxury, then he would one day order his finest horses to be harnessed in his

finest carriage, in which he would forthwith
drive down to Little St. Andrew Street and
carry off Lizzie with him as his bride.   O,
sweet visions, gilding with their refulgence
even the squalid every-day life of a London
slum ; and thrice sweet hope, which, blossoming most luxuriantly in the hearts of the
young, feeds with its rich fragrance every
ardent thought.   When the day came on
which he was to leave, he saw Lizzie go to
school and return as usual, watched her with
unwonted sadness in his eyes, was glad at
length when he received a smile and a nod,
and little thought that he had looked on the
queen of his imagination for the last time.

Mr. Tollady received him with his former
kind smile, and lost no time in making him
acquainted with the circle of his new duties.
The sphere in which he would henceforth
live was a very wide one.   Behind the little
shop, where, besides newspapers, prints,
cheap books, and general stationery were sold,
was the single room in which Mr. Tollady
himself lived, a darkish little place ; and
passing out of that by a side door, which led
to the foot of the stairs, one ascended to the
printing office, likewise a very small room,
smelling strongly of printer's ink, where one
man was generally employed as compositor.
It was easy to judge from these premises that
Mr. Tollady's business was not extensive.
Within this printing office a door led into

what had previously been an old lumber-room, some six feet square, lighted by a small casement. This had just been cleaned out and converted into a very neat little bed-room, henceforth Arthur's.

Arthur took his meals with Mr. Tollady in the little parlour at the back of the shop, breakfast, tea, and supper being prepared by the latter himself; the more important meal at mid-day, however, being brought in on a tray from a coffee-house in Goodge Street. For an hour each day one of the girls, in a poor family next door, came into the house and did what household work was required. It was distinctive of Mr. Tollady, that, though his opportunities of giving employ-ment were not large, yet he was most judicious in the choice of those he did employ, invariably finding those who were really in want of work, and holding that, *cæteris paribus*, those who come most closely within the circle of your every-day relation-ships, have the most claims upon you for assistance. Arthur did not fail to examine closely the details of his new abode, and more particularly the parlour, which was to him the most interesting room. The window certainly had no tempting prospect. It looked into a paved back yard, with a cistern in one corner of it, the principal variety in the scene being afforded on those days when the yard was thickly hung with newly-washed linen. Immediately opposite was a window, apparently that of a darkish parlour, much like Mr. Tollady's, and attached to the sill of the window was a long box containing various flowering plants. The circumstance of this box being carved and painted in front so as to represent the broadside of a man-of-war, gave a certain originality to its appearance, and afforded Arthur Golding frequent subject for observation during the first few days.

One side of the parlour was occupied by a large book-case, which contained the whole of Mr. Tollady's library. It was not extensive, but select in the choice of works. Here were the principal English classics, most of them evidently having been purchased second-hand, and also a few French and German books. The library was evidently that of a man who had known how to cultivate judiciously the emotional side of his nature; the only books really bound with any degree of richness were the poets. Theological works there were none, and natural science was alone represented by a few works on botany; but the collection of histories was complete and good. The lowest shelf was occupied by the Penny Cyclopædia, an old folio edition of Johnson's Dictionary, and a number of large volumes laid flat, one on the other, the contents of which could not be guessed at. Around the

walls hung a few good prints of works by the
old masters, and a bust of Shakespeare and
Milton stood at either end of the mantel-
piece. Opposite was a large chest of drawers,
which at night time was converted into a bed
for Mr. Tollady's own use. On the window-
sill outside bloomed one or two geraniums,
fuchsias, and lobelias.

One of Arthur's first duties in the morning
was to be standing at the corner of Charlotte
Place and Goodge Street at half-past six in
order to catch the bundle of daily papers
thrown to him from the news-agent's cart,
which passed by at that time, after which he
was first of all engaged in separating out and
folding the papers, and in pasting the placards
on to the boards to be exhibited outside the
shop; after that he had to go the round of
the regular customers, of whom there were
some fifty, delivering to each the daily
newspaper. On the first morning he was
accompanied as a guide by the boy whom Mr.
Tollady had previously employed in this
work, and returned shortly before nine.

He found Mr. Tollady sitting at his desk,
over his ledger. He did not seem to be
engaged in working at it, but, though his eye
was fixed on the page, he was clearly wandering very far away in his thoughts. He did not
notice Arthur's entrance, but continued, sunk
in his reverie till the clock of the Middlesex
Hospital, hard by, suddenly struck nine, and

brought him back, with a deep sigh, to actual
life. Raising his head he saw Arthur and
smiled, but sadly, and then seemed to make
an effort to return to his wonted manner.
There was something in this which even a
boy, particularly a boy of Arthur's intelligence, could not help being struck with.
Arthur felt his master was not happy, and a
feeling of sympathy began to be added to
that gratitude and reverence which he had
from the first conceived towards him.

Mr. Tollady came from his desk and proceeded to give Arthur a task which would
occupy him some little time, namely, to sort,
make up into bundles, and ticket a great
heap of miscellaneous papers which lay in
one corner of the shop, and which, for some
reason, it was desired to preserve. The boy
had not been engaged thus more than a few
minutes when two men entered the shop
together, both hatless and in slippers, as if
they had come from next door. The appearance of these individuals merits a slight
description.

The one who advanced first was a very
short man, quite bald, with meagre but
strongly-marked features, and with eyes
rather blood-shot. His nose was very much
hooked, and his gums, which he frequently
displayed in speaking, almost toothless. He
had a decided stoop in the shoulders, and
bandy-legs; in short, it was not difficult to

judge from his appearance that he was a tailor by trade. His companion was tall, also very bald, and of morose aspect; his left cheek was marked with a large wine-coloured stain which gave a decidedly unpleasant look to his countenance. He seemed affected with habitual nervousness, at times almost amounting, in his hands, to St. Vitus' Dance; he was perpetually biting first his lower, then his upper lip, with a fierce persistency which seemed to betoken some constant excitement in his mind. His dress was of the shabbiest, but gave no indication of his trade. He was, in fact, a seller of new, and a restorer of old umbrellas. Both of these individuals lived in Charlotte Place, and both every morning just at this hour entered Mr. Tollady's shop in company.

Each advanced to the counter, deposited his penny, and received his morning paper, but, instead of at once departing, they took possession of two chairs which stood in front of the counter, and began to unfold their papers.

For a quarter of an hour no one spoke (at their entrance they had confined their morning salutations to a friendly nod, which had been similarly replied to by Mr. Tollady), at the end of that time, the bald little man suddenly broke silence by reading, without preface, a paragraph which seemed particularly to have attracted his attention. He did so in an emphatic, here and there in a fierce voice. The paragraph ended thus :—

" The Magistrate replied that, if what had been said were true, it was evident that scandalous injustice had been done. The perpetrator of that injustice had not, however, brought himself within reach of the jurisdiction of that Court, and the only course open was to institute a civil suit. Under the circumstances, he could not advise the appellants to do this, inasmuch as the suit would probably be of long duration, and, as he was a poor man, might end in his ruin."

The reading of this was received in silence, but with looks which very clearly intimated the sentiments of the listeners. The reader, after noting the impression on the faces of the other two, began to speak in an excited manner.

" There, there it is again ! Precisely the words the Magistrate used to me the day I first asked for advice. He warned me, and my friends warned me. They said, one and all : ' Mark Challenger ! begin this suit, and you're a ruined man.' But I wouldn't be warned. I said : ' If there's such a thing as law in this country, if there's such a thing as justice in England, I'll have it, cost what it may !' For three years I was at law, and then the suit wasn't at an end. But I was. Ha, ha, ha !"

And he burst into a long fit of savage laughter.

"Am I right, Sam Tollady? Am I right, John Pether?" he continued, in his exasperated tone. "When do I take up a paper that I don't find in it an instance of what I'm always saying: 'For the poor man there's no such thing as law or justice in England.' Is it going to be always so? Are we going to be always ground beneath the money-bags of these smooth-tongued publicans and sinners? Which are in the majority, I should like to know—the rich or the poor? *Why*, I say, do we endure it?"

"Because we are cowards, Mark Challenger," replied John Pether, his voice sounding almost sepulchral after the shrill fierce tones of the former speaker. "Because we are cowards, one and all. Why did I let the tax-gatherer take the last penny out of my house when my children were dying for food? Because I had not the courage to strike the man dead, and offer myself a martyr to the cause of justice. That's why, Mark Challenger."

"You wouldn't have done much good, John," interrupted Mr. Tollady, his voice and manner a strong contrast to the wild excitement of the one, the concentrated ferocity of the other of his companions. "The tax-gatherer did you no wrong. It was the system, not the man, that was at fault. Strike dead at a blow the passions and the vices

and the pestiferous creeds of Society—then
let them make a martyr of you if they can!"

"It's all very well for you, Sam Tollady,"
jerked in Mark. "I often say to myself:
'How is it,' I say, 'that Sam Tollady can be
so calm and so quiet over all his wrongs and
his sufferings, when John Pether and me get
so savage over ours?' And I've always come
to the conclusion that it's because you've
only suffered in yourself, Sam; you've never
had either wife or children to share your
wrongs, and that's made it easier for you to
bear them. But John Pether and me has
had double suffering. We've borne our own
share, and, besides that, we've had to watch
our wives and children hunger and die at our
sides. Isn't that enough to make us wild,
Sam Tollady? Am I right?"

Mr. Tollady replied with his usual calmness, but in a voice full of sympathy; and for
half an hour the conversation continued very
much in the same strain, fresh excitement
being derived from the newspapers if ever it
lapsed for a moment. Then the two friends
rose to depart; but Mark Challenger, noticing Arthur for the first time, pointed to
him—

"A fixture, Sam?" he asked.

Mr. Tollady nodded, smiling.

"Train him up in the way he should go,
Sam!" he exclaimed fiercely, grasping the
printer's arm. "Make a Radical of him—a

Revolutionist! Teach him his wrongs, Sam; let him see the cause of his miseries, and the cure! You can do it, Sam; you can do it!"

"I dare say he might make an apt scholar," said Mr. Tollady, in a low voice. "He seems to me by no means an ordinary boy."

"Good!" replied the other; then, turning to Arthur, cried to him : "Come here, my lad!"

Arthur obeyed, and Mark grasped him by the coat collar.

"Boy!" he exclaimed in his usual excited tones, "have you known a single happy day in your life?"

"I—I think so, sir," stammered the boy, half frightened at the other's manner, and scarcely understanding the question.

"Have you ever been hungry?" persisted Mark Challenger, in irritated tones; "hungry, and without means of buying bread? Hungry —fiercely, savagely hungry, like a wild beast, till you could gnaw wood or shoe-leather? Have you ever felt like that, boy?"

"Yes, sir; often," replied Arthur, and with much truth.

"I knew it!" cried Mark. "See!" he added, pointing to Mr. Tollady. "He'll tell you why you were hungry! He'll tell you who it is robs you of the means of buying food and clothing! Mind what he tells you,

my lad, that's all; and when you grow up
make use of it."

And, flinging the boy almost angrily from
him, Mark Challenger nodded to Mr. Tollady
and left the shop, followed by John Pether,
who had fallen into a fit of moody abstraction.

"Did he frighten you, Arthur?" asked
the printer with a smile, when the men had
gone.

"A little, at first, sir."

"You mustn't mind his strange ways,"
replied Mr. Tollady, returning to his desk.
"Mr. Challenger is a good man at heart, but
he has had severe hardships, and they have
almost driven him mad. Now let us get on
with our work."

And as he turned away he sighed to himself—

"For the night cometh, wherein no man
can work."

A great part of the day Mr. Tollady spent
upstairs in the printing office, where he himself worked in connection with his assistant.
The extent of his business was not great, but
that which was entrusted to him he performed, according to the rule of his life, with
the utmost perfection his abilities rendered
possible. When he came down to partake of
his meals in company with Arthur he talked
kindly and pleasantly, as his habit was, and
was evidently exerting himself to win as

speedily as possible the confidence, and even the affection, of his young assistant.

Samuel Tollady was not one of those men who have so worn off the keen edge of their spiritual perceptions by rough jolting and jarring against their fellow men that any stranger they happen to come into contact with is of as little interest to them, except in so far as he serves their ends, as the very stones they tread upon in the street. To his new master Arthur was more than a piece of human machinery which had been taken in and set to work, and was only to be spared excessive toil or capricious brutality that his powers of future exertion might not be unduly injured. He was, rather, a young and promising bud on the great tree of humanity, a child of human pain and sorrow, but also with human needs and aspirations, the latter very possibly, as Mr. Tollady began already to perceive, in a higher degree than the majority of mankind. He had lived many years amidst terrible degradation, and yet was not degraded; had associated with those whose ends and aims were for the most part of the basest nature, and yet he had already shown signs of a yearning for the fruits of knowledge. Mr. Tollady's interest grew rapidly in Arthur; he watched him, tested him, and studied him with the utmost care. And as yet he found nothing to make him believe his interest was misplaced.

Looking upon the boy as a human soul, and not as a mere piece of useful machinery in his shop, Mr. Tollady soon conceived the idea of using his leisure to continue the very imperfect education which Arthur had as yet received. Accordingly the evenings—when the printing office was closed, and only a few customers had to be attended to in the shop— soon began to be spent in the mutual giving and receiving of instruction. Mr. Tollady had ideas of his own on the subject of education, and felt a keen pleasure in being able to put them into practice. Life seemed very soon to acquire a new value, a new significance for him. He was not so often absorbed in fits of melancholy brooding as previously.

And if the teacher benefited by his work, the pupil did so even in a higher degree. Appreciating intensely the consistent kindness of his master, Arthur progressed wonderfully under his instruction; his zeal for his work knew no bounds; where other boys of his age thought of nothing but their tops, their marbles, and their hoops, Arthur was uneasy when away from the tasks which had been set him. Now and then his thoughts returned to Lizzie. What would he give to be able to acquaint her with his progress!

But the direct instruction which he received from his master was not the sole

benefit for which Arthur was indebted to
him. To live with Mr. Tollady and observe
his actions from day to day was in itself an
education.

In ministering to his bodily needs the
printer was frugal almost to asceticism,
partly, perhaps, owing to the habits bred in
him by a long struggle with poverty. He
was a vegetarian on principle, and water was
his only drink. It would, indeed, have gone
somewhat hard with Arthur if he, too, had
been confined to such a diet, but Mr. Tollady knew what was due to a growing boy,
and stinted him in nothing. By dint of
severe economy he succeeded in keeping a
small sum of money always by him, only to
be drawn upon for purposes of charity. He
was charitable in the true sense of the word,
not giving his pence indiscriminately to a
beggar in the street, but following patient
misery into its secret hiding-places, and
coupling active assistance where he saw it
would be useful with strong, manly, wise
words of advice and comfort. Not a few
young girls living in the gloomy neighbourhood where his shop was situated had to
thank the hand of Samuel Tollady for having
checked them on the precipice of ruin; not
a few toiling wives and mothers, cursed with
husbands whose lives were spent alternately
in the gin-palace and the gaol, were indebted
to his benevolence for the help which kept

them from the workhouse. But so secret was
his alms-giving that it is doubtful whether
any but the recipients had any knowledge of
it; the neighbours generally looked upon
him as a quiet, agreeable sort of man, but
not unfrequently hinted at his having miserly
habits. Mark Challenger and John Pether,
who were very old acquaintances of his, had
a suspicion of the truth, but were themselves
too retired in their habits of life to spread
reports concerning it.

At five o'clock each morning, whatever the
season of the year, Mr. Tollady rose, and for
two hours was engaged in reading. He read
little besides the works in his own library,
and with these, thanks to many perusals, he
had obtained a thorough acquaintance, such
as it is to be feared, even few professedly
learned men can boast, with the standard
works of our literature. Throughout the day
he spoke little, the words he exchanged with
his two constant visitors each morning, and
the instruction he gave to Arthur at night constituting the chief part of his conversation.
Yet he was never morose; only at times very
sad in appearance. Whomsoever he spoke
to, it was with a gentleness of tone which
never varied; harshness he seemed incapable
of. Nevertheless he was not what we understand by a loveable man; he had too few
social qualities for that. In all with whom
he stood on ordinary grounds of acquaintance-

ship he never failed to inspire respect; it needed that he should unfold himself in the closest intimacy that he might be regarded with affection.

I have said that his shelves held a few works on botany, and this had always been the favourite study of his lighter hours. In his youth he had lived much amid the beauties of nature, and had been an ardent botanist. He had ultimately collected a herbarium which had been of considerable value in the eyes of men of kindred taste, but at one period of his life, overtaken by the direst poverty, he had disposed of this for a slight sum, only retaining a small collection in the shape of duplicates and imperfect specimens. It was this collection which filled the large volumes which have been noticed as lying on the lowest shelves of his book case. Every Sunday evening it was his habit to lift these volumes on to the table and go over them with a longing hand and a fond look, as each plant recalled to his mind the scenes amidst which it had been gathered. When late in the night he replaced them, after carefully shaking out the dust and seeing that the leaves were sprinkled with camphor to preserve them from insects, it was often with trembling hands and a moist eye.

CHAPTER IX.

STILL WATERS.

I⊤ will scarcely be imagined that Mr. Norman allowed his *protégé* to disappear so suddenly and mysteriously from the Rectory without instituting an active search for him. He was in reality deeply grieved and concerned, for he had already began to conceive an affection for the child, and had not unfrequently laid to rest his conscience, which sometimes troubled him on the score of duties neglected, with the subtle reflection that in adopting this little outcast of society he was performing a service to his fellow-men capable of counteracting many short-comings. But now all at once this opportunity was snatched from his hands. In vain the whole country-side was searched for more than a week. It scarcely occurred to the rector that Arthur could have returned to London; the distance was comparatively great, and he knew that the boy had no money. But when at length all inquiries had failed, the labourer of whom Arthur had inquired his way on the morning of his flight, suddenly came forward and gave his testimony to that fact. The matter was put into the hands of the

Metropolitan police, who forthwith made inquiries at Mrs. Blatherwick's abode. By this time, however, Arthur had gone to live in Little St. Andrew Street, and no tidings of him were forthcoming. Accordingly the Rector was at length obliged to surrender all hope of recovering his charge. With a sigh of regret he settled down again to the epicureanism of his wonted life—epicureanism, that is, in its truer and less ignoble sense—and the episode formed in the life of the Rectory by the arrival and the departure of little Arthur Golding passed away as the bubbles pass from a pool into which a stone has been cast.

For a short time after this unfortunate occurrence Mr. Whiffle was disconsolate. Though latterly Arthur's progress under his tuition had been very far from satisfying his requirements, the curate had still clung to the hope of being the instrument whereby that somewhat intractable young nature should be modelled into that form of spiritual and intellectual nullity most adapted to ecclesiastical preferment. To instil his favourite doctrines into the mind of an apt and ready listener was Mr. Whiffle's ideal of happiness, and to have such a chance as this suddenly withdrawn was grievous, to say the least of it. In speaking to Mr. Norman of their mutual loss, he waxed eloquent on the glowing future which he had planned out in his own thoughts, tracing in imagination the whole life of his former pupil from a curacy upwards, and well nigh weeping when he came back to the sad reality. Mr. Whiffle had somewhat of a fondness for theatrical display, and it is not at all improbable that he used the present occasion to the profit of his eloquence long after his veritable chagrin had worked itself off.

"Such a boy, sir!" he exclaimed, on one occasion. "Bishop was written upon every line of his countenance! What an opportunity for putting into practice the precepts contained in my (as yet unpublished) pamphlets on the Principles of Education, and on the Rudiments of Ecclesiastical Training! I assure you, sir, I could sit in sack-cloth and ashes for the loss of that child. He was already more than a son to me."

"And yet you have sons of your own, Mr. Whiffle," interposed the Rector. "Would it not be easy and natural to transfer to your eldest boy the care you would have bestowed on poor Arthur?"

"My eldest boy?" exclaimed Mr. Whiffle, as if in astonishment. "That—that young scamp? Upon my word I never thought of it."

This was doubtless very true. In all likelihood the curate did not think of his family once in a month. The most distant object of interest had a closer claim upon his attention than the inmates of his home.

"Upon my word, that's quite a new idea to me!" he cried. "Ah! now suppose I were to tackle young Augustus. I don't know. He might turn out something, with a little care.

"I think it very possible," replied Mr. Norman.

"You do really sir? Well, very possibly you are right. Young Augustus! Ha, ha, ha! The young dog!"

Mr. Whiffle laughed heartily, rising the while on his toes and falling back again on to his heels alternately. The idea had evidently all the charm of novelty for him.

"Upon my word, I think I shall try. When I come to think of it, I believe the youngster has brains, if only he can be made to use them. And if he won't take his learning patiently, why it can be licked into him, like doses of physic. An admirable idea!"

From that day Mr. Whiffle took his eldest son in hand, and proceeded very vigorously with his education, which had hitherto been entrusted to a village schoolmaster of no very distinguished abilities. Master Augustus, whom we have already seen receiving personal chastisement at the hand of his father, was a lanky, overgrown lad of some twelve years, bearing a rather striking resemblance in outward characteristics to Mr. Whiffle himself.

He was by no means destitute of ability, but
had acquired the unfortunate habit of employing it in the service of a somewhat impish
disposition, the result being that he was in
constant trouble, at home and abroad.   It
was to the young gentleman's considerable
surprise, and very little to his satisfaction,
when he became aware of his father's intention to devote an unusual degree of care to
his future progress in the paths of literature.
The first few days of the new *régime* were
stormy in the extreme.   As Mr. Whiffle had
feared, young Augustus took by no means
kindly to the strong food thus suddenly
administered to him, and in consequence the
curate, to use his own expression, "licked it
into him."   The lessons took place in Mr.
Whiffle's study, whilst the rest of the family
were assembled in the usual manner in the
parlour.   Mrs. Whiffle, whose nerves were
sadly out of order, had a tremulous anticipation of the character of these interviews in
the study, and sat, with her attention on the
alert, to catch the least sounds which should
issue from thence.   As a rule she was rewarded
at the expiration of the first ten minutes,
when Mr. Whiffle's shrill tones, and Master
Augustus' still shriller piping, would be heard
rising to an ominous pitch.   These sounds
would increase, till at length both attained
the character of a prolonged and piercing
squeal, amid which would be heard the pecu-

liar *wish* produced by the sharp descent of a cane upon tightened clothing. At this point poor Mrs. Whiffle would burst into tears, and, when at length she could bear her suffering no longer, would step sobbing to the study door and knock. As a rule her knock was either unheard or unheeded, and she would hurry back with her fingers in her ears, throw herself in her chair, and, encircling all her brood within her arms, weep till the termination of the lesson. When that moment happily arrived, the study door opened and Mr. Whiffle came into the parlour, followed, at a slinking pace, by Master Augustus, carrying his books and slate under his arm, both perspiring and both very much out of temper. Then, as a rule, Mr. Whiffle would set out on a walk, to restore his habitual calm, and Master Augustus would be pressed in his mother's arms with the rest of the brood, sobbing out the while that "it is a jolly shame to be so hard on a fellow," and that "I wish there was no such thing as a church in the world," whereupon Mrs. Whiffle would cast up her eyes in horror, or ask him where he expected to go to after his death, if he allowed himself to give utterance to such sentiments.

Evidently affairs could not long rest at this stage, which was, in the nature of things, transitional, Mr. Whiffle persevering, for a wonder, in the task to which he had applied

himself. Master Augustus did not lack the
wit to observe that he would gain very little
save beatings by an obstinate persistence in a
refractory course of behaviour, whereupon he
gradually adopted a more conciliatory attitude, and before long discovered that he
could, at the expense of very little trouble,
master such tasks as were daily set him,
earning in consequence a degree of liberty
during the remainder of the day to which he
had by no means been accustomed. Finding
that the show of interest and attention was
what his father principally required, and
seeing how easily he was pleased with the
recitation of a few stock phrases and *formulæ*
which it was by no means difficult to remember, young Augustus ere long progressed
very considerably in the art of hypocrisy. If
before he had been a noisy, careless young
imp, it took only a year or so of Mr.
Whiffle's discipline to convert him into a
demure-faced, canting little rascal, always
ready on the sly for freaks quite remarkable
for precocious villainy, but always preserving
before his father and mother a sobriety of
demeanour and a facility in the quotation
of text and rubric which constituted the delight of Mr. Whiffle's soul. Verily, he said
to himself, the seeds of his sowing were
already bearing fruit.

In the meantime the Rectory was also the
scene of parental instruction—instruction

however, somewhat different in its character and its aims. However much Mr. Norman might feel justified in neglecting the duties of his care of souls, his constitutional idleness never led him to neglect the intellectual welfare of his little daughter Helen. When she reached the age of nine, Mr. Norman took her away from the school in which she had been taught to read and write, and devoted himself henceforth to her education, as to the main object of his life. During certain hours every day the two were alone together in the study which looked out upon the lawn, the little girl reading aloud, her father commenting upon what she read, and smoothing away all difficulties.

In pursuance of a clearly defined theory, Mr. Norman directed his efforts mainly towards the development of the emotional part of the child's nature, paying no attention whatever to many of the " branches " esteemed vital in the ordinary seminaries for female youth. Above all, first and foremost in his scheme of instruction, came the reading, marking, learning, and inward digestion of the poets. To know the poets, those who are unquestionably great in all ages, to read them with facility in the tongue they wrote in, this was the great end of his educational scheme. For inasmuch as poetry represents the highest phase of emotional activity, in that degree does it deserve to take a foremost place among the influences which may be relied upon for the moulding of the female character into the noblest form of which earth has knowledge. Not a day was allowed to pass on which Helen did not commit to memory, and carefully repeat to her father, certain verses, which the latter always chose with judicious consideration of the learner's age and disposition. But when she had attained her eleventh year, Helen had already stored up in her mind a veritable thesaurus of English poetical gems, had brooded over them till they had become a part of her rich nature, till they seemed to endue her very form with the essence of their own rhythmic grace and sweetness.

For Helen Norman was a wonderfully beautiful child, and seemed to bear promise of a womanhood fertile in all perfection of female loveliness. By her eleventh year the light gold of her many curls had deepened to a rich chesnut hue, the face had developed to a perfect oval, the nose had become Grecian in type and of exquisite delicacy, the lips and chin were adapting themselves to an expression at once infinitely sweet, and indicating a character far above the more distinctly female feebleness in energy and decision. She was already tall for her age, and gave promise of a figure little less than stately; her walk was upright, her step at once light and firm, her face ever looking upwards. Her fingers, already skilled either to hold the needle, direct the pencil, or touch the keys, were models of fairy delicacy; the flowers which she loved to train in the garden were scarcely more beautiful, they seemed to revive always, instead of drooping beneath her touch. Already she was the directing spirit in the household, inspiring involuntary respect even in so respectable a retainer as Mrs. Cope. The poultry-yard owned her as its mistress, and to no one did the shaken orchard trees yield a more abundant shower of ripe autumn fruit. She had two especial pets, the one a parrot, the tale of whose years was lost in the backward abyss of time, the door of whose cage stood always open that its tenant might remain within or sally forth to pace the room as it saw fit; the other, a magnificent Angora cat, who was on very excellent terms with the parrot, and whose place was at Helen's feet, whether she was sitting in the parlour, in the study, or in the garden. Master Augustus Whiffle, who occasionally visited at the Rectory and appeared to entertain a high esteem for Helen, had once brought her a lark of his own capture, securely fastened in a small cage, and offered it as a highly acceptable present; but Helen had cried at the sight of the poor bird's struggles for freedom, and, instead of accepting it, had begged that it might be set loose again, which Master Augustus, immensely surprised, accordingly did. Ever since that Helen had declined to keep a caged bird. The parrot could not be regarded in that light, for if it had ever been free, it must have forgotten it, and ceased to regret freedom centuries ago; and, moreover, the joyous loquacity which it perpetually indulged in appeared to denote anything rather than painful restraint. Helen used to call this bird the Genius of the house, and it was indeed always the centre of domestic activity. There was no end of its good-natured merriment. Tom was the name of the Angora cat, and Polly learned to call its name in tones so exactly like those of its mistress that it was no unfrequent thing for puss to come running into the room in response to the call, only to be greeted by a loud "Ha, ha, ha!" from within the cage. Tom, however, bore no malice. If he appeared sulky for a moment, he would, immediately after, approach the parrot's cage and put his head close against the bars, whereupon Poll would gently scratch it with her beak. After that Poll would in turn bow down her greyish-blue head close against the bars, and Tom would return the compliment by scratching it with his paw. This comedy was so frequently repeated that Helen came to observe it, and would often hide behind a curtain in the room to watch its occurrence. Sometimes

she was unable to restrain her laughter to
the end, and then her silvery voice would be
echoed by a gruff " Ha, ha, ha ! " from
Polly, whilst Tom ran up to his mistress
as usual, and crouched at her feet to be
stroked.

To any child less wisely guided than
Helen, and less blessed with natural gifts,
this life at the Rectory would have been intolerable in its loneliness and monotony.
Very rarely indeed did visitors cross the
lawn, the most frequent stranger being Mr.
Whiffle, with whom, as may be imagined,
Helen could feel but little sympathy. Once
a year, however, as a rule, the dull uni-
formity of the rector's existence was broken
very agreeably by a visit from his best, and,
indeed, only friend. This was Gilbert
Gresham, an artist by profession, and a
gentleman of considerable talent, yet more
pride, and very comfortable income. The
two had become acquainted first at the
University, and a congenial laziness of disposition, a certain feeling which they possessed in common, that, belonging to the
aristocracy of intellect, it was beneath them
to trouble greatly concerning the inferior
ones of the earth, had bound them together
in a firm friendship. Each of them could
appreciate the excellent qualities which lay
at the root of the other's character, and
perhaps none the less because they felt their

mutual similarity. Like Mr. Norman, Gilbert Gresham had married early, and had now been for several years a widower; also like his friend he had a daughter for his only child, a girl some two years older than Helen, named Maud. These children looked forward to the yearly meeting with mutual delight, which increased as they grew older. Young as they were, there were developed in both, to a rather remarkable degree, features of character which already bade fair to be the true index to their respective lives. In many respects widely different, there was yet sufficient similarity between their mental dispositions to ensure much sympathy for each other. Helen Norman was already an enthusiast, her heart on fire with noble thoughts which it had been her father's constant care to nourish in her; her mind filled with all manner of lofty images, each one magnified and made glorious by the ardent imagination of generous childhood. Living so remote from the every-day life of the world she had never learned to talk of things which, as a rule, engross the thoughts of other children; the contents of her books, the simple pleasure of her home life, the rare delights of woodland, meadow and hill, these were her main subjects for conversation, and, since she conversed almost exclusively with her father, her turn of thought naturally acquired a reflective and mature character much beyond her years. Of the world, in the ordinary sense of the word, she knew absolutely nothing. Mr. Norman himself received a daily newspaper, but he purposely kept it from his daughter's sight, being unwilling that she should so soon darken the cheerful brightness of her fancy with an infusion of that saddening gloom which broods over the life of cities. Thus she was growing up almost entirely ignorant of the pains and the passions which convert earth's sanctuaries into dreary realms of chaos and black night. True, as we have seen, she was aware of the existence of poverty and ignorance, and, pursuing the bent of her nature, often looked forward with an eager delight to the possibility of one day combating both. As was to be expected from her wonted surroundings, the young ideas on such subjects were patriarchal; she knew of no suffering so severe that it could not be allayed by earnest individual effort. Compared with the views of life held by poor Arthur, her late companion, for Helen the world had reverted to the golden age.

Maud Gresham being two years older than her friend, it was natural that she should entertain somewhat shrewder views of life; but her natural disposition was by no means endued with so large a share of enthusiasm as Helen possessed. She had been born and bred in London, moreover, and being a

spoilt child in a well-to-do house had seen
already a good deal of the life of the world.
By nature she was quiet and observant,
rapid and shrewd in her judgments, with a
tendency to epigram which might in time
develope into causticity, displaying, moreover, at all times, and under all circumstances, certain good-humoured egotism,
which was, indeed, the basis of her character.
Her education was being cared for at a
London ladies' school of irreproachable
standing, with results, however, far from as
thorough as those which marked Mr.
Norman's instruction. Possibly Maud was
not so quick to learn, but at the age of
thirteen she fell considerably short of Helen
at eleven in the foundations of culture. But
what she lacked in depth she made up for in
externals. About the same height as Helen
—who was tall for her age—she possessed
all that grace of manner which is the result
of a dancing-master's care, and which was so
different from the purely natural grace of the
younger child. Whilst Helen's conversation
was delicate and thoughtful, and refused to
flow save on such subjects as held possession
of her heart, Maud had the easy and spontaneous manner of a town-bred young lady,
chattering gaily on all subjects whatsoever,
and, though never affected, seldom very deep.
Her face was pretty, rather than beautiful,
but the assistance of her maid enabled her to

make an appearance which was decidedly prepossessing, and gave promise of considerable charms in future years—charms of a nature, however, which it would have been quite impossible ever to imagine Helen Norman in possession of. The two made a delicious picture, as, with arms twined around each other's waists, they wandered on the lawn or through the orchard in the bright summer weather, Helen wearing a dress of pure white muslin, only ornamented with a pale pink sash, Maud displaying a rather more elaborate toilet, her face shadowed with a large straw-hat which set off her charms admirably. Little wonder that Mr. Norman and Gilbert Gresham often sat long in silence behind the white curtains of the breakfast-room, gazing in delight at the unconscious children.

The difference between the character of the two children was very well illustrated on a certain occasion during the present visit, an incident which deserves narration on account of the unmistakable influence it was to exercise on the future growth of Helen's mind. The two had strolled together one remarkably fine morning rather beyond their usual limits, and quite alone. To the north of Bloomford, on the crest of the gentle hill whereon the Rectory stood, a large wood commenced, and spread for several miles, abounding in game and strictly closed against all trespassers. The owner of the land, an easy-tempered country gentleman who attended Bloomford parish church as regularly as his gout would permit him, made exceptions to this rigorous rule in the case of several of his friends, Mr. Norman among the number; and consequently, as often as her walks took her in that direction, Helen had no scruple in entering the wood and seeking her favourite flowers amidst the tangled copse-wood and short stretches of open lawn which alternated for miles around. Hither she had led Maud Gresham on the morning in question, and for nearly an hour they had wandered in the cool shadow of the trees, till a fallen trunk, overgrown with lichens and moss, and half-buried in years' deposit of dead leaves, offered them a tempting seat. Helen never went for a walk without taking some book as a companion, which she could either open or not as the humour took her, and now when they were seated side by side she opened on her knees a volume of Leigh Hunt's "Stories from the Italian Poets," a book which possessed a wonderful charm for the child's romantic fancy, and, opening at the chapter on Boiardo, she began to read of the loves of Orlando, whilst the melodies of a thousand birds and the continuous rustling of the branches overhead made a fitting accompaniment to the sweet fancies of the story.

" I shall ask papa to buy me that book,"
said Maud, when Helen paused and asked
for her opinion on what she had been
reading.

"I'm so glad you like it!" replied the
other, with enthusiasm. " I have read it
again and again, and should never get tired
of it."

" When I grow up," said Maud, " and when
I've got rid of all the stupid lessons and
stupid teachers, I mean to do nothing but
read nice books. I shall have a room of my
own, and I shan't allow any one to disturb
me from morning to night. Won't it be
delicious ? "

" I hope to read a great many books when
I grow up," replied Helen, after a moment's
thought, " but I shouldn't like to do nothing
but read. Wouldn't that be a rather selfish
life, Maud ? "

" What is the good of having money,"
retorted the elder maiden, with true womanly
inconsequence, " if you're not to make yourself comfortable with it, and do as you like ? "

" But that wouldn't be what I should like,"
urged Helen, with native directness.

" Then what would you like ? " asked the
other, a little pettishly.

" Father always says," replied Helen, " that
we must think of duties before pleasures.
A woman has a great many duties. I am
going to keep a school when I grow up, and

then I shall have to attend to my pupils all day."

"Keep a school!" echoed Maud, with comical horror. "Do you mean you'll marry a schoolmaster! Oh, the horrid things!"

"No, I don't mean that," said Helen, decisively. "I mean never to be married. I shall have a school of my own, and the pupils shall be all poor children, who can't afford to pay much, you see. And if they're good, I shall often give them money to take home to buy everything they want. Oh, how I hope I shall be rich some day, to have a lot of money to give away!"

Maud broke into a long laugh.

"I shall be rich," she replied, with something of pride in her tone, "but I'm sure I shan't give my money away. Those nasty poor people! I can't bear to see them in the streets, they look so horrid. I'm sure I think one ought to look after oneself before anybody else. There's the Workhouse for poor people to go to."

They had risen and were walking away. Suddenly Maud, who was a little in advance, on forcing her way through some bushes uttered a little scream and started back. Helen ran forward, and perceived the cause of her companion's fright. In a hollow on the other side of the hazel they were passing lay a man, fast asleep. He was dressed in the most miserable rags, which were clotted all over with the dirt of the roads, seeming to indicate that he had been tramping the country for a long time. His face was hideous in its hairy and cadaverous squalor, and one arm, which appeared bare through the torn sleeve of his coat, was wasted almost to the bone. As Helen's eyes fell upon this object her breath stopped short, and for a moment she was deadly pale.

"Oh, look, look, Maud," she whispered, clinging to the other's arm. "I'm sure this man is suffering and in want. Oh, how I wish I had some money with me!"

"Come away!" replied Maud. "I don't like his look at all. He might hurt us if he woke."

"Oh, I'm sure he wouldn't, Maud, dear! I wish it wasn't so far home; I would run and fetch something to give him."

"Come away!" repeated Maud, in a frightened whisper. "I have often heard tales of these men doing people harm. He looks like a gipsy!"

The children exchanged a frightened look, but little Helen seemed to gain courage whilst her companion grew more timid.

"Have you a penny in your pocket, Maud, dear?" she asked. "Please let me have it. I will give it you back when we get home."

"No, no! How silly you are, Helen! I shall go, whether you do or not!"

But Helen persisted, and at last succeeded

in inducing Maud to take out an elegant little
purse, and open it to see if it contained the
desired coin.   Just at this moment the man
opened his eyes and started to his feet. Maud
darted away in terror, dropping her purse
at Helen's feet.   Helen's face was very pale,
but she showed no signs of running away.
She and the tramp stood looking at each
other in silence.

"Could yer tell me the time, miss?" asked
the tramp at length, passing his hand over his
mouth and grinning, whilst he eyed the purse
which Helen had picked up.   "I doubt I've
overslep' myself."

"I don't know the exact time," replied the
child, "but I think it is nearly one o'clock. I
—I am so sorry I disturbed you."

"Don't matter, miss, as I knows on. I've
got maybe a twenty mile to walk afore night."

"That's a long way," said Helen.   "Will
—will you take this to buy something to eat
with?"

And she handed him a sixpenny-piece out
of the purse, the smallest coin it contained.

"Thankee, miss," replied the fellow, looking cautiously round.   "You won't be alone
'ere i' this wood, I should think; eh, miss?"

"No; there is another little girl with me;
but—but she has walked on."

"I wonder at yer comin' into the wood
alone; it's lonely like.   An' couldn't yer
spare me a little more, miss, out o' that there

purse? I ain't eaten nothin' for four days, s'elp me God!"

"I—I really would if it was my own," replied Helen, looking about to see where Maud was; "but it isn't."

Whilst she spoke the tramp had also carefully reviewed the ground, had bent quickly forward, and, before Helen knew what had happened, had snatched the purse from her and escaped into the thicket. For a moment she stood looking after him in mute astonishment; then, as Maud came running to her from a short distance, where she had watched the whole episode, burst into tears.

"There now!" exclaimed Maud. "I told you so, didn't I? I was sure he was a bad man. I could tell from his face."

"And I have lost your purse, Maud, dear!" sobbed little Helen. "You will never forgive me!"

"Of course I will, you silly child!" exclaimed the other, who was not averse from an occasional show of magnanimity. "I have only to ask papa, and he will buy me another as soon as we get back to London. Don't cry so, Helen. That won't bring the purse back."

"But how cruel of him!" sobbed the injured little girl. "How ungrateful! When I offered him as much as I could afford! I couldn't have believed any one would have been so ungrateful!"

All the rest of the walk home she was very sad, and indeed all the rest of the day. When the story was told to Mr. Norman and his friend they laughed, and told the children to be more careful where they wandered to, and so dismissed the affair. But little Helen was far from forgetting it so easily. Long years after the occurrence was still fresh in her memory, and who can gauge the exact weight of its influence on her future life?

CHAPTER X.

CHANGES.

"POOR Golding!" exclaimed Mr. Gresham, during a conversation in which his friend had been recalling the strange incidents of little Arthur's history. "I was not so intimate with him as you were, Norman, but I always looked upon him as a good-natured fellow, and rather a clever fellow, too, if I remember aright. But I'll be hanged if I can spend so much sympathy on his fate as you do. He fell too low. However dissipated a man becomes, let him at least remain in respectable company. If a poor devil runs over head and ears in debt through living in too high a style, and then blows out his brains comfortably in his dressing-room—well, I can spare him some sympathy. But to let oneself be starved to death in a noisome garret—bah!"

Mr. Gilbert Gresham was a man of some thirty-six years of age, of tall and well-proportioned figure, and blessed with features, to adopt the easily-comprehended phrase, of an aristocratic cast. There was something in his tone and manner a trifle too supercilious to be altogether agreeable to one who did not know him intimately, but from time to time, as he grew warm in conversation, he would cast aside this manner and allow the indications of a warm heart and acute brain to make themselves pleasantly conspicuous. In his talk he mostly affected extremely aristocratic sentiments, the cause of this doubtless lying in an exquisitely refined taste which could not tolerate anything savouring of coarseness. And yet the listener could not help suspecting that these sentiments were *only* affected, an impression aided by the somewhat theatrical air and gesture with which he was fond of delivering them. It was this that led Mr. Norman to smile as he listened to the above utterances with regard to Arthur's father.

"I don't know that it matters much where such a man meets his end," he replied, with a slight sadness in his voice. "He has been equally a sinner against the great law of the fitness of things, and has equally broken loose from the bonds of that duty which *should* bind us all, and which, I fear, in reality binds so few."

"Why, my dear fellow," interposed Mr. Gresham, "what *is* duty, after all? If it be not the impulse to reconcile gratification of our most ardent longings, whatsoever they may be, with at all events a tolerable measure of respect for our fellow-creatures, I confess I scarcely know what to understand by it."

"I can tell you what duty is *not*, Gresham," returned Mr. Norman, earnestly. "It is *not* to continue year after year the paid servant of masters whom you despise or detest, masking with a hypocritical countenance your disgust for the offices which you only half perform."

Mr. Gresham looked sharply at the speaker, and there was silence for a moment.

"You take this matter too much to heart, Norman," he said, at length. "Do you think you are the only clergyman in the Established Church who goes through the prescribed routine with only half a heart? What paragraph of the rubric have you violated? I maintain that you fulfil your duties to the letter."

"To the letter, perhaps; but by no means in the spirit. Do you know what I ought to do, Gilbert Gresham, if I would earn the privilege of considering myself an honest man? I should walk down to the church next Sunday morning, mount the pulpit as I am, devoid of ecclesiastical mummery, and proclaim aloud to the congregation: 'Behold! Here am I, Edward Norman, who have been your pastor for so-and-so many years, preaching the Gospel to you day after day without in reality believing a word of what I preached! Now I come to show myself in my true colours. Find some one else who will preach to you with more conscientious earnestness

—if you can. For my part, I have done with preaching for ever!' That is what I *should* say, and what prevents me from doing it?"

"A most prudent distaste for the interior of lunatic asylums, my dear Norman," replied the other, smiling.

"Say rather," returned Mr. Norman, bitterly, "a most clinging taste for the income of my benefice."

"I tell you, Norman, you altogether deceive yourself. Do you imagine that you would deserve any credit for adopting the insane line of conduct you have just depicted so graphically? Why, you would merit the laughter of the universe! You forget that you live in the England of the nineteenth century, when 'only not all men lie.' I tell you, the world is not worthy of such self-sacrifice. Morality, remember, is but comparative; and the most moral man in an age like ours is, I repeat it, he who best reconciles enjoyment of life with external decency."

"I wish I could persuade you to think seriously of this question, Gresham; but you are always full of satire, even though it be at a friend's expense. Why, even, according to your dictum, I am a most immoral man, for my life affords me anything but the maximum of enjoyment. I grow more miserable every week. Now look at Whiffle, the curate. What would I give to have that man's energy and interest in his work!"

"Whiffle!" exclaimed Mr. Gresham, with a burst of laughter; "that sophisticated ass with an ecclesiastical bray! Why, do you for a moment imagine that he is any more convinced of the dogmas of his Church than you are yourself?"

"I don't know," replied the other, with a sigh. "At all events, he has the appearance of being whole-hearted in his work."

"Now I tell you what the matter is, Norman," said Mr. Gresham, more seriously. "You are very far from well in bodily health. You want a thorough change. What do the doctors say?"

"They allow me some four or five years of life yet," returned Mr. Norman, with a melancholy smile.

"Under the present circumstances, yes. But you are fretting yourself away, my good fellow. I tell you, you must have a change."

"It is too late, Gresham, to hope for any considerable prolongation of my life. I am perfectly well aware that the old ladies are already beginning to finger the shears with an eye to my especial thread, and only one thing in the prospect troubles me. What will poor Helen do?"

"Do you think, Norman," replied Gilbert Gresham, with a touch of nature in his tone, "that my theories extend to my conduct when a friend's wishes or a friend's interests are concerned ? You know I make no great account of the majority of the tasks I imposed upon myself when I became godfather to your child, and I believe a somewhat modest computation would suffice to calculate the quantity of Catechism I have exerted myself to teach her; but as long as I remain in the land of the living, don't distress yourself with regard to Helen's future."

Mr. Norman pressed his friend's hand with a satisfied smile, and the sound of the dinner-bell very shortly terminated their conversation.

On the following day the visitors were to depart, and the consciousness of this made the dinner somewhat less lively than usual. But the dessert was destined to be relieved from the unusual silence, for as Mr. Whiffle happened to call whilst it was being placed upon the table, he was immediately invited to join the company, which he did without hesitation.

It soon appeared that the cause of the curate's arrival was a weighty one. He stated it thus, directing his conversation to Mr. Gresham, as to one who would be more likely to be impressed with its novelty than his usual auditor, the Rector.

"You see, sir, my mind is at present perplexed on what I may venture to call, perhaps, a not unimportant question of ecclesiastical discipline. To state the matter in a few words, the proposition has been made by the congregation's churchwarden that we should, in future, employ for the purposes of the offertory small bags—if I may so express myself—in preference to the open plates which have hitherto received that portion of treasure which the congregation desire to lay up out of the reach of moth, rust, and—ahem !—thieves. You will at once observe, Mr. Gresham, that the proposition involves momentous issues. As you are doubtless, well aware, the passage in the rubric having reference to the points at issue runs thus : ' Whilst these sentences are in reading, the deacons, churchwardens, or other fit person appointed for that purpose shall receive the alms for the poor, and other devotions of the people in a decent basin, to be provided by the parish for that purpose,' and so on. We have here, you observe, explicit mention of a *basin*, which, if I may trust my technical knowledge, always conveys the idea of a vessel hollow on the inside to the depth of not less than, let us say, one inch and a half. Should the depth be less than this, the vessel, in my humble opinion, Mr. Gresham, falls more properly in the class of those domestic utensils which we are wont to designate as *plates*. Now, as it happens, it is a *plate* which has hitherto been used in the Church for the offertorial purposes, and, if I mistake not, the church of St. Peter, Bloomford, is not by any means singular in this country in the use of such a vessel. Hence, Mr. Gresham, we arrive at the logical conclusion that, although the Rubric expressly stipulates the use of a *basin*, it has become customary in the Church of England to substitute a *plate* therefor—doubtless owing to considerations of conveniency into which it is at present scarcely necessary to enter."

Mr. Whiffle delivered the last remark in a half apologetic, half interrogatory tone, shuffling on his seat as he arrived at the period, thrusting his fingers repeatedly through his thick masses of red hair, and looking first at Mr. Gresham, then at his rector, then at the children, with an air of undisguised satisfaction. Never was the curate so thoroughly at home as when suffered to enter at length upon the discussion of a question such as the present.

" Certainly unnecessary, Mr. Whiffle," said the rector, suppressing a smile. " Mr. Gresham follows you with attention."

" And with pleasure, allow me to add," put in the artist. " Your exposition, sir, is lucid in the extreme, as becomes the importance of the matter."

Mr. Whiffle bowed, and continued with a gratified smile—

"Having arrived at this conclusion—viz., that the strict prescription of the rubric has already submitted to modification in obedience to the dictates of conveniency, we have, as you will recognise, Mr. Gresham, established a precedent—a precedent, sir." The curate dwelt on the word with satisfaction. " So far then, sir, there is nothing whatever objectionable in the proposition that Mr. Vokins, the churchwarden, has felt called upon to make; that I must in fairness admit. But when we examine the motives which Vokins urges as in favour of the substitution of—so to speak—a bag or wallet, in the place of the present *plate*, it appears to me that we trench upon very debateable ground. Mr. Vokins—ahem!—makes the statement, Mr. Gresham, that many members of the congregation who would be glad to contribute their mite on the occasion of collections are restrained from doing so by the fear of public opinion; in other words, they prefer not to give at all to depositing on an open plate, in the full view of their neighbours, for the time being, a coin which, by its diminutive value, would seem to lay an imputation either upon their liberality, or, what is still worse, upon the condition of their finances. Now, gentlemen, this is a frame of mind singularly human, it must be confessed, and one which, though raised above those ordinary frailties of the flesh by our position as servants in that glorious Temple which we denominate the Church of England as by law established, it behoves us to take into consideration. I, individually, still hold my judgment in suspense, though I confess to having spent considerable thought on the subject. On the one hand we must weigh whether it is consistent with the dignity of The Church to make concessions to human weaknesses, such as those so acutely observed by Mr. Vokins; on the other, I opine that we ought to consider whether such concession may not appear justified by the, doubtless, not inconsiderable accession of voluntary offering which would accrue to St. Peter's in the event of *bags*—so to speak—beings substituted for *plates*. Might I venture to ask your opinion, Mr. Gresham, as that of a disinterested observer ?"

"You do me too much honour, Mr. Whiffle," responded the artist, in a tone of fine sarcasm, wholly unrecognisable as such by the vanity of the curate. "There is, doubtless, much to be said on both sides; but, if I may express an opinion, I think it just possible that history, if well searched, might afford a precedent—a precedent, sir—for the dignity of the Church giving way before such very important considerations as those which we, in worldly phrase, denominate pecuniary."

"I think you are right, sir!" exclaimed the curate. "Allow me to compliment you on your delicate penetration in so nice a matter. And, possibly, since you have so expressed yourself, I may venture to declare that I rather incline to Mr. Vokins's opinion in this matter. We are well aware, Mr. Gresham, that twelve of those humble coins called halfpence amount to the value of a silver sixpenny-piece; as also that twelve of the but slightly more dignified pennies represent the value of a silver shilling; and I have yet to learn, gentlemen, that the current value of a fixed sum of money diminishes with the denomination of the factor in which it is expressed. Mr. Gresham will forgive the figure in the lips of one who once boasted himself something of a mathematician."

The conversation continued in the same strain for some half hour longer, Mr. Whiffle taking upon himself the main burden of it. At the end of that time Mr. Norman rose from the table and dismissed the subject with the remark that he would give it his consideration, upon which assurance Mr. Whiffle retired, excellently well pleased at having had such a remarkable opportunity of displaying his ingenuity and eloquence.

The church of St. Peter's, Bloomford, was conducted on Low Church Evangelical principles. The interior was very plain, and the service was totally without those adulterated reminiscences of Romanism with which most of the churches in that part of

the country were then seeking to enliven the
zeal of not too ardent congregations. This
had been the state of affairs throughout
the period of Mr. Norman's incumbency, in
the early years owing to his convictions,
later on account of habit and carelessness
rather than anything else. But it was a
state of affairs by no means agreeable to
Mr. Whiffle, who had for a long time been
doing his very best to breathe something
of the spirit of Ritualism into the rector's
Gallio-like disposition. His efforts had,
naturally, been unsuccessful, greatly to the
curate's chagrin. Had Mr. Whiffle had his
will, St. Peter's would have been immediately converted into a model of advanced
High Churchism. Thus it was that every
subject of discourse connected with the
service of the church was seized upon by
him with eagerness, if only for the sake of
averting stagnation.

In the meantime he consoled himself with
the imagination of what he would do when
the presentation, to which he never ceased
to look forward, should ultimately realise
itself.

And, indeed, it was just now nearer than
Mr. Whiffle's most ardent hopes could have
conceived. Mr. Norman, whose consumption, though working but slowly upon his
frame, was none the less surely wasting him
away, would long ago have resigned his

living and gone to live in a more suitable climate, had it not been that the income of his rectory was quite indispensable to enable him to live in accordance with his usual habits. During the last half a dozen years he had twice spent several months of the winter at Mentone, each time to the manifest improvement of his health, and a not inconsiderable lengthening of his life might reasonably be hoped for were he able to establish himself permanently in that grateful climate. He would also have desired to live for some time on the Continent on Helen's account, for he was, of course, unable himself to give her the thorough instruction in the modern languages which he had set his heart upon her having. Reflection on these matters had often made him unusually melancholy of late, and a decided advance of his malady also made itself apparent.

He had almost resolved once more to obtain leave of absence for a few months, and this time in company with Helen, to revisit Mentone, when he received one morning, early in November, a letter bearing the seal of a firm of London solicitors. Upon reading it he became so nervously agitated as to bring on a severe fit of coughing, followed by spitting of blood. For the rest of the day he was quite incapable of maintaining any calmness, but paced his garden for several hours with the letter in his hand, constantly referring to it; and, on entering the house, walked in uncertainty between his study and the parlour, totally neglecting all food, and even Helen's lessons. Early on the following morning he came down, after a sleepless night, dressed for a journey, partook of a very slight breakfast, and walked to the railway station, where he took one of the first trains to London, having merely left a message behind for Helen, saying where he was gone. On arriving in town he went straight to the abode of his friend Gresham, in the neighbourhood of Regent's Park, but was so unfortunate as to find Mr. Gresham and his daughter from home. Thereupon he drove to his usual hotel in Oxford Street, and was very much engaged during three days, principally within the precincts of Gray's Inn. At the end of that time he returned to Bloomford. The excitement of his business had been so very unusual that it operated most unfavourably on his delicate state of health, and for several days he was confined to his room. On the last of those days he wrote the following letter—

> " Bloomford Rectory,
> " November 13th, 1863.

" MY DEAR GILBERT,

" I dare say you will have learnt by this time that I made a very unexpected descent upon your dwelling some ten days ago, and found it vacant. Since my return to Bloomford, I have suffered from some confounded nervous complaint or other, which has rendered me incapable of penning you a line. But I must no longer delay letting you hear a piece of news which I doubt not will rejoice you.

"The occasion of my going town was no other than this. I received a letter from Messrs. Connor and Tweed, of Gray's Inn Square, acquainting me with the fact that my brother William had recently died in San Francisco, intestate, that he had left behind him possessions to the amount of some £50,000, and that in default of a nearer heir, the whole of this fell to me! I think I have often told you of William's peculiarities. Nothing at all like a disagreement ever took place between him and myself, but as he went out to California some ten years ago, and has ever since been a desperately bad correspondent, we may be said to have become almost total strangers. I had no notion that he had become so wealthy, but as I fully believe that, had he made a will, he would have left, at all events, the bulk of his wealth to me, I have no hesitation whatever in availing myself of my legal rights in the matter.

"I need scarcely say how welcome such a windfall as this is. During the last few days I have reflected much on my future course, and, subject to any little modifications my friends and advisers may suggest, I think it will be pretty much as follows. As I am about as unfitted as it is possible for a man to be for my position in the Church, I shall as soon as possible resign my living, and bid adieu for ever to creeds and catechisms! Congratulate me on this, my dear Gilbert. Then, as I feel that my days are numbered, and, for the sake of Helen, I should like to remain still as long as possible in the land of the living—which I have found on the whole remarkably agreeable—I shall forthwith transplant myself to some more congenial climate, say to Mentone, or some such place, and there seek to enjoy the remainder of my life in that quiet manner of which, I flatter myself, I have so well learnt the secret. In doing this I contemplate no waste of time. Helen will of course go with me; I should like her to have a Continental education.

" And now, my dear Gilbert, let me see you as soon as possible. Come down on Monday, if you can, and bring Maud with you. It may be some time before she and Helen have another opportunity of seeing each other. I must not write any more, as I feel my head-ache approaching. Farewell for the present.

" Yours, ever affectionately,
" EDWARD NORMAN."

Mr. Gresham obeyed the call, and the following Monday saw him and his daughter once more at Bloomford. They only remained two days, during which long conversations took place between them, and many matters of importance were decided. First of all it was determined that Mr. Norman should, as soon as it was practicable, resign his living and quit Bloomford; that thereupon he should take up his abode with Mr. Gresham in London till all necessary arrangements for his leaving England could be completed; and that as early in the following year as possible he should remove with Helen to Mentone.

Never, it seemed to Mr. Norman, had he known what real happiness was till now, never had he yearned more eagerly for any day than for that which would fairly set him loose from the bonds of his clerical position, for years intolerably galling. The condition which had been the dream of his life, he had at length lived to realise; he found himself henceforth at liberty to enjoy the remainder of his days in that absolute freedom from official restraint which was naturally the ideal of his epicurean nature. Henceforth he had but one serious care, the education of his daughter Helen, and that indeed was so completely a task dictated by ardent affection and the loftiest emotions of which he was capable, that it was anything but a drawback upon his freedom. This duty, however, excepted, his days were his own. No longer need he rise with a sigh from his beloved poets, to turn in disgust to the compilation of an insipid sermon; no longer would the calm peace of his Sundays be broken by the necessity of presiding at ceremonies which he loathed in every detail. Above all he would no longer be oppressed by that hideous nightmare of hypocrisy, so inimical to his instincts, but which he had been compelled by weakness and the force of circumstances so long to hug to his bosom. What mornings would now be his in the glowing atmosphere of southern lands, what ambrosial nights would it be his happy lot to enjoy, watching the full moon scatter silvery beams on the smooth surface of a tideless sea! Oh, ye gods, was not the cup of bliss too full? What if he were slowly but surely sinking to the grave beneath a remorseless disease; at least he would derive the maximum of enjoyment from those suns which would rise upon him, and what more could he wish? Man is mortal, and sufficient for the day is the evil thereof.

By Christmas, Mr. Norman had already resigned his living, and had left Bloomford. For several weeks speculation was rife in the village with regard to his successor, and many were the prayers breathed up that he might be a young unmarried man. Whether agreeable or not, mattered little; for Bloomford was a rich living. Mr. Whiffle was elated with all manner of hopes, it being principally *in votis* that the new incumbent might be a man of strong High Church sympathies. And so indeed he ultimately proved to be. For Mr. Norman, who cherished some degree of good feeling towards his old curate, and was perhaps infected with that fever of generosity which often possesses sudden heirs to a fortune, exerted his influence with the patron of the living, and without much difficulty secured the presentation of it to Mr. Whiffle himself.

I shall not attempt in this place to describe the state of mind into which the *quondam* curate was thrown by the communication of this piece of intelligence. For the present it may safely be left for the reader's imagination to depict. It is not unlikely we may have other opportunities of observing Mr. Whiffle with his honours fresh upon him.

In the meantime Mr. Norman and Helen were residing at Mr. Gresham's, in Portland Place. The little girl had never before been in London, and now went the round of the sights, accompanied sometimes by her father, sometimes by Maud and Miss Wilson, Maud's governess. She enjoyed it all in a quiet, self-contained manner, very rarely breaking into childish delight; a circumstance which somewhat surprised her father, who knew so well her ardent temperament. The fact was she was rather oppressed by the multitude of

Q

novel scenes, and by the strange sensation
of living amidst so much life. It was only
in the calm intimacy of the home circle that
Helen could open her heart and speak freely
all her impressions ; a natural shyness kept
her reserved in the presence of strangers.
Only once did the stately little maiden allow
herself to be betrayed into strong delight,
and that was on the occasion of a visit to
Westminster Abbey together with her father
and Maud. At the sight of the tombs bearing names which she knew so well, and which,
young as she was, she had already learned
to love, she almost cried aloud with rapture,
and when she issued from the solemn gloom
of the Abbey into the open air, Mr. Norman
noticed, not without pride, that her eyes were
dim with moisture.

Mr. Gresham's house was for ever full of
gay company, but of this neither Helen nor
her father saw much. The daily lessons were
continued as usual, and Miss Wilson's skill
was called into requisition to continue the
musical instruction which had hitherto been
superintended by the organist of St. Peter's
church, a young man of only moderate
abilities. And so the time passed till the
commencement of February, when at length
all Mr. Norman's preparations were complete,
and the day was appointed on which he would
leave England. Mr. Gresham and Maud accompanied the two as far as the boat which

was to take them across the Channel, and here bade them farewell.

A week after, Maud Gresham received the following letter—

"Mentone,
"Feb. 8th, 1864.

"MY DEAR MAUD,

"I promised to write to you as soon as possible, and let you know that we got here safely. The passage was a little rough, and I was a little ill, but it soon passed away when we reached land. I like Mentone *very* much, dear Maud; but I should like it better if you were with me. Papa says he is much better already. I am so glad, for you know how much I love dear papa. I enjoyed myself very much at your house, and I shall never forget the beautiful sights of London, and above all that dear Westminster Abbey. Try to remember me and write when you have time. I will write again soon and let you know everything that I do. Papa has got me a teacher for French and German. I like her very much, but she has a queer name which I cannot pronounce. I am very happy, and I hope you are. Good-bye.

"From your loving Friend,
"HELEN NORMAN."

CHAPTER XI.

A DOUBLE LIFE.

CALM, uneventful were the years which succeeded Arthur's establishment under Mr. Tollady's roof. Uneventful outwardly, that is; for
as regards those unseen circumstances, those
silent conquests, defeats, and revolutions
which succeed one another in the hidden
depths of an expanding mind, these years
from twelve to eighteen were fruitful to a
degree of which we can only convey a partial
idea by dwelling on a few of the visible
results. Samuel Tollady had had no occasion
to regret the attention he had paid to
Arthur's intellectual training. The boy from
the first picked up knowledge with an almost
incredible facility; so quickly, indeed, that
his master began before long to fear that his
own knowledge would soon be insufficient to
guide the boy's mind in those paths which it
pursued with such eager delight. The
printer was a most indulgent master, per-
mitting to Arthur every practicable moment of
leisure time, and not unfrequently himself
performing tasks which were the boy's proper
work, in order that the latter might enjoy
the fruits of an extra hour spent over the

book he happened to be reading. Indeed it would be scarcely correct to speak of the two in the mutual relationship of master and servant, for a very few months sufficed to create between them a feeling of mutual affection, which, as time went on, was strengthened on Arthur's side by growing respect, at times almost veneration, and on that of the old man by genuine admiration of, and pride in, the powers which he saw developing beneath his fostering care. By when Arthur had reached his fifteenth year, an actual son of his own could scarcely have been more to Mr. Tollady than he was; and if ever Arthur endeavoured to recall to his mind the aspect of that father whom he had so bitterly mourned years ago, he was quite unable to dissociate the dim memory of his features from the look of those grave, kind eyes which so often rested upon him during the day with affectionate interest.

About this time Mr. Tollady began to give Arthur his first lessons in the art of printing, on which occasion he addressed to him a few words in a more serious strain than he had hitherto ever made use of to the boy. It was shortly after one New Year's Day, as the two were sitting in the back parlour after supper, listening to a furious storm which seemed ever and anon to shake the foundations of the house. The printer had been unusually sad that day, and as Arthur glanced up at him occasionally from gazing thoughtfully at the live coals, he thought he had never seen him looking so old.

"Arthur," said Mr. Tollady, suddenly, "do you think I am a rich man?"

"Not—not exactly rich," began Arthur, after some slight hesitation. "But—but, indeed, I have never thought about it at all."

"I dare say you never have, for you are still in the happy years, Arthur, when the thoughts run but little on riches or poverty. Should you be surprised if I told you that I was a poor man—a very poor man?"

"I should be surprised if you told me you were very poor, sir."

"You would?" repeated the other, smiling. "Would you be sorry to hear it?"

"Very sorry, for I am sure you do not deserve to be poor, sir," replied the boy with a proud firmness of tone beyond his years.

There was silence for a few moments, when the printer began again in a grave tone.

"I am indeed very poor, Arthur; so poor, that even the slightest expenses beyond our mere necessaries are a great burden to me. Do you remember how many newspapers you used to take out each morning when first you came to me?"

"I think about fifty, sir."

"Just so. And how many do you take out now?"

" Twenty-three, sir."

" Just so. Can you see why I ask you that, Arthur ?"

" Yes, sir," replied the boy, sinking his head and speaking sadly.

" The papers used to be the best part of my business," pursued the old man ; " but it was to the office that I looked for the greater part of my income. But that, too, has fallen off sadly during the last few years. Do you notice that James has not been here since Christmas ? "

James was the printer whom Mr. Tollady had long employed in his office. Arthur replied in the affirmative.

" I have been obliged to do without him, though it grieved me sincerely to part with him. I had no longer business enough to keep him at work, Arthur. I can manage it all myself now-a-days, with your help."

" I am very sorry to hear it, sir."

There was again silence for several minutes, when Arthur suddenly broke out.

" Then why do you let me be a burden to you, sir? I'm sure I don't anything like earn my food and the money you give me ; I have thought so for a long time, and wished to speak to you about it, but I was afraid you might be offended. Pray let me find some work somewhere ! I am sure I could earn fifteen shillings a week, sir, and—and that would be a little help—though not much."

He added the last words blushingly, as he met Mr. Tollady's eye fixed upon him with its kindly smile.

"Don't be ashamed of your generous nature, Arthur," replied the latter. "No doubt you could earn what you say, and more; but it would be very much against my wish. I fear I have done wrong in telling you all this; you will distress yourself about it. No; I said that all expenses beyond those necessary for our support were a burden; but I am glad to say that there is still no difficulty in providing what we absolutely need, and, I trust, never will be. This is the reason I spoke to you about such things. You are now beginning to learn a business, one that has supported me for the greater part of my life, and which, if you master it thoroughly, will always stand you in good stead, for a first-class printer can always find employment. Now the very best way you can help me, Arthur, is to become a good compositor as soon as possible. Then you will be able to take James's place, and who knows but what you may bring us good luck. I am afraid I am getting too old to push ahead, as I ought to."

"You shall have no reason to complain of me, sir," replied Arthur. "I shall not sleep till morning for eagerness to begin."

"I wish you could bestow on me a little of your life and energy, Arthur," said Mr.

Tollady, with a sigh. "It often rather grieves me to be able to provide no better field for their exercise than this musty old shop and office. But keep well in mind what I have said to you, my boy. I teach you to become a printer because I think that in so doing I shall best fulfil my duty towards you; I shall have given you knowledge by which you can always live. Do not suppose that I think you capable of nothing higher; had I the means I would spare nothing to give you the best advantages in whatever profession you should choose; but you see how it is with me. Have you done any more at your drawing to day?"

Arthur started to his feet with a joyful look, and ran to a corner of the room where a large and much-worn portfolio was leaning upright against the wall. This he carried to the table, and then laid it open. It contained a large number of drawings, on paper of various shapes and sizes, but at the top lay one on which Arthur was at present engaged.

For he had not forgotten the old fondness which had first been awakened by the mendicant lodger at Mike Rumball's. Very shortly after he had begun to live at Mr. Tollady's he had recommenced his rude attempts on any scraps of paper which he found lying about, and this time, when he was at length discovered, he met with every encouragement to cultivate his taste. The printer was himself not without some facility in the use of the pencil; or at all events such had once been the case; and he now brought out several old sketch-books which he had filled years ago, and showed them to the delighted boy. Henceforth Arthur divided his leisure time pretty impartially between his books and his drawings, and with Mr. Tollady's occasional suggestions to aid his natural instincts, he made perceptible progress in the art. With what scorn would he now have viewed that portrait of the parrot which he had laboured at so earnestly, and which he had offered with so much pride to his goddess, little Lizzie Clinkscales! For, indeed, he began to acquire not a little facility in copying from pictures, or from objects which the printer set before him as models. One copy of a cut in an old *Illustrated London News* Mr. Tollady had liked well enough to have framed, and it now hung over the parlour mantelpiece—a group of horses with legs a trifle too long, and manes of astonishing luxuriance. The drawing which he now brought forth from the portfolio was a more ambitious attempt. It was a copy in pencil of Giotto's portrait of Dante, which he had found engraved in one of Mr. Tollady's books. The profoundly sad, and somewhat weird expression of the face was very finely caught, and expressed in a few bold lines which gave considerable promise for the future skill of the hand which drew them.

Mr. Tollady sighed as he looked at the drawing. He was wishing that he had it in his power to provide adequate instruction for such exceptional talent. As he held it up in his hand, Arthur had left the room, and in a moment returned, holding something out of sight behind his back. He came and stood before Mr. Tollady with a smile on his face.

"What have you got there, my boy?" asked the latter, answering the smile.

"Something that I am half afraid to show you, sir," replied Arthur. "I know it is very bad, but it is only a first trial. You won't make fun of it?"

"You know it is not my habit to make fun of anything well meant, Arthur."

The boy drew his hand from behind his back and brought forward a small piece of paper on which he had made his first attempt in colours. It was a copy from nature of a sprig of holly, thickly clustered with berries.

"Ha! Water-colours!" exclaimed Mr. Tollady. "Bravo, Arthur! very good, upon my word, very good! When did you do it?"

"This morning, sir."

"Very well. Persevere, Arthur, and you will do something worth putting in the window yet. Where did you find your colours?"

"I bought a blue, yellow, and red for two-pence, sir."

"Why did you choose those three?" asked Mr. Tollady, smiling.

"I read the article on 'Colours' in your Cyclopædia, sir, and found that those were the three out of which all the others were made."

"Very well, Arthur. Try one or two more little things like this, and we will see whether we can find you a box of colours somewhere or other."

So the days went on. Arthur had worked away at "case," and was making evident progress in the art of printing. Not that he took any pleasure in the work for its own sake; being merely manual dexterity he very soon grew disgusted with it. But he never failed to fulfil his hours destined to this employment conscientiously, for he knew that in so doing he was affording pleasure to his master, and had, moreover, the expectation of being very shortly absolutely useful to him.

He had grown to be a tall, handsome boy, with blue eyes full of light, and a countenance open and glad. His surroundings were by no means of a joyous character, and yet such is the natural ardour of youth, and especially of youth animated by the celestial gift of genius, that his life at this time was, as it were, a continual hymn of gladness, the joyful exuberance of a lofty soul breathed upwards, under unseen impulses, to the eternal source of life and light which we feel, but know not. The miserable little outcast of Whitecross Street had, thanks to the strivings of his inborn spirit, assisted by the never-ceasing teaching of his friend and guardian, developed into a youth of rich promise, his mind already stored with no despicable harvest of knowledge, his heart throbbing with generous sympathy with all that is most beautiful in the world of nature or imagination. As he grew older he felt within himself the stirrings of a double life, the one, due to his natural gifts, comprehending all the instincts, the hopes, the ambitions of the artist; the other, originating in the outward circumstances of his childhood, and not a little in the instruction directly afforded him by Mr. Tollady, or indirectly caught from the conversation of such men as Mark Challenger and John Pether, which urged him on to the labours of the philanthropist, showing him in the terribly distinct reflex of his own imagination the ever-multiplying miseries of the poor amongst whom he lived, and painting in entrancing hues the glories of such a life as his master's, self-denying even to a fault, bent solely on the one object of making the world less wretched, even though he died in the effort. These two distinct impulses seemed to grew within Arthur Golding's

mind with equal force and rigidity; he experienced neither of them any the less for
being more and more convinced, as he grew
in self-knowledge, that their co-existence
was incompatible with the perfection of
either. To which of the two should he
wholly devote himself? As he drew on
towards his eighteenth year he spent many
and many an hour in vain efforts to decide.
Already he began to feel that this would be
the struggle of his life, that upon the solution
of this inward problem would depend the
happiness of his existence.

At times he was wholly the artist, especially
when he had been working long at one of his
drawings, or when he had been reading one
of his favourite books on art, to procure him
which Mr. Tollady had subscribed to a circulating library. His favourites were Cun-
ningham's " Lives of British Artists," and
Vasari's " Lives of the Painters." These he
read and re-read with an enthusiasm which
set at defiance the weariness of nature and
made night tributary to the supply of hours
of which the day had too few.

The second half of his nature grew strongest
at those times when he took his weekly walk
in Mr. Tollady's company. Sunday evening
was invariably spent thus, when, that is to
say, the weather was not so intolerably bad
as altogether to forbid outdoor exercise.
Starting from the shop about four o'clock,

they would walk in a direction already agreed
upon, and, by fetching a lengthy compass,
regain home towards nine. On such occasions
Mr. Tollady was more talkative than at other
times. The exercise appeared to do him
good, and not unfrequently in his flow of talk
he would make mention of scenes and events
which led Arthur to think that in his early
days the printer must have seen a great deal
of the world. But on his putting questions
on this subject, or indeed on any other in the
least personal to his companion, the result
invariably was to turn the conversation immediately into other channels. Arthur soon
observed this, and carefully avoided touch-
ing upon such points, but he nevertheless
nourished a great curiosity to know more
of Mr. Tollady's life, feeling sure that it
must be interesting far beyond ordinary life
stories.

One of these walks Arthur ever after remembered, partly on account of the energy
and freedom with which Mr. Tollady that
evening gave utterance to his opinions, partly
from an event which followed upon the walk,
and which we shall have shortly to relate.
The direction they had taken was City-wards.
After crossing Smithfield Market, they passed
along Little Britain, and over Aldersgate
Street into Barbican. When in Smithfield,
Mr. Tollady said, looking round with a peculiar smile—

"You remember the associations connected with this place, Arthur, don't you?"

"The burning of the martyrs, you mean!"

"Just so. When you read history, don't fall into the error of skipping over those parts affecting religion as too uninteresting to hold your attention. To my mind, Arthur, history of religious beliefs has always been at once the saddest and the most interesting of studies. It is nothing less than the struggle of the human mind from the black depths of ignorance and brutish fear up towards that glorious heritage of freedom to which, I cannot but believe, it is one day destined to attain. You can afford to smile at those writers who would have you reckon religious creeds among the influences which tend to exalt humanity. Never believe it! These faiths, one and all, great and small, from the most grovelling superstition of the cannibal to the purest phase of devotion nurtured in the mind of a Christian, trust me, they are nothing but remnants of the primeval darkness, *clinging* to man as he toils laboriously upwards, clinging in spite of all his efforts to shake them off. And woe to such as hug the darkness to their bosom!"

"Can you, then, feel no admiration for those men who suffered such fearful agonies in the cause they considered holy?"

"Admiration—no, Arthur; profound pity, if you like. Why should I admire a man because he knits up his bodily frame to the patient endurance of suffering, and all for the sake of error? Shake off that prejudice, I beg of you. Admiration! It is only the body that is in question, and how can I spare admiration for the body? As well ask me to admire the porter who carries easily upon his head a weight which would crush me or you to the ground. That, too, is a wonderful exertion of bodily force. You will say, perhaps: 'Never mind whether their belief was right or wrong; admire it because it was so unshakable.' I tell you, nonsense! There is no abstract merit in *that*. Call it pig-headedness, and will you admire it then?"

"But," interrupted Arthur, "you do not actually despise them for the part they took?"

"Do not misunderstand me," pursued the other, eagerly. "I argue merely against the absurd claim for admiration and reverence. Despise them! No, certainly not. I despise absolutely no man, and simply because I esteem all alike as involuntary agents in the hands of a great power which most call Providence, but which I prefer to call the inexplicable spirit of the world. History pursues its path, using us as its agents for the working out of prescribed ends. To think that we men can modify those ends is the delusion of ignorance or of madness. Why then should I despise the martyrs? They performed their part in history, and could

not otherwise. But do not ask me to
actually admire them. Admiration I can
only spare for those whom fate has ordained
as instruments to *advance* humanity. Those
who are so unfortunate as to represent the
retarding forces in the life of man, I can only
infinitely pity them."

" Does not this lead to a state of mind in
which one despairs of being able to benefit
the world, and let one's hands lie idle out of
mere fear of doing harm ? For you hold that
we are merely agents, that we have no power
to direct the course of human life."

" Wrong, Arthur. I did not say that we
had no power to direct the course of human
life; but, that we have no power to direct it
otherwise than in a certain path which has
been fore-ordained, and which experience
proves to us it will most certainly pursue."

" Yes; but if we are sure the world is
going to pursue this path, why trouble ourselves to help it on, why not sit and watch ?"

" I will tell you, Arthur; because we *cannot!*
The course of the world includes the course
of each man's thoughts. These pursue a
path which is fore-ordained in each individual
case ; how, I do not pretend to say. Now,
you who propose to me to sit down and
watch, *could* you follow your own counsel ?"

" I certainly could not."

" No, I am sure of it. If you could—well,
that would be your part in the world, to be

an obstruction, and even then you could not otherwise. You feel within you something that says : 'Rise up, and do so and so.' You may choose *your own way* of doing it, mark; and this is what we mean by free-will; but further than that you have no choice. This is quite distinct from the petty conventional distinctions of right and wrong, which, as the vulgar say, tempt one alternately. It is quite possible for a man to do wrong, in that conventional sense, and yet to be helping on in the noblest manner, and very likely unconsciously, the spirit of mankind ! "

" Then is this inward feeling of a duty all that we have to guide our actions ?"

" Not all. We have experience. The feeling which urges you to advance the world, at the same time takes the form of a craving for knowledge ; thus affording you materials for judging as to the best of many courses for fulfilling your life-task. In the history of the past you read the history of the future, and learn to judge of the significance of cause and effect."

Talking thus earnestly they had passed out of Barbican into Beech Street, and so to the foot of Whitecross Street. Here Arthur suddenly stood still.

" You asked me what Smithfield was memorable for," he said, with a peculiar smile. " Can you tell me the association connected with Whitecross Street ?"

" Do you mean the Debtor's Prison ?" asked Mr. Tollady.

" By no means. I think I have never told you, but this was the place where several of my earliest years were spent."

Mr. Tollady looked into the young lad's face with a look at once of pity and curiosity.

" Let us turn up here," said Arthur ; and they walked up the street.

It was a moderately fine summer's evening, and in front of all the doors, and in the mouths of the courts and alleys, groups of people were standing talking, driven by the warmth out of the pestilential air of their houses. Along the middle of the narrow street hundreds of children were playing, making the air resound with their laughter, shouts and screams.

" I must have been like one of those," said Arthur; " and listen ! Ha ! what remembrances that brings to my mind."

Coming towards them was a band of little girls, hand in hand, who, as they skipped along, joined in a chorus, and the words were :

There is a happy land, far, far away.

Mr. Tollady, surprised at the broken tones in which his companion had spoken, looked up into his face and saw tears starting to his eyes.

"Aye, aye!" said the old man, sighing. "There had need be a happy land somewhere, for it is but little happiness that these poor creatures are fated to meet with on earth. 'Far, far away!' Alas! how far!"

They had come to the entrance of Adam and Eve Court, the appearance of which was fouler than that of any they had yet seen. Dirty whitewash covered the lower half of the houses, such at least, as the narrowness of the court would permit of being seen. The stench which reeked into the outer street was overpowering.

"There, there!" exclaimed Arthur, excitedly. "In that very court, that very house, the last you can see, my father died!"

Mr. Tollady said nothing, but turned away and walked on rapidly. His features were working violently with an inward emotion he could scarcely suppress. Arthur, hurrying on by his side, gave vent to one audible sob. On issuing into the more open neighbourhood of Old Street, they paused and looked around them once more.

"Let us stand here for a moment," said Mr. Tollady, "and watch the faces of these people who go past. Is there one upon which vice and crime are not written as legibly as if put there in words? Do not only look at their faces, look at their bodies also. Look at that old woman, scarcely three feet high. What a monster of deformity! What generations of toil-worn, vice-blasted, hunger-nipped wretches has it taken to produce a scion such as that. Do you notice the faces? That lad, now. He is more than half drunk, but never mind. It gives him an advantage if anything. Have you not seen many a dog with a far more intelligent face? Look at the brutal cast of his nose and lips, the hideous protuberance of his jaw-bones. Or that young girl, about fifteen years old, I suppose. Is it possible to imagine a more perfectly hideous countenance? See the cat-like green eyes, swelling over with unutterable infamy; see the hair, coarse and foul as mud-growth. Listen, oh, for the sake of humanity, listen to her words! Nay, do not be ashamed, Arthur! Better men than we are, are not ashamed to employ thousands of such, and sigh at the most, when they hear their talk. Look at that puppy, with a cigar in his mouth which will make him sick before he reaches the end of the street! He is a draper's clerk, or something of the kind, and that girl with him is a miserable slave-of-all-work from next door, whom he is bent on seducing. Would the brains in that boy's head weigh as much as those of a cat, or be of equal reflecting power? Never believe it. Oh, Arthur, I could die of pity for them all! You have the hand and the eye of an artist. Paint a faithful picture of this crowd we have

watched, be a successor of Hogarth, and give
us the true image of *our* social dress, as he
did of those of his own day. Paint them as
you see them, and get your picture hung in
the Academy. It would be a moral lesson
to all who looked upon it, surpassing in value
every sermon that fanaticism has ever con-
cocted!"

They turned homewards, and so exhausted
was Mr. Tollady by the force of his emotions
that for some distance he was obliged to lean
upon Arthur's arm.

"Is it not hideous," he continued, after
proceeding a few moments in silence, "that
half a nation should travel from the cradle
to the grave in a gross darkness of ignorance
and bodily misery such as is not surpassed by
the condition of an old hack that toils its life
away in the depths of a coal-mine! Let us
disregard for the moment the absolute want
of education for the millions of wretched
children whose parents are either too poor
or too careless to send them to school. [There
were no school boards as yet in England.] Let
us assume, what one is tempted to believe in
places such as this, that they have no intel-
lects, and only bodily wants. Is it not hideous, I say, that places such as those courts
off Whitecross Street should be suffered to
exist, places where not even a litter of pigs
could grow up healthy? Is it not a disgrace
to humanity that generations of servitude, as

real and degrading as that of the negroes, should be suffered to produce in the centre of our proudest cities a breed of men and women such as those we have been observing, absolute Calibans, for the most part, in respect of a pure type of human strength and beauty? All my life I have given way to bursts of indignation at these monstrous scenes, and my reward has always been laughter and ridicule. 'What is the use of your railing thus?' they tell me. These things are an absolute necessity; it is as absurd to charge any human being with the fault, as it would be to throw upon mankind the blame of a droughty summer or a severe winter. Even you, Arthur, are perhaps saying in your mind that I am inconsistent, inasmuch as I one moment advocate the powerlessness of man to alter the course of history, and the next moment rail at the existing state of affairs, and protest that it might be better. But it is not so. Who is it effects the changes of history, if not man himself, acting, as I insist, in obedience to a law of which he knows not the author, but which he cannot resist? Now the mere fact that indignation, such as this, subsists in my bosom, and in the bosoms, I am glad to say, of thousands of my countrymen, is itself a sure sign that what we yearn for will ere long come about. We are the makers of history, Arthur, and it is the shooting of the seeds of future events which makes us restless. Only when *the past* is concerned is it foolish to say : ' That should have happened otherwise, for otherwise it *could* not happen.' The future is our own, and if we truly follow out those impulses which make our hearts burst with their impetuosity, we may be sure that we are truly working out the will of fate. There may be men at this day who long for a return to the despotism of the Inquisition as fiercely as I do for unlimited freedom of conscience. Well, let them strive their best to gain their ends. It is their allotted part. I shall oppose them to the utmost, for I know that to do so is *my* allotted part ; but even in opposing them I shall understand them — a fact which I flatter myself will conduce to some degree of charity on my side. No ! Let them maintain that these horrors are a necessary condition of the present moment, if they please ; but never that we have it not in our power to alter them ! What is a Government, forsooth ? Will any one attempt to persuade me that the duties of a Government are composed in the narrow bounds of paltry diplomacy ; that the etiquette of courts should take precedence in the minds of statesmen of a people's wail for food, food for body and food for mind ; that the only status of the poor, from our ruler's point of view, should be that of so much horse-power, to be employed

either in the production of luxuries for the
wealthy, or in the slaughter of hostile
wretches, poor and ignorant as themselves?
But if we despair of Governments, so long
inured to views such as these, and scarcely
capable of shaking them off till they feel the
fierce fingers of the maddened populace tearing at their very throats, what shall we say
of private wealth and influence, rotting in
pestilential idleness, or active only in schemes
for the still further brutalisation of the mob?
Did you ever reflect that there are men in
England whose private wealth would suffice
to buy up every one of the vile slums we
have just been traversing, and build fresh,
healthy streets in their place, and the men
still remain wealthy? To me it is one of the
most fearful marvels of the time, that among
such countless millionaires scarcely one arises
in a generation actuated with the faintest
shade of philanthropic motives, and *not* one
worthy of the name of a true philanthropist.
It is in the air they breathe, Arthur! These
gold-cradled monsters—monsters, verily,
from a human point of view—have every
seed of benevolent or large-viewed impulse
crushed in their hearts by the weight of
barbarous luxury heaped upon them from the
hour of their births. By the eternal truth,
what opportunities do these men cast aside
and neglect? Suppose a Rothschild, with his
millions, actuated only by the purest love of

his fellow-creatures, only waking to do good, and going to rest to devise fresh plans of philanthropy for the morrow! Imagine such a man calling into his counsels the wisest, the noblest, the bravest of a nation, and sitting down with them to devise schemes for the amelioration of his country! Do not ask what such a man could perform, ask rather what he could *not* ! He could not make mankind wise, or learned, or good, in an instant, but what aid could he give them in their united struggle towards wisdom, learning, goodness! What help could he afford in a million cases to struggling, suffering, despairing merit; how could he lessen the inmates of hospital, gaol, asylum; what glorious service would he perform in the cause of humanity by the mere spectacle of such enlightened benevolence! And your preachers! I declare, I wonder how our preachers can walk the streets at the present day and not shrink in confusion and shame from the sights which meet their eyes on every hand. How many of them are there who in their sermons dare to speak out to the rich members of their congregation and rebuke them manfully for neglect of their opportunities? Jesus of Nazareth dared to do it; but then He received no payment for His sermons; and they would tell you that He was a god, which clearly explains why He could be bolder than ordinary men! If I needed any proof, beyond that afforded by my reason, of the emptiness of their preten- sions, this listlessness and incapacity of theirs in the face of such problems as press upon us to-day, would be quite sufficient. Priests of the Almighty, forsooth! Nay, rather the hypocritical augurs of a wasting superstition, the very wrecks of which will in a few more centuries be hidden amidst the undistinguish- able chaos of things that were."

During the rest of the walk both were silent. Twilight was just verging into the darkness of a summer's night as they entered the house. Mr. Tollady preceded Arthur into the parlour, and was just taking up a box of matches off the table to strike a light when the latter, in the dim light which still came through the window, saw him suddenly press his hand against his left side and fall back, with a slight sigh, into an arm chair. Arthur called to him, but received no answer. Hastily striking a match and lighting a candle, he approached the light to the old man's face, and saw that it was deadly pale. The fit lasted but for a minute; then Mr. Tollady's eyes again opened, and with a slight effort he rose to his feet.

"You are ill, sir," exclaimed Arthur, in- sensibly falling back into the expressions of earlier days in his anxiety.

"Nothing, Arthur, nothing!" replied the other. "Give me a glass of water, my dear boy. There, that's all right again. It was nothing."

Arthur saw that he was unwilling to speak of the incident, and accordingly maintained silence, but nevertheless it made him very uneasy. The action of pressing the hands to the heart previous to the fainting-fit had impressed itself on his mind, and gave him much matter for anxious thought during that night and for days after. But for the moment the weakness seemed to have passed. The old man appeared perfectly recovered and ate a little supper in his usual manner before retiring. They then parted, and Arthur went upstairs to his little bedroom.

The brightness of the full moon rendered it unnecessary for him to strike a light, and throwing open his window, for it was a little close in the house, he sat down to breathe the fresh air for a few moments. It was rather later than usual for him to be out of bed; the clock at the Middlesex Hospital was just striking eleven. His brain had been excited by the unwonted energy of Mr. Tollady's conversation, and by the circumstances of the latter's fainting, and the cool breath of the night air was grateful to his forehead. For more than an hour he sat thus, thinking of a multitude of things. First he thought of the old man, of his apparently failing health, and of what would happen in the event of his dying; and his eyes brimmed over with tears

of affection as his heart warmed at the thought
of all he owed to this noble benefactor. He
reflected how little he used to understand
Mr. Tollady in the earlier years of their
acquaintance; how, little by little, an appreciation of the beauty and serenity of his
character had grown upon him, till to-night
he had obtained a more complete knowledge
than ever of all the wonderful purity and
lofty dignity concealed beneath the every-
day details of that simple life. Then his
thoughts wandered to the features of his own
mind and character, and for some minutes he
indulged in that self-examination which is
beyond the power of ignoble natures. He
thought of his beloved art, and wondered
whether he was in reality born with the
genius of a great painter, or whether it was
mere talent which led him to pursue that
course so eagerly. Rapidly emerging from
such reflections he passed into his wonted
current of thoughts, surveying in his mind a
long panorama of glorious pictures which he
firmly hoped one day to execute, and the very
imagination of which made his blood leap in
its courses, and his heart swell almost to
bursting with the fervid yearnings of a noble
ambition. Then his dream was checked, as
such dreams always had been of late, by the
thought of the far different aims to which
Mr. Tollady was always directing his attention, whose end was a life of quiet usefulness,

sacrificing all the claims of self to active
exertion for the benefit of one's fellows. Was
such a life consistent with the tumultuous
aspirations of the artist which so often filled
his mind? A vague fear seized him lest the
two should be utterly incompatible. Yet not
so, if he followed Mr. Tollady's advice and
used his heart for the purposes of social reform. Was not that a way out of the difficulty? He tried to think so, but felt in the
depths of his soul that it was not, for the art
to which he was devoted was not the same
in which Hogarth had excelled. He felt that
it would be impossible for him to take up
his pencil for the delineation of such varieties
of hideousness. Beauty was the goddess that
he worshipped at the inmost shrine of his
being, and to the bodying forth of visible
shapes of beauty his life must be devoted, or
he must cast aside the pencil for ever. Not
the most inspired productions of human
genius satisfied the criterion of excellence
which he had established for himself, not the
majesty of Angelo, the purity of Raphael, the
glow of Titian approached that celestial ideal
of the beautiful which was ever before his
thoughts; and how should he go for his
models to the slums and the hovels amidst
which his wretched childhood had been
passed? So it was with a sigh of despair
that he rose from the mental conflict, post-
poning the decision, as he had so often done

before, to a time when riper wisdom and experience should have come to his assistance. Nevertheless he was unable totally to destroy an apprehension that the decision might never be reached, that the doubt and hesitation would form the burden of his life, and that a future entered upon without the ardour of conviction could not fail to teem with perplexity and suffering.

CHAPTER XII.

MORE CHANGES.

> "London,
> "July 4th, 1867.

"My Dear Helen,

"You are positively the most wretched correspondent it was ever my lot to encounter. Three months, and not a line. Papa has heard from *your* papa once or twice I believe during that time, but you had not the grace to enclose a line to your very respectable friend and monitress. Now this morning when I woke at about four o'clock I said to myself: 'Positively I must get a letter from Helen Norman to-day, and if I *do not*—well, I renounce her acquaintance till we meet on the shores of Styx, on which occasion I shall certainly find an opportunity of disputing precedence with her in the matter of embarking upon old Charon's boat.' And why should I be so positive of a letter to-day? For no less a reason than because it is *my birthday!* To-day I attain the dignity of *seventeen!* You who are still at the kittenish stage of sixteen, do you not involuntarily bow before my grandeur, and wonder how you can have been so neglectful

of your duty as to leave me ungreeted under
such circumstances ?

"Yes, I am seventeen. Papa has made me a
wonderful present, nothing less than the most
delightful little pony you ever saw in your
life, an absolute darling of a pony ! When he
gave it me he said, in his usual way : ' Now,
Miss Maud, I am not throwing away money
on you for nothing, you understand. If I go
to the expense of buying you a pony, it is
that you may ride about and show yourself.'
' And why should I show myself, papa dear ?'
' Why ? To get a husband as quickly as
possible, Miss Gresham, of course ! You
don't think I'm going to have you upon my
hands till you're an old maid, do you ? '

"That is papa's way of talking, you know.
I really am afraid I don't quite understand
papa sometimes. Now when he was saying
that to me, he was so serious in face and
tone that anyone else could not but have
believed that he quite meant it. And yet I
know, of course, that he was only in fun.
The idea of my being married just yet ! Of
course I shall be married some day, you know,
Helen ; that I have very firmly decided in
my own mind. But who it is to be, I am
very far from knowing. Indeed I am not at
all sure that I have formed an *ideal* yet. Let
me see. I think the man I shall marry will
be rather old ; yes, notwithstanding your
horror at such an idea ; I think he must be

oldish. You see I am rather old for my age, myself, and I could never endure a husband who would seem to me younger than myself, as I am quite sure any man would do who was not at least thirty. Then he must be a staid and sober individual. No Romeo or anything of the kind will do for me. For you know, Helen, or you ought to know, that myself and Miss Lydia Languish are as unlike as possible. If a suitor wrote a piece of poetry to me, it would ruin his chance for ever. No; he must be, as I said, a grave and sober gentleman, with *not less* than ten thousand a year, subscribing freely to public charities and all such useful institutions, a chairman at numerous committees, a member of Parliament, in short a highly useful man in every sense of the word. Ornamental he by no means need be, though of course I should not care to have an absolute Bruin. On the other hand I should detest an Antinous. In the first place I should be jealous of every lady he spoke to, and secondly I should be much too proud of him and make him most horribly conceited. It is my idea of married life to exist in a perfect calm; all such things as *scenes*, of any kind, I should avoid to the utmost. All this, I must tell you, is not quite original, for the husband I have sketched is just the kind of man that papa has frequently said I ought to choose when the time comes. But, as I said, I have such dreadful difficulty in determining, at times, whether papa is in earnest or not.

" But what a foolish girl I am to be writing on such subjects to a mere child. No, Helen, you shall not deceive me. For all that your portrait represents you as being as tall as myself and just about twenty times as good looking, and that your letters read as though written by an experienced novelist of I don't know how many years old, you shall not persuade me to consider you as more than a child. Remember it is not many months since you were sixteen, think of that and be humble.

" Talking of portraits, papa has just finished painting mine, and—what do you think?—seriously talks of sending it to the Academy next year! Unfortunately it was too late for the present exhibition. I will describe the picture to you. I am sitting at a solitaire-board, to begin with, my right hand just raised in the act of moving a glass marble from one hole to another. My dress is a very light blue, and, as I am painted in full length, shows my taste in such matters very admirably. I tell papa, too, that, if he exhibits the picture, he ought to charge Mdlle. Gateau, of Regent Street, a handsome sum in return for the advertisement, having it stated in the catalogue by whom the dress was made. I confess I look very creditably. My fingers, to which, of course, special attention is attracted, are of absolutely wonderful delicacy, almost transparent. Then my hair is a marvel of ingenuity. I did it up in imitation of Miss E——, the celebrated singer, and flatter myself that I improved upon the original. Altogether the picture is, I am assured, and well believe, a highly attractive piece of work. A gentleman last week offered papa two hundred pounds for it! But the gentleman is not after my taste, though *my* picture seems to suit his. He is a great fop, and only twenty-two!

"Now I know what your first remarks will be when you read all this. You will say: 'What a dreadful thing to be painted in such a frivolous attitude! Why not be represented as drawing, or reading, or at least embroidering?' Well, it was papa's choice. He always says that if women are not ornamental they are nothing, and that they should always be associated with the hours of relaxation, and not those of work. He has no belief whatever in the heroic woman, laughing to scorn women's rights, and speaking almost as disrespectfully of that *schwärmerei* of which you are yourself such an exalted instance.

"But I must conclude, and, as usual, reserve for the last paragraph the little quantity of sense which my letters contain. Be assured, dear Helen, that though papa makes fun of a woman's enthusiasm, I am, in reality, very far from doing so. Though I consider worldly

prudence and good sense my strong point, yet
I am by no means without moments in which I
realise much the same feeling as those that
you so admirably express in your, alas! too
short letters. I hope you take it, as I mean
it, for one of the truest signs of my friendship that I write to you the first things that
come into my head, leaving you to divine the
background of serious feeling which they
conceal. But you really must write a line.
Surely you are not so absorbed in your
French, and your German, and your Italian,
and your I-don't-know-what, that you cannot
spare a few minutes to pen a word or two!
Now I calculate upon a speedy reply.

"Your loving friend,

"MAUD GRESHAM."

On the morning following the despatch of
this letter, Maud received a short note from
her friend, enclosed in a longer letter to Mr.
Gresham—

"Mentone.

"DEAREST MAUD,

"I have only time to write a
line. Papa has suddenly been taken most
seriously ill. He caught a severe cold the
other day by an unfortunate accident, and I
fear this is the result. He has asked me to
write to Mr. Gresham, begging him, if

possible, to come to us at once. I am afraid to think why he makes this request. Pray urge your papa to come.

> "With love, dear Maud,
>> "HELEN NORMAN."

The letter to Mr. Gresham was written in most pressing terms, and admitted of no delay. Maud added her entreaties, and Mr. Gresham set off the same evening for the South of France. On arriving at Mentone he found that he had not come a moment too soon. Mr. Norman, it appeared, had been pursuing his favourite pleasure, that of boating, and had, through some carelessness or other, been capsized. He had saved himself by swimming, but was almost immediately after attacked by a most violent cold, which all precautions had been unable to prevent. This, acting upon his already almost worn-out constitution, rapidly laid him prostrate, with little hope of ever rising from his bed again. In this condition the artist found him, so reduced that he could not stir, and quite unable to speak above a whisper. The sight of his old friend seemed to revive him, and in a private interview he informed the latter that, with characteristic procrastination, he had put off from time to time the making of his will, but that he desired to perform the duty immediately, being convinced that he was upon his death-bed. Mr

Gresham undertook to fulfil the office of executor, and the will was forthwith made.

Two hours after completing its dictation, Mr. Norman sank into unconsciousness, from which he never revived, save very partially for a few moments at a time. Before the end of the third day after his friend's arrival he died.

The greater part of his property he left, of course, to Helen, who was to become the ward of Mr. Gresham, seeing that she had none but distant relatives on her mother's side, and those in very humble circumstances, whilst on her father's side absolutely no relation remained living.

Under these circumstances, Helen might very fairly consider herself an heiress. There were also legacies to Mr. Gresham and his daughter Maud. Last of all came an item very characteristic of the testator. He made over to his executor the sum of £5,000 in the 3 Per Cents., with the following instructions :—

He desired Mr. Gresham to do his best to discover whether Arthur Golding was still living, and, if by any chance he should find him, to pay to him on his attaining the age of twenty-one the said sum. Till such date the interest was to be drawn by Mr. Gresham, to cover any expenses that might be involved in the search ; in the event of Arthur having been already discovered, might, if the executor saw fit, be applied to his use. If by the end of the year 1875 (to leave a fair margin), all efforts had met with no success, the sum to be employed for the benefit of any charity to which his executor might think fit to devote it.

Thus did Mr. Norman satisfy his conscience by bequeathing to another the performance of what he had always considered as a duty, and yet had never possessed sufficient energy to undertake.

It now remained to decide with regard to Helen's future. The poor girl was severely afflicted at her father's death, and begged to be allowed to remain a few months at least amid scenes which had hitherto possessed such happy, and had now acquired such mournful associations.

As her health seemed to advise this course Mr. Gresham readily acceded to the request, and it was arranged that Helen should live in the house of a very agreeable French family with whom she had long been acquainted. In the course of the autumn she was to return to England, when her future movements could be discussed at her guardian's house.

Early in October Mr. Gresham returned to Mentone to fetch Helen back to England, and this time Maud accompanied him. They remained in the South of France about a fortnight, and then started back.

It was rather more than four years since Helen left her old home, and she had greatly changed in the interval. If anything, she had slightly the advantage of Maud Gresham in height, and her excessive slimness made her appear even taller than she was. She had never been a robust child; but during the last few months grief had wasted her to a shadow. Her face was more beautiful than ever, for hers was a style of beauty which gained rather than lost by a marble paleness.

As she entered Mr. Gresham's drawing-room in the long black dress which she had travelled in, and, throwing back her veil, disclosed a face suffused with tears and smiles, which the excitement of the moment called forth, no one could have supposed her younger than the very compact yet elegant young lady who stood at her side; when they stood together it was Maud who appeared the child.

Upon Helen's face rested a sweet serious-ness which bespoke a nature at once exquisitely refined, susceptible to keen emotion, and strong in the power of suppressing its outward signs when it appeared most fitting to withhold them from observation. Her forehead bore the unmistakable impress of thought superior to her years; her eyes had a clear directness of expression which seemed to pierce to the truth through all barriers of form, and irresistibly claimed respect from all upon whom they rested; her lips were rich in the grace of female modesty and tenderness. Her walk had not altered; it was, as it had always been, that of a queen. Unconscious dignity was present in every movement.

To a stranger her bearing might at first have appeared haughty; those who knew her soon learned that this was the mere outward expression of a loftiness of soul which made itself manifest in every word she spoke and every act she performed.

Maud soon discovered that a great change had passed over her friend's mind in the period since her father's death. A few minutes' conversation sufficed to show her that this was not the same Helen who had written such ardent letters, brimful of enthusiasm for all that is beautiful, and good, and true. The ardour was now suppressed, and it was something more than grief that had effected the change. Maud was not long in discovering the explanation of this. Helen had become devout.

In one of our earliest chapters we had an opportunity of seeing the kind of religious instruction which Mr. Norman was in the habit of affording his child as often as her eagerness in questioning compelled him to touch upon the subject. Otherwise, if not compelled by her curiosity, he avoided the

subject, fearing somewhat, if the truth must
be told, her premature power of thought and
observation. The result of this was, that up
to the time of her father's death Helen had
thought little, if at all, on religious subjects.
The fact that she had never known a mother
doubtless contributed to make this possible,
and the completeness with which her days
were occupied in various studies gave her
abundance of matter for thought in her leisure
hours. But, as might reasonably have been
anticipated, the suddenness of her bereavement
acted as a powerful stimulus to those seeds
of devotional piety which are present in the
heart of every woman, and which usually
receive numberless impulses by fructification
long before the age at which Helen had now
arrived.

What sectarian Christians would style a
conversion took place in her mind. Of a
sudden she became discontented with the
occupations of her life. It came upon her
with the force of a revelation that she had
hitherto lived in absolute neglect of the
veritable end of existence, namely, devout
prayer and praise to the all-powerful Being,
upon whose existence she had as yet scarcely
reflected, but whom she now conceived of,
with all the energy of a powerful imagination, as the distinct and personal God.

This attitude of mind was confirmed by the
circumstance that the French family with

whom she went to live were strictly religious.
That their religion was Roman Catholic did
not prevent Helen from being strongly impressed with their zealous fervour, and she
forthwith commenced the performance of
the duties of her faith with an ardour which
marked her conduct whatever she undertook.

Her friends, who had long known her intimately, clearly observed the change, and
were inspired with an eager hope that it
might be the means of affording them the
power of converting her to their own faith.
To this end they forthwith began unobtrusively to exert themselves, and also secured
the aid of a *curé* in their self-imposed
task.

But the girl remained firm against their
persuasions, which even had the result of
rendering her more ardent than ever in the
cultivation of her Protestantism. Her days
were passed in the perusal of religious books,
in self-rebuke for her sins of omission and
commission in the past, in the contemplation
of a future to be devoted to charitable deeds;
whilst her nights were passed in prayer, the
early dawn sometimes finding her still upon
her knees, or bending over her Bible.

No wonder, under such circumstances,
that she grew thin and pale. The old child-
like enthusiasm had by this time well-nigh
forsaken her; her excess of zeal compelled

her to look with disapproval on the subjects which had occasioned it. The energy of her nature now exhaled in ecstasies which none were witness of, save her midnight lamp.

Mr. Gresham and his daughter agreed in strongly condemning this state of affairs, and before many days had passed began to unite in an attack upon what they esteemed Helen's self-destructive asceticism. They knew well that to attack it openly would only defeat their own object, so they proceeded by means of distractions to which Helen could scarcely refuse to consent without appearing ungrateful.

They arranged excursions into the country, in which they were joined only by one or two quiet friends; they spent mornings all together in the museums and the art-galleries; they induced Helen to read aloud occasionally in the evening from books which Maud knew had once been favouritse of hers, and Mr. Gresham began to give her lessons in oil-painting.

Concession in these particulars at first caused the pious girl acute pain, and many secret hours were spent in tears after some unusual backsliding; but by degrees the remedy began to prove effectual, and those who practised it were rewarded by seeing a very gradual, but still very evident, improvement in Helen's spirits, an improvement which before long began to affect her bodily health.

Helen had at length become so far weaned from her habits of solitude as to voluntarily request that she might pay a visit to Bloomford. She had in reality secretly longed to see the place of her birth ever since she had been in England; and now that the spring had once more come round, she was quite unable to resist the vivifying influence of the fresh west winds and the attractions of all those green country scenes, which the sight of the parks coming into life, again called so strongly to her mind. As the distance was comparatively short, it was arranged that Helen and Maud should undertake the journey alone, going early in the morning and returning the same evening.

At about eleven o'clock they found themselves before the gates of the Rectory. The house had not altered in outward appearance; but a group of young children playing, or rather squabbling, together on the lawn, reminded the visitors of the change in its occupancy. Passing up the walk, they rang the door bell and requested to see Mr. Whiffle.

They were shown into the drawing-room, which was furnished precisely as Mr. Norman had left it, but which was scarcely as tidy as it might have been, and as it always was in the days of Mrs. Cope's dominion.

Whilst waiting for the rector's appearance Helen kept her veil down, and Maud could hear her in vain endeavouring to suppress a sob, occasioned by the memory of old times. She had just time to give her friend's hand a reassuring pressure when Mr. Whiffle entered.

He looked shorter than ever, probably because he had begun to contract a somewhat portly habit of body, and his hair was just as red and just as stubborn as ever. He wore spectacles now, and strutted about with a more dignified gait than he had previously exhibited; but he still retained the old habits of running his fingers through his coarse red hair, and of rising and falling on his toes as he discoursed. His voice had acquired a slightly nasal twang, probably due to attempting to make his crow-like note subservient to the purposes of intonation.

On entering the room he bowed, and requested to be informed in what way he could serve his visitors.

Maud was somewhat more prepared for a speech than Helen, and accordingly replied—

"We are two old acquaintances, sir, who, I much fear, have outgrown your recollection. Of me you had never more than a slight knowledge; but my companion is a very old friend of yours, indeed. Her you will probably recognise."

The rector gazed in a puzzled manner from the speaker to Helen and back again, and for some moments was entirely at a loss. But the sight of Helen's mourning seemed at length to stimulate his memory, and his face gradually brightened as the idea gained power over his mind.

"Upon my word!—Ha!—No!—Yes! It must be. I *do believe* this is Miss Norman! And this—? Upon my word I cannot recollect."

"You are right as far as I am concerned, Mr. Whiffle," said Helen, who had now recovered her self-possession. "And this is Miss Gresham, whom you several times saw at the Rectory."

"Upon my word, and so it is! Miss Gresham, I am heartily glad to see you. Miss Norman, you have delighted me by this visit! Ladies, I beg you to consider yourselves both heartily welcome to Bloomford Rectory. Upon my word! This is one of my happiest days since that eventful one upon which I entered The Church! You have experienced a sad loss, Miss Norman, a very sad loss; but I feel sure that I need not remind the daughter of my sometime rector, whom I ever loved and revered, of the consolations which The Church offers for those similarly afflicted. And you have come down from Town, I suppose. Ha! I get to Town, myself, more frequently than I used to do,

Miss Norman, in the by-gone days. You
see, it behoves the pastor of a congregation
to keep his mind thoroughly in contact with
the movements of the day. I was in London,
in fact, so recently as three weeks ago, when
I had a little business in Paternoster Row,
concerning the publication of a small pamphlet on the subject of "Church Ritual," a
reply to certain calumnies which have of late
been circulated with regard to my method of
conducting our services in S. Peter's. I
trust, Miss Norman, you favour the High
Church form of worship?"

"I have been so long abroad," replied
Helen, after a moment's hesitation, "that I
doubt whether I am quite aware of the distinctions existing between the different forms
of worship in England."

"Indeed! Ha! We must discuss the
whole matter. You will, of course, take
dinner with us? We dine at one."

"We shall have pleasure in doing so," replied Helen.

"Ha! Delighted! Upon my word, I must
call Mrs. Whiffle—and the children. They
will all be charmed!"

So saying, the Rector hurried out of the
room. In a moment a confused whispering,
and shuffling, and pushing, and whimpering
began to be audible in the drawing-room,
which seemed to indicate that the whole
Whiffle family was already gathered outside

in the hall. A moment after a baby set up a terrific screaming, whereupon, as at a signal, Mr. Whiffle again marched into the room, with Mrs. Whiffle leaning on his arm, followed by nine children, the eldest girl bearing an infant in her arms. In the midst of agonising yells from this youngest member of the family circle, Mr. Whiffle introduced them all to the visitors.

" This is Master Peter," he concluded, taking the squalling brat in his arms, " so called because born on the day sacred to St. Peter, the patron of the church of which I have the honour to be rector. He is our latest arrival, and as yet somewhat of a care to Mrs. Whiffle. I often pity those people, Miss Norman, who have large families. The care of even a few children is something of which you, happily, can as yet form no conception. Augustus, my eldest, is not here, being at present a student at King's College, London, where he is preparing for the time when he shall have attained the years necessary for ordination."

There was something peculiar in Mr. Whiffle's tone, when he spoke of his eldest son, which might have led an acute observer to surmise that he was not altogether satisfied with that young gentleman's progress. But the thoughts of his visitors were elsewhere, and they did not notice this.

All through dinner Mr. Whiffle talked in-

cessantly, expatiating on the details of the
discussion going on between himself and a
neighbouring vicar on the subject of his
ritualism. With merciless detail he described
the points at issue in the contest, went back
for his authorities to the early ages of the
Church, gave citations in Latin which he did
not take the trouble to translate, described
diagrams on the table with knives and forks to
represent the Church ornaments of which he
was speaking, and in short gave the young
ladies an insight into the foundations of
ritualism calculated to send them back home
somewhat wiser than they came. And all
this amidst such a hubbub of juvenile
chatter, such a breaking of plates and overturning of glasses, such a thumping, and
squalling, and threatening, as would inevitably have driven anyone but Mr. Whiffle
frantic when engaged in the discussion of
such engrossing topics.

Maud and Helen did their best to appear
interested in all this talk, and with such
success, that Mr. Whiffle was jubilant.

" I must take you into my study," he exclaimed, as they all rose from the dinner
table, " and show you certain works which I
have in progress, works which I flatter myself will open the eyes of certain degenerate
sons of The Church, whom I could name, and
may perchance make the name of Orlando
Whiffle somewhat more widely known than

it at present is. Ahem! I have in contemplation, Miss Norman, amongst other things, a series of Tracts not unlike those issued by the Tractarian Party during the years 1833 to 1841. I have likewise pamphlets on hand on very various topics, among them—this way, if you please, Miss Gresham—treatises on 'The Orthodoxy of Stained Glass Windows,' 'Pews or Stalls?' 'Confession from the Point of View of Expediency,' 'Interpretations of the Thirty-nine Articles,' and many others of a similar description. I really must get you to read a few, Miss Norman, and give me your opinion on them; likewise you Miss Gresham. You can have but little notion of the way in which work accumulates in the hands of a rector, or parson, as perhaps he should be more properly called : *persona ecclesiæ*, the representative of The Church, a proud title, Miss Norman."

They were now in the study, the room in which Helen had sat day after day at her lessons with her father. In those days it had been always in the most admirable order, at present it was rather in " admired disorder." Books of all shapes and sizes were recklessly piled upon the shelves, and heaped upon the tables or the floor. There was scarcely a chair free to sit down upon. Everywhere was a litter of torn manuscript, old numbers of Church magazines, daily and

weekly papers, tracts by the thousand, even
the backs of books which had been rent off
in the struggle for existence. Certainly the
dust could never have been once removed
during the four years of Mr. Whiffle's incumbency. Maud could not repress a smile as
she looked round; Helen with difficulty repressed a tear.

"I wish I had an opportunity, Miss Norman, of directing your reading. You intend
to remain in England now? Ah! I certainly
should advise it. Nowhere have you the
benefit of such an enlightened movement in
the matter of Church ritual as our country at
present enjoys. Now suppose I were to
suggest a few books for your perusal, Miss
Norman, sterling works which you can easily
obtain in London, works of sound, practical
information. Here is a piece of paper, Miss
Norman, and a pencil; possibly you would
like to take the names of a few. Now here,
for instance is Rogers's 'Practical Arrangement of Ecclesiastical Laws,' containing very
much that is absolutely necessary to be
known; here is Hook's 'Ecclesiastical
Biography,' an extremely interesting work;
here, again, is Lathbury on 'The History
of Convocation,' very needful. You have
got Lathbury? Here, now, is Palmer's
'Origines Liturgicæ,' which I am sure you
will enjoy. Here we have Maskell's
'Ancient Liturgy of the Church of Eng-

land,' very sound. Got Maskell, Miss Norman? Here are the 'Monumenta Ritualia Ecclesiæ Anglicanæ,' admirable; don't omit that. Here is Neale's 'Tetralogia Liturgicæ.' Possibly those might be enough to begin with, and when you have perused them if you would so far honour me as to intimate the fact by letter, or, still better, by coming down again to see me, I will have another list assorted. By-the-bye, you might of course add Burn's 'Ecclesiastical Law,' a compendious work."

At this moment Mrs. Whiffle appeared in the doorway.

"My dear," she said, "here's that man Potts come again about the burial of his child. He says he *must* see you."

"Ah! Does he? Well, show him in here. A very refractory parishioner, young ladies. You shall see how I will deal with him."

The man thus announced then appeared at the door. He was a rude countryman in labour-stained clothes, and with a sun-burnt face. The latter, however, was marked by signs of suffering, and Helen noticed that the hat he held in his hand was bound with a scrap of black ribbon.

"Well, my man?" asked Mr. Whiffle, as he appeared.

"Well, sir," replied the man, pulling his forelock respectfully, "I's come to ask whether you won't be so good as bury our little Tom. It 'ud be a great kindness, sir, if you only would this one time, an' we shouldn't forget it so quick, neither."

" I told you this morning, Potts," replied Mr. Whiffle, with dignity, "that it is impossible for me to read the service of the Church of England over your child, seeing that he was never baptized. Is not that enough ?"

" Well, sir, if *you* can't see your way to do it, *would* you let Mr. Sykes do it, the one as preaches at t' chapel, you know ? He's a Dissenter I know, but he's got no 'bjections to do this bit o' kindness for us, and we'd rather have him than no one. I'm sure as it'll kill his mother if our poor little Tom, as never did no 'arm to no one, no not a fly, is put into t' ground like a dog, without Christian burial. Would you let Mr. Sykes read over him, sir ?"

At the first mention of the obnoxious schismatic, Mr. Whiffle's eyebrows had risen, and his eyes actually glared through his spectacles at the audacious speaker.

" Mr.—Mr.—Mr. Sykes ! " he stuttered, scarcely able to speak. " Allow *him* to read a service in a burial ground belonging and appertaining to the English Church as by law established ! I'll see Mr. Sykes in—his pulpit first ! I tell you the child must be buried in silence, Potts, so there's no use in further discussion. The ordinances of The Church do not permit me to read the service in such cases. Do I not know the ordinances of the Church in which I am a rector? Do you wish to insult me, man?"

"I's no wish to hinsult you, sir, or any one else," returned the man, "but I think it hard, that's all I's got to say; I think it hard, I do! It'll be the death of my poor wife, I know as it will; an' it's a blow for me myself. But I s'pose I must bide it. Well, sir, it's a queer Christian Church, that's all I's got to say, an' what's more—"

"Now that will do, Potts," broke in Mr. Whiffle, majestically, pointing to the door. "You've heard my answer, and you may go. Any attempt to infringe my rights as rector of the parish of Bloomford will meet with condign punishment; that's all *I* have to say, Potts. You may go."

The man retired with a terribly downcast look, far too sad at heart to give ear to the scorn with which his rector treated him.

"This seems very hard for these poor people," said Helen, as soon as he was gone. "Surely the severity of such a rule must sometimes be relaxed."

"I grant you it is sometimes neglected, Miss Norman," returned the rector, "by those who have but an imperfect sense of their own dignity and their duty to The Church."

He was proceeding to a long discussion on the subject of Church ordinances when he was again interrupted by the presence of Mrs. Whiffle at the door, who requested to speak with him for a moment. Mr. Whiffle was absent for a few minutes, when he returned and announced that his eldest son, Augustus, had quite unexpectedly made his appearance at the Rectory. His face, when he made this announcement, once more presented the mingled expression which it had worn when he first spoke of his son. Immediately after, the young man himself appeared in the study.

The outward aspect of Augustus Whiffle was scarcely that which we are accustomed to associate with a student of divinity. His dress was decidedly "loud" in tone, cut in the extremity of the existing fashion, and the ornaments which he wore were in excessively bad taste. In short he precisely resembled the typical counter-man out for a holiday. In person he was very tall, with a face in which it was difficult to determine whether folly or vice predominated, and his hair, though kept in strict order by means of a liberal allowance of bear's grease, was of exactly the same hue as his father's. He wore a gold *pince-nez*, had his hands covered with flashy rings, and carried a demonstrative cane, with which, as he stood in the doorway, he tapped his shiny boots, as if to draw attention to their exquisite finish. Such was Mr. Augustus Whiffle, whom his reverend parent had destined to become a shining light in the Establishment. It was far from improbable that he might even yet attain to that distinction.

On being introduced to the young ladies, this young gentleman bowed with a mixture of superciliousness and awkwardness generally observable in those men who are won't to spend a considerable portion of time in the society of females who neither exact nor receive any great amount of deference. He muttered a few remarks with regard to the weather, and something to the effect that it was a long time since he had seen either of the visitors, after which he beat an awkward retreat, almost overturning his mother, who had stood behind him with an expression of countenance which seemed to indicate that she scarcely knew whether to admire or sigh over her son's appearance and behaviour.

Augustus having disappeared, Mrs. Whiffle, with a look of intelligence at her husband, invited the young ladies to take a stroll in the garden, which being agreed to, they all three went out on to the lawn, accompanied by the nine young Whiffles. Scarcely were they gone than Augustus Whiffle again made his appearance in the study, where his father had been thoughtfully awaiting him. He closed the door behind him, and assumed the only vacant chair, cocking his hat on one side, and assuming the greatest possible extent of space for his legs, one of which, with an affectation of careless grace, he flung over the other, all the time continuing to tap his boots with his cane.

"Well, sir," began Mr. Whiffle, with a make-believe severity which his tremulous tones belied, "I thought I had expressly forbidden you to absent yourself from your duties again before the long vacation?"

"Very possibly," returned Augustus, drawing a gilt toothpick from his waistcoat pocket, and applying it to his teeth, which he smacked loudly with his tongue. "But if you tell a fellow to go and live in the society of other fellows, who are gentlemen, you must give a fellow the means to be a gentleman too!"

"What do you mean, sir?" asked the rector, still severely, though his hands were nervously twitching behind his back.

"I mean what I say. A fellow can't live like a gentleman unless he has the means!"

"Do you mean to tell me you have again run short of money?"

Augustus smacked each one of his pockets in turn—and he had a great number of them—but did not deign to make further reply.

"And what has become of the thirty pounds you had at Easter, sir? Where—

where are your accounts? Show me an account of your expenditure?"

"Don't keep any," returned the other, coolly, changing the position of his legs.

"And why not, sir, when I so expressly instructed you to?"

"Devilish ungentlemanly. No fellow that calls himself a gentleman keeps accounts."

"Indeed! And you swear too, sir! Is that indispensable to a gentleman?"

"Deucedly prevalent habit," replied Augustus, with a sarcastic smile.

Mr. Whiffle turned away from his son and made an attempt to pace the room in thought, but at the first turn he tripped over a folio and had difficulty in recovering himself with dignity. Augustus continued to pick his teeth and smile.

"I tell you what it is, sir!" exclaimed the rector, suddenly, in exasperation, "you'll have no more money from me till the long vacation comes—not a penny! And what's more, if you show your face again at the Rectory before that period, I will give orders that you are not to be admitted. You shall be turned away like a beggar from the door, sir!"

"Very well," replied Augustus, rising. "Then I shall at once throw up the College, and look out for something that'll bring in the needful. In the meantime I shall live on tick, and you'll have the bills."

"I'll write to your lodgings immediately, sir," cried Mr. Whiffle, in wrath, "and warn them to turn you out of doors to-morrow!"

"No difficulty in the world in finding another place. Lots of gentlemanly fellows that will go bail."

"I will forbid you to come near the Rectory again, as long as you live! You shall no longer be in any way related to me! I'll advertise in the newspapers, and warn tradesmen against trusting you!"

"Oh no, you won't—by no means!"

"Why not, sir?"

"Because you don't care to make yourself ridiculous. Now what *is* the good of calling a fellow over the coals in this way? You know a fellow can't get on without tin, and as long as you've got it, why not let a fellow have a reasonable supply?"

Mr. Whiffle wrung his hands in desperation.

"*What* have you done with all your money, Gus?" he asked, in a tragi-comic tone, which he, however, meant to be perfectly serious.

"Well, a good lot's gone in books," replied Augustus, who, it must be confessed, had very much the air of a studious youth. "They come so devilish high, you see."

"Don't swear in my presence, sir!" exclaimed the rector, stamping his foot. "What books have you bought?"

"Oh, I don't know. All sorts."

If this was meant to comprise a copious collection of very bad novels, it was certainly true.

"Have you got through the 'Origines Liturgicæ' yet?" asked the rector, after a pause, his wrath, never of long duration, perceptibly cooling.

"Very nearly," replied Augustus, who had never opened the book.

"You have!" exclaimed the credulous father, in delight. "Ha! Let me ask you a few questions."

"Well, I'm sorry," returned the young man, pulling out his watch, "but I really haven't time. I must positively get back to Town to-night. I have a lecture early to-morrow morning."

"Go back with Miss Norman and Miss Gresham," said the rector. "They go by the 5.30."

"Not a bad idea," replied Augustus, who felt rather uneasy at the prospect, for all that. "And, by-the-bye—did you write the cheque?"

Mr. Whiffle looked at his son, sighed, paused a moment, then left the room and returned very shortly with a folded cheque in his hand.

"Augustus Whiffle," he said, solemnly, as he handed it over. "This is the last money I can let you have before the long vacation.

As it is, I shall have to pinch myself and the children. There, take it, and make a proper use of it."

Augustus unfolded the cheque and glanced at it.

"Only twenty!" he exclaimed. "I say, governor, you're getting awfully shabby, you know."

At this moment the tea-bell made its clanging heard in the hall, and Mr. Whiffle, glad of an excuse, hurried away. Augustus followed, inserting the cheque in his pocket-book.

"What the devil's the good of this?" he muttered to himself. "Won't pay a twentieth part of a fellow's debts, let alone keeping a fellow in toggery and cigars. What an old screw the governor is!"

CHAPTER XIII.

EMANCIPATION.

THE journey home that night, as Mr. Whiffle had suggested, was travelled in the company of the divinity student, who, as soon as he had succeeded in vanquishing to some degree his awkward bashfulness, entertained the young ladies with descriptions of sundry adventures which he had at various times experienced in the company of congenial spirits, always denominated as "fellows." Maud listened with a well-affected interest, partly because she was in reality amused by the character being displayed before her, partly because Maud always paid deference to the *convenances*, and would not even have appeared rude to a chimney-sweep. Helen sat with her veil lowered, in absolute silence. She was unwilling to betray the disgust which she felt, but at the same time quite incapable of affecting an interest which she did not feel.

"I say, Miss Norman," exclaimed Augustus, at one point in the conversation, or rather monologue, "it seems an awful time since we used to know each other so well, don't it?"

"It does indeed seem a long time since I left Bloomford," replied Helen.

The quiet, ladylike tone of her voice, having nothing in the least childish about it, somewhat repressed the young man's conversational ardour. He gnawed the top of his cane for a moment, then renewed the attack.

"I say, Miss Norman, you remember the old parrot and the cat we used to laugh at?"

"Very well," replied Helen. "The parrot still lives. I have brought her back to London with me."

"I say, now! Think of that! It 'ud puzzle a fellow's brains now to calculate that old beast's age; wouldn't it, Miss Norman?"

"The bird must be very old."

"I say, Miss Norman," pursued the undaunted Augustus, after a little more gnawing of his cane, "do you remember that rummy little fellow that lived at the Rectory with you once—a rummy-looking cove, that bolted one morning, you know?"

"I remember him, quite well."

"I say, did you ever hear any more of him, Miss Norman? He used to have lessons from the governor, I remember."

"He was never heard of, I think," replied Helen.

"What a rummy go! Drowned, I always said."

Helen made no reply, and Augustus, after

in vain endeavouring to renew the conversation, again turned to Maud, whose attention he continued to engage to the end of the journey. At the station he assisted his companions into a cab, and lingered about the door with some wild notion that he might be invited to accompany them home. Being deceived in his hope he walked away somewhat disconsolate; but rapidly recovering his spirits, as he reflected on the brilliant conversational powers he had exhibited, he forthwith made for the lodgings of a certain "fellow," in whose company he spent the greater part of his time, and proceeded to detail in confidence the circumstances of his *tête-à-tête* which he professed to have held that afternoon with the charming daughter of "an awfully rich old cuss," the termination of which had been the acceptance of an offer of his heart and hand. On the strength of this, the pleasant "fellow" in question, who did not believe a word of the story, made bold to borrow a sovereign, which Augustus was ashamed to refuse, but the sure and certain loss of which he bitterly regretted.

"Well, Helen," said Mr. Gresham, as the three sat together the same evening, "how did you find Bloomford?"

"Very much changed I thought, Mr. Gresham," replied the girl.

"Or was the change in yourself, do you think?" pursued the artist.

" Possibly a little, but certainly not altogether."

" How was it changed ? "

" Bloomford itself was as beautiful as
ever," replied Helen, with some appearance of
reluctance, " but the Rectory I scarcely recognised as my old home."

" Ha! Has Mr. Whiffle been making
alterations?" asked Mr. Gresham, who perfectly understood Helen's meaning, but had
a perverse delight in drawing her into more
definite expressions.

" Oh, no ; at least none that I noticed.
I—I can scarcely say how it was changed. I
think it is hardly as quiet and homelike as it
used to be. There—there are many children
about."

" You went into the church, of course ? "

" No," replied Helen, sinking her head.

" Not ! Now that was a pity. According
to all accounts, Mr. Whiffle has made some
charming alterations. I believe it is almost
as pretty as a theatre," he added, carefully
watching Helen from beneath his heavy eyebrows.

" I feared it," she replied, in a low voice,
adding almost immediately, " I feel rather
tired after the journey. Will you permit me
to leave you to-night?"

" Certainly, Helen. You must not overtire
yourself. Good-night."

Helen rose in her wonted graceful manner,

shook hands with her guardian, kissed Maud, and left the room with a firm step, yet so light that it could not be heard.

Mr. Gresham was silent for a moment after her departure, apparently engaged in reading a periodical. Maud continued to work at a pencil-drawing which had held her attention from the foregoing conversation.

"Pallas seems a trifle out of sorts to-night," said the former at length, throwing down his paper and speaking in the tone he usually adopted with his daughter, a half serious, half trifling tone very well adapted to the sceptical character of his remarks.

"Why do you call her Pallas?" asked Maud, quickly.

"Is she not in eye, in gait, in mien a young Pallas Athene? Let me tell you, Maud, if you practised before your glass a couple of hours a day you could never acquire the graceful dignity which Helen has from nature."

"It is very unlikely that I should ever make the attempt," replied Maud saucily. "But if I lack dignity I suppose I have something to make up for it. If Helen is Pallas Athene, what am I?"

"Neither Here nor Aphrodite, child, but just plain Maud Gresham; a girl not too pretty to be useful, not too witty to be talked to by a plain man of the world, and far from possessing too much reverence for the good-natured father who spoils her, like a fool as he is. You are not much like your mother, Maud."

"So you often say, papa."

"She was an angel, which you—I hope— are far from being ; and the only mistake she ever made was in visiting earth to marry a man who had always been sceptical with regard to the existence of supernatural beings ! You, I am glad to say, Maud, are decidedly of the earth earthy."

"You are not flattering, papa."

"I never am, my dear. But to return to our muttons. Why is Pallas out of sorts ?"

"Can't you guess ?"

"Possibly I can, but I wish for your opinion."

"I will give it you then, papa. She went to Bloomford with a mind full of images of her past life, images which a reflection from the happiness of childhood made to glow with an unnatural splendour. I think the appearance of the country disappointed her a little, after the scenes she has been accustomed to, but still more the people she saw there. She expected, I fancy, to behold her ideal of a country clergyman, an exalted combination of Chaucer's and Goldsmith's good parsons. Instead of that she found a—but you know Mr. Whiffle, papa."

"Never mind, Maud. What did she find ?"

asked her father, regarding her with a malicious shyness.

"I say, you know Mr. Whiffle, papa, or, at all events, once knew him."

"And I say never mind, Miss Gresham. What *did* she find?"

"Well, if you *will* have me say it, a ridiculous old busy-body, possessed of about as much common-sense and good-feeling as the hassock he kneels upon, and as much entitled to the epithet of reverend as—as I am."

"You progress in the art of epigram, Maud," said her father, looking rather pleased. "Did old Whiffle discuss the Rubric at large?"

"He favoured us with not a few remarks thereon."

"And Pallas appeared disgusted?"

"Supremely so."

"Pained, too, no doubt, poor child. However, I hoped it would happen so. A few more visits to a few more such parsons and she would be almost cured of her mania, I fancy."

"You speak too disrespectfully of Helen, papa. Her convictions are independent of such influences as those."

"You think so? Why, you are becoming an idealist all at once, Maudie."

"I have much more of the idealist in my temperament than you dream of, papa," returned the young lady, rising with a smile.

" Pray don't think I am so sunk in the mud
of scepticism as you are."

" Ho, ho ! What are your ideals, Maudie ? "
cried Mr. Gresham, with jocose mockery.

" A calm domestic life, in which the
passion of love interferes as little as that of
hate ; and at the end of it a sudden, unan-
ticipated and painless death."

Mr. Gresham looked up at his daughter with
something of natural surprise, not being quite
sure whether she were in earnest or not.
She seemed to be so.

" I tell you what it is, Miss Gresham," he
returned, as he rose from his chair, " I shall
begin to fear presently that I have been
nurturing a species of female Mephistopheles.
Do you entertain any opinions on the subject
of patricide ? "

" The subject has not yet come within my
thoughts," returned the girl, with a slight
shrug.

" Indeed ! When you begin your speculations thereon perhaps you will be so good as
to favour me with notice of the fact. The
prospect of being kept rather too long out of
her inheritance might excite curious designs
in the mind of such a very idealistic young
lady."

" Oh, don't fear, papa," called out Maud,
as they parted at the door. " When the time
comes, your death shall be as painless as that
I hope for myself."

During the next few weeks Helen lived an extremely retired life. Mr. Gresham had assigned to her use an elegant little parlour, and from this she sometimes did not stir from morning to night, having the slight meals she partook of brought to her there.

In music, as indeed in everything she had undertaken, Helen showed precocious talent, and, on the few occasions when she was induced to play before strangers, manifested a taste and skill which filled her hearers with admiration. Mr. Gresham had procured her an excellent teacher, and those hours which were not devoted to solitary reflection were now usually spent in practice at her own piano. In music she found almost her only relief from the pressure of those distressing thoughts which had again assailed her with renewed force after her visit to Bloomford. For several months she had scarcely read at all. Her dainty little library, consisting of beautiful bound editions of the poets, novelists and historians, such a library as her father considered best adapted to the needs of a young lady, and which he had selected with the utmost care, now stood ranged in a couple of handsome book-cases on one side of her parlour ; but the glass doors had remained unopened since her return to England. Her Bible, which had but lately been her constant companion, now lay upon the table, unopened from day to day. Those agonising doubts and obstinate questionings which so seldom assail a girl's mind, thanks to the atmosphere of enervating pietism in which females usually grow to maturity, if, indeed, they can ever be said to reach that stage, those torturing thoughts which every intellectual youth has sooner or later to combat with, now held Helen at their mercy. Now, more than ever, did she bitterly mourn her father's death, which had deprived her of the one person to whom she could lay bare her mind in perfect confidence. As she had no longer her father's living voice to advise her, she took refuge in reflection upon his life, striving to wrest from her memory of his acts and words, an explanation of the creed by which he had lived. As yet she could arrive at few satisfactory results. Her practical knowledge of life was too limited to afford her the necessary means of observation and comparison, and little by little, under the guidance of bitter suffering, she was led into that path which could alone afford an exit from the gloomy regions into which she had strayed.

One morning Maud had been engaged for an hour, reading in the library, and was just rising to leave the room, when she was in turn visited unexpectedly by Helen, who walked softly into the room.

" You here, Maud ! " exclaimed Helen. " I thought this was your usual drawing hour ?"

"So it is," replied Maud; "but I seem to have no taste for it this morning. And you—I thought this was your usual music hour?"

"So it is," returned the other, smiling; "but Mr. Walsh is unable to give me my lesson this morning. You won't let me drive you from the room?"

"You came very opportunely to warn me that the morning is drawing on. I have an appointment with the housekeeper at eleven —more's the pity. I had quite forgotten the time over an interesting book."

As she spoke she closed the book that lay open before her, and left it there upon the table.

Whether she had drawn Helen's attention to it purposely or not may remain a question; but as soon as she had left the room the latter at once took up the work to examine it.

It was the English translation of Strauss' "Leben Jesu," the popular edition. With a throb of the pulses, as if in anticipation of what the book contained—though as yet she had no knowledge of it—she assumed the seat Maud had just left, and began to read.

She did not appear at luncheon; but this was such an ordinary occurrence that it attracted no attention; but when the dinner hour had arrived, and she was still absent, Maud sought her, first in her own sitting-room, and then, failing of success, in the library.

Helen had lit the reading-lamp, and was still bending over the pages of Strauss.

She started as Maud entered the room, and rose from her seat.

"Are you resolved to become an absolute chameleon, my dear child?" cried Miss Gresham. "But," she added immediately, "I see that air has not been your only sustenance all day. Do you like my book?"

"Is it yours?" asked Helen, who had closed the book at the other's entrance, and now stood with her eyes cast down, for a moment uncertain how to act.

"Yes; papa gave it to me when it was first published, three years ago, and when, as you can imagine, I had but little taste for it. Do you like it?"

Helen paused for a moment, without replying.

"I cannot say yet," she returned, in a low voice. "I—I cannot say till I have finished it."

"Shall you have the resolution?"

"I think so," replied Helen, looking up into her friend's face with a seriousness of expression, now unmixed with doubt or shame.

"I read it a year ago," said the other. "Perhaps you would like to take it away with you?"

" If you would kindly lend it to me, I should."

" Take it, by all means. But, in the meantime, are you aware that the dinner bell has rung ?"

" I did not hear it."

" So I supposed. Come, I can only allow you three minutes."

" I should be glad if I might be excused to-night, Maud," said Helen. " I really have no appetite. Would you ask Mr. Gresham to excuse me ?"

" Certainly, if you wish it. But I am not going to allow you to macerate yourself. I shall send you something up."

" Thanks, Maud ; you are very kind."

So Helen ran quickly upstairs, carrying Strauss with her, and sat down to her reading-desk with a true, though solemn, gladness of heart to which she had long been a stranger, which, perhaps, in its present form, she had never before experienced.

And long after the rest of the house was in darkness and quietness, when the noise had died away in the street below, and the striking of the bells in the neighbouring steeples was almost the only sound to be heard, Helen still sat at her reading-desk, bending over the pages of him whose eyes saw with surpassing clearness through the mists of time and prejudice, whose spirit comes forth, like a ray of sunshine in winter, to greet those toiling painfully upwards to the temple of Truth.

Mr. Gresham's library was rich in German authors, a language of which Helen had as yet no knowledge. Overmastered by the eagerness of curiosity, which the reading of Strauss had awakened in her, she now procured a German grammar, and began, with painful earnestness, the study of the language.

Through many a long summer day she toiled at the grammar and dictionary, manifesting a strength of endurance which the frailty of her frame scarcely seemed capable of supporting.

But, after all, her progress was too slow to keep pace with her eagerness.

One morning, about the middle of July, just when Mr. Gresham was beginning to make arrangements for a tour on the Continent, she came downstairs prepared with a report which she had long meditated.

Mr. Gresham was seated in an arm-chair as she entered. Maud had not yet made her appearance.

After the usual greeting, Helen took a chair by her guardian's side, and requested his attention for a moment.

" I have for some time wished to ask a favour of you," she began. " Will you let me go to Germany ?"

" Why that is just what we are all thinking of doing, Helen," replied the artist. "We shall certainly include the Rhine in our tour."

"You misunderstand me. I mean that I should like to go to Germany to study there for a year or two. I have a great anxiety to learn German thoroughly."

"Why didn't you tell me? I could have found you a teacher."

"A teacher would scarcely answer my purpose," pursued Helen. "He could not give me such a thorough knowledge as I require."

"But whatever has got into your head, Helen? Are you going to run away from us and look out for a place as a governess?"

"You are too kind to me for that. I fear I can hardly explain to you why I feel this desire."

At this moment Maud entered.

"What do you think, Maudie," said Mr. Gresham. "Here is Pallas threatening to desert us, and favour with her omens some synod of tobacco-wreathed professors in the land of the Teutons."

"I must beg you to speak somewhat less figuratively, papa, if I am to understand your meaning," replied the young lady, whose fresh complexion contrasted markedly with Helen's habitual paleness.

"In language suited to your intellect, then, Miss Gresham, she asks me to let her go to Germany for a short time, to study the language."

"And then?" asked Maud.

"Yes. And then, Helen?" repeated Mr. Gresham.

"I cannot look so far forward," replied Helen. "At my age, every day brings changes which one would have thought years could not effect."

She adhered firmly to her purpose, and her guardian, as usual, gave way to her wish.

It remained to decide upon the town she should go to reside in, and here her choice was influenced by her eager interest in Strauss.

She had discovered that at Tübingen Strauss had taught, and to Tübingen accordingly she decided to go, doubting not that her master's influence would there be most pronounced.

This determination of Helen's involved a few necessary changes in her guardian's plans; but ultimately all set out together, and together enjoyed a Continental tour of nearly two months' duration. In the course of this Mr. Gresham procured some good introductions to the professorial circle in Tübingen from one or two artist-friends, with the result that when he and Maud returned home, they left Helen behind them in the old university-town, comfortably established in the house of the widow of a recently-deceased professor.

Helen took leave of them in excellent spirits, looking forward to a long period of study with the utmost enthusiasm; and as for Mr. Gresham, he was in reality by no means sorry to be freed for a while from the task of caring for a young lady whose disposition appeared so little congenial to his own.

CHAPTER XIV.

MIND-GROWTH.

" October, 5th, 1868.—My guardian and Maud left Tübingen last evening, finally abandoning me, as the former characteristically expressed it, to my own devices. What these devices may be, I think neither of them has a very clear idea; possibly they look upon me as a hare-brained girl, possessing a desperate will of my own, and determined to gratify every whim, great or small. Doubtless it is partly my own fault if I am misunderstood by them, for I have never in reality opened my heart to them and exposed all the irresistible yearnings which have driven me to this step. These yearnings, it must be confessed, are as yet a trifle vague; yet there is one definite cry which my heart gives forth day after day, and that is— knowledge, knowledge, knowledge! It is for knowledge that I have come here, and knowledge I will pursue with all the energy my nature is capable of.

" Whither that knowledge may lead me, I cannot as yet tell. Never mind; at least it will lead *somewhere*, give me, sooner or later, some definite convictions, such as my soul hungers for.

" This is the first time I have ever begun to keep a diary, and I wonder the thought never occurred to me before. The following pages are not to be filled with pretty sentiments, hysterical wailings, or scraps of verse —I will not say poetry—I write for my own benefit, that I may more clearly gauge my own progress, and not for the amusement of others.

" I am such a poor hand at conversation that it is really only fair I should be permitted to soliloquise a little. Who is there in the world with whom I can talk confidentially ? Not a soul. I once thought that Maud would make a true friend, but I have long felt her companionship terribly unsatisfying. I wonder whether I shall make a friend here in Germany ? I fear not ; I am too timid and retiring, and adapt myself with such difficulty to the usages of society. Here in the silence of my own room I am comfortable ; I wish there were no necessity for me to ever leave it. But I must really force myself to become acquainted with people, if only for the sake of learning to speak German.

" Frau Stockmaier, with whom I am living, seems really a very agreeable woman, and, I should imagine, cultivated to a very fair degree. She cannot speak English, but is well acquainted with French, and in the latter

language we have hitherto for the most part
conversed. But, of course, as she reminds
me, that will not do. I must reconcile myself to the first serious plunge into the
troubled waters of German conversation, and
the sooner the better.

"One thing, however, I do not like in Frau
Stockmaier. She really treats me too much
as if I were still a child. She asked me my
age this morning, and on my telling her that
I was seventeen last April, she smiled and
expressed a wonder that my guardian should
have ventured to leave me here alone. I
confess I felt a little piqued, for, if I may
trust my glass, my personal appearance is not
very childish, and as regards my mind—.
But here I should perhaps whisper to myself
a caution against spiritual pride.

"As yet I am far from clear as to the order
of studies I shall pursue; but perhaps that is
of no immediate consequence. My first task
is to become thoroughly acquainted with
German, and how long that will take me I
dare not think.

"Frau Stockmaier is to be herself my instructress for the present. I think she will
not exercise too strict a despotism in intellectual matters, for that would be intolerable. I cannot as yet make out whether she
is orthodox and conventional in her beliefs;
at any rate, she does not appear to be intole-
rant, and for that I must be thankful."

" Oct. 10th.—A delightful walk this morning with Frau Stockmaier, through lovely autumn scenery. How I wish I had taken up my abode here earlier in the summer, and how I shall long, all through the coming winter, for the return of sunny weather.

" After walking through the town, crossing the Neckar, and taking a turn through the beautiful Platanen-Allee, we passed over the bridge and went in the direction of the Oesterberg, passing the house of the poet Uhland. At present I am purposely abstaining from all reading of poetry, but some day I hope to know Uhland; Frau Stockmaier speaks of him with much enthusiasm. We climbed the Oesterberg, passing between vineyards and orchards, and, on reaching the summit, were richly rewarded for our efforts. On the point known as the Wielandshöhe, we stood for fully an hour, enjoying the glorious view. Below us lay the whole valley of the Neckar, the river flowing along it like a green cord, and also the valley of the little river Ammer, on the banks of which are the Botanical Gardens, and, near them, our house. In the distance stretched the Swabian Alps, one could see the Castle of Hohenzollern, making a fine object against a background of clear sky. We returned home tired but delighted with our walk.

" Already I am becoming very fond of Tübingen. I wish Mr. Gresham had remained long enough to paint views of the beautiful old place from several points which I could point out. I think I shall be tempted to exercise my own slight skill before the rich autumn hues have quite died away from the trees and the hillsides. I should like to sketch the whole town as it creeps in terraces up the mountain to the grey old towered and moated stronghold of Hohentübingen.

"The mountain-scenery around, without being absolutely imposing, is excessively beautiful. Especially the form of the Oesterberg, seen from a distance, is wonderfully graceful.

"And then there is such a delightful air of peace and quietness throughout the whole country, as if these pleasant hills shut out all the troublous noises of the busy world. I like to pass the University in my walks, to dream over its four hundred years of existence; to go back in fancy to the days when Reuchlin and Melanchthon taught within its walls. In the University the air of peace, of which I have spoken, is especially noticeable, for here, side by side, are a Protestant or a Roman Catholic institution, the *Stift* and the *Convict*, each nursing its own disciples undisturbed by the neighbourhood of a creed essentially different.

"It strikes me that this state of affairs must very greatly conduce to liberality of thought among the students, at all events among the Protestant students. And yet I cannot forget how Strauss was rewarded for his labours ; but I suppose it would be too much to demand toleration for such a spirit as his.

" Frau Stockmaier is very agreeable company on a walk, and yet I cannot shake off my habit of very much preferring to be alone. During the last few days I have been especially thoughtful, finding a constant delight in wandering about alone, especially— and this would, to some, seem childish—in watching the golden leaves fall one by one to the ground. A favourite resort, when I am alone, is the fine ' Platanen-Allee ' on the other side of the river. The trees run in two noble rows over against the houses of the town, forming, as it were, a natural temple. When I walk alone here an inexpressible longing comes over me to take up some of our dear old English poets and revel in them once more ; but I do not permit myself to yield. For the present I must give myself wholly to stern facts ; imagination must be laid aside till my mind is more at ease. But if I only *could* once throw aside this eternal trouble of my thoughts which does not let me rest, how delightful would it be to yield to the impressions of this lovely nature and dream away my life. But that is a dangerous thought."

" Nov. 30th.—As winter draws on, and there is less and less temptation to wander about the hills, I am able to devote myself to severer study. Already I have made very noticeable progress in my German, and can now understand and make myself understood on every-day matters with very tolerable facility. I have determined that at the beginning of the new year I will commence a theological course, and, perhaps, at the same time, peep a little into philosophy. I begin to associate rather more freely with the friends and acquaintances of Frau Stockmaier, and have already been introduced to several gentlemen who would be willing to act as my tutors. Frau Stockmaier recommends me to choose a certain Dr. Eidenbenz, who is a *Stiftsrepetent*, that is to say, one who has completed his University curriculum, and is now engaged in directing the studies of undergraduates. Dr. E. is a youngish man, of rather pleasing appearance, and said to be remarkably clever. Though essentially a theologian, he would also be able to direct my philosophical reading, since, I am informed, all the students of the *Stift* are compelled to study philosophy for two years before commencing their theology. Of course I am, as yet, very ignorant in these matters, but it appears to me, from what I have heard and read of German philosophy, that those two years must be a somewhat

dangerous side-path into the high-road of
orthodox religion.

"I am prepared to find my tutor rather un-
congenial at first, for I hear he is a stout op-
ponent of dear old Strauss. Yet, on that
very account he will be very useful to me. I
want to see orthodox Christianity vigorously
defended, not on the ground of mere sentiment, with which I am but too familiar, but
with sterling arguments which will bear
criticism of the light of superior knowledge.
I trust I am by no means bigoted, though
prejudiced I certainly am. Something warns
me that the end of my intercourse with Dr.
Eidenbenz will be mutual dissatisfaction ;
but probably he will have more ground for
dissatisfaction than myself. At all events,
he will serve to conform me in the beliefs I
have embraced. And then, if his theology
is barren to me, possibly his philosophy may
stand me in better stead.

"In addition to my German, I have commenced to study Greek for a few hours each
day ; also to read a little Latin occasionally.
I wish my poor father had lived long enough
to give me the solid grounding in Greek that
he did in Latin. I found the grammar
horribly difficult, but it *must* be acquired.
First of all I wish to be able to read the New
Testament in the original ; then, when I have
got through my period of doubt and see my
life float once more into calm waters, I know

well what glorious regions a knowledge of
Greek will open to me. If a mere transla-
tion could inspire such a sonnet as that of
Keats, what must Homer in the original
be!"

"Feb. 1st, 1869.—For a month I have
been working with Dr. Eidenbenz, and with
what result? I think I may already safely
say that my prophecy has fulfilled itself. In
a word, the doctor is an unmitigated sophist.
At first he followed my request, and adhered
strictly to a critical examination of the
origins of Christianity, and in his treatment
of the subject there was little to find fault
with. His knowledge seemed deep and extensive, and some of the information he gave
me proved extremely interesting. But by
the end of the second week I noticed a decided change for the worse; he began to be
polemical, and polemical to an alarming degree. Oh, how learned he has already made
me in modern sects and schisms. And to
maintain his position he has recourse to
sophisms which a healthy-minded child could
at once see through, though I grant he seems
to be sincerely their dupe. It is evident that
he will never turn my mind back from the
course into which Strauss irresistibly pro-
pelled it. I have, however, no intention of
ceasing these lessons as yet. It is only fair
to hear him to the end."

"March 1st.—To-day ends my second month with Dr. Eidenbenz, and, to tell the truth, I am heartily tired of him. As I foresaw, I am merely strengthened in my rationalism; no argument I have heard advanced has sufficed to shake it. For several hours after he had left me yesterday, I sat reflecting earnestly upon these matters, endeavouring to ask myself, with all the solemnity of which I am capable, whether I am a really conscientious disbeliever, or one merely from caprice, affectation, or any other unworthy impulse. I convinced myself that no such impulse has power over me; I disbelieve because my reason bids me do so. It may be my mind follows a hereditary tendency on this, for, looking back in memory to those last years of my father's life, I now feel convinced that he, too, had yielded to the force of doubt; a suggestion which explains much in his conduct to me which I was never able to understand.

" In truth, I have fed to repletion on comparative estimates of Petrine and Pauline Christianity, and the like, and I have resolved to cease these theological studies, for my object is gained. But the philosophical readings I shall still persist in, for I find them vastly more interesting. True, the question now and then arose in my mind : ' Of what avail will all these metaphysical systems be in helping me to lead a happier and a better life, or in enabling me to make the lives of others happier and better?' But I suppose such doubts are really too profane. Dr. Eidenbenz is an enthusiastic metaphysician, and it puzzles me sadly to explain the co-existence of this enthusiasm with that mania for religious dogmas. The other morning I actually ventured to ask him to justify himself, and he replied with the curious statement that this philosophy was a mere matter of abstract speculation, a highly-amusing mental employment which could not in the least interfere with his more serious views of life. I could have made a rather startling reply, but wisely held my peace.

"A letter from Maud to-day. It seems to me sadly empty and unsatisfying. Why does she never send me her serious thoughts? Perhaps she would ask me the same question."

"April 18th.—The last few days have witnessed a most curious, and rather alarming event here, which Frau Stockmaier tells me is by no means uncommon in the spring-time. The whole valley of the Neckar is flooded. All the beautiful walks which I had again began to visit with delightful anticipations of spring sunshine, are deep under water, which rises even to the boughs of the linden and plane trees. This morning I ascended the Schlossberg, from whence the view was very extraordinary. All the lovely stretch of green meadows on the south side of the Neckar up to the foot of the hills, was converted into a vast rolling sea. I thought irresistibly of Dr. Eidenbenz and of the Deluge.

"The doctor has remained here during the Easter vacation, and we have been busy for some weeks investigating the fearful and wonderful theories of Messrs. Fichte, Schelling, and Hegel, and I protest I am sick to death of them all. It is a habit of mine to listen very patiently for a long time to my tutor's expositions, and then suddenly to astound him by some startling question. I know he regards me as a veritable daughter of the Philistines; but I follow the bent of my nature, and better to do that than to play the hypocrite. For the life of me, I cannot help interrupting him now and then, and exclaiming: 'What is the use of it?' In reply to which he merely smiles contemptuously, pitying my lack of appreciation. But I am not so sure that a contemptuous smile is a satisfactory answer to my question. If he asserts that such philosophising is of use, inasmuch as it sharpens the human intellect, keeps active speculation alive, and strengthens habits of independent thought, then I will grant that he is right. But surely the same results might be obtained by exercise upon very much more satisfactory topics. What is it to me whether I *am* or I am *not*, whether the internal world really *exists*, or is a mere creation of my fancy? Such speculations do not and cannot influence my practical life, which is the most serious consideration to me. I may be a young, un-learned, inexperienced girl, but still there is that within me that says that such questions as these are unanswerable, that to endeavour to ascertain the ultimate foundation of our knowledge of existing things, is, as men now are, an impossible task. And, such being the case, I confess I am rapidly losing all in-terest in metaphysics. Possibly if I were reading with a man who really held one of these theories, and could press it on me with all the energy of true conviction, I might see it in a different light; but Dr. Eidenbenz does not pretend to hold one of them.

" I was rather surprised last night to find Frau Stockmaier reading a German transla-tion of Darwin's ' Origin of Species.' I have never read the book, though I heard father speak of it occasionally. I am sure it must be immensely interesting. A hunger for it seemed to seize me as I looked over the pages. I almost think natural science would be a study admirably adapted to my taste."

" May 2.—I have read the ' Origin of Species ' in German, and it has created an enthusiasm in me such as perhaps no other book, except the 'Leben Jesu,' ever did. How delightful it is to receive fresh, strong support when one is at war with one's own mind. Here is a theory which recompenses me a thousand fold for my loss of the old Biblical superstitions. What immense labour, what a wonderful intellect does it represent! Yes, yes, this is real, solid food, no insubstantial cloud-shape or chimera. Here is a theory built up on solid facts, facts one can grasp, handle, examine with the eye or the microscope. Oh, how dear hard, plain facts have become to me since I have been wandering in the dreamlands of philosophy. I wonder whether Dr. Eidenbenz has read Darwin. I must ask him.

"Beautiful spring weather is once more breathing upon the face of the land, making field and land lovely past description. I begin to look forward eagerly to long summer walks in the woods, lonely walks, when I can indulge to the uttermost in that self-communing which I delight in. With the impulse of a great delight, born, perhaps, of the season, I have cast aside, for a while— perhaps for ever—both theology and philosophy, and returned to poetry and romance. Long, long have I panted for them, 'as the hart panteth for the water brooks.' I have begun to read Goethe and Schiller both at once. Uhland, too, I have

at length peeped into, and with much delight.
Frau Stockmaier loves Uhland, and often
warms eloquent to me with regard to him.
What I know of his life and personal
character pleases me much. A great poet is
a fine subject for thought, but surely a great
poet who also takes a noble part in the
practical life of the world is fit for the admiration of the gods. Henceforth I shall
always pass his house with a fresh interest.
This morning I made a pilgrimage to his
grave in the cemetery.

" I made a new acquaintance last night, a
certain Dr. Gmelin, Frau Stockmaier's
brother-in-law, who has been living as
privatgelehrter in Stuttgart, but is now come
to settle in Tübingen. It is probable he will
have rooms in our house, and I sincerely
hope so, for even at the first aspect I conceived a strong liking for him. He may be
some forty years old, and has a wonderfully
intellectual countenance, marked, moreover,
with a rare benevolence. Frau Stockmaier
smiles when she speaks of him; he seems a
favourite of hers. She tells me he has never
filled any professorship, though several have,
from time to time, been offered him. He
has very independent ideas on many subjects,
and would never consent to hamper his free
development by submission to official responsibilities and restraints. I admire him
for his consistency."

"May 10.—I have definitely ceased my connection with Dr. Eidenbenz, and rejoice that I had the resolution to do so. Really, to relinquish Dr. Gmelin's conversation for Dr. Eidenbenz's prelections was rather too much. I admire Dr. Gmelin more every day, and am flattered at the interest he appears to take in me. Frau Stockmaier tells me he has always been esteemed a misogamist, but that he ever really was such I cannot believe. He's all courtesy; certainly I never associated with a truer gentleman. And then his conversation is so fresh, so genial. Since he has come to reside in our house, he and I frequently take long walks together, and never run short of matter for discussion. Dr. Gmelin is a philosopher, without doubt, but, it appears to me, not committed to any definite system. In our conversation this morning he made frequent mention of Comte, whose name I have frequently seen, but of whom I know nothing. I must seek for information regarding him, for he evidently exercises much influence over Dr. Gmelin's mind.

"Dr. G. has lent me Häckel's 'Natürliche Schöpfungsgeschichte,' a work inspired by Darwin. I shall read it greedily."

"June 20th.—I have had a delightful walk with Dr. Gmelin over the hills, through woods and orchards, to Bebenhausen, where the cloister is. The building is one of the finest remnants of Gothic architecture in Germany. It lies buried in a deep valley, appearing suddenly at one's feet as you issue from the thick beech-wood. The foliage was glorious, lighted up by the warm June sun. Exquisitely peaceful did the old cloister look, wonderfully attractive for an imaginative mind wearied with the combats of life. Dr. Gmelin told me that he had often wished his conscience would allow him to turn Roman Catholic and enter some such retreat as this; and indeed I am not surprised at his experiencing the desire, for his character has much of gentle and poetical mysticism in it. Yet at other times I see him give signs of such an earnestly practical temperament, that I can hardly reconcile the two sides of his nature. Doubtless it is this wavering and undecided bending of his mind which has prevented him from ever doing any important literary work. I, too, fear very much the same conflict within me at times; perhaps it is the same with all people in a greater or lesser degree. But for the cloister I can now feel little but horror, I can only see the dreadful side of this seclusion from the world's life. Even the life I lead here in Tübingen, though far from monastic, often somewhat irks me. I often think I should find a truer field for my exertions in the turmoil of some great city, such as London.

But how I should employ myself I cannot yet clearly see. Possibly I may some day.

"We talked of a multitude of things on our way—of fate, of predestination, of the basis of morals, of the future of society, of woman's place in the history of the world, in short of almost every important question which either of us has ever thought of. Dr. Gmelin holds many strange theories, some of them wonderfully at variance with his practice. As we stood looking at the cloister, the conversation turned on the subject of asceticism, and he thereupon unfolded to me a dreadful theory of life. The substance of it was this : That the origin of all evil is to be found in the desire for life, and that he is the perfect man who succeeds in altogether uprooting this desire from his mind, losing the sense of his own identity, fixing his thoughts eternally in an absolutely passionless calm. The desire for life being the root of all evil, it follows that the world, by virtue of its very existence, is hopelessly corrupt, that there is no hope for it in the future, nothing but condemnation for its past. Hence, if every man were truly wise, he would mortify all his passions, settle down to a condition of absolute inactivity, and so overcome evil by the complete extinction of life. On my expressing myself pained and shocked at such a philosophy, Dr. Gmelin laughed and told me that it was his favourite theory. Subsequently I learned from him that it was the teaching of the philosopher Schopenhauer, whom hitherto I have only known by name. Dr. Gmelin confesses that, with him, it is nothing more than a theory, that it does not in the least influence his practical life, as indeed I know from experience. Yet it is strange to be pessimistic in theory and optimistic in practice; such a contradiction would be impossible in my own nature. I suppose the truth of it is that his holding such a theory is a mere matter of sentiment; his mind, I know, has a natural bent towards asceticism and mysticism.

"Dr. Gmelin has just knocked at my door and brought me two rather large volumes. He handed me them with a smile, and, on examining the titles, I found they were a work of Schopenhauer, called 'Parerga und Paralipomena.' In them, he tells me, I shall find the kernel of the philosopher's theories. I shall read them at once."

"August 3rd.—I have read through the two volumes of Schopenhauer twice, very carefully. I confess I have been agreeably disappointed. From what Dr. Gmelin had told me, I expected to find a misanthrope, but I have found the very opposite. The reading of these volumes has given me the utmost pleasure, and I am sure they will exercise a lasting influence upon my mind. Am I then a convert to the doctrine of pessimism? Not by any means, for, after all it appears to me that his pessimism is the least valuable part of Schopenhauer's teaching. The really excellent part of him is his wonderfully strong sympathy with the sufferings of mankind. Again and again he tells us that we should lose the consciousness of self in care for others, in fact identify ourselves with all our fellows, see only one great *self* in the whole world. For this doctrine alone I thank him heartily; it chimes exactly with the principle which has long been yearning for expression in my own mind."

"August 10th.—Having acquired some knowledge of Schopenhauer, Dr. Gmelin is now very anxious that I should read Comte; he asserts that I should like him immensely. When he first proposed it, I declared that I was weary of philosophy, and had begun to wander at my will over the fields of poetry. But he presses me so earnestly that I shall be obliged to yield. Indeed, from what he tells me of Comte, I feel rather attracted. It seems it is Comte's principle that the true destination of philosophy must be social, practical, and herein I heartily agree with him. He, too, insists strongly upon the development of sympathetic instincts for the human race at large. The latter principle I have thoroughly imbibed from Schopenhauer.

What if Comte can afford me some idea of the manner in which the principle may be practically worked out? That would be just what I need."

"Dec. 1st.—For nearly four months I have been hard at work upon Comte's 'Philosophie Positive.' Yes, Dr. Gmelin was indeed right when he said this would suit me. I could not have conceived a system so admirably adapted to secure my sympathy. First and foremost, Comte discards metaphysics, thereby earning my heartiest approbation. He shows that metaphysical systems are a thing of the past, something which had its inevitable place in the history of mankind, but which has served its purpose and may be cast aside for something better. How delighted I am with his masterly following of the history of mankind through every stage of its development. There is something entrancing to me in these firmly-fixed laws, these *positive* investigations. Comte is for me the supplement to Darwin; the theories of both point to the same result, and *must* be true! What encouragement he gives to ardent work! How grand to feel that one is actually helping on the progress of humanity, as every one is doing who seeks earnestly to learn and to propagate the truth. Comte hopes for a speedy rectification of all the errors of our social system, not a rectification of arbitrary means, but one which follows naturally and necessarily upon the whole course of previous history. He holds that the first step towards this improvement is the re-discussing and re-modelling of all social theories in a purely scientific spirit, and their disposition in a systematic whole with all the rest of human knowledge. This is a noble theory. I feel convinced that Dr. Gmelin in reality holds these views; I must bring him to confession."

"Dec. 10th.—It has been decided between Dr. Gmelin and myself that our conversation shall henceforth always run in practical grooves. Our metaphysical and religious discussions we will henceforth throw aside as done with. Every day I feel the longing for active life growing stronger within me. 'What can a woman do in the world?' I asked my friend this morning. His reply was wise and encouraging. I have already told him that I am possessed of considerable means, and it is his belief that, under these circumstances, if only I have the courage to despise vulgar conventionality and to pursue what I consider the path of duty, I can do considerable good. In early life, he travelled a good deal in Europe, and made it one of his special objects to observe the condition of the poor. Even now it is one of his favourite occupations to plan schemes for the relief of the poverty which burdens the world. In the course of a long conversation he made me acquainted with some of the theories of social improvement which are beginning to be advocated in Germany. Most of these involve an entire re-organisation of society, and that, though it will come in time, I fear neither Dr. Gmelin nor I shall live to see. Putting aside these extensive plans, we agreed that what was especially needed just now was the earnest exertion of private individuals. Let only private individuals do their utmost to relieve misery, let them keep the subject constantly in discussion, let them never lose sight of the *need* for improvement, and radical improvement will come as soon as is consistent with the progress of destiny. I am ashamed to think how little I know practically of the misery of great cities. Often I think that I shall cut short my proposed two years' stay in Germany, and return forthwith to London, to learn how I may perhaps be useful. Yet I am very loth to lose Dr. Gmelin's society. He has already done me vast good, and is capable of benefiting me still more."

"January 3rd, 1870.—A new year has began for me. Never before had this commencement of a new division of time such significance for me as now. Oh, how eagerly I long to get away into the midst of active life, there to play my part in the service of that true religion, the Religion of Humanity. What wonderful changes has my mind undergone since I have been in Germany, and how I shall always love to look upon Tübingen, upon this dear *Schwaben* where I have seen so much and been so happy.

"Yes, how much have I to thank Germany for. I came here with a mind rudely enough ploughed by the ploughshare of anguish, a mind lying in readiness for the sower, and here did the furrows receive these seeds which were to spring up into a harvest of peace and joy. How distant now seem those days which I languished out in bondage to the power of darkness, bondage of the spirit, far sterner and more deadly than any veritable bondage of the flesh could be! How well I remember the day when I took up Strauss' 'Leben Jesu' as Maud left it on the library table at home. The book was to me like the first ray of heavenly light piercing the darkness of a night of anguish, and striving, and woe unutterable. And yet how strange it now seems to me that I should ever have gone through such suffering, and so young, too. But it was terribly real at the time, and, but for happy circumstances, might have terminated very differently. I might even now have been telling my beads in a convent, hard-bound in the conception that thus I was fulfilling my own destiny and propitiating the favour of an avenging deity.

"No one can ever know how near I was becoming a Catholic during those days of bitter, bitter sorrow after my poor father's death. Even when I appeared to those who reasoned with me, most stubborn on my own faith, even then I was often on the point of raising my eyes to Heaven with a wild cry of rapture at my release from the agony of doubt, and for ever after bending before the crucifix in a sunless contrition of soul. Thanks to the unknown hand which guides suffering humanity through the storms of intellectual growth, safely leading it at length into the predestined haven, thanks to that mighty hand, which at times I feel pressing upon my heart, and moulding it into the forms to which its energies adapt it, I survived the struggle, and live to look back with a smile of pity upon all that I endured. Of pity— by no means of contempt. At no stage in its struggles is a human mind contemptible; for as long as it *does* struggle, it asserts its native nobility, its inherent principle of life.

"For some months I have read the *Times* regularly, day after day. I have been wrong to neglect newspapers so long. What an apocalypse of human mystery is here set before my eyes! And yet how little conscious of it seem those whom good fortune has raised above the fear of cold, hunger, and the diseases they engender. I read the reports of a sitting in Parliament, and find that hours have been spent in the angry discussion of some absurd point of national etiquette, or on the clauses of a Bill the object of which seems to be merely to enrich a body of most undeserving men, and when I afterwards turn to the police reports, and read, as long as my nerves will permit me, the heart rending stories which abound there, I am compelled to marvel that humanity is content to suffer so uncomplainingly."

" May 12th.—I have had many a long talk lately with Dr. Gmelin on the course I propose to pursue when I return to England, and he has given me many practical hints which I am sure will be useful. In religious matters he is wonderfully tolerant; almost too tolerant, I think ; and he never ceases to impress upon me what great and useful schemes of private charity are carried out by the religious sects. With some such sect he would have me enroll myself, merely for the purpose of having a better field for my work. But I fail to see how this would be possible without a degree of hypocrisy to which I could never reconcile myself. Doubtless I shall see my way much more clearly when I am once more actually in London ; I shall be able to gauge the existent misery with my own eyes, and I am sure some good plan or other will not fail to suggest itself. Something I am determined to do. To live the life of an ordinary wealthy lady, the life of " society," either altogether heedless of the sufferings of the poor, or occasionally satisfying my conscience with a perfunctory contribution to one or two ill-conducted charities —that would be quite impossible for me. I wonder whether I am what is generally known as a 'strong-minded' woman? It is possible; for I certainly feel but little sympathy with those many pitiful weaknesses generally pronounced to be the amiabilities of my sex. Well, I can only hope that my strength of mind, if it exist, will stand me in good stead, and enable me to make my life not altogether useless.

"Dr. Gmelin asked me the other day whether I did not intend to write at all on the subjects which interest me ; write, that is to say, in the periodicals and daily papers. On reflection, I think not. In the first place I am not by any means sure that I possess a spark of literary ability, and then it is my firm belief that such work is not woman's true sphere. If I were to write, it must be something of genuine scientific value, something which would hasten the advent of vast social reforms; and to do that is certainly beyond my power. What ideas may sooner or later occur to me I shall employ myself in putting into practice; doubtless I shall have abundant opportunities. Nature appears to me to have ordained that woman's sphere should be that of personal influence, and the influence of my own personality, such as it is, should be brought face to face with the horrors of helpless poverty. My ideas may be extravagant and unpractical, but I have faith in humanity. The results of my determination may not be great, but at all events they shall be real."

"May 15th.—My time in Germany grows short. As regards those I shall leave behind me here in dear old Tübingen, I shall depart with unfeigned regret ; as regards the prospects before me, I am all eagerness to be gone. I have compelled Dr. Gmelin to promise that he will pay me a visit some day in England, but I very much fear such a journey would require too much resolution for him. Years of motionless existence have so bound him down to his books that I believe it would break his heart to have to leave them.

"Of late I have departed from my strict principle of reading none but German works, and in favour of one who I am surprised has not long since tempted me to forbidden fields. For a week I have been poring over Shelley, reading him to the exclusion of almost everything else—Shelley, whom when I was a child I read without understanding, yet with such delight, carried on from page to page by the magic of his verse, and occasionally the glimpse of a thought which dazzled my feeble eyes. Of all the poets—yes, of all I have ever read—Shelley is my chosen one. Poets such as Keats, who live for art alone, regardless of the stream of human life, which makes fresh the meadows and the woods where they sing their songs, these have their irresistible charm, but they cannot always satisfy the heart. It is that glorious band of which Shelley is the foremost spirit, who, not content with for ever hymning poems at the altar of beauty, echo in their noblest songs the accents of that unceasing woe which writhes in the heart of the universe—it is before these that I will fall down and worship with a devotion which shall only fade when the fire of life is quenched in my soul. They recognise that poetry is not alone the voice of joy, but rather the noblest utterance of humanity clamouring for vengeance against its oppressors at the door of Fate. Nature has forbidden that I should join this noble choir, but I can at least assert my privilege to listen when others are deaf, and feel my heart stirred to action by the inspiring harmony.

" Schopenhauer, Comte, and Shelley—these three have each in turn directed the growth of my moral life. Schopenhauer awakened within me the fire of sympathy, gave a name to the uneasy feeling which made my life restless, taught me to forget myself and to live in others. Comte then came to me with his lucid unfolding of the mystery of the world, showed me why the fire of sympathy burned so within my breast, taught me the use to which it should be directed. Last of all Shelley breathed with the breath of life on the dry bones of scientific theory, turned conviction into passion, lit the heavens of the future with such glorious rays that the eye dazzles in gazing upwards, strengthened the heart with enthusiasm as with a coat of mail. Can I ever count myself an atheist when I worship such gods as these?"

"May 30th.—A few more days, and farewell to Germany! Farewell, also, to one phase of my life, that of sitting still and reflecting. When I again step on the shores of England I shall be no longer a girl; but, I trust, a woman whose sufferings and struggles have not been without profit to herself, and may, perchance, be the means of good to others."

CHAPTER XV.

THE EX-CLERGYMAN'S BEQUEST.

As the summer of 1870 began to draw near, the Greshams once more looked forward to having Helen Norman back in London, and not a little conversation took place between father and daughter with regard to the probable future relations betwen themselves and their ward. It was indeed a subject admitting of some little speculation. Would Helen come back a confirmed religious devotee, prepared to spend her life in alms-giving and in the discharge of the duties of a hospital nurse? Judging from her prevalent mood two years ago this did not seem an unlikely contingency. On the other hand, her residence on the Continent might have banished these morbid notions from her mind, and, whilst adding to her intellect and accomplishments, have introduced a mixture of worldliness into her nature that would make her rather more like an ordinary daughter of Eve than she had hitherto shown herself. Maud was inclined to adhere to the former supposition, considering it not unlikely that her friend would return a Roman Catholic. Mr. Gresham, however, sceptical, as usual, in all that concerned human consistency, held to the opinion that she would return very much like any other girl of eighteen, possibly already engaged, or at all events anxious to be so, and no doubt eager to make the most, from a worldly point of view, of her position as a heiress. How far either of these acute observers was right, the reader has already had an opportunity of determining.

They had very little means of judging of any alteration Helen's character might have undergone, except by their recollection of what she had previously been. For in her letters to Maud, written about once a month, she had confined herself entirely to remarks on the purely outward circumstances of her life, very often writing only of past times and of people she and Maud had known, at other times filling her letters, which never ceased to be affectionate, with descriptions of the scenery she beheld in her occasional excursions from Tübingen. She had purposely refrained from making Maud her confidant in what concerned her inward life; for, though still retaining the affectionate feeling which she associated with Maud, even back to her earliest childhood, she had grown sensible, during the months they had lived together, that Maud could no longer be regarded by her as a friend, in the sense of one with whom she might safely share every secret of her bosom. Much in the characters of both Maud and her father had repelled her when she came to observe them closely, as indeed was but natural when we compare their studied indifference to most of the loftier aims of life with Helen's fervour of mind and heart. It was thus with something of apprehension, on her own side, also, that Helen looked forward to her return to England.

The Greshams had not greatly altered during the past two years, either in appearance or habits of life. Mr. Gresham's reputation as a successful artist had continued to grow, and had brought him an increase of wealth, which he regarded by no means the least important of its consequences. I have not hitherto made any remark with regard to his stand-point as an artist, for the reason that there was very little to be said thereupon. He pursued multifarious branches of painting, never making an absolute failure, or at all events keeping them secret if he did make any, yet never, on the other hand, rising to productions which bore the unmistakable stamp of genius. He was possessed of considerable talent, without doubt, and took a pleasure in his profession, partly sincere, partly the logical outcome of his professed philosophy. He had a keen sense for the direction of popular taste, and was troubled by no subtle scruples with regard to the dignity of his art which might have withheld him from availing himself of popular favour. Probably few artists of his time were more successful, judged by the criterion of that substantial approbation which finds expression in the expenditure of pounds, shillings, and pence.

For Maud Gresham, now in her twentieth year, the intervening time had brought an event of some moment, which, however, found no place in the gossipy letters with which from time to time she favoured Helen. Maud was engaged. It would be scarcely possible to conceive of a young lady who had passed through the days of wooing with a less fluctuating appetite, or who looked forward to her approaching marriage with a less fluttering heart. Her future husband, by name Mr. John Waghorn, she had been acquainted with for some two years. Her father had originally met him at his Club, had found him a gentlemanly kind of man, and one apparently possessed of means, and had ultimately invited him to dinner. It then became known that Mr. Waghorn was a railway director, and the suspicion of "means" became a satisfactory certainty. Mr. Gresham had intimated to his daughter that here was a very eligible match for her; Maud had reflected upon the matter and came to a similar conclusion; and an extremely gentlemanlike proposal had even-

tually made it clear that Mr. Waghorn
entirely coincided with the views of his
friend. Should nothing happen to prevent
it, the marriage would be celebrated during
the August of the present year.

During all the time that had elapsed since
the death of Mr. Norman, his friend and
executor had not once made an effort to
fulfil the request made in the ex-clergyman's
will with regard to Arthur Golding. Deem-
ing such a search impracticable, and sure to
remain void of result, Mr. Gresham had constantly procrastinated the performance of
this duty, always in the intention, however,
of some day easing his conscience by the
execution of some such measure as forward-
ing a communication to the police, or inserting
advertisements in various newspapers. And
these steps he did at length take, though not
till the commencement of May in the present
year. As sometimes will happen in similar
cases, the event he had esteemed well-nigh
impossible actually occurred on the very day
when he had roused himself to such a perfunctory discharge of his obligations, and,
after all, by a pure piece of chance. On that
day, as Fate would have it, he discovered
Arthur Golding.

Returning homewards on foot from the
Strand, he took a short cut out of Oxford
Street by way of Rathbone Place, which
brought him into Charlotte Place and past

Mr. Tollady's shop door. Glancing up by chance into the printer's window, he saw a neatly-framed water-colour picture hanging there for sale, marked at the modest figure of five shillings. The execution of the drawing was in some respects remarkable, but this would hardly have sufficed to detain him without some other source of interest. This, however, he found in the picture itself, its subject and outline; for it was a copy of a picture of his own which had recently been exhibited in London, and had attracted some attention. It was a copy, and yet not a copy; for while the attitudes and countenances of the figures were precisely as in the original picture, the colouring was altogether different, and indeed much more effective. Mr. Gresham regarded it with curiosity for some moments, and, after a slight hesitation, entered the shop. Mr. Tollady was sitting there alone, and he rose as the stranger entered.

"Could you inform me by whom the drawing in the window was executed?" asked Mr. Gresham, speaking with that touch of aristocratic haughtiness which usually marked his speech when directed to those less wealthy than himself.

"It is by a young man who acts as my assistant, sir," returned the printer.

"Is he in the habit of selling pictures?"

"He occupies most of his leisure time in drawing and painting; but this is the first

I have succeeded in persuading him to try and sell."

"Then you can, possibly, tell me how this copy was made? I mean, was it taken from the original picture, or otherwise?"

"It was made, sir, from an engraving in the *Illustrated London News*, which seemed to strike my young friend's fancy. He purposed first to make a copy in crayon, but afterwards decided to make it a study of colour. He has often expressed a wish to see the original, but has had no opportunity."

"I think I could afford him that," said Mr. Gresham, with a slight smile. "Will you take the picture from the window and let me look at it again?"

The old man obeyed with sincere joy. The picture had been hanging for more than a month, and as yet no customer had offered. The artist took it in his hands and examined it closely.

"May I ask your opinion of its execution, sir?" asked Mr. Tollady, closely watching the artist's face.

"It is not bad," returned the other, looking suddenly into his questioner's face, as if he half resented the liberty. "There are a few faults in the drawing, and many signs of inexperience in the colouring. Where has the young man received his instruction?"

" He has had none whatever, sir," replied
Mr. Tollady, in a tone not unmixed with
pride. " The merit is solely his."

Mr. Gresham looked up for a moment in
surprise, but at once changed the look to a
somewhat supercilious smile.

" And the demerits likewise, then," he
said. " I am glad no one else is responsible."

" Do you know the original, sir ?" asked
Mr. Tollady, after a moment's silence.

" I myself painted it," replied the other,
without looking up from the drawing.

The old man's heart throbbed high. The
way in which Mr. Gresham regarded the
picture began to inspire him with hopes he
had scarcely dared entertain.

" If you will put this in paper I will be the
young man's first patron," said the artist, at
length, after apparently hesitating. " And,
what is his name ?"

" Arthur Golding," replied Mr. Tollady,
as he took the picture and began to fold it in
brown paper.

" What did you say ?"

" Arthur Golding, sir," repeated the other,
in some surprise at the earnestness of the
question.

Mr. Gresham knitted his brows in a puzzled
look, and regarded the printer closely.

" Arthur Golding, eh ? " he said at length.
" Excuse my curiosity, but has he long been
your assistant ?"

"Nearly eight years, sir," replied Mr Tollady, smiling.

"But how old is he?"

"About nineteen."

"H'm.   Then he was a mere child when he
came to you?"

"Little more."

Mr. Gresham turned from the counter,
walked into the doorway, and stood there for
some moments in reflection.   Making up his
mind, he again faced the printer.

"The name you have mentioned," he said,
"is one very familiar to me, and has raised
my interest in an especial degree.   Would
you have any objection—I leave it, of course,
entirely to your own discretion—to tell me
what you know of this young man's history
previous to his first coming to you?"

Mr. Tollady's turn for reflection had now
come, and he was a minute before he replied—

"I think I can have no objection to do so,
sir," he then said.   "Arthur Golding is at
present out, and will not return for at least
an hour, or I should have much preferred to
ask his permission.   But as I know he is
altogether free from false pride, and as you
have shown so kind an interest in his work,
I will freely venture to tell you what I know.
It is included in a very few words.   He came
to me originally in reply to a notice in my
window that I wanted a boy.   He referred

me then for a testimonial to his character to
a bird-dealer in St. Andrew Street, whose
name I have forgotten. From him I learnt
that the boy had been found by a friend
of his destitute in the street one night, and
had him brought home and put to bed; after
which he had continued to lodge there, earning his living by working as errand-boy, or
something of the kind at a neighbouring shop."

"But before he was picked up in the
street?" asked Mr. Gresham, seeing that the
other paused.

"Of that I know very little, for he has
always been reticent on the subject of his
earliest years, and I should be loath to pain
him by asking unpleasant questions. All I
actually know is that he suffered the severest
misery, and that he lived at one time in one
of the most wretched alleys off Whitecross
Street, in the City."

"Ah, he did!" ejaculated Mr. Gresham,
who saw Arthur's identity confirmed by this
last particular. "Well, it is a somewhat
singular thing, but I have for some time had
an interest in discovering an Arthur Golding, and have, not an hour ago, sent advertisements to various newspapers, addressed
to him, if he should be living. From what
you tell me, I feel pretty sure that you have
saved me further trouble. Did he ever speak
to you, bye-the-by, of a gentleman called Mr.
Norman?"

" I have no recollection of the name."

" Nor of a town called Bloomford ?"

" I think, never."

" Very possibly not; it was merely an idea that occurred to me. May I trouble you for your own name ?"

" My name is Samuel Tollady, sir.

" Very well, Mr. Tollady; I will leave my card with you, and I shall feel obliged if you will allow your assistant, Arthur Golding, to call and see me, any time after six this evening. I may possibly show him the original of his drawing. Bye-the-by, you might give me some idea of his character. Pretty fair ?"

" I have regarded him as my son, sir," replied Mr. Tollady, " for so many years that I feel as if it were hardly right for me to praise him. Nevertheless, I will say that I have never known him guilty of a mean or dishonourable action, and I believe that he would lose his life sooner than commit either."

" Strong expressions, those, Mr. Tollady," replied the other, with his sceptical smile. " I am glad you told me that you regard him as a son; otherwise I might have—well, have given less credit to your judgment than I am still disposed to do. Good morning."

Mr. Tollady, left alone, pursued his work with a lighter heart and a more cheerful

look than had been his for many years. I
say pursued his work; but during the hour
which intervened between Mr. Gresham's departure and Arthur's return from his absence
on a business matter, he was indeed scarcely
capable of applying himself to anything. He
walked up and down the shop rubbing his
hands together in his delight, knitting his
brows in the puzzle of wondering what could
be the artist's hidden connection with Arthur,
and turning over and over in his pocket the
five shillings which Mr. Graham had paid for
the picture.

How should he announce the news to
Arthur? He knew very well that the absence
of his picture from the window would at once
strike the young man on his entrance, and
this would exact an immediate explanation.
Yet he scarcely knew how he should preserve
the calmness necessary to give it. Be it
noted, that in contemplating the consequences of this event, Mr. Tollady only
thought of their advantages to Arthur.

During the last two years, since Arthur
had been able to take an active share in the
business, things had looked up again at the
old printing-shop, and prospects were now
much brighter than they had been for many
years. In pondering on the morning's event,
it appeared to Mr. Tollady as quite a natural
thing that Arthur should forthwith leave the
shop; but nothing was further from his

mind than the least thought of selfish regret
on this account.   Such was not Samuel
Tollady's nature.

After a delay which seemed several hours
instead of only one, Mr. Tollady's anxious
ear caught the sound of a well-known, light,
quick step on the pavement outside, and the
next moment Arthur Golding entered the
shop.

He had grown to be tall for his age, and
the promise of his boyhood was already fulfilling itself in his appearance as a young
man.   An abundance of hair, which was
still light and wavy, hung about a face in
which handsome and manly outlines blended
with an expression of serious thoughtfulness
which at once struck one as remarkable.   It
was not the face of a robust and healthy
youth, but decidedly pale and a trifle thin,
and the ceaseless motion of his large blue
eyes gave him somewhat of the restless
appearance of one who is urged to constant
activity and exertion by impulses from
within.

"Well," he exclaimed, in a full, joyous
voice, as he entered the shop, " it is all
right, Mr. Tollady. I have got the order !"

" Have you, my dear boy ? I am glad of
it—I am glad of it."

The old man kept pacing up and down the
shop, laughing inwardly, and quite surpris-
ing Arthur by the vividness of his delight.

He had never seen him so pleased before at the mere acquisition of an order, and could scarcely understand it.

Mr. Tollady himself kept glancing towards the window, where the picture had hitherto hung, in the hope of attracting the young man's attention thither, but still without success.

"Well, come!" he exclaimed, at length. "As you have got the order, Arthur, it is only fair you should have some commission. What shall it be? Suppose we say five shillings—five shillings, eh?"

As he spoke he took the two half-crowns from his pocket, and pressed them into Arthur's hand.

Then a sudden idea of the old man's meaning flashed across the other's mind. He turned rapidly towards the window, and at once perceived that his drawing was not there.

"It is gone! You have sold it!" exclaimed Arthur, with boyish delight, pressing one of Mr. Tollady's hands in both his own. "To whom? Tell me! How did it happen?"

For a few moments the old man was unable to speak; but at length he summoned the resolution to begin his story.

As he proceeded, Arthur's astonishment kept pace with the narrator's delight, and when he knew the whole a serious expression rested upon his countenance.

"What do you say the name on the card is?" he asked. "Gresham?"

"Yes, Gresham. Can you recall it?"

"Not in the least," replied Arthur, plunged in thought.

"Do you recall the name of Norman?" asked Mr. Tollady, after a slight hesitation.

Arthur raised his head suddenly.

"Yes, I do; I recall it perfectly. For years I have lost it. Mr. Norman was a clergyman."

"I suppose you knew him some time before you met with me?"

"Forgive me, Mr. Tollady," exclaimed Arthur, "for never having told you of this. I imagined it was an incident buried away in my old, miserable life, and little dreamt it would ever be spoken of again."

Arthur then related, in few words, and as well as he could remember the details, the story of his brief acquaintance with Mr. Norman at Bloomford, naturally exaggerating much which he barely retained of the far-off memories of childhood, but giving a true and vivid account of that uneasy yearning in his child's heart, that longing for a sight of his dead and gone father, and all the vague restlessness to which it gave rise, which had ultimately led to his running away from Bloomford.

Having completed his confidence, Arthur

then went to work for a few hours at "case," leaving Mr. Tollady to his reflections.

At the stated hour, Arthur took his way towards Portland Place, discovered the number, and rang the visitor's bell. It was not without much natural tremulation that he found himself standing in the imposing doorway of what was a palace compared to any house he had ever entered. One moment he almost hoped they had not heard his ring, and that it might be possible to retreat unobserved to his life of happy obscurity ; but bolder thoughts soon came to his assistance. The democratic education he had received told him that though this man might be wealthy, he was not necessarily an object of awe, or even of respect. As an able artist he might command deference, and that Arthur felt it would be no indignity to show. But as for his big house and his portentous door-bells, pooh! "A man's a man for a' that!"

A servant in livery at length opened the door, and, evidently apprised of Arthur's expected arrival, at once requested him to walk in. He then led the way upstairs, treading noiselessly with slippered feet, till he arrived before a door concealed behind a heavy green curtain. The curtain he drew back, and requested Arthur to step in, informing him that he would apprise Mr. Gresham of his presence.

" What a dreadful house to live in ! " was
Arthur's first thought, when left alone. The
very air seemed oppressed by the weight of
the luxury through which he had passed
merely in ascending the stairs. The absolute
silence which reigned throughout, scarcely
broken by the affected whisper of the footman, seemed to assail his ears more painfully
than the most intolerable noise. And now he
looked around and surveyed the room he
found himself in. The first glance showed
him that it was a studio. An artist's studio !
How the recollection of all the studios he had
ever read of flashed across his mind, dazzling
his perceptions with unnumbered rays of
glory. How often had he seen studios in the
spirit—the studios of the great masters, to
his imagination more sacred than any holy of
holies reared by human superstition ; but
with how faint a hope of ever sating his
bodily eyes with the appearance of an actual
one.

Eagerly he gazed round at the multifarious
objects which met his look. The room was a
spacious one, round in shape, and lighted from
above, where there was a species of glass dome,
shaded on one side by a movable curtain,
which allowed no ray to pass in that direction. Three or four large easels stood in the
centre, each bearing an unfinished picture,
one of a considerable size. On the walls
hung a number of looking-glasses, also an

abundance of framed sketches, studies, oil and water-colour pictures.

In one corner lay a heap of armour, very brightly polished, together with a few sheathed swords, and one or two enormous feathers. Against the wall, in another corner, hung a quantity of various-coloured robes. Everywhere were canvases, either finished, about to be finished, or never to be finished —canvases, as it seemed to Arthur, by hundreds.

As for the multitude of small articles of luxury which were scattered about the room on every available space, his eyes refused to take note of them individually. The furniture of the room consisted of massive antique chairs and tables, and the fire-place was surmounted by a lofty mantel-piece of dark oak, marvellously carved in elaborate foliage, the whole a masterpiece. Then, standing on a small table near to one of the easels, he observed the colour-boxes, pallets, sheaves of brushes, together with a multitude of small appliances of which he knew neither the name nor the use. His mouth watered at the sight.

Surveying in turn the pictures hanging on, or leaning against the walls, he came at length to one at the sight of which he started in surprise. It was the picture which he had copied by means of the engraving; the subject, Arviragus coming forth from the cave with the corpse of Imogen in his arms, whilst Belarius and Guiderius regard him with surprise and grief. As he stood earnestly examining every feature and each tint, to compare it with his own execution, he was startled by a cough close behind him. Turning, he found that Mr. Gresham had entered unobserved.

" You have discovered the ' Imogen,'" said the artist, extending his hand to his visitor, and regarding him at the same time with a critical look.

" I was thinking how little I understand of art, and how I had spoilt the picture for want of skill in colouring."

The speech was very well adapted to secure favour, but it was in no calculating spirit that Arthur uttered it. He spoke, as he always did, the veritable thoughts of his heart.

" Perhaps you underrate your skill," returned Mr. Gresham, disposed to be gracious; " but it is not of that we have first to speak. Let us sit down. Now you will, in all probability, be prepared for my first question. Have you any objection to tell me precisely what you can remember of your life previous to your acquaintance with that bird-catcher, bird-trainer—whatever the man was—who lived Seven Dials way ?"

Arthur replied that he had no objection whatever, and proceeded once again to relate those painful passages of his early years with

which the reader is well acquainted. When
he had finished, Mr. Gresham reflected a little.

"You have not heard of Mr. Norman since
you left him in that—that somewhat abrupt
manner?" he asked at length, with the
touch of sarcasm seldom absent from his
speech.

"Never," replied Arthur.

"Very well. Then I must tell you that
Mr. Norman died some three years ago,
abroad. I was with him at the time of his
death, and one of his last requests to me
was that I should endeavour to re-discover
you."

Arthur looked up in the utmost surprise.

"I have no doubt," proceeded Mr. Gresham, "that I have now fulfilled his wish, so
far. May I ask you what is the nature of
your plans as regards the future?"

"I have never reflected much upon them,"
replied Arthur, "for I have grown accustomed to regard my future as inseparably
connected with Mr. Tollady. I have learned
printing from him, and, if he should die, I
have always the means thereby of earning my
living."

"*If* he should die," repeated the artist,
with a rather unfeeling emphasis. "He
appeared to me rather an old man."

"He is an old man," said Arthur, with
some sadness in his tone.

There was silence for some moments,

during which Mr. Gresham cast side glances at his companion, and seemed to be in some doubt how to proceed.

" What made you first think of drawing ? " he asked, at length.

" I can scarcely say. I have always been fond of it, as long, almost, as I can remember."

" You have never received lessons of any kind ? "

" None at all."

" Should you be inclined to take advantage of the opportunity of obtaining instruction, in case it presented itself ?"

" I should be glad to do so," replied the young man, with warmth.

Again Mr. Gresham paused, and this time he rose and paced the room.

" Mr. Norman," he began again, resuming his seat, " appears to have taken considerable interest in your welfare, Mr. Golding ; so much, indeed, that in his will he left some little provision for you, in the event of my being successful in the search."

Arthur gazed at the speaker with unconcealed astonishment.

" You are surprised ! Well, it remains with you to justify the hopes which seem to have prompted Mr. Norman's kindness. We will say nothing at present of the details of the bequest. Suppose I were to undertake to supply you with sufficient money to live upon, without the assistance of your own work, and to superintend your studies during an hour or two each day here in my own studio, would you be content to devote yourself entirely to art, and to pursue it in the manner I should suggest?"

For several minutes Arthur remained silent, experiencing sensations which deprived him of the power of rational thought. Conceive his situation. A youth of high spirit and lofty ambitions, inspired, though he knew it not, with the breath of genius, whose life hitherto had been hemmed between the narrowest bounds, who had pictured for his pleasure the most glowing futures, without the hope of ever rising above a scant subsistence, procured by persevering manual work, for him to be thus suddenly, and without warning, presented with the chance of realising his most rapturous dream—a life devoted exclusively to the study of his beloved art; it was, indeed, too much for his brain to encompass. He stood unable to reply.

"Well, what do you think?" said the artist, reading with amusement the thoughts which impressed themselves on the young man's ingenuous features.

"I fear I could not reply without—without reflection," said Arthur; "but no—I know I could not fulfil these conditions. If I were to withdraw from our business, Mr. Tollady would be unable to carry it on alone."

" But he might obtain some one else."

" No one else, I fear, who—who would suit him.   No, sir ; in any case I should be unable to devote myself entirely to art."

" Could you spare some two or three hours each morning ? "

" I—I fear not.   It would be impossible for me to say without consulting Mr. Tollady."

"Is Mr. Tollady's business extensive ? " asked Mr. Gresham, with a smile.

" It is not very large, sir ; but I am glad to say it has been improving lately."

" Bye-the-by, where did you receive your education—reading and writing, you know?"

" I owe it almost entirely to Mr. Tollady," replied Arthur.   " He has been my father ever since I have known him.   It would be impossible to over-estimate my indebtedness to him."

" I fancy Mr. Tollady must be a somewhat notable man," said Mr. Gresham, with his peculiar smile.   " Well, I think we have talked enough for the present.   The best thing you can do will be to return home and acquaint Mr. Tollady with the propositions I have made to you.   Talk the matter over together.   Then come to see me again to-morrow, at the same time, and let me know the results you have arrived at.   Will you do so ? "

" I will, sir."

" And, bye-the-by, bring me up a few of

your drawings—your ordinary work, you know. I shall be better able to judge of your ability from them."

So the interview ended, and Arthur returned to Charlotte Place, so distracted with contending emotions that he was quite unconscious of the streets he passed through, several times missing his way, and being roused at length by surprise when he heard Mr. Tollady speaking to him from the doorway of the shop.

Meanwhile Mr. Gresham had left his studio and descended to the library, where he found Maud writing a letter in the twilight, for it was after seven o'clock.

" To Helen ? " he asked, standing on the hearth-rug with his hands behind him.

Maud nodded, but did not look up.

" Have you told her of my discovery ? "

" I am just doing so. Has he been yet ? "

" Just gone."

" Well ?"

" Well ? " repeated Mr. Gresham, feigning not to catch her meaning.

" What is the verdict ? "

" Rather favourable, on the whole. Indeed, considering his antecedents, I should say that he bears a wonderful resemblance to a gentleman."

" Without, of course," returned Maud, " exciting the least suspicion that he really may be a gentleman ? "

"I wouldn't commit myself to a decided opinion yet," returned her father, smiling.

"And what do you intend to do with him?" asked Maud, after writing on for a few minutes.

"To tell you the truth, Maudie, I find it a trifle difficult to decide. At all events, I have offered him the chance of taking lessons here, and I fancy he will be much tempted to accept."

"It doesn't ever strike you, papa, that you may be doing a very foolish thing?"

"How so, Miss Gresham?"

"Wouldn't it be much better for this young man to keep to his tailoring, or shoemaking, or whatever else it is he has been brought up to, without having his head disturbed with fancies which can never come to anything?"

"Pray be accurate, my dear. In the first place he is neither a tailor nor a shoemaker, but a printer; secondly, I beg to tell you that he possesses a most uncommon talent, and the fancies, as you term them, may not improbably result in something very substantial indeed."

"Oh, I have no desire to damp your philanthropy, papa," returned Maud, with a sly look. "It is somewhat novel to find you taking such an absorbing interest in a *sans culottes*."

"You are severe, Miss Gresham."

"Not at all, papa. Do you authorise me to tell Helen what you say with regard to—to the foundling?"

"Just as you please. It will help to fill up the letter."

"Do we dine alone, papa?" asked Maud, rising at length from her seat.

"Waghorn promised to drop in. I saw him at the Club this afternoon."

"Oh, bother the man! He is here perpetually."

"In a month or so, Maud, you are likely to find his society still more perpetual."

"Pooh! That will be a different thing. Don't stand all night in the dark there, papa. You seem unusually thoughtful to-night, and it doesn't become you."

CHAPTER XVI.

THE STUDIO.

NOTWITHSTANDING Maud's parting injunction, Mr. Gresham still remained for some time in the gathering darkness of the library, plunged in thought of a description somewhat unusual to him.

The subject of his meditation was Maud herself. That last remark of hers in reference to her future husband had, he scarcely knew why, jarred most unpleasantly upon his ear. For the first time he asked himself seriously whether this marriage of his daughter with Mr. Waghorn was a prudent one, or likely to be a happy one. In vain he represented to himself that Waghorn was undoubtedly a highly respectable man—a railway director, to boot—and that Maud had exhibited no repugnance whatever for the match; indeed that she had been left to her own will entirely in the matter. He could not restore his mind to that state of calm indifferentism which it was his habit to pursue. He reflected upon his own marriage. It had been a happy one, he thought; yes, he certainly thought so; for the truth of the matter was, that his wife had been a helpless, good-hearted, inoffensive child, with whom scarcely the most refractory husband could have had the brutality to quarrel.

In all probability, he thought, Maud had no particular affection for her intended husband ; but what matter, so long as she did not absolutely dislike him ? It was a highly respectable match.

" Pooh, pooh !" exclaimed Mr. Gresham, at length, and went to dinner. The mood had passed away.

Mr. Gresham had been more favourably impressed with Arthur Golding than, in accordance with his usual habit, he had seen fit to declare. He looked forward with some pleasure to his return on the ensuing evening, and, when he arrived, was awaiting him in the studio. Arthur had a large portfolio under his arm.

" You have brought me some drawings to look at ?" said the artist. Let me see."

He took the portfolio, laid it open upon the table, and proceeded to examine the contents, whilst Arthur stood regarding the pictures on the wall, from time to time stealing a glance at Mr. Gresham in an endeavour to observe the effect the drawings were producing upon him.

" Some of these are by no means bad," said the latter, at length, " considering the circumstances under which they were produced. Well, did you discuss the matter with Mr. Tollady?"

Arthur replied that he had done so. He did not say, however, that in doing so, he had made no mention of the pecuniary circumstances, and had merely spoken of Mr. Gresham's offer to give him lessons for an hour or two each day.

"And what was the result?" asked the artist.

"We fear that it would be impossible for me to cease working in the office altogether; but Mr. Tollady is very anxious that I should accept your kind offer to direct me in my studies."

"Well, I will tell you, Mr. Golding," said the artist, "precisely my opinion on this affair. I have carefully examined your drawings, and I feel sure that you possess ability, which, if rightly directed, will make you an eminent and successful artist. But you no doubt understand that ability alone is of little good without careful training. Your drawings are very clever, there is no denying it; but, if I chose, I could pick holes in them after a manner you wouldn't thank me for. And this merely because your taste has not been trained properly. Now if I undertake to instruct you in these things you lack, you understand it would be with the intention of making an artist of you. That to become an artist, you must be able to devote *all* your time to your art. Now, what is to be done?"

"Then I am sorry, sir," replied Arthur, "but I fear it is useless for me to think of becoming an artist. My duty must come before my inclinations."

"But is it not one's first duty to consider one's own future?" asked Mr. Gresham, looking at Arthur from under his eyebrows.

"Not in such a manner as to inflict injury upon others," replied Arthur, firmly.

"And you would be content to resign the glories of a successful artist's life merely because your preparation for such would give Mr. Tollady a little inconvenience?"

"You do not know Mr. Tollady, sir," replied Arthur, with a touch of indignation in his tone. "He would gladly submit to any inconvenience if he thought it for my benefit; but I could not accept such a sacrifice. It would not merely be inconvenience to him if I were to desert his business now, it would be a serious loss; for circumstances have made me very useful to him. I must not think of taking such a step; I could not."

"You are young, Mr. Golding," said the artist, with his peculiar smile. "If you live another twenty years your views of life will change."

"Never, I trust, in this particular!" exclaimed Arthur.

"I see a number of drawings from casts

here," said Mr. Gresham, turning suddenly round to the portfolio. " Did you purchase the models ?"

" Mr. Tollady has bought me them from time to time, sir."

" And when do you work at them ?"

"In the evenings and early in the morning."

" When do you usually rise ?"

" At five, sir."

" And go to bed ?"

" Generally a little before midnight."

" Have you any design upon your life, Mr. Golding ?"

" Habit has made those hours easy to me," replied Arthur, with a smile.

" Yesterday," resumed the artist, after a short pause, " I referred to a legacy of Mr. Norman's. I think it is time to speak of it in detail. Mr. Norman left you in his will the sum of five thousand pounds."

Arthur kept his eyes fixed upon the floor, and made no reply.

" The money," pursued Mr. Gresham, " is invested in Three per cent. Consols, and produces accordingly a hundred and fifty pounds a year. You could almost live on that, Mr. Golding ?"

Probably Mr. Gresham had no intention of looking fiendish when he spoke these words ; but an observer could scarcely have helped associating his expression of face with that of a diabolical tempter.

Arthur still held his eyes down and made no reply.

"Discretion is left to me in the will," pursued the artist, "with regard to the disposal of this money till you reach your twenty-first year. If you think it desirable, I will direct that the half-yearly dividends shall be paid to you henceforth."

Still Arthur made no reply.

"Perhaps I am taking you at an unfair advantage," said Mr. Gresham, after watching the young man with an amused face for several minutes. "Suppose you were to ask my advice on this point. I am in a certain sense, you see, your guardian."

"I should gladly listen to your advice, sir," said Arthur, raising a pale and anxious face to his questioner.

"It shall be sincere, then. Listen! As you conceive that to give up your printing would be an unjustifiable injury to Mr. Tollady, suppose you reconcile your doubts in this way. Say to Mr. Tollady: 'I find it is very desirable that I should have all my time to devote to my art studies. In place, therefore, of working myself in the business for the future, I will become a sleeping partner, advancing towards our joint expenses of every kind the sum of a hundred and fifty pounds a year. With this we shall be able to employ another man in my stead, and I shall esteem my board and lodging as quite adequate interest upon my money.' I am well aware that this would be a peculiar arrangement under ordinary circumstances, but between yourself and Mr. Tollady it might possibly exist."

"Nothing would please me so much as to use my money for Mr. Tollady's advantage," replied Arthur: "but I very much fear he could not be brought to accept it."

"Mr. Tollady has, probably, maturer views of life than yourself, Mr. Golding," said Mr. Gresham, smiling.

"I am sure, sir," replied Arthur, "it is quite impossible for any man to be more nobly disinterested in all his views. Had he been of a less benevolent nature he would be a far richer man than he is."

"Do you mean he employs much money in charity?"

"More than he can afford to. I know his life would be valueless to him if he lost the means of relieving suffering."

"I fear there are not many such men," said the artist, with concealed irony.

"It is impossible there should be," replied Arthur. "The world would not be so miserable as it is."

"Do you find it miserable? On the whole, it appears to me a sufficiently agreeable spot."

"You view it as a wealthy man, sir," replied Arthur, surprised at his own boldness, but feeling impelled to speak. "You see only the bright side of life; into the darkness which envelopes the majority of mankind you never penetrate, the scorn or disgust which it excites in you is too strong. Could you view a tenth of the hopeless depravity, the unspeakable wretchedness, which we who live in a poor quarter have daily before our eyes, it would render you unhappy for the rest of your life."

"I must not detract from your estimation of my humanity," replied Mr. Gresham. "But let us stick to the matter in hand. Do you think it would be of any use if I saw Mr. Tollady personally, and endeavoured to bring him round to our plans?"

"But I beg," interposed Arthur, "that you will not consider me to have given my absolute consent. In any case I must necessarily have a few hours of leisure time during each day, and you would not object to my employing these in Mr. Tollady's affairs?"

"That will, of course, be your own business. I think we shall find a way out of the difficulty. In the meantime, will you do me the favour of dining with me? Then we will go together and see Mr. Tollady after dinner."

Arthur started at the unexpected invitation, and was on the point of making a hurried and awkward excuse, when Mr. Gresham, who was by no means deficient in agreeable tact, when he chose to exercise it, perceiving his embarrassment, hastened to reassure him.

"My daughter and myself are alone tonight, and dinner under such circumstances is apt to lack conversation. You have no pressing engagement?"

Arthur could not allege that he had, and Mr. Gresham turned to show the way from the room.

"Bye-the-by," he remarked, as they passed out of the studio, "do you remember Miss Norman, the little girl at the Rectory, as she was in those days?"

"I remember her distinctly," replied Arthur. "One circumstance has especially fixed itself in my memory, that of our having once looked over a book of engravings together, which gave me great delight."

"You were an artist even then?" returned Mr. Gresham. "Miss Norman will be with us in a short time. She has been studying in Germany for a couple of years."

As he spoke they entered the dining-room, where Maud awaited them. Arthur was duly presented, and got through the business in a very creditable manner. His natural grace of demeanour never suffered him to be absolutely awkward in his movements, but the deep blush upon his features told how keenly he felt the unwonted nature of his position.

"How delightfully you have altered papa's

picture !" exclaimed Maud, as they assumed
their seats at table, the wonted expression of
the corners of her lips rendering it uncertain
how she meant the remark to be interpreted.
" I really scarcely recognised it in your beautiful little water-colour."

" The alterations were due to my not
having seen the original picture," replied
Arthur, in his tone of manly modesty. " I
made the copy from an engraving, and had to
trust to my imagination for the colouring."

" Our imaginations are wonderfully useful; are they not, papa?" proceeded Miss
Gresham. " Life would be scarcely tolerable
without them."

" I thought, Miss Gresham," said her
father, " you rather prided yourself upon
your actuality."

" Very possibly," replied Maud, " but that
does not exclude a very useful employment
for my imagination. By means of it I gauge
the sufferings of those whose imagination is
too powerful, and derive consolation from the
contrast."

Conversation was maintained with more or
less vivacity till the dessert was being laid,
when a servant announced that Mr. Waghorn
had called.

" Oh, ask him to come in here," said Mr.
Gresham. " He is just in time for dessert.
Mr. Waghorn is one of our especial friends,
Mr. Golding."

Mr. John Waghorn entered. He was rather
a tall man, partly bald, and, to judge from
his features, about thirty-six or thirty-seven.
The appearance was intensely respectable,
from the scanty locks carefully brushed forward on each side of the forehead, down to
the immaculate boots which made no sound
upon the carpet. He was in evening dress,
and wore an exceedingly massive gold chain,
supporting a wonderable number of valuable
seals. In body he showed a tendency to
stoutness, and one observed that his fingers
were short and chubby. He had a very full
beard, but no moustache. The outlines of
his face could hardly be called agreeable;
and there was an expression in the dull eye
and the rather thick lips which denoted a
sensual temperament; whilst the narrow and
retreating forehead was suggestive of no very
liberal supply of brains. For all that, Mr.
Waghorn's appearance was intensely respectable. He bore the stamp of a wealthy man
on every part of his person. A certain habit
he had of drawing in the lips and suddenly
shooting them out again somehow conveyed
an impression of the aftertaste of good
dinners. Stepping up to the table with an
astonishingly polite air, he shook hands with
Mr. and Miss Gresham, and bowed to Arthur
Golding, then assumed the seat indicated by
Mr. Gresham, which was over against Arthur.

Why did this man's face appear familiar to

Arthur ? He felt sure that he did not now
see it for the first time, but, though he racked
his brains to discover when he and Mr.
Waghorn could by any possibility have met,
the effort was quite in vain. The countenance
excited in him feelings of intense repulsion,
though he had no idea why. He felt instinctively that beneath that smooth outside
of immaculate respectability lay hidden secret
depths of foulness and all impurity. He felt
uncomfortable in the man's presence, and
when he discerned, as he soon did, that closer
relation than mere acquaintanceship existed
between him and Miss Gresham, he experienced, involuntarily, a keen sensation of
pity for the young lady.

Mr. Waghorn's conversation was, like his
appearance, eminently respectable. His
object in looking in this evening, he said, had
been to request his friends' company in his
box at the opera. " Lucia di Lammermuir "
was to be played, he informed them, and
thereupon gave utterance to a number of
most respectable criticisms of the piece, such
as may be heard in the mouth of any respectable gentleman during the opera season.
Here Miss Gresham made a diversion by
asking Mr. Golding if he liked Scott, and
upon Arthur replying that he read Scott
with exceeding pleasure, Mr. Waghorn broke
in, if so boisterous an expression may be
applied to his velvety-tongued discourse, with

the remark that he supposed his hearers knew that the Waverley Novels had remained for a long time anonymous, and how very curious it was that such should have been the case. Upon Mr. Gresham's entertaining the company with a few rather more interesting remarks in reference to the same subject, Mr. Waghorn said that he had heard on very good authority that Lord So-and-So had just completed a novel, which he seriously thought of publishing; and upon Maud's observing, somewhat satirically, that she was glad his lordship was reflecting upon the point before coming to his ultimate decision, Mr. Waghorn replied that he echoed Miss Gresham's sentiments, for the reading public were so deplorably inappreciative now-a-days. And so the conversation continued to the end of dessert, when, Mr. Gresham excusing himself from the opera, Maud proposed that she should despatch a note to a friend a few doors off, begging her to make up the trio. This was accordingly done, the friend yielded her gracious assent, and she, Miss Gresham, and Mr. Waghorn drove off in the latter's carriage to the opera.

Mr. Gresham and Arthur Golding then set out to walk to Charlotte Place, where they found Mr. Tollady standing in the doorway of his shop, awaiting Arthur, whose long absence somewhat surprised him. All retired to the back-parlour, and there discussed the proposition which Mr. Gresham brought forward. Mr. Tollady would not at first listen to the proposal that Arthur should surrender his money to him, but on the latter and Mr. Gresham's representing to him that it was in reality an investment in the business which Arthur wished to make, in return for which he obtained the necessaries of life in any case, and, perhaps, some share of subsequent profits, the printer, though reluctantly, ceased his opposition. He showed to Mr. Gresham that, considering the modesty of Arthur's wants, the hundred and fifty pounds a year would quite suffice to supply them all and to pay for the services of a new assistant as well, and would only consent to the arrangement in case Arthur would make a definite stipulation to accept a certain percentage upon the profits that might result. In this way, at length, the matter was settled, and Mr. Gresham, after bidding Arthur to visit him in Portland Place at ten o'clock on the following morning, took his leave.

"I don't like it, Arthur; I don't like it," said Mr. Tollady, after pacing the little room for some time in silence. "I shall become a dead-weight upon you, holding you back from no one knows what advantages. You will regret having thus disposed of your money; I fear you will, Arthur."

"Never," exclaimed the young man. "You know well, Mr. Tollady, how often we have said that a little capital in our business was what we chiefly wanted. It will be a gain in every way. Do not think that I shall desert you, even when you get the new man. I shall find many an hour to look after office work; and you have often said that I had good ideas in business matters. And then I shall every day be making progress in my art. I feel like a new man to-day! Oh, how I will work, work, work! When shall I have my first picture in the Academy? It shall not be long, I assure you. Why, have I not already begun to earn money for my pictures? Here, Mr. Tollady, take these five shillings you gave me to-day. Take them and do anything you like with them; I beg you to! I will make a resolution that all the money I henceforth earn by my paintings I will put into your hands, to be used as you think best. I could not dispose of it better!"

"Stop, stop, my dear boy!" cried Mr. Tollady, with a smile, at once pleased and pained. "Why, Arthur, you will never get on in the world if you give away all your money in that fashion. You would always be miserably poor, and if there is any curse which I would fervently hope and trust may be averted from you, it is that of a weary, grinding, life-long poverty. Besides, you speak as if I should live for ever. You forget that I am close upon my sixtieth year, and that I cannot hope to share your hopes and your triumphs for very much longer."

"Nonsense!" exclaimed Arthur, who was in wonderfully high spirits. "You shall live to see me R.A. yet! Don't shake your head, Mr. Tollady; I tell you, you shall!"

"Arthur," began the old man, in a grave voice, the smile dying away from his worn features. He seemed on the point of communicating something which lay upon his mind, but suddenly he ceased, and shook his head.

"What were you going to say?" asked Arthur.

"Nothing, my dear boy, except that I am heartily glad of this piece of good fortune that has befallen you. I feel sure it will only be the prologue to a series of such scenes, each brighter and happier than the other. No, Arthur, I shall not live to see your richest rewards; but I can imagine them, and the rest of my days will be the more peaceful for the prospect. Make a good use of your fortune, Arthur. If you ever become wealthy, do not let your wealth pervert you. It is a furnace through which few can pass unscathed; but if youth holds forth any promise of manhood, I think you may be one of those. For my own part I am getting a little tired of life, though I hold with the old philosophers that no man should desert his post till Fate calls him from it. Life has not been over kind to me, on the whole, though in the sight of your happiness, Arthur, in the hope of your future I find rich amends for all I have suffered. Still I am tired, and I am not sorry to feel that Fate is preparing the summons. I feel that any day I may fall into my last sleep, and from that I hope and believe that no one will ever wake me."

Arthur could not reply in words, for the solemn pathos of the old man's last words affected him too strongly. But he caught his friend's right hand in both his own, and pressed it fervently. Then, according to his habit, he went upstairs into the printing office and worked an hour at case, till Mr. Tollady called him down to share his supper. It was eleven o'clock when they parted for the night, and for several hours after this Arthur paced his room, unable to go to rest. His forehead was hot and feverish with the ardent thoughts which wrought tumultuously in his mind. Now for the first time, in the dead stillness of the night, he seemed fully to realise the extent of his good fortune. He possessed for the future a yearly income amply sufficient for all his moderate wants, if Mr. Tollady's sad forebodings should prove true, and he should find himself dependent on his own resources. A hundred and fifty pounds a year represent nearly three pounds a week, a fortune to one brought up among the hard-working classes of London life. How many have to live and support a family on not more than a third of that sum. And, in addition, all his thoughts arose before a background of calm delight, the consciousness that henceforth it would be possible to devote himself entirely to his art. Not for the present was his mind disturbed by those uneasy conflicts between the varying elements of his nature which we have already described. To-night he was all artist; the thought of living for anything but art never occurred to him during these hours of enraptured reverie.

Strange that in the midst of his thoughts an old recollection should come back with startling vividness, and he should see himself as a child in Bloomford Rectory, sitting by the side of another child, a little girl, and gazing with delight at a large volume of pictures. Then he remembered what Mr. Gresham had said to him with regard to Helen Norman, and immediately his mind began to picture her as she must appear now that she was grown up. He retained, of course, no recollection of her face as a child, but he had never ceased to associate with her memory a distinct consciousness of wonder, partaking of reverence, from which he concluded that she had been, in all probability, a beautiful child. Should he ever see her at Mr. Gresham's? If he did, would she pay any attention to him, or show any sign of re-

membering his name? There was but little
chance of her doing so, and yet he felt he
should very much like to see her, to know
what she had become in the years since he had
sat by her side. Doubtless she was now a
tall, handsome, proud young lady, whom the
recollection of such an incident would cause
to blush and be annoyed.

As the clock at the Middlesex Hospital
sounded two he put out his lamp and threw
himself, still dressed, upon the bed. He
never had felt more wakeful; sleep was altogether impossible for him. For half-an-hour
he made vain endeavours to rest, and then
once more rose and re-lit his lamp. Over his
bed hung a small book-shelf, on which were
ranged the few favourite books which he had
been able to buy, and one of these he now
took down and began to read. Tiring of this,
he took up his drawing-board, and, having
fixed the light in a suitable position, commenced to work at a crayon copy of a cast
which he had hung for the purpose against
the wall. And at this he worked with
desperate energy till at length the change in
the position of the light and shade on his
model told him that daylight was beginning
to make its way into the room. Putting aside
his work, he washed and made some alterations in his dress, stole gently downstairs,
and took a brisk walk till the hour for fetching the newspapers arrived, when he opened

the shop and made the preparations for the
day's work in the usual way.

For a couple of hours each morning after
this, he worked in Mr. Gresham's studio, and
the greater part of the rest of the day he
spent in studies which the former suggested,
working with an energy begotten of the intense love he had for the work. Several
hours, also, he continued to devote to Mr.
Tollady's service, disregarding all the latter's
remonstrances and his earnest entreaties that
he would have more regard to his health. In
the course of the following month he executed
too little water-colours, the fruit of two days
spent in excursions to spots some miles up
the Thames, and these being placed by Mr.
Gresham's recommendation in the window of
a picture shop in Oxford Street, were very
shortly sold for prices which Arthur laughed
at as extravagant.

One morning Arthur had gone as usual to
Portland Place, and, on being admitted, had
ascended to the studio. It was Mr. Gresham's habit to enter the room some ten
minutes after his pupil's arrival, so that the
latter always opened the door and went in
without the precaution of a knock. This
morning, on doing so, he found that the
studio was not empty. Standing before one
of the large easels, examining a picture which
was still incomplete, he saw a young lady,
tall and graceful in figure, robed in a morn-

ing-dress of dark material, which fitted tightly
round her perfect shape, her hair gathered
into a simple knot behind her head, around
her neck a plain collar and a narrow violet
coloured tie, which made a small bow in
front, but with that exception devoid of
ornaments. So easy, and yet so naturally
dignified, was the attitude in which she stood,
so marvellous was the chaste beauty of her
countenance, lighted up with a look of pleasure as she gazed at the picture, so impressive was the extreme simplicity of her attire,
that the first glance almost persuaded Arthur
that he had before him the real person of one
of the goddesses whose forms made beautiful
his day-dreams and flitted in ghost-like
silence across the vacancy of his sleep. So
intensely was his artistic sense impressed by
the beauty of the vision that he with difficulty suppressed an exclamation of delight
which had risen to his lips. The next
moment, the lady's clear, deep eye had turned
upon him, and his sunk before its gaze.

For a moment there was silence, during
which both stood still. The lady was the first
to speak.

"Mr. Golding, is it not?" she said ; and
the voice thrilled upon every nerve in the
hearer's body, so wonderfully sweet did it
sound to him.

Arthur bowed, but could find no words.

"I had forgotten the time," pursued Helen

Norman, "and must request you to pardon my intrusion. I knew that you came at ten, but the delight of looking at these pictures has kept me here too long."

"Pray do not let me disturb you, Miss Norman," said Arthur, venturing at length to raise his eyes.

"You know who I am, then?" said Helen, speaking in the absolutely natural and un-affected manner which had always been characteristic of her, containing as little of self-consciousness as her beauty did of the commonplace. "I scarcely thought we should need a formal introduction."

Arthur's heart swelled with a mingled pain and delight at the kind tones in which he heard himself addressed. The pain might be partly excess of pleasure, partly it was caused by the recollection of how very different his relations to this beautiful girl *might* have been had Fate suffered him to grow up at Bloom-ford Rectory. Almost in spite of himself an expression of these thoughts rose to his lips.

"I should scarcely have thought you would have remembered my name, Miss Norman. My childish folly and ingratitude certainly rendered me unworthy of recollection."

"It is not my habit, Mr. Golding," replied Helen, "to judge the motives of others. One's own are often scarcely to be understood. My father never ceased to speak of you."

"My thoughts have often turned in gratitude to Mr. Norman," said Arthur, with sincerity in his voice. "It pains me that I was not able to see him again and express the feelings with which I remembered his kindness to me as a child."

"My guardian speaks to me in high terms of your talent as an artist," said Helen; "I hope I may soon have the pleasure of seeing one of your pictures. But I am keeping you from your work. Good morning, Mr. Golding."

She bowed and passed out of the room; and though by looking up to the ceiling of the room the summer sunshine could be seen playing athwart the blue vault of heaven, it seemed to Arthur as though she had left the room in darkness.

"She is indeed a goddess!" he exclaimed to himself, as, for the first time in his life, perhaps, he began with reluctance to work. "And she is as far superior to me as a 'Madonna' of Raphael is to this miserable smudge which I call a picture!"

END OF VOL. I.

Printed by REMINGTON & Co., 5, Arundel Street, Strand, W.C.

WORKERS IN THE DAWN.

A Novel.

IN THREE VOLUMES.

BY

GEORGE R. GISSING.

VOL. II.

London:
REMINGTON AND CO.,
5, ARUNDEL STREET, STRAND, W.C.

1880.

CONTENTS.

WORKERS IN THE DAWN.

CHAPTER I.

A HAND TO THE PLOUGH.

WITH a heart full of the noblest phantasies, the most lofty aspirations ; purified of the last trace of that popular egotism which makes the self-conscious striving for one's own salvation antecedent to every other aim of life ; beating high with an all-embracing affection for earth and the children of earth, bred of a natural ardour of disposition and nurtured upon the sweet and mighty thoughts of all great men ; with a heart yearning for action of some kind, weary of a life bounded within the lines of self-study and introspection, desirous of nothing more than to efface the recollection of self in complete devotion to the needs of those million sufferers whose voices had long cried to her with ever-growing pathos, Helen Norman had set foot once more upon the shores of England. Commencing upon that day a new page in her

diary, she headed it with the lines of Long-
fellow, as an appropriate motto :

> Let us then be up and doing,
> With a heart for any fate ;
> Still achieving, still pursuing,
> Learn to labour and to wait.

The first few days were spent in walks
alone, which she planned each morning by
reference to a map of London, choosing in
preference those districts which she knew by
reputation as mean and poverty-stricken. As
yet she had never seen poverty in its worst
shapes, and she now for the first time became
acquainted with the appearance of a London
slum.   With a thin veil drawn close over her
face, often with a step quickened by involuntary horror, or even fear, she walked in turn
through the worst parts of Soho, through
Seven Dials, and the thoroughfares which
spread themselves around that reeking centre,
through Drury Lane and Clare Market,
through all the unutterable vileness which is
to be found on the other side of the river,
then through everything most heart-breaking
that the wide extent of the East End has to show.
In this way she learnt from actual experience
what she had hitherto only been able to see
in fancy, and it is but slight reproach to the
powers of her imagination to say that never
in her most fearful visions had she attained
to a just appreciation of the reality.   As she
walked hurriedly along she would now and

then behold sights which made the hot tears
of pity or of indignation start to her eyes;
but for the most part the ardour of a
righteous wrath, to think that such things
could be permitted to exist, dried up the
fountain of tears, and only left her
strengthening herself in firm resolve that
what one determined heart and mind could
effect towards the alleviation of all this hellish
misery, that should be her aim as long as her
life lasted.

Before setting to her task she deemed it
necessary to procure her guardian's assent to
what she was about to do, and, for the purpose of acquainting him with the designs, requested a quarter of an hour's conversation
with him in the library. This opportunity
being obtained, she laid before him all her
aims and aspirations in clear, direct language,
every word of which seemed to burn and glow,
as fresh from the anvil of her thought; and
then requested his permission to enter upon
this mode of life. Mr. Gresham manifested
no surprise, it was part of his philosophy
never to be surprised at anything, but he
allowed several minutes to elapse before
making any reply.

"And how do you purpose setting about
such a work, Helen?" he asked, at length,
gazing at her with a half-suppressed ironical
smile, which, however, could not hold its
place upon his lips before the earnest, open

gaze of his ward. " I suppose you must have some definite plan for—for getting rid of your money ? "

" I beg that you will not think that I am going to be recklessly extravagant, on pretence of charity," said Helen, in reply to the last phrase. " I shall indeed give money when I see it is needed, but I have already convinced myself that money can by no means be the principal instrument of one who sincerely wishes to benefit these poor people. On this point I have my own ideas."

" But would it not be better, if you are determined to trouble yourself so much about these tatterdemalions, to give your relief in the form of subscriptions to well-known charities, which have much better opportunities of doing good than any single individual can have ? "

" Doubtless they *have* better opportunities," returned Helen, " but what I have already seen convinces me that they do not use them. The efforts of bodies are commendable and excellent—in their proper places. But for the work I see before me, individual effort is alone fitted ; of that I am convinced."

" But, my dear child," said Mr. Gresham, with a smile of indulgent pity, " you surely have not got the idea into your head that you are going alone the rounds of these pestilence-breeding slums ? Have you the remotest notion of the kind of beings by whom they are inhabited ? "

"Only too exact a notion. I have spent the last few days in penetrating the worst districts. I know precisely the nature of my task."

Mr. Gresham looked into his ward's face, where exquisite beauty was heightened by a flash of generous ardour, and he felt, though he yet would not confess it, that here was a nature for which in his classification of mankind he had left no place.

"But you altogether lack experience in such affairs," he urged, compelled, in spite of himself, to assume a tone of serious argument very unusual in him. "You will be robbed and pillaged wherever you go."

"For my lack of experience I must try to find a remedy. It is my present intention to apply to some clergyman in one of these neighbourhoods, and to offer him my services in the capacity I have chosen for myself, asking him to afford me the benefit of the experience he must naturally have obtained in the fulfilment of his duties."

"Then you will become what they call a Bible-reader."

"I shall not willingly class myself under that head," replied Helen, "but if I am convinced that good might in some instances be done by reading the Bible aloud, I shall have no hesitation in doing so."

Mr. Gresham smiled, with an expression of humorous despair, and began to pace the room.

"May I hope to have your consent, Mr. Gresham, to what I propose?" asked Helen, when some minutes had thus elapsed.

"If you proceed as you suggest," said her guardian, "and act strictly under the advice of some clergyman, whom, bye-the-by, I must see and have a little talk with, I shall make no further objection, for I am perfectly convinced that a very brief trial will give you a wholesome distaste for these abominations. Would you like to know my opinion of the people you are going to endeavour to benefit?"

"I should, if you please, sir," replied Helen, calmly.

"Very well. In my opinion, then, they are not to be classed with human beings, but rather with the brutes. Persistent self-brutalisation, through many generations, by all the processes of odious vice which the brain of man has ever invented, has brought them to a condition worse, far worse, than that of the dogs or horses that do their bidding. It is my firm belief that their degeneration is actually and literally physical; that the fine organs of virtue in which *we* possess all that we have of the intellectual and refined, have absolutely perished from their frames; that you might as well endeavour to teach a pig to understand Euclid as to teach

one of these gaol-birds to know and feel what
is meant by honesty, virtue, kindness, intel-
lectuality. That they have become such is,
I say, the result of their own vices. Unless
you can take all the children, one by one, as
they are born in these kennels, and remove
them to some part of the New World where
they shall grow up under the best influences
of every kind, so, by degrees, letting the old
generations rot away in their foulness, and
then, when they are all dead, set fire to the
districts they inhabited, totally rebuild them,
and fetch back to their renovated homes the
young men and women who have grown to
maturity, healthy, clean, and educated—unless
you can do all that, you need never hope,
Helen, to better the condition of the poor of
London."

"That, I fear," replied Helen, with a sweet
smile, "would be beyond my power; and yet
I will venture to persevere in the belief that
I *can* better the condition of at least a few.
This belief depends upon the view I have
formed of their condition, and it is this:
Without denying that their vices may have
had very much to do with the misery they
suffer under, I firmly believe that this misery
is in the greatest degree the result of the
criminal indifference and the actual cruelty
and oppression of the higher ranks of society,
those ranks out of which come the leaders of
popular fashion and the actual governors of

the country. And even those vices are in a very great measure the result of this indifference and oppression; for does it seem credible that not until this very year have the governors of England made any effort to provide adequate education, even of the simplest kind, for the poor of this country? I should not tell the truth if I denied that these wretched creatures excite horror and disgust in me as often as they excite pity, but I am glad to say that my reason outweighs my mere emotions, and the allowances it makes for them forbid me to regard them with absolute contempt. I will grant that they often seem mere beasts, but I cannot, I *will* not believe that this is more than seeming. The greatest men that the world has known have ever retained to the last a vivid faith in humanity. If ever I feel disposed to fall into doubt and despair I shall seek consolation in their words, and I doubt not I shall find it."

"Very well, Helen," replied Mr. Gresham, with a slight shrug, "far be it from me to act the domestic tyrant. Only acquaint me with your exact plans."

"I will not fail to do so as soon as they are formed," returned Helen. And so the interview concluded.

After a few more days spent in investigation, in which she had no aid, Helen obtained the names of three clergymen to whom she determined to write, offering her services in their respective parishes for charitable and educational purposes. Two of these were Church of England clergymen, the third was a Dissenter. To the first she wrote as follows :—

"Portland Place,
"30th July, 1870.

"SIR,

"Having considerable leisure and some little means at my disposal, it is my desire to employ both in an effort to improve the condition, physical, moral, and intellectual, of at least a few among the multitudes of poverty-stricken people that inhabit the worst districts of London. But as I am quite without experience in such work, and have no adequate knowledge of London, I should be glad if I could place myself under the direction of some clergyman whose acquaintance with such scenes of misery is extensive, and who would be glad of an earnest volunteer to give him some little assistance in his charitable endeavours. It is in consequence of this wish that I venture to address myself to you.

" I must, however, refer to one point which is of essential importance to me. Though my age is but little more than nineteen, I have for some years devoted myself to serious study, one of the results of which has been that I am no longer able to conscientiously consider myself a member of any of the Christian Churches. Nothing is farther from my thoughts than a desire to press upon you the reasons which have led me to this attitude. I must merely say that for the present it is unalterable, and I could not undertake to devote attention to arguments intended for my conversion. Under these circumstances you will think it strange that I make these offers to a clergyman. My reason is, that as I am myself, I trust, quite free from bigotry in my beliefs, I can also hope that a minister of the Church will bear with what he may consider my errors, and not allow them to stand in the way of any usefulness of which I may be capable. I need hardly say that I should confine my attention solely to the bodily and mental condition of the poor, seeing that I believe it is their bodies and minds that most pressingly call for attention.

"I trust, sir, that the earnestness of my motives may prove an excuse for my freedom in thus addressing you, and beg to remain,

"Yours respectfully,

"HELEN NORMAN."

Alas for the *naïveté* which could lead a high-minded girl to despatch such a letter to a minister of the Church of England! Two days after sending this to the clergyman who stood first on the list, she received in reply the following note :—

" MADAM,

" I am in receipt of your letter of the 30th July, but I may not say that I regret I cannot accept your offered services. Should I do so, I should be a traitor to the Church and to my God, introducing into my flock a wolf in sheep's clothing, who would devour their souls as surely as Satan will devour the souls of all who, resting on their pride of intellect, reject the authority of Holy Scripture and are guilty of the sin against the Holy Ghost.

" I may add, however, that as money offered for good purposes does not lose in utility from the fact that the giver is devoid of that grace of God which passeth all understanding, and may possibly plead before the throne of the Almighty for the soul of such giver, if you shall be willing to allow me to add your name to the enclosed subscription list for the restoring St. ——'s Church, I shall with pleasure receive your subscription, and have it acknowledged, with other names, in the daily papers.

" In conclusion, I trust you may soon be brought to see the error of your ways, and to wash away in the blood of the Lamb their sins which, I am sure, must be as scarlet. I regret that the extent to which my leisure is occupied does not allow me time to engage in the work of your conversion.

" Yours, in hope and trust,
"————."

This letter caused Helen not a little mirth, and, on being communicated to Mr. Gresham, brought to his face one of those sarcastic smiles which were the best expression of his ordinary mood of mind. He read the present effusion with gusto. It so thoroughly confirmed his view with regard to a very large portion of mankind.

Undaunted, Helen despatched the same letter to the second name upon her list, but, after waiting more than a week, she received no reply whatever. The Dissenting clergyman still remained ; and to him at length she wrote. She received, almost by return of post, a note, requesting that she would appoint an hour at which he might have the honour of waiting upon her. Having immediately replied, Helen awaited the stranger's arrival with some interest.

At the appointed hour she repaired to the library, where she was shortly apprised, by a card, of the arrival of Mr. Edgar Walton Heatherley, who was accordingly introduced.

Helen had exerted her imagination considerably in endeavours to depicture Mr. Heatherley's personal appearance, and, strange to say, the original did not rudely overturn her preconceived notions. She liked the man as soon as she saw him. He was evidently young, and his countenance slightly florid in complexion, with but a moderate growth of rather reddish whiskers and moustache, had an open, pleasing, intelligent air, though its lines were not regular enough to constitute a handsome face. Its expression bespoke, moreover, considerable firmness. The eye was honest and cheerful, proclaiming immediately the total absence of all cant, hypocrisy, or bigotry. He was decidedly tall and almost athletic in frame, holding himself as upright as a soldier. It was apparent at the first glance that Mr. Heatherley was no town growth, but had drunk in health and spirits during his earlier years from the fresh breezes of meadow, wood and hill. He was a man whose character could at once be determined from his face and form. Inspiring confidence himself, he had the hearty manners of one who was wont to thoroughly confide in his acquaintances. Here there was no trace of the execrable theory of believing every man a rogue till he be proved honest. Rather was it written in plain characters upon his open brow, that he never suspected without overpowering cause, and, even if deceived seventy times seven, would not cease to cling to his gospel of eternal trust and hope.

Helen advanced to meet him with her wonted open smile. They were friends from the first glance. After exchanging the ordinary greeting, they resumed seats, and Helen introduced the subject of the conversation.

"My letter will have acquainted you with almost all that I wish to say," she began.

"Your reply contained nothing beyond the request for an interview. May I suppose that you look favourably upon my proposition?"

"The character of your letter, Miss Norman," returned the other, speaking in very firm and rather quick tones, "from the first inclined me to do so. But I am now not so sure as I was."

"Indeed? Why not?"

"I am but little acquainted with the West End of London," replied Mr. Heatherley, "and I did not know Portland Place at all. I fear that residence in the midst of such refinement is hardly a good preparation for work among our East End courts and alleys. Have you any idea, Miss Norman, of the character of the task for which you volunteer?"

"A very exact idea, I believe, Mr. Heatherley."

"You have seen the worst part of the East End?"

"I believe so."

"And you think you possess the courage to face their horrors day after day?"

"I am sure of it, sir."

Mr. Heatherley examined the girl's face for an instant, dropped his eyes, bit his lower lip and mused.

"You will excuse my cross-examination, Miss Norman. Whatever I undertake it is with my whole heart. If I thought this were an idle fancy of a wealthy young lady, possessed of rather too much leisure, I should grieve that I had wasted time over it."

"I like your frankness, Mr. Heatherley," replied Helen, smilingly. "As far as I know my own character, I think I may say that I, also, whatever I undertake, do it with my whole heart. My energy has as yet had no fields for exercise but those of learning, it is true; yet I have there learned some confidence in my own powers of perseverance."

"So far, so good," said the clergyman, who had keenly watched Helen's countenance as she spoke. "But I believe you told me you were a minor, Miss Norman. Have you parents living, may I ask?"

"Neither parents nor any near relatives. I am living with my guardian, Mr. Gresham.'

"And have you informed Mr. Gresham of your intention to undertake this work?"

"I have, and have obtained his consent, with the proviso that he should see and become acquainted with the clergyman under whose direction I placed myself."

"Good," replied Mr. Heatherley sententiously; then sunk into reflection.

"You have not yet touched upon the second portion of my letter," said Helen, at length, looking with some timidity into the clergyman's face. The latter raised his eyes, and they gazed at each other for several seconds, neither faltering.

"Am I right in concluding from the tenor of your letter," asked the clergyman, "that you have no intention of propagating your special views among the poor people you visit?"

"You are, Mr. Heatherley."

"Would you oblige me by stating exactly in what light you regard the matter of religious teaching?"

"I will do so as well as I can. My own religion teaches me to confine my thoughts to the present world, and it appears to me that one of the most pressing needs under which the world suffers is that of attention to the bodily and mental state of the poorest classes. For my own part, I regard the necessity of their having enough food, and being able to read and write, as much more urgent than the necessity of their being taught religious dogmas, which, in my belief, would exercise a scarcely appreciable influence upon their lives. You, Mr. Heatherley, are, of course, of a different opinion in this matter. You exert yourself to the uttermost to make them religious; and, whilst you may do good in this, you certainly do no active harm. For the comprehension of my creeds, considerable culture is necessary, and it would be madness to attempt to make poor ignorant working-people understand them. Under these circumstances it appears to me that I cannot do better than devote my attention to clothing, feeding and in some degree teaching them; to the former two on the score of compassion, to the latter because it is the only true way of rendering the results of charity enduring."

"Very well, Miss Norman. At least your position is intelligible. Such being the case, I suppose it would be impossible for you to join any of the charitable associations founded on a religious basis?"

"If you think it possible, I had rather— at present, at all events—work alone."

"You have plans, doubtless? You have thought out methods of procedure?"

"I have thought much on the subject, but shall require much advice from you."

"Well," returned the clergyman, after a slight pause, "it would perhaps be the best way for us to walk over my neighbourhood together."

"Certainly. When might I come to you?"

"Could we say to-morrow at ten?" asked Mr. Heatherley, in his decisive manner.

"I shall be punctual," replied Helen, at once. "And now, if you will excuse me, I will inform Mr. Gresham that you are at liberty to see him."

They shook hands, Mr. Heatherley smiling pleasantly, as Helen repeated—"To-morrow at ten." She then disappeared, and the next moment Mr. Gresham entered the room.

Had Mr. Gresham been a sincere man, even to himself, he would have inwardly confessed that the applicability of his law of universal doubt had now found a second exception. In the depths of his heart he knew that Helen Norman was truth incarnate; and now on first beholding Mr. Heatherley he felt instinctively that here was a man in whom he could absolutely trust. But the yoke of old habit was too strong for him, and he commenced the conversation with that ironical smile which betokened distrust of all things human or divine.

"You must understand, Mr. Heatherley," he began, "that I have given my consent to this freak of Miss Norman's simply because I wish her to be cured as quickly as possible of certain girlish fancies that have taken possession of her lately. She has just returned from a two years' stay in Germany, and she appears to have come back a trifle eccentric. Vigorous treatment, I imagine, is the best for this ailment. Let her by all means disgust herself with a peep into these eastern dens of yours. I only hope she won't bring us some infectious disease here, that's all."

"Miss Norman has not long exhibited these philanthropic tendencies, sir?"

"Pooh!—of course not. Only let her have a few days' experience. She will perhaps throw away a little money, but that is fortunately of no great consequence. We shall have her back cured, and then an end of it."

"Are you sure you gauge this young lady's character quite correctly?" asked the clergyman, who had hitherto regarded Mr. Gresham's face with an observant eye.

"Do you imagine the contrary, Mr. Heatherley?"

"I do, sir."

"From anything in particular she has said to you?"

"From her countenance and the tenor of her discourse. I fancy the trial will last longer than you imagine, Mr Gresham."

"Well, well; we shall see," said the artist, with careless good-humour. "I confess to but little faith in enthusiasm of any kind."

"And yet, sir, it has been the most powerful operative force in the world's history," returned the clergyman, in his decisive manner.

"That, of course, is a matter of argument," said the artist, turning slightly away. "But having seen you, Mr. Heatherley," he pursued, "I have fulfilled my object, which was merely to be sure that my ward had placed herself in the care of a responsible man. Possibly you could find time to see me again, say this day week? We shall then see more clearly the course that events are likely to take."

"I shall have pleasure in doing so," returned the clergyman.

Whereupon they parted, Mr. Gresham ascending to his studio, whistling a subdued air, and smiling the while; Mr. Heatherley turning his face eastward, musing much with serious countenance.

CHAPTER II.

WAYS AND MEANS.

MR. HEATHERLEY lived in a pair of agreeable rooms on the ground-floor in a street a short distance from the City Road. Here Helen Norman arrived on the following morning, after some little difficulty in discovering the address, and was admitted by a most unusually neat servant girl, the sight of whom impressed her with the feeling that this neatness was directly or indirectly due to Mr. Heatherley's presence in the house. On entering the parlour she found the clergyman seated at the table, side by side with a very shock-headed youngster of some twelve years old, who appeared to have been reading aloud from an open book before him.

"Well, that will do for this morning, James," said Mr. Heatherley, after rising and requesting his visitor to be seated. "Rather better than usual, I think. Look over *bonus*, *niger*, and *tristis* again for Monday's lesson. Good-bye."

The lad collected his books together and went off at a sort of trot, turning towards Helen, as he went out, a bright though rather ugly face.

"A little pupil of mine," said the clergyman, by way of explanation. "His parents are unable to give him more than a very poor education, and as he is a sharp little chap I have got into the way of teaching him a little at odd times. On Saturday he doesn't go to school, so we have our lessons rather later than usual. I am glad we have a fine morning, Miss Norman. I almost think we had better take our walk first of all, then return and discuss your plans with the work fresh in our minds. Do you approve?"

As he spoke, he arranged a few books which he took from the table in their places in a well-filled book-case. Helen replied to his proposition with a cheerful assent, watching him the while.

"Latin, I suppose, you have not attempted to subdue?" he asked, turning a curious face towards his visitor.

"I can read Virgil and Horace with tolerable ease," replied Helen. "But I am afraid my knowledge of the niceties of the language is very imperfect."

"And Greek?" said Mr. Heatherley, without affecting surprise.

"Of Greek I have a very trifling knowledge."

"Young ladies usually devote more attention to modern than to ancient languages, I believe," said the clergyman.

"And I am no exception to the rule," replied Helen.

" You know Italian ? "

" Pretty well."

" Ha ! I envy you. I have a desperate desire to read Dante in the original—but time, time, time ! "

" You would very quickly learn sufficient of the language for that," said Helen, smiling slightly.

" You think so ? Ah, well, I must make an attempt one of these days. In the meantime we have our work before us, Miss Norman. You are ready ? "

" Quite."

" Good. Then we will set out."

As they issued into the street, Mr. Heatherley consulted a small note-book, in which appeared to be jotted memoranda concerning the poor he visited daily. Conversing agreeably as he walked—always in the same pithy, energetic language, showing considerable information, both as regards books and men, and always such a healthy freedom from mere conventionality that Helen felt herself more and more at home with him—he led his companion by degrees into dark, dirty, narrow streets, where low-browed arches frowned on either side, leading off into courts and alleys of indescribable foulness, and over-running with a population as horrible to view as their own abodes.

" Now," said the clergyman, as they paused for a moment to gaze down a court

not more than three feet wide, the entrance
into which was down a flight of broken stone
steps, and at the other end of which was
just visible another low archway precisely
like the entrance to a kennel, "I should
neither advise nor permit you, Miss Norman,
to venture into places such as that. The
worst of these courts are the haunts of such
unutterable brutality and wickedness that it is
often dangerous for hardy men to venture
into them. For a woman to do so would be
folly. It would be quite impossible for her
to do good there at all adequate to the risk
she ran. I trust that you will confine your
visits to these wider streets. God knows
there is enough wickedness everywhere in
this neighbourhood, but you are not so remote
from assistance in the open streets. And
here we come to our first place of call. If
you will follow me I will enter here."

They stood before a second-hand clothes
shop, the front of which was quite open to
the street, where an old woman and a young
girl sat on the floor amidst heaps of ragged
clothing, stitching remnants together to form
saleable articles. They looked up as the
clergyman entered, and the old woman
nodded a palsy-stricken head, the total bald-
ness of which gave her a hideous appearance,
and began to mutter unintelligibly between
her bare gums.

"What does your grandmother say,

Kitty?" asked Mr. Heatherley of the young girl.

The latter bent her ear close to the old woman's mouth before replying.

"She says she's better to-day. She's been a wearin' the flannel you giv' her for her rheumatics, and she thinks as how it done her good."

"That's right. I'm glad to hear it. Is your mother in, Kitty?"

"She's gone to the station," replied the girl.

"What now? More trouble between her and your father?"

"Father come 'ome this mornin' drunker than ever," said the girl, in a matter of fact way, continuing her stitching as she spoke. "Mother got up, and they begun to 'ave words; an' then father 'it her on the 'ead with his boot-heel, as he'd just took horff. And mother's 'ead bleeded—my! how it did bleed! An' so she's gone to the station for another summons, you see."

Mr. Heatherley glanced at Helen to see the effect of this city-idyl upon her. She was rather paler than usual, but listened attentively to what was said.

"And where's your father?" pursued the clergyman.

"Well, father got mad like, you see, at some words as mother used to him about 'Arry as used to lodge 'ere. She said as 'ow

he'd have been a better 'usbin to her than
father ever was. So father got mad like, an'
he said as he'd go and murder 'Arry this
mornin'. An' he's gone to do it."

The calm *naïveté* with which the girl
uttered these last words chilled Helen's very
blood. The clergyman, more accustomed to
such remarks, reassured her with a look, and
proceeded with the conversation.

"Any new lodgers yet, Kitty?"

"Yes, there's one—a young woman in the
third floor back. Leatswise so mother tell'd
me. I ain't seen her."

"What does she do?"

"Don't do nothink, mother said."

"How does she pay for her lodging then?"

"Don't know."

"I suppose she's out now?"

"No; she ain't comed out this mornin'
yet, cos I's been here sen' seven o'clock."

"Is she ill?"

"Very like."

"Could we go up to see her?"

"Why not? Don't suppose as you'll
steal nothink, Mr. 'Eatherley!"

Leave thus graciously granted, Mr.
Heatherley led the way through the shop into
a pitch-dark passage, where he was obliged to
strike a match, a box of which he fortunately
carried in his pocket, before he could venture
to lead Helen up the mouldy staircase. The
walls, Helen observed, had once been papered,

but they now so recked with damp that only
an old strip or two still hung loose to indicate where the paper had been. She could
feel the stairs often bend beneath her feet, so
rotten were they. On reaching the third
floor they tapped at the back-room door, and
received permission to enter, delivered in a
shrill, childish voice.

In a garret, empty but for a small iron
bedstead and a wooden stool, sat, upon the
latter article, a child, whose age the visitors
at first put down for some twelve years. She
was dressed in rags which scarcely concealed
her nakedness, and on her lap lay an infant
sleeping. The elder child's face was thick
with grime, the only places where the original
colour of the skin could be discovered being
narrow streaks from the corners of the eyes,
a sufficient indication that she cried long and
frequently. She seemed frightened at the
entrance of the strangers, and quickly stood
up, gathering the infant carefully in her
arms.

Mr. Heatherley instinctively yielded place
to Helen. She seemed the more suitable
person to commence the conversation.

"They told us down-stairs," said Helen,
"that there was a lodger here who was in
want of employment. Is it you, my poor
child?"

"Yes, mum. I's got no 'ployment. I
on'y wish I 'ad."

" But are you quite alone here ? "

" Yes, mum."

" Have you no father or mother ? "

" Both doin' six weeks, mum."

Helen looked interrogatively at Mr. Heatherley, who whispered that she meant to say her parents were both in prison for six weeks.

" But how do you feed your little sister ? Is it sister or brother ? "

" It's my child, mum," said the little creature, with perfect simplicity, without a trace of shame.

" What ! your child ! "

" Yes, mum," returned the other, surprised at the astonishment her remark had excited.

" But—but how old are you ? " asked Helen, blushing as she spoke.

" Turned fifteen, mum."

Here Mr. Heatherley came forward.

" If you will speak to this poor child for a few minutes, Miss Norman," he said, " I will return directly. There is another lodger below I should like to see."

He left the room, and Helen, after a brief pause, continued her questions.

" Are—are you married ? " she asked.

" No, mum, not yet," returned the child.

" Does the father of your child support you now ? "

" No, mum, not yet."

" Who is he ? What does he do ? "

" He's a butcher-boy, mum."

" Does he mean to marry you ? "

" Some day, mum. When he gets fifteen shillin' a week, that is."

" How much does he get now ? "

" Nine an' six, mum."

" But how are you going to live for the present ? " asked Helen, bending down to stroke the miserable little baby's face, at which a look of pleasure and pride lit up the young mother's countenance.

" He's big for his age, an' he grows every day, mum, he does," she remarked.

Helen could scarcely restrain the tears from rushing to her eyes.

" How are you living now ? " she repeated.

" I've got four shillin's as mother give me the night afore she was locked up, mum, an' that'll last me a few days. And when that's gone, I—I—oh, I really don't know what I'll do, mum ! "

Here, for the first time, her fortitude broke down, and she wept bitterly. The baby set up a piercing shriek out of sympathy, and Helen's tears at length refused to be held back. At this moment Mr. Heatherley again entered the room.

" Are you quite well ? " asked Helen, hastily brushing away her tears with a handkerchief.

" Yes, mum, thanke, mum."

" Take this, then, for the present," she

said, pressing two half-crowns into the child's dirty palm, " and buy better food. Would you like me to come and see you again in a day or two to see how the little baby gets on ? "

" O yes, mum; I should, please, mum! " exclaimed the child, a radiant look upon her dirty face which Helen felt to be a heavenly reward for her little kindness.

" I will do so then. And I will tell the people below to find some clothes to fit you, as soon as possible, and some for the baby, too. Have you no wash-hand basin ? "

" No, mum."

" Where do you wash, then ? "

" The tap in the wash'us, mum."

" If I send you a jug and basin you will promise me to use it twice a day till I come again ? "

" I'd be glad to, mum."

" Very well. Good-bye for the present, then."

And, bending once more to pat the baby's cheek, she left the room, followed by Mr. Heatherley. On reaching the shop she soon made arrangements with regard to the clothing and the utensils, after which they bade the old woman and her grand-daughter good-bye, and issued again into the street.

" I must warn you, Miss Norman," said the clergyman, as they walked on, " against being too easily caught by affecting stories.

I believe this is a really deserving case, but you will often be seriously imposed upon. I should advise you never to give much money at once. In any cases where you think more extensive relief desirable we will always appoint a meeting at the chapel with the people. It is often easier to arrive at a correct judgment of the poor when they are away from their ordinary horrible surroundings."

After this they paid many visits, passing from one haunt of abominations to another, from one scene of heart-rending sufferings to another, till the morning had worn away. Everywhere Helen admired Mr. Heatherley's kindness and readiness of speech, his thorough acquaintance with the circumstances of those he visited, his broad charity when faults seemed to call for reprobation, his entire devotion to the work of alleviating wretchedness. When she began to feel weary and weak in consequence of the long walk and the excessive pressure upon her sympathies wherever they went, she admired and envied, too, the robustness of frame which rendered such a morning as this but child's play to her guide.

On their return to Mr. Heatherley's, they found a light lunch ready laid for them. Helen did not disguise her need of rest and refreshment, and frankly accepted the clergyman's friendly attentions. For a time she was very silent, her thoughts busy with the

morning's experiences, and with the devising
of plans for future efforts. The clergyman
was the first to commence the conversation.

"When we remember our Poor Laws, our
hospitals, all our great efforts of public
charity and private benevolence, one who had
not visited these poor neighbourhoods could
scarcely believe that such misery existed."

"It is an all-sufficing proof," returned
Helen, "that neither the public nor the
private charity is well conducted. And yet
it is, perhaps, unjust to speak so of the
latter. In the midst of a social chaos, such
as ours, individual effort must necessarily be
poor in results. Is it not a disgrace to our
civilisation, Mr. Heatherley, that such exertions as ours should be needful?"

"It used to be a favourite mental exercise
with me," replied the clergyman, smiling,
"to originate schemes of future Utopias.
But I fear I now see only too clearly the
futility of all such dreams. The powers of
Government are slight, Miss Norman, when
weighed in the balance against human
passions."

"Then you cannot hope for a state of
society in which disgraceful poverty, such as
that we have witnessed this morning, will no
longer exist, in which the will to earn a respectable livelihood shall be equivalent to
success?"

"My *hopes* are unbounded," replied Mr.

Heatherley, rather sadly, " but my expectations, when confined to this life, are of the most modest character."

The phrase " this life " jarred terribly on Helen's ears. Enthusiastic as she was for the future of humanity, she could scarcely restrain a hasty answer; but good taste withheld her from rudely shocking the clergyman's ears.

" Well," she replied, with a smile and a slight sigh, " it is *this* life in which I am principally interested, and doubtless you would laugh at me if I expressed to you all my expectations regarding it. When in Germany I thought and read much on social matters, and in the end formed my own theories as to the future constitution of society. But as such hopes have by no means reference to any immediate future, I may say that my stand-point is one with your own, Mr. Heatherley, in all practical matters. Whilst I *know* that even at this moment history is bringing about such changes for us as we cannot dream of, I am content in the meantime to do my little utmost towards rendering the transition somewhat easier. I have not much patience with those who look so much to the future, and stop their ears against the groans of the present. I tell you this, Mr. Heatherley, that you may understand more clearly the source of my eagerness to be a worker, that you may feel more

convinced that my conduct is something beyond mere caprice, as you expressed it yesterday."

The clergyman watched Helen calmly as
she spoke, and then sank once more into
thought.   He seemed to be endeavouring to
get at the bottom of her character, and the
task appeared to be a troublesome one.

"You have studied in Germany, Miss
Norman ?" he asked at length.

"For about two years; I only returned a
little more than a fortnight ago.   I think,"
she continued, after a short silence, " that I
ought to give you some slight information
with regard to myself; I am sure you think
me somewhat *bizarre*; perhaps you even condemn me for being too forward."

"You interest me much, Miss Norman,"
replied Mr. Heatherley, in his frank way,
"but, as yet, I have seen nothing in your
conduct to warrant condemnation."

"The truth is," pursued Helen, "I have
always lived a rather solitary life, my only
companions being people very much older
than myself.   My father was a clergyman ;
he died nearly four years ago.   I have never
been to a school in the ordinary way, but
have studied privately with tutors and professors.   For several years before my father's
death I lived with him in the south of France.
We hardly mixed with society, and saw rarely
anyone except one or two literary friends.

In Germany, too, I made very few acquaintances, and those were grave, thoughtful people. These influences may, in some degree, explain to you my habit of mind."

" Was your father a clergyman of the English Church ? "

Helen replied affirmatively, and there was again silence.

" There is also another matter," resumed Helen, " not without importance at present. My father left me at his death considerable wealth, and, though I am still a ward, my guardian allows me great freedom in disposing of this. I mention this, not for its own sake, but because I am bent upon carrying out one or two rather extensive schemes. I could not be satisfied with merely relieving a few individual cases of distress; when my means enable me, I trust, to do much more."

" Would you let me hear a few of your plans ? "

" Naturally they are at present mere outlines," pursued Helen, her eyes glowing with pleasure, and her tones becoming more rapid as she unfolded her thoughts. " I shall depend very greatly upon your suggestions in the practical details. First of all, then, I shall visit these haunts of poverty day after day, and do my best to become acquainted with the most pressing needs, and to learn the best ways of meeting them. I shall endeavour to gain the personal confidence of these poor people, so that they will freely impart to me their difficulties, and allow me to help them in the most effectual way. Then, as I am firmly convinced that no radical change for the better can take place in these people's condition till they are educated, I shall endeavour to establish a free evening school for girls, principally for those who are engaged in earning their living, and who have never had the opportunity of being taught anything. Then, again, it has seemed to me that some good provision might be made for those suffering from illness. You tell me that the public hospitals are by no means sufficient to deal with these wants, so I would suggest something of this kind. Suppose I were to establish a good dispensary in the centre of this district, and to find one or two earnest physicians, who would be willing to attend there for certain hours every day—of course receiving adequate compensation for their work—the poor who wished to avail themselves of the dispensary could then apply either to you or to me, and we, if we thought fit, would give them tickets entitling them to gratuitous advice and medicine. The physicians would report to me any especially noticeable cases, and I should then be able to provide needful things which would be beyond the people's own power to purchase. Do you think this a practicable scheme, Mr. Heatherley?"

"With care I think it might be made so,"

replied the clergyman, after a moment's thought, his tone and countenance showing that he derived much pleasure from these suggestions.

"I fear I shall burden you with work," went on Helen, "if you are good enough to undertake to assist me. But, above all, I wish everything to be done with the utmost quietness. Publicity of my efforts would be the very last thing I should desire ; for, of course, they will be nothing *more* than efforts for a long time. But I should like to lose no time in putting my theories into practice. Doubtless you could at once name several girls who could be induced to attend an evening class ? "

"I think I could," replied Mr. Heatherley, cautiously ; "but the hour would necessarily have to be late. I should think eight o'clock would be the earliest practicable. Your pupils would, for the most part, be engaged in work-rooms, and they rarely regain their liberty before half-past seven."

"Oh, I would arrange for any hour, of course. And do you think I could find a physician to undertake the dispensary work ?"

"I do not myself know of one," replied the clergyman, reflecting. "Probably we should be obliged to have recourse to advertisement. In the nature of things it would not be a very difficult matter."

"Then I may conclude that you approve these two plans ? "

"I do, heartily; and will help you with my utmost power, Miss Norman."

"Thank you, thank you," returned Helen, fervently. "Oh," she continued, "I have many more plans, some even more extensive still, but at present they are too immature; I must gain experience. But, in the meantime, promise me, Mr. Heatherley, that you will never let a deserving case of poverty go unrelieved as long as I have the means of charity. Charity! I hate the word! It is *justice* to these poor sufferers to share my wealth with them! What right have I to such a superfluity?"

The conversation lasted for some half hour longer, during which many plans were discussed and some details of work arranged. When at length Helen rose to go, Mr. Heatherley, on shaking hands with her, said, solemnly—

"Miss Norman, though you deny the authority of Christ, you nevertheless are eager in His service."

It was with a joyous heart that the noble girl returned home. The same evening she wrote to her friend, Dr. Gurelin, a long account of her plans in a letter where every word throbbed, as it were, with fine enthusiasm. When she retired late at night it was only to spend many long wakeful hours, rendered restless by impatient longing for the new day.

CHAPTER III.

THESE were happy days for Arthur Golding,
destined, indeed, to be the happiest of his
life. Whilst he was hard at work all day
with crayon or brush, studying theoretical
works till far into the night, or rising with
the sun to convert the theory into practice—
whilst his thoughts between sleep and sleep,
and all the happy visions which circled around
his mind during the hours of repose, had their
origin in but one idea, that the result of all
this delightful labour would before long
declare itself to the world in the shape of
fame and fortune—he little knew that this
labour must be its own reward, or look for
none at all; that the happiness he yearned
for was now absolutely existent, that the
future held for him no single day that would
not appear gloomy by the side of these
glowing hours.

Similarly Helen Norman was progressing
day by day in the struggle upwards and
onwards, but in her case there was more
consciousness of effort, and less of advance.
Though she seemed to have chosen between
two paths, resigning the constant care of her

own intellect in favour of weary, and often
seemingly ungrateful, labour in the cause of
others, there was in reality no one of her
thousand acts of sweetness, charity, and
perseverance but reacted with tenfold effect
upon her own nature, rendering her day by
day more patient and enduring, as well as
bolder, in the campaign against the mistakes
and the vices of society upon which she had
entered.   For her, too, in all likelihood, this
was the happiest period of her life, though
she was as little conscious of the fact as
Arthur.   In these days, when the energy of
young enthusiasm wrought up her strength
to the performance of any severe or disgusting toil, when as yet she could see nothing
but the bright results of her efforts, and
firmly believed that every new day would
add to this brightness, she did indeed experience true happiness.   When Mr. Heatherley
met her from time to time in the course of
her daily visits, and saw her lovely features
aglow with the fire of boundless benevolence,
and that active virtue, which is so very
different a thing from the mere passive
virtue upon which her sex, for the most part,
prides itself, he could not but marvel in his
mind that any impulse other than that of
religion could give the spur to such wonderful
exertions.

On the other hand, the more Helen saw of
the clergyman the more she respected him.

If he marvelled at the inspiration which Helen derived from her natural religion, the latter, in her turn, could not but admire Mr. Heatherley's abounding charity. For, with a generous divergence from the *letter* of his creed, the latter held that the merit of good works was not solely dependent upon the faith of their performer; there was such a thing, he maintained, as unconsciously fulfilling the Gospel; and, far from esteeming error damnable, he looked upon it as deserving the most tender pity and consideration. So, from the first, Helen Norman, with her noble and generous freethinking, had been to Mr. Heatherley an object of wonder, at times almost of reverence. Was it not a truth that the ways of God are not the ways of men, and could he for a moment believe that the eternal law of justice would permit the co-existence in one bosom of such heavenly purity of intention with heresy in doctrine nothing less than blasphemous? Surely this was but one phase in the life of a soul struggling towards the truth.

Despite all this, Helen was frequently made to feel those other points, besides mere intellectual attitude, upon which there was no contact between them. Whereas her own nature was richly poetical—esteeming poetry the perfection of the noble faculty of speech, as the highest outward expression of that law of perpetual striving which alone she worshipped—Mr. Heatherley's, she soon learnt, was only in a very moderate degree appreciative of anything apart from the hard details of social life. They agreed in believing that, for the present, their scene of duty was the earth, their work amidst the misery with which it abounded; but whilst Helen idealised everything she looked upon, he viewed all things alike in the light of common day; where she saw higher significances, he saw merely facts. Such was indeed the necessary result of their difference in religious views. The man who convinces himself that he has ever at his elbow the key to the mystery of the universe, whose profession it is to make manifest to the world that he *has* this key, and to apply it for everyone's behoof, who conceives that the great laws of duty have long ago been written down in black and white for the use of man, and are not capable of discovery otherwise; such a man *cannot* but regard the world in a more or less prosaic light, compared with the point of view of one who recognises no patent key as in existence, for whom the mystery of life and death begins and ends with a vast doubt, whose every thought is the fruit of, and leads to, boundless conjecture, and who is compelled at length to confess with the poet, that

> Beauty is truth, truth beauty, that is all
> Ye know on earth, and all ye need to know.

Some such thoughts as these had occupied Helen's mind on her way homeward one afternoon early in August, when in body she was fatigued almost past endurance, though her reflecting powers were no less vivid than ordinary. On her arrival in Portland Place, instead of mounting to her room she repaired forthwith to the library, which she knew was always empty at this hour, after giving orders that a cup of tea should be brought to her there. Throwing off her hat, she allowed herself to sink into the luxury of an easy chair, and was continuing her reflections, when the door opened suddenly and Maud entered, equipped for riding.

"You here!" she exclaimed to Helen. "I was that moment imagining you in some frightful cellar, or else garrett, scattering your gold like a beneficent fairy to a whole family of destitute drunkards. But really, Helen, you are as pale as a ghost. You are working yourself to death, depend upon it. If I were an Irishwoman, I would add that you will acknowledge I am right when you actually are dead. I just came in to have a look at my pistols. I think you haven't seen them yet?"

With that she proceeded to open one of the drawers in the centre-table, of which she took the key from her pocket, and to take from it two small American revolvers, holding one in each hand, and regarding them with the peculiar ironical smile which she had learnt from her father.

"They're both loaded," she said, calmly.

"Do you say they are yours, Maud?" asked Helen, in surprise.

"Yes; I bought them in the Strand, last Monday."

"But whatever for?"

"What for? Why, you know I am on the point of being married."

"And what is the connection between the two circumstances?" asked Helen.

Maud shrugged her shoulders, once more examined the pistols carefully, replaced them in the drawer, and locked them up.

"One can never foresee what may happen," she said at length. "Supposing robbers broke into one's room at night. There are a thousand contingencies rendering the possession of such little defenders very desirable."

Helen was silent and thoughtful. At this moment a servant brought in her tea.

"Bring me a cup, too, will you, Mary?" said Maud. Then, turning to her friend, "It will strengthen me to endure my ride."

"Where is your ride to be to-day?" asked Helen.

"Where, my dear child? Why, in the Row, of course. Where else can a civilised person ride, I should like to know. Waghorn calls for me at four."

"Do you enjoy your ride in the Row?"

" Enjoy it ? My dear Helen, you grow more *naive* every day. Is it meant to be enjoyed, think you? Do you suppose that any soul ever does enjoy it ? "

" It is somewhat difficult to account for their persisting in the practice if it brings them no enjoyment," returned Helen.

" Duty, Helen, duty. Do not suppose that you philanthropists monopolise that article. We go to the Row to show ourselves, and purely from a sense of duty. Society requires it of us. Who would venture to question the dictates of society ? "

" But I suppose the dictates of society are sometimes one with those of pleasure ? "

" Give me a single instance in which they are," returned Maud, " and I'll—allow you to congratulate me on my wedding-day. Which, bye-the-by, I herewith seriously forbid you to do, Helen Norman."

" You mean it ? "

" I mean it."

" May I ask why ? "

" Because I esteem you too highly, my dear girl, to allow you to make a hypocrite of yourself out of deference to these same social rules of which we have been speaking."

There was silence for some time, which Helen was the first to break.

" You could hardly regard the concert last night as disagreeable," she said. " Mr. Gresham told me that it was admirable."

"Never trust papa," returned Maud, "especially when he praises anything or anybody. He does so purely out of deference to your optimistic views; for, you must know, papa is a trifle afraid of you. I assure you the concert was fatiguing to the last degree."

"Do you ever enjoy anything, Maud?"

"Yes, Helen."

"What, may I ask?"

"Why, talking with you. It seems to do me good to mingle my insipid ideas with your vigorous, healthy thoughts. It refreshes me to come into contact with your genuine nature, after feeding my littleness upon the affected admiration of fools. You see I can be severe in a downright manner when I chose, Helen, and upon myself, too."

Helen did not reply, but enjoyed her tea with gravity.

"Do you know, Helen," pursued the talkative young lady, "I have only seen one person in my life *very much* like you. Can you guess who it is?"

"I fear not."

"You will be surprised. I mean Mr. Golding."

Helen looked up with a surprised smile.

"What are the points of resemblance?" she asked.

"Many. You are both grave habitually, and enthusiastic upon occasion. You are

both furious advocates of what you will
permit me to call the *canaille*, their rights
and wrongs. You have both a manner of
smiling quite peculiar, and which, to atone
for the other expression, I may perhaps be
permitted to call angelic. Also you are
both, in conclusion, extraordinarily good-
looking."

"How can you know all this of Mr. Golding?" asked Helen, smiling.

"Oh, I frequently have a little conversation with him in the studio of a morning. I
find him rather interesting."

"Upon what subjects has he waxed enthusiastic to you?"

"Principally upon the merits of an old
gentleman with whom, it seems, he has lived
for many years, but whose name is a trifle
uncouth, and I forget it. Oh, I know!
Tollady—Mr. Tollady. To hear Mr. Golding
speak of him, he must be an angel, before
whom even you, Helen, must veil your wings.
He impoverishes himself by giving to the poor,
and has been known to walk home shoeless
at night that a beggar's feet might be shod."

Helen listened with an expression of the
most lively interest upon her features, but
made no remark.

"But I shall cease my connection with Mr.
Golding," pursued Maud.

"Why?"

"His enthusiasm is contagious. If I

talked to him for an hour every day during a week he would scatter my calm philosophy to the winds."

Helen made no reply.

"It is very unfortunate," said Maud, "that his position is so ambiguous."

"In what sense ambiguous?" asked Helen.

"Why, you know, he is not, to begin with, what the world calls a gentleman."

"Indeed! Has he been rude to you?"

"Far from it."

"What has he done, then, to forfeit the title of a gentleman?"

"He never owned it, Helen. He must have been as poor as a church mouse all his life, and Heaven forbid that he should disclose how he got his living always."

"Are you speaking seriously, Maud?"

"Quite seriously, Helen, as the mouthpiece of the world, which you know is the character I love to adopt."

"But as the mouthpiece of your own thoughts?"

"Why, what is your opinion?"

"I never saw him act, or heard him speak otherwise than as a gentleman, on the two occasions I had for speaking to him."

"Well, when I speak of his ambiguous position, I mean to say one is not quite sure whether one ought to talk to him as an equal or not."

"That I consider an unworthy doubt, Maud."

"You have no scruples in the matter?"

"I confess that I have not. If I wish to do so, I shall speak with as much freedom to Mr. Golding as to Mr. Gresham."

"You consider him an equal?"

"In many respects, my superior," replied Helen, unconsciously straightening herself, as was her habit when desirous of speaking with special force. "As an artist he has shown that he possesses genius, and that is a property I bow to wherever I meet it."

"The genius Mr. Golding owns is, unfortunately, not always so useful as its namesakes of the "Arabian Nights." Genius is highly agreeable company in the world's estimation as long as it is able to keep a carriage; but genius in rags is the most objectionable of mendicants."

"And can you rank yourself, Maud, on the side of a world with principles such as these?"

"Don't say *can*; the proper word is *must*. Depend upon it, the world is too strong for an individual will to combat. It will conquer, sooner or later. The difference between you and me, Helen, is, that whilst you are determined to fight out the struggle to the bitter end, I, rather more sensible, I flatter myself, calculate the chances to begin with, and give in at once."

" Well," said Helen, with a sigh, " if I am
fated to be beaten, I still think it will be a
consolation to me to remember that I
struggled.   But why do you always practise
this insincerity with me, Maud ?   I know
quite well you think far other than you
speak."

" You know that ? "

" I am sure of it."

" Well, well.   Then you know more of me,
Helen, than I do of myself.   But here is
John.   You are very late, sir."

These words were addressed to Mr. John
Waghorn, who just then entered the library,
looking, if possible, even more respectable in
his riding clothes than he had done in evening
dress.

There was, however, to-day, a certain
sallowness in his cheeks, and a slight heaviness about the eyes, which, in any less respectable man, would have awakened a
strong suspicion that he had been " making
a night of it " the evening before, and had
but very lately risen from bed.   In Mr. John
Waghorn's case this supposition was, of
course, inadmissible.   Doubtless the " seedy"
look could be attributed to undue strain in
business matters.

" May not we have the pleasure of Miss
Norman's company ? " he asked, in an accent
of much politeness.

" Thank you," returned Helen, with a not

altogether successful effort to conceal the dislike she had of the speaker; "I never ride."

"Pity, that," remarked Mr. Waghorn. "The Row is a loser by your absence."

"I thought you had already learnt that Miss Norman does not care for compliments," put in Maud. "Besides, all your *esprit* in that direction should be reserved for me. Are you ready?"

"I wait your pleasure," returned Mr. Waghorn, turning to Maud with a smile of remarkable insipidity, very different from the bold look of genuine admiration with which his eyes had rested upon Helen.

They walked together to the front door, where their horses awaited them, and rode away in silence, with a distance of ten feet between them. Strangers viewing them as they passed took them for man and wife.

Helen, when left alone, took up her hat with a sigh, and ascended to her room. As she passed the studio she saw the curtain drawn aside from the door, which stood wide open.

"Maud!" cried Mr. Gresham's voice from within.

"It is I, Mr. Gresham," said Helen, entering the room. "Maud has this moment gone for her ride."

"Ha!" returned the artist, in an abstracted tone. Then added, with an affec-

tation of indifference, "Did you see Waghorn ? "

"For a moment."

"He—he wasn't quite well, was he ? "

"I didn't hear him say so," replied Helen;
"but I thought he appeared to have a headache."

Mr. Gresham was standing at his easel,
pallette and brushes in hand, and between
his words he hummed a tune carelessly.
Suddenly he faced Helen.

"I suppose I shall have to give you away
next ?" he said, smiling in his old manner.

"I think there is no present prospect of
that," returned Helen, with a slight laugh.

"What sort of a man will it be, Helen,
when the time does come ?—anything like
Waghorn ? "

He added the last words after a scarcely
perceptible pause, and in a slightly lower
tone.

"I cannot say that I have ever thought
on the point," returned his ward, calmly. "I
should not be surprised if I never did."

"Shouldn't you ? But I should. Do you
think your beauty should serve no better
purpose than to be cast away in drunkards'
dens and reeking hospital wards ? When
do you mean to tire of your silly whim,
Helen ? "

The girl looked with surprise into his face.
She had never heard him speak with so much

energy, with so little of his habitual irony of tone.

But he seemed to be himself immediately conscious of this, and coloured slightly as he relapsed into indifference.

"Haven't you had enough of it yet, Helen?"

"It would be a sad thing for me, sir," she replied, "if I were already weary of the work of my life."

Mr. Gresham shrugged his shoulders and smiled, continuing to add touches to the picture before him. His ward turned to go, but he recalled her.

"Will you allow me to paint your portrait some day, Helen?" he asked, still keeping his eyes fixed upon the picture.

"To exhibit at the Academy, like Maud's?" she asked in reply, with a touch of irony.

"Psha!" exclaimed the artist. "To hang up in the drawing-room, or, better still, over the mantel-piece, here in the studio."

"I fear I could not spare the time to sit," returned Helen. Changing the subject, she added immediately, "I think you know the gentleman with whom Mr. Golding lives, do you not?"

"Know him?" said the artist, in surprise. "What about him?"

"Maud made some remarks with regard to

him to-day which excited my interest. Do you know whether he is a very charitable man ?"

"I think I have heard something to that effect from Golding; but I fancy he is not possessed of too ample means for the bestowal of charity. It must be in a very small way."

"And therefore the more creditable to him," said Helen. "You would have no objection to my making myself known to him, with a view to his acquainting me with any particularly deserving case of want which he may not be able to relieve himself ?"

"I suppose if I were to refuse my consent you would do so without it ?" said the artist, keenly examining Helen from under his heavy eyebrows.

"Certainly not," replied his ward. "I trust I shall always have a proper respect for your wishes, Mr. Gresham, as I should for those of my father, were he living."

Her guardian's face softened wonderfully as she spoke these words. He continued to regard her, as she stood with downcast eyes.

"Helen," he said, in a lower tone, "you must not take everything I say too much *au sérieux*. I should not like always to be judged by my words."

"And yet," returned the girl, simply, "it

is generally by that criterion that we judge and are judged."

And nodding a pleasant adieu she left the studio, closing the door behind her, whilst Mr. Gresham, with an expression upon his countenance somewhat strange to it, went on with his painting.

Helen had scarcely had time to doff her walking dress and assume that in which she ordinarily sat down to study, when a knock at her door disturbed her, and a servant informed her that she was inquired for by two ladies, who had declined to send their names on the plea that they were perfect strangers.

She descended to the drawing-room in some surprise, and, on entering, saw two ladies, one about her own age, one middle-aged, who rose to meet her. They were both very richly dressed, but rather too showily, and their countenances were wonderfully meaningless.

"Oh!" exclaimed the younger lady, before Helen had time to speak. "Oh! you really must excuse our unceremonious call, you know. But we have heard so very much of you, Miss Norman, that we really couldn't resist the *quite too* delightful chance of seeing you, you know. Could we, Mrs. Hopper, now?"

"No, indeed, Miss Norman," put in Mrs. Hopper. "We are only *too* glad to find you at home.   We really hope that you will excuse our freedom, really."

" Oh, yes, Miss Norman!" exclaimed the voluble young lady.   " We have heard so much, so very much of your *too* beautiful charity, you know.   And oh! Miss Norman, what church *do* you attend?"

" May I ask what your purpose is in asking the question?" said Helen, who had at first been somewhat disconcerted by the enthusiasm of the pair, but soon recovered her calmness, and felt considerably indignant at their intrusion.

" Oh, Miss Norman!" exclaimed the young lady.   " We do *so* want to know, if you would tell us, you know.   Of course you are *high*, Miss Norman?"

" I am afraid I do not quite understand you," said Helen, doing her best to show her distaste for this conversation.

" Miss Pitcher means, Miss Norman," explained the elder lady, " that you are, of course, devoted entirely to the High Church service?"

" Really, ladies," said Helen, distantly, "I fail to see how my religious opinions can interest you.   May I request that you will state the object of your visit?"

The elderly lady seemed somewhat abashed by the speaker's calm dignity of manner, but the younger returned to the attack, not at all discouraged.

" Oh, Miss Norman, we ask, you know, because we are so *awfully* anxious to get you to attend *our* Church, St. Abinadab's, you know. You *could* be so *very* useful there, you know, Miss Norman ; a person of your *too* charitable disposition !   There is so *much* work to be done in the Sunday schools, and with regard to the bazaars, and the tea-meetings, and—and so *awfully* many things, you know. And we have got such a delightful new incumbent, such a *quite too* dear man, Miss Norman.   It is such a *pity* he is married, and has thirteen children !   And his name's Mr. Whiffle, Miss Norman.   Oh, I'm *sure* you would so like him ! "

" Miss Pitcher is quite right," interposed Mrs. Hopper, the young lady being out of breath.   " It would be such a great blessing if we could secure your services for St. Abinadab's.   We have heard so much of your indefatigable charity. And I'm sure you would *so* like poor Mr. Whiffle."

Helen started slightly as she heard the name of the new incumbent of St. Abinadab's. She could scarcely doubt that it was the Mr. Whiffle with whom she was acquainted, She was about to speak when Miss Pitcher cut her short.

" Oh, yes ! *Poor* Mr. Whiffle, Miss Norman. You can't think how he has been persecuted by that *quite too* dreadful man, his former bishop ! And all because he was so devotedly *high*, Miss Norman, and altogether refused to become either *broad* or *low!* Is it not shocking? But I am *so* thankful that friends have obtained St. Abinadab's for him. Oh, what sermons! and oh! what singing, Miss Norman!"

"Mrs. Hopper," said Helen, as soon as a pause came, turning to the elder lady, "if I rightly understand that is your name—I must really request that you will tell me whether you had any serious object in visiting me. If not, I must tell you that I do not feel justified in wasting more of my time in hearing of matters which do not at all interest me."

"Oh, yes, Miss Norman," said the elder lady, shrinking a little before Helen eyes, "yes, we had a very serious object in view. It is this, Miss Norman. Finding that our new incumbent, Mr. Whiffle, suffers severely at times from rheumatism in the right leg—poor man!—we have decided to raise a subscription to purchase him a very handsome leg-rest; and—and, we have really heard so *very* much of your extreme charity, Miss Norman, that—that we have ventured to call upon you in the hope that you would add your name to the subscription list."

As she spoke Mrs. Hopper drew out of her pocket a small note-book, which she opened at a page headed, "The Rev. Mr. Whiffle's leg-rest," and handed it to Helen together with a pencil.

"Oh, yes, Miss Norman!" exclaimed the younger lady, "and for something quite handsome, you know. Something worthy of you!"

Indignation burned fiercely in Helen's breast. Stepping to the bell-cord, she pulled it sharply, whilst she spoke in decided tones.

"I see," she said, "that we scarcely agree in our opinions as to what a serious object is. That which you are pleased to call such, I can only term, with no desire to offend you, frivolous and impertinent. I wish you good afternoon, ladies, and hope that you may before long find a more worthy occupation for your abundant leisure. Kindly let these ladies out, James," she added, as the footman knocked and entered.

Not even Miss Pitcher's audacity was proof against this. The two departed with blank countenances, and without uttering a word. As soon as she was alone, Helen gave way to irresistible laughter, and ran up to her room again.

On the following day, Arthur Golding, entering Mr. Tollady's shop at two different times, met on the door-step two very different people, both of whom, however, excited surprise in him and one a somewhat different emotion also.

The first of these occasions was about noon. As he was returning from making a few purchases of colours, he met, just issuing from the shop, a gentleman whom he immediately recognised as Mr. John Waghorn. At the same moment he recalled to mind how it was that, on meeting Mr. Waghorn in Mr. Gresham's dining-room, he had been so strongly impressed with the feeling of having seen him before. He now felt sure that it was here he must have seen him, indeed, thought he remembered the very occasion. In the present instance Mr. Waghorn's eyes fell upon Arthur for a moment, but were immediately removed. He either did not recognise the young man, or did not wish to appear to do so.

On entering the shop, Arthur found it empty, and, on stepping into the parlour at the back, found the old man sitting with his head leaning forward and his face hidden in his hands. He had not heard Arthur's approach, and raised his head with a start when the latter spoke.

" Are you ill, Mr. Tollady ? " asked Arthur, in an anxious voice.

" No, no, Arthur," replied the printer, in rather tremulous tones, which he strove to make firm. " No ; I was only thinking."

" Of no pleasant subject, I fear," returned Arthur, sitting by the other's side, and looking concernedly into his face.

Mr. Tollady seemed to reflect for a moment, but then his face cleared up, and he smiled in the old benevolent way.

" Perhaps I am not quite as well as I might

be, Arthur," he said. "Never mind, we will have a walk into the country on Sunday, if it's fine. That will set me up."

"Who was that who just left the shop as I entered?" asked Arthur, not content with this dismissal of the subject.

"Someone I had a little business with, Arthur," replied the old man, calmly.

Arthur knew the tone in which these words were spoken, and respected Mr. Tollady's wish to avoid further explanation. But he went up to his work with an uneasy mind.

The second meeting occurred about five o'clock in the evening, when he was returning from an errand in connection with the printing office, for he still insisted on finding time to do much of this work. Just as he had met Mr. Waghorn, he now encountered a tall, veiled lady, whose identity his heart at once revealed to him by a sudden leap. Even had he not discerned her features faintly through the veil, he would have known this lady to be Miss Norman. The form, the bearing, the walk could belong to no other.

She recognised him, bowed, said—"Good-evening, Mr. Golding," and passed on. It seemed as though she had held a whole conversation with him, so sweet and lingering in his ears was the voice which uttered the commonplace words.

Mr. Tollady was in the shop, and wearing an expression of countenance far other than that he had worn in the morning.

"Why, whatever was Miss Norman doing here?" cried Arthur, as he bounded into the shop.

"She has been here nearly half an hour," replied Mr. Tollady, smiling.

"And I was away!" exclaimed Arthur, in a tone of disappointment. Then, observing the old man's clear eye fixed searchingly upon him, he affected to laugh.

"Whatever was her business? Is it rude to ask?" he said.

"Not at all," replied Mr. Tollady. "She has made me the happiest man in London, bless her kind heart! You remember, Arthur, how bitterly I was regretting only this morning that I was unable to help poor Sarah Thomson, whose husband died last week?"

"Yes."

"Well; even whilst I was brooding over the poor woman's lot and making myself quite miserable, who should come in but an angel with the very succour that was wanted! Upon my word, I shall believe henceforth in angels, Arthur."

"I don't quite understand you," said the young man, amused at Mr. Tollady's unusual enthusiasm. "Have you known Miss Norman long?"

"Not till half an hour ago. Then sh came and introduced herself, saying that you —silly boy!—had been telling tales about my poor efforts to help a few needy people, and begging to be allowed to contribute from her purse if ever I should know of a worthy person. I at once told her Mrs. Thomson's story, and—see the result!"

He held up a five-pound note, with almost childish glee.

"Yes!" he exclaimed. "And more to follow if it be necessary. And sewing for the poor thing to employ herself with, too! Yes, Arthur, I shall believe henceforth in angels. Her very voice has done me good. If there were but more like her!"

For a moment an unworthy feeling arose in Arthur's mind—he felt half ashamed that Helen should have seen the poor place in which he lived. It was only for a moment; the next, he had crushed the base thought, as he would have done a poisonous insect beneath his foot. He felt that, for the future, the shop would seem brighter and more cheerful, glorified as it was by the reminiscence of her presence. What if it were a poor place? Would not Helen think all the better of him that he had conceived the idea of making himself an artist under such discouraging circumstances? It was but the third time he had set eyes upon Miss Norman, and yet he felt it a matter of inexpressible importance that she should think well of him. The idea that she might not think of him at all did not enter his head; his feelings were not sufficiently developed for that. At present the mere thought that she had been beneath this roof invested the whole house with a vague sanctity, as with a perfume. With a day-dream of lovely forms and faces dazzling before his eyes, he mounted the stairs, and once more set eagerly to his work.

CHAPTER IV.

MARRIAGE À-LA-MODE.

ANOTHER week has elapsed, and it is the eve of Maud Gresham's wedding-day. Before, however, paying a visit to Portland Place, to see how Maud conducts herself on the last evening of her maiden life, let us visit the rooms of a certain student of divinity, situated in the humbler neighbourhood of University Street.

This student has, it is true, only a very indirect connection with the forthcoming marriage; but, for all that, the consideration of his movements on the evening in question may not prove altogether inappropriate.

The student was no other than Mr. Augustus Whiffle. Pending his attainment of the age at which the law permitted him to be ordained to the service of the Church, Mr. Whiffle still continued to hold the position of an occasional student at King's College; but his attendance at the lectures was very occasional indeed.

When Mr. Whiffle, senior, removed from Bloomford to become incumbent of St. Abinadab's he naturally made the proposition that his eldest son should live with the family, for

the sake of economy, if for no other reason ;
and this proposition Augustus, also quite
naturally, declined to consider. He found
himself extremely comfortable in lodgings,
and had no desire to alter his mode of life.
On the whole, it may be considered as somewhat to Augustus' credit that he declined to
transfer himself, with all his companions
and his habits of life, to the house wherein
dwelt his mother and his young brothers and
sisters.

Mr. Augustus Whiffle's sitting-room was a
tolerably comfortable one, of the ordinary
lodging-house type, situated upon the first
floor, and from the windows could be caught,
on the right hand, a glimpse of University
College; on the left, a peep at the busy
traffic of Tottenham Court Road ; whilst the
Hospital loomed darkly over the way. The
occupant of this room has altered considerably since we caught a glimpse of him a little
more than two years ago. In those days,
with all the will to be a thorough-paced
rascal, neither his age nor his knowledge of
life was sufficiently advanced for that ; with
just a tinge of recently acquired profligacy,
he was, on the whole, what nature made him
—a fool.

But he has learned much since then. Bitter
experience has taught him how easy it is to
be duped by those a little older, a little
shrewder, a little more wicked than oneself,

and mature reflection has convinced him that it is just as easy to live on others as to permit others to live on you, and far more agreeable to boot. Any little compunction in a course of villainy, which might once have clung to him, has now been entirely shaken off, together with the outward and visible symptoms of his folly. For Augustus is not a fool now—at all events not in his own conceit. He is shrewd, long-sighted, devoid of feeling; he has a quick hand and a clear brain for cards or dice, and a mind stored with unquestionable lore on the recondite subject of horse-racing. If Augustus were to keep accounts and to reckon how much he makes in a year, nett, out of these various pursuits, the total would represent a very respectable sum. But he is not reckless, far from it. Is he not still an occasional student at King's College, and does he not ever keep in view the day on which he will become eligible to receive a " cure of souls ? "

Even in personal appearance Augustus has altered of late considerably. Curious to tell, his hair, whiskers, and moustache, instead of being what nature made them, an emphatic red, have taken to themselves a hue of glossy brown, a deep, rich tint, which ladies might envy. Then his face has by no means that empty, would-be-wicked expression which it wore when he sucked the top of his cane on the way home from Bloomford

with Helen and Maud.   With the very least
stretch of the imagination, it could even be
pronounced handsome, for though nothing
less than intellectual in mould, the lines
are fairly regular, and the nose has even an
aristocratic bend.   The habitual expression
it wears, too, is one of thoughtfulness, which
produces an effect altogether independent of
the subject of thought.

Augustus was just turned twenty-one, and
had grown of late several inches, so that he
now stood not much less than six feet.   His
dress, it is almost superfluous to state, was
in the latest fashion, exhibiting not inconsiderable care and conveying an impression
of wealth.   On the whole, Mr. Whiffle was
unmistakably an attractive young man to
anyone with whom he might choose to display
only the amiable side.   It had taken him
some little time to learn all this, it is true,
but his progress in *savoir vivre* had been
very wonderful when contrasted with his
progress in letters.   At present he was
still studying the former ardently.   Mr.
Whiffle, senior's, position at the aristocratic church of St. Abinadab's had thrown
open to him a circle of society very superior,
in worldly possessions at least, to any he had
hitherto moved in; and though on but indifferent terms with his father, Augustus had no
scruple in using the latter's prestige to procure an entry into the same circle.   He felt

it was necessary for him to obtain the acquaintance of a few wealthy families, and as he always presented himself under the character of the divinity student, he was remarkably well received.

At half-past seven, then, on the present evening, Augustus was sitting at his open window, smoking a cigar. Meantime his eyes found employment in watching the streams of girls who at this hour pour out of the work-rooms in which the neighbourhood abounds, on their weary way home.

The occupation was a congenial one. Not unfrequently he would see one pass with whom he had, or desired to have, some kind of acquaintance, and at such times a loud cough or a low whistle on his part would attract the girl's attention, when he would smile graciously, or wave his delicate hand. Augustus had evidently a good taste in such matters, for the girls whom he appeared to know were invariably the prettiest that passed.

Once he went through the usual pantomime, and, in addition, took a little piece of paper from his waistcoat pocket, rolled it up, and let it fall, as if through carelessness, on to the pavement. The next moment it was picked up by the person for whom it was meant, and Augustus smiled contentedly.

He was interrupted in the midst of these delights by hearing a double knock at the front door below, and on bending forward out of the window he recognised an acquaintance who now and then called for him. Hastily putting one or two things in order in the room, he closed the window and was ready to receive his visitor.

The latter is already known to the reader as Mr. John Waghorn. Though his dress was, as usual, extremely genteel, and his hair arranged with the ordinary care, for some reason or other he had by no means a respectable look this evening. It seemed as though he had the power of altering his face to suit the occasion. At present he looked what he really was, brutish, sensual, ugly.

"Game for a night of it, my boy, eh?" he asked, as he flung himself carelessly into an arm-chair.

"Don't mind," returned Augustus. "Are you?"

"Yes; for the last time."

"What do you mean?" asked Augustus. "Going to give up wine and women, and turn moral in your old age? Bye-the-by, how old are you, Waghorn?"

"Turned six and thirty," replied the other, lighting a cigar. "Think of that."

"Sound in wind, too. You won't begin to knock up for another ten years. Let's look at your teeth old boy."

Mr. Waghorn seemed to resent the refined joke.

" Teeth be damn'd !" he exclaimed. "Sound or not, I've come to the end of my tether. I mean to have a frisk to-night, and for the last time, I tell you."

" For God's sake, why ?"

" For a very good reason. I'm going to be married to-morrow."

" What !" cried Augustus, in amazement.

" Fact !" said Mr. Waghorn.

" And who the devil has been fool enough to have you, Waghorn ?" asked Augustus, with friendly frankness.

" That's nothing to do with the matter," returned the other. " You don't know her."

" How do you know I don't ? What's her name ?"

" Well, if it interests you particularly, her name's Maud Gresham."

" Maud Gresham ! The devil ! Daughter of an artist ?"

" Do you know her ?"

" As well as I know you !" exclaimed Augustus, with trifling exaggeration. " Well I'm damn'd ! Uncommon fine girl, and heaps of tin, I believe. I say, old fellow, I must be best man !"

" Impossible ! My brother's volunteered for that. Must have a respectable fellow, you know."

" Thanks for the compliment," returned Augustus, laughing. " After all, the affair would be a good deal too tedious. But, I say, Waghorn, you'll invite me to dinner before long? How long shall you be away?"

"Couple of months, perhaps."

"Continent?"

"Suppose so. What a damned slow life it will be!" exclaimed Mr. Waghorn, with agreeable anticipation of the delights of the honeymoon.

"Do the other fellows at the Eau de Vie know?"

The institution thus referred to was a club which both our friends much frequented, the proper name of which was the Young Men's Conversational Club, but which, in relation to the beverage principally consumed there, was chiefly known by the *habitués* as the Eau de Vie, sometimes shortened, with a punning reference, to D. V.

"Don't think so," replied Mr. Waghorn, in reply to the question.

"Mean to tell them, eh?"

"Why yes, I think so. May as well let the boys have a joke."

"Waghorn married!" exclaimed Augustus, leaning back with a roar of laughter; after which, by way of being facetious, he imprecated curses upon himself for several minutes.

As soon as it began to grow dark, the two issued forth to fulfil their purpose of making a night of it. We shall not endeavour to follow their nocturnal wanderings, in the course of which they picked up several congenial acquaintances equally bent on spending a jovial evening; but let it suffice to say that a popular music-hall, an indecent exhibition, numberless restaurants, the green-room of a second-rate theatre, and a notorious casino enjoyed in turn the honour of a visit from these choice spirits.

In the last-named resort several equally choice spirits of the opposite sex were selected to join the company, and eventually they all repaired to some supper-rooms of unsavoury reputation, where they disported themselves till closing time, the performance of a *pas seul* by one of the ladies on the centre of the table being a prominent feature of the merriment.

On leaving the house the attractions of their female companions drew in different directions the majority of the choice spirits, and Mr. Waghorn and Augustus repaired alone to the Young Men's Conversational Club, otherwise known as the Eau de Vie. Here the sweet of the night was but just commencing.

Around a number of small tables some twenty or thirty young men were engaged at cards, each supplied with his glass of the eponymous beverage, the odour of which was perceptible even in the street.

Owing to Mr. Whiffle's care, the great event to take place upon the morrow soon became generally known. It created a *furor*. One young man, more than half drunk, sprang on to a table and proposed the health of the bride and bridegroom, suggesting in conclusion that every member of the club should turn out on the following morning to conduct Mr. Waghorn from his residence to the church, a proposal which was vigorously cheered, but received a polite refusal from the prospective bridegroom, delivered in the form of a speech from behind the drinking-bar, whither Mr. Waghorn had betaken himself to avoid his companions' too boisterous congratulations.

The greater part of the conversation ensuing upon the proclamation of this piece of intelligence was of that description which the newspapers call "unsuited for publication." Mr. Waghorn was evidently a highly popular member of the club, and, moreover, owing to his advantage in years over the majority of the members, a constant source of jokes of the most approved "Eau de Vie" flavour—which was high.

When the excitement had cooled a little, Augustus, as was his wont, proposed a little play to while away an hour or two, which Mr. Waghorn, being already weak in the legs, readily agreed to; the result being that Augustus rose from the table towards four o'clock in the morning appreciably richer than when he sat down. But these little losses were nothing to Mr. Waghorn. During the day he was always a sharp-eyed, hard-hearted, close-fisted man of business ; and if he occasionally relaxed by making a brute of himself at night, why, he could afford it.

Leaving Mr. Waghorn to celebrate in appropriate style the eve of his wedding-day, we return to Portland Place and to respectability. Mr. Gresham of course intended that his daughter's wedding should be marked with all the *éclat* which became his own position, and frequent had been the visits paid by milliners and outfitters of every description during the past month. Maud found a good deal of pleasure in all this. To pay attention to such matters was to fulfil the world's requirements, and this, in Maud's philosophy, constituted the only serious business of life. Never had she been so caustic and sceptical in her conversation as during these last few weeks. With Helen in particular, it seemed as though she felt bound to show herself absolutely consistent in what is normally considered one of the most momentous epochs of life, to make it clear that she regarded the whole affair in the light of a more or less tedious farce, even as she regarded all the every-day occurrences of her existence. To Helen this mental attitude of her friend was painful in the extreme. Day after day she studied Maud's manner and countenance, and always with a growing conviction that there was nothing genuine at the bottom of all this cynicism, that it was merely acted. It seemed to her, also, that it was a part of which the actor was beginning to grow weary. Very closely did she watch for any sign of sincere emotion, any indication, however slight, of a growth of seriousness as the eventful day approached. Nothing of this kind was perceptible, Maud seemed only to harden in her indifference. It was with deep apprehension that Helen looked forward to a union entered upon in such a spirit.

Helen had not failed to notice the peculiarity in Mr. Gresham's manner when last he spoke to her of Mr. Waghorn, and she had observed since then that her guardian did not greet his future son-in-law altogether as heartily as he was wont to do. She noticed all this, and it made her uneasy, though it was as impossible for her to conjecture causes as it was to conceive remedies. She had observed, moreover, that Maud and her father had seemed to shun each other of late. They spoke but seldom in her presence, and Maud never now visited the studio when her father was at work there, as she had previously been in the habit of doing. Was it possible that this marriage was distasteful to one or other of them? If so, to which?

On the present evening Helen made a point of visiting Maud's chamber, ostensibly to view her friend's *trousseau*, but in reality to seek the opportunity for a serious conversation which had never yet presented itself. Helen was not to take any formal part in the ceremony, and that at Maud's earnest request. Mr. Gresham had wished his ward to be first bridesmaid, but to this Maud had strenuously objected, though altogether without reasons, and her father had yielded. But Helen yearned for a few sincere words from her friend of so many years, and could not but hope that this evening would see her desire satisfied.

Waiting till she knew Maud was in her chamber, Helen knocked at the door, and entered. Maud was sitting in the midst of an immense quantity of magnificent equipments, her hands crossed upon her lap, her face thoughtful, even sad. But as soon as she saw her friend enter, she rose with a brisk movement and greeted her with an ironical smile.

"Have you come to obtain food for future meditation upon earthly follies and vanities?" she said, glancing scornfully around at the muslin and lace. "Don't spare me, Helen. Lecture me soundly, and with as little remorse as if I were the fool in the Proverbs. Now if all the money that has here been wasted upon knavish drapers and milliners,

had only been put into Helen Norman's
hands for distribution among her multifarious
pensioners—isn't that how you are going to
begin?"

Helen sighed in disappointment. Maud
seemed more frivolous than ever.

"Why do you sigh and look miserable?"
pursued the bride. "Surely it is I who
should have the monopoly of such performances; and yet I am in excellent spirits,
as you see."

"But why should you have the monopoly
of misery, Maud?"

"Why? Am I not about to be married
to-morrow? Am I not about to play the
fool on a broader stage and before a larger
audience than I have yet had experience of?
Am I not about to exchange liberty for
slavery?"

"But surely, Maud," replied Helen, with
much gravity, "you cannot mean what you
say? If you look forward to marriage as only
a state of misery, why do you marry at all?"

"Why, my dear Helen? Doesn't everyone get married sooner or later? Depend
upon it you yourself will be no exception to
the rule."

"I trust I shall never marry with such a
disposition," returned Helen. "I should be
deeply grieved if I thought you were in
earnest, I should indeed. Have you lost all
confidence in your old friend, Maud?"

" Confidence ? How can you ask me the question ? I protest, Helen, I have this moment been more confidential to you with regard to the state of my mind than I would or could be with anyone else."

" And you seriously tell me, Maud, that you look for no happiness from this marriage ? That you have no love for your future husband ? That you enter upon married life merely because it is conventional to do so ? —I *cannot* believe you ! "

Helen had risen as she spoke, and trembled with the excess of her motion. Maud continued sitting, and smiled in her wonted manner.

" And could you believe me," she began, in turn, speaking in a hard, inflexible voice, " if I were to tell you that I not only look for no pleasure but for intolerable wretchedness —at all events till I have got used to it ? That, so far from *loving* my future husband, I hate and despise him ? That I am altogether unable to say *why* I am going to be married, except that papa wishes me to be, and that I know I may as well marry this man as any other ? Do you believe all that ? "

" If I must believe it," replied Helen, " I can only say that you are acting very wrongly, Maud, and that I should not be a true friend if I did not tell you so."

Maud suddenly rose to her feet with a flash

of anger in her eyes, an expression which
Helen had never before seen on her face.

"And what is it to me," she cried, in a
voice shaken with passion, "whether you are
a true friend or not! Do you think I have
any faith in friendship of any kind? What
does it matter to me whether I am doing
right or wrongly? Who commissioned you to
come here and tell me so? Am I a child to
be lectured in this way?"

Helen trembled like a leaf before this display
of most unwonted passion; she was scarcely
able to realise that Maud had spoken. She
saw, however, that the latter had turned her
back to her, and, looking straight before her
into the glass, could see the girl's face all distorted by a thousand conflicting emotions,
among which anger still held the supremacy.
Bursting into tears, she quitted the room and
sought the quietness of her own chamber.

As soon as she saw that she was alone,
Maud sank into a chair and sat there in the
same attitude as before. But her face soon
lost its angry expression. Before many
minutes had passed tears rose irresistibly to
her eyes, and began to trickle down her
cheeks. She made no effort either to check
them or dry them as they fell, but sat as
motionless as a statue, weeping, weeping.
And even so she sat and wept till far on into
the night.

When it was nearly one o'clock, her father,

on his way to his room, paused at her door.
He could see that there was a light within,
but could hear no sound. For a moment
his hand sought the handle, but the next it
dropped again to his side. Once, twice he
moved away from the door and returned to
it. But not a sound came from within, and
he walked softly away.

Early next morning bustle and bell-ringing
was the order of the day. The usual stately
quietness of the house in Portland Place
was violated by innumerable unwonted intruders, who drove up in carriages or cabs,
and vied with each other in showing un-
doubted appreciation of the dignity and
felicity of the occasion. The Greshams had
few friends, but a very great number of
acquaintances, and as Mr. Gresham was
determined to spare no means to ensure the
brilliancy of the festival, invitations had been
issued in the most liberal and open-hearted
manner. Mr. Gresham himself, perhaps a
trifle paler than usual, as if from a bad
night, undertook the duty of receiving
the guests, and went through the task
with that perfect gentility of demeanour
which he prided himself upon, never allowing it to be mistaken, however, that he hid
beneath this outward complaisance a serene
contempt for the whole affair which was
extremely edifying. Now and then he would
whisper in a friend's ear some sarcastic

remark on social conventionalities, the next moment he would delight his inward soul by discussing ironically to this or that lady, perfectly sure that his listener understood him in the literal sense. There was a pleasure in all this for Mr. Gresham. Perhaps the only real pleasure he had experienced in life had been this successful blending of outward respect for society with never-ceasing internal ridicule of its vanities. Mr. Gresham had not met with much affection in the course of his three and forty years, and had been equally sparing in imparting it to others. Thus there was probably not one among this crowd of strangers for whom he entertained anything approaching frendship. They, for their part, regarded him with considerable admiration, as a perfect gentleman, a man of money, a man of talent; but beyond that, little, if anything. Maud Gresham excited even less real interest in those who had come to witness her marriage. With a contempt of society equal to that entertained by her father, she exercised less care in glossing it over with external forms and graces, and had seriously offended not a few of her so-called friends by her carelessness in this particular. Under these auspicious circumstances it was hardly to be expected that conversation amongst the visitors should greatly turn upon the chief business of the day. There was a little chat with regard to the dowery with which it was probable Mr. Gresham would make up for lack of sweet disposition in his daughter, a little subdued scandal with regard to the bridegroom, with whose habits of life a few of the gentlemen present were rather more acquainted than Mr. Gresham was; also a few instances of sweetly spiteful vaticination on the part of certain ladies in regard to the probable relations of the couple a year hence; after all which they turned their attention principally to their private affairs, discussed matches likely to come about and talked scandal with regard to others already effected. Truly, Mr. Gresham and his daughter had some grounds for their attitude of mind as regards this world of society.

There was, however, one point of interest common to most of those present, curiosity with regard to which had not, as yet, been satisfied. It soon became evident what this was when at length Helen Norman unobtrusively joined the company. A few of the guests were altogether unconscious of Helen's existence, but the greater part had, notwithstanding her retired and simple life, both heard and talked very much of her lately. I should but display my incapacity to deal with the mysterious problems of the world of fashion if I attempted to explain how intelligence of Helen's so-called eccentricities

had permeated the walls of her guardian's
house and filtered through a great variety of
social strata; creating an itching sensation as
it went, an eager curiosity to know more of
this strange beast in woman's form that Mr.
Gresham sheltered beneath his roof. If I
might hazard a very private conjecture, I
might possibly be disposed to imagine that
certain unusual gratuities which had of late
found their way into the pockets of Mr.
Gresham's servants were not unconnected
with this phenomenon. We know that when
the gods of old quarrelled they were wont to
tell each other somewhat unpleasant truths,
and we likewise are aware of the portentous
fact that, in our own day, rival editors of
rival papers have in anger charged each
other with procuring their "fashionable" intelligence by the means here hinted at. As
I say, I must not, however, venture to
account for mysteries such as these. It is
certain that neither from Mr. Gresham nor
his daughter did the information proceed, for
both of these cherished in the depths of their
hearts too sincere and involuntary a respect
for Helen Norman to permit of their making
her a common subject of conversation. Be
the matter how it may, it is certain that
reports concerning Helen, often widely
exaggerated, were very rife among all who
knew the Greshams, and the main inducement of not a few to honour the house with

their presence this morning had been the hope of seeing this peculiar creature in the flesh. The ladies, in particular, were prepared to be scandalised. The idea that a young, handsome, and unmarried lady should think of benefiting her poorer fellow-creatures was, to begin with, altogether shocking; and how disgracefully immodest must any young lady be who could visit the East End—positively, it was asserted, the East End—and there mix with people whose very aspect ought to be enough to create loathing, if not still worse feelings, in the mind of any properly trained young person. But there was even worse behind. It was whispered—who would have dared to speak it aloud?—it was actually whispered, with bated breath and blanched lips, that Mr. Gresham's ward *never went to church!* Though the very monstrosity of this accusation was sufficient to deprive it of all credit, save among those whose attendance at the same church as the Greshams has enabled them to be personal observers, yet the mere fact that the accusation could be made pointed to the existence of moral depravity in the unfortunate individual in question, scarcely inferior to that which would have been implied by habitual absence from church.

Helen had reflected much upon the part it became her to take in the day's proceedings. If she had obeyed the truest impulse of her heart she would have proceeded with her usual work and have kept entirely aloof from the wedding. This, however, she had felt to be impossible. Ordinary respect for her guardian demanded that she should pay some attention to his guests, and, disagreeable as the duty was, Helen faced it like every other duty, and resolved to be present. Accordingly, when she made her appearance in the drawing-room in Mr. Gresham's company, she was dressed with considerably more attention to effect than usual, but still in a very plain manner compared with those who surrounded her; and her countenance wore its accustomed expression of calm self-possession, though perhaps with a trifle more colour in the cheeks than they were wont to show. Her manner displayed just as little of *gaucherie* as of immodest effrontery. Helen was indeed, as she always was, beautiful, unaffected, queenly.

The first effect produced by her appearance upon those who had already arrived was one of disappointment. After all, her likeness to the Scarlet Woman of Babylon was faint in the extreme. But, before long, more positive feelings began to assume the place of mere disappointment. Glances of undeniable admiration were exchanged between the gentlemen; little shrugs, smiles and sneers began to indicate the emotions of the ladies. But, however bold the man who was favoured with an introduction, his eyes fell involuntarily before Helen's calm, frank look; however envious the ladies, they had to confess to themselves an influence in her face and tone which made their miserable little souls shrink and pine within them. This made many of them absolutely vicious. They could not bear to be made to feel their vast inferiority by one who spent her days distributing charity in the East End, and—did not go to church.

It is none of my purpose to give a detailed account of this notable wedding. Let the curious in such matters refer to the account in the *Times* of the marriage between Sir Horace Good-for-Nothing and Miss Lydia Rake-at-Heart, which made so much fuss last week. The description of the proceedings will apply equally to the present case. The same singular ceremony was gone through; the same wonderful vows were plighted between John Waghorn, immaculate in his Sunday dress of respectability, and Maud Gresham, impassive and slightly smiling; the same tears were wept by hysterical bridesmaids (the only appropriate part of the entertainment); the same benedictions were pronounced by a similar priest in a similar hurry to get home to lunch; and then—Glory to God in the Highest! Maud Gresham is no longer Maud Gresham, but Mrs. Waghorn; and all go away, charitably hoping that the result of it will be more

children, who will in turn, if parental affection spare them, take their part in a similar
pantomime.

Helen passed through this day of benedictions and congratulations with sorrow in her
heart. As soon as she saw Maud in the
morning she had turned towards her, hoping
that she would come forward in her wonted
easy manner, and show that the scene of the
previous evening had been forgotten. But
Maud evidently avoided her among the company, and Helen saw but little good in pressing upon her friend in this mood. Her
friend ? Helen asked herself whether Maud,
no longer Maud Gresham, would henceforth
be her friend, and she experienced keen
pangs as she thought that the marriage might
be the means of severing their intimacy.
She cherished a sincere affection for the
strange girl, notwithstanding the slight sympathy which appeared to exist between their
respective thoughts and aims. She could not
but believe that beneath the cold surface of
Maud's character lay seeds capable of bearing at least the ordinary fruits of human
kindness. Even till the last minute she endeavoured to afford her opportunities of
speaking one friendly word before they
parted, but Maud would not avail herself of
them.

When, at length, the carriage stood at the
door waiting to take Mr. and Mrs. Waghorn

to the railway station, and when farewells were being exchanged all round, Helen received a kiss just like that Maud gave to her bridesmaids, but not a direct look, not a pressure of the hand. She was on the point of whispering an ardent wish for her happiness in the bride's ear, but her voice failed her, and the chance was past. Mr. and Mrs. Waghorn were already on their way to Italy.

CHAPTER V.

In a dark corner of the church, whilst the marriage ceremony was going on, sat one spectator who had no eyes for the magnificent toilette of the bride, the starched respectability of the bridegroom, or any of the follies attendant upon the occasion. Arthur Golding's sole purpose in coming had been to obtain, if possible, a glimpse of Helen Norman. He had seen her hitherto only in her simple morning dress, or in her neat, but plain walking costume, and he was curious to observe the effect her beauty would produce when arrayed in the costume appropriate to a wedding. This, at least, was the excuse he made to himself for giving Mr. Tollady to understand that he was about to take an ordinary walk, and then hurrying off to the church where he knew the marriage was to take place and securing a " coign of vantage " before the strangers began to arrive.

It was purely an artist's fancy, he had thought, a piece of study which might give him new ideas.

But never did artist gaze upon mere model

with the fervour which led Arthur to seek eagerly for Helen's face in the crowd, and, when he had found it, keep his eyes fixed upon its beauty till the very moment when it again disappeared from the church. For him the place was vacant of other forms and features, so intensely was his interest centred in that one alone. He had no need to compare her appearance with that of the other ladies present; for him her beauty was something absolute, a type of perfection which, in the nature of things, could not be compared with other types. He did not notice that her dress was much plainer and simpler than of those all around her; he merely knew that it was richer than that in which he had previously seen her, and that its adaptability to her loveliness was perfect. The strength of his admiration almost amounted to frenzy. He gazed at her till an actual halo, a visible aureola, seemed to glitter about her, and he feared to turn away his eyes for a moment lest the beautiful effect should vanish.

When at length he suddenly found the church empty, and rose to go away, he was not conscious of any one of his actions. So visibly did he retain Helen's features in his memory, that they floated before him in the air as he walked, still surrounded by the aureola.

He regained his bedroom, which served

him for a studio, and sat down before a picture he was then working at, intending to paint. It was impossible. Even as a vision of the sweet-faced Madonna may have floated before the eyes of Fra Angelico, and held his mind in a state of pious rapture till he took his pencil and, almost without the exertion of his will, embodied the tender outline in a tangible form, so Arthur sat, brush in hand, gazing into vacancy, unable to think of anything but the chaste features of Helen Norman, till, scarcely knowing what he did, he took up a fresh sheet of paper and began slowly and lovingly to outline what he saw. In ten minutes the sketch was finished, the likeness was complete, and with a loud cry of delight Arthur sprang to his feet and held it at arm's length to sate his eyes upon it. He dared not add another touch, erase a line, lest the exquisite resemblance should be destroyed. What if it were but a rough outline in crayon? His imagination filled it out with the hues of life; it seemed to him to breathe, to smile. He had drawn it with the eyes directed full upon his own, and he now thought with rapture that Helen, *his* Helen, made his by this portrait, would for ever gaze upon him with that sweet, tender smile. No one could deprive him of this joy. However great the gulf that wealth and social dictates spread between himself and the original, however little Helen might think of him, she could not prevent her lifelike image from gazing upon him as he sat at work, breathing into his blood a rapture of enthusiasm for love, for beauty, for art, which would urge him to the achievement of great things. Henceforth Helen must be his Muse, his tutelary goddess. For a moment he had a glimpse into those regions of immeasurable exaltation which genius alone admits to; he felt that the world was within his grasp.

The sketch was too precious to be put away with the others. Repairing to a stationer's hard by, he purchased a piece of mill-board, and upon this carefully mounted the drawing. He then emptied his best portfolio, henceforth to be reserved for the idol alone, and, having carefully tied the strings, put it away in a safe place. This done, he was too over-wrought to proceed as usual with his work. Seeing the afternoon to be very fine, he slung over his shoulders the little bag containing his sketch-book and pencils, and set off on a walk to Hampstead Heath.

Meanwhile, the house in Portland Place had assumed its wonted quiet air, but with the departure of the newly-married couple and, very shortly thereafter, of all the guests, a sense of loneliness had come upon those left behind which they did not ordinarily experience.

Mr. Gresham was in his studio, making

believe to paint, for his hand refused to work
as usual when his thoughts were straying he
knew not where.   Helen was in her room,
busy at some correspondence which arose
out of her work in the East End.   Upon the
completion of this, she endeavoured to
study, but wholly without success.   The
thought of Maud too completely occupied
her mind, and made her sad.   It was a relief
to both guardian and ward when at length
the dinner bell rang, calling them from the
cheerless company of their own reflections.

"Well, Helen," said Mr. Gresham, as they
took their seats at table, "now that Maud has
left us to our own devices, I suppose the
first thing to be done is to decide how we are
to spend the next two months.   What do you
propose?"

"My time will be quite fully occupied," replied Helen, in a tone of natural decision;
"but no doubt you purpose taking your usual
holiday?"

"And no doubt you purpose doing the
same," said her guardian, with good-
natured mockery.   "Do you imagine I shall
permit you to remain in town all through the
autumn, and come back to find you worn to a
skeleton?"

"You need not anticipate the latter extremity," said Helen, smiling; "but it will
be impossible for me to leave town."

Mr. Gresham had learned the significance

of the quiet but decisive tone in which his ward delivered these words. He glanced at her furtively, and read the same significance in her undisturbed features.

The rest of the dinner, which was quickly finished, passed almost in silence. Only when the dessert was on the table, and the servant who had been waiting had retired, did the artist renew the conversation in earnest.

"Bye-the-by, Helen," he began, "did it ever strike you that, now we have lost Maud, I must have some one to look after my house in her place?"

"Yes, I have thought it might be necessary," replied Helen.

"You have? I never thought of it till Maud brought up the subject the other day."

Mr. Gresham played with his walnuts as he spoke, and from time to time glanced timidly at Helen from beneath his eyebrows.

"Do you know," he said, at length, smiling as he always did when about to advance some particularly audacious proposition, "I have been thinking that, rather than go to the trouble of hunting up such a person from among my list of distant relatives, I would sell the house and emigrate to the farm in Dorsetshire. I might live there in rural peace and happiness for the few remaining years of my life. Might I not, Helen?"

"The *few* remaining years!" exclaimed

Helen, smiling. "I trust that you may reasonably hope for more than a few, Mr. Gresham."

"Think so? Well, perhaps I may. Do you know my age?"

"I am a bad judge of such questions."

"Well, I am just forty-three. Upon the whole, one is rather young than otherwise at forty-three. Don't you think so, Helen?"

"At all events, far from old."

"Yes," said the artist, as if reflecting, "I was married at twenty-two, when I was a boy, and didn't know my own mind."

Helen looked curiously at him; but, meeting his covert glance, again dropped her eyes.

"Upon my word I have a good mind to carry out the scheme. Do you think I should make a good gentleman-farmer, Helen? Should I be apt to learn the price of grains and bullocks, think you?"

"Not very, I fear."

"Indeed! But why?"

"It is merely a guess," said Helen; "but I fancy you would never be so much at home in the country as you are in the city."

"Upon the whole, I think you are right," exclaimed her guardian, laughing. "No, the Dorsetshire farm is in very good hands, and doubtless had better remain as it is. But then we revert to the old question, Who is to take care of my house?"

"You spoke of distant relatives," said Helen; "do you know of anyone who would suit you?"

"Only one. That is an aunt, a sister of my mother, who, I believe, is very little older than myself. She is a widow without children, living in Birmingham."

"Do you think she would like to come to London?"

"I really have no idea, but I might ask her."

There was again a short silence.

"But I had hoped there would be no need of that just yet," he pursued, in a disappointed tone. "I imagined you would leave town till at least the end of September, and then it would have been time enough to think of my aunt. It would be the easiest thing in the world to make up a party. The Leighs are just thinking of going to Ireland, and they would be delighted if we would join them. You would have Mrs. Leigh with her two daughters to chaperon you. Surely you do not mean, Helen, that you intend to stay at home?"

"I seriously mean it, Mr. Gresham."

"But why? Are you too ascetical to permit yourself a holiday?"

"At present I really have no need of one," replied Helen. "Then next week I begin my evening school. You would not wish me to disappoint the poor girls who are looking forward to a chance of learning to read and

write? Mr. Heatherley thinks I shall have
at least a dozen to begin with."

Helen ceased, and her guardian made no
reply. His brow lowered slightly as he heard
the clergyman's name mentioned.

"Mr. Heatherley," pursued Helen, in unconsciousness of the last movement, "has
had no holiday for three years. I heard so
from an old lady whom I occasionally meet
at his house."

"Do you go often to his house?" asked
Mr. Gresham, cracking a walnut somewhat
fiercely.

"Not very frequently. If I wish to see
him we generally meet at the chapel. Indeed
he is very seldom at home. I should not
have thought it possible for anyone to work
as hard and as continuously as Mr. Heatherley
does."

The artist rose suddenly from his chair.

"Then I understand," he said in a rather
husky tone, which caused Helen to look up in
surprise, "that it is impossible to persuade
you to leave town?"

"I really must not," returned Helen, rising
and looking at her guardian with a smile
which was not returned.

"Then I remain at home myself," said the
latter.

"But not, I trust, on my account?" said
Helen. "Mrs. Thomson—the housekeeper—
is quite capable of seeing—"

"No, no," broke in Mr. Gresham, turning away his head, "of course not only on your account, Helen. I have a picture or two that I must get off my hands. Yes, I shall stay at home."

"I am sure you will alter your mind," urged his ward. "You really require a holiday. I hope you will alter your mind, Mr. Gresham."

"You are anxious to get me away?" he said, and immediately feeling that the words had been spoken unguardedly and with some rudeness, reddened a little and laughed. "Yes, yes," he repeated, in a jocular tone, "you are anxious to get rid of me, Helen."

"I am anxious that you should not break an agreeable custom solely on my account," returned his ward. "It would distress me to think you did so."

"It would? Then I shall think the matter over."

Helen nodded, smiled, and left the room.

"What the devil did she mean by that?" muttered her guardian to himself, when he was left alone. Then he struck the table a blow with his clenched fist, drank off what remained in his wine-glass, and walked away, seemingly in no very good humour.

What could be the matter with Mr. Gresham? All the next day he paced up and down, first in the studio, then in the library, quite unable to settle to anything. Several visitors who called were dismissed with the reply that he was not at home; he had no taste whatever for conversation. At meals he spoke very little, but, as often as Helen was not looking, watched her from beneath his eyebrows constantly. When she asked him whether he had decided to go to Ireland, he replied that he was thinking the matter over. If so, it appeared to occasion him more reflection than so slight a matter had ever done before. He could scarcely be well.

In the evening he decided to take a walk. Just as he issued from the door into the street, the postman was about to put some letters into the box. He took them from his hands instead, and examined the addresses. Two were for himself, and one was for Helen. Mr. Gresham altered his intention of going for a walk, and went into the library.

He was in no hurry to open his own letters; that directed to Helen seemed to absorb all his attention. On looking at the post-mark he saw that it had been posted in the east of London. That, and the fact that the address was written in a bold male hand, satisfied him that it was from Mr. Heatherley. It was a pity that Mr. Gresham had not just missed the postman on leaving the house.

Holding this letter in both hands behind his back he once more began to pace the room. Mr. Gresham was, without doubt, a gentleman as far as ordinary manners and social

condition went, but it was unfortunate for
him that he had decided to live without the
guidance of any such thing as principle, that,
indeed, he did not think the business of life
serious enough to require more than *tact* in
its transaction. This state of mind would
have been still more unfortunate had Mr.
Gresham been so unhappy as to be a poor
man ; being, on the contrary, a rich man, he
had never yet met with any temptation sufficiently strong to call for firm principle to
resist it. Without a doubt he would himself
have conceded this to you in argument, and,
for the same reasons, would have looked with
the most liberal tolerance on a poor man
whom temptation had caught unawares and
led into mischief. This was one of the better
points in his character. But the fact remained that Mr. Gresham had not principle.
Had he possessed it, he would, in the present
instance, have thrown Helen's letter on to
the table, rung the bell, and ordered it to be
taken to her. As it was, for some cause or
other, he seemed wholly incapable of letting
it escape his hands. The expression which
rested upon his face, meanwhile, was half a
frown, half an ironical grin—a smile it could
hardly be called—just as if there were at
that moment two voices speaking within himself, the one a rather angry and serious one,
the other an ironical, bantering voice, very
much like that in which he usually spoke.

Several times he gave utterance to exclamations, such as "Pooh! psha!" evidently part of the internal argument. Then he again looked at the letter, and it seemed to decide him.

Quickly he tore it open and came to the contents. They were these—

"DEAR MISS NORMAN,

"You will be glad to hear that I have a list of thirteen girls, all more than fifteen years old, who will gladly attend your class on Tuesday and Saturday evenings. I have told them, as you instructed me, that next Tuesday would be the first evening.

"Faithfully yours,
"E. W. HEATHERLEY."

Mr. Gresham quickly crushed the letter in his hand, and then thrust it into his pocket, with an extremely unpleasant expression of countenance. He seemed disappointed that he had not found more. The next moment he broke into a low laugh.

"And I have made a damned fool of myself for that! Pooh! I need not fear Heatherley. He's only a parson."

Muttering this he resumed his intention of taking a walk, and left the house.

This little event formed an epoch in the life of Mr. Gresham. Had he been told, but a very few months previously, by some plain-speaking and clear-seeing cynic, that he would one day commit an act which the polite world has agreed to brand as dishonourable, he would have listened to the prophecy with silent contempt; had he been further told that he would commit this act under the impulse of an ignoble jealousy, he would have laughed the idea to scorn. For all that, he had to-day been both shamefully dishonourable and unmistakably jealous. The effect of the unconsidered act could not but prove most disastrous to himself. If previously he had renounced the guidance of principle, he had at all events been tolerably well led by pride and prudence in the same paths in which the former would have guided him; now that he had absolutely set principle at defiance, his pride would henceforth be his evil genius, bidding him look with contempt upon the rules of morality he had hitherto observed, whilst his prudence would only serve him in keeping secret the outrages of which he might be guilty. Had he been twenty years younger, it is just possible that this act of dishonour with its altogether futile results might have proved such a salutary lesson that, with the help of that new and strong passion which was for the first time taking possession of his being, it might have effected a wholesome revolution in his views of life. As it was, such a result was impossible. The man was too hardened in his career of eternal scepticism. For the future, instead of being a mere sceptic, he would be a hypocrite, a character still more despicable. But nature, whose dictates he had so long violated, had prepared a severe punishment for him. Henceforth, Mr. Gresham is rather a subject for pity than indignation.

When he and Helen met at dinner on the following evening, the latter's first remark caused him acute suffering.

"It is a curious thing," she said, looking directly at her guardian, "Mr. Heatherley tells me that he posted a letter for me yesterday, about noon, which I ought to have received by one of the evening posts. Yet it has never come."

"Very curious," replied Mr. Gresham, forcing himself to return her direct gaze. "Have you made enquiry of the servants?"

"Yes. They tell me we had no letters yesterday except by the morning post. No doubt it is the fault of the post office. Have you ever failed to receive letters?"

"Once or twice, I think, at long intervals. But never anything of consequence. I hope your letter was not important?"

"Oh, no; not at all. Merely a note in reference to my evening classes. I begin on Tuesday, Mr. Gresham."

"What sort of pupils shall you have?" asked Mr. Gresham, relieved at length, and smiling in the usual manner

"Mostly grown up girls. Girls who are hard at work all day, poor things, and have never had the opportunity of learning to read and write."

"What are your hours?"

"From eight to ten, using a room in the chapel for school-room. You cannot imagine the pleasure with which I look forward to these lessons. As the attendance is of course purely voluntary, I know I shall have some capital scholars. And then I hope by degrees to be able to find better situations for those who show themselves able and industrious. Mr. Heatherley is doing his best to interest several ladies in the scheme, whose help will be very useful."

"But eight to ten!" exclaimed Mr. Gresham. "That is horribly late, Helen. You won't be home till eleven. Do you consider it altogether ladylike to be travelling about London, alone, at such hours?"

"I certainly see no objection to it," replied Helen, "when one's engagements make it necessary."

"H'm. You are aware, I presume, that young ladies do not, as a rule, permit themselves to indulge in such night excursions; that, in fact, it is hardly considered *bon ton?*"

"The ordinances of so-called society concern me very little, as you know, Mr. Gresham. As yet I am unconscious of having in any way neglected propriety. It is only between the chapel and the station that there could be any real danger for me, and in that walk Mr. Heatherley will always be kind enough to accompany me. It happens to lie in his way as he goes home."

Mr. Gresham flinched visibly at these words, and endeavoured, by raising his glass to drink, to conceal the expression which rose involuntarily to his countenance. He made no reply, and the meal continued in silence.

As they rose, at its conclusion, Helen asked whether Mr. Gresham had yet decided upon leaving town.

" I find I have too much work on hand," he replied. " I shall not leave town at all."

" Indeed ? I am sorry."

" I wrote last night to my aunt, Mrs. Cumberbatch," he continued. " In all probability I shall have a reply to-morrow morning. I hope it will be favourable."

Helen said nothing, but left the room, pondering on the possible character of Mrs. Cumberbatch. Mr. Gresham, unable to find rest at home, went out very shortly and passed his evening at the theatre.

On the following morning the anticipated letter arrived, bringing the news that Mrs. Cumberbatch, after mature reflection, had decided to accept her nephew's proposition. As it happened, she was just then on the point of removing from her house, so that it only remained for her to dispose of her furniture and come at once to London. In all probability she would present herself at the house in Portland Place in not later than a week.

After hearing her guardian read this letter, Helen went up to her sitting-room. She purposely left her door slightly ajar, and when at ten o'clock she recognised the footstep of Arthur Golding passing by and entering the studio, which was on the same landing, she left her room and followed him.

"Have you heard anything from Mr. Tollady lately," she asked, "with regard to Mrs. Thomson?"

This, as the reader will perhaps remember, was the woman Helen had assisted at the printer's request.

"Yes," replied Arthur, who had been startled by Helen's entrance, his pulses throbbing with delight at the sound of her voice. "Only this morning Mr. Tollady told me that she was getting better every day, and able to do more work. She is very anxious to see you, Miss Norman, and to thank you with her own mouth for your kindness to her."

"I am so glad to hear she is better!" exclaimed Helen. "I must see Mr. Tollady again very shortly; perhaps he has found some other poor people for me."

"I am afraid he is himself far from well,"

said Arthur, only venturing to glance for a moment at the face before him.

"Not well!" exclaimed Helen, in a tone of pained surprise. "What is he suffering from?"

"I hardly know. A short time ago, after we had been a rather long walk together, he fainted as soon as he entered the house. The same thing happened again last night, and this morning I left him seeming very depressed."

"But has he seen a physician?"

"I think not. He makes light of it, and says that it is only what he must expect now he is growing old. But it makes me very uneasy."

"But he must certainly have advice, Mr. Golding," urged Helen, earnestly, "I am sure his life is of far too much value to be lightly risked. Pray tell him this from me, will you? Say that I beg he will consult a doctor."

"I have myself frequently urged him to do so," replied Arthur, feeding his eyes upon the speaker's beauty, thus heightened by emotion, "but he always puts me off with a good-natured excuse. Perhaps your request will weigh more with him. It is very kind of you to express so much interest in his welfare."

"I must see him," pursued Helen. "Though I have only spoken with him once, I feel as if I had known him all my life. It is only noble natures that can inspire such confidence."

"And only noble natures, Miss Norman, that are so quick to recognise nobility in others. You do not exaggerate Mr. Tollady's goodness. I have not seen a day pass for several years without some act of kindness on his part to those who were in need of it."

For a moment their eyes met. The sincere feeling with which the young man spoke gave to his countenance a striking vivacity, and Helen saw in its expression a spirit in closer sympathy with her own than any she had discerned elsewhere. When Arthur turned his head away, she followed his look, and her eyes fell upon the picture he was then working at. It was a copy of a small Rembrandt which Mr. Gresham possessed. She bent forward to examine it.

"You are making wonderful progress," she said, frankly. "To my uncritical eyes this piece that is finished seems scarcely inferior to the original. I envy you your talent, Mr. Golding."

The last words were spoken warmly, with a look which avouched their genuineness. Arthur's reply followed rapidly, and in eager tones—

"You envy me, Miss Norman; you, who are so richly endowed with every excellent quality, envy another's trifling facility in handling a brush or a pencil? It may excite your wonder, perhaps, but never your envy !"

"That is hardly fair, Mr. Golding," said Helen, smiling. "I spoke truth, and you reply to me with flattery. Let me advise you, if it is not too great a liberty, never to depreciate your art. In your estimation nothing should excel it. You will be more zealous for its claims some day, when you become one of its foremost representatives."

And nodding a pleasant good-morning she left the studio. For some seconds Arthur remained gazing at the door through which she had disappeared, with passionate longing and regret depicted upon his countenance, then, with a deep sigh, passed his hand over his eyes, as if to prepare them for their ordinary functions, and hurried to his work.

It happened that the studio had two doors, the one ordinarily used, which led out into the landing ; the other, at present concealed behind an easel supporting a large canvas, which communicated with Mr. Gresham's dressing-room. Through this latter Mr. Gresham had passed a few minutes before Arthur entered the studio, and had left it very slightly ajar, but quite sufficiently to admit of his becoming acquainted with every word of the conversation between his pupil and his ward. He had no scruples in listening ; in his present state of mind would have had none even if the act had been far more

objectionable, than, considering his relationship to Helen, it in reality was. What he had
heard, innocent and meaningless as it
would have sounded to any less interested
auditor, inflicted upon him the keenest
torture. That Helen should so far transgress the bounds of conventional propriety as
to enter into conversation under such circumstances at all, was alone sufficient to
aggravate his new-born intolerance ; that the
conversation should terminate in what he
regarded as unwarrantable familiarities
exasperated him almost beyond endurance.
For a full half-hour he sat in his dressing-
room, exerting his utmost ingenuity in the
devising of self-torment. Doubtless she was
in the habit of indulging in these morning
interviews. No doubt, also, she saw Golding at other times, when he knew nothing of
it ; for what considerations could restrain a
girl who openly defied all social regulations.
These same social regulations which he had
hitherto looked upon with such scorn, how
he now respected them in his heart, how
convinced he was of their propriety and
necessity ! Yet how was it possible for him
to begin to assert his authority as guardian
for the purpose of compelling Helen to observe them. It would be to stultify himself,
nothing less. He thought with exasperation
of her spending all the day in going from
place to place alone, making acquaintances of

which he knew nothing, meeting with respect and admiration which he had no means of checking. For, had he possessed the power, he would have reduced her to the condition of a Turkish slave, allowing her to see, and be seen by no one ; so fiercely had his involuntary infatuation begun its operation upon him.

That morning he did not visit the studio at all, sending a servant to excuse him to Arthur on the ground of other engagements. He felt it would be impossible to face his pupil with any degree of calmness, and an acute feeling of shame, which was but a little less strong than his jealousy, withheld him from any risk of self-exposure.

The same evening Helen fulfilled her intention of visiting Mr. Tollady. Arthur was again away from home, and Mr. Tollady, when he had submitted to his visitor's pressing interrogations with regard to his health, turned the conversation by asking what she thought of Arthur's progress in the studio.

"It is impossible to speak too hopefully of it, Mr. Tollady," she replied. "I have been delighted with what little I have seen of his work. I suppose you have many pictures of his here ? "

"A great many drawings," replied the old man, with that air of justifiable pride which always marked his tone when he spoke of Arthur. "It is possible you would like to see a few, Miss Norman ? "

"If it would not be taking too great a freedom in Mr. Golding's absence," replied Helen.

"It is one of the greatest pleasures my life affords me to look over his work," said the printer. "I frequently take down his portfolios when I am alone. But it is so seldom that I have the opportunity of looking over them with anyone capable of appreciating their merits that you will confer a real favour on me, Miss Norman, by allowing me to show them to you."

He went up accordingly to Arthur's room, and brought down the portfolios which held the young artist's work. The first they opened was full of copies, some in crayon, some in sepia or Indian-ink, of celebrated pictures by old masters.

"It is Arthur's habit to make copies such as these," said Mr. Tollady, as he turned them over with a loving hand, "whenever he meets with engravings of old pictures in books or elsewhere. His collection will soon be a large one. Ah! Here are his copies of Raphael's Cartoons. Are they not admirably finished? There is a Madonna of Correggio; the original is in the Museum of Parma. I always think he has caught the expression of the child's face wonderfully. Here are a series of pen and ink copies from Albert Dürer, grand old pictures, and finely drawn."

They passed on to another portfolio.

" That is a copy of an etching by Nasmyth, 'The Alchemist.' It took Arthur more than a week's hard work, there is such an immense amount of detail in it. You like it? I knew you would. Ah! Here are a few water-colours. I like that copy of Rosa Bonheur; the sheep are admirable. I often laugh at my learning in these matters, Miss Norman. Arthur has made quite a connoisseur of me."

The next portfolio was a smaller one, and contained only a few drawings, most of them in pencil.

" These," said Mr. Tollady, with a smile of peculiar delight, and with a confidential lowering of his voice, " these are his original designs. He has made a great number at different times, but there are only a few that he has cared to preserve. Indeed he often destroys drawings which I think admirable. These are a series illustrating Shelley's 'Witch of Atlas.' It was a bold flight to undertake, but I notice that Arthur is most at home at regions farthest removed from the earth. It seems to me there is much of delicate fancy in these drawings. What is your opinion, Miss Norman?"

" I should say they were quite admirable. I certainly never saw illustrations of the poem which at all approached them. I know they are defective in drawing here and there," she added, " but the ideas are wonderful in each case."

" Here again," went on Mr. Tollady, his face beaming with pleasure, " are a few sketches of subjects from Scott. There is Rob Roy's wife challenging the invaders from the top of the rocks. There is astonishing force in that woman's attitude. That is meant for a portrait of Habbakuk Mucklewrath. Ha, ha! I always think that capital. There is the Master of Ravenswood on his last ride."

And so the old man went on, pointing out all the merits of the drawings—and indeed the merits were not few—delighted whenever Helen put in an assent or expressed herself pleased. When they came to the last of the four portfolios, he exclaimed—

" What have we in this other ? He has been making some changes here lately. It is a portrait, carefully mounted, too. Why, it is—"

Indeed it was no other than Arthur's memory-drawn portrait of Helen. She saw it, and blushed deeply.

" I did not know you had favoured him with a sitting," said the old man, regarding Helen with wonderful *naïveté*. " But it is an admirable likeness, though so slight."

" I never did," replied Helen, in some confusion. " It—it must be some picture he has copied which bears some slight likeness to me. Have we seen all, Mr. Tollady ? "

" Those are all his finished drawings. He has an abundance of crayon studies from casts, and of sketches from nature, but those I know he does not like to be seen.   He calls them his *chips*."

And Mr. Tollady laughed with a quiet gaiety of heart which only appeared when he spoke of Arthur.   A little conversation followed with regard to the poor people in whom the printer was interested, and then, leaving half-a-sovereign for one of these, Helen took her leave.   She walked thoughtfully homewards, not unfrequently smiling to herself, as if her reflections were far from disagreeable.   Throughout the evening she was *distraite*, being wholly unconscious that her guardian scarcely averted his eyes from her during dinner, and replying to his few questions in an absent manner which goaded him to hardly repressible irritation.   But Helen was not aware of his feeling.   When she retired to her room, it was with the intention of reading a new volume of poems she had just purchased, but the lines seemed to her lacking in inspiration.   There are certain moods in which even the loftiest verse seems poor to us compared with the odes and poems which nature is chanting within our own hearts ; and in such a mood Helen Norman found herself to-night.

The next day was Sunday.

" Will you read to me for an hour or two this morning, Helen ? " Mr. Gresham asked, at breakfast.

It was a scheme which had just entered his head for keeping his ward near him.

Helen assented, and they shortly met in the studio, which was Mr. Gresham's favourite room at all times. After looking round the room as if in search of something, as soon as she entered Helen asked—

"Did Mr. Golding take away his picture yesterday?"

"I suppose so," replied Mr. Gresham, averting his face, and endeavouring to speak with indifference. It was only a few minutes ago that he had taken the picture in question from the easel and placed it with its face leaning against the wall, because he could not bear to have it before his eyes.

"I am sorry," said his ward. "I wished to look at it again."

Then she proceeded to tell her guardian of the treat she had enjoyed on the previous evening in looking at Arthur Golding's drawings. Every word of praise she uttered was torture to her hearer, but he mastered his feelings with a great effort and succeeded in keeping the slightly sneering smile upon his features unbroken.

"Golding will never make an artist," he said, with all the calmness of a habitual calumniator, though such had hitherto by no means been his character. A somewhat contemptuous universal toleration had always marked his criticisms; and in Arthur's case, that portion of genuine artistic feeling which he undoubtedly possessed had made him at first even sincerely laudatory. But the change which had for weeks been developing itself within him now began to make itself openly seen, and imparted a sincerity to many of his remarks which could hardly be mistaken.

On hearing him speak thus of Arthur, Helen looked at him in surprise.

" Never make an artist, Mr. Gresham ? "

" Not he. He has no perseverance. He takes offence at my slightest corrections, and not unfrequently shows hastiness of temper. I shouldn't be surprised if he thanked me for my trouble and went off about his business one of these days."

He had begun to speak with his eyes firmly fixed on Helen's, but could not support her gaze to the end. In his heart he trembled lest her clear intelligence, of which he had always stood in awe, should see through his narrow disguise of words and pierce down to his inner purpose. Helen made no reply, however, save a pained look of infinite surprise. At Mr. Gresham's request she began to read, and continued for about an hour, the former standing at an easel the while and painting. At the end of that time he suddenly laid down his pallet and brushes, and stood with a satisfied smile upon his face till a pause came in the reading.

" There," he said, " we have had our

first sitting. Will you inspect the result, Helen?"

Helen rose, surprised, and, on looking at the canvas at which the artist had been engaged, saw the first outline of her own face. She did not know whether to appear pleased or annoyed, for, in truth, she was neither; the matter was indifferent to her.

"Does it please you?" asked Mr. Gresham.

"Any opinion would be premature," she answered. "Besides, I am, in any case, the worst person to consult with regard to my own portrait. Shall I continue to read, Mr. Gresham?"

For a moment the artist's lips worked, as if under some keen inward emotion, and once he raised his eyes with a serious expression, seeming about to speak. But a momentary paleness, followed by a flush, was the only result of this hesitation. He nodded merely, and Helen resumed her book.

When Arthur entered the studio on the following morning Mr. Gresham was in his dressing-room, purposely. The door was left slightly open, and an easel arranged in front of it so as still to permit a clear view of all that the artist desired to see. The first object that met Arthur's eyes on entering was the newly-commenced portrait. He could not help seeing it, one person well knew. He started as he recognised the likeness, then gazed at it long and intensely. Not one of the shades of expression which passed over his countenance escaped the notice of the watcher in the dressing-room.

Five minutes after Mr. Gresham entered the studio as usual. His reply to Arthur's " Good-morning" was a trifle curt, and he continued throughout the morning somewhat abstracted in manner. Not unfrequently he glanced searching looks at his pupil, when the latter was closely occupied with his work, and each look was more lowering than the last. When Arthur requested his assistance he replied in the briefest possible manner, scarcely turning his head whilst he spoke; and whilst it yet wanted nearly half an hour to the usual time for the former's departure, he consulted his watch and excused himself on the plea of an engagement.

Arthur, whose temperament was keenly sensitive to the least slight, noticed these changes and did not cease during the rest of the day to distress himself in searching for an explanation of them. On the following morning, Mr. Gresham's inattention was yet more marked; it amounted to plain incivility. It was Arthur's way to be explicit in matters that nearly concerned him, and just before he left he could not resist speaking out the thought that had troubled him.

" I fear, sir," he said, speaking in decided, though respectful tones, " that I have been so unfortunate as to offend you. May I beg you to tell me how?"

"Offend me, Mr. Golding?" returned the artist, with a curl of the lip. "I scarcely understand you."

"Your altered manner to me yesterday and to-day," pursued the young man, and somewhat irritated by the ill-concealed contempt of the other's manner, "appeared to me only to admit of that explanation."

"Do you refer to my correcting a mistake in your colouring?" asked Mr. Gresham, without turning from his canvas. "I have noticed that you seemed to resent my interference of late. Perhaps it would be better if you finished the picture without consulting me, and then allow me to criticise it at the end."

"I certainly was not aware that I received your remarks otherwise than with gratitude, Mr. Gresham," replied the young man, with quiet dignity. "I much regret it if I should have given you reason to think me disrespectful."

"I am sorry I have not time to discuss terms with you," said the artist, consulting his watch. "I find I must leave you, for the present, to the guidance of your own genius. And, bye-the-by, I am sorry I shall not be able to see you to-morrow. I am engaged during the morning."

So saying he left the studio, and Arthur

retraced his way slowly to Charlotte Place, half-grieved, half-angry, and altogether astonished at what had occurred. He scarcely knew whether he should return to the studio again. At all events he would tell Mr. Tollady what had happened, and ask his advice. Something must have occurred to annoy Mr. Gresham, in which case the next meeting would be sure to bring with it an explanation from him. To this, at least, Arthur felt he had a right. He forgot that superiority of social standing brings with it a licence in the matter of insults quite unknown to those whose civil bearing is the only test of their respectability.

CHAPTER VI.

THE STORY OF A LIFE.

When Arthur reached the shop he found Mr. Tollady standing in the doorway with his hat on, as if prepared to go out.

"Could you sit in the parlour for about an hour, Arthur?" he asked; "I have to go into the City."

Arthur looked up and saw that the old man's face was much paler than usual and wore a haggard look. As he took out his watch to see the time his hand trembled perceptibly. He had the appearance of a man just risen from a bed of sickness.

"Isn't the business such that I could see to for you?" asked Arthur. "You don't look well, Mr. Tollady. It is too far for you to go this hot day."

"No, my dear boy; no, thank you," replied the old man, with a forced smile. "I must see to it myself—myself. I hope not to be long. Have dinner as usual, of course. I have just had a mouthful of lunch and that will serve me till tea-time."

Arthur brought down his drawing-board to the back parlour, and tried to get on with his work. But reflection upon his own sources of annoyance and on Mr. Tollady's evident suffering, the cause of which the old man persisted in keeping a secret, held his thoughts from the subject in hand. The time went very slowly; it seemed as though the printer would never return. When, at length, Mr. Tollady re-entered the shop, about three o'clock, it was in a state of exhaustion which he in vain endeavoured to conceal. Dropping his trembling limbs into the wonted chair, he let his head fall backwards, and sat gazing at the ceiling in a manner which seemed to bespeak lethargy both of mind and of body. Arthur walked to his side, when he had sat thus for a few minutes, and laid his hand upon his shoulder.

"Let me persuade you to lie down upon the bed for an hour," he said, in an affectionate tone. "It pains me to see you like this, Mr. Tollady. Have you no regard for me that you refuse to pay more attention to your health, though I every day beg you to? Your face is as pale as death; I can see you are suffering. I am neglecting my duty in allowing you to remain without advice. Will you let me go and ask a doctor to see you? I am determined to do so on my own account if you leave it later than to-night."

"You shall have your way, Arthur," replied the old man, smiling feebly. "I have such pains here on my left side; just now they are very severe. I will go to the hospital to-morrow morning; I shall have better advice there. Let me rest a little now. Can you continue to draw here?"

"No, I cannot, Mr. Tollady!" exclaimed Arthur, as he saw the other pressing his hand against his side, and turning his face away to conceal its expression. "I cannot do anything whilst I see you suffer so! I am sure that you are suffering in your mind as well as in your body. This business you have been seeing to has distressed you, it has been burdening you for a long time. Are you sure that you do wisely in keeping it from me? Are you sure I could not help you in it? Yo do not still consider me a boy, in whom you cannot confide?"

Mr. Tollady held down his head in reflection for some moments, then he took Arthur's hand and pressed it.

"I believe you are right, Arthur," he said. "It is not because I have not the fullest confidence in you that I have hidden from you this burden on my life; I kept it to myself to spare you needless trouble. But, perhaps, it was not wise to do so; sooner or later you must know, and I have several times been on the point of telling you lately. Go upstairs to your work as usual, Arthur, for the present. After tea we will have an hour's talk together. The pain has gone for the present; I feel better."

Accordingly, when tea was over, Arthur

remained downstairs in the parlour, where
Mr. Tollady also sat, the door being left open
in case of customers entering the shop. For
a long time the old man remained buried in
deep reverie, the expression of his face
changing as it was in turn lit by a gleam of
pleasure or darkened by the shadow of
gloomy recollections. Unfortunately the
shadows predominated, and from time to
time a slight sigh broke from between his
lips. At length the entrance of a customer
called Arthur away for a moment, and when
he returned Mr. Tollady had roused himself
from his abstraction, and was prepared to
speak.

"I have been thinking, Arthur," he commenced, "that it would not be amiss for me
to tell you the complete story of my life, now
that I have made up my mind to let you
know the trouble that has weighed upon me
for the last few years. For very nearly forty
years it has been a far from eventful life;
during that time I have always lived very
much as you have seen me. But my early
years were neither so quiet nor, I think I
may say, so profitably spent. As I look back
from my sixty-fifth year upon those far-off
memories, I can, at times, hardly believe that
it is my own history I am reviewing, so
utterly do I now find myself out of accord
with all the impulses which then guided me.
It is not, then, from any sense of pleasure

that I go back to my early days, but because I think there is a lesson to be learned from them. Every thoughtful man is capable of receiving benefit from the contemplation of other men's lives, and I feel sure you will see what warning may be derived from mine. It is, indeed, little less than a homily against a special vice that I am about to recite to you."

Arthur gazed at the speaker in surprise as he heard these words. It seemed so impossible to him to conceive of his deeply-respected friend as capable of being under the dominion of any vice. It was with a sense of pain at his heart that he listened whilst Mr. Tollady went on.

"I was born," he said, "at Ipswich, in 1805. It seems a long time ago, doesn't it, Arthur? In that year Scott published his 'Lay of the Last Minstrel'; then Byron was still at Cambridge, and Shelley, a boy at Eton. Can you believe that I was nine years old when 'Waverley' first appeared, and that I distinctly remember the delight with which my dear father then read it? It is like looking back upon a glorious dream to think of my boyhood, spent amid such wonders, both of peace and war. I remember hearing our friends talk of Wellington's victories in the Peninsula as matters of yesterday; it may be self-deception, but I have always been convinced that I could recollect my father's enthusiasm at the result of Bonaparte's Russian campaign, when I was seven; and Waterloo, with all its wild excitement at home and abroad, is yet vivid in my mind. For you, Arthur, these are all matters of history, for me they seem dear and precious remembrances of a happy time that has gone for ever.

"My father was a bookseller, and, if only he had possessed the means, would have been an excellent publisher. With him, his trade was something far more than a mere mechanical occupation, the chief end of which was to secure daily bread. Rather, he regarded it as a means for the elevation of himself and all those with whom he had business or friendship. There was not a book in his shop of which he did not possess some accurate knowledge, quite distinct from those technicalities of the trade which a bookseller usually possesses. His books were living souls in his eyes, and on me, his only child, he never ceased to impress that to damage a book was to commit a sin. 'Books are men's brains' he would say, and I shall never forget a favourite quotation of his from Milton, often uttered to me when I was a child, and intended, of course, to be taken by me in the literal sense: 'As good almost kill a man as kill a good book. Who kills a man, kills a reasonable creature, God's image; but he who destroys a good book kills Reason itself; kills the image of God, as it were, in the eye. Many a man lives a burden to the earth; but a good book is the precious life-blood of a master-spirit, embalmed and treasured up on purpose to a life beyond life.' I had to write that passage out ten times for him on one occasion, when I had wantonly torn to pieces an old volume of 'Don Quixote,' which had strayed out of its proper place.

"I was sent to a day-school at Ipswich, where, I am sorry to say, that I did not learn much besides Greek and Latin; in those days they were alone thought worthy of being seriously taught; but I learned at home what a multitude of other things the world contained of vastly more interest than Virgil and Homer, and I had in after life to add to my education by pursuing such courses of reading as my tastes naturally led me to. For beyond the age of fifteen I did not remain at school. When I was so old my father died.

"He had been far too charitable and too generous to his own family to have saved much money, and one of the first things I learned after the funeral was that I should not return to a school. I cannot say that I was sorry to hear it; in those days the fervour of boyhood was added to a naturally adventurous disposition, and I felt decided pleasure in looking forward to so great a

change as was involved in beginning to work
for my living.

"The sale of the house and business
brought my mother a little money, with the
aid of which she established herself as a dress-
maker, whilst I was apprenticed to a printer.
When my time was out I became assistant to
the same man, and thus I worked on till I
reached my twenty-first year.

"Those six years were among the most
miserable of my life. I detested my business, and would gladly have run away if I
had had the least idea where to go or what
to do. Day after day I made my poor mother
wretched with my selfish complainings, whilst
she was all the while working hard to keep
us both in some degree of comfort. I was
but a boy, and had no eyes for my mother's
sufferings.

"I think it would be impossible for any
youth to be more selfish than I was during
these years. I had no thought but for my
own annoyances, my own wishes and plans,
and many an evening did I embitter for my
mother by spending it in unceasing com-
plaints of our poverty, and descriptions of
the indescribably selfish things I would do
if I were once rich. All my dear father's
lessons seemed to have passed away from my
mind. I hate myself when I look back at
these years. How heartless, how despicable
I must have been!

"But at last came my twenty-first year, and with it came the news from my mother that an uncle of mine, who had died two years before, had left me a thousand pounds. I thought I should have gone mad when I heard this. A thousand pounds was for me a fortune. My visions were realised, and I was rich.

"In vain did my poor mother try to make me sensible, to advise me as to the use I ought to make of this money, to put before me, though in no selfish manner, the help it would be to her if I were to settle down in a business of my own, live with her still, and do my best to thrive. I was utterly deaf to all this. One idea alone possessed me, and that was a desire to see the world. For years this had been my ardent wish, and now I had the power of fulfilling it.

"When my mother heard this purpose she sighed and went away to her own room, doubtless to weep. I thought nothing of her grief. I do not believe that even then I was base and hard-hearted. The truth was that I did not realise my mother's position; I knew nothing of the world, and could not deem it possible that she had serious need of my assistance, though such was indeed the case. She was too fond of me to hold out long against my determination, and so, with many promises to write frequently, and not to be away more than a few months, I set off to see foreign countries. Was there ever such a young madman?

"I was away three whole years. I saw something of most countries of Europe, of India, and of America. Everywhere I lived as cheaply as possible, and in one or two cases I worked my passage from country to country. Often do I re-travel in thought over all that I saw in those three years, and, separated from the other circumstances of my life, how delightful is the memory of it to me.

"The mountains and the valleys of Switzerland became familiar to me, the grand old Italian cities, the vineyards, the blue Mediterranean, each place I came to I thought I should stop there for ever; but my eager and restless spirit drove me away. I walked through the streets of Athens, rushing thence to Constantinople, and thence again to the banks of the Ganges. I lived for a month at Benares, and can still see it as well as if I had been there yesterday; its bridge of boats across the river, its ghauts where I lounged and bathed, its numberless mosques and temples, its sacred bulls which roamed at will through the streets and bazaars, and over all that fierce Indian sun which so baked my skin that I often fancy it is still darker than that of most Europeans.

"Many other cities I wandered through, and I even saw the everlasting snow on the crests of the Himalayas. Thence I came back once more to Europe, passed over into Africa, saw the Nile. In Cairo I lived some weeks. How distinctly I can see its red-and-white minarets, its dark and narrow streets, and hear the eternal shouting of the hucksters and beggars. And the view from Mount Mokattam! There, as you looked eastward, stretched the long line of tombs, where the old caliphs sleep. To the west you saw the Nile, like a streak of silver, and, far away beyond, the distant Pyramids rising dim and ghostly out of the desert. Oh, the walks and rides at evening around this city, through the groves of fig-trees, of tamarisks, and acacias!

" After this the dream seems suddenly to change, and I find myself in Spain, rushing with an enthusiasm, that was almost frenzy, over the scenes I had learned to love years before in ' Don Quixote.' I was now comparatively near home, but I had not as yet been away two years, and not a thought of returning crossed my mind. I wrote occasionally to my mother, but did not expect to hear in return, so uncertain were my movements.

" The Atlantic was now before me, and I crossed it, working my passage in a French vessel from Marseilles. On arriving in the States, impatient of towns and all the evidence of civilisation, I plunged at once into the wilderness. For a long time I lived with an English family which had established itself in a spot nearly two hundred miles distant from any other settlement, and here I worked in the labour of clearing till I got weary of it. Then I visited Niagara, the vision of which still, at the distance of more than forty years, occasionally haunts my sleep; I saw the great lakes, and thence passed into Canada. But already I was growing weary of my mad restlessness.

"Very shortly I made my way back to New York, and arrived there just as my money came to an end. Now the business I had learned, and which I had formerly so much despised, stood me in good stead. For nearly half a year I worked as a printer, saving up till I should have enough money to return to England. That day at last came, and I once more crossed the Atlantic.

"I found myself again in Ipswich, after an absence of almost precisely three years. During my voyage homewards I had reflected much, and already a change was working in my inward nature; already that repentance for my folly was beginning which was to last to the end of my life.

"I reached my native town with a heart full of uneasy apprehensions. Should I find mother in health? Should I find her well-to-do, or poor? For the first time I reflected seriously upon her position, and asked myself how she had endeavoured to live during these years of my absence. Had it been wise in me to leave her so completely alone? For she had no relative of her own, and my father's relations all lived in other parts of England. A terrible uneasiness, the beginning of a dreadful self-reproach, seized upon me by degrees. Between my disembarkment at Liverpool and my arrival at Ipswich I neither ate nor slept; and in those days, you must remember, travelling was a very different thing from what it is now.

" I went to our old house, and saw at once that it was inhabited by strangers. I went thence to the house of my father's most intimate friend, and I found him dead. In an agony of apprehension I hurried to the house of another acquaintance, and here at length received intelligence. It was nearly a year and a half since my mother had left Ipswich for London, hoping to earn a better living than she was able to at home. I was told her address, and, after only an hour's pause for refreshment, started for London.

" Arthur, may you never suffer in your mind as I suffered during that journey. It is sufficient if I say that my punishment was proportionable to my fault, and *that*, as you have learned, was almost unpardonable.

" The address I sought was in a poor quarter in the East End, and, when I found it, appeared to be an ordinary lodging-house.

A girl who came to the door knew nothing of the name I asked for, but, on my requesting that she would make further inquiry in the house, she called down the landlady. This woman remembered my mother well enough. Mrs. Tollady, she told me, had lived with her about half a year, only occasionally paying her rent, and, to all appearances, making next to nothing out of her sewing. It was now some months since she had suddenly been taken with a serious illness, had been removed to the infirmary—and there had died."

Mr. Tollady again paused and sat long in silence, struggling with the bitter emotion which his story had awakened in himself.

Arthur knew not how to console him, and, a customer entering the shop, he was glad to withdraw from the room for a few minutes. When he returned, the printer roused himself from his depression, and smiled sadly.

" I did not think it would have cost me so much to tell you all this, Arthur," he said. " I had thought I could speak of it aloud with as much calmness as I have grown accustomed to go over the horrible story in my own mind, for there is not a day passes without its being all acted over afresh before me. Now you know the worst, and I feel relieved. I hope the pain it has given you will be compensated by the lesson my conduct teaches.

" I shall not endeavour to describe to you my state of mind during the months, nay, the years that followed. At first I seriously believe that I was as near suicide as ever man was who did not actually yield to the temptation. I woke night after night from hideous dreams, in which the figures of my father and mother appeared to me in all kinds of situations; now on the precipices overhanging Niagara, now on the top of one of the Pyramids, now in the dreadful silence of a western prairie, always with angry faces, cursing me for my selfish cruelty.

" How often I have dreamt that I fled before these terrible images, and, as the only means of escape, leaped wildly into the chaos of a terrific cataract—and then awaken only to bitterly regret that the dream was not true, and that I still lived in my agony.

" Well, by degrees my suffering lessened, as all suffering, sooner or later, must, and I began to think of how I should expiate the crime of a mother's murder, for of that I sincerely accounted myself guilty. At length I came to the resolution simply to do all the good in my power for my fellow-creatures, never to let a day go by without having assisted by word or deed someone who was in suffering and want.

" I was then earning my living as a journeyman printer in this very house. I did not earn very much; but out of that I forced myself to save enough to always have a few coppers in my pocket for charity. By degrees, too, I bought myself, a few second-hand books, among them most of the historians and the poets that you see now on my shelves, and, in what leisure time I could get, worked hard to improve my very defective education. And very thankful I am that I did so, as it has enabled me to help you a little, Arthur, in your own self-education.

" Well, well, all that happened a long time ago, long before you were born, and probably there is not a person now living who remembers me in those early days. I shall not trouble you with the story of my life from year to year; it was very quiet and uninteresting, for I never again left London, or this house, except for a long country walk now and then on Sunday, when I returned to my dear botanising, and by degrees made the collection we have so often looked over together.

" I must hurry on to the matter which just now most concerns me, the trouble which has led to my telling you the story of my life. You must know that for fifteen years I was employed by the same master, an excellent man, whom I truly loved and honoured, at the end of which time he took me into partnership with him. Our business was then a very good one, and seemed to promise constant improvement. Five years after becoming a partner, we were in a position to purchase together the house we worked in. Not two months after the completion of this purchase my dear old friend died—he was then sixty—and by will bequeathed his share in the house to me. So that the house became my own.

"For some years I continued to prosper in my business. I used to employ five men and a boy, and I even thought at times of removing to a larger place. But then, almost before I knew it, my profits began to decrease. I don't know whether it was that I was already growing old and losing my energy, or whether several other large printing-offices that had opened round here took away my customers. At all events, within three or four years I had dropped down to one man and a boy, and had scarcely employment for these. I was obliged to let the top part of the house, and, shortly after, to turn my office here into a shop, and become half newsvendor, half stationer, still, however, continuing to do whatever printing I could get.

"It was very shortly after this that you came to me, and I have no need to tell you how the business went on in succeeding years. One thing, however, happened, that you, of course, know nothing of. Seven years ago exactly I was visited by a man in a wretched state of poverty, who gave as his reason for calling on me the fact that he had had an uncle of my name. A little talk showed me that he was the son of my mother's brother, who had for many years been dead, but whose name I recognised at once when mentioned to me. He told me that he had been a publican, but had fallen on ill-luck, and had now nothing but the workhouse before him unless I could afford him help of some kind. It was impossible for me to give him any employment, but it was no less impossible to refuse assistance to a relative of my poor mother.

" I felt that I *must* do something for him ; I was not in very good health at the time, and conceived a sort of superstition that this man was sent to me as a means of atoning in some poor degree for the sins of my younger years. Giving him all the ready-money I then possessed, which was a very paltry sum, I requested him to see me again on the following day.

" In the meantime I went to the only wealthy acquaintance I possessed. This was Mr. Henry Waghorn, an elder brother of the Mr. Waghorn who has just married Miss Gresham. I had done a good deal of printing for him from time to time, and had found him a pleasant, straightforward, generous gentleman. Summoning all my boldness, I went to Mr. Waghorn, stated to him my need and asked him whether he would lend me a hundred pounds on the security of my house. Before he consented, he went on to question me in a most friendly manner about my own business. I told him frankly my position, and thereupon he offered to lend me three hundred pounds, so that I might have the advantage of a little capital for myself, with the assistance of which he thought I might revive my business. This I refused, but I was at length persuaded to accept of two hundred. This was secured by a mortgage on my house, by the terms of which it was arranged that the principal should be repaid in five years, during which time I was to pay at stated intervals a certain rate of interest.

"With the money I went off rejoicing. I spent half of it in establishing my relative in a coffee-house in Holborn, for he seemed best fitted for this, and he still does an excellent business. For a few weeks after I had so assisted him, he visited me occasionally, then he ceased to come entirely, and for more than six years he has never been near my shop."

"The ungrateful fellow!" exclaimed Arthur, indignantly. "And you say he prospers! 1 wonder you ever gave away another penny in charity."

"Not so, my dear boy," replied the old man, calmly. "Such cases of ingratitude are, happily, very rare, and a long life among the poor has convinced me that real gratitude is pretty certain to reward the vast majority of one's efforts do good. But I must hasten to the end of this miserable business. I continued to pay my interest regularly; but the prospect of having to pay the principal lay as a terrible burden night and day upon my mind. Notwithstanding the hundred pounds, my business showed no signs of improvement; I could not imagine how the money was to be paid.

"As the period drew year, I one day visited Mr. Waghorn and told him I feared he must take possession of my house, as I saw now no possibility of paying more than a small portion of the debt. But he behaved to me with noble generosity: 'We will say nothing about the principal when the time comes,' he said. 'You shall just continue to pay the interest, as you have been doing, and also pay a portion of the principal whenever you are able. Don't trouble your mind about it. I am rich, and can very well wait for my money.'

"After this he exerted himself to procure me customers, and with some success. That was just the time when you were beginning to be of great service to me, Arthur, and you remember our business throve better than it had done for a long time. To cut the tale short, I paid off portions of the principal by degrees, and by the beginning of last April owed only one hundred. But just then Mr. Waghorn died.

"His death has been a serious misfortune to me. Nearly all Mr. Henry Waghorn's property, it seems, has gone to his brother John, Miss Gresham's husband, and amongst it this mortgage on my house. Mr. John Waghorn is sadly different from his brother. Though he is now very wealthy, he has taken advantage of the fact that the period for the payment of his principal has gone by without any definite renewal, and yesterday he announced to me that the whole must be paid within three months from the present date, or, if not, he claims the house. There, you have the secret of my misery, Arthur. You know that I am utterly unable to pay this money, and—"

The old man did not finish the sentence, but sank back again into a state of sad reverie.

Arthur sprang to his feet, his blood·boiling with indignation.

"The mean rascal!" he exclaimed. "I felt sure that that was his character, even from the little I knew of him. I *knew* that his visits here were the cause of your suffering, that that mean face of his could bring nothing else! Will he not wait a year, half a year?"

"Not a moment longer than the three months. And he takes credit to himself for being so generous as to allow that, though I believe the law would compel it."

"A hundred pounds!" cried Arthur. "Why, it is nothing, after all. The miserable fellow shall have his hundred pounds, with interest and what not in the bargain, and then we will hiss him out of the shop. Do you forget that I am a rich man, Mr. Tollady?"

He laughed gaily as he spoke, endeavouring to cheer the old man; but the latter rose from his chair with a grave expression upon his face, and took Arthur's hands in his.

"I was prepared for this, Arthur," he said, "and prepared to resist it. If it had been possible to hide the affair from you completely I should have done so, but it was not. I could not allow you to try and obtain this money. I could not, indeed, Arthur."

"But why not?" cried the young man. "You know we have agreed that my interest, as Mr. Gresham pays it me quarterly, goes to our common expenses of whatever kind. Where is the harm in forestalling two or three quarters in order to keep a roof over our heads? Surely that is a very necessary expense, Mr. Tollady?"

"No, no. It is not just that you should suffer for my debts. We must not speak of it, Arthur."

"Suffer!" cried the other. "Whether do you think I shall suffer most, of the loss of a little money, or by seeing you driven out of house and home, and having myself to look out for a dwelling in a strange place when I love this old house so well? It is you that are unjust, Mr. Tollady! Will you not allow me to do this little service for you? Is it fair or right that you should keep the power of conferring kindnesses to yourself, and not allow me to exercise it when I can? I insist upon seeing Mr. Gresham before I go to bed to-night; you *must* allow me!"

Mr. Tollady still resisted, but was at length obliged to yield to Arthur's vehemence. Without a moment's delay the latter started out for Portland Place. Once or twice on the way he thought of what had occurred when he last saw Mr. Gresham, but that was a matter of such little importance compared with what he now had in hand that he dismissed all thought of it from his mind. He had not a doubt with regard to the success of his mission. His heart throbbed with the pleasure of being able to benefit his old friend.

At the same time Mr. Gresham was sitting alone in the library, in no very pleasant mood. As it was Tuesday night, Helen had gone to her evening school, a circumstance very distasteful to her guardian, who could now scarcely suffer her to be out of his sight. It irritated him to think that he was of so little account in her daily life, that her principal friends were people entirely strange to him, that her aims were of such a nature as altogether to exclude him from any participation in them. Every day, as his own uncontrollable passion continued to grow in vehemence, he clearly perceived that Helen became constantly more distant in her intercourse with him. He half suspected that he had betrayed his secret, and that his ward was adopting this method of discouraging him. The effect upon his temperament of this unceasing agitation—agitation all the more severe because he had never hitherto experienced anything of the kind—was to convert his equable cynic's mood by degrees into harshness and irritability. He was intensely angry with himself for nourishing a sentiment which he had hitherto ridiculed with such persistent sarcasm, and, with the injustice of a man whose only philosophy is founded on habitual deception of himself and the world, visited his bad temper on whosoever had the misfortune to be a safe object of insult. Love performs very curious metamorphoses on different characters, but perhaps its operations are almost always for the better. In the present case, however, this was not so. Whereas, Mr. Gresham had previously been only rather cold in temperament and a good deal affected, love had now made him mean and despicable.

When Arthur's visit was announced to him, he first bade the servant say he was from home, but the next moment altered his mind and ordered that he should be admitted. Accordingly Arthur appeared in the library.

"You come at an unusual time, Mr. Golding," said the artist, in a distant tone. "What can I do for you?"

"A great kindness, Mr. Gresham," returned Arthur, somewhat abashed by his reception, but determined to do his utmost. He then went on to relate the chief circumstances connected with Mr. Tollady's loan, and to describe the difficulties in which the printer at present found himself. The artist suddenly cut him short as he approached the end of the story—

"And the object of all this, Mr. Golding?" he said, abruptly. "Excuse me, but your tale is a trifle long and not as interesting as it might be."

"My object, sir," returned Arthur, preserving his calmness with a great effort, "is to endeavour to spare Mr. Tollady the severe suffering which is threatening him. It can be done so easily. If you would so deeply oblige me as to allow me the use of the sum I need, advancing it upon the interest which will fall due to me this year and next, this claim could then be satisfied, and a very deserving man would be freed from the danger of being driven out of house and home. Mr. Tollady is sixty-five years old, and in very feeble health. I dread to think of the result of his having to seek a new home, and perhaps a new occupation, under such circumstances as these."

The young man paused, and, keeping his eyes steadily fixed on Mr. Gresham's face, waited a reply with a throbbing heart.

"I am very sorry, Mr. Golding," returned the artist, with a rather malicious sneer, "but I am altogether unable to comply with this request. I must beg you to remember that your legacy is not, strictly speaking, due to you till you become of age, which you will not do for about a year and a half. Thinking the money might be of use to you I took upon myself the responsibility of paying the interest before you could really claim it. I have no objection to continue doing so, but I should not feel justified in advancing large sums to you. It is quite impossible."

A sudden chill passed over the young man's frame as he heard these words pronounced, but the next moment he flushed hot with righteous anger at the insulting manner in which he had been reminded of his dependent position. Close upon the anger followed intolerable shame. For a moment he turned away, and with difficulty kept back the tears from rushing to his eyes. Then again came the memory of Mr. Tollady, and bitter disappointment took the place of all other feelings.

"I am sorry you cannot do this kindness for me, Mr. Gresham," he suddenly exclaimed, "but perhaps I should not have ventured to ask it, it was requesting too much. But you have it in your power to help us in another way, if you will. I cannot think that you will refuse to do so. Mr. Waghorn is now your son-in-law. Will you ask him to put off this claim for another year? I am sure you will do me this kindness, sir? Mr. Waghorn has no need of this money. A hundred pounds are scarcely as much to him as one pound is to Mr. Tollady. Will you ask him to give us a year longer. I am sure we can pay off the debt in that time. Only a year!"

Arthur forgot everything in the eagerness of his pleading. He felt that this was his last resource. Should this fail him, he knew not what evils might ensue. His impassioned tones and the glow which mantled his fine features as he spoke would have vanquished any ordinary obduracy. But Mr. Gresham's jealousy was by no means an ordinary obstacle. It showed no sign of yielding.

"I am really very unfortunate, Mr. Golding," replied the artist, "in my utter inability to serve you. Though Mr. Waghorn, as you remind me, is now my relative, I have absolutely no concern in his private affairs. He is at present on the Continent, too, and I could not apply to him if I wished. I am sure you will see that it is impossible for me to do what you wish."

Arthur was beginning to speak again, but Mr. Gresham interrupted him.

"I regret that I have no time at present for further conversation, Mr. Golding," he said. "Indeed I have already allowed you to detain me too long. I must really say good-night. Bye-the-by, you remember that I am engaged to-morrow?"

Arthur rose to his full height, looked for a moment sternly into the artist's face with a look before which the latter dropped his eyes, then bowed and left the room without a word, with the same stern expression on his countenance. With set lips, clenched fists, and throbbing veins, he walked rapidly along the streets homewards. Already he had made up his mind what to do. The very next morning he would say good-bye to his painting for ever and henceforth would devote himself to his dear benefactor. His exact plan of conduct this was no moment for deciding. Sufficient that he knew his duty and was determined to perform it.

When he reached Charlotte Place he was surprised to find that the shop was not lit up as usual, for by this time it was quite dark. Stepping quickly inside he saw that the parlour at the back was also in darkness. All at once every drop of blood in his body seemed to rush to his heart, he gasped for breath. Manning himself with a desperate effort he stepped to the parlour door and

called Mr. Tollady's name. There was no
reply. He ran to the foot of the stairs and
called repeatedly and loudly, the perspiration
breaking out upon his body in the intensity
of his nameless dreads. Still no reply came.
Hurrying back through the darkness into the
shop, he groped for the matches in their
usual place and hurriedly struck a light.
With this burning in his hand he entered the
parlour. He had just time to see that Mr.
Tollady was sitting in his arm-chair, when
the match went out. He struck another, and
with it lit a candle that stood on the mantel-
piece; then drew near to the printer, and,
thinking him asleep, laid his hand upon his
shoulder to shake him. As he did so, the
old man fell forward into his arms. Arthur
hastily raised him, and held the candle close
to his face, calling his name the while in loud
and rapid tones. But not a breath stirred
the flame; there was no intelligence in the
clear eyes which seemed to regard their questioner: Mr. Tollady was dead.

CHAPTER VII.

THE SHADOW OF DEATH.

SPEECHLESS and horror-stricken, Arthur Golding stood for full a minute, holding with his right hand the dead man upright in the chair, while the candle, still close to the pale features, trembled in his left. Involuntarily he had endeavoured to give utterance to a cry of pain and terror, but, though his lips were widely parted, no sound escaped them. The eyes of the corpse were still open, and seemed to gaze upon him with a resemblance to life which held him fixed as with a horrible charm. At length he forced himself to turn away and put down the light upon the table; then he once more leaned his ear close against the breathless lips, and, suddenly seized with terror at the dreadful silence, fled from the room out into the street. A minute brought him to the shop of John Pether, the umbrella mender, into which he burst with breathless haste.

John Pether was sitting in the little room which formed his shop, upon a low stool, closely engaged in divesting an old umbrella of its last strips of tattered silk. A small oil lamp stood upon a very ricketty table, and

its light fell strongly upon his features, showing all their grim and sallow meagreness with
hideous effect against the dark background
of the rest of the shop. The wine-coloured
stain upon his left cheek seemed more than
usually distinct to-night, and as he sat working he bit his lips with a species of ferocity.
His face was strongly smeared with grime,
and his long, skeleton-like hands, which rent
the silk as if they took a pleasure in destruction, were black and hairy like those of a
gorilla. The effect of his eyes, as he turned
them upon Arthur's sudden entrance, was
that of two very small black spots in the
centre of two spheres of gleaming white.
On hearing the young man's stammered
words of explanation, he rose from his stool,
interlacing his long fingers, and stood leaning
forward with an expression upon his face as
if he not yet understood what had happened.

" Mr. Tollady ill, you say?" he asked, in
the slow, hollow tones of one who is not accustomed to speak much.

" He is dead!" cried Arthur. " I can see
no trace of life! Come with me and look!"

John Pether followed him immediately, and
they entered the dark shop together. There
in the back parlour they found the corpse
sitting upright in the chair, the candle faintly
illumining the room. The umbrella-mender
took the light, and, as Arthur had done,
approached it to Mr. Tollady's face. In a

moment he set it down again and faced his companion.

"Dead," he remarked, with hollow emphasis. "How did it happen?"

Arthur recounted the events of the evening as far as Mr. Tollady was concerned, whilst John Pether still kept his eyes fixed upon the corpse.

"Heart-disease, no doubt," added the latter, when the young man had finished. "I have expected it for years. Help me to lay him upon the bed."

Together they lifted up the old man's body and laid it down again upon the bed, which they previously opened out.

"He had an easy death," said John Pether, gloomily, regarding the calm and noble countenance. "May we die as easily."

Again he bent over the prostrate body, and Arthur, half awed at his gloomy impassibility, stood regarding him. As he watched he saw a change come over the seared features, passion seemed to convulse them and to pass over the man's entire body, making him tremble in every limb. Then the hollow voice once more broke the silence, but speaking with a terrible concentration of energy which almost froze the hearer's blood.

"Another gone," it said. "Another trodden down into the grave in the struggle against the tyranny of kings and princes, of idle lords, and all the pestilent army of the rich, whose rank breath poisons the bitter crust they throw to us! How many more, how many more of us shall perish before we learn the courage of the dog which leaps at its tormentor's throat? Year after year I have watched you, Samuel Tollady, starving yourself that half a dozen of us feeble wretches should creep on a few paces longer before we dropped into the gutter and died; year after year I have known you a friend to those of us whom hunger and despair had made worse than savage beasts, always bidding us remember we were men and hope that we should some day have our rights; year after year you have toiled without ceasing for others, and at last despair of helping all you could has killed you. How many more, how many more? You fought it out well to the end, Samuel Tollady, but you have lost. You were too kind, too good, too tender for a fight like this. Your voice was as little able to call back freedom or justice to the earth as this candle that lights up your dead face would be to take the place of the sun and light up the whole world! Your struggle against our tyrants was like a pebble thrown into the sea, it could make no more impression! Year after year I have told you the truth, but you refused to believe me. It is not gentleness and kindness and forgiving words that will end our miseries, but swords and cannon-balls and every river of the earth red with blood. It is good you are gone; the fight that is coming would have been too stern for you; your heart would have been moved to pity by the shrieks of dying wretches when the hour came for killing, and killing without mercy, man, woman and child. We will make the earth fat with their thick blood, and it will grow us better bread! We will pull down their palaces which shut out the air of heaven, and build houses out of the ruins, for we are tired of creeping into dens for our rest!"

Here he turned suddenly and seized Arthur by the hand.

"Come," he cried hoarsely, working himself with each utterance into fiercer excitement, "come and swear over the body of this good man! Swear that when the hour comes—and it may be nearer than you think—you will take a sword with the rest of us and kill without mercy! Swear that never till you lie stiff and cold, like this man, will you make peace with the tyrants of the earth! Swear that you will never be the friend of a rich man, that you will never enter the house of one but to destroy it! Swear all this, in the presence of Death, who shall be our only king!"

Despite himself, Arthur became imbued with a portion of the speaker's enthusiasm as he listened to his fierce words; the touch of the man's hands seemed to send a current of hot passion along all his veins. With face deadly pale and voice almost as hollow and ghostlike as that of John Pether himself, he solemnly pronounced the words: "I swear." At the same moment he thought of Mr. Gresham, and felt capable of fulfilling his oath to the letter. His companion then pressed his hand with a force which seemed intended to crush every joint in it, and strode in silence out of the house.

Thus, left alone, Arthur first of all closed the shop in the usual manner, then returned to the parlour and lit the lamp. This illumined the room more completely and deprived it, in some degree, of its ghostly horrors. By this time he had shaken off the nervousness which hitherto possessed him, and he could now bend over the face of his dead benefactor with no feelings save of affection and sorrow. As he stood carefully perusing every lineament, as if he wished to impress the countenance firmly upon his mind for ever, a natural emotion at length got the better of his firmness, and, sinking on his knees by the side of the bed, he burst into a flood of tears. All the dead man's unspeakable goodness to him passed through his mind, heightened by that intense light of sudden conviction which so frequently breaks upon us in similar situations. He saw himself coming into the printer's shop eight years ago, a struggling, hard-worked child, trembling in doubt whether his services would be accepted ; he saw again with perfect distinctness Mr. Tollady's friendly smile of encouragement, that smile which for sweetness he had never seen equalled on the face of any other man, and heard his voice speaking in tones so different from those of harsh vulgarity with which alone he had been familiar. Then the many, many hours spent in delightful study by the old man's side passed before his mind's eye, each illumined with bright sunshine. He could not believe that any one of those hours had been otherwise than hours of sunshine. Then, still later, came the first serious awakening of the artist's genius within him, and he remembered, with tearful gratitude, how Mr. Tollady had noticed its first manifestations and had fostered it by all the means in his power. Surely it was impossible for any man to excel this one in all perfection of tender virtues. In this moment of supreme grief Arthur felt the full grandeur of the dead man's character, and experienced an ardent desire to emulate his goodness. Still kneeling by the bed-side, he took a solemn, though a silent vow, henceforth to devote his whole energy, even as his friend had done, to rendering more happy the lives of others. Henceforth he would be dead to art, for it seemed to him useless labour, devoid of benefit to the struggling masses of mankind. He would work for his living, but only in his trade of printer; thus, he conceived, he would be benefiting the world even by the toil which brought him his daily bread. All his leisure hours he would devote to works of charity and goodwill, to the utmost that lay within his power. How much even a very poor man can do, if only actuated by a sincere spirit, Mr. Tollady's memory would never fail to remind him.

But before he threw aside his pencil for ever it must perform for him one more service, secure to him one more everlasting pleasure. Once more lighting the candle, he went upstairs to his room and fetched a sheet of drawing-paper. With this he descended again to the parlour, and, having tenderly raised the dead man's head into a suitable position, he commenced to draw the outlines of the high and noble forehead, the closed eyes, the lips even now wearing the half-smile which gave so much attractiveness to the face during life. Slowly and carefully he continued the portrait, lingering with affectionate hand over every trail, not omitting a wrinkle or the slightest gradation of shade. For three hours he bent over the drawing, never satisfied that he could not add yet another touch to render it more complete. When at length it was finished, Arthur wrote the date and his own initials in one corner, and laid the drawing aside. It was one o'clock. Turning the lamp out, he took the lighted candle in hand, and, bending over the corpse, tenderly kissed its forehead. Then he drew the counterpane of the bed carefully over the body, and went to his rest.

He slept soundly till six o'clock, for the violent emotions of the evening, so various and succeeding each other in such quick succession, had resulted in deadly fatigue. Though still longing to sleep, he resolutely rose from his bed and dressed. At eight o'clock the man whom Mr. Tollady had employed in the printing office would come, and it would be necessary to apprise him of what had happened, to pay and dismiss him. There was moreover one task which must be performed before Arthur could have peace of mind. As soon as he had risen he took a sheet of paper and an envelope and addressed himself to its fulfilment. After some reflection he succeeded in penning the following letter, directed to Mr. Gresham :—

" Sir,
        " I grieve to have to inform you that Mr. Tollady died suddenly last night. I found him lifeless in his chair on returning home from my interview with you.

" This event confirms a resolution I had all but determined upon when I left your house last night—never to enter it again.   I have no doubt whatever that Mr. Tollady's death was hastened by trouble consequent upon the circumstances you learned from me ; and though we now see that even your assent to my request would have been powerless to save him, yet it would be impossible for me to continue to feel myself indebted for the slightest favour to one who would not open his lips in behalf of a man he knew so worthy.

"I am altogether unaware what can have caused the strong signs of disfavour which you have shown to me during the last few days ; but as I have already once begged an explanation and been refused, it is needless to express any regret at having offended you. It only remains for me to say that I shall, of course, cease from this day to receive the money which you last night told me I could not really claim. I sincerely regret even having accepted a penny of it. If I live to my twenty-first birthday it is possible I may then address you again on the subject, but till then I trust I may never be compelled to intrude upon your leisure.

"ARTHUR GOLDING."

This letter was despatched at once, after which Arthur breathed freely once more. He could not conceal from himself that he had a double object in writing it, however. Whilst his main wish was doubtless to express to

Mr. Gresham that righteous indignation which took irresistible possession of him whenever he thought of the latter's manner during their last interview, and also to free himself from what he now regarded as merely an encumbrance in entering upon his life of labour and self-denial, viz., the money he was to receive quarterly; there was a second impulse, likewise very powerful, the desire that Helen Norman should become acquainted with his loss. For he felt sure that as soon as she heard of it, her first thought would be to visit the shop. It would be hard to say how much of the sincerest love is pure egotism, and Arthur, though he would never have acknowledged it to himself, had even some degree of pleasure in thinking that his sad position would be sure to create the strongest sympathy in Helen's heart. To be regarded by her with tenderness of any kind was, however much he might endeavour to suppress the feeling, still one of the strongest desires in the young man's breast.

Having completed this task, and having concluded his business with the man when he arrived, Arthur secured all the doors and went once more to John Pether's to consult with him on the necessary steps to be taken with regard to Mr. Tollady's burial and the settlement of his business affairs. Finding that Pether was altogether unacquainted with the story of the mortgage, Arthur related it to him, whilst the former sat and listened with an ever-dispersing gloom upon his forbidding features.

"Has he left a will?" he asked, when at length the story was finished.

"I have no idea," replied Arthur.

"Then I think you should look. There is pretty sure to be one."

"Come with me, Mr. Pether," said Arthur. "Can you spare the time?"

The umbrella-mender shrugged his shoulders, and, rising without a word, left the shop, locking the door behind him. Arrived once more in the parlour where the corpse lay, they went at once to the desk where it was known that Mr. Tollady kept all his important papers. Among the first they turned over was a sheet of foolscap, at the head of which was written, "My Will." It was dated April 3rd, 1870, and was signed and witnessed quite formally. The document ran thus :—

"As I have been warned repeatedly of late by signs which I cannot mistake that I am suffering from an affection of the heart, which I fully believe may result in my death any moment, I esteem it prudent, now that I am in possession of unimpaired faculties, to make known my last will with regard to the disposal of such property as I may own at my death.

"All property that I die possessed of I bequeath, without exception, to Arthur Golding, who has grown up from childhood in my house, and for whom I cherish the affection of a father. Should he be in a position to afford it, I trust that he will continue to bestow small gifts, from time to time, on such poor people as he knows I should like to have assisted. I beg, moreover, that he will never fail to confer any benefit in his power upon my friends John Pether and Mark Challenger. Had I been rich, both of these should have received bequests from me, but as I know that I shall die poor they will forgive my inability to do all that I gladly would. I should like them, however, to choose some book or other slight article out of what I leave behind me, and preserve it as a memento of my friendship.

"To Arthur Golding I leave, moreover, my most fervent good wishes for his future happiness, and my gratitude for the pleasure his true affection has ever afforded me. I trust that he will never forget what was the main object of my life, and that he will do his best to continue that work as long as he lives."

Arthur read this with difficulty, on account of tears which filled his eyes, and even John Pether's hard countenance betrayed signs of emotion. After a short pause they continued the work of examining the papers in the desk. There was very little of importance, the chief articles being several bundles of letters neatly tied up and docketed, and one or two old manuscript volumes, which appeared to be a diary kept abroad many years ago. Having fastened up the desk again, the two went out together and spent the rest of the day in the transaction of necessary business.

On the third day after his death Mr. Tollady was buried. A very favourite walk of the old man's, on Sunday evenings, had been by Highgate Cemetery, and here Arthur resolved that he should have his last resting-place. Arthur still possessed sufficient money to cover the expenses of the funeral. In consultation between John Pether, Mark Challenger and himself, it was determined that the ceremony should be of the simplest nature, or rather that there should be no ceremony at all. The deceased had never made any secret of his religious opinions, though no man could have been less fond of making a display of them, and the three friends knew well that a simple burial, devoid of the affectation of a service which could have had no significance for him, would be the best way of testifying their deep respect for his memory.

The news of Mr. Tollady's death had spread rapidly throughout the neighbourhood. So very little was he known by the

more well-to-do of his neighbours, that the
majority of them had long thought him mad.
There was a very general opinion, too, among
these worthy people, that he was immensely
rich, in short an absolute miser, and some
little conversation now arose with regard to
the manner in which his money would be
disposed of, if anyone should be so lucky as
to find it. Most of them, however, heard of
his death with a shrug of the shoulders, and
some such exclamation as, " Poor old bloke !
I wonder he lived so long. Never left his
'ouse for ten years, have he ? " But there
were great numbers of the miserably poor
round about to whom the news of the
printer's death was a veritable affliction. It
meant to them the sudden loss of frequent
kindly assistance, of help and advice in sickness, of consolation in trouble, of a friend in the
best sense of the word. Many was the boy
and girl, the children of drunken or criminal
parents, who had to thank Mr. Tollady for
getting them a situation, when they could
find no one else who would "speak for
them " to employers. Many an ill-used wife
remembered him gratefully for services performed on her behalf with a brutal husband,
words spoken in scorn which went with forcible
directness to the wretch's heart and made
him either ashamed of his cowardice, or at
least afraid to repeat it. Many an honest-
working-man had found in him an earnest

friend whose advice was invaluable in restoring something like domestic quietness to a
home which was threatened with destruction. How often had he paid a trifling fine
for some pennyless victim of drunken folly,
and so saved him from the imprisonment
which would, in all probability, have proved
his ruin. Not a few families there were with
whom it had become quite a custom to seek
out Mr. Tollady if a boy or girl had shown
signs of going the wrong way, trusting im-
plicitly to his influence to check them while
yet there was time, and seldom disappointed
in their hopes. With such poor people as
these, victims of the world's vices much more
than of their own, the good old man had
stood on terms of the most intimate familiarity. He, a man who had been at great
pains to provide himself with a good education, had the completest sympathy with the
most brutal forms of ignorance ; he who was
to the day of his death absolutely pure and
chaste, did not feel himself repelled from the
vilest of the vile if he felt that he could do
them good. And all this good work had been
performed so quietly, so unpretentiously,
with such an extreme regard for the feelings
of those who were its objects, that now when
their benefactor's death became the subject
of common talk, the people were surprised at
the revelations in which the talk resulted.
" Why, and did *you* know him, Mary ? " one

woman would ask of a neighbour, as they stood gossipping on their respective doorsteps. "Know him! Sure I did," would be the reply. "Why, when my Billy were down wi' fever six weeks after Chris'mas who else paid the doctor as come and give him medicine?" Many such little sentences were exchanged during the day when Mr. Tollady lay in his coffin in the back parlour. And when at length the day of the funeral arrived a very large crowd of women and children had assembled round the shop door to see the coffin brought out. Many were there who wept unrestrainedly, perhaps even then they lacked their dead friend's assistance or advice, and when at length the simple coffin was borne out and deposited in the plain hearse, it was in the midst of an absolute silence, only broken by a sob here and there.

The three friends were the only mourners who followed the coffin to the grave. They rode together in a cab behind the hearse, all along the noisy thoroughfare of Tottenham Court Road, and its continuation, Hampstead Road, and so out to the Cemetery. Here in a retired corner, which they had previously visited together, they stood around the open grave whilst the body of their friend was lowered into it. Not a word broke the solemn silence. Only when the hollow sound of the first sods fall-

ing in made itself heard did Arthur's tears
refuse any longer to be withheld, whilst Mark
Challenger, who stood close by his side,
broke into unrestrained weeping. He was a
good and tender-hearted fellow, who had
suffered much from wrong of many kinds,
and it was his wont, as we have seen, to rail
on all occasions with unsparing bitterness
against the injustice of his oppressors, but
had the occasion presented itself he could not
have found it in his heart to hurt one of
them. As he walked away with his companions from the grave, he recited to them
in inarticulate tones the long story of Mr.
Tollady's many kindnesses to himself personally, charging himself with all sorts of
ingratitude, of which he had never been
guilty, and protesting that he had lost in the
printer his best and only friend. Arthur and
John Pether maintained silence, the former
so sad that he was unable to utter a word,
the latter seeming to brood with a savage
intensity, which had already become in him
a species of madness, over the wrongs and
sufferings which afflict the world.

Very shortly they parted, Challenger and
Pether going back to their day's work, whilst
Arthur, seeming to derive consolation from
the bright, warm sunshine, continued to
linger about the walks of the Cemetery,
pausing here and there to read an inscription
half-mechanically, and ever returning in the

direction of the grave, which the men were
still at work filling up. At last he saw their
labour completed, and with a deep sigh he
walked up the hill-side to the highest point
of the grave-yard. It was a perfect day, just
at that period of the year when summer is
gently fading into autumn. One or two
white clouds alone flecked the deep blue
above, and the intense clearness of the
atmosphere rendered the colours of the trees,
the grass, the flowers, and the whiteness of the
marble monuments almost painfully brilliant.
Reaching the top of the hill, he turned and
beheld the view over distant London. At
this moment it seemed to him that the dim,
smoke-capped city was a veritable abode of
misery, and that only here, in the midst of
those who had left it for ever, was true peace
to be found. A weight of melancholy, a
suffering distinct from that of sorrow, pressed
upon his heart, filling him with a sense of
dreary and hopeless misery which he had
never hitherto experienced. The future
seemed dull and hopeless, the past bright
with a gladness which could never return.
In vain he endeavoured to shake off the intolerable load, to breathe in fresh hope from
the breeze and the sunlight, to look forward
to the life of energy and usefulness which he
had promised himself, and in which action
would be its own reward; he could not
succeed in freeing himself from a gloomy

presentiment that his period of gladness had
gone bye for ever. His thoughts, wandering
at will over the whole field of his past
existence, frequently rested upon the image
of Helen Norman. She had never called at
the shop, though she must know that Mr.
Tollady was dead; and this omission on her
part added to his misery. Then he burst into
an exclamation of self-scorn, asking himself
what reason he had to expect that Helen
would take any interest in his loss. There
was a whole world between them. It had
only been as a promising artist that Helen
had ever taken any interest in him, and now
that he had done with art for ever he had at
the same time done with her and all recollection of her. What business had he—the
foundling of a London slum, henceforth to
work hard for his living as a common
journeyman—what business had he to be
thinking of a wealthy and beautiful young
lady who might one day not improbably
become a striking ornament of the fashionable world? And, at this last thought, his
blood worked itself into a very whirl of
democratic ferocity. The world, forsooth!
And he, and such as he, were of no account
in this " world," formed no fraction of it!
He thought of the insults he had received
from Mr. Gresham; and all the lessons which
life had taught him concerning the relations
between rich and poor, seemed all at once to

bear fruit within his heart and to make him another man. He looked back with scorn at the calm life he had hitherto led, with double scorn upon the art which had absorbed his energies and kept his mind from troubling itself with all-important questions. But he assured himself that that period of his life was at an end. The hours of grief following upon his old friend's death had wrought a development in his moral being. When at length he turned from the Cemetery the west was already beginning to glow with the hues of evening, he walked with a firmer step, saying to himself that he was no longer a boy.

It is not improbable that the constant companionship of John Pether during the last few days had been not a little effectual in bringing about this mood of mind. That gloomy fanatic never allowed the sense of his wrongs to sink to rest for a moment; all his waking hours were spent in exciting himself to fresh passion; and during many years of such perpetual brooding he had at length fanned the fire of wrath within his breast to such an intense glow that it only lacked some special accession of fuel to make it burst forth in all the violence of raging insanity. John had always shown a marked inclination for Arthur, and, but for Mr. Tollady's careful and judicious interference, would have long ago made the youth a confident of his gloomy imaginations. During the past year his visits to the printer's shop had not been as frequent as before. He had contracted increased habits of solitude, and continual privation at once added to his sense of unmerited suffering and the brooding passions aroused by it. His trade had fallen off by degrees till he had scarcely the means of livelihood, for in the neighbourhood his terrible aspect had confirmed the impression that he was a lunatic, and most people had some fear in approaching his shop. Amidst the congenial occupations of happy days Arthur had had but little leisure or inclination to busy his thoughts much with this strange man and his eccentricities, but now that grief and mortification had rendered his mind susceptible to gloomy impressions he found a decided pleasure in the umbrella-mender's society. Each evening since Mr. Tollady's death they had spent in company, Arthur sitting a silent listener whilst John Pether, with unwonted fluency, had recounted circumstances in his life, at times working himself into paroxysms of passion terrible to witness.

To-night they met again in the back-parlour, and sat there till it was very late. Pether was not much disposed for conversation this evening, but Arthur was unusually talkative. He related to his companion many events of past years which he had hitherto told to no one but Mr. Tollady, and passed on to an account of his relations with Mr. Gresham, of which his hearer as yet knew nothing beyond that he had been receiving instruction from the artist. Arthur spoke of Helen Norman, too. John Pether was a somewhat strange confident for such topics, but the young man had no other acquaintance with whom he could speak, and at present the abnormal activity of his mind rendered it absolutely necessary that he should give utterance to what he thought. He spoke of her as any stranger might have done, making mention of her kindness to the poor, and the reciprocal friendliness which had at once grown up between her and Mr. Tollady.

"Tollady was always too ready to trust to appearance," put in John Pether, gloomily.

Arthur bit his lip and paused. Even now he could not bear to hear Helen spoken of slightingly.

"She has not been here since his death," he said, after a moment's silence, as if speaking to himself. "And yet she knows of it."

"How could you expect it from a woman?" returned the other, sitting with his elbows resting upon his knees, and his face between his long, hairy hands.

There was a long silence, and then John Pether suddenly raised his face, and asked—

"Did you ever know your mother?"

"She died before I was old enough to really know her," replied Arthur.

"So did mine," said Pether, speaking in slow, deep tones, and as if he had a grim pleasure in the recollection to which his thoughts were turning. "Did I ever tell you of my mother?"

Arthur looked into the speaker's eyes, which were blood-shot to-night, and almost shuddered at their expression. He shook his head.

"She murdered a man she had lived with —perhaps my father—and she was sentenced to be hung for it. But at that time she was on the point of giving birth to me, so that her execution was put off for a month. Then they hung her, and I was brought up in the workhouse."

Even before he had ceased speaking, he had relapsed into abstractedness, and was apparently forgetful of what he had said. But his words had thrilled Arthur with horror. During the hour that followed neither spoke a word, and at the end of that time Pether rose in his usual manner and left the house in silence.

The next day but one was Sunday. During the morning Arthur went out to keep an appointment with a man to whom he had offered his services as compositor, and in his absence John Pether sat before the counter in the shop. The door was slightly ajar, admitting a long streak of sunlight, which also made its way through two round holes in the shutters. The umbrella-mender was meditating as usual, his eyes watching the moats which were making merry in the sloping shafts of light. He was in a quiet mood this morning, influenced doubtless by the cheerful weather, and beyond an occasional twitching of the fingers, as they rested upon his knees, he exhibited no sign of internal agitation. All at once the shop door was pushed open, and the veiled figure of a lady entered. Raising her veil, she stood for a moment unable to discern objects in the gloom. When at length she became aware of John Pether sitting close in front of her, she started slightly and gazed at him with surprise.

"Is Mr. Tollady at home?" she asked.

Pether regarded her countenance closely before replying, and for a moment something like a grim smile rested on his lips.

"He is," was his answer.

"Is he at liberty? Can I see him?"

"Scarcely."

"How am I to understand your answer?" repeated the visitor, shrinking a little before Pether's ill-omened eye.

"He is at home," said the man, sternly, "but neither you nor anyone else can see him—unless you take a spade and a mattock

to Highgate Cemetery and disturb the dead,"
he added, with a slight shrug of the shoulders.

" Do you—do you mean he is dead ? "
stammered the lady, with the utmost astonishment depicted on her face.

" I do. Are not the dead at home ? What
better home can a man have than the grave?
There no tax-gatherer comes to trouble
you, no hunger, no oppression. You look
surprised. Your home is not so poor and
comfortless as to make you look forward with
pleasure to the grave."

" I look surprised because I had no idea
that Mr. Tollady was dead, that he had even
been ill. When did it happen ? "

" Last Tuesday night. What is your interest in him ? Are you Miss Norman ? "

" I am. How is it you know me ? "

" I have been warned of you."

" Warned ? By whom ? "

" It is no matter. You have asked for Mr.
Tollady, and I tell you he is dead. What
more do you want? "

" Is Mr. Golding still living here ? " asked
Helen, after a slight pause, and with some
hesitation.

" He is."

" Is he at present in the house ? "

" It is unnecessary to say whether he is or
not. He warned me of your coming. You
cannot see him."

" Do I understand you to say that he has determined not to see me in case I call ? "

" You may do so. He has taken an oath never again to speak to you. Are you satisfied ? "

Helen stood for almost a minute regarding the speaker's face. Not a muscle on his seared countenance moved, but his eyes spoke a struggle with inward emotion. Helen was turning to leave the shop when he suddenly rose and caught her by the arm. Her nerves were firm, and she looked into his face undismayed.

" I have been told," he said, speaking in hollow tones and more calmly than usual, " that you try to do good to the poor, to satisfy their hunger, and to clothe their nakedness. Stop, if you are wise, and don't trouble yourself with what does not concern you. What are the miseries of the poor to you ? You have your great house to live in, and your fine clothes to wear ; what do you know of suffering ? Do you lack amusements ? Haven't you your theatres and your balls, your carriages and horses to show yourself with in the park ; can't you eat and drink of the best from morning to night ? Isn't this enough, but you must look for new excitement in gaols and hospitals and the holes which such as we call homes ? You help the poor ! Do you know that every penny you give in charity, as you call it, is poison to the poor, killing their independence and that sense of liberty which is the only possession they can hope to boast of? Do you know that you accustom them to think of you rich as the lawful holders of all the fruits of the earth, from whom they must be glad to receive what scanty crumbs it pleases you to throw to them, when they ought rather to rise as one man and demand as an eternal right what you pride yourself in giving them as a boon? Go home, go home!" he added, in a softer voice, "you have a pretty face, and perhaps a good heart, but you are only a woman. The work that you make your play, the amusement of your leisure hours, is not for women's hands. Men will set to it before long, and you will see then how it ought to be done. I should be sorry to see you, or such as you, suffer for the faults of your fathers, but it is the curse of wealth that you are born under, and it will prove your destruction. Don't you know some far-off country where there are fewer people and happier, where you can play with your toys all day long and wrong no one? If you do, go there, go there quickly. Who can tell what morning you may wake and see these streets of London running with the blood of your friends and relatives. There are knives sharpening now that will before long set right the injustice of centuries, set it right far more quickly than all your gold, if you scattered it all day long about

the slums and alleys.   Have you studied
history?   Did you ever read of the French
Revolution?   Take warning by it, and see to
your safety while you have time."

Helen stood for a few moments uncertain
whether to speak in reply, but seeing that the
man had resumed his seat and was apparently
lost in gloomy meditation, she again drew
her veil over her face and left the shop in
silence.   Grieving and wondering much at
what she had just seen and heard, she took
her way homewards.   As she entered the
house and was going upstairs to her own
room Mr. Gresham called her into the library.

" Are you busy this afternoon, Helen? " he
asked.

" Not at all," she replied.

" Then you can give me a sitting? "

" Yes," said Helen, absently.   Then she
suddenly asked, " Have you heard that Mr.
Tollady is dead, Mr. Gresham? "

The artist looked up at her for a moment,
then replied in the negative.

" He died last Tuesday," she resumed.
" That will account for Mr. Golding's continued absence."

" In part, possibly," said her guardian,
looking at her askance.

" Do you know any other reason? "

" Oh dear, yes," he replied, with a slight
shrug, " but I did not imagine the matter of
sufficient interest to you to be worth talking

about. I think I told you that he had shown signs of a spirit of independence which was not very promising for his progress. Eventually he became impertinent, and one morning wrote me an indignant letter which opened with the statement that he had resolved never to enter my house again, and went on to say that he had no present need of the money I offered him, but could well afford to wait till it became legally his !"

Helen looked at him in astonishment.

"But did you not reason with him, Mr. Gresham?" she asked. "Did you not try to show him the folly of acting so?"

"You know, Helen, that I am but a poor hand at moral dissertation."

"But in so sad a case! Mr. Golding cannot have known what he was writing. Perhaps it was immediately after Mr. Tollady's death, and he was distressed with grief. You certainly answered his letter?"

"*A quoi bon?*"

"Surely it is worth an effort to keep a young man of such talent from throwing away his best chances, perhaps before he knows the value of them? Have you no intention of trying to bring him back?"

"Do you think my efforts would be successful? What is the result of your own visit this morning, Helen?"

He spoke with a slight bitterness of tone, though still with a smile on his face.

" My visit was not originally meant for Mr. Golding, but on hearing of Mr. Tollady's death from a strange man in the shop, I naturally asked for him. I was told that he refused to see me."

" Indeed," exclaimed the artist, with a short laugh of pleasure. " Then you have experienced his mettle. And what is your opinion of his politeness ? "

" I am wholly at a loss to understand why he has taken this course. I sincerely hope he may yet see his true interests and continue to be as before. It is altogether so extraordinary, this sudden change of character."

" You are very much interested in him," said Mr. Gresham, with an unpleasant look from beneath his eyebrows.

"It is natural I should feel interested in his welfare," replied Helen. " When he was a child my father brought him home with the intention of educating him as his own son, only to be disappointed. Now that he has been so strangely discovered again, and has given promise of such a bright future, I think it would be unkindness in those more experienced than himself if they did not do their best to show him his errors."

" My studio is open to him if he chooses to return," said the artist, half averting his face.

" But will you not write and tell him so, Mr. Gresham ? Write a note and let me take it to him."

"Helen," said her guardian, with some sternness, "you occasionally go too far in your disregard of conventionalities. It would be entirely improper for you to do any such thing."

"I am at a loss to see why," replied the girl, surprised at the most unusual tone and sentiment of Mr. Gresham's speech.

"If you don't see why, I can hardly explain it to you. I beg, however, Helen, that you will on no account visit that place again, or hold any kind of conversation with this Mr. Golding if you should meet him. His behaviour has not been at all such as I can approve."

An observer of manners would have been amused to hear Mr. Gresham speak these words. To hear the habitual polite mocker at everything, which others esteem serious in this life of ours, adopting the emphatic tones and language of a martinet of the first water, was indeed singular. Mr. Gresham himself, moreover, was painfully conscious of the unreality of his utterances. The very sound of his own voice made him angry.

"Do you intend to pay attention to *this* request of mine, Helen?" he asked, after a brief silence.

"What other request have I neglected, Mr. Gresham?" asked his ward, justly hurt at the tone in which she was addressed.

"I do not at all approve of the manner in

which you spend your days, and I have frequently intimated as much."

This unkindness following upon the previous agitation of the morning, proved too much for Helen. As she stood facing her guardian, he saw great tears well to her eyes and fall upon her cheeks. These, and the expression of sorrowful astonishment which her countenance had assumed, touched him profoundly. In his heart he cursed his precipitance.

"Why, Helen, do you think I meant what I said?" he exclaimed, taking one of her hands in his own. "Pooh, pooh! I must have acted uncommonly well. That would get me a fellowship in 'a cry of players,' as Hamlet says. I would give a fortune if your face could remain just as it is now till I had conveyed it to canvas. Such a picture would make an artist's reputation. But you do not bear malice for the joke?"

"There are some subjects, in my opinion, too serious for joking on," replied the girl, hastily passing a handkerchief over her eyes. "Must I understand your injunctions with regard to Mr. Golding as also a jest, sir?"

"No, not that part of our scene," replied the artist. "There I was in earnest. You forget that I am responsible for you, Helen. If you err, I am blamed. Do you think I would lay any injunction upon you that was not for your good?"

"I am sure you would not bid me do anything that you did not *think* for my good."

"Which is as much as to say that I am an old fool and had better mind my own business?"

"I am sorry you should attribute such a thought to me. You are unusually severe to-day, Mr. Gresham."

"Only because I mean to be unusually kind."

"May I go?"

The artist still held her hand in his, though he did not venture to exert the least pressure on it. He found it an impossible task to retain it, however, and made no reply.

"Have you further business with me?" Helen asked, looking into his face with perfect ingenuousness.

"You will give me the sitting this afternoon?"

"I have promised."

"You have forgiven my ill-timed jest?"

"Entirely, though it grieves me that you should insist upon the other prohibition."

With a muttered exclamation the artist loosed her hand, and Helen left the room.

"Damnation!" exclaimed Mr. Gresham, as she closed the door behind her; and for the next hour he paced the library in the worst possible temper.

CHAPTER VIII.

A WORKING-MAN'S CLUB.

For many days Arthur's mind was almost entirely occupied with troublous anticipations of Helen Norman visiting the shop. John Pether had said nothing with regard to the interview between the latter and himself, and Arthur still felt convinced that Helen would come.

Almost certainly she would hear of Mr. Tollady's death from her guardian; but, even if she did not, a still small voice whispered flatteringly in the young man's ear that his prolonged absence from the studio would cause her to try and see him, for she had always manifested a frank interest in him, which, he felt, could not all at once give way to indifference.

If she should interrogate him on the subject, how would Mr. Gresham explain his pupil's sudden desertion?

Arthur trembled as he asked himself the question. So indignant had he become with Mr. Gresham that he could believe him guilty of almost any disingenuousness, even to an entire misrepresentation of what had taken place between them. When a week had passed, and still he had not seen Helen, the belief that the latter event must have occurred began to take firm possession of him. Doubtless the artist had so far defamed him in conversation with Helen that the latter could no longer experience any solicitude on his account. Who could tell what Mr. Gresham might not have accused him of? For it was plain to Arthur that, for some inscrutable reason, the artist had suddenly conceived a dislike to him. It was pain unspeakable to think of Helen viewing him in the light of false accusations, and losing all that interest in him which his talent—was it his talent alone?—had excited.

When the week had passed, and still he was disappointed, his mind entered upon another mood. What was Helen Norman to him, or he to Helen Norman? There was slight enough connection between them under the most favourable circumstances, and if Helen had so poor an opinion of him as to credit the first calumny she heard, then, indeed, she was of less than no account in his life.

Could he persuade himself that he had ever had especial interest in her? Impossible. That he had ever been on the point of loving her? Monstrous! Ignorant as he was of Helen's daily life, her schemes and her aspirations, he had little difficulty in so representing her character to himself as to persuade himself that there was nothing to regret in losing her from sight. What if she had given a few pounds to Mr. Tollady to distribute among the poor? There was no great credit in that, seeing that she had most likely thousands at her disposal. Very likely this had been a solitary instance of charity, induced by some momentary curiosity, some lack of occupation.

She was beautiful; that he could not endeavour to deny; but what was physical beauty to him, a man with a serious life before him and no ignoble aims?

Thus he argued with himself sophistically, and thought he was convinced. But the very currents of his life-blood, had he been calm enough to listen to them, as they throbbed along his veins, gave the lie to every one of his arguments.

In an evil moment he took her picture out of the portfolio, with the intention of destroying it; but at the first glimpse of that pure and noble countenance, he fell on his knees before it with a sob of pain. After all, she was his idol, the embodiment, to his heart and mind, of all that is loftiest and most worthy of pursuit in life. With an irresistible rush all the poetry of his nature seized upon and swelled his anguished heart; he wept violently. No, no, he would never destroy her picture! To the end of his days it would remind him of a time of real, though foolish, happiness, and would be capable of awakening the purest emotions of his breast.

He was now anxious to leave the old house as soon as possible. Since Mr. Tollady's death the shop had not been opened, and notice of the cessation of business had been forwarded to the few regular employers of the old man's printing-press. It remained to dispose of all the moveables, with the exception of Mr. Tollady's books, and the few articles of furniture which Arthur resolved to retain for his own use. The books he would not have allowed himself on any consideration to part with, so intimately were they connected with the happiest memories of his life; and with the furniture he proposed fitting up a little empty room somewhere in the neighbourhood of his work, wherever that might happen to be.

This matter of employment was naturally one of the first to be attended to. With the assistance of a few respectable tradesmen, with whom his work in former days had brought him into connection, he succeeded, after the lapse of a couple of weeks, in obtaining a situation as compositor in the office of a daily newspaper. During one week his work would occupy him throughout the day, during the next throughout the night, alternately.

This point happily gained, he was proceeding to look for a lodging, when a visit from

Mark Challenger spared him the trouble. Mark (who had some time since given up his shop in Charlotte Place, and gone to work as a journeyman), occupied a bedroom in Gower Place, a small thoroughfare running out of Gower Street into Euston Square, and in the same house happened to be a small room, to be let unfurnished. Mark begged so earnestly that he would not go quite out of the neighbourhood, and represented with such sincerity what a delight it would be to him to have his young friend's companionship, that Arthur consented to take the room.

On the following day his bed, table, and two or three chairs were transported thither, and the old house in Charlotte Place was abandoned for good. At the same time it was intimated to Mr. John Waghorn that, as it was impossible to pay the remaining hundred pounds on the mortgage, the property was waiting for him to take possession of it as soon as he chose.

Arthur was now to have his first experience—that is, since early childhood—of the ordinary London lodging-house.

His landlady's name was Pettindund, and, besides her own family of grown-up sons and daughters, she had her house always full of lodgers. When Arthur grew to know these people with some degree of familiarity, they excited in him a feeling of unutterable disgust. Enthusiastic as were his hopes for the amelioration of the poor and ignorant, he saw at once that here he had come into contact with a class of people from whom it was vain to expect improvement save by the agency of time. They could not be called poor, since the weekly earnings of the family amounted to no small sum, the whole of which they regularly squandered in surfeit and vice; and their mental and moral debasement was to them no pain whatever. To attempt to influence these people by any powers of example or persuasion, which an individual could exercise, he saw at once would be waste of time. They were too completely sunk in their hoggish slough to be capable of rescue by any single hand. Many an hour did he spend in contemplating their condition, and not without good results to himself. He got thus by degrees truer views on the subject which most interested him. He had glimpses in time of the great truth that education, and education only, working perhaps through generations toward the same end, gaining here a point and there a point, could be the instrument of the redemption of the well-to-do labouring classes.

But, in the meantime, events occurred which were the instruments of bringing him into active spheres of life such as he longed for.

One evening, very shortly after the two had gone to live together in Gower Place, Mark

Challenger announced to Arthur that he had joined a club of which he should like his friend also to become a member. He proposed to take Arthur to a meeting which would be held on the ensuing Sunday evening.

"It's a club of working men," he said, when describing it; "but men that are unmarried and have no one to support but themselves, and who come together just to do what good they can. Every man pays just what he likes every week; we have a box with a slit in it hung up in one corner, so that no one sees what you put in. And this money goes to form a fund, you see, out of which any member can have help if he really needs it. It isn't like a public club that almost anyone can join. We mean to have no more than twenty in it, at all events just at present, and all those twenty, Arthur, must be men that feel the wrongs of the poor and are sworn to work tooth and nail for bettering them. You see, it's more like a sort of committee for real working purposes. If any one of us knows someone that's badly in want and deserves help, he's only to tell the rest of the club, and they inquire into the matter. If they find it all right they either give help out of the funds of the club, or have a special subscription. We're all teetotallers, mind you. If we drank away half our money every week we shouldn't be able to contribute much; but as it is we make up a good purse, and, I can tell you, it goes to good uses."

"It seems to me a grand idea, if only it can be well carried out," said Arthur. "But how much is it usual to contribute each week?"

"The best-to-do sometimes give two shillings. I earn thirty shillings a week, and out of that I manage to give five. But then, you see, I've no one dependent on me now, and I only pay six shillings rent."

"Five shillings, Mr. Challenger!" exclaimed Arthur. "You indeed show yourself in earnest. I honour you for it."

"Bah! It's nothing. I have all I want to eat and drink, and before I get too old to work there'll be better times coming, see if there won't."

"How many members have you at present?"

"Why, only twelve. You'll make the thirteenth, if you join. You see, where there's no fixed contribution, and where there's serious work meant, we have to be quite sure of our men. Most working-men when they join a club just do it for their own advantage. But, as I've told you, that isn't our aim. We help each other if we need it, but most of us have very little fear of wanting much as long as we've our heads and our hands on, and our object is to help those poor

devils that haven't had the strength or the
good luck to hold out against the rich that
we have.   I should have been one of that
sort still if it hadn't been for old Sam Tollady.   Aye, aye, Arthur Golding, we must
never forget Sam.   Gad! what a chairman
he'd have made for us if he'd only been alive
now!"

"What do you do at your meetings?   Is
there one every Sunday night?"

"Yes, every Sunday night, and sometimes
an extra called in the week, when there's any
case to be considered. I'm told it was started
by Will Noble.   He's a printer, like yourself,
and a grand fellow. You must know Will.
Will had an idea that we working-men have
waited too long for other people to help us,
and it's time we turned to and helped ourselves.   So he began to look round him, and
before long he found half-a-dozen other men
who were not miserably poor, but who had
the same ideas as he had about doing what
they could to help others.   You'll know them
all if you'll come down to-night, and I can
tell you they're worth knowing.   What do
we do at our meetings? Well, we have some
settled subject for discussion, you see, each
Sunday night.   Last Sunday was my first
night there, and then Will Noble got up and
spoke what he thought about the best way of
helping poor people without making them
lose their independence.   Will said some un-

commonly good things, and the best was that it's the poor must help the poor. The rich will never do it—till the day comes when they're made, and that won't be so long, either! He said that we working men had the best chances of going about and seeing just what people wanted and what they didn't want. And when Will Noble had done, one or two of us got up and said what we thought, you see. The subject to-night is: 'How are the poor to get possession of their rights?' A man named Hodgson, a carpenter, will speak first. I don't know him at all, but I'm curious to hear what he's got to say."

"Does Mr. Pether belong to the club?" asked Arthur.

A look of perplexity rested for a moment on Mark's countenance.

"Well, no, he doesn't," he said at length, hesitating slightly in his speech; "and, to tell you the truth, Arthur, I shouldn't care for him to know about it. Poor John Pether has suffered more than any of us, and his wrongs have driven him half mad like. I'm getting almost afraid of John, he's so terribly fierce at times; I often fear he'll do either himself or some one else an injury. You see, he has brooded year after year in solitude, always growing poorer and poorer, till he couldn't get his thoughts away from that one subject, however much he tried.

John won't hear of any other way of righting things except by violence, and it's just that that our club won't have anything to do with. Now you'll hear to-night what Hodgson says, but I'll warrant there won't be a word about blood in the whole of his speech. So you can see the reason why John Pether couldn't very well be a member ; and things being so, I wouldn't have him know of it at all. It would seem unkind, you know, to keep him out, and I wouldn't have him think me unkind to him for the world. John and I have known each other hard upon thirty years, and we've been good friends all the time. I only wish he'd let me help him a bit now and then, but he gets into one of his fearful moods if ever I mention it. Poor fellow ! I often wonder what'll become of him."

Eight o'clock was the time at which the club met, and about half-past seven Arthur and Mark set out together. Mark led his companion down Tottenham Court Road and across Oxford Street into Crown Street. Near the lower end of this they passed before the closed shop of a tin-worker, over which was written the name, " Isaac Spreadbrow." Knocking, they were almost immediately admitted, and passed through the shop into a little yard at the back. It was a sort of small timber-yard, one side of which was occupied by a long carpenter's shed. Here it

was that the meetings of the club were held
pro tempore.

Half-a-dozen men were already present in
the yard, walking up and down, engaged in
conversation. They were all hard-faced,
hard-handed men, dressed with a decent care
which betokened the tolerably well-to-do
artisan.

Amongst them Arthur's eye at once
singled out one who, he felt sure, must be
the leader. He was not mistaken. To this
tall man Mark at once led him, whispering
that it was Will Noble.

"Mr. Noble," said Mark, "I've ventured
to bring you a friend of mine, one I've known
ever since he was a lad of ten or eleven. He's
heart and soul in this work of ours, I assure
you, and he'd feel proud if he was made
a member of the club. Wouldn't you,
Arthur ?"

"I should indeed," replied the young man,
returning the hearty grasp of the hand with
which the tall man greeted him. "There is
nothing I feel so much interest in as efforts
such as yours, and I should think it a privilege to work with you. Mr. Challenger
forgot to tell you my name. It is Golding."

"Well, Mr. Golding," said Will Noble, in
a full, deep voice which spoke the heartiness
of the man's nature, "I like the way in which
you speak. You must know it is our rule
that a new member must be introduced by

at least two old ones who know him personally. You are one, Mr. Challenger; who is
the other ?"

"Why, it's rather awkward," returned
Mark, looking round at the other men, who
stood in a group apart. "I am afraid there
isn't another of us that knows Arthur personally. But I'll tell you just how it is.
Arthur has lived and worked from a boy up
with an old friend of mine called Tollady.
You didn't know him, Mr. Noble; I only
wish you had, but—ha! here comes Spreadbrow. He knew him. Isaac !" he called out
to a stumpy little man who was shaking
hands with the members of the other group,
"Did you know Sam Tollady ?"

"Know him, by God !" exclaimed the
tin-worker, energetically; "if I didn't know
Sam Tollady show me the man who did.
Damn me if I didn't !"

"Well, did you ever hear him speak of one
Arthur Golding, who had lived with him ?"

"Many a time, and a good lad he must
have been, though I didn't know him at
all. Where's he gone now that poor Sam's
dead ?"

"Why, here he stands," replied Mark,
pointing to Arthur. "I want him to be a
member, but unfortunately I'm the only one
who knows him."

"I know him, Will Noble," cried Isaac, in
a squeaking voice which he might appear to

have caught from his trade. " Damn me, I'll go bail for him. Now I see him, I remember his face too. I must have seen him in the shop. But I'll go bail for whoever was Sam Tollady's friend, damn me if I won't!"

" Then I think that's quite enough," said Noble. " Wait till we're all together, and we'll have you elected, Mr. Golding. Mr. Challenger will take you to sign the book. Isaac, I wish you could get out of that habit of swearing. I'm no Puritan, as you know; but it don't fall pleasantly on a man's ears. Couldn't you make shift to do without it, don't you think?"

" I tell you what it is, Will Noble," returned the little man, stroking a scrubby beard, " you're about right in what you say, as you always are for the matter of that. I've had many a damned hard struggle with this habit; but, by God! it's always been too much for me yet. But I'll try again, if it's only to please you, Will. I'm damned if I don't!"

Will Noble turned away with a good-natured laugh, and Mark Challenger took Arthur into the shed, which was now illuminated by half-a-dozen tallow candles. The litter of the shop had been all pushed away into corners, and in the centre of the shed stood a long deal table, round which were placed benches. A chair was at the head, for the chairman, and on the table in front of it lay a small book containing the rules of the society, written out in Will Noble's own bold hand.

Every member had to read these rules and sign them. They recapitulated pretty much what Mark had already told Arthur, the principal being—" That every member must be a *bonâ fide* working man; that every member must be a teetotaller; that each must contribute something every week, the amount to be left to his own discretion."

As Arthur put his name after Mark Challenger's, for Mark had been the last admitted, the men began to assemble in the shed, and to take seats round the table. Counting Arthur, exactly thirteen were present.

The office of chairman, it appeared, was held by all in turn. To-night, Isaac Spreadbrow assumed the head of the table. On his right hand sat Hodgson, the man who was to introduce the debate, if such it could be called where there was no opposition. Hodgson was the owner of the shed, and worked in it on weekdays.

As soon as all were seated, Isaac Spreadbrow rose.

" Gentlemen," he began, " the first thing we have to do to-night is to vote for a new member. I know you'll be glad to hear that, and I'm glad to tell it you. You know we've set our limit at twenty, this one makes the thirteenth. His name is Arthur Golding, and he's worked for years with an old friend of mine as is just dead—that's Sam Tollady, one as would have been a member if he'd lived. I knew Mr. Golding through Sam Tollady well enough, though I never exactly talked to himself before to-night. Mr. Challenger has known him ever since he was a boy, too; and it's Mr. Noble's opinion as we may introduce him as a new member. So I'll ask your vote on the point. Those who are in favour of electing Mr. Arthur Golding hold up their hands, please."

The vote was unanimous.

"Then," continued Isaac, "Mr. Golding makes our thirteenth member. And now, before we listen to our friend Mr. Hodgson, I've got something more on my paper to speak of. And it's this. Most of us here, I think, are men as do a good bit of reading when we get the time, but most of us could do a good bit more if we'd only the books to read. It's a great shame we haven't a good public library to go to, where we could get books out for a small subscription, which we should all be able to pay. But as we haven't that, we shall have to fall back on an old rule, the rule as proves our guide in everything we do, and try to help ourselves. Now, Mr. Noble, who, you know, has our work thoroughly at heart, and constantly puzzles his brains to see how things can best be managed, has suggested to me that we should have a small weekly subscription of a stated amount, which is to go to buy a good book now and then, and one, you see, that would be too dear for each one of us to buy for ourselves. When we bought the book, whatever it was, it could go the round of us, each keeping it a certain time, and after that we'd put it somewhere to be kept for the benefit of the club in general. In that way, you see, we should get a library by degrees. Now, any one that's got anything to say to this idea, I should like him to speak."

A short discussion followed, two or three difficulties being raised with regard to the choice of books. This, however, was ultimately arranged, and the Book Club was unanimously voted for. The weekly subscription was arranged to be threepence.

The chairman then called upon Mr. Hodgson to deliver his address, which lasted some twenty minutes, and was listened to most attentively, several of the hearers making notes of what was said.

There was nothing very original, but at the same time nothing absurd or exaggerated in the speaker's ideas, which were principally that providence and co-operation were the best resources of the poor. He dwelt upon the evils of drink, maintaining that it was one of the most serious drawbacks to advancement; that it brutalised the poor and made them necessarily the servants of the rich, who had more command over their passions, or, at all events, had more means of concealing their results. He held that it was only a question of time, this restoration of the poor to their rights. In conclusion, he hoped that such working men as had votes would always use them in behalf of such candidates for Parliament as bound themselves to protect the interests of the poor.

One or two members having made remarks on this address, there ensued a pause, in the midst of which William Noble rose, and was received with much slapping of the table and clapping of hands. He looked round at his fellow-members with an earnest glance, and, after collecting his thoughts for a moment, began to speak in a slow, emphatic voice.

" Our friend Mr. Hodgson," he said, " has made a good and sensible speech, and I have had very much pleasure in listening to him. With what he said about the evils of drink I entirely agree. We are all here teetotallers simply because we see such terrible results ensue from the abuse of liquor that we choose rather to go without it altogether than to run the risk of becoming its slave. I only wish all working men could be induced to do the same. I know very well there is many a working man who drinks a glass or two glasses every day without its doing him the least harm; but these are the exceptions, I am sorry to say. We working men, on the whole, are a lot of poor, weak, ignorant fellows, who have next to no command over ourselves, whether it's in anger, or whether it's in any kind of enjoyment, and in my opinion we must try to remedy our weakness by strong means. Our disease has gone too far for a moderate treatment. We must set our faces firmly to the task of cutting away the whole habit, just as if it was a limb, and I think that if even moderate drinkers set the example of altogether going without their drink, it will be an aid and an encouragement to those who have a harder struggle to undertake. In all things we must help each other, and in this way I think we, by being teetotallers, are helping the drunkards."

The speaker was interrupted by applause, after which he continued in more rapid tones—

"But I didn't mean to talk much about this matter just at present. In all things I like to go to the very bottom; if it's geometry I study, I like to know what a straight line is; if it's arithmetic, I must know the multiplication table; and so in this matter we're discussing to-night, I want to ask myself *what* are these rights that the poor desire to win? Friends, I have heard men speak in the cause of the poor who seemed as if their object was nothing more nor less than to take away all the wealth from the rich and give it to the poor, as if that would mend matters. Now, I'm not one of these men. I think I have seen very well, from my own experience and from the books I've read, that as long as this world is a world, there will be in it rich people and poor people. That I feel sure of, and I feel that it's no use grumbling about it. Some men are born with more brains than others, and, even if there was no such thing as hereditary wealth, these men with the brains would have ten chances to one against the men without in the struggle for riches. Well, then, I say I am convinced there *must* be a rich class and a poor class. But shall I tell you what I am *not* convinced of? I am not convinced that, of these rich and poor, the one must be a class of brute beasts—of ignorant, besotted, starving, toil-worn creatures—whilst the other must be a class of lords and princes, spending in profitless luxuries—luxuries which perish with them and are of no further good to the world— riches which would suffice to put every poor man at his ease, which they obtain without labour, which serve only to rear generation after generation of vicious prodigals. I am *not* convinced that it is a necessity for the rich class to spend their days in refined selfishness, as careless of the miseries of the poor at

their palace-gates as if these poor lived in
another world; or that it is right for them
to sit in judgment daily upon wretches who
have committed a so-called crime to save
themselves from starvation, and to condemn
them to horrible penalties. Of all this I am
far from being convinced, and that is why I
did my best to form this club of ours, and
hope to see it number before long twenty
men who are as far from being convinced as
I am, and who will work with me to remedy
what they think wrong."

Murmured approvals. All the listeners
hang upon the speaker's lips with rapt attention.

"And now shall I tell you *why* I am far
from being convinced that these things are
necessary? For that is the next point in an
attempt to get to the bottom of the matter.
For these reasons then. At their birth all
men are equal, all are helpless, young creatures, dependent upon the care of parents for
existence. These parents have to find sustenance for the children as they grow up,
sustenance and clothing. These are the
essential needs of man. Now nature has
ordered that the infant's sustenance should
first of all come from the mother; after that,
that it should come from the earth. Now
suppose a mother finds herself unable to
afford milk to her new-born child, what do
we say of her? Do we not say that the

mother is diseased, that there is something wrong in her system, that things are not as they ought to be? Very well. Now if at a later period the child, or the grown-up man, finds himself unable to obtain that sustenance from the earth which nature prescribes, oughtn't we also to say that here too something is most clearly wrong? And worse wrong, friends, than in the other case! For whereas the diseased mother *could* not afford milk, the earth offers abundance of food, but certain men monopolise it, and do not allow their starving brothers to have their share. Mind you, I say their *share*, and their share is a sufficient quantity properly to sustain life. I have already told you that I believe some will always have more than others, but I hold that it is a wrong against nature to say that some shall have *none at all !*

"But you will perhaps say to me, why do you talk so much about nature? We are no longer in a state of nature. We are no longer savages, but men living in a social order. And I have even heard men say that it was one of the necessities of this social order that certain men should starve, they said they could prove it by political economy! But I tell you, friends, that, as far as food, clothing and shelter go, we *are* still in a state of nature, and must be, as long as we are men. We require all these as much as any savage, although we boast of being civilised.

In spite of their political economy I venture to assert that my argument has proved man's *right* to these necessaries. If the human family increased so much that the earth could not afford food for them all, that would be a very different thing. Then no one but the earth would be to blame, and the maker of the earth, whoever that is. But we know this is so far from being the case that untold millions could yet be added without exhausting the capacities of this old earth!

" Now I think I have shown you *what* these rights are that Mr. Hodgson has spoken of, and also *why* they are rights. These are two important points gained. Now we pass to the harder questions of practical application. After all the men are right who say that, though every man is the earth's creditor for a sufficient quantity of food, it is impossible for everyone to go into the fields and gather it whenever he wants it. Of course he cannot, and the reason is because we live in an artificial state of society. (Mind, I don't imply anything bad of that word artificial. I should be crazy if I proposed that we should break up society and go back to the woods, to live as savages.) Well, it has been found necessary, through long centuries of experience, for men to do a certain amount of work for this food. As we can't all plough and reap we must do something to pay those men who do actually plough and reap for us. All men agree to this in theory, but strangely enough it has been found in practice that certain men refuse to work because they can obtain food without it, whilst others are willing to work their hardest, and yet cannot obtain food for all that. You will see that the fact of our being civilised does not in any sense take away our original rights, it only slightly alters the mode in which we are to receive them. So when the case is found to be as I have described, what shall we say? Surely not that a man must suffer because he happens to be a social being, but that there is something radically wrong in the social system which deprives him of his rights. I know very well that we find men now and then who starve because they are too lazy to work. Should I say that because these men *are* men, therefore they must be fed whether they work or not? Certainly not, and for this reason. If it is bidden by nature that every man should be fed, it is equally bidden by nature that every man should take the trouble of reaping his food. Now one way of reaping our food now-a-days is by working for it, and if a man refuse to do this he must suffer just as a savage would who should lie down on the ground and refuse to take the trouble of plucking fruit or killing animals. Nature would not drop food into his mouth.

" I assume, then, that nature bids the construction of a social order. But then comes a question which it is left for man to decide : ' How shall this social order be best arranged for the benefit of all men ?' And here we are, friends, at the centre of the problem. We grumblers don't complain that nature will not feed us without our working, but we complain that this rich class, this class which has the main voice in the formation of society, has managed things so badly that they could scarcely have been managed worse; and, further still, that these rich men are altogether careless about the result of their bad management, trouble themselves not the least about anything, so long as they have their fine houses, their fine clothes, their fine dinners.

"Mr. Hodgson ended his address by reference to politics. Now what do we mean by politics? The science of government, I should say. In other words, the sum of what men know of the best rules for managing this social machine of ours. Now, because it is impossible for every man to have a hand in this management, we have what we call a government. Never mind that our form of government, monarchy, is in theory the most absurd the mind of man could conceive; for in reality we are not governed by a monarch, we merely pay for maintaining one because it looks generous, I suppose, to do so. But this parliament which really governs us, what has it to say to these frightful evils we have hourly before our eyes, these outrageous wrongs to which the poor have to submit? Friends, does it not in reality say: ' Well, I see the evil, I am very sorry for it, but I really don't know how to remedy it?' I maintain that all its acts amount to such a speech. But, I ask, what right has a government to exist, except as long as it successfully does its duty, the managing of the social machine? If a government no longer does this, it is *no* government. It should be swept from the face of the earth!

" But, friends, I am sorry to say that we cannot do this. We are not strong enough. In numbers we poor constitute a vast majority, but in influence you know we are very weak. The weakness is partly due to our poverty, partly to our ignorance. Before we can get a government such as we wish we must become as influential as the rich. How to bring this about, then, was the question Mr. Hodgson asked to-night. In my mind there is only one answer: *We must get taught*! The rich domineer over us not only because we are poor, but still more because we are too like the animals, we have too little of that grand intellectual power which, by taking entirely the place of bodily strength, distinguishes civilisation from barbarism! Yes, we must get taught. You have seen the government this year grant a scheme of education which will be of admirable effect, and what is this measure but the result of that very spirit in the nation which collects us together here to-night? This is *our* work, the work of those known as the Radicals, never mind who were the immediate agents. Well, is not this an encouragement for us? Does it not prove that we shall by degrees gain our objects? Depend upon it, it is not the government that will originate such measures; it is us, the poor, who must struggle without ceasing to raise ourselves out of the gutter and make our voices heard by the rich. If our reasons are good, the rich cannot but listen to them; these reasons of ours will weigh heavily against their wealth, and will ultimately prevail. But first we must get our reasons! We must keep our brains clear from the fumes of drink, we must get books, read and remember them; we must lay hold of this boon of reading and writing for our children, and make it a stepping stone to still more! And in the meantime we must also do our best to aid those suffering from actual want of the necessaries of life. The rich will not do this to any purpose, so we must do it ourselves. We who are here form a club of men without any ties, and therefore we can spare something out of our weekly wages. To-night we have got a new member, that means new possibilities for doing good. Don't let us be discouraged, friends, if we seem to do only a little. Every little helps, and depend upon it our exertions will not be without their influence. And so I have had my say."

Noble resumed his seat amidst much applause. Arthur, in particular, had listened to him with admiration, and had warmed with him into enthusiasm. When a few more had spoken and, after the chairman had announced the subject for the following Sunday, as well as certain items of business for the week-day meetings, the assembly broke up, Arthur shook hands heartily with him, and expressed his gratification in a few words glowing with earnest sincerity. Noble returned the young man's warmth with interest.

"Well, Mr. Golding," he said. "I see no reason why we shouldn't be very good friends. We are both of a trade are we not?"

"Yes, I work at the case," replied Arthur, with a sense of pride. "But at present the death of Mr. Tollady has put me out of employment. I hope to find some, however, before long."

"I will keep my eyes open for you, if you like," said Noble.

"Thank you," returned the other, "I should be very glad if you would."

By Mark Challenger's advice, Arthur had said nothing about his interval of artist's

work, and indeed he felt there was no insincerity in altogether passing it over.   For in
his present mood he firmly believed that all
the time spent in the study of art had been
wasted time, and that he was only now beginning serious life.   His feelings were excited
to the highest pitch by the events of the
evening, and, on their return home, he and
Mark sat up together till a late hour ardently
discussing the prospects of the club.

CHAPTER IX.

If Arthur Golding had his days of uneasy
expectation, followed by the momentary
sickness of hope deferred, when Helen
Norman appeared to have renounced all
interest in him and his, Helen herself was
but little less hurt at the repulse she had
received upon her visit, the result, as she
could not but believe it, of Arthur's direct
instructions. Hurt she was, in the true sense
of the word, and not merely distressed, as
she had told her guardian, at the apparent
folly with which Arthur had thrown aside
his best chances of attaining to eminence in
the path to which his genius had directed
him. In the communings with herself which
followed her return home, and the short conversation with Mr. Gresham, she would fain
have persuaded herself that it was the latter
feeling alone which influenced her ; but that
sincerity of self-examination to which she had
long been accustomed told her that she
suffered an emotion quite distinct from this.
She was pained at the indifference to her
displayed by Arthur, grieved that she had

not been allowed the opportunity of expressing to him her sincere sympathy in his misfortunes. Subsequently she learned from
her guardian that Arthur had renounced the
benefits he might have received from her
father's will, and this made her anxious with
regard to his future subsistence. Nevertheless she was in no wise tempted to neglect
Mr. Gresham's injunctions and pay another
visit to Charlotte Place. Despite her loftiness
of character, Helen Norman was still a woman,
and instinct preserved her from exposing herself to still further slights.

But she too, like Arthur, had her refuge
from painful reflections in determined application to her daily work. The path she had
chosen for herself was no flowery one, and,
though never daunted in her onward progress,
she not unfrequently came to obstacles
against which she had to struggle with
unutterable sadness, or pity, or disgust in
her heart. To begin with, wherever she
went among the destitute poor, she was
almost always met with the most open
feelings of distrust and suspicion. She
found at the very entrance to her work how
terribly deep and wide was the gulf set
between the class to which she belonged by
birth and these poor wretches whom her
heart was set on benefiting. Too often her
kind words met with surly and ungracious
replies, and sometimes her benefits were

repaid with the basest indifference or even ingratitude. This subject was the occasion of numerous long and earnest conversations between her and Mr. Heatherley. One such took place on the day after Arthur's introduction to the club. The clergyman had met her by chance as she was returning homewards, and, reading in her countenance the signs of extreme fatigue, he had insisted upon her repairing to his house, which was but at a short distance, and partaking of some refreshment. Helen did not refuse, for she seriously felt the need of half an hour's rest. Seated in Mr. Heatherley's homely little parlour, she allowed herself to be persuaded to drink a glass of wine and eat a biscuit, and very shortly the wonted light of cheerful energy came back to her eyes, and the little colour she could boast of to her cheeks. The clergyman was unceasing in his attentions, and though at first she could only reply to him with a grateful smile, she soon found herself able to converse with her accustomed freedom.

" It always does me good to hear you talk, Mr. Heatherley," she said, as she sat in the arm chair by the table, and the clergyman on an ottoman in front of the window. " I have seldom felt so dreadfully exhausted as when you met me, but now I could almost go over my morning's work again, though it has not been very pleasant. You never seem tired.

There is always a healthy freshness in your words which does one good."

Mr. Heatherley reddened slightly, and laughed, a low but clear and genial laugh.

"I am heartily glad my conversation has such tonic properties," he replied. "Let us hope I lose none of it when I am in the pulpit. But you say your morning's work has not been pleasant, Miss Norman. Where have you been to-day?"

"To some of the worst places you permit me to venture into. But I spoke more particularly of some people I have never mentioned to you before. To tell you the truth I was very doubtful of what I had done for them, and wished to see the result. I find that I was not mistaken in my fear."

"Indeed? What do you refer to?"

"It is a family, named Crick, living in a cellar kitchen in an unspeakably foul alley. When I first visited them I found the man lying asleep on the floor, and his wife with three little children sitting about the room in a state of absolute idleness. Not a particle of furniture of any kind was to be seen in the place. The woman told me that none of them had tasted food for several days, that they had long ago sold all their furniture and spare clothing to keep themselves alive, and that her husband had just found work of some kind but was unable to begin because he had not a decent coat to appear in. I did not much like the appearance of the people at the time, for the man seemed a great strong fellow who ought long ago to have found some sort of occupation, and I felt sure that the cellar smelt strongly of spirits. But I could not refuse to do something for them, if only to see what effect my efforts would have, and to earn experience. So I gave the woman a few shillings to buy food, and then went with her to a shop close by and bought her a few articles of the cheapest furniture I could find, and also a suit of clothes which she said would fit her husband. She seemed extremely thankful, and when I went away I promised to call again in a very few days. Well, I went again, and this time only found the three children at home. They said their father had not been at home since I was last there, and that their mother was out looking for work. I noticed, however, that one or two of the articles of furniture had disappeared, and I had many misgivings with regard to the state of affairs. This morning I called again, and once more found the whole family at home, but this time the woman was asleep on the floor, the man was sitting in a state of drunkenness on the cellar steps, and the children were quarrelling for a jug of beer which the eldest of them was just drinking out of as I entered. All the furniture had once more disappeared, and the man was wearing the same clothes I had

first seen him in. It was impossible for me
to do any more, for they seemed hopeless
people, so I went away with a heavy heart."

"I have known only too many such cases,"
said Mr. Heatherley. "As you say, Miss
Norman, you acquire experience from them;
but I should advise you to be very careful
not to waste your money where there appears
but slight hope of its doing good. After all,
we have but very little power, except where
the recipients of our charity come half way to
meet us. Happily there are many such instances, and, as a rule, it is not very difficult
to discern between honest distress and a true
anxiety to take advantage of help."

"But the other poor wretches? Must we
then let them perish in their dreadful life?
Have we no means of raising them?"

"We individually have, I am afraid, none.
The most we can do is to lose no opportunity
of lending our aid in all reforms for the good
of the poor generally. The spread of education will do a very great deal, it is to be
hoped. But at the best, we cannot hope for
perfection in this life."

"It is only when you speak so, Mr.
Heatherley, that you are discouraging," said
Helen, with a smile. "You then make me
feel that, spite of all your activity and hope-
fulness, you in reality despair of the world.
It is not this poor earth of ours on which
your highest hopes are fixed, after all, and in

looking forward to that shadowy future world
I cannot but think that you must at times
lose interest in the present."

The clergyman looked at Helen with a
slight surprise. It was the first time since
their first meeting that she had alluded to
religion, even in the most distant manner.

"You are right, in a certain sense, Miss
Norman," he replied. "I can never hope for
the perfection of this world, but that does not,
I trust, in the least dishearten me in my work
here. The certainty of a future life of perfection is rather an inestimable incitement to
me. How much more glorious to know that
I am doing my best to prepare souls for
eternal bliss, than to be actuated by a mere
desire to lessen pain for a few fleeting years.
I know you will forgive me the comparison,
Miss Norman."

"Most certainly," replied Helen, smiling.
"Will you permit me, in return, to ask you
a question relative to your religious beliefs,
Mr. Heatherley? Pray do not have any hesitation in refusing if you think me impertinent."

"I shall have the utmost pleasure in
answering any question, Miss Norman," replied the clergyman, who heard Helen enter
upon these subjects with a pleasure he could
scarcely conceal.

"It is this then. Do you believe in the
doctrine of eternal punishment?"

" What means an all-powerful and an all-merciful God may, in His wisdom, adopt for the purification of all souls and rendering them worthy of everlasting life, I am unable to say, Miss Norman ; but that all souls *will* ultimately be likened in purity to their Creator and live for ever in His presence, I firmly believe. So you see that the doctrine of eternal punishment has no place in my creed."

" You relieve me," replied Helen, " Shall I confess it ? I always feel a little uncomfortable in the presence of those who I know are possessed with this idea of the damnation of their fellow-creatures."

" Had you," asked Mr. Heatherley, " any other object in asking the question besides the desire of relief ? "

" Merely that I might more thoroughly understand the spirit in which you labour among the depraved and the wicked. Under such circumstances as these, why weary yourself in efforts to bring about an end which is already predetermined ? "

" How do I know, Miss Norman, that I, humble creature as I am, may not be an indispensable instrument in the hand of the Almighty ? I work in obedience to the spirit which most distinctly pervades the revealed will of God, to do good to others, even as I would that others should do unto me. But I fear you do not comprehend my religion. It is not a matter of calculation and reasoning to me, but an unmistakable conviction. I follow an impulse which irresistibly actuates me, an impulse which I feel to be the will of my Creator. I do so because I cannot do otherwise."

"And I am afraid, Mr. Heatherley," replied Helen, "that it is just as impossible for you to understand the hopes and fears which actuate us who look to no other home but this present one. You can have no idea of the intense desire to be *doing* which possesses one who is firmly convinced that, if this life and its opportunities are neglected there will be no other chance. If you regard each one of these wretched beings as an immortal soul, and work to render them worthy of immortality, I for my part regard them as lives which are burning away like a candle, being extinguished for ever, losing day by day the million glorious possibilities which humanity sees before it, perishing without having ever known one noble thought, one worthy impulse, one hour of human happiness. Is not that a prospect capable of exciting sympathy, the deepest that can be born of human heart? Are there not here motives— frightfully urgent motives, for action? But I grant that you have the advantage over me in sources of consolation when you feel your weakness. It is dreadful to me to see that I can do so little! Can you not advise me,

Mr. Heatherley, some better way of winning the confidence of these poor? That is what I want, their confidence. They will not trust me. My speech, my dress, perhaps, revolts them. They think that I do not belong to their class, and, though they take my money, it is with suspicion of my motives. I have made my dress as plain as it possibly can be, to be respectable. If I could, I would even speak in their uncouth tongue. There is always that horrible difference of caste between us. Can it ever be removed? Will they ever learn to look upon me as a human being like themselves?"

Mr. Heatherley's eyes had remained fixed on the girl's face as she spoke, and they involuntarily expressed admiration as all her lineaments glowed with a richer beauty begotten of enthusiasm. When he replied, it was after hesitation, and in a low voice.

"You ask me, in effect, Miss Norman," he said, "to do what you have forbidden me to do—to impress you with the truth of my religion. I fear there is much reason in what you say. I fear you find your superior position a sad obstacle. It is necessarily so. There is but one thing—the influence of Christianity—sufficiently strong to remove this obstacle; and of that you are unable to avail yourself. I grieve profoundly that it should be so."

The emphasis with which he pronounced

these last words impressed Helen. She looked into his face, and, meeting the full gaze of his earnest eyes, averted her head again.

"I *cannot* think you are right, Mr. Heatherley," she replied, after a moment's pause. "Have these people so utterly lost the reasoning powers of human beings as to be unable to see that all men are necessarily born equal, though wealth may make them different as far as attainments and outward appearance go? Are they so degraded as to consider themselves hopelessly inferior? Have they not sufficient insight to discern kindred hearts even in those whom the world exalts?"

"Possibly what you imagine to be an overwhelming sense of their own superiority," replied Mr. Heatherley, "is rather a proud and obstinate assertion of their equality. We must blame the dreadful social errors which have so long forced them to live the life of beasts, even whilst they felt and knew themselves to be men. No; they have *not* sufficient powers of insight to distinguish one wealthy person from another. It is their hereditary belief that the rich are their enemies, and how can we expect them to be suddenly converted from it? They will much rather attribute any extravagant motive to your charity than surrender the traditions of their lives by attributing it to true benevolence."

"And do you seriously believe, Mr.

Heatherley, that your religion materially assists you in gaining their confidence?"

"I do, Miss Norman. When I speak to them of God and their Saviour, when I tell them that one great Being has created all men alike, and that one Christ came down to earth to die for all; when I point to the future life, and tell them that there we shall all live again in the sight of our Father, no one of us superior or inferior to the rest, then indeed they see that I am only a man such as themselves, and they are willing to trust me. As well try to make their minds comprehend a metaphysical problem, as to put before them the fact of the equality and brotherhood of men as you understand it, Miss Norman, and expect it will aid you to win their confidence."

Helen rose to depart, and held out her hand to the clergyman.

"I thank you for your frankness with me, Mr. Heatherley," she said. "It shows that you rate my independence at its true value. What you have said will afford me matter for thought."

"If your reflection led you to see the truth of what I have said, Miss Norman," returned the clergyman, as he took her hand, "and to enter into the spirit of the faith which is my support, it would be the richest blessing of my life that God had made me the instrument to so great an end."

Helen thought, on her way home, that the more thoroughly she came to know Mr. Heatherley, the further removed from him did she feel in all the most essential of the principles by which her life was guided. If possible, she respected him more then ever after every conversation she held with him, as she came more fully to recognise his consistency, his sincerity, his powers of sympathy. But, great as were the latter powers, she felt that they were insufficient when applied to her own philosophy, and felt that in the nature of things it must be so. Mr. Heatherley did not even understand her motives, much less truly sympathise with them. All the more, however, did she respect his tolerance, and wonder at it. This, indeed, was the one feature of his character which greatly influenced her.

In listening to him, she herself became more tolerant. Hitherto she had taught herself to look upon the Christian religion as a gigantic mistake, every sign of which must be swept away from the earth as soon as possible. For individual Christians her good sense had already made her entertain the widest charity; but for the faith they professed she had been unable to preserve the slightest. Fresh from the study of ecclesiastical history, with all its hideous barbarities, its ghastly beliefs, its brutal condemnations of what is noblest in man, it was but natural that her young and enthusiastic mind should look upon Christianity as an enemy to be combated with and destroyed, of no possible use to the world, but rather of unutterable harm. But experience of life since she had been in London, and, above all, conversation with Mr. Heatherley, had greatly modified her opinions. Though her reason still forbade her as strongly as ever to relinquish her intellectual freedom for the bondage of dogmas, she was beginning to understand that Christianity has its reason for existence, and to doubt whether, even if it were possible, it would be wise to suddenly exterminate it.

After all, was there not a very close analogy between the mental condition of these denizens of the slums and alleys and that of the men of earlier ages, who found religion absolutely necessary for them, and so created it if they had not it ready to hand? Was not every child naturally impressed with religious beliefs, and was it not very possible that the history of the world was but a steady growth to maturity, corresponding to the growth of the individual mind? Theories such as these she had already met with in her reading, but had scarcely considered them with sufficient impartiality; and now they came upon her with the vivid reality of experience.

Helen was an example of that most enspiriting rule in the moral order of the world, that no one can endeavour to do good to others without at the same time actually benefiting himself.

When Helen reached home that afternoon she was rather surprised to see a cab standing before the door, from which the driver, aided by one of the servants, was lifting two large trunks into the hall. She knew of but one person who was expected to arrive about this time, and that was Mrs. Cumberbatch, Mr. Gresham's aunt. And on glancing at the first trunk that was set down in the house, she saw that it was labelled with that lady's name.

At this moment she was accosted by the housekeeper, who appeared in somewhat of a flurry.

"How very unfortunate, Miss Norman! I'm so glad you've just come. Mr. Gresham told me that this lady would be here to-morrow afternoon, and here she has come quite unexpected. There's been no fire lighted in her room yet, and hardly any preparations made, and, what's more, Mr Gresham went out about an hour ago, and I dare say won't be back till dinner. Whatever shall we do?"

"I suppose I must see Mrs. Cumberbatch," whispered Helen in reply. "Where is she?"

"I have taken her into the drawing-room for the present, ma'am."

"Very well, I will go to her. See that her room is put into some kind of order immediately. She will want to go to it at once. There must have been some mistake."

So saying, she passed into the drawing-room.

Sitting in an arm-chair, with a small travelling-bag upon her lap, was a middle-aged lady of no very striking appearance. She was short in stature, rather prim in countenance, and wore ringlets of greyish hair on each side of her face. She was dressed with scrupulous neatness, in garments which betokened widowhood. She rose as Helen entered, and listened with close lips and a peculiar smile, half gracious, half supercilious, whilst the latter apologised for Mr. Gresham's absence.

"You didn't expect me to-day, perhaps—h'm?" asked Mrs. Cumberbatch, in a subdued voice.

The assertion she first uttered was pronounced in a tone which seemed to take the point for granted, and the interrogatory "h'm?" came out with a sudden, unexpected start, which almost made the listener jump.

"Mr. Gresham was under the impression that you said Tuesday," returned Helen. "He must have made a mistake."

"No," said the lady. "He was quite right. I merely altered my mind."

The matter-of-course way in which she said this struck Helen as curious. Mrs. Cumberbatch spoke with her lips very close together, despite which Helen fancied that she had few, if any, teeth. She did not behave in the least like a stranger, but spoke and looked rather as if she had just come on a visit from the next street.

A servant knocked and entered.

"If you please, mum, the cabman says he has not been paid."

"I quite forgot," said Mrs. Cumberbatch, smiling calmly at Helen. "And I positively have no change. My dear, might I trouble you to lend me a couple of shillings."

Helen gave the servant the desired sum, still marvelling much at the stranger's matter-of-fact manner.

"You are Miss Norman,—h'm?" asked the lady, and, on receiving an affirmative reply, proceeded to examine Helen's face so closely, so much with the air of a mistress inspecting a new servant, that the latter's eyes dropped, and she began to feel uncomfortable.

"Scarcely what I expected to see," proceeded Mrs. Cumberbatch, as if to herself. "Mr. Gresham—he is my nephew, you know, but I have never seen him, and so I speak of him as a friend merely—Mr. Gresham has told me that you are much engaged in philanthropic works, h'm?"

" I should not venture to give my efforts so dignified a name."

" But still you don't mind others doing so? In connection with what religious community do you work, may I ask ? "

There was a touch of natural maliciousness in the first sentence. Helen began to wish that the duty of receiving the lady had fallen upon anyone rather than herself. She replied to the latter question that she worked in connection with no community of any kind.

" Indeed? I was in hopes you might have belonged to my own form of faith. I attend the meetings of the new branch of the Semi-United Presbyterio-Episcopal Church. Did you ever attend our services ? "

" Never," replied Helen, shortly.

" You know, of course, the nearest of our meeting-houses, h'm ? "

" I think I never heard of the sect before."

" Sect ! " repeated Mrs. Cumberbatch, with a smiling condescension. " So I have heard people speak of us before. Some even call our faith a schism. But, of course, you know, we are the only true Church ? After all I am not surprised that you are unacquainted with us. We do not care much to make converts. We alone are the elect, and if it pleases our Master to turn to us one of those who are going the broad way we accept the offering gladly. Otherwise, we can acquiesce in the Lord's will."

Helen could not restrain a smile at the cheerfulness with which Mrs. Cumberbatch acquiesced in the damnation of that not inconsiderable portion of mankind which did not belong to the new branch of the Semi-United Presbyterio-Episcopal Church. The latter answered the smile with one of her own. At this moment the servant re-entered and presented the change out of the two-shilling piece in coppers to Helen.

"Thank you," interposed Mrs. Cumberbatch, holding out her hand and taking the coppers coolly. She took out a purse from her pocket and deposited them in it with still the same self-approving smile upon her face.

"I think I may now take you to your room, Mrs. Cumberbatch," said Helen, rising. "As we did not expect you to-day it was not quite ready, but I think it will be in order now."

The lady accordingly followed, smiling graciously, with compressed lips, at the servant as she left the room. Helen departed to her usual occupations, and the two did not meet again till dinner-time.

When Helen entered the dining-room at that hour she found Mrs. Cumberbatch discoursing with her nephew as if she had known him from childhood, and when the little, black-robed woman with her grey ringlets assumed her seat at the end of the table opposite to Mr. Gresham it seemed as though she had always sat there. The same evening Mr. Gresham delivered over to her the management of his house. Henceforth she would be supreme in all matters of domestic arrangement. Mrs. Cumberbatch appeared pleased with the commission.

At seven o'clock Helen took the train, as usual, to the City. It was not a very long walk to the chapel, where she held her class, and on arriving there she found two or three of her pupils already waiting round the door. Helen produced the key and admitted them.

At this hour the interior of the chapel was already dark, so that the gas in the school-room had first to be lit. It was a moderate-sized room, fitted with benches, a few small desks, and a large desk for the teacher. Texts of Scripture ran round the walls in illuminated text, but the white plaster showed no other kind of ornament. Throughout the building prevailed a fresh, upholsterish smell, indicative of general newness. Indeed the chapel had scarcely been built three months, and parts of it were still unfinished.

Helen took her seat at the large desk and began to look over a few copy-books, making marks here and there with a blue lead-pencil. Whilst she was thus occupied girls continued to come into the room, each one upon entering hanging up her hat and cloak on pegs provided for that purpose and assuming her usual place upon the benches. Very shortly some ten or a dozen had collected, and sat rustling the leaves of books and whispering together quietly. Most of them appeared to be between sixteen and seventeen years old, and nearly all—as was to be expected when the class was purely voluntary—had faces indicating a certain degree of cheerful intelligence. Without exception they were dressed with extreme neatness. A glance at the hats hanging on the wall showed that they were not all above the temptation of a little cheap finery, but scarcely any wore ornaments on the dress, beyond a small blue or purple tie. The appearance of their hands sufficiently proved the manner in which their days were spent, the coarse stumpy fingers engrained with ineradicable dirt bespeaking toil of no delicate description. All their fingers bore the impression of the eternal needle, and not a few, on sitting down, had, by force of habit, taken a thimble from their pockets and slipped it on before beginning to spell.

Suddenly a clock in a different part of the chapel struck eight, and as the sounds died away in repeated echoes through the empty building, every girl drew herself up and sat with her book on her lap waiting for the commencement of the lesson. Helen began by calling over the roll. Two only were found to be absent.

" I have been thinking since last lesson," she then said, whilst the girls all regarded her with fixed attention, " that it would be wise to divide you into two classes. Some of you know the alphabet quite well, and are even able to read a little, whilst some do not yet even know the letters thoroughly. I wish you to understand that those who will be put in the lower class are not put there because I think them any worse than the others. In time, no doubt, they will make just as good scholars, but at present, through no fault of their own, they would keep the more advanced back if they continued in the same class with them. But for two classes it is clear that two teachers will be required, so I have asked Mr. Heatherley to endeavour to find someone to assist me. No doubt he will succeed before Saturday evening. To-night I must give one hour to each class, asking the class that I am unable to attend to at the time to go on studying by themselves."

As she concluded, Helen perceived a look of disappointment going round among the girls, and one or two whispers exchanged.

" Have you any objection to make to these arrangements ?" she asked, with the good-natured smile which had already endeared her to her pupils.

There was silence for a moment, but at length one of the girls sitting on the front bench ventured to speak.

"We know it's best whatever you say, ma'am," she said, "but we don't like to have any one else teach us but you."

Several voices made themselves heard confirming this remark.

"I'm sure I ought to be very proud of your confidence in me," replied Helen, with a glad light in her eyes; "but you see that it will be clearly impossible for me to take two classes at once. Suppose I say that I will take the classes by turns, the first class one evening and the second the next. Do you think that will do, Mary Walker?"

"That seems the only way, ma'am," replied the girl who had first spoken, and the rest also murmured their assent.

"Very well. Now I will call out the names of those who will form the first class."

When the two classes had arranged themselves upon the forms, Helen proceeded to give a lesson to those who did not yet know their letters, leaving the more advanced to study in silence. It was not easy work, but the earnest desire of the poor girls to do their best made it far from disagreeable. But how slow they were! With what immense difficulty they succeeded in comprehending the difference between n and m, between b and p! Helen's quiet patience

seemed inexhaustible. To the dullest she
would repeat the same thing over twenty
times, and the twentieth with no less of
gentleness in her tone than had marked her
first explanation. When at length nine
o'clock struck, she turned with a sigh of relief to the first class. Here there were one
or two who could read at the rate of five
words in as many minutes, but these were
the exceptions; most, though they knew their
letters well enough, puzzled in a hopeless
manner over the simplest word of two
syllables. There was something dreadful in
the sight of these faces bent with a determined, almost a desperate, energy over tasks
which every well-educated child of five or
six years old would think nothing of. The
efforts it cost them were painful in the extreme, they suffered with a physical suffering. But as soon as any one looked up into
the teacher's countenance, the courage which
had just been on the point of giving way
before apparently insurmountable difficulties
came back again. Helen's smile was a perpetual incitement to the most stupid.

At ten the classes broke up. For several
minutes Helen was engaged in answering
questions relative to the work for next lesson,
and then by degrees the school-room emptied
itself. She watched the girls as they took
down their hats and cloaks, and made internal comments upon their characters.

She had not noticed that for several minutes Mr. Heatherley had been standing in the doorway of the room, and by his side a girl of perhaps the same age as Helen, rather pretty in face, whose appearance rendered it probable that she was the daughter of a well-to-do working man. As soon as she perceived the two she advanced towards them, and Mr. Heatherley introduced his companion as Miss Venning.

"You desire to help me in my evening classes?" said Helen, as she shook hands with the girl, who was very timid in manner.

"I should not have ventured to think of teaching," replied the latter, a modest blush upon her comely features. "It is Mr. Heatherley who has persuaded me to offer myself. But I am really afraid that I have not ability enough."

"That's all nonsense, Lucy," said Mr. Heatherley, good-naturedly. "You don't mean to pretend that you can't read and write?"

The girl held down her head in silence, still blushing.

"I thought your impudence wouldn't go quite so far," said the clergyman. "Well, nothing more whatever is wanted, except a little patience. And that I know you have."

"Oh, please not to think I am unwilling to do what I can," said Lucy Venning, looking from the clergyman to Helen. "I really shall be very glad to help, if I am thought capable, very glad indeed."

"I have no doubt whatever that you will be capable, Miss Venning," replied Helen. "Patience is the principal thing needed. These poor girls are sadly ignorant, and want slow and careful teaching. Can you begin on Saturday?"

"Oh yes," said Lucy.

"Very well. I shall be sincerely glad to see you here. And now I must be off; it is getting late."

"Let me see," interposed Mr. Heatherley. "You pass Miss Venning's door, if I'm not mistaken. You must let me see you safe to the station as usual, Miss Norman."

And so they turned out the lights and left the chapel.

CHAPTER X.

A FOREGONE CONCLUSION.

SELDOM had Helen experienced so strong an aversion for any one as that excited in her by the words, the manner, and soon the very appearance of Mrs. Cumberbatch. In the latter's presence she suffered from continual irritation. And this was all the worse, seeing that Mrs. Cumberbatch seemed to take the utmost interest in her nephew's ward, and seldom allowed her to remain alone when in the house. On Sunday alone was there any rest from her persecution. Happily she had discovered a congregation of the new branch of the Semi-United Presbyterio-Episcopal Church, and the fact that it met at the extremity of Mile-end Road, was to her no obstacle whatever. Twice each Sunday did she attend the service there, going and returning by omnibus each time. Helen never knew her to manifest the slightest sign of fatigue. She was always the same close-lipped, smiling little woman, under every circumstance.

Under the pretence of requesting her to read to him, Mr. Gresham continued to engross much of his ward's leisure. Indeed, so strong was his infatuation becoming, that he could hardly bear her to be out of his sight. In the afternoons he always waited for her return home with childish impatience, and called her into his presence on some trivial pretext almost as soon as she had entered the house. His jealousy of a hundred imaginary rivals well-nigh drove him to madness, he plotted and schemed for hours how to put an end to her long daily absences. For all this he had not the courage openly to break his secret to her, and know his fate. Indeed, he felt that he already knew his fate only too well. He saw that Helen still behaved to him with the most perfect frankness, without a trace of embarrassment, in every respect treating him like a friend— and no more. At times he was driven into paroxysms of rage when he thought of the mean acts he had committed, the perpetual torture from which he suffered, all in consequence of this ill-advised but involuntary passion. He mocked at himself, he attacked himself with the fiercest sarcasms and ironies ; a thousand times he went to bed at night saying that in the morning he would rise calm and indifferent to the whole race of womankind, as he had been but a few months ago. And yet the morning found the invincible worm eating still deeper into his heart. He was beginning to despise himself as a coward, a creature devoid alike of honour and of courage.

He asked himself whether there was any real obstacle in the way of his offering his hand to Helen, and being either accepted or refused as the case might be. He could see none. He knew cases of men older than himself who had married wards of their own, under far less creditable circumstances. At least no one could think that he was actuated by a mercenary spirit; his own independent position forbade that. What, then, stood in his way? He knew very well that it was that stiff-necked pride, that empty vanity which had been the guiding spirit of his life. Could he, who had scoffed at all the passions, the sentiments, the principles which ordinarily rule the existence of men, who had trained himself into an affected cynicism which all his friends imagined to be real, could he now confess himself a convert to the gentle teaching of love, humble himself to entreat the favour of a girl? The thought was intolerable to him.

Helen's portrait was proceeding very slowly. Mr. Gresham lingered over it purposely; partly because he had an actual pleasure in the work, partly because it afforded him a good opportunity of frequently enjoying his ward's society; partly, again, because he felt that the completion of the picture would be the most appropriate occasion for opening his heart; and he dreaded the approach of the time. Soon it had been in hand nearly six weeks, and was all but finished. One morning he had requested Helen to sit, and had lingered for a couple of hours before the canvas, now and then adding a touch, but for the most part only pretending to paint, and keeping his eyes fixed upon the girl's face. At last he laid down his pallet, and threw himself with a careless air into a seat by Helen's side.

"And how goes the missionary work in the Oriental regions?" he asked, with a forced assumption of his wonted sceptical tone and look.

"As well as I could hope, I think," replied Helen.

"Then let us have statistics. How many have you converted to the doctrine of soap and water, say during the last week?"

"I wish the process of conversion were capable of being represented by statistics," said Helen. "We can only venture to look for decided results at the end of a comparatively long period. Ask me when I have been at work a year, Mr. Gresham, and I hope to be able to give you something tangible."

"A year! And you mean to say that your whim will last so long? Why, I was calculating that our Christmas festivities, at the latest, would celebrate its burial."

"You credit me with very little stability of character, Mr. Gresham."

"On the contrary, in giving you till Christmas I conceived I was crediting you with a most astonishing stability."

"I have already said that this will be the work of my life, and I say so in seriousness."

"Your life? And when you are married do you suppose your husband will allow you to spend your days in slums and ragged schools?"

"I think there is little prospect of my ever marrying," replied Helen, with a quiet smile.

"Indeed? Not Mr. Heatherley? You would make an admirable parson's wife, Helen."

Helen looked curiously at him as he spoke thus, and he met her gaze with one which conveyed much more earnestness than his words.

"Mr. Heatherley and I are, I hope, very good friends," she replied, "but the idea of our ever becoming more to each other than that is one for which you must yourself take credit, Mr. Gresham."

"But how and where will you live? I have been very seriously thinking of late of the Dorsetshire farm. Suppose I sell this house and go to live in the country; what will become of you then, Helen?"

"I shall take a lodging somewhere near to the scene of my occupation," replied the girl, calmly. "By so doing I should save much time and expense."

" Possibly you would like to do that at once ? "

" I should only do so if I had no near friends in London.   At present I enjoy living in your house, Mr. Gresham.   I should lose your society with regret."

" And yet there is not much similarity between us, Helen, is there ? "

" We often agree in our literary tastes."

" So we do.   But then you take the world so terribly *au sérieux ;* I look upon it as a farce, and amuse myself with the spectacle."

" That I am sorry for," said Helen.

There was silence for a while.

" Do you ever think about my character, Helen ? " asked the artist then.

" I have naturally sometimes thought of it, Mr. Gresham," returned his ward, with some little hesitation.   "Not to have done so would argue want of friendship."

" And what were your conclusions with regard to me ?   Is it indiscreet to ask such a question ? "

" Rather indiscreet, perhaps."

" You decline to make any comments ? "

" Would any useful end be served if I consented ? "

" Possibly by regarding my image in your clear mind, I might learn to know myself better than I now do."

" In that case I will venture to mention one thought which has sometimes occurred

to me. It is my belief, Mr. Gresham, that
people are not so sincere with each other as
they might, with great advantage, be. As you
have invited me to speak, you will not be
offended at what I say?"

"In no case."

"I have sometimes thought, then," said
the girl, looking into her guardian's face with
frank simplicity, "that it is a pity you do
not try to divest your words and your manner
of a certain unreality, insincerity—what shall
I call it?—which they possess. I sometimes
fancy that you are not naturally so sceptical
regarding the seriousness of life as you would
pretend to be. I have noticed indications of
this more particularly during the last few
weeks."

Mr. Gresham smiled. He seemed to experience a real pleasure in hearing these words.

"And why is it a pity that I am what I
am?" he asked. "Should I be more amiable
do you think—should I seem more agreeable,
say to you, if I were otherwise?"

"I am sure you would."

"But what would you have me do? How
can I evince sincerity? Shall I turn Ranter,
and harangue a crowd next evening from the
top of the nearest lamp-post?"

"I fear you are incorrigible, Mr. Gresham,"
said Helen, shaking her head and smiling.

"But, in sober earnest, what shall I do?
I am willing—I am willing to be savagely

serious, indeed I am. There shall be a proof of it."

He took out his pocket-book, and released from it a ten-pound bank-note.

"There," he continued, "take this, Helen, and spend it for me upon your unspeakable *protégés*."

Helen shook her head.

"But why not?" he pursued. "Take it, I beg of you. Shall I go down on my knees? Take it, Helen, and buy somebody a ton of soap with it—the very best brown Windsor!"

"You do not mean what you say, Mr. Gresham. You would regret it the moment the money had left your hands."

"Upon my word, no! I am in terrific earnest. Won't you take me at my word?"

"It is always so difficult for me to understand whether you mean what you say."

"But in this case I do. Take the ten-pound note, Helen. I mean it. Take it, and when it is spent, ask me for another. I wish to be serious. I wish to be amiable. I wish to please you, Helen."

"Indeed you do please me, Mr. Gresham, if you really mean this. I will take you literally." As she spoke she put the note in her purse. "You shall have an exact account of how this money has been spent. I think I have already a purpose for it in my mind. It is very good of you to make me your agent."

Mr. Gresham suddenly took one of her hands in both his own, and looked full into her face. Just as he was opening his lips to speak, the door creaked, and Mrs. Cumberbatch entered. Mr. Gresham rose with a savage look, which he vainly endeavoured to conceal, and walked to his easel.

"The picture near completion—h'm?" asked the intruder, turning first to Helen, who sat perfectly composed, then to the artist, who was leaning over his pallet.

"Almost finished," said the latter, in a low tone, and continued to paint.

Shortly, Mrs. Cumberbatch withdrew, and Helen at the same time. As the latter was leaving the room, Mr. Gresham recalled her for a moment.

"I shall add to it the last touches," he said, "before I go out, but in the afternoon I have an engagement which will keep me away till nearly nine to-night. Will you come up here when you return from the school and have a look at it? I shall be here then."

"Gladly," said Helen.

It was Saturday, and at eight o'clock Helen opened her classes as usual. Her new assistant, Lucy Venning, was punctual, and the room was soon a scene of assiduous study. Lucy, when she succeeded in overcoming her extreme diffidence, made a capital teacher. Her patience equalled that of Helen's, and her comprehension of, and sympathy with the pupils was perfect. From the first, Helen had regarded Lucy with much interest, and, now that she came to know her better, the interest began to develope into attachment. There was an excessive charm for her in Lucy's perfect simplicity of manner, her low, gentle voice, and her uniform sweetness of temper. As yet there had not been much opportunity of winning the girl's confidence, but each time she saw her, Helen felt more desirous of doing so. At present she felt that Lucy regarded her with somewhat of awe, knowing her to be wealthy, and in a high social position compared with herself. Despite this, she hoped before long to make a friend of Lucy.

Whilst Helen was thus engaged, Mr. Gresham was at his Club. His engagement, which was a real one, had terminated sooner than he had anticipated; and feeling by no means disposed for an evening in the company of Mrs. Cumberbatch—from whose invasions he knew no apartment was safe —he had dined at his Club, and proceeded to amuse himself for an hour or two with periodicals. He was almost alone there, for most of the other members were then out of town. Having finished his dinner, he retained a bottle of wine, out of which he hoped to imbibe something more than the mere juice of the grape. In fact he wanted courage. Helen had promised to visit the studio when she returned, which would be about eleven. At that hour Mrs. Cumberhatch would be, it was to be presumed, fast asleep; and the artist had resolved that to-night should decide his fate.

His attempt to read resulted in failure. He threw the paper away from him, and resolved to fight it out manfully with his thoughts. By degrees he finished the wine, and ordered another bottle. When he had also finished this, it was ten o'clock. He left the Club, called a hansom, and was driven home.

With a hand and head feverishly hot, he entered the studio. He knew it was too early to expect Helen yet, but he felt relieved when he saw that the studio was dark and empty. Having lit two or three large tapers, he began to pace the room in impatience. He thought over the morning's conversation, and succeeded in persuading himself that there had been something in Helen's manner towards him which he had not before observed, something more gracious, more affectionate even. He was determined to look on nothing but the bright side of things, and the most unusual quantity of wine which he had drunk doubtless aided him in his attempt. By degrees he lost himself in glowing hopes and fancies, and was at length startled at suddenly perceiving Helen by his side.

"Ah! you are here!" he exclaimed. "Did you come down the chimney?"

"In a far more prosaic manner. I came through the door, as I usually do."

"And you have come to look at the finished picture?"

"I promised that I would."

"There it is, then. Are you satisfied with it?"

"Mrs. Cumberbatch told me it is a very good likeness. As a painting, I think it admirable."

"And now what are we to do with it, Helen?"

"I have no idea, Mr. Gresham, what your intentions are with regard to it. I should myself suggest that it be put away into some corner till you take your threatened departure for the farm in Dorsetshire, then taken with you, and hung up in a shady corner of some quiet room."

"Is there no one you would like to give it to?"

"It is not mine to give, Mr. Gresham."

"But say it were yours. Is there no one you would give it to, in preference to all the rest of the world? Tell me seriously, Helen."

The girl looked at him with some surprise, he spoke so earnestly.

"I should give it to you, Mr. Gresham," she said. "There is certainly no one to whom I should give it in preference to you."

"You mean that Helen?" he asked eagerly.

"Certainly. I should like you to keep it as a memento of my friendship."

Helen still gazed into his face. The unusual brilliancy of his face struck her. She made as though she would say good-night and depart.

"Stay, Helen!" he said, catching her by the hands, the fierce beating of his heart almost choking his words. "It is mine, then. I thank you for the present, but grant me one more favour. Let me have it framed and hung up in my drawing-room as the portrait—of my wife!"

He was almost stunned by the word as it left his lips. It seemed to him to echo throughout the whole house. He appeared to himself to have shouted, rather than whispered it. At all events, the word was uttered, and he stood holding Helen's hands, waiting for her reply.

She said nothing, but replied to his burning gaze with one of amazement, almost of fright. He continued to speak, using tones such as, perhaps, had never before passed his lips.

"Yes, as my wife, Helen! I mean it. In this I am serious—in this, at least! Cannot you believe it? You have spoken to me of friendship, Helen, but it is with far more than friendship that I have long regarded

you, rather with affection which I feel is
sincere and true, affection such as I have
never before felt for living creature. Speak
Helen! Have *you* any such affection for me?
Could you accept me for your husband? Do
you believe in my affection?"

"You cannot mean what you say, Mr.
Gresham," Helen replied at length, drawing
her hands away.

"Every word. I love you devotedly,
Helen! Quick; free me from this wretched
suffering. I can endure it no longer. Will
you be my wife?"

"I cannot," replied the girl, in firm, but
gentle tones. "It would be impossible for
me to accept your offer, Mr. Gresham. I
entertain the sincerest friendship for you;
I regard you always as my adopted father;
I could not be your wife."

The answer fell with a calming effect on
Mr. Gresham. He took one turn up and
down the room, then suddenly stopped
before her with the old ironical smile on his
face.

"Why, so I anticipated, Helen," he said.
"And the picture has been painted in vain—
not an unusual thing in this world. And so
we may say good-night, I suppose, may we
not?"

"Was this a jest, Mr. Gresham?" asked
the girl, with something of indignation in her
tone.

"By no means," he replied, grinding with his teeth. "Oh no, not a jest, by no means. But yet it would be best to think of it as such. Do you know what I am going to do now, Helen?"

She looked at him in doubt, for a moment in fear, but reflection told her that the latter feeling was groundless.

"On Monday I shall begin the task of settling all my business affairs, and as soon as they are all settled, I shall leave England for a year, perhaps for longer. Do you approve of that?"

"It grieves me extremely that I should be the cause of it, Mr. Gresham."

"You the cause of it?" he exclaimed, with affected surprise. "My good child! not in the least. You the cause of it!"

"Then why impart this purpose of yours to me under such very strange circumstances?"

"You think them strange, eh? Ah! perhaps they are rather so. Never mind. My purpose holds good for all that. You can do very well without me for a year?"

Helen began to be convinced that her guardian had partaken of too much wine. She stepped towards the door.

"It is getting very late, Mr. Gresham," she said. "I must wish you good-night."

Suddenly he started to her, and seized her arm.

"You are not a chatterbox, are you?" he asked, in a low and rather fierce tone.

"I hope not," replied Helen, relieving herself from his grasp, and opening the door.

"Then you won't go and boast to people what a damned fool I have made of myself to you to-night?"

"I shall not speak a word of it, Mr. Gresham," replied his ward, regarding him with concern; "and I hope by the morning it will all have passed from your mind."

"Amen! Good-night, Helen."

"Good-night, Mr. Gresham."

The artist was absent from home all the next day, and also the whole of Monday. During that time Helen did not see him. On Tuesday they met at meals only, during which Mr. Gresham behaved quite in his ordinary manner, except that perhaps he spoke rather less than usual. Helen also did her best to show no sign of remembering what had happened, and succeeded in appearing quite at her ease. At dinner on Tuesday, Mr. Gresham announced his departure at the end of the week for the Continent.

"Do you propose to be long away, Gilbert,—h'm?" asked Mrs. Cumberbatch.

"Probably a month or two," was the reply. "I shall write to you, aunt, and tell you of my plans."

Mrs. Cumberbatch glanced from her nephew to Helen. She suspected something. For a wonder, however, she did not pursue her interrogations, and the subject dropped.

Mr. Gresham and his ward alike took care to avoid a private interview. On Saturday morning the artist was ready to depart, apparently in quite a cheerful mood. He shook hands with his aunt and with Helen, bestowing no more pressure in the one case than in the other, and stepped into his carriage. Helen sighed as she saw him depart, but whether with relief or not she scarcely knew. The incident which had apparently given rise to this departure affected her much; even yet she scarcely knew what to think of it. In any case, she did not see how she could have adopted any other course than that she had chosen. Nothing remained but to settle down to the companionship of Mrs. Cumberbatch, and to see whether Mr. Gresham would really fulfil his purpose of being away a year.

CHAPTER XI.

The Club of which Arthur Golding had become a member was only one of a great number of similar combinations which at this time the glorious spirit of Radicalism was calling into existence throughout the Metropolis. It is true that this association stood perhaps alone in the lofty and unselfish nature of its immediate aims. This was the result of the individual character of its founder, who, by gathering around him only single and moderately well-to-do working men, rendered practicable the noble scheme which he had long meditated before endeavouring to carry it into execution. The aims of other Radical clubs, which began to manifest activity towards the end of the year 1870, were almost exclusively political, though some comprehended in their scheme the advantages of a benefit-society for their own members when in need of assistance. It was a season of strong political ferment among the oppressed classes throughout the kingdom. As early as April of that year a great public meeting had been held in Trafalgar Square, at which resolutions were passed

demanding the attention of the Government
to the scandalous sufferings of the working-
classes.

The notes of the " Marseillaise " were occasionally heard in the open streets. Repub-
licanism of an advanced type was loudly
advocated on numerous platforms and in
open-air assemblies ; active associations, such
as the Land and Labour League, spread a
knowledge of the wrongs of the poor and the
tyranny of the ruling classes, far and wide
over the country ; men who were so crushed
beneath the burden of ceaseless, brutal toil,
that they had forgotten to raise their eyes
from the dull earth, now began to look eagerly
around them, to read the signs of the times,
and to rejoice that at length their voices would
be heard as they clamoured for justice.

The war between France and Germany
came to aid, with the impulse of a new excitement, the movement for justice and liberty.
With hopes of the downfall of tyranny in
France and of the establishment once more of
a Republic, the thoughts of the poor in England were naturally turned in the same direction more strongly than ever. One of the
ripest outcomes of the time was the London
Patriotic Society, whose meetings at the
tavern called the Hole-in-the-Wall, excited the
attention of rich as well as poor, and for the
suppression of which indirect efforts were
before long made by the Government. Great

was the excitement awakened among all these
humble, but not ignoble, advocates of freedom when the news of the glorious 4th of
September was read in London, when it was
known that Paris, the suffering high-priestess
of Liberty, had once again shaken off the degrading yoke of princes and proclaimed the
rule of the people.   That evening an extraordinary meeting was held by the club in
Crown Street.   Every-day business was for
once thrown aside, and the members joined
hands in mutual congratulation, in exalted
enthusiasm.   The speech of the evening was
made by Arthur Golding, for William Noble
saw that his friend was bursting with eagerness to pour forth his emotion in a flood of
words, and purposely withheld his own
eloquence.   After speaking of the event of
the day, as it concerned France in particular,
Arthur concluded with a glowing rhapsody,
wherein was set forth the hopes he entertained
for the future of their own country.

    " Between England and France," he said,
" roll but some twenty miles of sea.   But a
few hours' journey separates us from a
country where the gates of the temple of
Liberty have once more been thrown wide
open, never, let us hope, to be closed again.
Is it alone disinterested love for our fellow-
creatures in France that makes us rejoice at
their freedom ?   Let us hope that we duly
feel the claims for a common humanity which

links us to the oppressed in all quarters of
the globe ; but it would be vain to pretend
that we had not some yet stronger reason for
the delight this news has awakened in us. It
means that we shall henceforth have before
our eyes, and near at hand, an example of a
great people ruled by its own voice alone, of
a people that has known but too well all the
terrific evils of monopolised authority, and is
determined to banish them from its land for
ever. This example will be of inestimable
value, of incalculable aid to us in our struggle
here in England. For now nearly a hundred
years England has possessed such an example
in the United States of America, but this has
been of little effect. In the first place the
vast sweep of the Atlantic lies between us
and America, and though thousands of our
fellow-workmen go forth thither yearly,
as if to a land of promise, but few ever come
to return and bring to us the good tidings.
They settle for good and all in the States, exercising in a foreign land and under brighter
skies the strength of mind and body which,
had they stayed with us, would only have
proved their curse. Secondly, it was only
by means of a war with England that
America procured its freedom, and, though
I trust that we here are far above such
foolish prejudices, this may perhaps count as
one reason why Englishmen have seldom
sought for an incitement to progress in the

example of the enfranchised country. But with France it is different. France is a name dear to the present generation of Englishmen. In the last war which called to arms the greatest nations of Europe, France fought by the side of England, and by her side helped to conquer. France is close to our shores, her cliffs can be seen across the strip of sea which divides us. Despite her misfortunes, brought upon her head by the cursed descendant of a cursed house, France always has been, and always will be, a leading state in Europe. Her example will be unspeakably precious in the sight of us strugglers for right.

"She will teach us that the ability to govern is not alone entrusted to those whom centuries of wanton luxury have rendered the slaves of selfishness and ignoble pride, to those whose brains have been warped and narrowed by the hereditary burden of a crown ! She will teach us that the meanest beggar in the streets has as indefeasible a claim to justice and right as the pampered lord who flung him a curse instead of a coin ! She will teach us that men are not beasts, that light, and air, and cleanliness, and raiment, and food are what every man has a claim to, and what is the duty of those whom the people choose to represent their voices to see that every man obtains ! And she will teach us that the poor have brains and mental faculties as well as the rich, that from the ranks of the poor oft-times rise the geniuses of a nation, that consequently the development of the higher nature of the poor man's child by a course of enlightened education is as much the duty of the State as the establishment and endowment of schools and colleges for the heirs to wealth.

" France has seized upon her liberty in the midst of cruel anguish and misery. Whether we shall live to see England at the feet of a foreign enemy it is impossible to foresee, we can only stoutly hope not. But is such a position the only one in which a change of government is possible ? Is it only by the oppression of foreign conquest that a nation is driven to despair, and so wins the courage to cast aside its tyrants ? The end of the last century saw a revolution in France which turned her rivers of water into rivers of blood, and darkened the face of Europe with the smoke of conflagration. But surely we need not expect a revolution under any such circumstances as these. Is not our position one which will excite the laughter, if not the scorn of future eyes ? Here are we working classes, numbering who can say how many times more than the rich who oppress us, stronger in arm, firmer in endurance, more earnest in aim. Is it not indeed worthy of scorn that, despite all this, we suffer from day to day and see no way out of our

suffering?   Suppose every working-man in
England got up to-morrow morning, and, instead of going to his work, walked to the
great square in the town where he lives and
declared that he was sick to death of the life
he led and *would* have things otherwise. You
say that the army would be marched against
us, and violence would naturally result. Yes,
but are not the soldiers themselves working-
men, men hired to the despicable toil of
making themselves machines in order to be
able to slaughter their fellow-men with skill?
Why should these men be more afraid of
striking, of throwing up their wages with the
chance of bettering themselves than other
labourers are!   You can scarcely say that
their wages are so excellent they cannot hope
to earn more under other masters and at
other and better work.   Then what is to prevent these soldiers from joining us?

" Friends, the work for the future lies with
such clubs as this of ours.   Not content with
helping to keep our fellows alive, we must
teach them their power !   We know that the
lesson has already begun to be learnt, but we
must not cease in our effort for all that.   We
will teach these wretched poverty-stricken
crowds their strength, if only they choose to
exert it.   And henceforth we shall have the
example of France to point to, in proof of
our assertion that we are not dependent for
our existence upon kings and queens.   All

good wishes, then, to the new Republic. May she grow, may she thrive, may her future be all the more bright and glorious that her birth has been amid scenes of sadness and ignominy !"

This speech ended the meeting, and the members crowded round Arthur to shake hands with him.

"What do you think, Arthur ?" asked Mark Challenger, as the two walked home together. "Isn't this better than being a painter, and living at somebody else's expense ? Don't you feel that you are more of a man ?"

" You are right !" replied Arthur, " I feel utterly ashamed of myself when I think of those days. What can have possessed me to think of being an artist ? Then I should have spent my days and nights in useless labour, and after all been miserably dependent upon the rich and proud. If *they* had not bought my pictures, I should have starved—and serve me right, too, I think. Now I have the consolation of knowing that I work for a useful end. The newspapers I help to print spreads knowledge among thousands every day ; it makes me work with energy when I think of it. Hurrah ! We shall do something yet !"

Arthur possessed from nature the temperament which always accompanies genius. Undoubtedly at this period he sincerely believed the sentiments which we have just heard him express to his friend Mark.   Except on Sunday he allowed himself scarcely any time for calm reflection ; he lived in a perpetual ferment of activity.   If he was not at his work, he was engaged heart and soul in exertions connected with the club.   He became acquainted with the editor of a paper—one of many which were springing up about this time—which had for its object the spread at once of Radicalism and Free-thought, and not unfrequently he wrote a letter or a short article which was printed in its columns.   All such circumstances as these were incitements to fresh enthusiasm.   At the club he seemed already to take precedence of Will Noble himself, for he certainly excelled the latter in a certain fervid eloquence which he himself was surprised to find that he possessed.   But in solid force of argument he never equalled the founder of the club.   Had either of these two been of an envious disposition, they could not certainly have long continued friends under the circumstances.   But envy or jealousy were remote from the thoughts of both, their minds were engrossed with far other and higher feelings.   Every day cemented their friendship more firmly ; every act or word of the one only incited the other to a generous rivalry.

Both Arthur and Mark kept completely apart from the other residents in Mrs. Pettindund's house as far as any social intercourse is concerned. In the first place they were not much at home, and then the appearance of their fellow-lodgers was not such as to excite much interest. To this, however, there was one exception, at least in Arthur's case. Very shortly after he had taken up his abode in Gower Place, his notice was attracted by one of the lodgers on the floor beneath him. This was a young girl, of perhaps seventeen or eighteen, whom he had occasionally passed on the stairs, and once or twice in the street. She was very pretty, if not positively handsome, tall, with dark hair which she arranged in a tasteful way, and dressed in black which seemed to indicate mourning. Though her beauty was of a somewhat sensual type, and her features betrayed no special intelligence or good-humour, Arthur felt strangely attracted to her for all that. To a beautiful female face he was always especially susceptible, and in this case the natural ardour of his years was additionally excited by the occasional and brief glimpses he obtained of her, and by the fact that she resided under the same roof as himself. There was, moreover, a fixed paleness upon the girl's face, and now and then a look of suffering which excited his compassion. As week after week went by, he noticed that these signs increased. He thought she must be ill, and felt his interest in her grow yet stronger.

He knew that she took her meals with the landlady's family in the kitchen, for on several occasions when he had gone down early in the morning to pay his rent he had seen her at breakfast there, and had heard her addressed as "Carrie." He concluded that she was in some way related to the Pettindund's. He knew also from conversation heard on the same occasion that she went out to work every day with Mrs. Pettindund's two daughters, as a "mantle-hand." Before very long he learned her complete name, for, taking a letter out of the letter-box one night just as the postman delivered it, he found it was addressed to Miss Carrie Mitchell; and it was not probable that there was more than one young lady in the house. Arthur would have been glad to know more of her; but scarcely knew how the information could be gained. He was thinking of asking Mark Challenger if he knew anything of her, when another piece of chance threw a very unexpected light upon her history.

Arthur had risen one morning about six o'clock—it was drawing near to the end of October—and was engaged in dressing, when Mark Challenger's door, which was next to his, opened, and Mark having called out to know if his friend was up, Arthur opened his door and replied in the affirmative, whereon Mark entered his room.

" Read that," he said, holding out a sheet of paper which looked like a letter.

Arthur took it, and read this :—

" DEAR CARRIE,—

"My landlady tells me a girl has been calling at my lodgings several times lately, asking to see me. I have no doubt this is you, and I wish you to understand at once that you will have to stop bothering me. I have done all I mean to do for you, and now you will have to look out for yourself. You needn't expect I shall stump up anything even if you have a child, as you say you are going to. If you try to force it out of me, it's the easiest thing in the world for me to prove that you're nothing but a common girl of the town, and then you have no remedy. Do just take this hint, and leave me alone in future; if you don't, I shall have to do something I shouldn't much care to.

"A. W."

Arthur looked at Mr. Challenger in pained astonishment.

" Why did you give me this to read ? " he asked. " I thought it was something of your own. We have no business to have read this."

" Why, I'll tell you," replied Mark, scratching his head. " You know I came up late to bed last night, and as I passed one of the doors on the floor below I saw a piece of paper lying near it. I picked it up and found it to be this. After all, I don't think there's so much harm in our reading it. You see, if I'd given it back to the girl, she would never have believed that I didn't know all it contained. As it is she will perhaps never know she has lost it, and it's much better it should come into our hands than into those of someone who would talk about it all over the house."

" But what a rascal this fellow is ! " cried Arthur, burning with righteous indignation. " What a cold-blooded villain ! I declare, if there was only an address on it, I would seek the fellow out and tell him what I thought of him. Why, it's that poor girl underneath, called Carrie Mitchell, isn't it ? "

" To be sure. I have rather noticed her lately, and I half suspected there was something wrong."

" But do you think it likely the Pettindunds know of this ? "

" Can't tell ; but I don't think so."

" Bye-the-by, how is the girl connected with them, do you know ? "

" Oh, yes. I had the whole tale from Mrs. Pettindund one day. It seems that Carrie Mitchell is Mrs. Pettindund's niece. Her father and mother died not long since, and

the girl then came here to earn her living.
She pays no end of money for her board and
lodging, and she certainly can't get more than
fifteen shillings a week—poor creature."

" But this letter. However can she have
got into a scrape with a blackguard such as
this ? You see he writes a fairly good hand.
Some clerk, I suppose. I should like to have
my fingers on his throat ! "

" What shall we do with the letter,
Arthur ? "

" Burn it, by all means. As you say, it is
impossible to return it. I wish heartily we
could do something for the poor girl ! "

" And yet I don't see how we can," returned Mark. " We mustn't appear to know
anything about this affair, of course."

" Such a beautiful face she has," said
Arthur ; " but looks so terribly pale and ill.
No wonder ! I shouldn't be surprised if Mrs.
Pettindund turned her out of the house as
soon as she finds this out. I have very little
faith in her charity."

" Well, if she does that," said Mark, " we
might be able to help her ; but I really don't
see what we can do now."

" Nor I," added Arthur, sadly.

Throughout the day his thoughts were
busy with this discovery. It did not occur to
him for a moment that the girl herself might
possibly be to blame. He could feel nothing
but tender pity for her, passionate indigna-

tion against the heartless brute who had cast her off when she most needed his help.

For several days he did his best to catch sight of her, after listening at his door for several hours in hope of hearing her come up stairs.

One morning, just as he was returning from work through the night, he had his wish. As he entered the house he saw Carrie ascending the stairs with a large can of water, which seemed beyond her strength to lift. He ran forward at once, and begged to be allowed to help her.

As he looked into her face he saw she was crying. Not knowing how to express anxiety or condolence, he pretended not to observe her distress, and contented himself with carrying her can to her door. She thanked him in a low voice, always keeping her face averted.

Troubled beyond expression by the girl's sufferings, Arthur, instead of going at once to bed, paced his room for nearly an hour, vainly endeavouring to devise some method of giving her assistance.

Mark Challenger was already gone to business, so that there was no one at hand with whom he could take counsel. Emotions such as he had never felt surged within his heart. The sight of Helen Norman had but a short time ago been sufficient to exalt him to regions of enthusiastic rapture; but his love for

Helen, if love it were, had been a pure devotion of the spirit, a sentiment which called into play the highest energies of his intellect, the noblest impulses of his heart to the exclusion of all ignobler feeling.

But now it was the senses that had sway over him. His blood coursed hot through his veins, his pulses throbbed. One moment he burned with vehement anger at the unknown author of the poor girl's troubles, becoming conscious of a depth of resentful ferocity in his nature, the existence of which he could not have believed; the next, his being seemed to melt with excess of passion, as he thought of Carrie's beautiful face and form, and dwelt with unutterable tenderness upon the vision of her tear-reddened eyes, her pale cheeks, her feeble step. He suffered physically; it was as though some force were straining at his heart-strings, making him pant for breath.

Once or twice he was on the point of casting aside all doubts and hesitations, and of going to speak to her at her own room-door and to offer her what help he could—in the shape of money. But a sense of shame and of respect for her feelings retained him. Still he could do nothing but pace the room, now quite unconscious of the weariness which had possessed him when he entered the house, and dreaming of nothing less than of sleep. The contest forced groans from his heart;

he pressed his hands fiercely together upon his forehead, as if to force himself into calmness.

Just then he fancied he heard a voice speaking on the stairs. Starting to the door he opened it softly, and listened.

He was not mistaken. Someone was knocking loudly at a door below, and calling—"Carrie! Carrie!"

Then there was a pause, during which an answer seemed to come from within, though it was not audible.

"Ain't you well?" asked the voice again, which Arthur now recognised as that of Mrs. Pettindund's daughter. "We're just going. You'll be late."

Again no reply seemed to come from within, after which the girl who had spoken ran downstairs.

Still Arthur listened intently. Presently he heard a heavier step ascending the stairs, and, leaning over the banisters, he could perceive Mrs. Pettindund's portly person. The landlady also stopped before Carrie's room, and knocked loudly.

The key turned, and the door opened.

Arthur leaned forward still more, and listened with his utmost power of attention. He saw nothing dishonourable in so doing, under the circumstances; or, perhaps, more properly speaking, he merely obeyed an instinct, and did not think about it at all.

" And so you can't go to work, eh ? "
asked the woman, in a tone of repulsive
coarseness.

A reply was made in so low a voice that it
was inaudible.

" And d'ye think I didn't know all about it
long since ? " returned Mrs. Pettindund, who
seemed to be standing half in, half out of
the room. " Well, all I've got to say is
you've made yer bed and you must lay in it.
How d'ye think ye're goin' to live if you don't
go to work, eh ? "

Arthur could hear a sob for the only
reply.

" Yer don't think I'm sich a fool as to keep
yer, eh ? " pursued the kindly-hearted landlady. " An' lose the good name o' th'ouse
an' all ? If you do, you're mistaken, that's all
as I've got to say t'yer."

The listener's straining ears could just
catch the answer.

" You won't turn me out of doors, aunt ? "
pleaded the girl's sobbing voice. " Won't you
let me stay till it's over, and then work and
pay you all back ? "

" A likely joke that, too! *You* pay me
back ! Catch yer doin' of it ! I tell you,
you leave this 'ouse to-day, an' there's no
two ways about that. D'ye 'ear ? "

" But you've always been kind to me,
aunt ! " sobbed Carrie. " Won't you have
some pity ? If I've done wrong, I'm sorry

for it; and I shall have to suffer for it all my life. You've been kind to me till now, aunt; don't be so cruel as to turn me out. I've no home to go to."

"What I 'ave been, an' what I'm goin' to be now, is two very different things," returned Mrs. Pettindund, in her coarse, gin-thickened, over-fed voice, and always with that inimitable ferocity of the true London lodging-house keeper. "I'll trouble yer to pay me twelve-an'-sixpence, too, as soon as you get it; so you'd best go to work to-day, if it's only for the money. I'll have no ——— i' my 'ouse, an' so you 'ave it straight."

Mrs. Pettindund, exercising her discretionary powers in the matter of English orthoepy, pronounced the last word "stright." And, having delivered herself thus, she slammed the door to, and turned to go down stairs.

Guided by the irresistible impulse of the moment, Arthur darted down the stairs. As soon as Mrs. Pettindund saw him he beckoned to her to follow him.

With a look of surprise upon her pursy and somewhat bloated face, she ascended to his room, and entered it after him. Arthur closed the door.

"I have been listening to you for the last few minutes, Mrs. Pettindund," he said, with as much of contemptuous anger in his voice as it was capable of expressing.

"An' ye're goin' to give notice?" returned the landlady. "Just what I expected!"

"No, that's not my intention," pursued Arthur. "At all events, not just yet. I only want to ask you whether you really mean to turn that unfortunate girl into the streets in her present state?"

"Why not? Of course I mean it," returned the woman, with a look of the utmost surprise.

"You mean to do so, knowing that she has not a friend in London, perhaps not in the world—you, who are a mother, and living in comfort? You really mean that?"

"And why not, I say? I s'pose I can do as I like in my own 'ouse? Eh?"

Arthur surveyed her for a moment with a gaze of the most extreme disgust and detestation.

"You say—why not?" he said, at length. "But I should like to know, why? Whatever can be your reason for acting so cruelly —so mercilessly?"

"I don't see as I'm bound to give you a reason for all I do, Mr. Golding," answered the woman, with a snarl. "But if yer want to know so much, I'll just ask yer if it's reasonable I should keep a girl in the 'ouse, who can't pay no rent or money for her food, and isn't likely to do for Lord knows how long to come?"

She had modified the impertinence which

at first rose to her tongue, probably remembering that Arthur was very regular in his payments, and gave no trouble.

"And that is your sole reason? For the sake of a few shillings a week you will turn your relative out of doors when most she needs tenderness and care—turn her into the streets to beg, and starve, and very likely die?"

"I've nothing to do with all that. That's her own look out. If she hadn't done what she oughtn't there'd a' been no trouble come to her. She's made her own bed, and she must lay in it."

Not a sign of womanly pity, of human feeling even, could Arthur discern in Mrs. Pettindund's face.

He saw that to appeal to her feelings was totally vain. It only remained to appeal to her avarice.

"How much has she been paying weekly for board and lodging?" he asked.

"Twelve-an'-six, an' little enough, too. That's only because she's a sister's child."

"If I pay you this twelve-and-six each week," said the young man, after a moment's reflection, "will you allow her to remain in the house till she is able to earn her own living again?"

Mrs. Pettindund fell back several paces, in her amazement.

"Then it's you, after all, Mr. Golding,"

she said, "as 'as been an' got Carrie into this scrape? I couldn't have believed it of yer!"

"Keep your insults to yourself, woman!" exclaimed Arthur, with sudden passion, exasperated beyond endurance at having a crime attributed to him which he so much detested.

"And *you* keep *yourn* to *yourself*, Mr. Golding," retorted the other. "Woman, indeed! And why else, I should like to know, should you offer to keep the girl?"

"Never mind my reasons," returned Arthur, abruptly. "I make an offer—will you accept it?"

"D'yer mean what yer say, Mr. Golding?"

"Of course, I do. Be quick and reply. If you are not willing I dare say I can find another lodging for her."

Mrs. Pettindund looked alarmed.

"Well, I don't mind," she answered. "But I must always have it in advance, you know."

"So I suppose. When is Miss Mitchell's rent-day?"

"To-day, Friday."

"Then I shall pay you the next week's money at once. Sit down there and write me a receipt."

Mrs. Pettindund scrawled on a piece of paper, which Arthur gave her, for several minutes. Then she handed it to him.

"Received one week's rent for first flore
back for C. Mitchell from Mr. Golding. Also
for one week's bord.   In advance.   12s. 6d.
    "Oct. 26.   M. PETTINDUND."

"Very well," said Arthur, smiling at the
form.   "Then, you understand, she is to live
here just as she has been doing."

"I understand," said the woman.   "Is
that all, Mr. Golding?"

"Not quite.   You are to promise me that
you will not let Miss Mitchell know that I am
doing this.   You understand?   If I find that
she knows, I shall cease to pay, and offer to
find another lodging for her."

"But what shall I say to her about her
rent?"

"Say that you will allow her to repay you
when she is able.   Anything except the truth."

The idea of representing herself to a lodger
in such a very benevolent light, was so completely new to Mrs. Pettindund, that she held
her fat sides and laughed heartily.

"Well, well, I'll do as yer wish, Mr. Golding," she puffed.   "Is that all?"

"That's all at present."

The landlady left the room and hurried
downstairs.   That same night she related to
all her family that Carrie Mitchell had been
led astray by Mr. Golding, that the girl was
only about a month off her confinement, and
that Mr. Golding had undertaken to pay all

her expenses henceforth. But at the same
time she strictly exacted that this latter piece
of news should be kept secret from Carrie
herself. For she had no doubt whatever that
intimate relations existed between the girl
and her protector, and that the latter would
at once know if his conditions had been
broken. Why he should have made such
conditions she was wholly incapable of understanding. In truth Mrs. Pettindund's philosophy contained the key to very few problems save those of arithmetic in as far as was
required for the calculation of her weekly
income.

This matter settled, Arthur flung himself
on the bed for a few hours' rest, his whole
frame aglow with tremulous delight. To be
able to have served that poor, pale-faced, yet
beautiful girl, and to have done so, moreover,
at the cost of some sacrifice, was a joy of
almost fierce intensity. At this time he was
earning thirty-five shillings weekly. Out of
this he paid four shillings rent, and the remaining thirty-one he had hitherto distributed
thus : ten-and-sixpence for food (being eigh-
teen-pence a day), five shillings his weekly
subscription at the club, half-a-crown for
minor personal expenses ; the remaining
thirteen shillings were always put aside to
form a fund for clothing and unexpected requirements. They just covered Carrie Mitchell's rent, and for the present his clothing

would have to look after itself. In the midst
of all manner of delightful fancies, in which
he saw the future open before him, rich with
he knew not what vague joys and blessings,
Arthur fell asleep.

His light slumber was broken by Mark
Challenger, who had come home during the
dinner hour. He heard Mark pause at his
door, listening for any indication of his being
awake, and he called to him to enter.
Nothing was at this moment more foreign to
Arthur's mind than the faintest vanity as
regarded his act, but for all that he could not
help instantly revealing it to his companion
at once. The words overflowed, as it were,
from his heart. The secret would not be held
down. He felt bound to seek for some associate in his joy.

Mark, who was a man of some fifty years
old, smiled curiously as he listened to his
young friend's narrative. But at the end of
it he looked rather concerned.

"But," he said, "I was just going to
propose to you that the club should do this.
I fancy we could muster enough weekly. We
haven't many calls on us at present. You'll
rob yourself. You won't have enough to live
on."

"Trust me, Mr. Challenger," answered
Arthur, with a boyish gaiety seldom seen in
his manner. "I shall take no harm. I
wouldn't have allowed the club to do this

for anything.   And what's more, I beg you won't say a word of it to any one."

" I'll do as you like, Arthur," returned Mark, with some reluctance. " But it isn't really right that you should have the burden all on your own shoulders. Come, let me pay half. I can afford it easily."

" Not a penny ! So we won't talk about it any more."

Shortly after, Mark went to his dinner, looking rather puzzled and grave. Arthur, however, finding it impossible to rest longer, took down one of Mr. Tollady's books and applied himself to study. A piece of bread, cut from a loaf which he kept in his cupboard, was quite sufficient for his dinner. He felt just now as if he should never be hungry again.

The rest of October, and half a dreary November slid rapidly away. Whenever he was at home, Arthur listened at his door for signs of Carrie, but he neither heard nor saw her. At length he was almost tempted to believe that Mrs. Pettindund had in reality fulfilled her threat of sending the girl away, and was now taking his money under false pretences. He accordingly called the woman into his room one day to make enquiries. He learned that Carrie kept herself closely shut up, and would not even come out to eat ; all her meals had to be taken to her. This was the truth, as he found the same evening ; for on going into the back yard purposely to look up at her window and discover if her room was lighted up, he saw her form leaning out over the window-sill. On hearing his step she instantly withdrew, and closed the window.

It might have been nearly a week after this, that, as he was lying awake in bed one night, his thoughts wandering he knew not whither, but always returning to the pale, beautiful face of Carrie Mitchell, he suddenly thought he heard a noise, just as if something had been slipped under his door. It was past midnight, and the house had long been in perfect silence. Listening intently he heard another noise, this time in the house below, which he knew to be the slamming of the front door. The absolute darkness of his room would not allow him to see whether anything had really been pushed into his room. He concluded it must have been fancy; perhaps the scratching of a mouse. Yet the slamming of the door had been unmistakable; and who could be going out at this time of night? On the other hand, it might have been somebody entering, one of the Pettindunds, or a lodger out late. These suppositions, however, did not quiet his mind. He was sleepless and uneasy, and an indefinite fear was beginning to oppress his mind, a fear bred, perhaps, of the silence and gloom. From thinking of the noises his thoughts again took their own way, and suddenly conducted him back to Adam and Eve Court in Whitecross Street. He saw himself sleeping alone in the desolate room where his father had died, and, strangely enough, he almost convinced himself that he could hear children's voices, singing,

There is a happy land, far, far away !

He listened till the very silence seemed to throb around him, till he heard the beating of his heart. Then once more his thoughts reverted to Carrie Mitchell, and again came the vague fear. This was intolerable. He jumped out of bed and struck a light, thinking that he would read till he wearied himself out. With the first gleam of the candle something glittered close to the door; it was a piece of paper. For a moment he stood almost terrified; why, he knew not; but his nerves were so excited that the least thing proved too much for his fortitude. Then he picked up the paper with trembling fingers. He saw that it was written upon, and the writing was this :—

" I have heard that you have been paying my rent. My aunt is always telling me of my fault, and she has told me of this at last. I can't thank you enough for your great, great kindness ; but I can't stay any longer. My aunt and my cousin are too cruel to me ; they are always telling me of my fault. I couldn't go without thanking you ; I don't know why you did the kindness for me ; no one else has any pity. Please excuse my writing. I never had enough schooling to learn to spell properly.   CARRIE MITCHELL."

The hand-writing was extremely bad, so bad in places as to be almost undecipherable, and the orthographical errors were very abundant. I have chosen to correct the latter fault, lest the letter should excite amusement. It excited a far different feeling in Arthur Golding, as he read it by the candle-light. A dead weight seemed suddenly to fall upon his heart and press the very life out of it. He turned deadly cold, and trembled excessively.

The first thought was to dress hastily and run into the street after the fugitive. He remembered the slamming of the door, which he now saw must have announced her departure. But that had been at least half an hour ago ; it would be vain to pursue her now. His anguish was unspeakable ; only in this moment did he fully realise the powerful hold upon him which his passion had gained. He pressed the letter to his lips and kissed it madly. He read it over and over a hundred times, dwelling upon the words of gratitude to himself with a mixture of delight and pain, which amounted almost to frenzy. " I knew it ! " he exclaimed aloud, forced to give utterance to his anguish in sounds. " I knew that she was good as well as beautiful. Curses

on the villain that wronged her, and the base
wretches who have driven her from house and
home ! "   The tears rushed irresistibly to his
eyes as he noticed the bad writing and spelling.   The pathos of the last sentence touched
him deeply ; he read it over and over again,
sobbing as he did so.   He flung himself upon
the bed, still holding the note in his hand,
and buried his face in the pillow.   Never
before had he suffered from grief so intense.

The candle burned down to the socket, and
the room was once more left in darkness.
Arthur had sunk into an uneasy sleep, and
this, with the intervals of half-consciousness,
lasted till six o'clock.   At that time it was
Mark's habit to call him, and he accordingly
came and knocked at the door.   At the sound
Arthur at once started to his feet.

" Why, you are up ! " exclaimed Mark,
entering with a candle. " But, good Heavens !
What's the matter with you, Arthur ?   Are
you ill ? "

Arthur held out the letter, but did not
speak.   Mark read it, and looked at the young
man with curious pity.

" Damn them all," he exclaimed, alluding
to   Mrs. Pettindund and her daughters.
" Whatever will become of the poor thing ?
But you mustn't take on so terribly, Arthur.
Is she so much to you as all that ? "

" Oh, can't you see ?   Don't you know ? "
cried Arthur.   " Couldn't you guess how

much she was to me? It will kill me if I do not find her again!"

Mark, with a look of concern on his wrinkled features, did his utmost to calm the young man by assurances of their being able to discover Carrie, assurances in which, however, he had not himself much faith.

"At all events," he concluded, "we won't stay another day with these abominable brutes. I'll lose a morning's work and go and find rooms for both of us."

"No, no," returned Arthur. "We must stay here, in any case. She may return; most likely she will return. She can have no money at all. Whatever will she do?"

"Yes, yes," returned Mark, "I think she is pretty sure to come back. But don't put yourself out so terribly, Arthur. I can't bear to see you so. Have you been up all night?"

"No," groaned Arthur, throwing himself upon a chair, and covering his face with his hands. "I think I have slept—I don't know —I can't remember anything."

"Now don't, don't, there's a good fellow," said Mark. "Wash your face and come out with me. It's a fine morning for November. Come, that's right. We'll go and have some breakfast presently, and in the meantime we'll talk the matter over."

After some persuasion Mark induced his friend to dress and accompany him out. It was just becoming light as they issued into the street ; but the air was bitterly cold.

" I think we shall have snow," said Mark, looking up to the sky, where stars were still dimly glistening here and there.

Arthur shuddered. He thought of Carrie out in this terrible season, with no one to look to for shelter or a crust of bread.

CHAPTER XII.

WHEN Christmas Day was as yet a fortnight off, notes of preparation began to sound through the house in Gower Place. There was anxious reckoning-up of resources and eager devising of extra and unwonted means of supply, in order that the season might lack nothing of its due celebration. Let us see how matters stood, what chances there were of the god of gluttony and surfeit being gladdened with an appropriate sacrifice.

In the first place several of the members of the family were enrolled in the "goose club;" that is to say, they had each paid four-pence a week at a neighbouring public-house during the last half year, in acknowledgment of which patronage the landlord supplied each of them with a Christmas goose. Then Mrs. Pettindund and two of her daughters were in the "grocer's club;" that is to say, they had each paid the sum of threepence weekly since the month of May, in return for which they now rejoiced in the receipt of two pint bottles of port wine, of one or two large plum cakes, and of sundry pounds of tea, coffee and sugar. (It is curious, bye-the-by,

how incapable the working classes, as a rule, are of keeping their own savings. The public-house landlord, or the grocer, or the benefit society is quite welcome to a few shillings a week, provided they return occasionally something like a tenth of what they have received). These provisions were all very well as stop-gaps, but in the serious business of the feast they went for nothing. Accordingly, in each of the three weeks immediately preceding Christmas, Mrs. Pettindund had, with the utmost efforts, succeeded in putting aside the sum of one pound out of her regular receipts. That money would go towards supplying joints, and would not be any too much. Then, the eldest Miss Pettindund had paid repeated visits of late to a pawn-broker's shop at no great distance, in the course of which sundry coats and trousers, sheets and blankets, boots, watches, rings, necklaces, bracelets, &c., had become converted into a very respectable little sum of current cash. But neither was this sufficient, for it must be remembered that the Pettin-dunds took a serious view of the obligations of the season; anything less than deep carousal from Christmas Eve to the morning of the first day of January would have been desecration in their eyes. Accordingly Mrs. Pettindund herself paid a visit to a familiar loan office, where she procured, without difficulty, on the security of her house and furniture, the sum of fifteen pounds. And now at length, when this last sum had been carefully put away in the tea caddy, together with the three pounds before mentioned, and the harvest reaped at the pawnbroker's, the family quietly rested till the arrival of Christmas Eve. This pause was absolutely necessary. It was like the diver taking a long breath before he springs into the water, like the athlete reposing his sinews for a moment before he tries an enormous effort of strength.

Early on the eventful day which precedes Christmas the Pettindund family was stirring to some purpose. To-day were to be baked an utterly incalculable number of mince-pies, together with half a dozen very large plum-puddings, destined to be eaten cold on the morrow. *The* plum-pudding, the weight of which I dare not guess at, was now made and received its first boiling, but that would have to be reboiled on the following day. To-day were to be roasted some six or seven ducks, these also to be eaten cold on Christmas and the ensuing days. The turkey would not be boiled, of course, till to-morrow, and till then were reserved the two ponderous masses of beef, which, on account of their size, would be entrusted to the tender care of the baker. This morning, too, Mrs. Pettindund, happening to be quenching a momentary thirst at the public-house, purchased, as it were, *en passant,* a quart bottle of brandy and two similar sized bottles of the beverage known as " Old Tom."

" Now mind yer don't keep my Moggie a waitin' when she comes for the liquor to-night an' to-morrow," was Mrs. Pettindund's parting injunction to the landlord ; to which the latter replied with a wink of each eye, and the exclamation, " All serene ! "

That evening—Christmas Eve—only some two or three friends were expected. They arrived between eight and nine o'clock, and began by satisfying their hunger. I shall not endeavour to find a name for this meal and those that follow. At this period such purely factitious distinctions were lost sight of by the Pettindunds ; the tables were spread, and folks ate, all day and night. This evening, however, the mirth was kept within moderate bounds. All present knew by experience the folly of wasting one's energy in mere preliminaries. To be sure Mr. Pettindund got very drunk and passed the night on the kitchen hearth-rug, but that was a matter of course, an event which occurred so repeatedly that no one took any notice of it. By three o'clock in the morning the house was at rest.

At ten on the following morning—Christmas morning—the earliest guests began to appear. The very first to arrive was Jim Glibbery. Jim was a carter, and as good as

engaged to the eldest Miss Pettindund; so
that his arrival excited no particular attention, he being regarded as one of the family.
Jim took a seat by the kitchen fire, despatched
Moggie for a pot of "six ale," and undertook to
watch that the saucepans on the fire did not
boil over. When Mr. and Mrs. Tudge and
the three little Tudges came in, however, it
was a different thing. Here there was a
grand reception. The visitors were shown
into the best room and all the Pettindunds
crowded to greet them. Mr. Tudge was, in
fact, a very well-to-do oilman, and so could
not be neglected. It was this gentleman's
habit to flirt jestingly with the eldest Miss
Pettindund, to the vast exasperation of his
wife. Accordingly when this object of his
affections entered the room, he bestowed a
sounding smack upon her lips, and in return
received no less sounding a smack on each
ear, one from the maiden herself, one from
the angry Mrs. Tudge.

"Well, I'm damned!" he exclaimed,
without paying the least attention to these
marks of favour, "here's Sarah with a new
dress on! 'Ev yer wet it, Sarah, eh?"

"Not yet, Mr. Tudge," replied the damsel,
with a becoming leer at herself in a glass
hard by.

"Then, damn me!" cried Mr. Tudge,
"where's that Moggie o' yourn? Here,
Moggie, young 'un. Run for two pots of

'four ale' with a quartern of Old Tom in it! D'ye 'ear? Here's a two bob piece, and mind yer bring the right change."

The uninitiated reader must be informed that the "wetting" of a new garment means drinking the health of its wearer. Before many minutes Moggie returned with the prescribed compound in a huge tin can, into which each individual dipped his or her glass till it was all finished. But by this time numerous other visitors had arrived. Prominent among these was young Mr. Spinks, a grocer's counterman, who had an eye upon another Miss Pettindund. He was always the funny man of the party. As he entered the room he struck an attitude and exclaimed in a stagey voice—

" Bring forth the lush ! "

" Ain't got none ! " screamed *his* Miss Pettindund. " Just finished ! "

" So ! Then, Moggie, run and get me a 'alfporth o' four 'alf, and blast the hexpense ! "

This jest was received with perfect shrieks of laughter, which continued to be excited by sallies of the same nature till the house was quite full of visitors, and at length dinner was ready. Then indeed for a time there was silence, save for the unceasing clatter of knives and forks and the audible evidences of mastication ; it would be difficult to say which of these sounds predominated. The two

masses of beef disappeared like tall grass
before the scythe of a sturdy mower. If any
guest was incommoded owing to Mrs.
Pettindund's inability to carve quickly
enough, he amused himself with half a duck
or a considerable fraction of turkey till his
turn came. Those who were so unfortunate
as to have been beyond reach of these *entrées*,
solaced themselves with mince pies and celery
alternately. Poor Moggie's life became a
burden to her. Her duty it was to see that
every guest's glass was kept filled, in the
execution of which she rapidly emptied two
large cans, ordinarily used for carrying up
water into the lodgers' bed-rooms. When
these contained no more she hurried for a
fresh supply, and on her return was roundly
cursed for having been so long. Mr. Spinks
went the length of throwing a turkey's leg-
bone at the unfortunate child's head, and was
loudly applauded for the ingenuity of the
joke.

Gorged into silence, the guests at length
leaned back in their chairs, and for a few
minutes amused themselves only with picking
their teeth. It was the preparation for an
outburst of enthusiasm. When, after a few
minutes, two Misses Pettindund struggled
in under the weight of a mountain of plum-
pudding, which had been drenched with
brandy and then set on fire, each person in
the room arose and gave utterance to a yell

which must have been heard in Tottenham Court Road. The cry seemed to have aided the process of digestion; the capacity of all appeared renewed. By this time ale was no longer in request, but bottles of spirits circulated round the table, and Moggie was at hand with a kettle of boiling water. The scene now baffles description. Every one talked and nobody listened. Most of the men swore, not a few told disgusting stories, a few interchanged expletives or even blows, the women shrieked and squabbled indiscriminately. At this period Mrs. Pettindund, happening to go downstairs into the kitchen, caught Moggie—who had had nothing to eat all day, bye-the-by—in the act of demolishing some fragments of duck which had been left. With a howl of rage and a curse which it would defile the very ink to trace, she caught up the nearest object, which happened to be an empty bottle, and hurled it at the child. Luckily her aim was not very steady, and Moggie was only bruised on the shoulder. With a yell of pain, the wretched child darted past her mother and up into the street, where she waited out of sight till she thought the incident had been forgotten.

And so the short day darkened into night. Shutters were now closed, and blinds drawn down, and two or three rooms prepared for dancing. The fact that these rooms were only about twelve feet square was no obstacle.

The eldest Miss Pettindund then began to hammer a waltz on the piano, which had been carried out in the hall in order that its sounds might penetrate as far as possible, and dancing forthwith commenced. Before long the house seemed to shake and quiver to its foundations. Here a couple, whirling themselves into insensate giddiness, would fall with a heavy crash upon the floor, and two or three other couples stumbling over them, the whole room would become a mass of struggling, kicking and cursing humanity, if the latter word be not grossly inappropriate. At one point two young men became obnoxious to each other in consequence of their attentions to the same young woman. From expostulations they proceeded to recriminations, and thence rapidly to blows. Vain were the efforts of the bystanders to separate them. Unable long to stand, from the excess of liquor they had imbibed, the two rolled in each other's embraces from end to end of the room. They bit, they scratched, they tore, they kicked, had not their wonted vigour been somewhat enfeebled, one of them would without doubt have been killed. In a few minutes their faces were indistinguishable from streaming blood, their waistcoats were rent open, their collars and neck-cloths were scattered to the winds. At length they were both overpowered by pure weight of numbers, Mrs. Tudge, together with three stout women,

fairly falling upon the one, and Mrs. Pettindund with all her daughters actually sitting
upon the other. Most of the men present
were enraged at this result. Their ferocity
was excited, and they longed for the sight of
blood. They satisfied themselves, however,
with the anticipation of the match being
fought out on the morrow when there would
be no women to interfere.

Matters had been once more brought to a
pacific state, and Miss Pettindund had recommenced to hammer upon the piano, when
she suddenly stopped.

" What is it ?" yelled half a dozen voices.

" A knock at the door," was the reply.
" Fire away ! I'll go."

And she accordingly went and opened the
door. Outside in the black street a fierce
snowstorm was raging. The girl's breath
was stopped by the blast which blew into her
face as she held the door and peered out to
see who it was. A tall woman's figure, clad
in a ragged black dress which only showed
here and there through the cleaving snow-
flakes, and carrying some kind of bundle in a
large shawl, was all that Miss Pettindund
could discern.

" Why it's a beggar ! " she exclaimed, indignantly. " Get away with yer ! We've
enough to do to make our own living, these
hard times, without givin' to beggars. Now,
you be orff ! "

The woman stepped forward, reaching out with one long, bare arm, and saying something which the fierce blasts of wind and the riot within the house rendered inaudible.

"I've nothink to say to yer!" shrieked Miss Pettindund; and she was on the point of exerting her whole strength to slam to the door, when the beggar actually advanced into the hall.

"Sarah! Don't you know me?" she cried, in a hoarse voice.

As the light from the hall-lamp fell upon her face, Miss Pettindund saw that it was Carrie Mitchell. With a horrified scream she ran into the front parlour, calling out— "Ma! ma!"

"What is it, child?" screeched Mrs. Pettindund, in reply. "Ugh! who's gone an' left that front door open? I'm froze to death. Whatever's the matter, Sarah?"

"Oh, my God, ma!" cried the young lady. "Here's a go! Come and look here!"

In a moment, a dozen people had crowded into the hall, and were gazing with astonishment on the tall figure, half white, half black, from whom the melted snow was running like a stream on to the floor.

"What the devil's all this about?" blustered Mr. Tudge. "Here, get you out o' this 'ere 'ouse!"

"Aunt!" cried the intruder, struggling to make herself understood with a voice which exposure to the weather had made so hoarse and feeble that it could scarcely be heard. "Aunt! let me in!—Let me sit in the kitchen! My baby will be frozen to death!"

"Oh, God! she's got a baby!" screamed all the Misses Pettindund together.

"What! Carrie Mitchell!" exclaimed Mrs. Pettindund. "She a comin' 'ere in that way! Well, I'm blowed! Isn't it like her impudence! Now, come, trot! I've nothing to do with people of your class. Go somewhere else, and don't come to 'spectable 'ouses. *You* know well enough where to go, trust you! I ain't got nothin' for yer, I tell yer; go!"

One cry of despair came from the lips of the outcast, but even that was scarcely heard amid the yell of approval with which the guests greeted Mrs. Pettindund's determination. The latter, never blest with a very good temper, became a fiend when under the influence of drink. Laying a rude hand upon her niece's shoulder, she pushed her violently into the street, and slammed the door fiercely behind her.

"There!" she exclaimed, "that's how I treat them kind o' people!—Ha, ha, ha!"

The mirth was resumed, and sped on fast and furious. In five minutes the incident had been altogether forgotten. The piano rang out its discordant waltzes, polkas and gallops, and again the very house rocked and

reeled. Soon it was midnight, at which hour
Mrs. Pettindund proclaimed that supper was
ready. Accordingly the guests once more
crowded round the table. Cold provender
was there in abundance, and, in addition, the
two younger Misses Pettindund had just
completed the broiling of some half-dozen
pounds of beef-steak, which, smoking in
reeking onions, made a dish at which the
guests cheered. An hour was spent in the
consumption of supper, after which music
and dancing recommenced. All the time, be
it understood, the supply of liquids had been
unfailing. Shortly before the time at which
the public-house closed, Moggie had refilled
all the largest vessels, the contents of which,
it was hoped, would suffice to bring the
merriment to an end. And so they did.
Towards half-past three, signs of abatement
began to manifest themselves; by four o'clock
several guests were fast asleep, either on the
floor or on chairs. About this hour, the
movement of departure began. The party,
led by Mr. Spinks, went off arm-in-arm,
howling, " We won't go home till morning."
Mr. Tudge staggered into the street, with
difficulty supported between his wife and
eldest child; bevies of young damsels, who
were far from quite steady upon their feet,
rushed out into the snow-storm with shrieks
and laughter which made the night re-echo;
the two young men who had fought went off

with the young woman who had been the cause of the combat, and, before they had reached the end of the street, quarrelled again, came to blows, and wallowed together in the snow, whilst the female with them yelled like a vulture over a field of battle. Neither of the gentlemen reached their home that night, for the cries of the woman attracting one or two policemen, they were both dragged away to the police-station, and there allowed to sleep off the effect of their carouse. By five o'clock, there was silence throughout the house of the Pettindunds.

During the morning, Mark Challenger had been visiting some friends, but, as the short afternoon drew on towards night, he returned, and, before entering his own room, knocked at Arthur's door. Summoned to enter, he did so, but the moment he opened the door, such a tremendous shouting, yelling and screaming sounded from the rooms below, that Arthur started to his feet in sudden anger.

"Good God!" he exclaimed, "this is intolerable! Have they got half the inhabitants of the Zoological Gardens to dinner downstairs? Every five minutes I hear such a hideous roaring that I am almost driven mad. I have a headache to begin with."

"You may well ask whether they are beasts," replied Mark. "As I came along the passage, the front-room door was open, and I never set eyes on such a scene in my life. There must be twenty people there, and I'm quite sure they're all drunk. I had only time to notice one thing, and that was old Pettindund at one side of the table, and another man opposite to him, holding a goose, or something of the kind, by its legs, and ripping it in two between them!"

"Brutes!" replied Arthur, in a tone of disgust. "Do not such blackguards as these give good cause to the upper classes to speak of us working men with contempt? I warrant they waste as much money to-day in guzzling and swilling as would give twenty or thirty poor starving wretches a good dinner for a week to come. Mr. Challenger, I think I must leave this house. I do indeed. If this sort of thing is to go on all through Christmas week, as no doubt it will, I shall be driven mad. I seem to have become irritable of late, and nervous."

"I have thought of the same thing," returned Mark. "I don't feel justified in giving such people money for them to make beasts of themselves with. Shall we look out for another place to-morrow?"

"Let us do so, by all means. I want to get into new scenes. I shall hardly know myself if I am here much longer. I must forget everything that has happened here, and begin anew; that is the only way. I am fast losing all taste for every healthy kind of occupation. I can't read, I have no pleasure in speaking at the club, or in hearing others speak. This state of affairs will never do. I *cannot* live so any longer!"

"Have you had any dinner, Arthur?"

"No, indeed I haven't. I haven't felt hungry yet; is it dinner time?"

"It's nearly four."

"Nearly four? Then I suppose I must eat something. Luckily I have a loaf of bread and a bit of cheese in the cupboard here. Come and share with me, Mr. Challenger."

"Thanks; I had my dinner nearly three hours ago."

"You had! Then I must eat alone. And do talk to me about something, if you please. There must be a spider inside my skull, eating up whatever little brains there are, and spinning cobwebs in their place. Look! Gibbon's History has always been one of my chief delights, and yet I couldn't get through half-a-dozen pages to-day."

He ate his bread and cheese for some minutes in silence, then, filling a glass of water, held it up before drinking.

"It's Christmas Day," he said, "and we mustn't entirely forget to keep it. I won't drink your health in wine, Mr. Challenger, lest I should be too much like those shouting fools downstairs. So here it is in water."

"And none the less sincere for that, I

know, Arthur. Do you know what I've been thinking? We really ought to go and see poor John Pether to-day."

"So we ought; so we ought. I'm very glad you thought of it. When did you see him last?"

"A little more than a week ago. He didn't seem very well then; had a bad cold, and wasn't much in the mood for talking. I'm afraid he's gradually starving to death."

"I wish to goodness," exclaimed Arthur, "that we could find some way of helping him!"

"Yes, but how is it to be done? Whenever I've hinted at it lately, he's got quite fierce and angry. I don't know what will become of the poor fellow."

"Come, let's go to him at once," said Arthur, hastily finishing his meagre repast. "I'm afraid he's having a terribly lonely day of it."

Accordingly, in a few minutes they departed, hurrying out unnoticed through the noise and confusion of the lower part of the house. At that moment, some half-dozen people were engaged carrying the piano into the passage, whilst in the front parlour Mr. Tudge was standing on a chair, singing in a voice which shook the walls, a song wherein frequent reference was made to "Sairey Jane an' me," amid unceasing plaudits from the other guests. Once in the street, Arthur and

his companion struggled on in the gathering
darkness, bending forward against the fierce
storm of wind, sleet and snow. Snow lay
thick upon the streets, and clung to the fronts
of the houses, filling the corners of the
windows, and heaping itself up wherever it
could find a hold. Already the street-lamps
were lit, and threw their dim light upon the
comfortless scene, whilst streaks of pale grey
still held a place amid the else uniform gloom
of the sky. There were not many people
about, and the few vehicles which went past
made no noise. It was a desolate evening.

After casting a glance down Gower Street,
where the lamps seemed to converge in a
limitless perspective, the two friends walked
quickly along University Street into Tottenham Court Road, where a walk of ten minutes
brought them into Charlotte Place. They
both cast a glance at the old shop, over
which still stood Mr. Tollady's name, and
Arthur sighed. The shutters were up, and
the whole house showed no sign of life. Its
desolation seemed heightened by contrast with
the house next to it, all the windows of
which gleamed with lights, whilst from
within proceeded a tumult scarcely less
than that the companions had left behind
them.

"The shop isn't taken yet, is it?" asked
Arthur, as they paused for a moment in front
of it.

Mark shook his head.

" I suppose its owner has satisfied his base nature by getting possession of it," returned Arthur, " and now he cares little if it rots to pieces."

They arrived before the umbrella-mender's shop and knocked. After waiting several minutes without reply, they knocked again. Again they waited a long time, but at length heard a key turning in the lock. The door was partially opened, and John Pether, only showing his head, asked who had come to disturb him.

" It is only us, John," said Mark Challenger. " You'll let us in, won't you ? "

No sign of pleasure passed over John's dark countenance, but he opened the door a little wider and admitted the two. They found the shop quite dark, but a candle was burning in the room behind it, the door of which stood open. John, who, they saw, was naked all but his shirt, led the way into the lighted room, and there got into bed, whence he had come to open the door. As he lay with his head resting on the pillow, his eyes turned up towards the ceiling, his appearance was almost ghastly. His face was the colour of parchment, wrinkled and creased with hundreds of deep lines, and amid its pallor, the red stain upon his cheek showed with hideous distinctness. He paid no attention to his visitors, but lay at times shivering slightly, and moving his lips as if talking to himself.

" You're not well, John," said Mark Challenger, after one or two uneasy glances at Arthur. " Have you been in bed all day ? "

" Why not ? " asked the other, in a hollow voice which sounded almost fierce. " It's a holiday, isn't it. Haven't I a right to take a holiday as well as rich people ? "

" That you have, John," returned Mark, endeavouring to sooth his friend. " Aye, and a better right, too. The rich have holiday all the year round—curse them !— but you have to work hard for what little rest you have. And it's the same with Arthur and me, John. You don't think us enemies, do you ? "

" Enemies ! " exclaimed Pether. " No ; *you* never did me harm."

" You ought to have a doctor to see you, Mr. Pether," put in Arthur. " You look terribly ill."

" Doctor ! How am I to pay a doctor ? "

" Oh, if you haven't the money just now, Mr. Challenger and I will do that gladly, and you shall pay us back when you can. Do let us do something for you, Mr. Pether. It is dreadful to see you so lonely in your suffering."

" There it is ! " cried the man, half rising on his elbow. " There it is ! You want to

make a beggar of me, to make me feel my
poverty, to know even better than I do that
I am a miserable wretch. You'll tell me to
go into the workhouse next! I don't want
your money. It isn't friendship to offer it
me; it only makes me mad—mad—mad!
Look here; I have been reading a newspaper
to-day. Do you know how many paupers
there are in London? About seventy-
thousand! Do you want me to make one
more? I have held out these many years,
and why shouldn't I hold out a few months
more? It's coming, I tell you; I know it's
coming. I can feel it coming by the trouble
in my mind, like I can feel an east wind
coming by the pains in my body. A few
months and we shall have no lack of food.
These seventy-thousand paupers shall be dressing themselves in the garments of the rich,
and warming their frozen limbs in the blood
which shall stream like water along the
streets! I feel it's coming!"

Arthur shrank back before the man's
violence, but kept his eyes fixed upon him.
In his excitement John Pether had now fully
risen, and his almost bald head, his ghastly
features, his straggling beard, and his open
shirt, which displayed his bony and hairy
chest, gave him the appearance of a man in
delirium. Neither Arthur nor Mark spoke
in reply, and presently he again lay down
and fixed his eyes upon the ceiling; and then

his lips began to move, and he spoke as if unconscious of any one being present.

"I have been thinking of my mother to-day," he said. "She was tried and found guilty of murder, but her execution was put off because she was with child. I was born in prison, and then she was hanged."

Arthur shuddered with horror as he remembered where and when he had heard this before. Mark Challenger sat with his forehead resting on his hands, and showed no sign of attention. Probably he had heard it too often. After a few minutes of silence, John Pether continued to speak, still as if to himself only.

"I was brought up in the workhouse, and suffered cold, and hunger, and cruelty. Then they made me apprentice to a master who starved and beat me. One day he caught me taking a halfpenny which had dropped on to the floor. I thought I could buy a piece of bread with it, and the temptation was too strong. He had no mercy, and I was sent to prison. Oh, God! When I came out, I begged for days, sleeping at night in dark archways or in cellars with thieves and murderers. I prayed men to give me work, but they only threatened me with the gaol. One night I went to drown myself. It is a rare death, drowning. You feel the water, at first deadly cold, grow warmer and warmer, and a kind of music in your ears lulls you to sleep. I thought I might have drowned myself in peace, but I was saved and forced back to life."

Arthur listened eagerly to hear more of this strange and terrible history, but the speaker's lips ceased to move, and he was silent. So quiet was the house, that shouts from the revellers on the opposite side of the street could be distinctly heard. Arthur sat watching the breath of the sick man, which rose in a cloud through the freezing atmosphere of the room. At length Mark Challenger rose.

"And you won't let us do anything for you, John?" he asked.

John Pether started, look round, then shook his head with an impatient frown.

"Then we will leave you," said Mark. "Try to sleep John; you are tired. Do you sleep well at night?"

There was no reply, and Mark beckoned to Arthur to leave the room. The latter was obeying, with much inward reluctance, when John Pether suddenly turned on his side and tried to check him with his hand.

"You remember what you swore?" he asked, in a hollow voice.

"I do," replied Arthur, pressing the other's hand.

"The time is coming," returned Pether. "A few months yet, and our chance will show itself. I feel it coming."

He then once more averted his face as the two friends left the room and passed out through the dark shop.

"Aye," said Mark Challenger, sadly, as soon as they were in the street, "I fear John Pether's time is coming. He has had an awful life. Perhaps it wouldn't be much kindness to try and make it longer."

"He seems mad," returned Arthur. "It is scarcely safe that he should be left alone."

"Poor fellow!" sighed Mark, and they walked on in silence.

They had taken a short cut which brought them into Tottenham Street. The night had grown still more boisterous, and the snow lay very deep upon the ground. Hurrying arm-in-arm in the direction of Tottenham Court Road, they shortly passed by the Prince of Wales's Theatre. As they were going beneath the portico Arthur saw what appeared to be a woman's form crouching far back in the darkness against the steps to one of the entrances. Touched with pity at the thought of a human being preparing to spend a terrible night in such a place, he pointed her out to Mark, and they stopped. The woman, seeing them, rose to her feet and staggered forward. She carried something in her arms, pressed against her bosom. In a hoarse voice, expressive of agony unutterable, she begged of them to give her enough to pay for a night's lodging.

" Is that a child you have in your arms ? "
asked Arthur, unable to discern clearly in the
darkness.

The woman stepped out of the shadow of
the portico. A gleam from a gas-lamp on
the other side of the street illumined her
form, as she lifted her shawl and discovered
a young child's face. As she did so, Mark
Challenger plucked Arthur by the sleeve.

" Don't you see who it is ? " he whispered
hurriedly.

Arthur looked into the woman's face, and
at once in the ghastly pale and worn features
recognised the face of Carrie Mitchell. She
had no covering to her head but a coarse
handkerchief, tied around it. Her long dark
hair hung all dishevelled down her back, wet
with melted snow. Her feet were bare, save
for a pair of loose slippers which were no protection against the snow. Her countenance
displayed no sign of intelligence ; it was
fixed in an unutterable expression of pain.
She stood pointing at her child and muttering.

" Is your name Carrie Mitchell ? " asked
Arthur, overcome at once with emotions of
anguish and joy.

She nodded, but continued to point to her
baby.

" It is dead," were the words that struggled
from her frozen lips.

" Good God ! " exclaimed Arthur. " What

shall we do? Mr. Challenger! What shall we do? Where can we take her?"

As he spoke the girl tottered and would have fallen had she not supported herself against one of the columns of the portico. Arthur sprang to her side and encircled her with one arm.

"There is a coffee-house at the end of the street," said Mark. "Perhaps they have a room to let there. I will go and see."

"Quick! Quick!" cried Arthur. "She's dying."

The girl seemed indeed either to be dying or to have fainted. Arthur placed her in a sitting position upon the steps at the theatre door, and commenced to chafe one of her hands. The other hand was still fixed tightly around the form of the dead child. She had once more opened her eyes with a deep sigh when Mark came running back.

"I have got a room," he cried. "Let us be quick. Can she walk?"

With difficulty the two supported her between them. It was a very small coffee-house, and at present empty of customers. Only a young girl was to be seen, who, with wide-staring eyes, watched the three enter, and led the way to a small bedroom on the first floor. The two friends were obliged to carry their charge up the stairs; she was quite incapable of walking up herself.

"We should have done better to take her

to the Middlesex Hospital," said Mark, as
they laid her, apparently lifeless, on the bed.

"No, no!" cried Arthur, "she shall not
go to the hospital as long as I possess a
penny. Now will you fetch a doctor?
Where does the nearest doctor live?" he
asked, turning to the girl who had accompanied them upstairs.

Information of a vague kind was given,
and Mark hastened off on his errand.

"Light a fire here at once," cried Arthur.
"Have you any spirits in the place?"

"We mayn't sell 'em," replied the girl.

"Will you run to the nearest public-house
and get me some brandy?"

"I daren't leave," returned the girl.
They're all out."

With a hurried exclamation Arthur took a
glance at the form on the bed, and himself
darted down the stairs and out of the house.
In three minutes he returned with a small
bottle of spirits. Hot water was forthcoming,
and, whilst the girl was lighting the fire in
the grate, he tried to administer a little of
the mixture. But Carrie was now perfectly
unconscious, and her teeth were fast set.
Arthur was forced to content himself with
chafing her hands and arms, and bathing her
forehead with the brandy.

It seemed as if Mark had been gone an
hour already. Arthur fretted and fumed
with impatience, and his sufferings, as he saw

no sign of life returning to the girl's face, were intense. He was on the point of himself running in pursuit of aid when he heard footsteps upon the stairs, and Mark appeared, followed by a middle-aged man. The latter examined his patient forthwith, and looked serious.

" We had better remove her at once to the hospital," was his first remark. " Will one of you fetch a cab ? "

Mark posted off again at his best speed.

" She is alive, isn't she ? " asked Arthur, in an agony of apprehension. " Can't you bring her back to consciousness ? "

" She is alive at present," replied the doctor, " but I shouldn't like to promise that she will be so long."

As he spoke he disengaged the dead child from her arms with some trouble.

"The child has been dead several hours," he remarked, laying it by the side of the mother. He then proceeded to attempt the latter's restoration. In a minute or two he was interrupted by a shout from the bottom of the stairs. The cab was waiting.

Arthur and the doctor carried the patient down stairs, and placed her in the cab. After that Arthur returned to fetch the dead child. With a hurried charge to his friend Mark to pay whatever might be wanted for the use of the room, and then to follow to the hospital, he jumped in with the doctor and they drove off.

Mark Challenger followed almost immediately, and found Arthur in a waiting-room, where there was a huge fire, waiting till he should hear at least that Carrie had shown signs of life. They sat side by side, occasionally speaking to each other in a low voice for more than two hours. At the end of this time they heard that the patient was doing well. Satisfied perforce with this gleam of hope, and having obtained permission to make an inquiry in the morning, Arthur left the hospital, and walked home with his friend.

CHAPTER XIII.

A TOWN IDYL.

CARRIE lay ill in the hospital for nearly three weeks. Many a night did Arthur wander around the building till long after the clock had sounded twelve, ever and again pausing to gaze up at the window of the ward in which he knew she lay, picturing to himself, amid the silence of the dark streets, the beautiful face of the suffering girl lying with its background of rich dark hair upon the uneasy pillow. He liked to think of her as asleep, drinking deep of sweet and healthful rest after the misery of homeless days and nights, and the long agony of starvation in the streets. He never availed himself of the visitors' days to go and see her. It was extremely unlikely that she remembered his face, and to introduce himself to her by the memory of by-gone trouble would be the mere selfish gratification of his wishes. He knew that she continued to improve, and that was sufficient.

In the meantime he had succeeded in making an agreeable change in his occupation. The night-work to which he was subject in alternate weeks had grown extremely irksome to him, and was producing an evident impression upon his health. Accordingly, he had seized the opportunity of a tempting advertisement by a celebrated firm of printers, and had been happy enough to obtain an excellent place in their office, where his work would only occupy him in the day-time, and where he would earn more than hitherto. He began to work at the new place only a few days before Carrie was ready to leave the hospital. For the latter event he immediately began to make preparations.

He and his friend Mark had kept their resolution of relinquishing their abode in the house of the Pettindunds. At the end of their week's notice they had taken one large room in Huntley Street, at no great distance from Gower Place, where they for the present lived together, thus affecting a piece of economy very agreeable to both. In the same street Arthur now proceeded to look for a small furnished bedroom. Before long he found one precisely to his taste, at a low rent, and this he forthwith bespoke, saying that its occupant would come and take possession of it in a day or two.

Arthur was now somewhat puzzled how to proceed. He knew that Carrie was in a deplorable condition as regards clothing, and scarcely saw how he could make good the deficiency. He was troubled, moreover, to discover some plan by which he could make an offer of his assistance with suitable delicacy and then instal Carrie in her room without fear of endangering her reputation; the latter, especially, being a task which the fearful and wonderful complication of our social delicacies and pruderies renders always somewhat difficult. The world is so very slow to believe that connections other than of a certain sort can possibly exist between young people of different sex who see each other in private; it is so easy for corrupt imagination to picture situations completely familiar to themselves, so extremely difficult for them to conceive the existence of virtue and self-respect. After much reflection Arthur concluded that there was but one easily-practicable course; he must take his landlady into his confidence.

Mrs. Oaks was, as far as Arthur had hitherto been able to judge, a kind-hearted and motherly woman, not at all of the lodging-house-landlady type. She had several children, whose clean and respectable appearance had already struck Arthur as unusual under the circumstances, and as she had been a widow for several years she had no one but herself to consult upon a point of delicacy. She was, moreover, the only woman whom Arthur had at present any relations with. Arriving at a decision after a consideration of these various points, the young man re-

Y

quested an interview with Mrs. Oaks. In plain, straightforward terms he explained to her Carrie's helpless and friendless position —suppressing, of course, all mention of the circumstances which had led to this—and declared his interest in her. He stated that he had already taken a lodging for her, and then went on frankly to declare the difficulties in which he found himself, and to request Mrs. Oaks' assistance, should she be willing to give it. The good woman had listened with some signs of doubt and misgiving to the commencement of this narrative, but, as Arthur progressed in it, his frank, generous expression of face and the hearty earnestness of his voice and manner won her over to fully believe in his good intentions. Possibly Arthur's handsome features had not a little to do with the eventual conquest. Always agreeable to look upon, they became, especially to a woman, quite irresistible when lighted up with emotion.

" What I should ask you to do, then, Mrs. Oaks," said Arthur, " if you should be willing to help me, would be this. I should like you to go and see Miss Mitchell, to judge from her appearance what clothing will be necessary for her, and then to buy it for her and let her have it. I have no idea of the cost of such things. I can spare five pounds, however; do you think that will be sufficient ? "

"Well, sir," returned Mrs. Oaks, "it'll, at all events, get her enough to go on with."

"Very good. Then I understand, Mrs. Oaks, you will not mind undertaking this troublesome business for me?"

"Lord, no!" returned the worthy woman. "I never grudge a little trouble if I see as I can do *real* good to a body. I'm sorry to say it isn't so often I have it in my power."

"I should, of course, wish you to consider the time you employ for me together with the rent at the end of the week," added Arthur, after some little hesitation.

"Pooh! no such thing!" cried Mrs. Oaks. "Time's not so over val'able to me as all that. If I go and see the girl, my eldest daughter 'll buy all the clothing, and be glad of the job. She likes shopping, Lizzie does."

"Then there is one more thing to speak of, Mrs. Oaks, and I have done troubling you. Would it be too much to ask you to let me see Miss Mitchell in your parlour for half an hour before she goes to her own lodging? As I told you, she scarcely knows me, and some sort of explanation will be necessary."

"You're welcome, sir," returned the landlady, after a moment's thought. "I have confidence in you."

"I am glad to hear you say so, Mrs. Oaks," said Arthur. "I can never sufficiently thank you for your kindness; I can-

not, indeed ! When you see Miss Mitchell
in the hospital, please do not mention my
name. Say merely that a friend has sent
you—a friend that will come to take her
away on Saturday."

"Well, well," said Mrs. Oaks, laughing
quietly. " I'll do as you wish. You mean
to be kind-hearted, Mr. Golding. It isn't
everyone as 'ud do all this."

"And it isn't everyone that would give
such kind help to a stranger as you have
promised, Mrs. Oaks," replied Arthur.
" Once more, I thank you sincerely."

Everything went well, and at three o'clock
on Saturday afternoon Arthur had a cab
waiting before the Middlesex Hospital to
take away the convalescent. As he stood in
the waiting-room expecting Carrie's appearance, his heart beat fiercely in his bosom, he
was almost choked with the varied emotions
which struggled for the ascendancy within
him. And when at length he saw her coming towards him, tall, graceful, still deadly
pale, her thick hair done up tastefully yet
simply, the plain garments which Mrs. Oaks
had purchased for her giving her a fresh and
neat appearance, her step evidently feeble,
her eyes wandering in curious expectation,
the rushing flood of deep tenderness and
passion all but welled up from his heart into
his eyes. He could not speak, but beckoned
to her to follow him, and led her to the cab.

They drove off towards Huntley Street.
Seeing the expression of doubtful recognition
with which his companion regarded him,
Arthur bent forward and asked if she remembered him.

"I—I think so," she stammered. "You
lived at aunt's. I think it was you who paid
my rent, wasn't it?"

"And who had a note put under my
door when you went away," said Arthur,
smiling.

The recollection of her sufferings, blended
with her physical weakness and uncertainty
of mind, was too much for Carrie. She
burst into tears.

"Where are we going?" she sobbed.
"Where are you taking me? Not to
aunt's?"

"No, no, we will not go there," said
Arthur, taking one of her hands gently, and
chafing it like the hand of a suffering child.
"Are you afraid of me? Dare you trust
me?"

But still she continued to sob, and made
no reply. Arthur feared she would faint,
and was glad when the cab at length stopped.
There was a cheerful fire burning in the
parlour, and Mrs. Oaks was there ready to
pour out a cup of tea. After a few kind
words to Carrie, the good woman went away
and left the two to themselves.

Arthur waited till Carrie had in some degree recovered herself, and then, sitting opposite her on one side of the fire-place, he told his story in a kind, soothing voice. He related how he had seen her suffering and had felt his sympathy keenly aroused, how this feeling had become yet stronger when on the evening of Christmas Day he had found her dying in the snow; how he had her taken to the hospital, and how, now that he hoped she would before long be quite restored to health, he desired nothing so much as to be allowed to serve her. He spoke not a word directly of his passion ; natural delicacy withheld him. He merely represented himself as a sincere friend, and in conclusion he begged that she would not hesitate to use the room he had taken for her, and to accept of whatever assistance it was in his power to give.

She listened throughout as though she were in a dream, appearing to only half-understand what was said to her. When Arthur's voice had been silent for some minutes, she said, at length, with much hesitation—

" But how can I pay you back ? I am too weak to work yet, and even when I do work I shall never get money enough to pay you back. I—I don't know that I understand what you mean ? "

A vague look of apprehension marked her countenance. Arthur divined her thought from this and the manner in which she spoke. He hastened to reassure her.

"And yet it is very simple," he said. "I want to be a sincere friend to you, that is the whole of the matter. As to paying me back, I never dreamt of it; that is out of the question. All I beg of you, is that you will let me see you occasionally and ask you whether you are comfortable. That is all."

"But why do you do this for me?" she continued to ask, looking dazed and still a little apprehensive. "You know so little of me. Why do you do it?"

"If I promise you that I will answer that question in a month's time, will that be sufficient?" asked Arthur in return.

The girl looked still more puzzled.

"But you will do what I wish, won't you?" urged Arthur, scarcely restraining himself from falling before her and declaring that he loved her madly. "You will let me provide for you, for the present? You won't refuse?"

"If I do refuse," returned Carrie, after a moment's thought, "I must go back to the workhouse. I have nowhere to go. I have no money."

"Then you accept?" cried Arthur, springing to his feet in delight.

"You are very kind," said Carrie, looking with a smile through her tears. "I don't know why you do it all for me. As soon as

I am strong I can earn my own living, but
till then—"

"Not another word!" interrupted Arthur.
"And you will let me see you sometimes?
You will let me meet you somewhere in the
evening, and see how you get on?"

"You are very kind to me," stammered
Carrie, as her only reply.

"Then that's all. Now you shall go to
your own lodging. I have arranged with
them to wait upon you and buy whatever you
want for your meals. You will be able to do
that for yourself soon, but not just yet. I
have one or two other things to get you, and
those I shall send as soon as I can. But
however shall you employ yourself? Do you
like reading?"

"A—a little," replied Carrie, with hesitation.

"I must look for a few books then. Mrs.
Oaks, that's my landlady here, is going to
walk to the house with you. She's a kind
woman, and you needn't be afraid of her.
She only knows that you are a friend of
mine. You won't have far to walk, only a
few yards. And you will be careful of your
health, won't you? Whatever you do, don't
go out if it is cold or wet. I know you will
take care; that is one of your ways of paying me back, mind."

He spoke thus standing, and with his hand
on the door. It was agony to him to main-

tain such a calm and distant tone when his heart was burning in the desire to discharge itself of endless passion. He opened the door, but instantly closed it again.

"Your window looks into the street," he said. "If you see me waiting opposite about one o'clock on Monday, will you put your hat on and come to speak to me for a moment. I shall only come if it's fine."

"Yes, I will," she replied. "I will put my hat on so as to be ready, and watch."

"Only one thing more, then," said Arthur, taking a small purse from his pocket and handing it to her. "Let me know as soon as that is empty. You will, of course, pay the rent and everything else yourself. And now, good-bye for the present."

He held out his hand, and Carrie took it timidly. She seemed even yet to be uncertain as to his intention, and her dark eyes viewed him curiously and askance. He then opened the door and called Mrs. Oaks. That lady came up with her bonnet on, and at once set out with Carrie.

As the door closed behind them, Arthur hastened upstairs to his room, from the window of which he could watch them to the end of their walk. When at length Carrie and her guide completely disappeared, he sank upon a chair with a sigh, half of gladness, half of regret, and relapsed into deep thought.

As yet Mark Challenger knew nothing of all this. Arthur had feared that he would insist upon sharing in the charitable work, and he wished to have the whole delight of it for himself. But, now that it was completed, he saw no reason for further secrecy, and Mark was accordingly informed of everything the same evening.

"And what is to be the end of all this, Arthur, my boy?" he asked, gravely, as soon as the young man had completed his story.

"Who can tell?" returned Arthur, with a merry laugh.

"Who is to tell, if not yourself?"

"Ah!" sighed Arthur, "if it only depended upon me—"

Mark regarded his young friend with a shrewd look of inquiry.

"Well?" he asked.

"Why, cannot you guess?" cried Arthur, laughing. "Carrie would be my wife to-morrow."

"Your wife?" returned the other, as if relieved. "Well, well, there's no great harm in that. The world seems to have treated you fairly well, on the whole, Arthur; let's hope you'll never be worse off than you are now. I had a wife once, and a daughter. The one starved to death, and the other—well, well, I mustn't think of all that. It'll make me like poor John Pether, and I seem to have been getting quieter in my mind of late. I can wish you nothing better than a good wife, Arthur, after all. But don't be in a hurry, my boy; don't be in a hurry."

Arthur laughed, and, humming a merry air, sat down to one of his favourite books.

And where was the memory of Helen Norman—of that sweet ideal which had once allied itself with all there was of noblest and most aspiring in Arthur Golding's nature? It had passed away with the use of those noble faculties and the aspirations towards which they tended; passed away, that is, as far as any active influence was concerned, though it still lingered as a sort of vaguely remembered joy—a background of dim and fading gold to the rich, warm image of the reigning delight.

The responsibilities Arthur had taken upon his shoulders were the reverse of light. He was now compelled to become, in all that concerned his personal expenditure, an absolute miser. Luckily, during the last few months, he had saved every penny he could, always in the hope of being one day able to devote them to Carrie's needs; but these resources were now already drained, and it was only by the exercise of the most pinching economy that he could hope to keep Carrie in those circumstances of comfort which, in his eyes, befitted her.

It was not only her food and lodging which

had to be paid for, but he must succeed in
saving a little each week towards the purchase of clothing for her. As to her ever
returning to the daily drudgery of the work-
room and earning her own living, that he was
determined not to suffer. Sooner would he
divest himself of everything save the extremest necessaries.

Under these circumstances, there was one
step he felt bound to take at once. He must
relinquish his membership of the club. And
this caused him the more pain because the
club had of late been showing unmistakable
signs of decadence. In fact, whilst no new
members had joined it since Arthur, no less
than six of the old ones had recently fallen
off.

Enthusiasm, strongly sustained by
example, can do much ; but even Will
Noble's firmness and eloquence had failed
to keep in their posts all those whom his
strong persuasion had collected around him.
The men were but unenlightened working
men after all, and the temptation to find
other uses for their money than that of self-
denying charity were too strong for their un-
fortified natures. So it was with some sense
of shame that Arthur attended the club
meeting on Sunday, knowing that it would be
his last.

When it was over, he took Will Noble's
arm and asked the latter to walk a short way

with him. Then he related the circumstances which would lead to his defection.

Will listened without any sign of annoyance.

"If only the other men could know all this, Golding," he said at length, "you could still stay with us, for you are doing nothing but what it is our aim to do. But that, of course, under the circumstances, wouldn't be agreeable. Well, I suppose we must lose you, old fellow; but that's no reason why you and I shouldn't meet and have our chats as usual, is it?"

"None in the world. I am only afraid lest you should think less of me for having given up useful work for private ends."

"If the ends were selfish," replied Noble, "I should certainly think less of you, Golding, I confess. But when I know they are the opposite, I should be a fool if I did so. I value your friendship more than ever for this bit of kindness to that poor girl. I have a plain and downright way of looking at things, and it has always seemed to me that the man who saves one fellow-creature, however poor and miserable, from a life of degradation, deserves the utmost respect. We have such a lot of windy clamour now-a-days about doing good, but still so precious little of real individual effort. You talk of making this girl your wife. Well and good. You are the best judge in such a matter;

and you ought to know whether she will suit you. Marry her by all means, and make a good, honest woman out of her. If you succeed in doing that, I can tell you, Golding, the thought of it will bring you happiness to the end of your life."

They walked on for a little distance in silence.

"Bye-the-by, Noble," said Arthur at length, " I wonder you have never thought of marriage yourself. I know very well you have plenty of use for *your* money, and that you do as much good as a man in your position possibly could do. But don't you think of getting a home of your own one of these days ? "

Will turned away his head, though the darkness would not allow his features to be observed.

" What if I had thought of it for a long time, Golding ? " he said, with a nervous twitch of his arm, which Arthur felt.

" Why, I should be glad to hear it," returned the latter. "I suppose I musn't venture to ask if the person is decided on ? "

" Yes, you may ask." said Noble, with a laugh. "She has long been decided on ; but is not so ready to come to a decision herself."

" What ! Is it possible that a girl can hesitate to accept you, Noble—you, such a fine, generous, handsome fellow ? "

"Hush, hush, hush!" interrupted the other, laughing still. "You make me feel uncomfortable. For all those imaginary qualities your friendship gives me, Lucy doesn't seem to care much for me. Well, well!"

He sent a sigh from his broad chest which showed that Will had sorrows of his own to occupy him occasionally, in addition to those of other people.

Arthur was silent, wondering curiously who this Lucy could be who played the coquette with such a man as Will Noble. His thoughts were interrupted by the latter's voice.

"Will you come with me some day, Golding, and see Lucy?" asked Will.

"I should be delighted," cried Arthur. "Does she live anywhere in this neighbourhood?"

"No, in the East End. We'll go some Sunday, if you like."

Very shortly after this they parted, Will taking his way homewards with a gloomier face than he usually wore, Arthur returning to dream all night of Carrie. He did not go home without first walking past the house in which he had established her and looking up at the window. It was quite dark; no doubt she was in bed and sleeping.

With many a fervent thought stirring in his heart, he sighed and walked slowly away.

At all events, he would see her on the morrow.

Monday was frosty and fine. Punctually to his time, Arthur stood on the side of the street opposite to Carrie's window. For a moment he saw her face there, and a minute afterwards she came out of the front door and walked quickly towards him. He thought she looked stronger already, and flattered himself that the slight glow on her cheeks was due to pleasure at seeing him. They walked side by side out of Huntley Street towards the more quiet neighbourhood of the adjoining squares.

"And how have you occupied yourself since I saw you on Saturday?" asked Arthur, stealing side glances at her face as they walked slowly on. "Has the time seemed long?"

"No, very short," was the reply.

Arthur had hoped she would have said the opposite. He felt that the time had so crept with himself.

"Indeed? What have you been doing, then?"

"Oh, I have been putting my things in order, and doing some sewing."

"Sewing? But had you needles and cotton?"

"Oh, yes. I went out on Saturday night and bought them."

Arthur felt a sudden feeling something

like anger rise within him. She had gone out alone on Saturday night? He could not bear the thought. He would have liked to be able to lock her up from all the world, so intense was his passion, and, consequently, so acute his jealousy.

"Went out!" he cried. "But I begged you never to go out except when the sun was shining. I wonder you didn't catch your death of cold."

"Oh, I wasn't out long. I only went into Oxford Street and back."

"And how do you like your room?"

"It is very nice. I am very comfortable there. And the people are so nice. When I go to work again I'm sure I shall stay there."

"When do you think you will be able to go to work?" asked Arthur, inwardly irritated at the matter-of-course way in which she spoke.

"Oh, in a week or two. The landlady's eldest daughter goes to work, and she says she can get me a place with her."

Arthur fumed in his heart. Carrie seemed already quite changed from what she had been on Saturday. She was making friends already, and plans in which *he* had no part. He had never suffered so acutely in his life.

"Shall you be glad to get to work again?" he asked, with something of pique in his voice.

"I shan't be *glad*," replied Carrie, with a slight sigh. "But what else can I do?"

Arthur's equanimity was restored. After all she was dependent upon him. He had it in his power to relieve her from a disagreeable life.

"Well, well; we won't talk about that just yet," he replied, gaily. "What you have to do now is to get well as fast as possible. You are dreadfully pale yet."

They walked about the squares, talking thus, for nearly an hour. Then Arthur, looking at his watch, found that he had no time to lose. As it was, he had sacrificed his dinner for the sake of this conversation.

"Oh, must you go?" asked Carrie, in a rather sad voice.

"I must indeed. I must be at my work at half-past two. I shall have to run."

"And when shall I see you again?"

"Perhaps in two or three days," said Arthur, with a carelessness which he purposely affected.

"Not before that?" asked his companion, with evident disappointment. "I suppose you are very busy?"

"Well, suppose I said the same time to-morrow, if it is fine?"

"Oh, yes; I will be ready."

"But mind; if it rains or snows I shall not come. And you will promise me not to go out again to-day?"

" Yes."

" Then good-bye."

" Good-bye."

Arthur pressed her hand for a moment in both his own, and then forced himself to walk quickly away. At the first corner he turned. Carrie was still standing where he had left her, looking after him. He waved his hand, and went on with joy in his heart.

The fortnight which succeeded was one of internal perturbation such as paled Arthur's cheek, and gave his eye a restless, feverish look. With one or two exceptions, which he forced himself to make, he saw Carrie every day. Out of fear lest their regular appointments should be noticed from the house, he arranged that they should always meet at a certain spot in Torrington Square. Here he was, day after day, punctual to his hour, though it always cost him a hard walk and the sacrifice of his regular mid-day meal. He accustomed himself to satisfy his hunger with a few biscuits, which he ate as he walked, and often on reaching the square he was ready to faint with exhaustion. In his scrupulous delicacy and care for Carrie's reputation, he would not meet her after dark, but many a night he paced up and down Huntley Street, looking up at her window. As a rule, her light was burning there, and he imagined her sitting with her book or at her sewing. But once or twice her window was dark all the evening, and he tortured himself with divining all manner of explanations, good and evil. On the following days he endeavoured to discover where she had been, though he never ventured to tell her plainly why he asked. Perhaps she would say that she had been sitting with her landlady, and with this explanation he had to satisfy himself, though jealousy seemed to eat at his very vitals.

Notwithstanding his frequent requests that she would not leave the house at night, she several times showed in conversation that she had done so. But as she became more accustomed to his character, Carrie grew more careful, and, even if she had transgressed his rule, took care not to let him know it. Arthur pressed his injunctions upon her ostensibly on account of her health, but in reality because it was agony to him to think of her walking about the streets without his company and protection. This occasional disregard of his wishes was unutterable pain to Arthur. He said to himself that she *ought* to do as he desired, if from mere gratitude alone. But these momentary irritations would rapidly pass away, and be succeeded by a long conversation, in which each strove to give the other pleasure, and succeeded. It was a dreadfully transparent business, this affectation of mere friendship between the two.

But Arthur had resolved that, till the month was up, he would not transgress these bounds, hard as it was to keep within them. He argued with himself that it was only fair to let Carrie become well acquainted with him before he asked her to become his wife. To present himself as a lover so soon would have appeared too like taking advantage of the gratitude she owed him. He was resolved that he would treat this friendless girl with as much consideration as if she had been the child of wealthy parents. In what else, he asked himself, does the character of a gentleman consist but in this according of courtesy to such as are not able to exact it?

The commencement of the third week was marked by a painful incident. On Saturday night Arthur had walked past Carrie's window as usual, and had been troubled to see no light there. She had told him that she occasionally sat with the landlady and her daughter, and possibly she might be with them now. But an evil genius seemed to whisper suspicions in the lover's ear. He resolved to watch the house for a time, and see whether she entered her room. It was now seven o'clock, and a raw, disagreeable evening, but weather was nothing to him. The fire that ceaselessly burned within him forbade his suffering from the inclement air. For several hours he walked perpetually up and down the street, and round the adjacent streets, never daring to be out of sight of the window long, lest she should, during that time, enter her room and go to bed. As the evening went on, his anxiety increased. He worked himself up to fever-heat. Several times he had almost resolved to knock at the house-door, and ask to see her, but this his delicacy prevented. Was it possible she had gone to bed without a light? That supposition could not satisfy him. Eleven o'clock came, and, with a heart over-whelmed with bitterness, he was on the point of going away and demanding an explanation on the morrow, when he saw two female figures emerging from the darkness, and walking in the direction of the house he was watching. From the first sight he felt sure that one of these was Carrie. He recognised her tall figure and her walk, though it was impossible to discern features. The two were laughing and talking together also, and he persuaded himself that, as they drew near, he recognised her voice. Drawing back against the houses to escape notice, he saw them stop before Carrie's house and enter. He had not been mistaken.

He went home and crept shivering into bed, but closed not an eye all night. Should he kill himself at once?—that was the question that rang unceasingly through his brain. Better to do so than suffer the internal tor-ture that must be his lot if incidents such as this were frequent. Where could Carrie possibly have passed the whole evening? Once or twice during that night of agony, he determined that he would continue to assist her till she could support herself, and then say good-bye to her for ever. A resolution likely of fulfilment! Between three and four, whilst Mark Challenger was sleeping peacefully in his bed, which stood at the other end of the room, Arthur rose and dressed; then paced the room till day-break in perfect silence. He felt that another such night would either kill him or make him raving mad.

He was to meet Carrie at ten o'clock on the following morning, and, if the weather proved fine, they were to take a walk. But the dawn which broke on Arthur's eyes, as he sat in the cheerless room looking impatiently through the window for the first trace of daylight, was anything but promising. Thick, low, leaden-hued clouds kept back the morning till a late hour, and when first the street began to be visible, it was through a mist of hopeless, heart-breaking rain. The roofs opposite reflected the earliest rays of dawn in the dull, distorting mirror of dripping slates; the smoke which here and there began to show itself at the tops of the chimneys, faltered and sunk in a lifeless waver towards the ground; the feet of the passers-by on the pavement below, and the wheels of the occasional vehicles, went splash, splash, splash, revealing to the ear a waste of melancholy pools and snow of old deposit trodden and rained into sump; the cries of the milkmen seemed to come from afar off through deadening layers of fog.

As soon as he saw Mark Challenger beginning to stir and wake, Arthur, despite the weather, quickly put on his hat and hastened out. To have been spoken to, questioned, sympathised with, would have been intolerable. He was in no mood for any company but his own. He walked past Carrie's house. The blind was down at her window, as at every other window, and the sight of it roused within him so fierce, yet so unreasoning an excess of bitterness, that he wrung his hands together, and could scarcely hold his voice from crying aloud. He hurried on, walking he knew not whither, unconscious of everything save the slow progress of time. He had eaten nothing since noon on the preceding day, but if he at all felt the pangs of hunger, he did not recognise them. By degrees it grew lighter, but still the thin, hopeless rain came down from the leaden sky. Already it was nine o'clock. It was impossible for it to clear up that morning.

Ten o'clock came, and Arthur was at the place of meeting, feeling sure that Carrie would not come, and yet unable to return home. He had waited half-an-hour, and was on the point of moving slowly away, when he saw, at the further end of the square, a female form under an umbrella coming towards him. In a moment he saw that it was Carrie, and he ran to meet her.

"I suppose you didn't expect me?" she asked; then added, without waiting for an answer, "How queer you look in the face! Aren't you well?"

"I have had a bad night," returned Arthur, every limb trembling from physical weakness and the force of his emotions.

"I'm sorry to hear that. You shouldn't have troubled to come a dreadful morning like this."

"I always keep my promises, however difficult it may be," replied Arthur, with a steady gaze into her face. "But *you* don't look well. Did the landlady keep you up late again last night?"

"Oh, no," replied Carrie, carelessly.

"Did you pass the evening alone?" asked Arthur, affecting a like carelessness, though his eyes never moved from the girl's face.

"Yes. It was dreadfully lonely. I was sewing as usual."

"In your own room?"

"Of course. The people were all out somewhere last night."

Arthur stood aghast. Though he had already once or twice been tortured with a vague suspicion that Carrie was not always truthful to him, he had never caught her in so direct an untruth.

"Then you never went out of the house?" he asked, still endeavouring, though with poor result, to hide the interest he had in the matter.

"Why should I?" returned Carrie, biting her lower lip, and slightly averting her head. "You know you told me not to go out after dark."

Arthur could restrain himself no longer. For a moment a fierce combat raged within him, then he spoke in a low, trembling voice.

"In that case, Miss Mitchell, how was it that I saw you enter the house with one of the landlady's daughters at nearly midnight?"

Carrie blushed involuntarily, but only for a moment. Then her eyes met Arthur's full gaze. She stammered, but made no articulate reply.

"Where were you last night?" pursued Arthur, still holding her with his eye. Her colour went and came, and suddenly she spoke with angry emphasis.

"Well, I was at the Oxford Music Hall, Mr. Golding, if you *must* know. And what harm? Am I never to move out of my own room? I wish you had to live all alone as I do, you'd soon be glad of a little amusement!"

Arthur's passion caught fire at the spark. He replied with trembling lips, cheeks deadly pale, and a tongue that stammered from anger.

"What harm? A great deal of harm that you should go where I do not wish you, where I *will not have* you go—at least, as long as you accept my help!"

He could have bitten off his tongue the next moment for speaking such words. But they were beyond recall. Whilst yet they were ringing in his ears, he saw Carrie turn passionately from him, and walk hastily away.

CHAPTER XIV.

SHADOWS.

CURSING himself for a hot-tempered fool, and a mean-spirited one to boot, Arthur walked round and round the adjacent streets for several hours. For a while, indignation at Carrie's behaviour struggled for place against anger at his own lack of gentleness and patience.

Oh, was it not cruel of her to act so towards him? Surely, surely it was only some momentary whim that had taken possession of her. He could not think she would deliberately plan to deceive him.

But then came the hot blast of jealousy to keep up the fire of indignation. She had gone out on Saturday night, and, above all places, to a music-hall, the resort of the most abandoned of both sexes, a place in which no woman who valued her reputation would care to be seen. Was it she who had proposed to go, or was it her companion, the landlady's daughter, who had persuaded her? In either case she was culpable.

But this mood soon spent itself, giving way to one of apprehension and self-reproach. He had allowed her to leave him in anger, and who could tell what step she might take? The suddenness with which she had departed disclosed a hasty, impulsive temper, such a one as might lead to all manner of unconsidered follies.

Perhaps she would forthwith leave her lodgings and go where he had no means of discovering her. Clearly he must follow her to the house and see her there. Impossible to wait till to-morrow on the chance of her meeting him as usual. The anguish would be too unendurable.

He had turned in that direction, and was just entering Huntley Street, when, as he hurried on with his eyes on the pavement, he was stopped by a sudden hand upon his shoulder.

Looking up, he saw the short, stout figure of Mark Challenger before him.

"Where on earth have you been, Arthur?" he asked. "Why, I have been hunting for you all the morning. Are you ill, boy? Whatever is the matter with you?"

This sudden encounter seemed to recall Arthur to a sense of his physical suffering. He was wet to the skin, and exhausted with hunger. His eyes wandered over Mark's face as if he had not yet clearly recognised him.

The latter quickly seized his arm, and, in spite of a feeble resistance, forced him to walk quickly home. In their room Arthur found

a bright fire burning, and the table spread
with the simple breakfast they were in the
habit of taking together on Sundays. Mark
compelled him to change his clothes, after
which the warmth of the fire, combined with
the internal action of a strong cup of coffee,
soon restored him to physical strength.

As soon as he felt once more master of
his faculties he rose and was going out
again, with some muttered excuse, when
Mark once more caught him by the arm and
detained him.

"Now look here, Arthur," he said, "for
the present you don't budge. Dash my but-
tons! What's the good of my being something approaching three times your age, if
I'm not to exert a little friendly authority
now and then? There's something amiss, I
can see. Now can't you just tell me what it
is, and ease your mind?"

Arthur felt it would indeed ease him, but
he hesitated.

"Have you and Carrie been quarrelling?"
pursued Mark. "That must be it. Now,
tell me what's the matter, there's a good
lad."

Thus pressed, Arthur did at length confess
that there had been a little disagreement. To
confess the whole, even to Mark, he felt to
be impossible. Though the object of his love
might be lowered in his own eyes, he could
not bear that others should see her faults.

But he said enough to make Mark partly suspect the truth, and the latter shook his head and looked grave.

Then, by dint of questioning, he got Arthur to reveal the greater part of the circumstances, proceeding after that to reason with him, and to try to show how great a need of caution and deliberation there was in a matter which probably concerned the happiness of two lives.

But Arthur was an impatient listener, and scarcely replied to his friend's words. It was impossible for him to rest whilst he was yet uncertain about Carrie's movements. Very shortly he found an opportunity of leaving the room, this time unopposed by his friend, and hurrying into the street, he took the direction of Carrie's abode. Arrived opposite to it, he was rejoiced to see her face at the window. He motioned with his hand, and the face disappeared. A few minutes afterwards she herself appeared at the door, and walked across the street to join him.

It had now ceased raining, though the day continued as dark as ever. As Carrie drew near him, Arthur saw that her eyes were red, as if from crying, and immediately his heart went out to her in a gush of forgiving tenderness.

He took her hand as though they had not already met that morning, and together they walked on in silence.

" Will you forgive me for my angry words this morning?" asked Arthur, first breaking the silence in a timid voice, and without venturing to look into his companion's face. " I did not know what I was saying."

" Will you forgive me for doing what you didn't wish me to?" was Carrie's low-voiced reply. " I am very sorry. I will not do it again."

They were near their favourite place of meeting in Torrington Square. At the moment only one or two people were in sight at the farthest end of the square, and the distant roll of vehicles was the only sound which broke the stillness of the dull January afternoon.

" Carrie!" whispered Arthur, grasping her hand as he walked on, and feeling that it trembled.

She looked into his face with a sweet smile and a questioning expression. He went on in low and eager tones—

" Will you give me the right to guard and protect you, not only from a distance, as a friend, but by your side, for the rest of your life? Will you be my wife?"

" Do you care so much for me?" asked Carrie, the sweet smile mingling with a light blush, so that she looked yet more beautiful.

" I have loved you ever since I knew you, dearest," he returned. " Can you care for me a little?"

"I can love you with all the love I have," she replied. "Is that enough?"

The word "love," uttered for the first time by her lips, smote upon the finest chords of Arthur's being, and left them throbbing with an intensity that almost deprived him of consciousness. He could only once more press her hand, when several people appeared turning the corner of the square, and coming towards them.

What had these innocent strangers done that Arthur should curse them in his heart with the bitterest of curses?

All the afternoon, all the dull, sad, dripping afternoon, till the lamplighter began to hurry on his blessed mission along the sloppy streets, did the two wander side by side, absolutely ignorant of the places they passed; listening to nothing but the sweet utterances of each other's lips, seeing nothing but the glad looks upon each other's faces. The day of unutterable gloom and misery had set in such an outbreak of glorious light as neither had ever known. What was it to them that the rain had recommenced with the coming night, that a chill, bitter wind had begun to rock the leafless boughs in the middle of the square? Other pedestrians hurried by with nipped faces and wet clothes, eager to reach the warmth and comfort of home; but for these two there was no home possessing anything like the attraction of these hideous streets. When it rained they opened their umbrellas; but, finding them inconvenient, Carrie soon closed hers and made Arthur's suffice for both, availing herself of the chance to slip her little gloved hand delicately through Arthur's arm, where it was immediately pressed warm and tight against his throbbing heart.

Consideration for his companion was the only feeling capable of arousing Arthur from his delicious trance. At length he insisted upon her going home, and she, after much resistance, consented.

They were close to Huntley Street and to Carrie's abode when they passed the pitch-dark entrance to some mews.

" We had better say good-bye here," said Arthur. " Then you must run on home quickly."

He drew her gently beneath the archway, pressed her closely to his heart and kissed her.

" Will you always love me so, Arthur ? " whispered Carrie, sighing with fulness of joy.

" Always, darling," he replied, fervently; " as long as I have breath."

They then parted, Carrie running quickly home, Arthur turning to walk by a round-about way. He did not feel ready to face his friend Mark at once. It was nearly eight

o'clock when he at length entered, and he was glad to find Mark absent. In his excitement he had forgotten that the latter would be at the club as usual.

That night Arthur said not a word of his happiness. On the following day he found time, however, to visit the Registrar's Office and to give notice of an intended marriage between himself and Carrie. Neither of them had parent or guardian, so the fact that they were both under age was of no consequence. At the end of three weeks the marriage could be performed.

Wholly wrapped up as he was in one subject, Arthur would have been in danger of entirely forgetting the aims and aspirations which had so lately been the sole guides of his life, had it not been for the friendship of William Noble. Greatly as Arthur could not but admire the latter, he had grown of late almost to dread the frequent meetings with him and the long, earnest conversations into which Noble never failed to draw him. The secret of this uneasiness lay in the feeling that Noble's daily life contained a reproach, a protest against the habit of mind into which his friend had fallen of late, though Noble's own words and manner implied nothing less than a reproachful feeling. William's life was one of steady, patient, unremitting toil; toil, moreover, thoroughly fruitful for himself and those with whom he came into connection. The son of parents who had earned their daily bread by the coarsest manual labour, and who had been unable to give him any education beyond mere reading and writing, he had so wrought his way upwards by virtue of persistent labour, vitalised by a source of innate ability, that now, at the age of twenty-four, he found himself possessed of knowledge quite wonderful for a man in his position of life, and, what is better still, of an unflagging energy ever ready to operate in obedience to the dictates of a sound, healthy judgment, and a most tender, sympathetic, charitable heart. In the presence of this man Arthur felt his genius rebuked.

On the Saturday preceding his last week of surprise, Noble proposed that they should spend the following afternoon in a visit to the house of the young lady whom he had spoken of as " Lucy."

" But shall I be a welcome visitor?" asked Arthur, who could not help regretting a walk with Carrie. " A perfect stranger, you see—"

" Oh, you don't know them," interposed Noble, with a smile. " Mr. Venning, that's Lucy's father, is always glad to see me and any friend of mine. I have often spoken to him of you, and he is anxious to see you."

" But shall I not be in your way?"

" If you were likely to be, Golding, I shouldn't ask you," replied Noble, calmly.

" As I have told you, Lucy regards me—as yet—with nothing but friendship, and I always go there as a mere friend. Do you care to come ? "

"Oh, yes, I shall be very glad indeed to come," replied Arthur, ashamed of his hesitation as soon as he saw that a refusal would really pain his friend.

So the same evening he was obliged to inform Carrie that he should only be able to spend the Sunday morning with her, and not the whole day, the reason being that he was obliged to visit a friend.

"A friend ! What friend ?" asked Carrie, sharply.

Arthur, to avoid further questioning, explained the circumstances in detail.

" And you would rather go to see strange people that you know nothing about than spend the time with me ?" said Carrie, in a tone of annoyance.

"You know I would not rather do so, Carrie," replied Arthur. " I have explained the case to you. You must see that it is impossible for me to refuse."

"I don't see that it is. You could say that you were engaged. I *can't* do without you all day to-morrow. You must write and say you find you have another engagement."

" It is impossible to do so, Carrie," urged Arthur, in his quietest tone. " It would be unkind, it would be rude to do so."

" I'm sure I think it's much ruder to leave me," retorted the girl, separating herself some feet from his side as they walked along together. " You are getting not to care about me at all. That's the second thing you've refused me in one day. I asked you to take me to the theatre to-night, and you refused, and now you refuse to see me for a whole day."

" You shouldn't speak so, dearest," urged Arthur, drawing close to her again. " I don't refuse to see you for a whole day. I shall be with you all the morning, if it's fine; and then, if you like, I will see you when I come back at night. And as to the theatre, you know why I don't wish to take you. I can't afford to pay for a good place, and I don't choose that you should crowd in with a lot of vulgar people ; it isn't nice."

It was not the first time that Arthur had adopted this tone in speaking to Carrie. In his attempt to exalt her nature above the level on which it had hitherto moved, he, the democratic agitator, the ardent sympathiser with the most miserable of poverty's victims, waxed quite aristocratic in his conversation. In his heart he would rather have seen Carrie fall into the most complete snobbishness on the subject of riches and rank than continue at rest among the sympathies with vulgar life with which she had grown up. At present his passion was too earnest to permit of his playing the pedant, but already he looked forward to their marriage as affording him an opportunity of educating Carrie and rendering her, from an intellectual point of view, more worthy of his devotion.

After the above conversation they parted with rather less of their usual fervour.

" When shall I see you to-morrow morning, Carrie ?" asked Arthur.

" Oh, I don't know," replied the girl. " The usual time, I suppose."

" Of course if it isn't fine you mustn't expect me."

" Very well. You will have all the more time with your friend."

So saying, Carrie walked off, and Arthur returned home miserable to the heart's core. Luckily it was fine on the following morning, and something like a reconciliation was patched up between them, but still Carrie could not part from her lover at noon without speaking with some bitterness of his " friends," and Arthur was not sorry to look forward to Will Noble's society as a relief from these petty troubles which yet gave him such exquisite pain.

As it was a clear, frosty afternoon the walk towards the East End was agreeable. Noble was in excellent spirits, probably because he was about to see Lucy, and talked in his most cheerful vein all the way. In reply to Arthur's request for some infor-

mation with regard to Mr. Venning, he told
him that the latter was by trade a flute
manufacturer, but not in very flourishing
circumstances.   His wife had been long
dead and he had one child, Lucy, who was
employed as a " fitter-on," or in some such
capacity, in the show-rooms of a large East
End millinery establishment.   Hereupon he
diverged into a eulogy of Lucy, speaking
with delicate appreciation of her beauty, her
modesty, her cleverness.   Arthur was rather
amused to see his friend under this new
aspect, but at the same time it gave him
pain.   How unlike was his own passion to
this calm, deep, persevering affection.

On arriving at the shop they of course
found it closed, and knocked for admission
at a side door.   Mr. Venning himself replied
to the summons, and forthwith led them into
a small parlour.   He was a middle-aged
man, short in stature and with his left foot
distorted, so that he walked very lame.   In
face he was somewhat care-worn, but his
features wore a singularly sweet and amiable
expression.   In his eyes was a rather absent
look, indicating that he was addicted to
reverie.   When he spoke his voice was low
and musical.   He wore neither beard nor
moustache, the absence of these increasing the
female cast of his countenance.   His dress,
though very plain and showing signs of
poverty, was fastidiously neat, and Arthur

observed that his hands were of a wonderful delicacy.

"Mr. Golding," said Noble, as they all took seats in the little parlour, " is an intimate friend of mine, and I felt sure you would thank me for bringing him to see you. He has the same interests at heart as ourselves, Mr. Venning."

" I am always rejoiced to see any of William Noble's friends," returned Mr. Venning, looking at Arthur with his captivating smile, and speaking in a very quiet tone, which was still cordial. " And especially on Sunday afternoon when I have leisure to sit quietly at home. Next to the society of my good friends, Mr. Golding, I have no pleasure so great as that of sitting quite still and in perfect silence. Since two o'clock I have been holding a very pleasant conversation with the fire, its cracking seemed to make answers to my thoughts. How fond I am of the stillness of the Sunday! This street is never noisy, but on Sunday not a sound reaches this parlour."

In the low, sweet tones of the speaker's voice there was something singularly soothing, something which invited irresistibly to the same perfect calm of which he spoke. In making a reply, Arthur insensibly lowered his voice to the same pitch. Loud speech in this silent little room would have appeared profanation.

"It is wonderfully quiet, indeed," he replied. "One could almost imagine he was in a little country town, such remote, peaceful places as I have read of, but, I am sorry to say, have never seen."

"Does it make you think of that?" inquired Mr. Venning, with a quick look almost of gratitude. "Now that is the very feeling it awakens in me. And that is why I love it so, this Sabbath stillness, for it reminds me of the village I was born in. That was a little place close by the River Don in Yorkshire. You have read Scott's 'Ivanhoe,' Mr. Golding?"

"Yes, O yes!" replied Arthur. It was one of the first books he had read with Mr. Tollady, and the mention of it awakened pleasant thoughts.

"Then you will remember Conisboro' Castle. It is now a grey old ruin, and within sight of that I was born. Our house was a very small one, and was quite overshadowed by a huge elm. Hush! I can almost fancy that I hear the low whistling of its leaves on a midsummer afternoon, when (lazy boy that I was) I used to lie at full length in the warm sunshine on the floor of my little bedroom, and read. I think it must have been those afternoons that gave me my liking for quiet solitude."

He sighed slightly, but the next moment broke into a quiet laugh.

"It is a happy thing for me," he said, without looking at either of his companions, "that I can think of those dear old times with nothing but pure delight, though I know so well that I shall never leave London again. It used to be my ambition to work hard and make money—*just* enough to live upon, no more—and then to go back to my native place with Lucy and, in our Father's good time, be buried in the dear old church-yard. But now I know it is impossible, and, as I am sure that everything that happens to us is for the best, I do not sorrow over it."

There was silence for a few moments, broken at length by Noble.

"I suppose Lucy has not returned yet?" he asked.

"No," returned Mr. Venning, looking up with a smile. "She is still at the Sunday-school. But she cannot be more than a quarter of an hour now. How does the club get on, William?"

Noble shook his head with a rather sad smile.

"There are only five of us left," he replied. "Several have left of late from unavoidable causes, but others, I am afraid, have grown tired of the work. The other societies, which have amusement and politics for their chief aims, have attracted several."

"Well, well," said Mr. Venning, "perhaps it is too much to expect. There are not many that have your steady courage, William."

"Or perhaps it would be more correct to say," remarked Noble, "that the others are not so strongly impressed with the necessity of the work as I am."

As he spoke a light knock was heard at the outer door. Mr. Venning was to his feet.

"You recognise her hand, William?" he said, smiling. "She is so gentle, I don't think she could reconcile herself to strike even the door hard."

And he left the room, laughing in his quiet way. The next moment a light step sounded in the passage, and Lucy Venning entered the parlour. Very charming she looked in her simple walking attire, and the start and blush with which she noticed the presence of strangers were delightfully natural.

"You didn't tell me you had company, father," she said, turning to Mr. Venning with a tone of playful reproach.

"I quite forgot to mention it," replied her father, with a smile to the two young men. "One of my visitors, I fancy, is known to you, Lucy. This is Mr. Golding, a friend of William's."

Lucy offered her hand to Noble, and bowed to Arthur in a pleasant way.

"It is a very long time since we have seen

you, Mr. Noble," she said, without venturing, however, to meet his eye directly.

"I do not venture to disturb your Sundays too often," was Noble's reply, whilst the accession of colour to his cheek bespoke the pleasure with which he heard Lucy's regret.

"I'm sure it is anything but disturbing us," returned Lucy, affecting to have trouble in unbuttoning her glove. "We have scarcely another friend who comes to see us. You have of course asked these gentlemen to take a cup of tea with us, father?"

"I omitted to ask them, I am afraid, dear," replied Mr. Venning, whose eyes had been wandering with something of troubled interest between his daughter's face and that of William Noble. "But it was only because I took that for granted."

Noble and Arthur exchanged glances.

"We mustn't ask too much of your good nature, Miss Venning," said Noble.

"No, and therefore you mustn't ask Lucy to excuse you," put in Mr. Venning, with a quiet laugh. "Run up and take off your hat and cloak, Lucy, and I will see that the kettle boils."

With a smile at the visitors and a glance of affection at her father, Lucy left the room. In a very few minutes she returned, and proceeded to cover the round table with a white cloth. As she was engaged in placing the tea things, the ringing of a bell in the street outside broke the silence.

"There is the crumpet-man," said Mr. Venning; "we must levy a contribution upon him this evening, Lucy."

A few minutes after Lucy was engaged in toasting crumpets, and, when they were done, all drew up to the table. The room was now the image of home comfort. The heavy green curtains had been drawn close before the window, and though the bright blaze of the fire rendered it almost needless, a large oil lamp stood in the centre of the tea-table. The furniture of the room was extremely simple, but Arthur had already noticed that in one corner stood a small piano, and he wondered whether father or daughter played. On the side over against the fire-place stood a very high, old-fashioned chest of drawers, the top covered with a white cloth, upon which were ranged a few carefully-kept volumes. On the mantel-piece, which was also high and old-fashioned, stood several quaint figures of wood. On the walls were several pictures, all representing quiet country scenes—without doubt the choice of Mr. Venning. As Arthur seated himself at the table, he experienced a sense of delightful comfort such as he had never known. It was the first time in his life that he had enjoyed the sight of such a truly home-like picture.

"A good class this afternoon, Lucy?"

asked Mr. Venning, as he passed the cups of
tea to his visitors.

"Better than usual, father," replied Lucy.
"I hadn't the least trouble with any of the
children. Poor Nellie Wick was unable to
come again. Her mother sent a note to say
her cough was much worse to-day."

"Poor child! you must go and see her,
Lucy."

"I did as I came from school, and Mr.
Heatherley walked with me. Mr. Heatherley
says he is very much afraid there is no
hope for her. I fancy, father, if it were not
for him, poor Mrs. Wick would have been in
the workhouse long since."

"Mr. Heatherley is the clergyman whose
chapel we attend, Mr. Golding," said her
father. "He is a most excellent man, a man
who does endless good in the neighbourhood,
and all in the quietest way."

William Noble kept his eyes fixed on
Lucy's face whilst her father was speaking,
and for a moment she met his glance. Her
face reddened slightly, and she turned away
under the pretence of filling the tea-pot.
There was a short silence which Noble himself broke.

"Does the lady you told me of—I forget
her name—still continue to teach her evening
school?" he asked, addressing himself to
Mr. Venning.

"Miss Norman?" returned the latter.

" Oh, yes.   And what is more, she has taken quite a fancy to Lucy.   She makes quite a friend of her."

Arthur started as he heard the name pronounced, and with difficulty concealed his surprise.   Mr. Venning noticed something of it, and interpreted it into a desire for explanation.

" Miss Norman," he said, accordingly, " is a very wealthy young lady, who spends nearly all her time in efforts to help the poor, Mr. Golding.   She is a friend of Mr. Heatherley's, and I think it was very likely at his suggestion that she began free evening-classes for young girls who have never been taught anything in their lives.   She has nearly twenty pupils, hasn't she, Lucy ? "

" Twenty-one, father."

" And Lucy is her assistant teacher," went on Mr. Venning.   " I should like you to hear Lucy speak of her as she sometimes does to me.   You would both be as curious to see her as I am."

" Indeed, father," said the girl, earnestly, " she deserves everything I say, and much more.   I am sure there can be very few rich ladies like Miss Norman.   If there were, there would not be half so many poor.   And she is so unpretending, you would think she was not at all above the poor girls she teaches. They are all passionately fond of her."

Lucy paused suddenly, and blushed to find

the eyes of all three fixed upon her. In her enthusiasm she had spoken with a boldness very unusual in her. Arthur, who listened with eagerness to every word that was said, feared lest the conversation might turn to another topic, and was the first to speak.

"Does this lady live in the neighbourhood?" he asked, addressing Lucy.

"Oh, no," replied the latter, "she lives somewhere in the West End, and comes to this part nearly every day. I am afraid, father, she is doing too much. I have noticed her growing paler and more worn-looking of late. She has worked for half a year now without any rest. But nothing will keep her back when she thinks she can do good. You know, father, one of Mrs. Willing's children has got the small-pox, and all the neighbours are afraid to go into the house; but Miss Norman goes every day. I heard Mr. Heatherley begging her to leave the care of Mrs. Willing to him, but she said that her visits seemed to cheer the poor woman, and she could not bear to keep away."

"She would make Mr. Heatherley a good wife, wouldn't she, Lucy?" asked her father, smiling.

Lucy was then putting a piece of sugar into her father's tea-cup, and it suddenly dropped from the sugar-tongs into the saucer. She blushed and seemed embarrassed for a reply. Noble, whom none could exceed in delicacy of apprehension, relieved her by introducing some other subject. Tea over, all made a circle round the fire, and Mr. Venning rendered the little circle cheerful with his conversation. He kept up a quiet, genial flow of talk which pleased at once by its agreeable *naïveté* and the unmistakable desire to please which manifested itself in every word. At times he was witty, at others he showed a sincere spirit of piety which excited involuntary reverence in his hearers. But of whatever he spoke, his words indicated the calm, clear mind, a sweet resignation flowing from the belief that everything in this world is arranged for the best, though the reason for so much suffering and wrong is often difficult to acknowledge.

"You are not going to send us away without any music, Mr. Venning?" asked Noble, when the clock upon the mantel-piece showed that it was nearly nine.

Mr. Venning looked with a smile towards his daughter, then turned to Arthur.

"You must not think, Mr. Golding," he said, "that because I earn my living by making musical instruments, I am a skilled musician. I now and then play a little, however, on the piano there, and Lucy sings to my accompaniment. William always tells us he has pleasure in our music, and with him we have no feeling of hesitation. But I scarcely know whether you—"

Arthur interposed with a request that they would by all means give him the pleasure of hearing them, and Mr. Venning accordingly took his seat at the piano. Lucy took a place at his side, and sang several simple hymns, compositions which, like the overwhelming majority of English devotional hymns, had no special merit, but which acquired the interest they naturally lacked by virtue of Lucy's sweet voice and earnest feeling. Neither she nor her father used a book, and the performance had a perfectly spontaneous character which removed it altogether from the reach of criticism. William Noble's face, as he listened to Lucy's singing, expressed deep emotion. Arthur noticed that, after watching the girl's features for a few minutes, he turned his eyes away and appeared to suffer keenly.

Very shortly after this the two friends left, Arthur receiving a warm invitation from Mr. Venning to repeat his visit as soon as possible. He walked on by Noble's side in silence for some time; both too occupied with their very different thoughts to exchange words. Noble was the first to break the silence.

" I never can say whether these visits give me more pleasure or pain," he said. "If I were to act upon my present feelings I should never go there again; but I know very well that to-morrow I shall have nothing but pleasant remembrances, and desires to see them both as soon as possible."

"But why do you feel otherwise at present?" asked Arthur. "I really could see nothing but the utmost friendliness in Miss Venning's manner to you."

"Friendliness; aye, that is just it, Golding! It is real friendliness—but nothing more."

"Do you suppose, then, that she is attached to anyone else?"

"I will ask you another question," returned Noble. "Do you remember her dropping the lump of sugar at tea?"

"Yes! but what has that to do with the matter?"

"Ha, ha! You need a lover's eyes and ears to note those things, Golding. Why, it was at the moment when her father had said that Miss Norman would make the clergy-man a good wife."

"And—you suppose she is in love with the clergyman?" asked Arthur, in surprise.

"I feel sure of it. I have noticed her too closely and too frequently to doubt it."

"But what sort of a man is this Mr. Heatherley?"

"I never saw him, but I understand that he is young, handsome, energetic, good-hearted; all, in short, that a man can be to please a girl of Lucy's disposition."

"But — excuse the question, Noble — wouldn't he consider Miss Venning rather below his station?"

"Lucy is below no one," said Noble, de-

cisively; "and what's more, Heatherley is
the man to recognise that. He is a Radical in
politics and social views, and if he fell in love
with the poorest girl on earth he would see
nothing to prevent his marrying her."

"But this Miss Norman," urged Arthur—
"isn't that her name?—Mr. Venning seemed
to hint at some connection with her? Do
you think it possible?"

"I have not the least idea. Neither Miss
Norman nor Mr. Heatherley is known to me.
But I suppose it is not unlikely that a girl of
her sympathies should make such a man her
ideal. However, as I tell you, I know nothing
of the matter."

"I dare say you wouldn't be sorry," said
Arthur, "to hear that Heatherley was disposed
of in that direction?"

"I cannot say," returned Noble, holding
his head up as he walked. "I love Lucy
Venning with all my heart, and should be glad
to make her my wife because I feel sure she
could marry no one who would be more
devoted to her happiness. But if I find that
her love for Heatherley continues, and that my
position is hopeless, then I shall be glad if
her love is returned. It would be selfish to
feel otherwise."

There were thoughts at that moment in
Arthur's heart which made this high-minded
utterance sound to him like a rebuke. Their
talk was on other matters during the rest of

the walk, and when at length they separated, Arthur said—

"Bye-the-by, I think I haven't told you that I am to be married to-morrow?"

"Told me!" returned his friend, in astonishment. "Of course you never did! What the deuce do you mean, Golding, by stealing a march on me in that way?"

Arthur laughed and held out his hand.

"Where is it to be?" asked Noble, who returned the other's grasp.

"Oh, at the Registry Office, of course. As you know, I am no great friend to the Church."

"And when will you introduce me to your wife?"

"When you like," said Arthur, carelessly. "We shall live in my present quarters, as Challenger insists on turning out and getting another place. He's always a good-hearted fellow."

"Well, every wish for your happiness, Golding," said Noble; "you deserve the utmost.

Upon this they parted, and Arthur walked slowly homewards with a vague heaviness at his heart.

CHAPTER XV.

THE Waghorns returned to England towards the end of October, and forthwith took up their residence in a stately house in the neighbourhood of Regent's Park. The first intimation Helen Norman received of their presence in London was a personal visit. One day they drove up together in a brougham, and, as Mrs. Cumberbatch happened to be out, Helen had to receive them in solitary grandeur. It was not an enviable task, for, considering the terms on which she had last parted from Maud, she might reasonably be in doubt as to how she should behave towards her.

The commencement of the interview was formal. Mr. John Waghorn, respectable as ever, was profuse in expressions of interest. He feared that Miss Norman was not so well as when he had last seen her ; certainly she looked somewhat pale. He feared she over-worked herself in her never-to-be-sufficiently-lauded philanthropic undertakings. Helen, in her turn, manifested absorbing interest in her visitors. Maud was looking wonderfully well, and Mr. Waghorn appeared to enjoy something more than his usual robustness.

"And Mr. Gresham?" inquired the gentleman. "Have you heard from Mr. Gresham lately, Miss Norman?"

"We heard from Berlin about a fortnight ago," replied Helen. "Mr. Gresham was then in the enjoyment of good health."

"Would you believe it?" pursued Mr. Waghorn. "We became slightly acquainted, at Venice, with a gentleman who is one of Mr. Gresham's intimate friends, and who had left him not a fortnight before in Germany. That was the first intimation we had of his being on the Continent."

"Did he leave suddenly?" asked Maud, who was lolling back in a low easy-chair, going lazily over the patterns of the carpet with the end of her umbrella. She spoke in a somewhat affected and languid tone, and without looking up.

"Rather suddenly," replied Helen, somewhat at a loss for a reply.

"Ah, I feared his health would give way," put in Mr. Waghorn. "I sincerely hope, Miss Norman, that you may not experience a similar misfortune. Indeed you are too devoted. You do not consider yourself sufficiently."

"You don't live altogether alone, I suppose?" asked Maud, glancing up for a moment at Helen's face.

"No," replied Helen. "An aunt of Mr. Gresham's, Mrs. Cumberbatch, is living here now. I am sorry to say she is out at present."

The conversation dragged on in this manner for some ten minutes, when Maud suddenly turned round towards her husband (she had been sitting with her back to him), and said—

"Don't you think it would be as well to go on into Oxford Street, and call for me here when you come back?"

"Possibly it might, my dear," replied Mr. Waghorn, with a slight cough and a quick glance at Helen. "You might perhaps ask, however, if Miss Norman is at liberty just now?"

Helen affirmed that she was entirely so.

"In that case I might do as you propose," said Mr. Waghorn. "I shall perhaps be a little more than half-an-hour. I will say good-bye for the present, Miss Norman."

And he withdrew with much grace of manner. The moment the door had closed upon him, Maud suddenly jumped up from her seat and, with a laugh of delight, flung her arms round Helen's neck.

"Come, come and sit down by me, you dear old beauty!" she exclaimed, kissing her friend and laughing heartily between the kisses. "Here, on the sofa. Don't be afraid of spoiling my dress. It was all I could do to keep from bursting into fits of laughter whilst that man was by—it was so absurdly comical to see you receiving us with that stately dignity which becomes you so well, and to hear you talking polite small-talk in a way which didn't become you at all! Now confess, you didn't know whether to treat me as a friend or an enemy, did you?"

"It is true," returned Helen, "that I scarcely felt safe in speaking to Mrs. Waghorn as I had once been used to talk to Maud Gresham. I can't tell you how glad I am, Maud, to hear you speak in your old way."

"Yes, yes," cried the other; "call me Maud. Let Mrs. Waghorn go to—the old gentleman, as far as we two are concerned, Helen! That name is a mere outward garment, something I put on occasionally for show, as I do these silks and satins when I go out to pay visits. If you love me, Pallas, never a word of Mrs. Waghorn!"

Helen was pained to hear her friend speaking thus. It confirmed old fears, and once more clouded her countenance.

"Are you not happy in your marriage, Maud?" she asked, quietly.

"Happy? Oh, as the day is long! I have enough to eat and drink, a good house to live in, what I like to wear, and carriage to drive about to my friends. Why should I not be happy, O, goddess of wisdom?"

" But your husband, Maud. Does not Mr. Waghorn enter into your list of blessings?"

" What a delightfully innocent creature you are!" exclaimed Maud, passing her arm round her companion's waist. " Have you the felicity to think that a husband can by any possibility be a blessing? Now let us understand each other once for all. Waghorn is neither a blessing nor a curse to me, but something totally indifferent. He lives his life, and I live mine, and as long as that life of his doesn't encroach upon my peculiar privileges I have nothing to say to him good or bad. You understand?"

Helen looked into the speaker's face with pained surprise.

" Why bless you, Pallas!" cried Maud, " what is there in all this to trouble one's head about! Don't you know that this is marriage *à-la-mode*, the way in which every matrimonial establishment with any pretension to elegance is conducted?"

" I am very ignorant in such matters," returned Helen, " but it appears to me very dreadful."

" No doubt it does, my dear child. And to you it *would* be dreadful. But for me, who knew exactly what it would be like before I actually experienced it, I assure you it is the most natural thing in the world. You are as different from me and the million other women who resemble me, Helen, as chalk is

from cheese. Suppose I saw you suddenly
seized with an infatuation for a man like
Waghorn, and on the point of marrying him,
do you know what I should do? I should
hang upon you night and day till I had forced
you to break off the engagement; I would
let you have no peace; if I couldn't prevail
otherwise, I would bring out one of the
beautiful little pistols I carry about in my
dressing-case and shoot the man that was to
marry you. I would do anything rather than
see you plunge into such a gulf of misery!"

"But why would you take such pains to
save me from what you encounter yourself
with your eyes open?"

"Because I have got brains to recognise a
merit superior to my own, and a heart to
cherish affection for an old friend. And that
is what I want you to understand, Helen.
Come, will you make a compact with me?
Will you promise me that, however, you see
me behave before other people, however much
you learn to despise me, you will still keep
one little corner of your heart open to me?
Promise that you will come and see me often,
and that you will let me come and see you.
In all London I shall not have any one but
you that I can really call a friend; I know
very well I shall not. You must let me come
and talk seriously for a few minutes with you
when I am weary of chattering nonsense to a
houseful of fools. Now will you promise me
all this, Pallas?"

"But it seems very sad, Maud," replied
Helen, "that you should see so clearly into
all your errors, and yet lack the resolution to
correct them. Instead of making a friend of
me in your tired-out moments only, why not
let me be your friend at all times? Why not
throw away all this affectation of giddiness
—I am sure it can be nothing but affectation
—and settle down to a steady useful life?"

"Why not? Why, because I am not Helen
Norman, nor anything like her. That is the
reason, my dear girl. You must not try to
reason me out of my nature, Helen. The
leopard can't change his spots, you know.
But upon my word I speak the truth when I
say that I have a little bit of brain and a
little bit of heart still available. Possibly
they may be made to expand and grow
with judicious watering, I won't deliver any
opinion on the point. Shall we be friends on
these terms, Helen?"

"It is impossible for me to regard you
otherwise than with kindness, Maud," replied
her companion; "but how can real friendship subsist under such circumstances as
these?"

"Oh, never mind the name!" cried Maud,
impatiently. "Let us call it enmity, if you
will, provided you agree to live on these terms.
Shall I whisper a secret into your chaste ear,
Pallas. I feel within myself now and then
possibilities of wickedness which would startle

you if I dared name them.   How shall I
combat these ?   You know already that I have
no such thing as principle to fall back upon,
and as to the world's opinion, well, that can
be preserved under any circumstances by one
who possesses a little tact.   So the fact is,
Helen, I must look upon you as my principle,
personified.   I must have this friendship of
yours to stand fast upon if I feel that which
it used to be the fashion to call the *devil*
getting hold of me.   Do you understand ! "

Helen was on the point of replying when
suddenly the door opened and admitted Mrs.
Cumberbatch.   Helen had to perform the
ceremony of introduction, after which the
conversation once more assumed a common-
place character.   Mrs. Cumberbatch's sharp
little eyes never ceased to examine Maud's ;
whilst the latter seemed to find amusement in
" drawing out " her grand-aunt.   The conversation was chiefly carried on between these
two, as Helen was too much occupied in reflecting upon Maud's words to take much
part in it.   It was a relief to her when at
length Mr. Waghorn re-appeared.   Once more
the introductions had to be gone through,
after which followed a few more polite
commonplaces from each one present, and
then Mr. and Mrs. Waghorn rose to depart.
As Maud shook hands with Helen, she
whispered—

" Remember."

Helen's thoughts followed the two home in their carriage, wondering greatly whether Maud had not exaggerated the indifference between herself and her husband. We, who are privileged to intrude into the most private recesses of the heart, need hesitate little to take a seat in the brougham of a lately-married couple and overhear their conversation.

"Where to now?" was Maud's question, as Mr. Waghorn, after giving directions to the coachman, entered and took his seat opposite her. She did not look at him as she spoke, but occupied herself in rustling over the leaves of a novel from Mudie's.

"To the Edwards's," replied her husband, with something of a scowl upon his face.

There was silence for a few minutes, and Mr. Waghorn was the first to break it.

"I want you to pay attention to me for a minute," he said, bending slightly forward.

"Well?" returned Maud, without raising her face.

"Look at me!" exclaimed the other, stamping his foot.

"I can hear quite well," persisted Maud, still rustling her pages.

"Look at me!" he almost shouted, clenching his fist; "or, by God—"

Maud raised her face for a moment, and it was rather pale. But she did not speak.

"I want you to understand one thing,"

went on Mr. Waghorn, satisfied with having forced her to submit, and preserving in his tone but little of that suave politeness which distinguished him in society. " You may be as damned sulky as you please when we're alone together ; for that I don't care a snap. But when we're obliged to be seen in each other's company, I'll thank you to show me a little more politeness. Do you hear ? "

" I can hear quite well, as I said before. If you wish the coachman to hear too, why not beg him to take a seat here for a few minutes ? It would save you raising your voice, and I should feel somewhat safer with his protection to look to."

" If you give me any of your blasted impudence," returned Mr. Waghorn, his face livid with passion, " you'll have need for protection in earnest. You've heard what I said. Just heed it, or I'll make you ! "

And so the colloquy ended. It was not the first of the kind that had taken place between the two. In all probability it would not be the last.

Mr. John Waghorn had not been altogether wrong when he said that Helen did not look so well as she had once done, and as the year drew to a close she continued to grow paler. Her eyes seemed to lose something of their wonted joyous brightness, and oftener showed instead a dull and fixed intensity of gaze which unmistakably denoted over-application.

For several months now she had been working with an energy which only a strong man
would have been able to support long. Daily
she spent many hours in her toil among the
poor and miserable, breathing air charged
with all manner of foulness, omitting no
possible chance of making her work as complete as possible. As we have heard Lucy
Venning testify, she would not allow herself
to be withheld by any fear of evil consequences to her bodily health, penetrating
into sickness—haunted homes where others
were afraid to go, finding her sole reward in
the increased opportunities for exertion which
there lay before her. In several cases she
had already spent whole nights watching by
sick beds, fulfilling all the duties of a hospital
nurse, and deriving a sense of pleasure from
her increasing skill and knowledge. Then
she had her school two nights of the week,
on which she toiled with unceasing energy,
for here she felt that she was making clearly
visible progress, and every lesson well learnt,
every good habit inculcated, cheered her on
to renewed exertions. In addition to all this
she never failed to spend some portion of the
day in self-improvement, pursuing a course
of severe technical study which she had laid
out for herself. Most generally the early
hours of the morning were spent thus, for
she was never later than six in rising. So
completely was her life one of stern self-

sacrifice that, in her moments of calm reflection, she felt that she was growing to
understand something of the ascetic's zeal,
and asked herself with a smile whether she
might not possibly develope into a veritable
ascetic, loving to toil merely for the sake of
toiling and the sweetness of self-imposed
pain? Indeed it is not at all unlikely that to
the increasing sternness of her temperament
was due the course of thought she pursued
with regard to Maud. A year ago she
would hardly have met Maud's appeal as now
she did. Her affection had become less
effusive, her mind more used to stern combat
with the bitterest problems of life.

Though severe application of any kind has
a tendency to increase seriousness, it is only
labour which has in it very much of the distasteful and disappointing that embitters the
spirit. There was in Helen's character far
too much of genuine firmness, of exalted
purpose, of inexhaustible sympathy to permit
of her ever being soured by tasks of whatever distastefulness; and yet in all probability
it was the circumstance of her having so
often to encounter grievous disappointment,
and experience deep disgust in the course of
her work, which began by degrees to impart
to her perseverance a character of grim stubbornness where there had at first been only
cheerful persistence. Many times was she
obliged to confess in her inmost heart that,

prepared as she had been to combat with horrors, her imagination had been far from encompassing the full extent of hideous suffering and wickedness which it was her daily lot to strive against. When she confessed to Mr. Heatherley that she was often brought to a pause by ingratitude, stubborn lack of confidence, and similar evils among the poor, she was only on the threshold of her labour; when she passed over from the old year to the new she had grown inured to these evils, and, as I have said, they were gradually converting her cheerfulness into stubbornness. On New Year's eve she spent several hours in reflection upon the past half-year, and the result of it was a night made sleepless by discontent and fear—fear for the future lest her bodily strength should give way or her resolution faint. She concluded that her aims had been too high, that she must cease to hope for such great results, and be content if she made any progress at all. The dispensary had now been open for three months, and was doing good work—there was certainly satisfaction in that. Then again when she thought of her school she obtained a glimpse of true encouragement. There was toil enough there, it is true, but not toil of such a hopeless and repulsive kind as that among nature petrified by long years of vice and crime. Among the bright young faces which met her each Tuesday and

Saturday night, Helen always recovered
her cheerfulness and her hope, and it was in
thinking of these and in making plans for
their better instruction during the year to
come that she at length sunk to sleep.

Her life at home was a very lonely one.
With Mrs. Cumberbatch she had no sympathy
whatever, and, though the latter frequently
forced her society upon her, she regarded
this as an infliction rather than a relief.
From time to time she saw Maud, and
listened, half in wonder, half in pain, to
the strange revelation which that young lady
seemed to delight in making of her own
cynicism and frivolity, but it appeared so impossible to penetrate to any source of genuine
feeling that Helen grew somewhat weary of
these *bizarre* conversations. Very occasionally indeed she visited Maud's house,
but the certainty of finding it full of people
who excited nothing but disgust in her soon
led her almost entirely to cease these visits.
To one of these, however, we must refer
more in detail, seeing that it was the occasion
of her meeting once more with very old
acquaintances.

She had called rather early in the morning
and was shown by the servant into the small
drawing-room where she usually saw Maud
in private. After she had waited nearly a
quarter of an hour the door opened, but no
one immediately entered. Helen could dis-

tinctly hear Maud's voice chattering to some one, and interrupting her chattering with bursts of laughter.

"Come," said Maud, at length, pushing the door wide open, "we shall be safe from interruption here. But mind, you mustn't tell me any more of those ridiculous stories. I shall positively die of laughing!"

Helen had risen to her feet, and, before she was herself perceived, saw Maud entering with her face turned back towards a tall and elegant looking young man, who was smiling as if highly pleased with himself. When Maud a moment after turned her head and perceived Helen, she started and went suddenly pale. Her discomposure only lasted for a second; then she advanced towards her visitor in her usual manner, with both hands extended.

"Why, however long have you been waiting?" she asked, in a tone of the utmost surprise. "No one told me you were here."

"I have only been here a very few minutes," replied Helen, somewhat disconcerted by a consciousness that the young man present was not entirely unknown to her, though she could not exactly recognise him.

"How desperately provoking!" pursued Maud, in the voice which she was wont, in private conversation with Helen, to term her "society voice." "Well, you are an early

visitor, but you see I have another still earlier.
Of course you remember this gentleman ? "

"I fear not," replied Helen, glancing
slightly towards the young man.

"Oh, but I'm sure you must! It is such
a very old friend."

"I have doubtless altered much since
I last had the pleasure of seeing Miss Nor-
man," here put in the gentleman referred to.
"We met then, if I am not mistaken, in the
Rectory at Bloomford."

Helen was now freed from her doubts, but
surprise took their place. She could scarcely
believe that in this tall, handsome, elegant,
well-spoken gentleman she saw the eldest
son of the Rev. Mr. Whiffle, who had given
her so much amusement during the railway
journey by his raw affectation of polite
manners.

"I certainly thought I remembered your
face, Mr. Whiffle," she said, extending her
hand with the frank courtesy natural to her;
"but till you spoke I could not decide upon
your identity. I hope the elder Mr. Whiffle
is quite well ?"

"Oh, charming!" put in Maud, as she
pointed to seats for her visitors. "Why I
actually believe I never told you, Helen, but
we attend St. Abinadab's—Mr. Whiffle's
church, you know. You must really come
with us some Sunday; you would be delighted."

"You are living in London at present, Miss Norman?" asked Augustus.

"Yes," replied Helen, "I have lived here now almost a year."

"I think I understood from my father that you had been in Germany for some time?"

"Yes, I was there two years."

"Mr. Whiffle, you must know, Helen," put in Mrs. Waghorn, "is studying for the Church. Of course he could not adopt any other career, bearing in mind Mr. Orlando Whiffle's prominence. And the fact is he has inspired me with quite a zeal for ecclesiastical matters. The reason of his calling so early this morning was to make some arrangements with regard to a bazaar we are about to hold for the purpose of contributing towards the expense of wax tapers consumed in the church. You cannot conceive, Helen, how indispensable wax tapers are to the salvation of High Church souls. Other people's souls may possibly be saved by the light of vulgar gas or even tallow-candles, but for *us* wax tapers are absolutely indispensable."

Whilst Maud spoke, Augustus Whiffle kept looking from her face to that of her friend, and at last a smile rose to his lips.

"Mrs. Waghorn is rather fond of speaking satirically," he said. "Don't you find it so, Miss Norman?"

"Upon my word, not in the least!" exclaimed Maud, willing to spare Helen, who she saw hesitated how to meet such a question. "I really don't think I even know the meaning of that word 'satirical.' But as I said, Helen, Mr. Whiffle is studying for the Church. I constantly impress upon him that he must not let his zeal lead him to too severe study. I really think he begins to show the result of sleepless nights. What do you think, Helen?"

"Mr. Whiffle appears to me to enjoy very good health," replied Helen, who was suffering extremely from the nature of the conversation.

"You think so? I'm afraid you are too indulgent to people who over-work themselves. You must know, Mr. Whiffle, that Miss Norman is a severe student, quite a blue-stocking."

At this moment a servant knocked and entered.

"The Rev. Mr. Whiffle wishes to know if he can see you, ma'am."

But apparently the Rev. Mr. Whiffle could not wait to receive the permission, for his voice was immediately heard close behind the servant, calling out in a tone which at once announced the fashionable clergyman.

"Oh, tell Mrs. Waghorn that I won't detain her a moment. A matter of considerable importance. Am unable to wait very long, and regret that I cannot call at a later hour."

At the first sound of the voice Augustus Whiffle and Mrs. Waghorn had at once started to their feet, interchanging a glance of something very like consternation. Scarcely had they risen when Mr. Whiffle's form followed his voice, and he pushed into the room past the servant. He was dressed in the ordinary clerical suit, which indicated, however, in several places, that his old habit of personal negligence had not altogether deserted him. His ruddy hair, which had begun to grow much scantier than of old, still asserted its inherent stubbornness, and his eyes still had the droll wide-open expression which had marked them when their possessor was a curate at Bloomford. But in person he was becoming quite stout, and, whether it was due to the physical cause, or adopted as an appropriate indication of importance, he had acquired a habit of puffing between his sentences, which, bye-the-by, were spoken in a much louder and more consequential voice than of old. For all this, Helen would have known him anywhere, and at present his appearance afforded her such unutterable relief that she really felt glad to see him.

As Mr. Whiffle's eyes fell upon his son and heir they became wider than ever, and he paused in the middle of a loud greeting to Mrs. Waghorn.

"What! You here, Gus!" he continued,

putting a gold-rimmed *pince-nez* upon his nose. "I had not the remotest knowledge of the fact that you were acquainted with Mrs. Waghorn! I protest, it is an entire surprise to me! Mrs. Waghorn, I rejoice to see you looking so wonderfully well. This is trying weather, dreadfully trying weather; I can scarcely remember such weather since first I entered The Church, and I dare not think how many years ago that is. Ha! But whom have we here? Upon my word, I believe I have once more the pleasure, the delight, of seeing Miss Helen Norman, the daughter of my dear departed rector! Miss Norman, how *do* you do? Really I am overjoyed to see you! Been to old Bloomford lately, Miss Norman?"

"I have not seen Bloomford since I last called upon you there, Mr. Whiffle."

"You have not! Well, upon my word! Ah! there are sad goings on down at Bloomford, Miss Norman, very sad goings on, I assure you. During the period in which I enjoyed the inestimable honour of succeeding my dear departed rector in the incumbency of St. Peter's, I did my little utmost, Miss Norman, to establish a pure form of ritual, but I fear with little enduring result. I endured persecution, Miss Norman, which amounted to little less than martyrdom. You remember old Isaac Simpson, the retired tallow-chandler?"

" Very well," said Helen, smiling at the recollection.

" Well, would you believe it ? that man was churchwarden during a portion of my incumbency, and he made it the object of his life to thwart me in my endeavour to establish a pure form of ritual. I placed a cross upon the communion table, following what I consider to have been the practice of the primal Church. Old Simpson took the first opportunity of removing it. I replaced it ; old Simpson took it away again ! Can you believe, Miss Norman, that old Simpson, the retired tallow-chandler, would have the unspeakable audacity to beard a rector of the Holy Catholic and Apostolic Church as by law established in the performance of his ecclesiastical functions? I wrote a letter to the *County Chronicle*, wherein I spoke wrathfully, I confess, Miss Norman, and—can you believe it ?—old Simpson was on the point of commencing an action for libel ; fancy, an action against a clergyman of the Church of England ; against a parson, *persona ecclesic*. But I persevered unto the end, Miss Norman, and I won the victory. Old Simpson died—I discovered that he had never been baptised—I refused to read the Burial Service over him ! "

" But those days are happily gone by, Mr. Whiffle," interposed Maud. " At St. Abinadab's there are no such obstinate schismatics.

There we have the purest of rituals, absolutely free from adulteration. But oh! how thankful I am that you triumphed over that odious Simpson! How delightful to be able to refuse to read the Service! Oh! what an admirable Church is the Church of England!"

"Thank you, Mrs. Waghorn, thank you," replied Mr. Whiffle. "If all my congregation were as ardent as you, I should indeed have little to wish for, and could at any moment intone the *Nunc Dimittis* with a clear voice and a quiet conscience. But I grieve to say that there is yet a drop of bitterness in my otherwise overflowing cup. Would you believe it, Mrs. Waghorn? I have only this morning received this anonymous letter, doubtless from some ill-guided member of my flock."

He pulled out an enormous bundle of letters from an inside pocket, and, after rummaging over them for some minutes, at length hit upon the one he sought.

"Now let me read you a paragraph or two from this letter, Miss Norman," he said. "You will marvel at the audacity of this fellow. Bear in mind, always, Mrs. Waghorn, that this is addressed to a clergyman of the Church of England—nay to the Incumbent of St. Abinadab's. Hum—hum—hum— Ah! I will begin here. 'I beg to call your attention to the fact that on six

successive Sundays'—so and so, so and so,
and &c.—'you have made use of lighted
candles upon the communion table, where
they were evidently not needed for the purposes of light.' The paltry fellow ! He ought
to be thankful to anyone who lightens the
darkness of his perverted soul—ha ! ha ! ha !
Now he goes on, observe, Miss Norman :
'Moreover, that you are in the habit of
wearing unlawful ecclesiastical vestments, to
wit, an alb, a chasuble, and a biretta.'—The
audacity of this creature !—' Furthermore,
that you illegally administer to your com-
municants wafer-bread. Again, I must remind you that to adopt the eastward position, as you habitually do, is unlawful, as
also to make the sign of the cross towards
the congregation, to omit kneeling during the
Confession, and to have a cross upon the
communion table.' And so on, and so on.
And then he concludes—' I shall certainly
esteem it my duty to make representation to
the Bishop of these deviations from the
ritual prescribed by the Church of England.'
—The presumptuous blockhead ! The fellow, Miss Norman, has the unparalleled impudence to assert that he is better acquainted
than the Incumbent of St. Abinadab's with
what is, and what is not, allowed by the
Church ! He positively includes in his letter
a long argument on the subject, which I, of
course, have not done him the honour to read

through, but in which I see mentions of the words *Rubric, Common Prayer*, and *Reformation*. Since he is so familiar with the Rubric, I should have imagined that his idiotship would have known that in the Rubric at the end of the calendar it is written : ' that such *ornaments* of the Church and of the ministers thereof at all times of their ministration shall be retained and be in use as were in this Church of England by the authority of Parliament in the second year of the reign of King Edward VI.'—Ha, ha! Miss Norman, he'd better not come the Rubric over me! I imagine I know it as well as most men, as well as the ritual of the Church in the reign of Edward VI. ' Unlawful ' and ' illegal,' forsooth ! Where is the Act of Parliament to restrain me, I should like to know? Ha, ha, ha! An excellent joke ! "

By this time Mr. Whiffle had talked himself completely out of breath, and into such a perspiration that he was obliged to wipe his face all over with an immense silk handkerchief.

But in the operation he was repeatedly overcome with his sense of amusement at the audacity of the letter-writer, and broke into little bursts of scornful laughter.

" But I entirely forgot to state the purpose of my visit, Mrs. Waghorn. Bye-the-by, Miss Norman, have you seen my pamphlet on ' Religious Teaching in Public Schools'?"

"I am sorry to say I have not," returned Helen.

"Indeed! Of course, I need not ask you, Mrs. Waghorn?"

"I deeply regret it has never come into my hands," said Maud.

"Not!" cried Mr. Whiffle, elevating his fat hands in horror. "You astound me! Not seen my pamphlet? I must send you a copy this very day; I will send you half-a-dozen copies! And you, too, Miss Norman, I will send you as many copies as you like, to distribute among your friends. It is only signed ' O. W.' I should be loath, you know, to take undue advantage of my position as incumbent of St. Abinadab's. In controversy I always like to allow my adversaries fair play, you know, Miss Norman. O, Mrs. Waghorn, I know you will be delighted with the pamphlet. In it I preach an absolute crusade against the godless policy of our School Boards. Miss Norman, you must certainly attend St. Abinadab's next Sunday. I am preparing a sermon which I know will please you. Promise me you will come."

"If nothing occurs to prevent me, I shall have pleasure in doing so, Mr. Whiffle."

"Of course, of course! And, bye-the-by—but, upon my word, I am still forgetting the object of my visit, Mrs. Waghorn. Did it ever occur to you that—that one or two of my

portraits on the stalls at the bazaar might not
be in bad taste? You see, it is so natural
that the congregation of St. Abinadab's
should like to possess a photograph of their
minister. Suppose, you know, we sold them
for half-a-crown a piece? I shouldn't wonder
if they added materially to the profits."

" A delicious idea!" exclaimed Maud. "A
perfectly dazzling idea! What a stupid
creature I am that it never occurred to me
before. Of course, it is the very thing—so
tasteful, so delicate. And especially on Mrs.
Whiffle's stall they will be appropriate."

"You think so? My very idea! I am
overjoyed."

" Oh, I hope you will sit especially for the
occasion."

" Will you believe that I have already
done so—and in full canonicals? Upon my
word, I believe I have one with me. Yes—
no—yes, here it is!"

He produced a portrait and handed it to
Mrs. Waghorn, and, skipping behind her like
an excited child, peeped over her shoulder as
she examined it.

" Do you think it good? Do you think it
worthy of the incumbent of St. Abinadab's?"
he asked breathlessly.

" Oh, delicious!" cried Maud. "How
stately, how reverend! I vow I should have
taken it for an archbishop if I had not known
the features!"

"You would? No! You mean it? I am overjoyed! Miss Norman, pray what is your opinion?"

"I think it very like," and then, feeling that graceful condescension to human weakness required more than this, she added, "It is a very excellent portrait, indeed."

"I am delighted! I am entranced!" cried Mr. Whiffle, skipping about. "It is the happiest day since I entered The Church! Mrs. Waghorn, you shall have ten dozen for your stall. I'm sure you could easily dispose of that number, don't you think so?"

"Oh, ten times as many!" cried Maud, with enthusiasm.

"You shall have them!" exclaimed Mr. Whiffle. "But, I protest, I have been here nearly half an hour. I must run. Miss Norman, remember your promise for Sunday. You must come and see Mrs. Whiffle. Pray come and dine with us, any evening you like. Bye-the-by, Mrs. Waghorn, did you see my letter in the *Times* the other morning on that poisoning case, you know?"

"I did," returned Maud, "and was entranced with the argument."

"Oh, the mere thought of an odd moment!" exclaimed the clergyman. "But, good-bye all. Good-bye, Miss Norman, good-bye, Mrs. Waghorn; I will look in again very shortly. Gus, are you going my way?"

" I think not," replied his son, somewhat coolly.

" Very well. Once more, good-bye all."

And, clapping his soft hat on his head, he hastened from the room and from the house.

" I do believe that father of mine grows more absurd every day !" exclaimed Augustus, as soon as they were alone. " Didn't you admire Mrs. Waghorn's satirical replies, Miss Norman ? I thought them admirable."

" You disrespectful boy !" cried Maud. " You do not only venture to say that your father is absurd, but also that I openly ridicule him ? I'm ashamed of you !"

At this Mr. Augustus and Maud laughed heartily in chorus. Helen rose, eager to be gone.

" Are you really going ? " asked Maud, in a tone of purely affected regret. " Again, I am dreadfully sorry for having kept you waiting for me. Pray come again soon. Mr. Whiffle, excuse me one moment."

Helen, having bidden adieu to Augustus, left the room, and was followed into the hall by Maud.

" Come again to-morrow morning at the same time, there's a good girl," whispered the latter. " Forget all this nonsense. You ought not to have seen me in this mood at all."

"Having seen you, Maud," returned Helen, "I sincerely wish I never had. Would it not be better if I ceased coming to you? I could not bear to be subjected to such an hour again."

"Pooh, pooh! Foolish child! I tell you, I am not in my grave mood, Pallas. I may regret it, but can't help it. Will you come to-morrow?"

"I fear I must not promise. I have much to do to-morrow."

"Well, well; whenever you like. Good-bye. Don't think too hardly of me, Helen. You know what power you have over me."

"I wish I felt that I had any," replied Helen.

And with these words they parted.

END OF VOL. II.

Printed by REMINGTON & Co., 5, Arundel Street, Strand, W.C.

WORKERS IN THE DAWN.

A Novel.

IN THREE VOLUMES.

BY

GEORGE R. GISSING.

VOL. III.

London :

REMINGTON AND CO.,

5, ARUNDEL STREET, STRAND, W.C.

1880.

CONTENTS.

WORKERS IN THE DAWN.

CHAPTER I.

MARRIED LIFE.

ARTHUR's life was now pent within a narrower course than ever hitherto. With the exception of Mark Challenger and William Noble he saw no friends, and even these very occasionally. During the day he worked hard for his living, but throughout those hours of labour, as at every other moment of his working time, his thoughts revolved around the petty circumstances of his home life. All wider aims and aspirations seemed to have perished from his mind; if ever his thoughts recurred to them it was to dwell upon them as the vanished joys of a past life. For six months the single room which he occupied with his wife was the sole scene of his existence. It becomes our duty now to trace out as rapidly as is consistent with clear delineation the drama which was there played.

Arthur brought his wife home in an in-

B

toxication of joy and hope. Carrie was now his, his to guard, to foster, to cherish; his, moreover, to lead into higher paths than her feet had yet known, to develope, in short, into the ideal woman that his imagination had for years loved to depict. He resolved that this should henceforth be the main task of his life. In long conversations with William Noble he exposed all his plans and hopes, asking and receiving advice in detail, and always deriving encouragement from this clear-headed and warm-hearted friend. From Noble he concealed nothing. The assurance of the latter's sincere friendship was invaluable to him, and helped to support him in many an hour of what would otherwise have been despair.

He lost not a day in commencing the plan he had conceived for Carrie's education. She must first be taught to read, write and speak with correctness. When on the first day of their married life, Arthur drew Carrie to his side, and in a gentle but firm tone of explanation told her of his intention, she listened with a peculiar expression of countenance, partly amused, partly astonished, partly apprehensive, but wholly incomprehensive. Notwithstanding the seriousness of Arthur's demeanour she evidently felt convinced that it was some curious joke he was playing on her, but a joke of which she was not quite able to understand the fun.

"For how long did you go to school at home, Carrie?" asked Arthur, holding her upon his knee and caressing her long dark hair as he spoke.

"Two years, 1 think," she replied.

"And what did they teach you at school?"

"Why, what do they always teach at schools? Reading and writing, of course."

"Nothing else?"

"What else is there to be taught?"

"No geography, or history?"

"I don't know what that is," she replied, with a somewhat contemptuous smile on her beautiful features. "No, they didn't teach me that."

"But I am sure you would like to know all these, and to be a clever woman, wouldn't you, dearest?"

Carrie shrugged her shoulders a little, but made no immediate reply. Arthur was about to proceed in his coaxing when she interrupted him.

"Do you ever earn more than forty-five shillings a week, Arthur?" she asked, passing her fingers through the hair upon his forehead.

"Oh, never mind that at present," he said, laughing. "Let us talk a little about your education. Will Carrie promise to do as I wish her and spend a few hours a day in teaching herself to read well and write without mistakes?"

" I shan't never be able to do that," she replied, shaking her head and evidently thinking of something widely different.

" Shan't *ever*, you mean," corrected Arthur.

She looked at him in surprise.

" You won't mind me correcting you when you make mistakes in speaking, will you, dearest ? " said Arthur.

" Oh, then we shan't be able to talk at all," returned Carrie, rather pettishly. " You say I make so many mistakes, and I'm sure I shan't never be no better, however much you trouble."

Arthur thrust his fingers into his ears and made a wry face as though something had hurt him.

" Shan't *ever* be *any* better, you mean," he said.   " Never mind, Carrie; you will get better for all that ; I am determined you shall. Now, here's a book. Let me hear you read a little."

Carrie took the volume and inspected it for a few moments, then, in all probability finding it beyond her powers, gave it back to Arthur.

" Oh, what's the good of it all ? " she asked, impatiently. " It won't make me cook dinners no better."

The conversation was long and curious, but, by the exercise of wonderful patience and good-humour, aided, of course, by the deep love he bore her, Arthur succeeded at length

in persuading Carrie to let him set her brief
and easy tasks, which she faithfully promised
she would perform in his absence from home
during the following day. There were a few
words of which the spelling was to be learnt,
half a page to write in a copy-book, and a
short piece of poetry to get by heart.

On the following evening Arthur returned
home with a glad and hopeful heart. Hoping
to give Carrie a pleasant surprise he stole upstairs in the completest silence. The door of
his room was closed, but he could perceive
that a light burnt within; though he listened
he could heard no voice. He knocked, in the
manner of a stranger. In a moment Carrie
opened the door, and, peering into the darkness, instantly saw who it was, then with a
joyful cry sprang and threw her arms around
his neck. The room was in nice order; the
few additional articles of furniture which
Arthur had procured for Carrie's special
pleasure were neatly arranged round the
room, and the cloth spread upon the table
gave hopeful promise of dinner. But what
gave Arthur still more joy was the sight of
Carrie's copy-book lying open on the side-
table, as if she had just been occupied at it.

Resolved not to become a pedantic bore,
Arthur ate his dinner with vast enjoyment,
and then devoted half an hour to lover's-
talk with Carrie, before he broached the
subject of lessons.

"Has the day seemed long, darling?" he asked at length, by way of getting round to the delicate topic.

"Oh, very long," she replied. "I don't know what I shall do without you always, Arthur."

"But I see your copy-book there. That's a good sign. Come, let me look at what you have done, Carrie."

"Oh, not to-night," she answered. "I haven't done much, and its dreadful bad."

"Never mind, let me see. You are not afraid of me, Carrie?"

At length he persuaded her to bring him the book. Two lines were written, and it was no exaggeration to say they were "dreadful bad."

"There, I knew you'd only make fun of me," said Carrie, snatching the book from his hand, as she noticed a slight elevation of the eyebrows which he could not resist.

"1 shouldn't dream of making fun of you, darling," he replied earnestly. "It is too grave a matter for joking. Now let me show you how you can do it better next time. Come and sit by me at the table, love, and bring your pen."

"No, not now," she persisted impatiently. "I'm tired to death. If you'd had a room to clean up and a dinner to cook, you wouldn't want to be bothering with reading and writing."

Arthur was silent for a moment, sitting with downcast eyes.

"But I have been hard at work all day, Carrie," he urged gently, as soon as he could trust his voice. "I think my work is at least as hard as yours; and yet I am anxious to do more now for your sake, dearest. Besides yours has been only work with the hands. You can listen to what I say, and rest at the same time: Come and sit by me, Carrie."

With some hesitation she took a chair at his side. Carrie had a slow, sidling way of walking which was never very agreeable to see, and the ungracious way in which she now obeyed his request gave Arthur acute pain.

"Where are the other books?" he asked, quietly. "Have you learnt the spelling and the poetry?"

She looked away from him and made no answer.

"Weren't you able to do it, dearest?" he asked, passing his arm affectionately round her. "Did you try, Carrie?"

"Yes, I tried," she returned. "But the words were too hard, and I couldn't understand the other stuff a bit."

"The other stuff" signified the first three verses of the "Ancient Mariner." Arthur felt annoyed to hear a favourite poem so designated.

"But it is very simple, dear," he urged. "Let us read it together, and I'm sure you will understand it."

"Oh, what's the use of bothering!" she returned. "I'm tired now. I'll look at it again to-morrow."

Then she added, directly, "Arthur, where do you keep the money you save?"

This was agony to him. It is all very well to say that on the second day after his marriage he ought to have been as much in love with his wife as to care for nothing but listening to her heedless talk and to think everything worthy of detestation which caused her the least annoyance. Arthur's nature being what it was, such love as this was impossible to him. What he intensely loved, he could not but wish intensely to respect. The pity which had originated his love was in itself a species of respect; he had convinced himself by force of emotion that Carrie could not deserve the suffering she endured, and he had almost reverenced her as an instance of unmerited misfortune. Then of course her striking personal beauty had forced him to look up to her as something superior. He could not believe that such outward perfection could exist with a common-place and sterile nature. When he openly declared to her his affection, the warmth with which she reciprocated it had added another link to his chain by convinc-

ing him of the strength of her feelings. He
felt that an indifferent, passionless woman
would have been intolerable to him. But
now a vague dread began to encroach like an
unnatural darkness upon his heart, a terrible
fear lest he might have deceived himself not
only with regard to her intelligence, but also
as to the extent of her affection for him. He
could not bear the suspicion. At all costs he
must throw it off. Possibly it might force
itself on him later, gain ground surely and
with the pitiless persistency of fate, but as
yet it was too, too early. Why, he had
scarcely tasted the fulness of his joy ; should
the cup already be dashed from his lips ?

"There, never mind the books to-night,
Carrie!" he exclaimed gaily. "Throw away
the copy-book! we will think of them again to-
morrow. Look cheerful again, darling. Come
and sit on my knee and tell me how much
you love me."

Carrie was all radiance at once, and as
pretty a lovers' tattle followed as novelist
might wish to chronicle; but—somehow or
other I have no taste for it. Perhaps the
shadow of coming events falls already upon
me and makes me gloomy.

A week elapsed. The first lesson had at
length been struggled through, though with
little good result as regards Carrie's temper.
In the ensuing week Arthur had calculated
that he would be more exacting. He began

by persistent correction of his wife's speech, which was indeed faulty enough. The speedy result was that he brought about an outbreak of temper such as he had never conceived possible.

"Why don't you let me speak as I'm used to?" cried Carrie, starting up with flashing eyes, one night when Arthur had interrupted her in every sentence for a quarter of an hour. "What's the good of tormenting me in that way. If you wanted to marry a grammar-machine you should have looked somewheres else, and not have taken up with me! You can understand what I mean, well enough, and what more do you want, I'd like to know? I shan't speak at all, that's what I shall do, and then maybe you'll be satisfied."

And she flung herself into a chair by the fire-side, with her back to Arthur.

Arthur's temper was severely tried. For some minutes he bit his lips to restrain the angry words which all but made their way. His face burned and his throat was so dry and hot that he could scarcely breathe.

"You are unkind and unjust to speak so to me, Carrie," be began at length, "Do you think I do it to annoy you? Do you think I take a pleasure in it? I assure you I do it as a duty; I force myself to correct you when I would gladly think of other things."

"Then why do you give yourself the bother?" retorted Carrie, without moving. "No one wants you."

"But you *should* want me to," persisted Arthur, drawing near to her, and speaking in a calm though forcible tone of explanation. "Can't you see, Carrie, that it is for your own good? Do you *like* to make mistakes in speaking?"

No answer.

"Do you wish to render my whole life miserable, Carrie?" he pursued. "It lies in your power either to make me completely happy or completely wretched. Do you prefer to make me wretched?"

It was an important sentence. Had Arthur been cool enough to reflect on the experience he had already acquired of woman's illogicality, he would never have ventured to speak thus.

"Oh, I make you miserable, do I?" she said, starting up from her chair. "I can precious soon take myself off. Perhaps you'll be happy then. Let me go past! I've earnt my living before now, and I dare say I can do it again. I won't stay here any longer to make you miserable."

Arthur was in despair. With trembling fingers Carrie was putting on her hat and jacket, and seemed in earnest in her purpose to depart. He felt that he had not deserved this treatment. A burning sense of injustice raged within his heart, and withheld him from confessing that he was wrong, and begging for pardon. Doubtless, also, there was something of stubbornness in his disposition. Though Carrie was a long time in dressing, much longer than was necessary, he did not stir to prevent her. He stood with his eyes fixed upon the floor.

She was dressed, but did not move towards the door. After a few moments of absolute silence, she moved towards him and held out her hand.

"Good-bye, Arthur," she said. "I don't want to make you miserable longer than I can help."

The last word was broken with a sob. Arthur looked up and saw that the tears were coursing fast down her cheeks. This was too much. In a moment he folded her in his arms, and kissed away the tears with passionate warmth.

"Why *will* you so cruelly misunderstand me, darling?" he whispered, as she leaned her head upon his shoulder. "Do you think I take a pleasure in annoying you? Some day you will see the reason of all I say and do, and you will thank me for taking such pains with you. It's terrible for me to make you so angry. Promise me, dear Carrie, that you will try to understand me better, that you will try to do as I wish. Indeed, indeed, it is for your good. Will you believe me, darling?"

In this way at length the quarrel was made up, but the same night Arthur, with great difficulty, succeeded in getting permission from Carrie to visit William Noble, and to him he made known all his afflictions. Noble listened attentively, but with a pained expression on his countenance.

"This is very soon to begin quarrelling, Golding," he said, when his friend had done. "Don't you think you are too peremptory, too exacting? You must remember the old proverb, that Rome wasn't built in a day; and I can assure you there is nothing requiring so much tact, patience and quiet perseverence as the education of a grown-up person, especially a woman. You must not expect too much you know."

"Good God!" exclaimed Arthur, impatiently, "is it possible for a man to entertain more humble pretentions than I do? Is it too much to beg and pray her to write and read for half-an-hour a day? Am I too exacting when I rejoice if she learns to spell only one word of two syllables, or corrects some single outrageous error in her pronunciation? Do you think this too much to expect, Noble?"

"It doesn't appear very exorbitant, does it?" returned William, smiling. "But there is a great deal in manner, you know. Do you think you are gentle enough? Don't you lose patience too quickly, and correct her harshly?"

"How can you ask me such questions, Noble? Isn't she my wife, and haven't I told you that, spite of all her imperfections, I love her passionately, and would not retract my steps for the world! How is it possible that I could speak harshly to her? I use the gentlest persuasions. I put it to her in every possible form I know, that she ought to do this for her own sake."

"How does she employ her days?" asked Noble.

"Oh, women always find enough to do," replied his friend. "She sews a good deal, she has the meals to prepare, and walks out now and then when it is fine. But all that would leave her plenty of time to do what I ask of her."

"Has she any kind of society besides your own?"

"Most unfortunately not," replied Arthur, "and that is one of the sore points. The landlady is a very decent woman, and would willingly afford her company now and then, but Carrie has conceived a most inexplicable dislike to her. I can't persuade her from it; in this, as in many other matters, she is terribly self-willed."

"You must confess, Golding," said Noble, "that this loneliness is a very bad thing for her. When one spends day after day in solitariness, one loses energy, and acquires a distaste for everything."

"True, but how can it be avoided? It isn't likely I could permit her to return to her old acquaintances of the work-rooms, and her relatives she will certainly have nothing to do with. You see, I am such a lonely fellow myself; I cannot boast a female acquaintance except my wife."

"Well, well, we must hope for better things," said Noble, encouragingly. "Depend upon it she will find suitable friends before very long. In the meantime, Golding, you must exercise the utmost forbearance. Remember what a tremendous responsibility you have taken upon yourself. I don't think you are the man for shirking a duty, however disagreeable, Golding. Your way is clear before you, and, so long as you don't stray from it, I fear you must be content at present with scarcely perceptible progress. Whatever you do, you mustn't make your wife miserable; better she should be ignorant than unhappy. To make her happy is the first aim of your life, the second is to train her to prefer a higher kind of happiness to that she has always been content with."

Arthur was silent for some moments, reflecting. Then he rose to depart, and held out his hand, which his friend grasped.

"You are always a true comforter," he said; "you give encouragement of the highest kind, Noble. I am afraid I make but a poor figure compared with a man of your grand energy. Do you know, I have often felt lately as if I were out of place in the world, as if the work I had before me wasn't my true work. I don't know whether you can understand this?"

"Partly, perhaps," said Noble, with a sigh. "I know the feeling occasionally myself, but I always struggle against it. The true philosophy is to consider whatever work you *have* to do as the true work, and to do it with all your might. Depend upon it the feeling is not a symptom of health, Golding."

Arthur was just going, when he again turned.

"Noble," he said, with some little hesitation, "have you mentioned my marriage to any of your acquaintances?"

"To no one."

"May I ask you always to be as silent— with everyone?"

"I will be so."

"Thanks, Noble; you will oblige me. Good-night."

It would be a tedious and unedifying task to relate the daily life of the new-married couple in persistent detail. The days which I have described are a fair example of every day during the first month. Arthur continued to exert himself to the utmost for Carrie's education, but always with insignificant result. Once or twice he all but made up his mind that the task he had set himself was vain, that it meant nothing but life-long misery to Carrie and himself, and that it would be infinitely better to cease to care for these matters, and to preserve domestic quietude at the expense of his wife's advancement. But to this he could not reconcile himself; it would have been to relinquish too much, to render himself degraded in his own eyes, and immeasurably to lessen the love he had for his wife. He asked himself what their marriage would become if he once despaired of raising Carrie to his own level. He would lose all that had rendered it most delightful to him, that precious sense of the performance of a lofty task which seemed necessary to his existence. If it were to degenerate into a mere vulgar connection, subsisting mainly upon sensual emotions, he felt that it would hang upon him like a crushing weight, a veritable degrading weight of fetters. What did it mean then, this love which he still felt convinced of? If he had loved his wife merely for her own sake, surely he would have been happy with her under any circumstances which gave her happiness? But what, he asked himself, trembling at the very thought, what if it were but a false love after all, a passion like that of Ixion for a mere insubstantial fancy? What if he had fallen in love with an ideal, clothing it with Carrie's outward beauty? If the soul of the ideal vanished, could he love the frame for its own sake; or, if at moments he felt he could, was it not the hot blood of youth which spoke, instead of his sober reason?

He had no reason to think Carrie particularly extravagant in the expenditure of the money he allowed her weekly for house expenses, but still he could not prevail upon her to keep any kind of accounts. Any mention of the desirability of doing so was sure to awaken that acute spirit of suspicion which seemed ever lurking in her mind.

"So you can't trust me!" she suddenly replied one night, when he had brought home a neat little account-book, and begged her to try and make use of it. "Do you think I make waste of the money? If you think so, you'd better not give me so much."

Remonstrance was quite in vain. She appeared hurt at the idea of being asked to keep an account of her expenditures; so that Arthur was fain to drop all mention of it, and sigh in secret over another defeat.

One morning, as he was walking quickly down Huntley Street in the direction of his work, he was surprised at finding himself suddenly stopped by the landlady of the house in which he had established Carrie previous to their marriage. She was standing in the doorway, and called out, "Eh! eh!" at the same time making signs to him as he went along the opposite side of the street.

He crossed over, wondering much what the woman could want with him.

"Could you let me 'ave 'alf-a-minute's talk?" she asked, beckoning him to enter the house. Arthur had never much liked her appearance. At present she was slatternly in the extreme, and had the look about the eyes which distinguishes persons who have but lately slept off a debauch. He noticed that her hands trembled, and that her voice was rather hoarse. When he had stepped into the passage, she asked—

"Do you know as your wife owes me five shillings?"

"For what?" returned Arthur, in surprise. He had not even been aware that this woman knew him as Carrie's husband. "I thought all expenses were paid when she left."

"No, no, they wasn't," replied the woman. "Far from it. There was five diff'rent shillin's owin' me for brandy."

"For brandy!" exclaimed Arthur, aghast.

"Yes, for brandy. She used to say as how a drop did her good when she felt weak, an' so I s'plied her, yer see—five diff'rent shillin's-worths."

"But did you ask her for the money?"

"Oh, yes; an' she said as how she'd pay me soon, for she couldn't at the time. But I've been to see her at your 'ouse three or four times, an' she always puts me horff. So

I thought as how the best plan 'ud be to arst you for it."

"Well," said Arthur, "of course I can't pay you without making some inquiry into the matter. I will speak to my wife about it to-night, and if she admits the debt I will pay you to-morrow. Good-morning."

And he hurried off, leaving the woman looking after him with a hideous grin upon her face. The thought of this affair destroyed Arthur's peace throughout the day. If this brandy had been in reality procured for medicinal purposes why should Carrie hesitate to tell him of the debt? But if there were no truth in this assertion. That was a supposition upon which he durst not dwell. He remembered, however, the intimacy which Carrie had spoken of as existing between herself and that woman, and this, when he considered the latter's appearance and manner, was anything but an agreeable thought. The moment that the day's work was over, he hurried anxiously home, resolved to lose no time in solving his doubts.

Carrie met him as usual with open arms and an affectionate kiss.

"Carrie," he said, holding her slightly away from him, "how is it you always eat so much peppermint?"

"Do you notice it?" she returned, colouring very slightly.

"Notice it! I have frequently been overpowered with the smell of peppermint."

"Oh, I always have some by me," she cried, gaily. "These are my favourite eating. Look, you shall have some yourself."

And she fetched a small paper of lozenges from the mantel-piece.

"Taste them," she said. "They're the best I ever bought, and only three halfpence an ounce. Take some."

"Not before dinner, thanks," replied Arthur, his thoughts too much fixed on one matter to join in his wife's gaiety. He resolved to say nothing, however, till dinner was over. Carrie's sharp eyes at once discerned that something had occurred to annoy him, and occasionally she watched him through the meal. Had Arthur regarded her in turn he would have noticed that her eyes were unusually bright, but he kept his own fixed upon his plate, and spoke very little. Carrie scarcely ate anything at all; she said she had no appetite.

After long reflection as to how he should broach the subject which monopolised his thoughts, Arthur resolved that the best way was to proceed to the point without circumlocution.

"Carrie," he said, steadily regarding her across the table, "is it true that you owe your old landlady five shillings?"

Carrie returned his look with one of alarmed surprise. But it only lasted a second, as well as the sudden blush which had risen to her cheek.

"Who has been telling you that?" she returned, with an affectation of *nonchalance* which did not sit well on her.

"Never mind who has told me. Is it true that you owe the money?"

"I suppose she has told you herself, has she?" said Carrie.

"Yes, she has."

"And she told you I owed it her for brandy?"

"She did, as I passed her house this morning," replied Arthur, regarding her gravely.

"Did you pay it?" asked Carrie, after a brief pause, in which she seemed hurriedly to reflect.

"Certainly not. The demand appeared to me so extraordinary that I couldn't think of paying it till I had asked you about the matter. Whatever did you want with five shillings worth of brandy?"

"Well, I'm glad you didn't pay it," she replied. "It's all a lie. I don't owe her five shillings at all."

"But what is the foundation of her claim then?"

"I'll tell you how it is, Arthur. Several times whilst I was there, I was ill and faint, and I asked the landlady to let me have a little brandy. When I was going away I asked her how much I owed her for it, and she said five shillings. Then I told her I wasn't such a fool as all that, and I didn't owe not nearly as much, more like one shilling than five. But she wouldn't take one, so I said I shouldn't pay at all."

There was so much of sincerity in her tone and manner as she gave this account, that Arthur could not but believe it. It raised a terrible load from his breast, and his face brightened up wonderfully.

" Then," said he, " I shall go and offer her two shillings to-morrow morning, and if she isn't content with that she must do without payment."

" You needn't trouble to do that," replied Carrie. " She came here whilst you were away this morning and told me she had asked you for this money. So to save bother I paid her half-a-crown, and she was satisfied."

Arthur looked surprised.

" She has been here several times lately, hasn't she ?" he asked.

" Once or twice."

" But why not have told me of it, Carrie ? It would have saved a great deal of trouble."

" Oh, I didn't like to bother you about it," she replied, beginning to remove the plates from the table.

She was in a wonderfully good humour all that evening, and delighted Arthur by being the first to propose that she should have her usual reading lesson. She read aloud to him from " Robinson Crusoe " for half an hour, making not more than four or five blunders in each line, and being corrected with the utmost patience. Then she wrote a line or two in her copy-book, whilst Arthur sat, pretending to read, but in reality watching her. It needed very little to re-excite hope in his breast, and he felt to-night that he had been foolish to despair so early. The full tide of love once more deluged his heart, aad he was perfectly happy.

In the morning Carrie took the opportunity of bright sunshine to propose that she should accompany Arthur for a short distance on the way to his work. Her proposal was joyfully accepted, and the two set out together rather earlier than usual. They did not take the nearest way, directly down Huntley Street, but, in accordance with Carrie's wish, made a circuit by Tottenham Court Road. For this she made some idle excuse, and Arthur, far too happy to spoil her pleasure, yielded without a thought.

When Carrie returned alone, she did not go straight home, but stopped and knocked at the door of her old abode. The landlady opened to her.

" Oh," began the latter, " so you're come at last."

" Yes, I have, Mrs. Pole," returned Carrie, with an indignant air. " And I'd like to know what call you had to go telling my husband about that money you make out I owe you."

"Come in, come in," said Mrs. Pole, closing the door, and leading the way downstairs into the kitchen. "Why, there's no call to have words over it. I only did what I told you I'd do, and what anyone else i' my place 'ud a' done. It ain't likely as I could afford to lose five bob, is it now? An' so you're come to pay, I s'pose?"

"I haven't come to pay five shillings, Mrs. Pole," returned Carrie, "and nothing like it; so you needn't think I'm such a fool as to do it. I don't owe you so much, and what's more you know I don't."

"So help me God!" exclaimed the woman, "you owe me every penny of five bob, and you know it. There was 'alf a quartern o' brandy that day as you come an' told me you was too lazy to fetch it yourself; there was another 'alf quartern that day as you got wet and come into this very kitchen to dry your boots before the fire; then there was a 'ole quartern that night as you went with my Ann to the Hoxford—"

"Oh! How can you say so!" broke in Carrie. "In the first place that wasn't brandy at all. It was gin hot, and there wasn't even half a quartern of it, so don't tell lies whatever you do, Mrs. Pole."

Mrs. Pole recriminated, and the conversation—if conversation it can be called—endured nearly an hour and a half. The end of it was that Carrie paid three and sixpence, and received a receipt for it.

" Well, we're not goin' to part hunfriendly, I'm sewer," said Mrs. Pole, when the business was thus satisfactorily arranged. " You've drove me 'ard, but I don't mind standin' somethink for all that. What's it to be? A drop o' brandy?"

" No, no," replied Carrie, laughing. " No more brandy. If it must be something, say a drop of whiskey hot."

" Well, I likes whiskey myself, for a change," said Mrs. Pole, and forthwith dispatched a girl to fetch the required amount. The consumption of this beverage took up another hour, after which Carrie hurried home.

One evening, shortly after this episode, Arthur returned home at the usual time, and, as usual, very hungry. Carrie had been growing somewhat careless of late in the preparation of meals, frequently being nearly half an hour behindhand with the dinner. To-night was a case in point. When Arthur entered, the table still exhibited the remains of that morning's breakfast, and a fire almost out gave little promise of the speedy provision of a meal. It had been a dark, miserable, rainy day. Arthur was wet through and weary, and had been looking forward all the way home to a bright fire to warm and cheer him.

" Really, this is too bad, Carrie! " he exclaimed on entering. " What ever have you been doing all day? Have you been out?"

She was apparently occupied in regarding something which lay on the side table, and for the moment made no reply.

" Carrie ! " he repeated, with more emphasis, " why do I come home and find the room in this state ?"

" Well, there's nothing to make a noise about," she replied, slowly turning towards him. " You can't always expect to have everything ready the minute you want it."

Arthur knew not how to speak. These little scenes had become so frequent of late, starting in every imaginable petty case, that he dreaded to do anything to provoke one. The constant recurrence of such annoyances operated upon his nervous nature with terrible effect; he would have undergone almost any privation rather than have suffered all the agonies of these vexatious quarrels which were so often forced upon him. At present, therefore, he made no reply, but began to take off his wet things, watching in silence for Carrie to prepare the meal. But she was still regarding the same object on the side-table, and showed no sign of leaving it.

" What are you doing there?" Arthur asked, with sudden impatience, moving towards her.

She caught up a sheet of paper from the table and held it behind her back.

" What have you got ?" he repeated. " Why don't you speak ?"

There was a peculiar look upon her countenance such as Arthur had never seen there
before, and which he did not in the least
understand. Suddenly she drew the paper
from behind her back and held it out for him
to look at. With surprise and pain he saw
that it was his memory-portrait of Helen
Norman.

"Who is that?" she asked, a light gleaming in her eyes which Arthur now recognised
as that of jealousy. He replied to her with
another question.

"How did you find it?"

"I found it in your box."

"And what were you looking for there?"
Arthur asked, angry to think of all the dear
remembrances of his past life being turned
over by one who could neither understand
the drawings themselves nor the feelings
which they represented. "I thought I left
it locked."

"So you did, but I have a key that fits
it."

"Then I ask you, what were you looking
for there?"

"Can't I look over your things if I choose?"
returned Carrie. "It's a nice thing if one
can't be trusted by one's own husband! It
doesn't look a very good sign when things
are hidden away out of sight and kept secret.
Who is this?"

It was impossible for Arthur to reply to

this question; not merely because he was angry and indisposed to yield a point, but because he felt that to have mentioned *her* name under such circumstances would have been profanation.

"It is an imaginary face," he answered. "Are you satisfied?"

"A what face?"

"An imaginary face—a face drawn from my own fancy. Give it me at once!"

This was altogether beyond Carrie's understanding. To her mind every picture *must* be a likeness; how else could it have come into existence? She smiled with angry scorn, but on meeting Arthur's eye, in which real anger was now beginning to burn, she hesitated before proceeding in her taunts.

"Give it me at once!" repeated Arthur, in a sterner voice than he had ever yet used to his wife. It was torture to him to see her sneering at the picture; it was desecration for it to remain in her hands.

"If I give it you will you tear it up?" asked Carrie, holding the drawing close to her.

"Certainly not!" replied Arthur. "Why should I destroy it?"

"That shows; that shows!" cried Carrie, tauntingly. "I knew it was somebody. It was put away carefully by itself. I know very well it's someone!"

"And even if it were," said Arthur, angrily, "what does it matter?"

"There, I knew!" cried Carrie. "You *shan't* keep it; I'll tear it first!"

Pale with rage he felt compelled to suppress, Arthur suddenly stepped towards her and seized the drawing from her grasp. In a moment she sprang forward, and, even as he held it, rent it fiercely in two. Without speaking a word, Arthur gathered up the remnants, folded them carefully, and with them in his hand walked from the house.

CHAPTER II.

PEPPERMINT.

IT was none of Arthur's intention to quit his wife for good. Angry as he was, his was not a nature which could allow itself to be led wholly astray by blind passion, and, as he descended the stairs, he said to himself that he would be absent for a few hours, trusting to the interval both to calm his own outraged feelings and to effect a salutary change in his wife's bad temper.

It still rained, and the February wind swept the streets with cutting severity. Strong emotion had stilled the sense of hunger as effectually as a meal would have done, and although all his clothes were so wet that they clung about him, Arthur did not feel it.

Heedless of what direction he took, he walked at a rapid pace along the main streets of the neighbourhood, seeing nothing that he passed, merely obeying the impulse which led him to quick motion. As he turned the corners the cold rain lashed his face, and he felt it soothing rather than disagreeable, for his whole body burned violently. The inside of his mouth, moreover, as is usual after moments of strong anger, was terribly parched; his tongue felt like a piece of leather.

As he passed the coffee-houses, he felt that a cup of coffee would have been a great luxury to him, but he had no money with him. So completely did he place confidence in Carrie, that he always entrusted to her the whole of the money for the week, applying to her whenever he needed any, and so few were his private needs, that it was quite usual for him to be without a coin in his pocket. So he was obliged to turn his eyes from the warm interiors of the coffee-houses and to take a long, cold draught from the first drinking fountain which he passed. There also he bathed his forehead, and the moisture seemed to refresh him.

When he had so far recovered himself as to be able to reflect, he drew aside from the crowded thoroughfares into narrow and darker streets, and at length, pausing in an entrance above which hung a gas lamp, he drew the torn drawing from his pocket, and, holding the two halves together, once more regarded it.

For a long time it had lain in the very bottom of his box, for he had placed it there purposely, lest by being too near at hand it should tempt him to look at it. It was a most unfortunate circumstance that Carrie's ill-governed curiosity should have led to its discovery to-night, for all through the day Arthur's thoughts, despite his strongest efforts to turn them in another direction, had been running on Helen Norman. He had thought of the drawing, and had half persuaded himself that there would be no harm in taking the opportunity of some moment when Carrie was absent to gaze upon it once more.

What harm? he had asked himself. Was not Helen Norman as far removed from him now as if she were dead? and what harm could there be in giving himself the pleasure of looking at her picture? Then Arthur's sterner good sense had come to the rescue, and had urged that the mere fact of this being a pleasure proved that the wish should not be indulged. His honour spoke, and told him that not even in thought should he deviate from the undivided attention which he owed his wife.

Upon his return home, had he found the room neat and bright, had Carrie been in her best humour, and received him, as usual, with a kiss, then the victory would have been complete, and Helen Norman would have rested undisturbed in the portfolio at the bottom of the box.

In this way he reflected as, piecing the portrait together, he viewed its sweet outlines by the lamp-light. Insensibly he passed on to a comparison between Helen and his wife.

Supposing he had married Helen, and she had one day come across a piece of evidence proving indisputably that her husband had once loved another girl, would she have acted as Carrie had done? Would she not rather have made it a subject for merry laughter and jest, have asked questions about the buried love, have sincerely sympathised with any little sadness which the recollection might have aroused, and then, after all, have set a seal upon the real and living affection with tender caresses? But he felt in his heart that such behaviour was impossible in Carrie; it was vain to expect from her the gentleness, the intelligence, the fine discrimination of such a nature as Helen's. And thereupon a fierce rush of wild regret swept over his soul, and in a burst of anguish he pressed a thousand kisses upon the mutilated face.

Intruders forced him to once more fold up the picture and pass on. But Helen's countenance had stamped itself upon his imagination, and he saw it gleaming in the darkness as he hastened along the narrow bye-ways. Helen and Carrie! O God! How could he bear to reflect upon the two together? In these moments every loveable look which he had ever seen on Helen's face, every tone which he had heard from her lips, every wise, good, tender word she had spoken in his presence, was as real to him as if he had been subject to its influence but a moment ago.

What a spirit of sweet and noble intelligence breathed from her whole person. Intelligence—intelligence ! That, after all, was what Arthur most worshipped in her ; that godlike property in virtue of which man becomes " a being of such large discourse, looking before and after."

Aye, had she been endowed with the grossest ugliness that ever weighed upon human creature, Arthur, in his present mood, felt that he should have made a goddess of her for her intelligence alone. But poor Carrie—alas ! What was all her outward beauty when she utterly lacked all trace of that divine fire, that heaven-aspiring flame which, when it burns upon the altar of the heart, permeates and sanctifies it with its glow. Who was this that he had married ? What beast's nature encased in a human form ?

In this hour of agony he felt that the struggle had begun ; that while he aspired to highest regions of pure air, this weight to which he had immutably bound himself was dragging him down, down into the foul atmosphere of a brutal existence.

Wandering on with limbs already stiffening under fatigue, and with a mind well-nigh exhausted by the violence of his emotions, he found himself at length in Leicester Square, and mingled with the crowd of reeling revellers and painted prostitutes which is always to be found here after nightfall. Such company was dangerous to one in his mood, for how easy is it for the nature weary with struggling after an exalted ideal suddenly to fall into the opposite extreme, and find no depth of degradation sufficient for its cravings.

Before him blazed the lights of the Alhambra, and for the first time in his life he burned with passionate eagerness to see the inside of a theatre, a delight he had never yet experienced. But he was without money. Eager to relieve his thoughts from the insufferable oppression to which they had yielded, he turned his attention to the female faces which he saw passing and re-passing. How hideous were most of them! The eyes encircled with rings of dark red, the drawn lips, the cheeks whereon the paint lay in daubs of revolting coarseness, the bodies for the most part puffed into unsightly obesity— surely there was little to invite in all this. But Arthur's passions were awakened, and he found a pleasure in the novel sensation of witnessing such scenes.

At length a young girl passed him, very different in appearance from those other women, yet none the less evidently a *fille perdue*. Her shape dainty and slim, her walk marked by that delightful spring which gives an impression of staginess, and her face unmistakably lovely. Without thinking why he did so, Arthur turned and followed her.

Possibly she heard his step behind her, for suddenly she stopped, turned round with a fascinating smile, and spoke to him in French. Arthur, at once abashed, turned hastily away, and walked quickly from the square.

It was past ten o'clock, and he felt that it was time to return home. Making his way slowly in the neighbourhood of Soho Square, the quietness of the street was suddenly broken by the sound of a barrel-organ which proceeded from a court close at hand. Music of any kind had always the utmost attraction for Arthur, and for a street organ he entertained the utmost liking, partly because it was almost the only kind of music he ever heard, partly because it recalled to him many happy hours of his childhood, when his toil in Little St. Andrew Street had been lightened by some heaven-sent organ-grinder's strains.

He now approached the court where the music was, and saw a little band of miserably clad children availing themselves of the Italian's good offices to enjoy a dance on the pavement. Hidden in the shadow of a wall Arthur stood and listened for nearly a quarter of an hour, whilst the organ played through a long string of hackneyed street ditties, the favourites of the day on the lips of errand-boys, the latest melodies of the music halls or the theatre. Be they what they might, to listen to them was soothing for Arthur.

Gradually his thoughts reverted to Carrie, and he felt himself able to think of her with more kindness, before long even with pity. What sort of a night had she passed alone ? Doubtless she was yearning for his return. After all, she certainly loved him ; for what was this outburst of absurd jealousy due to if not to the very strength of her affection, which could not brook the mere suspicion of a rival ? Yes, she loved him, and what an ungrateful wretch was he to return her love with anger. Had she forced him to marry her ? Had it not been by his own free will that he had taken her home as his wife ? Was it not his bounden duty to bear with the fullest consequences of his own act—nay more, to exert himself to the utmost for the poor girl's happiness ? Aye, poor girl ; for was she not worthy of the profoundest pity ? Was it her fault that she had never been educated, that she had been born with such a small portion of intelligence ? Surely not, and he was a brute, lacking in reason no less than in humane sympathy, to think of her as he had done. He would make full reparation ; he would bear with her utmost humours. Above all he would never do her the wrong to despair of her elevation to a higher stage of culture.

He hurried homewards, now eager to arrive. As he turned into Huntley Street he had to pass a public-house, about the door of which was collected a little crowd. From the midst came the shrill voices of two women, high in dispute. Drawn on by curiosity, he caught a glimpse of the wranglers, and—horror! he saw that Carrie was one of them, the other being her old landlady, Mrs. Pole. Carrie was hatless, her hair streaming in wildest disorder, her dress torn in places, her face swollen and tear-stained. Even as Arthur stood gazing, struck into momentary paralysis, the other woman rushed at her with the violence of a fury, and the language of a Billingsgate fish-wife, and struck her repeatedly about the head. In a moment Arthur had violently forced a passage through the crowd, and, how he knew not, had dragged Carrie from the midst of it into the open street. She seemed incapable of walking, and only leaned against him, gasping out his name with hysterical repetition. Calling to the crowd to keep back the woman, who had begun to pursue, he lifted Carrie bodily into his arms, and, with a strength he could not ordinarily have exerted, bore her rapidly along to their own door. He entered, and supported her up the stairs to their own room.

As soon as he had lit a candle, Arthur saw that the room was just as he had left it, in cheerless disorder. He could not for a moment doubt what had led to the hideous scene he had just been in time to interrupt. Carrie was quite unable to stand, and her breath filled the room with the smell of spirits.

Seating her with difficulty upon the bed, he held both her hands, and gazed into her face with unutterable anguish.

" Carrie ! Carrie ! " he repeatedly exclaimed, " for Heaven's sake tell me what this means ! What have you been doing ? Where have you been ? "

She made no reply, but sobbed hysterically, and floods of tears streamed from her eyes. To his repeated questions she at length muttered some kind of unintelligible reply. She evidently had no clear knowledge of her situation. It was vain to endeavour to make her understand or answer.

Arthur passed the night in watching, distracted with remorse which almost drove him mad.

Carrie was sleeping just as he had placed her—a heavy, drunken sleep, interrupted by struggling sobs, by starts and cries. As the candle by degrees burned down into the socket, Arthur extinguished it and lit the lamp. Any thought of rest was impossible, though his limbs ached intolerably, and his whole body was oppressed with a deadly faintness. With the exception of a very slight lunch, he had eaten nothing since breakfast during the day. At length he was compelled to rise, and, going to the cupboard, cut a slice of bread from a loaf which he found there. This and a draught of water somewhat refreshed him, but only to become more sensible to the fearful pictures of his mind. His wife a drunkard, engaging in a low brawl before a public-house—surely this was a degradation of which he could not have dreamt. What would this be the prelude to ? Was it but the commencement of horrors such as he had witnessed in the homes of wretched creatures whom he had visited for the purpose of relieving, horrors which he had often thought it would drive him mad to suffer in his own home ? He durst not turn his eyes to look at Carrie ; the disgust and terror which the sight of her awakened were too painful.

He endeavoured to read, but in vain gazed upon the page; not a line could he understand. He went to the window, threw it up, and looked out into the night. It still rained a little, but otherwise the night was calm ; the only wind was a warm and gentle one from the south-west, doubtless betokening more rain. As he stood thus gazing into the darkness, he was startled to hear a deep-toned bell begin to strike the hour with the utmost distinctness. Not till it had struck three or four times could he remember that it

must be Big Ben at Westminster, whose
tones were borne so plainly to his ear by the
wind. The hour was midnight. It seemed
as though the deep-mouthed bell would never
cease to toll, and every stroke bore with it
echoes which sounded like moanings of woe.
It brought hot tears to Arthur's eyes, and for
many minutes he wept like a child, quite
overcome by the anguish of his mind. He
turned to look at Carrie, who had just uttered
a groan, and, approaching her, he gazed long
at her face, letting his tears drop upon it.
Then he arranged the pillow under her head
so as to render her more comfortable, and,
having kissed her forehead, he returned to the
window.

In a garret on the opposite side of the
street a dull light was burning, and it was
now the only light visible in the houses
around. Arthur began to find employment
for his thoughts in speculating as to the
cause of the light. Most likely some one
was lying in the garret ill, perhaps dying ;
or perhaps it was only a husband or a wife
sitting in all but hopeless expectation for the
loved one to return, even though it were in a
condition which it was agony to picture.
With such watchers as these Arthur felt that
he should henceforth have a keen sympathy.
Then, as he thus pictured imaginary scenes,
a far-off shriek, piercing even though so distant, seemed to cut through the night. Here

was a fresh horror, a fresh exercise for the thoughts. Was it the mere yell of a drunken woman being dragged through the streets? Was it a scream to awaken the neighbourhood to the terrors of fire? Or was it midnight murder? He heard the policeman who had been tramping steadily along the street below suddenly pause and listen. But there was no second cry, the policeman continued to tramp on, and Arthur's thoughts wandered away to other themes.

One and two he heard sounded by the great bell, and after that his frame began to yield to exhaustion. Carrie still slept; she seemed rather quieter, too, moaning and struggling less. Taking one of the pillows from the bed, Arthur placed it on the floor, spread out by it a few articles of clothing, and, turning the lamp low, lay down to rest. But very few minutes had passed before he sank into a deep sleep.

When he woke it was pitch dark; apparently the lamp had burnt itself out. Striking a match he found it was half-past six. Already there were signs of waking life in the streets. Though his head ached so dreadfully that the light in his hand seemed to swell his brain to bursting, Arthur had no inclination to sleep again. His whole body was shivering with cold, his face and hands felt clammy with a strange perspiration. Having lit a new candle, he occupied himself in making a fire, and, as soon as the blaze began to shoot up cheerfully in the grate, he made some water warm and washed in it. Feeling revived, though still suffering intensely in his head, he proceeded to make tea. As he completed this, he perceived by motions upon the bed that Carrie was sleeping less soundly. She appeared to be in the agony of a fearful dream; her eyes were wide open, her hands convulsively clenched. Shaking her, and calling her name, Arthur at length succeeded in partly awaking her. She sat up on the bed and looked round the room with only half-conscious eyes.

"Carrie! Carrie!" said Arthur, sitting beside her, and holding a cup of tea in his hand, "wake, dearest!—try and drink this."

She took the cup from his hands and drank the contents eagerly.

"More," she said, holding it out to him again.

He refilled it, and this she also drank off.

"Are you well, dear?" he asked. "Can you go to sleep again?"

"My head, my head!" she moaned, sinking once more upon the pillow. Then, a moment after she asked, "What is the time?"

"Nearly seven o'clock. Do you think I may leave you to go to my work?"

"Oh yes," she moaned; "leave me, leave me. Why do you ask?"

"I cannot leave you if you are not well."

" You didn't mind leaving me last night,"
she returned, sobbing " why should you
now ? "

With a thousand self-reproaches, Arthur
exerted himself to calm her ; he caressed
her, spoke to her with loving words, only
speaking to her of his own fault, not a
syllable of hers. That must in time be
spoken of, but not yet; not now that she
was suffering so terribly from its consequences. Neither did she refer to it in the
few sentences she uttered. She was still
heavy with sleep, and Arthur saw it would
be better to let her have quiet rest. Promising that he would return at dinner-time, he
watched her once more fall asleep, and then,
as soon as it was time, set out as usual.

When he returned about mid day he found
Carrie sitting over the fire, her face resting
upon her hands, her long hair falling loosely
about her shoulders. All his anger had now
left him, and he felt for her nothing but the
sincerest pity. When he entered she did not
stir, but when he bent over her and laid his
hand soothingly upon her head, she looked
up at him for a moment. Her eyes were red
and swollen, and her cheeks had lost all their
natural colour. She had evidently been
crying, but was doing so no longer. To his
enquiries as to whether she felt better she
replied in the affirmative, but with very few
words. Evidently something was upon her

mind, and Arthur naturally concluded that she was suffering from remorse. Thinking it best to leave her undisturbed, he swallowed a mouthful of lunch, and again approached her to say good-bye; he had a long distance to go, and not a minute too much time.

"I will be back early, dearest," he said, bending over her and pressing his cheek to hers. "Don't trouble to get any dinner ready. I will bring something in with me that will do. Shall I find something nice for Carrie, to surprise her with?"

At other times she had always welcomed such a suggestion with a childish delight. Now she only shook her head and said, "Don't trouble."

"Oh, we shall see," he returned; and he was on the point of going, when she suddenly moved to face him and asked—

"Where is that portrait?"

In the pain of the result all memory of the cause had escaped Arthur's mind; he started when he heard this sudden question, for he knew the torn drawing was still in his pocket. It smote through him, moreover, like a piercing blow, the sudden disclosure of the true cause of Carrie's depression. It was not sorrow for her fault which weighed upon her, but a brooding jealousy which nothing could dispel from her mind. In a second Arthur's resolution was taken, and he answered firmly—

" I destroyed it last night ; I threw it away in the street."

Something like a smile rose to Carrie's lips, and she resumed her attitude over the fire. Without further adieu, Arthur left the house.

In the evening, before returning home, he made a hasty call at Noble's lodgings. Noble had just arrived from his work.

" I wish to ask a favour of you," said Arthur.

" Ask a hundred," returned Noble.

" No, only one. Will you take this little parcel of mine, and guard it for me as if it contained something more precious than gold —guard it till I ask you to give it me again ?"

" I will," replied his friend, with a slight look of surprise.

" But are you willing to do so without knowing what it contains ? If I do not wish you to know it, Noble, you may be sure it is a secret which is far better kept by myself alone."

" I am willing to do so," replied Noble. " Let us say no more about it. Look; I will lock it in this little drawer, which I do not use for anything. You will find it there when you want it."

" Many thanks."

" How is your wife ? " asked Noble, as Arthur was on the point of going.

" As usual, thanks," replied the other ; and, waving his hand, departed.

Arthur had been at first uncertain whether he should impart to Noble what had happened at home, but at the last moment he found it impossible to do so. The degradation was too great; far better that no one else should be cognisant of it. And then if, as he devoutly hoped, it was a single case which would never find a repetition, there would be an injustice to Carrie in making it known to his friend. Certainly it would be unjust to relate Carrie's error without at the same time making the cause fully known, and this Arthur was not disposed to do. In the parcel he had entrusted to his friend was, of course, the torn portrait. But the perfect confidence he possessed in Noble's honour was a guarantee that the parcel would never be looked into. Otherwise, he could not have given it to Noble to keep; for the thought that the latter should even suspect the secret which the portrait contained was intolerable to Arthur. He felt that his high-minded friend could not but regard him with less respect if he knew this secret, and Noble's respect was a necessity of his life.

On his way home he fulfilled his promise of purchasing a delicacy for Carrie. As he ascended the stairs to their room, he wondered what effect his last sentence at dinner-time would have had upon Carrie. Without a doubt she would have ransacked his box once more, but she might suspect that he was carrying the picture in his pocket; he resolved to give her an opportunity of seeing that even this was not the case. Perhaps by this means he should restore peace to his home.

He was not surprised, on entering, to find the room once more in tolerable order, and Carrie neatly dressed, standing to receive him before a cheerful hearth. She was still pale, but otherwise all traces of her illness seemed to have passed away. He did not speak, but took from his pocket the newly-purchased delicacy and opened it upon the table. A smile lit up Carrie's face, and, stepping a foot or two towards him, she held her arms open. In a moment he met her embrace.

"You are sure it is thrown away?" she whispered, as he pressed her in his arms.

"Suppose it were in my box again?" he returned.

"I don't think it is," she replied, and Arthur knew that his supposition was confirmed.

"Suppose it were in one of my pockets?" he continued, willing to remove all suspicion from her mind. He asked himself, as he spoke the words, whether she would trust to his word alone, or whether that would be insufficient.

"Let me look," was Carrie's reply; and she instantly began to rummage his pockets.

Arthur sighed, but asked himself what

right he had to demand that his mere word should suffice; had he not already deceived her?

"You won't tell me who it was?" asked Carrie, when she had satisfied herself that the odious picture was nowhere to be found.

"No one at all," repeated Arthur, laughing. "I copied it from an old picture, long since."

Carrie was fain to put up with this answer, though it was clear she did not believe it. She immediately set about preparing dinner, and the meal passed smoothly over. When it was finished Arthur made Carrie sit by him, and spoke gravely.

"Now I have satisfied you, Carrie," he said, "I think it is fair that you should satisfy me. How did you pass the time when I was away last night?"

"I don't remember anything about it," replied she, laughing and shaking her head.

"But you mustn't laugh, dear," urged Arthur, "I am very serious. You have pained me more than I ever was pained in my life. How was it that I found you with that woman, Mrs. Pole?"

"Oh, I forget all about it," returned Carrie. "Talk about something else."

"No, I wish to speak of this. Please to attend, Carrie. Did that woman come to you, or did you go to her?"

"Why, if you go away in a bad temper

and leave me," returned Carrie, rather sharply, "I suppose I must get who I can to talk to. Any one's better than no one."

"There you are wrong," said Arthur, firmly. "Far better to have no one at all to associate with than choose such a woman as that. I had no idea of her character when I took a room for you in her house, or I certainly should have had nothing to do with her. Then you went to her, Carrie?"

"What if I did?"

"Why, this. That I beg you will never do such a thing again as long as you live, on any pretence; and if she comes here you must refuse to see her. Do you understand, Carrie?"

"I don't care much for Mrs. Pole," replied Carrie, a little awed by Arthur's firmness; "but who else have I to talk to?"

"I know quite well that it is disagreeable to live so entirely alone as you do," pursued Arthur; "I would give anything to be able to find you suitable friends. But whether you find such or not, it is clear that you must make no friend of Mrs. Pole. Will you promise me, Carrie, never to speak to her again upon any pretence?"

"Well," returned Carrie, averting her face, "there's Ann Pole; she isn't so bad. She doesn't drink at all."

"That's the daughter?"

"Yes; she's a very nice girl, I'm sure."

"I know nothing of her," replied Arthur, "and do not wish to. But if you associate with her, it is impossible to avoid coming in contact with her mother. So I must ask you to have nothing to do with anyone in that house."

"Who *am* I to talk to then?" asked the girl.

"Why don't you make a friend of Mrs. Oaks? She is a very agreeable woman, and her conversation would do you good. You seem to have some unaccountable dislike for her—how is it?"

"Oh, how can I talk to Mrs. Oaks? She's so stiff, and never has anything to say to me."

"I have never found her so," replied Arthur. "She is kind and good-hearted in the extreme, and a far better educated woman than I have ever known in her position. I'm sure it is a foolish prejudice you have against her."

"I don't like her," exclaimed Carrie, "and so it's no use talking."

Arthur rose from his chair and paced the room, fearful lest he should be betrayed into angry expressions.

"Whether you like her or not, Carrie," he said, after a few minutes' silence, "she is the only woman you know who is at all fit for you to associate with. She has several married daughters, who, I dare say, are very respectable women; and you might get to

know them. But, in any case, I must insist
upon your having nothing to do with Mrs.
Pole. If your own good taste does not keep
you from her, you must please to remember
that you are my wife, and endeavour to do as
I wish. Do you think I have no ambition?
Do you think I shall all my life be as poor as
I am now, and with as few friends? Some
day I hope to be able to introduce you to very
different people from those you have yet
known, to people in a far higher position in
life. And how will you be prepared to associate with such people if you train your tastes
to sympathise with none but Mrs. Pole and
her like? This is why I so earnestly wish you to
occupy your spare time in attending to your
education, to do your utmost to become better,
to know more, to understand more. Have
you no ambition for yourself? Would you be
willing to continue absolutely ignorant to the
end of your life?"

Carrie had reassumed her position over the
fire, and the dull smile upon her face indicated
clearly that she understood but little of what
Arthur was saying, and sympathised with his
eloquence not at all.

"Look at me, Carrie," he continued, approaching her and laying his hand upon her
head. "My youngest years were far more
uncared for than yours. I was a wretched,
ragged, half-starved child, playing in the
gutter. When I was quite a little boy I had

to begin to earn my living, and earn it by downright hard work. But I soon felt that I could not bear always to be such an ignorant creature as I was growing up; with desperate efforts I succeeded in going to an evening school once or twice a week, and I occupied every spare moment in learning to read and write. Then by chance I got a place as shop-boy under a most excellent master, a man whom I have to thank for nearly all the knowledge I possess, without whom I might still have been a mere ignorant, rude-speaking workman. Now, Carrie, what he did for *me*, it is my earnest wish to do for *you*. I am not as clever as he was, I do not know anything like as much, but still I am able to teach you much, very much that you do not know, and that you will be better for. To train your mind in this way, to give you a hand and help you up to a higher kind of life, and to devote my whole existence to making you better in every way —that has been my ambition since I knew you, Carrie! Will you do your part in the work? Will you not make just the few efforts I require of you? Will you promise to do so in future, dearest? I am sure you will."

There was silence for several minutes, and when Carrie replied it was in a manner which showed that the appeal had been altogether lost on her.

" It's all very well to ask me to do more,"
she said. " If you only knew how much
house-work I have to do every day whilst you
are away, you wouldn't ask me to find time
for a lot of other things."

" But half an hour, Carrie. Surely you can
find *half an hour* in a day ? "

" Well, well, I'll think about it," replied
the girl. " Don't talk no more about it now.
You make my head ache with talking so much.
I don't feel very well as it is."

Arthur sighed deeply. He saw that further
conversation would only lead to another scene,
and that he dreaded too much voluntarily to
excite. So he took a volume from among
Mr. Tollady's old books, and endeavoured to
read.

When he had lived together with Mark
Challenger in this room, he had been accustomed to spend several hours in serious
study every day; but since his marriage he
had scarcely opened a book. This was but
one of many circumstances tending towards
his unhappiness. Another was the constant
longing which he experienced to take up a
pencil and see whether he had lost his old
skill in drawing. Though he had succeeded
in lulling the voice of this internal monitor
by force of numerous occupations, he could
never completely silence it.

Only by years of neglect and oppression is
it possible utterly to stifle those inborn im-

pulses which we personify as genius, if, indeed, it be possible at all to do so, and Arthur, though he had accustomed himself to regard his artistic yearnings as something which it was his duty to suppress, had never been able completely to quell them. They came upon him at times with dreadful force, operating like an inward pain, a gnawing at his very vitals which would not let him rest.

The incident of Helen's picture had awakened them to their utmost energy, and to-night, as he sat endeavouring to read, he looked upon his daily life as a dreary waste, a perpetual, arid desert, to which he was condemned, though his eyes never lost sight of a delicious country, fair as the land of Beulah, so near to him that it seemed he could attain it by a stride.

Now, too, he began to think more frequently of the approaching day when he should be able to claim Mr. Norman's legacy. Hitherto this thought had been crushed down with the others, as something which was in any case of little consequence to him. For he had resolved that the possession of comparative wealth should make no difference in his daily life.

In the society which he had frequented of late, that of men such as William Noble— strong, earnest minds so terribly convinced of the curse of wealth that they advocated a system of society in which no man should live upon money which was not the exact representation of his own labour—among men such as these Arthur had grown to the determination never to abandon his daily toil, however easy it might be for him to live independently of it. Daily labour was one of the fundamental principles of the gospel he had adopted, and had himself earnestly sought to spread, at the club and elsewhere.

Holding such views, he had long since resolved that, when he became possessed of his money, every farthing of it should be employed in the cause of the poor, in direct charity, and in aid of movements which he approved. No single coin of it should go towards his own support; rather than that he would toil unceasingly for the sufficiencies of life.

But since his marriage Arthur's feelings had undergone a considerable change. He thought of Carrie, and he would have been less than human could he have long resisted the temptation to raise above a life of sordid cares the woman whom he loved, or at all events whom he had bound to himself as his wife, the possible mother of his children.

And then came the perpetual whisper within him, bidding him contemplate a life spent in devotion to art. What was to prevent his entering upon such a life when the time came? Nothing—except principle, except that the voice which whispered that it would be shame to desert the cause he had embraced, to afford to his companions one more example of wealth corrupting a generous nature.

But the time had not come for reasoning on these matters. As yet there was only a question of vague impulses, which, on account of their very sweetness, must surely be wrong and on no account to be followed. For all that they sufficed to render Arthur's life even more unhappy, by degrees to darken the brightness of his eyes, and to impart an aspect of enduring trouble to his countenance.

For some days Carrie was in unvariable good humour, and Arthur was too glad of the change to ever touch upon one of the subjects likely to disturb the peace of his home. He said to himself that Carrie's education was not a matter to be completed in a day; he must commence by degrees, humouring her idleness at first, and not insisting upon a sudden correction of all her faults. So he again occupied himself chiefly with her pronunciation, and Carrie was good enough to receive his corrections with equanimity. Hope once more dawned upon Arthur.

It was nearly a week after the dreadful night that Arthur, on returning home, once more noticed the strong odour of peppermint in the room. He said nothing about it; but, in spite of himself, strange thoughts were awakened by it in his mind. So engrossing were these thoughts that they kept him very silent during the evening. Carrie, on the other hand, was quite unusually talkative.

He observed her closely, and thought he perceived an unnatural glow in her eyes which he had at times noticed there before, and that also on occasions when she had been eating peppermint. He was distressed by an uneasy fear, a dread of an uncertain kind, which made him turn sick at heart.

About nine o'clock Carrie went out to buy something for supper. Another time Arthur would not have let her go alone. To-night he had a special purpose in doing so.

As soon as she was gone, he went to the cupboard in which she kept all her crockery and other articles of household use, and rapidly examined its contents. After some little search he discovered an empty corked bottle, of the use of which he had no idea. Taking out the cork, he smelt it, and sickened as though the odour had been deadly poison, for he clearly recognised that the bottle had contained spirits.

The dreadful suspicions he had entertained with regard to the peppermint were fully confirmed. For a moment he hesitated as to how he should act. It was clear that

the shortest course was the best. He had to
do with a disease which required the most
decisive of measures, and any weakness on
his part would be culpable.

Placing the bottle in the middle of the
table, he sat down and awaited Carrie's return with an anxiety so intense that it rendered him physically feeble.

She entered at length, with a heightened
colour, laughing gaily, and immediately went
to the paper of peppermints on the mantel-
piece and put one in her mouth. She then
began to lay the cloth for supper, and, in
doing so, had of course to move the bottle.
She started at the sight of it, and paused for
a moment, as if endeavouring to remember
whether she could have left it there by mistake or not. She turned her eyes cautiously
in Arthur's direction, and saw at once that
he was watching her closely.

"No," said the latter, divining her
thoughts, "it was not there when you went
out, Carrie. I found it myself in your absence and put it there."

She muttered something and was putting
the bottle into the cupboard again, when
Arthur stopped her.

"What do you use that bottle for, Carrie?"
he asked.

"Oh, for all sorts of things," she replied,
readily, though her face had gone pale. "I
used it to fetch some brandy in to-day. I felt
very faint, and was obliged to have it."

" In that case," said Arthur, persistently gazing into her face, "why didn't you tell me of it ?"

" Oh, it was nothing," said Carrie, trying to turn away. "It wasn't worth bothering you about."

But Arthur held her hand, and would not let her go.

" Was that all, Carrie ? " he asked. "Why then, do you trouble to eat peppermints, that I mayn't smell the spirits when you kiss me ? "

She reddened again for a moment, then laughed, still struggling to free herself.

" What an idea ! I'm sure I don't do it for any such reason ! I eat peppermints because I like them, that's all. If you grudge me them you've only to say so. They don't cost so much as all that."

" No, you are getting angry without a cause, Carrie," returned Arthur, " and that is a bad sign. Tell me this : Have you ever had spirits before to-day because you felt faint ? "

" No, never."

" Never ? " he repeated, with the utmost gravity.

" And what if I had ?" cried Carrie, suddenly breaking away from him, and speaking angrily. " I suppose you'd rather come home and find me dead than allow me to spend a little money when I want it."

" You have no right to speak so to me,

Carrie," returned Arthur, severely. " When have I shown disregard of your health, or grudged you anything I could afford that would give you pleasure? You are angry because I have found that bottle. I tell you plainly, it is not true that you got the brandy because you felt faint! If that had been the reason you would have told me of it. And why should you feel so faint as to require such a restorative? You are quite well, you are not overburdened with hard work, you have nothing to make you faint. A cup of tea would have refreshed you much better, if you had been in need of more refreshment. You have not told me the truth."

" Very well," retorted the girl, with terrible passion in her eyes, " tell me I have been a liar at once ! "

Arthur turned away with a suppressed expression of disgust. There was no doubt that Carrie had been drinking again. Her features denoted it clearly, and the fierce passion with which she spoke could only have been excited by drink.

Taking both her arms firmly in his hands, Arthur forced her to stand facing him before he spoke again.

" Can you understand what I am going to say to you ? " he asked, in a low, firm voice. " Have you still enough of your senses left to listen to me and heed what I say ? "

She persisted in turning away her head, and made no reply. In spite of her struggles to free herself, he held her with unshaken firmness.

"It is evident," he went on, "that I allow you too much money. You have more than what you need for our every day expenses, and instead of saving, you spend the superfluous money in poison which will soon render you worse than brutal. Mark what I say, Carrie, for I am determined to save you, whether you will or not; at all events, I am determined to do my utmost before it is too late. From this day I shall give you much less money to spend, and of that money you will have to keep a strict account. Every penny you pay away you will set down in the book I have given you. You have shown me that it is impossible to have *absolute* confidence in you; I trust you will not force me to believe that you are not to be confided in *at all*. Do you understand me?"

She only replied by a wild effort to free herself, and, succeeding in her object, darted to the other end of the room. There she stood, looking at him with her unnaturally bright eyes, but saying nothing.

"Have you no regard for me left, Carrie?" Arthur pursued. "Must I look upon you as an enemy in my home, instead of a wife who returns my love? Are you determined to make me wretched, to leave me no moment's peace, day or night? What peace can I have if I know that, in my absence, you are taking the surest means, day by day, to degrade yourself and render yourself altogether unworthy of my affection. In Heaven's name, what has driven you to this fearful vice? Is your home miserable? Do you want for anything? Am I habitually unkind to you? Carrie, Carrie!" he cried, in a voice of agony, again drawing near to her, "open your eyes, and see what a hideous path you are entering on! Surely it is ignorance which allows you to act in this way, you cannot know what fearful dangers you are encountering. Promise me that you will never drink spirits from this day. Promise me that, Carrie—will you?"

"There's no call for me to make any such promise, as I see," replied the girl. "I don't drink them only when it's necessary. I don't know what right you have to call me all those names."

"As long as you are well and strong, it is *never* necessary," returned Arthur. "You don't understand me, Carrie. You seem to think I am doing something for my own selfish interest in forbidding you to drink; you cannot see that I have your own happiness, and nothing but your own happiness, at heart. How shall I make you understand what I mean? Will you come for a walk with me?"

Carrie looked up in surprise at the apparent inconsequence of the request, but on Arthur continuing to urge that she should go out with him, curiosity persuaded her to consent. It was Saturday night, and already the hour was late. Leading her through the crowded streets of the neighbourhood, Arthur took his way towards the meanest quarters he knew of, into courts and alleys swarming with the riotous life of the last night in the week. He made her pause near the beggars on the edge of the pavement, pointing to their foul rags, their hideously-distorted features, their bodies tortured with nameless diseases. He made her stand by the entrance to pawn-shops, and watch the men, women and children who entered and came out, made her watch the mother pawning her infant's very rags, after already robbing herself of more than decency could dispense with, the dissipated boys running with frightened faces to turn stolen articles into money, the tottering old men and women pawning the few remains of miserable clothing which they should have kept to make shrouds. He led her to the doors of the most crowded gin-palaces, showed her hundreds of women in appearance too ghastly for description, made her listen to language which should have rotted the tongues which uttered it, stood by with her whilst human creatures, mad with liquor, tore each other with their claws like wild beasts. No sight,

no sound, no most terrible experience which
Saturday night could afford did he spare her,
and at every fresh horror he made her observe that drink was, ten to one, at the
bottom of it. And at length, when the church
clocks were striking one, he led her back
home, wearied and sobbing, and before she
sought rest, he made her solemnly promise
that she would drink nothing that could
harm her from that day. She promised, with
tears; after which, Arthur kissed her, and
she fell asleep like a child.

CHAPTER III.

A CLIMAX.

ARTHUR pondered much during the days which followed as to whether it would be wise to acquaint Carrie with the wealth that would become his early in the following year, or not. At times he was strongly tempted to do so, urged by the hope that this expectation might awaken in her a stronger feeling of self-respect than his own exhortations and instructions had hitherto availed to excite. But, on the other hand, if he meant to persevere in his severely unselfish plans with regard to the disposal of the money, it would be scarcely prudent to make Carrie a party to them, for Arthur was beginning to recognise only too clearly that she had but little of that high-mindedness which would be required to achieve such renunciation. She would not be able to comprehend his views; who could say that she would not attribute to him in her own mind the meanest motives instead of the highest? But then came the question—Did he really mean to persist in his purpose? Would it be wise? Would it be just to himself and to Carrie? As yet he was not prepared with an answer for these questions. There were yet many months before an absolute decision would be required of him. For the present he would let the matter rest. Possibly in the end he might find it prudent to consult William Noble, who himself knew nothing of his friend's fortune, and it was very difficult to foresee in which direction Noble's advice might tend.

If he was reticent with regard to the future, Arthur was almost as silent about the past, as far, at least, as it concerned Carrie. Once or twice he did venture to ask her a question about her life during the period in which he had lost sight of her, but she showed such reluctance to reply, that he ceased to mention the subject. Indeed, there was very little to learn. Carrie's experience had been that of the numberless girls in a similar destitute condition whom London nightly pillows in her hard corners, the only peculiarity being that she had found a way out of her misery without having recourse either to the workhouse or the river. Of one thing, however, Arthur felt certain, and it was that this period of wretched vagabondage had done Carrie considerable moral harm. True, he had scarcely spoken to her before the night on which he saved her from death in the streets, but he felt sure that she had previously been much gentler, and, to speak plainly, more innocent. Above all, he believed that this fatal habit of drinking had had its source in that prolonged nightmare of homeless agony. Doubtless his own unsuspecting heedlessness had contributed to its development, for he now saw clearly that the woman called Mrs. Pole had exercised a strong influence for evil over Carrie's mind, an influence that endured even now that he thought he had removed his wife from her reach. One experience which he had now acquired, tortured him ceaselessly; it was that Carrie was by no means to be trusted. She seemed to have no innate respect for truth, and had acquired a facility in deception which made it all but impossible to arrive at the truth by questioning her. The knowledge of this terrible flaw in her character gave Arthur many sleepless nights. How could he tell what ruinous schemes were ripening in the brain of the girl who slept so peacefully by his side? And this evil only grew by time, for his suspicions never ceased to be fed with only too substantial evidence. *Distrust* haunted him like a phantom. It constantly stood between himself and Carrie, chilling her kiss, and little by little estranging her from his embrace. At times he asked himself, with a shudder, whether he could any longer pretend that he loved her.

For, in spite of her solemn promise, she continued stealthily to gratify her passion for drink, and Arthur knew it but too well. Often he detected it in her breath, and openly charged her with her broken faith, but she denied the charge so boldly, with such shameless persistence, that he stood aghast before her, and was unable to say another word. He had so strongly insisted upon her keeping accounts, that she was obliged to make a show of it; but Arthur, by inspecting her book, saw clearly that the expenses were constantly falsified. Before long he resorted to the plan of giving her money every day, barely sufficient for the expenses he knew to be legitimate; but, nevertheless, he continued to find her upon his return either excited to an unnatural gaiety, or plunged in dangerous moroseness, and always with the gleaming eye which were the infallible index of her wrong-doing. He could not understand how she managed to procure liquor; but before long he began to notice the disappearance of sundry articles from the room, and he had no more wonder on the subject.

They had soon been married six months. The pretence of Carrie's education had long since gone to add another stone to the paving of Hell; no word was ever heard of reading or writing now, and Arthur had even ceased to correct her errors in speaking. All day long he worked with an overburdened heart, and a brow which began to show distinct signs of hopeless trouble. His foot began to lose its lightness, he began to stoop as he walked, never looking about him with the old joyous, hopeful glance, but with eyes fixed upon the ground, ever thinking, thinking.

He acquired the habit of talking aloud to himself, and occasionally gesticulated as he walked. He had grown to dread his wife's face. Affectionate expostulation was altogether thrown away upon her, or only met with a return of sickening hypocrisy; and to angry utterances she only replied with passionate retorts. Arthur fancied that he could observe her features growing coarser, and he felt convinced that her voice had no longer the clearness of tone which had once marked it. Yet of none of these signs did she herself appear conscious. Not the most impassioned pleading on Arthur's part had force to awaken her to the unavoidable consequences of her course of life.

One morning, early in July, as Arthur was leaving the house to go to his work, he was stopped by his landlady, Mrs. Oaks, who requested him to step into her parlour. The good woman had a troubled expression on her face, and was evidently preparing to speak on a subject she found disagreeable.

" I'm afraid, sir," she began, " that I shall be obliged to ask you to find other lodgings."

" For whatever reason, Mrs. Oaks ? " asked Arthur, in the utmost surprise.

" Well, to tell you the truth, Mr. Golding, the character of my house is being damaged. These girls that come so often to see your wife have such a very—unrespectable appearance, I might say, that the other lodgers don't at all like it. One has given me notice already, an old lady on the first floor who has been with me a year. And then the neighbours are beginning to talk about it, too. I shall have my house empty if it goes on."

Arthur turned deadly pale as he listened. He looked round to see if the door was closed behind him, and then sat down, as if overcome with sudden weakness.

"Aren't you well, sir?" asked Mrs. Oaks, disturbed at the sight of his countenance.

He waved his hands to signify that it was nothing.

"I know nothing of these visitors you speak of," he said. "When do they come? Who are they?"

"They come at all hours of the day, sir; and as for what they are, I don't exactly know, of course, but I am afraid they're no good. But didn't you know they came for Mrs. Golding?"

Arthur shook his head.

"Well," took up the old lady, "and I asked her only the other day if you knew about it, and she said that you knew well enough, and that there was no call to complain of anything, as they were respectable friends of hers."

"I assure you, Mrs. Oaks," said Arthur, solemnly, "I know nothing of them. How many come?"

"Oh, perhaps not more than two or three; but they are here so often, and they dress in such a flashy way, that nobody can help noticing them. They must stop coming here, that's very certain."

"So they shall, Mrs. Oaks," returned Arthur, rising. "I am very much obliged to you for telling me of this. I hope that is your only objection to me remaining your lodger?"

"Oh, I've nothing else in the world to complain of," said the old lady. "I'm sure I should be very sorry to lose you."

Arthur went upstairs again forthwith. It would result in his missing half a day's work—perhaps losing his place—but that he could not help. For him to be absent all day with this weight upon his mind would be intolerable.

"Carrie," he began sternly, as soon as he re-entered the room, "who are these girls that visit you so often in my absence?"

"I don't know of any girls," she replied, shaking her head.

"You do!" replied Arthur, with sudden violence, every fibre in him thrilling at the bare-faced lie. "You know very well that you are constantly visited by girls during the day. Tell me who they are at once!"

"Oh," she replied with an affectation of indifference, "I suppose you mean Lily Marston, as come to see me once last week."

"And who is she?"

"One of the girls I used to work with. What harm if she did come? I suppose I'm not to be caged up like a wild beast, am I, and not allowed to see any one?"

" Do you mean to tell me that this girl is the only visitor you have ever had ? "

" The only one as I remember. Who told you about her ? "

" Never mind who told me. I know perfectly well that you have had frequent visitors during the present week. It is useless to try to deceive me."

" I know who told you," returned Carrie, her eyes flashing. " It's that spiteful old cat of a landlady ! She's got a spite against me, she has, because she knows I don't like her. She threatened to tell you."

" And she has done so. And she has also told me that the nuisance has become so great we shall be obliged to leave if it continues. Once more, I ask you : Who are these girls who visit you ? "

" Is it likely," returned Carrie, " as I can live day after day without seeing no one ? And I'm not going to do it, that's plain. If I have one or two friends come to see me, they come into my own room and don't disturb anybody, and the landlady's a spiteful old cat to say as it isn't so ! "

" Then you own that you have visitors, and without my knowledge ? Well, it must cease at once. You understand me ? I forbid you to see any one at this house without my consent."

He paused to see the effect of his words. Carrie turned away, and said nothing.

" Do you mean to obey me ? " he asked.

She said nothing, but appeared engaged in covering over something which lay on the dressing-table, something in front of which she had been standing since he entered the room. Arthur stepped up quickly to her, and, seizing her hands, disclosed a large jet necklace, a gold brooch, and a silver bracelet. For some minutes he was unable to speak with surprise.

"How have you obtained all these?" he asked at length, his voice quavering from the conflict of emotions.

"They're mine!" cried Carrie, passionately. "Leave them alone!"

"Yours!" he exclaimed. "How have they come into your possession?"

"They've always been mine."

"Always yours! But you have not had them here in this room."

"I know I haven't. They've been at my aunt's all the time. I went and fetched them yesterday."

He looked into her face for some moments, desperately endeavouring to determine whether she spoke the truth. Possibly she did, but, as Arthur too well knew, it was quite as possible that she did not. Yet how else could she have obtained these ornaments? He dared not ask himself the question, but forced himself obstinately to believe that she had told him the truth.

"What are you going to do with them?" he asked, after standing with his eyes fixed upon the objects for several minutes, almost stunned by the weight of trouble that was pressing upon him.

"What should I?" she asked, putting them away into a drawer. "Wear them, of course."

He stood still, gazing at the place where the things had lain, unable to determine upon a course of action. Suddenly he spoke.

"You didn't answer my question about the visitors," he said. "Do you mean to obey me, or must I look for other lodgings?"

"Oh, I'm sure I don't want to drive you away," retorted Carrie. "If you're tired of having me with you, I can look for a room for myself. That's very easily done."

It was not the first time that Carrie had expressed herself ready to leave him, and to hear her speak thus was always intensely aggravating to Arthur. Regarding his marriage as a solemn bond which nothing but death could break, it was torture to him to hear it spoken of so lightly, as if it were capable of dissolution at will. It may be that in this feeling there was something of the indignation with which an upright mind regards a tempter. So when she spoke, the taunting coldness of her words irritated him once more into stern anger.

"What do you mean, when you speak so to me?" he exclaimed. "Do you understand the words you use? Do you mean that you hate me, that you are weary of owning me as your husband? Would it please you if I took you at your word and bade you go and earn your own living?"

"I could force you to support me," replied Carrie, with a short laugh.

The utter heartlessness of these words checked his further speech. What good was it to exact a promise from her that she would obey him? Neither was her word to be trusted, nor had she the slightest trace of affection for him left. With a glance of burning scorn he walked out of the room. On reaching the ground floor he knocked at Mrs. Oak's parlour, and was admitted.

"I am sorry to say that in any case we shall be obliged to leave, Mrs. Oaks," he said. "I suppose you will not require more than a week's notice?"

The old lady replied in the negative, surveying Arthur's pallid features with a look of pity. Possibly she divined the trouble from which he suffered. He did not leave her time to make any further remark, but walked at once from the house.

The rest of the morning he spent in wandering aimlessly about the streets, his brain throbbing feverishly, his body oppressed with an intolerable lassitude. He had taken his resolution. At the end of the week he would move to an entirely different part of London, where Carrie would be out of the reach of these companions who were leading her to her ruin. Once in a new abode, he would again attempt the work of reformation. But even as he resolved thus in his mind, he was struggling with the heart-sickness of perpetual disappointment. He could not bear to keep his sorrows any longer to himself. As yet he had not said a word of them to his friend Noble, but now, at length, he felt compelled to make him his confidant, and seek counsel in his dire straits.

During the afternoon he worked as usual. His appearance readily lent itself as a proof of his statement that he had been kept away in the morning by sudden illness. When the day came to an end he gladly left the toil which was ever becoming more odious to him, and set out in the direction of Noble's lodgings.

These were near the Strand. In crossing that thoroughfare he had to run before a hansom which was coming along at an unusual speed, and, even in the moment of its passing him, he distinctly saw Carrie seated in it by the side of a tall, finely-dressed young man. Was it possible he had made a mistake? As soon as the thought had flashed through his mind he started and ran at his utmost speed in pursuit of the vehicle. He had it distinctly before him amid the great crowd of traffic, and he gained upon it visibly. Suddenly it drew up to the pavement and stopped. The next moment he was standing by it—only to see a grave old gentleman step out with a carpet bag in his hand. In his agitation he had evidently pursued the wrong hansom.

No thought now of visiting Noble. Arthur was mad, and the very thought of his friend's calm conversation was insufferable to him. Homewards—homewards! that was the sole idea which filled his brain. It was just possible that he had deceived himself in the hasty glance which the speeding vehicle had allowed him; if so he should find Carrie seated at home as usual. But if he found her absent, then—there would be time enough to decide how to act. As he ran along the swarming streets between the Strand and his home he did his best to persuade himself that his eyes had played him false, but all the time he was convinced that they had not. He knew Carrie's face and form too well; he felt sure that he had even recognised the gold brooch and the bracelet.

He reached Huntley Street and rushed panting upstairs to his room. He flung the door open. The room was empty.

He sat down to think. Was the fact of Carrie's absence a proof of his having seen her in the hansom? By no means, for she had of late frequently been absent when he returned in the evening, employed he knew but too well how. But were the ornaments still here? He stepped to the chest of drawers. All the drawers were open, and in none were the ornaments to be found. There was no other place in the room where she could have put them away. He went to the cupboard in which she was in the habit of hanging her dresses. It was empty, with the exception of one cast-off garment and the hat she generally wore. Her best hat was gone. He turned to examine other parts of the room, and, in doing so, his eye fell upon half a sheet of note-paper which lay on the table amidst the remnants of the morning's breakfast. He took it up with a trembling hand, and read, written in Carrie's well-known scrawl and with all her favourite errors of spelling, this :—

"Don't expect me back. I've gone for good. I shan't trouble you any more, though I am your wife."

When he took up the paper it had shaken in his fingers like a leaf in the wind, but, having read it, he put it down with perfect steadiness. The certainty of what he feared seemed to have cured him of his feverish anxiety. For a moment he felt cold in every part of his body, but, after that, he was calm. He began to pace the room, repeating to himself in a low voice the trenchant sentences of the note: "Don't expect me back." "I've gone for good." Several times he stopped in his slow walk and looked out of the window. He faced the west, and could see

the sky over the houses opposite still glowing
with the rich colours of sunset. From one
chimney ascended a thin stream of smoke,
and very beautiful it looked as its transparency
was permeated with a tinge of the hues behind it. Arthur's thoughts wandered off to
a translation of the Odyssey which he had
once read aloud to Mr. Tollady, and he could
not help connecting the vari-coloured smoke
before him with his imagination of the smoke
rising from a Greek altar in some sea-girdled
isle made beautiful under an Ionian sunset.
There was calmness in this hour. The streets
seemed unusually quiet, and an organ being played in the distance sounded like delicious music. He found himself wandering
off into day-dreams, and had the greatest
difficulty in forcing his thoughts back to the
present hour. To do so, he still kept repeating the note half aloud. What was this feeling so strongly resembling pleasure which
crept further into his heart at each repetition? How was it that he unconsciously
drew himself more upright, as if some great
burden had suddenly been taken from his
shoulders?

So Carrie was gone. Well, nothing more
natural than that she should go. Was it not
rather wonderful that she had stopped so
long? He had not been mistaken; it was
really Carrie whom he had seen in the hansom. And who could the elegant-looking
young man be who was with her? How had

she made his acquaintance? Might it not even be the " A. W." upon whose identity he had so often reflected?

He found himself thinking of Carrie's future lot as if she had been someone with whom he was slightly acquainted, and no more. Would her new friend trouble himself about her grammatical faults, her errors of pronunciation? Most probably not. How foolish he himself had been to trouble, either. Of what consequence was an *h* omitted or foisted in where it had no business, what mattered a few violations of the rules of syntax in this most irregular of worlds? Certainly there was passing annoyance caused by the neglect of such little conventions; but then there were other girls quite as beautiful as Carrie who spoke quite grammatically and had no trouble with their *h's*. Would it not be possible to find such?

The scene of unwonted freedom quite perplexed Arthur. Carrie was gone, and, as she herself said, "for good." This would necessitate some little change in daily habits, probably. Well, that could be thought of to-morrow; how was the present evening to be spent? Should he go out and entertain himself with the comedies and tragedies of the streets. Why not? It no longer mattered if he returned home a little late; there was no one to blame him. Or should he sit at home and read—aye, read in the delicious stillness of this July evening? It was long since he had read anything; there had been no leisure for that of late. Yes, certainly he would stay at home and read. It was nearly nine o'clock, and dusk was beginning to deepen into gloom, so that he must have a light to read by. Accordingly he drew a table close up to the open window, through which was blowing a warm, delicious breeze, then he lit the lamp and placed it upon the table. Now what should he read? There was but one book in which at that moment his soul delighted. He would read Vasari. Why should one deny oneself any procurable pleasure in this most uncertain of worlds?

He sat down by the table, just where the soft night air could fan his cheeks and awaken his so long-sleeping fancy, and, leaning one volume of his author against the rest, began to read. Oh, joy! It was like a draught of cool spring-water to one panting in the desert; like a fresh breeze upon the sea-cliffs to one whose energies have wasted in the hateful gloom of a manufacturing town; like the first ray of fertilising sunshine to one who long yearned in the wilderness of winter for the sweet, flowery days of spring; like the first kiss of returning health to one who has travelled even within sight of the very valley of the shadow of death. Ten, eleven, twelve boomed upon the south-west wind from the great bell at Westminster, but this evening Arthur did

not hear; one and two sounded with greater
distinctness through the silence of midnight,
but still he was feeding his soul upon stories
of the world-artists, those grand workers of
old to whose unpolluted sight was revealed
Heaven and all its glories. And so Arthur
read on, till at length sleep overcame him,
and his head sank upon the book.

He woke out of a troubled dream. He
had been enacting over again the horrible
events of that night on which he first became
aware of Carrie's fatal passion for drink. He
was on the point of rebuking Carrie in bitter
anger when he suddenly woke.

It was morning, and the sun had just
risen. Rising as quickly as his stiffened
limbs would permit him, he endeavoured to
recall the events of last night. There was
moisture in his eyes, and he still trembled
from the overwhelming passion which had
disturbed him in his dream. The first
object his eyes fell upon was the half-sheet
of note-paper containing Carrie's farewell.
He took it up, read it, looked hurriedly
round the room, and immediately burst into
tears. He wept passionately, the great sobs
bursting from him as though they would
have burst his heart. Till this moment he
had not realised the fact that Carrie was
gone, and now he thought her absence would
kill him. He wrung his hands together,
giving utterance to his agony the while in
terrible cries and moans. He uttered wild

prayers, he knew not for what or to whom; and then he ceased his exclamations to whisper in scarcely audible tones every endearing epithet he could imagine, coupling all with Carrie's name. He reproached himself in the bitterest terms for every stern word he had ever addressed to her, he blamed himself, himself only, for this terrible misfortune. Why had he not been patient? Nay, why had he not exercised ordinary kindness to his wife? It was his cruelty, his base heartlessness that had driven her away, and driven her—Oh, God!—to what?

Exhausted with his anguish he fell back upon the bed, and lay there with the hot tears streaming down his cheeks. Never till this moment did he know how he had loved Carrie. He would have given years of his life to see her once more enter the door, to have thrown himself upon the ground at her feet and begged her to forgive him. What were all her faults, seen through this haze of bitter, maddening regret and remorse? They were not faults, mere mistakes, venal and needing only the gentleness of a loving voice, the tender pressure of a loving hand, to banish them for ever. These means he persuaded himself he had never tried; no, he had endeavoured to exert a brutal authority, nothing else, and—fool that he was!—had been rightly punished. Oh, how differently would he act if only Carrie once more returned to him!

But, no ; that he must not expect. She had found someone who would love her better than he had ever done, whose affection she could return with less fear of being slighted. And hereupon the fire of a consuming jealousy broke out fiercely within him, and drove him mad with torture. Forgetful of what he had just thought, he raved against Carrie's ingratitude, her base forgetfulness of all he had done for her, of all he fain would have done if she had permitted him. But she would regret him, she would re-proach herself bitterly for having thus deserted him, and that before long. This well-dressed fop whom she had preferred to him would amuse himself with her as long as the fancy lasted, and then would fling her aside without pity. And then perhaps she would return. Oh, with what an overflowing heart would he welcome her again! But, no, she had said she would not return, and there was little hope that she would not keep her word. And then he pictured to himself her future career ; how her passions, now set free from every restraint, would scourge her on from degradation to degradation, till she met her end in some abyss of unspeakable horror. If it was fated to be so, might the end come soon !

Arthur did not leave the room during the whole day. What was daily work that he should heed it under the weight of an affliction such as this ? And, thinking of his work, he suddenly rose and went to the box in which he kept his few valuables, the same box in which Carrie had discovered Helen Norman's picture. Unlocking this, he took out a cash-box, which, on examination, he found to be untouched. He was glad that Carrie had not taken any of his money, for it showed some lingering self-respect, perhaps some regard for him still holding a place in her heart. After this he ate a few mouthfuls to still the feeling of faintness from which he had begun to suffer; then, unable to occupy himself in any way, once more lay upon the bed. At intervals he continued to weep, but for the most part he lay with dry, red eyes, looking fixedly up at the ceiling, only the constant clenching of his hands giving outward evidence of the anguish within.

It must have been nearly seven o'clock in the evening when he was startled by a knock at the door. He had risen from the bed some time since, and, after eating a little dry bread and drinking a glass of water, was bathing his face, in the endeavour to remove the startling signs of his suffering. Hastily arranging his dress, he went to the door and opened it. Mark Challenger stood outside.

"Are you alone ?" asked Mark, then added a moment after, "what on earth is the matter, Arthur? What have you been doing ?"

"Nothing at all," replied Arthur. "I

have had a little headache, that's all, and have been sleeping it off."

"I should think you have had a considerable headache," replied Mark, "judging from your appearance. Is your wife out?"

"Yes, she is away for the day," returned Arthur, after a scarcely perceptible hesitation.

"Will she be back to-night?"

"Not till to-morrow morning. Why do you ask?"

"Why, I was going to ask you to go somewhere with me—but you look so horribly ill."

"It is nothing," said the other hurriedly, "nothing! I shall be glad to go with you. It will make me think of other things, and so cure me. Where are you going to?"

"I was going to ask you to come with me to see poor John Pether. I'm afraid it's near the end with him."

"You mean that he is dying."

"I fear as much. I've had a doctor to see him these last few days, and he makes light of it. But I know John better than the doctor does. He has been lying still on his bed since yesterday morning, and hasn't spoken. I lost a day's work to-day to stay with him. You see, poor John has no one else in the world to look after him, and I'm afraid he won't trouble us long."

"I'll come at once," exclaimed Arthur, glad of any distraction. "If it seems necessary I will stay with him all night. You don't look very well yourself, Mr. Challenger."

"Why, to tell you the truth, Arthur, I was up all night with him, too, and I should take it very kind of you if you could sit with him a few hours whilst I get a nap."

They set out at once, and soon reached Charlotte Place. The umbrella-mender's shop was shut up, and, as usual under such circumstances, looked gloomy enough. Mark opened the door with a key which he drew from his pocket, and the two passed through the shop into the parlour behind.

John Pether lay in bed, his gaunt face and scanty black hair strongly relieved by the whiteness of the pillow. His features had altered so since Arthur had last seen him as scarcely to be recognisable. Their expression was ghastly ; the jaw-bones seemed almost to pierce through the skin; the lips were shrivelled and somewhat drawn back over the clenched teeth. He lay looking straight upwards, if indeed he could be said to look with eyes which were but half open, and showed no sign of intelligence. Only his right arm lay outside the clothes, and the hand was clenched so firmly that the tips of the knuckles were pure white compared with the colour of the skin elsewhere. By the side of his bed was a great heap of newspapers, those at the top lying open as though they had been lately read, those underneath carefully folded up.

"He has been reading since I left," whispered Mark as they entered. "The last thing I did was to fold up all the newspapers."

"Why does he keep such a heap by his side?" whispered Arthur in turn.

"They are papers with accounts of the Communist rebellion in Paris. He has done scarcely anything but read them for several months."

Arthur shuddered involuntarily as he pictured to himself the sick man's thoughts, how they must teem with dreadful images of slaughter. Doubtless these reports realised to John Pether the dreams of the coming revolution on which he had for years persistently dwelt.

"Is he asleep?" asked Arthur, regarding the half-open eyes with something of awe.

"I think not," whispered Mark back, "but I don't know whether he sees us. I'll speak to him."

Accordingly he approached and said some words in a low voice, to which the sick man paid no heed. He lay as though in a trance.

"Has he eaten anything to-day?" asked Arthur.

Mark shook his head.

"He ought to take a dose of the medicine on the table there about ten to-night. But I don't know whether he can be made to do it."

They exchanged a few more whispered

sentences, and then Arthur urged upon Mark to go home for a little rest, whilst he himself sat and watched. This Mark consented to do, promising, however, to return shortly after midnight and relieve his friend, who, as he said, seemed also to have much need of sleep. After a few directions with regard to the treatment of Pether, Mark left the house, and Arthur locked the shop door behind him.

Returning to the parlour, he sat down at some distance from the bed and again resigned himself to his misery. But he felt that his thoughts were more endurable even in company such as this than they would have been had he remained alone all night. Before long his mind began to occupy itself with the past history of John Pether. What glimpses he had had of this were so terrible that his imagination could scarcely err in imparting the gloomiest colours to those long years of whose events he knew nothing. What a life had been this man's even during the un-eventful period in which Arthur had known him. What terrible brooding over a hideous past, what fierce internal maledictions on that society to which his miseries were mostly due, what maddening visions of a revenge he would live to enjoy had filled up the monoto-nous days spent in the work of the gloomy little shop. He tried to recollect John Pether as he had first seen him, and he was con-scious of how great a change had come over that strongly-marked countenance during the past nine or ten years. Most rapid, however, had been the change since Mr. Tollady's death. The latter had been a true friend to John Pether, as he was to every one whom he knew to be suffering and in need of help, either in word or deed, and his friendship had kept the lonely man's mind from sinking into that hopeless abyss and madness in which it had since been overwhelmed.

He stirred slightly once or twice, showing Arthur that he was still alive, of which there might otherwise have been doubts, for the colour of his skin was like that of a dead man's, and his breathing could not be heard. Arthur would gladly have taken up one of the papers near the bed, to while away the dreary moments, but he had a fear lest his doing so should offend the sick man. So he was forced back upon his thoughts, and these were anything but enviable companions, as at length twilight deepened into gloom. The window of the chamber looked out upon a wretched little yard, in which at this moment newly-washed clothes were hanging, and these waved hither and thither in the gathering darkness with a ghostly motion. Scarcely a sound from the street could be heard, except that dull, unbroken rumble which seldom quits the ear of one sitting in a London house. Unable to bear the stillness, Arthur at length rose, stepped past the bed and lit a small lamp which stood on the mantel-piece, making a noise as he did so, in the hope of rousing Pether's attention. He was not successful in this effort, so, after leaning across the bed to draw the one dingy curtain which darkened the window, he laid his hand on the man's shoulder and spoke to him. A look of recognition seemed to rise to Pether's face, and he spoke in a low whisper.

"Put the light nearer. It is almost time. I must look again to see how *they* began."

Arthur put the light on a chair by the bed, and Pether, taking up the first newspaper which came to his hand, began to read, muttering passages half aloud. The way in which he did this sent a chill through Arthur's veins. He knew that it was mere delirium and not healthy consciousness which stimulated Pether.

He re-assumed his chair, and his thoughts once more flowed irresistibly back into the gloomy channel of his own griefs. But this time thought seemed to bring with it so great a weariness that before long the lids of his eyes sank as under weights. His slumber of the previous night had been brief and disturbed, and strong emotions had worn out every nerve. In vain he made great efforts to keep himself awake, walking up and down at one time, as well as the small chamber would permit, and trying to fix his thoughts on Pether, who had ceased to read and lay holding a paper in his lank hands. Spite of

all, his utter weariness was not to be resisted.
He fell asleep.

It appeared to him to be hours after, but
was in reality little more than ten minutes,
when he was awakened by a fearful cry which
sent all his blood rushing back upon his
heart and left him marble with terror. A
heavy hand was upon his shoulder, under the
pressure of which he in vain tried to rise.
Staring straight before him with such consciousness as he had left, he saw that it was
John Pether whose hand he felt. The latter
was standing in front of him, dressed only in
a long white shirt, in his left hand the little
lamp, and with his face so close to Arthur's
as almost to touch it. All his features seemed
red and swollen with a sudden access of
blood, and his dark eyes flashed with a fearful fiery radiance in the lamp-light. His
breath, hot and quick, came full upon the
young man's forehead, and from his lips proceeded a stream of wild and fierce eloquence,
delivered in a voice which at times all but
yelled.

"Wake!" he cried. "Wake! Can you
sleep whilst the drums are beating and the
bells are ringing so loud? Wake, and join
yon whilst you have time! We are fifty
thousand strong, and already half London is
in our hands. Everyone who is ragged or
hungry or oppressed, everyone who knows
the bitterness of long and hopeless waiting
for justice, everyone whom wrong has driven

into crime, everyone whom tyranny has made *mad*—all are with us! Hark! Now the drums have ceased, and the firing has begun. They will fight desperately, these rich men, for their bags of gold and their palaces overflowing with luxury. But what can they do against the millions of us slaves who have cast away our fetters, and know our strength? Cannon, too; not a house shall be left standing, not the latest-born of our tyrants shall live another hour!"

He raised his heavy hand from Arthur's shoulders and held it up, in an attitude as if of listening. At the same moment Arthur started to his feet. He would have fled, but he had not the strength.

"Here! Here!" yelled the maniac, a minute after. "This way! Follow me! I have a right to lead, for none have suffered more than I have. Fire these houses, and kill every living creature that flees from them! It grows dark, but the fires will light us to our work. No pity! No mercy! Aye, the women and children, too! Kill, kill, kill!"

Uttering terrific cries, he waved the lamp wildly above his head, then flung it with violence upon the floor. In the same instant he sprang forward like a wild-beast and seized Arthur around the throat. For a moment the two struggled in the dark, but for a moment only. Then the oil from the lamp suddenly igniting flamed up to the very ceiling. Instantly the great heap of newspapers had taken fire, and the conflagration spread thence, quick as thought, to the bedclothes. Arthur was conscious of the fierce glare, the terrific heat, and, very shortly, of blinding smoke; but terror had deprived him of the power of reasoning, and he knew no guide save the blind impulse to struggle for his life. It could not have been but a few minutes that he writhed beneath the madman's terrific grasp, but it seemed to him that he struggled with fury for at least an hour. He could no longer see anything but a blood-red glare swimming before his eyes, his brain seemed bursting with agony—in a moment he would have lost consciousness; but before that happened the grasp upon his throat suddenly relaxed, and he found himself free. The same instant found him wrapped in an immense cloud of stifling smoke, whilst he became aware for the first time that his clothes had caught fire. Rushing wildly in the direction of the shop, he succeeded in finding the door, and, forgetting that it opened inwards, threw himself with all his force against it repeatedly. Whilst he was doing so, the door was suddenly thrust open from without, and he found himself rushing into the open street, among a crowd of people who were shouting " Fire ! "

Still speeding onwards, he suddenly found himself seized and clung to, whilst the voice of Mark Challenger sounded in his ears.

" Good God ! " cried the latter. " Stop ! Where is John Pether ? How did it happen, Arthur ? "

For some minutes Arthur was unable to speak, then he gave in a few hurried words an account of all that had happened. Even as he spoke the cries of " Fire ! " continued to ring through the street ; and a great crowd forced the two quite away from the spot whither they were struggling. The narrow court was already filled with volumes of smoke. Mark, leaving his companion, struggled with difficulty towards the shop, and was rushing in through the open door when a policeman seized and detained him. It would have been impossible by this time to penetrate to the inner room, and Mark was compelled to stand back amid the throng, and wait the result. Before long the firemen arrived, and within an hour the fire was got sufficiently under to permit of the shop being entered. Two firemen essayed the task in company, and at the end of five minutes returned, bearing between them an unrecognisable corpse.

CHAPTER IV.

REACTION.

THE whole of the following day Arthur was bound to his bed by illness. A slight access of delirium during the night had been followed by prostrating weakness, and a headache so severe that it was agony even to move. Throughout these long hours of pain he was haunted perpetually by the memory of last night's horrors, only broken at intervals by a burst of passionate grief when he painfully raised his head and looked round the desolate room. One of Carrie's dresses still hung behind the door, and so distressing did he find the constant reverting of his eyes to this object, that he rose for a moment and removed it out of sight. He tried to sleep, but wholly in vain ; he endeavoured to read, but the letters struck in through his eyeballs upon his brain with the painfulness of a violent blow. His only resource was to lie and think.

The next night he again slept little. Rising early, he packed his large trunk with what clothing he possessed, adding a few of his favourite books, and one or two small remembrances of Carrie. This done, he sat down and wrote a brief letter to Mark Challenger, merely saying he was compelled to leave London very suddenly, and begging that Mark would take away and retain till it should be re-demanded all the property left behind in the room in Huntley Street. The letter sealed and directed, he went down and gave Mrs. Oaks notice of his intention to leave immediately, making some plausible excuse to explain his wife's absence. After that he removed his boxes by means of a cab to the nearest railway station, depositing it in the left-luggage office till he should have found himself another lodging. This object he effected before the afternoon, and the evening saw him seated in a garret which he had taken in a dreary part of Islington.

No criminal in fear of the gallows could have effected a more complete escape from the eyes of all who knew him; yet Arthur was urged to this step by no sense of guilt, merely by overwhelming shame and a blind, unreasoning desire to re-move himself entirely from the scene of his sufferings. Once established in the wretched garret, which on account of its quietness and security seemed a very haven of refuge for his storm-beaten soul, he breathed more freely. Even his body seemed to benefit by the change, for a long night of profound sleep left him altogether free from fever and with a more temperate pulse than he had known for many days. He rose shortly after six o'clock, and, throwing open

his lattice, drank in the fresh breath of the
July morning with an effect upon his spirits
almost exhilarating. The narrow street
below, bordered on either side with neglected
gardens, was absolutely still, and grass growing here and there between the paving
stones seemed to show that traffic was
almost unknown. For the moment Arthur
felt that he would ask nothing more than
to live and die, unknown, in such retirement
as this.

First of all it behoved him to consider
how he should find employment. To return
to his old place was, of course, impossible.
He had absented himself too long, and, even
had this been no objection, he was determined to shake off completely every trace of
his former life. In his purse, moreover, he
had five pounds still, and he calculated that,
by exercising economy, he could live nearly
ten weeks on this sum, for he only paid
half-a-crown a week for his garret. The
prospect of so long a period of absolute
freedom was so delightful to him that he
embraced it forthwith. Why should he
trouble to seek for work immediately? When
the time of need came a good workman like
himself could have no difficulty in finding a
place. For a while, at least, he would allow
himself to taste the rare sweets of liberty.

Throughout the day he occupied himself
pleasantly enough in reading. He was surprised at the sudden calm which had come

over him, which allowed him to put aside all
his gloomy and painful thoughts and drink
once more of his old delights, finding the
draught the sweeter from his long abstinence. Then, towards evening, he issued
forth and wandered about the back streets
of Islington, quite sure of meeting no one
who would recognise him. When it grew
dark he found himself irresistibly attracted
towards the thronging life of the larger
thoroughfares. He experienced a delight in
mingling with the crowd greater than he
could have conceived, a delight of which he
had enjoyed but a brief foretaste on the fatal
evening when Carrie's voice first became
known to him. By degrees he drew towards
the City, into the Strand. Here the glitter-
ing doorways of the theatres began to
attract him, and, after standing near one of
them for a long time, exciting his fancy by a
perusal of the play-bill, he yielded to the
voice of the charmer and entered. A comic
opera was being played, one of those thrice-
warmed French *ragoûts*, slightly unspiced to
suit the less discriminating English palate,
a dazzling *mélange* of tinsel, and dance and
song, where lovely English faces come and
go against a background of roses and melody,
and taper limbs whirl gracefully hither and
thither amid a mist of muslin. To Arthur,
who had never even witnessed the legitimate drama, this was the veritable cup of
Circe; his senses were rapt; without a

thought of resistance he yielded to the intoxicating influences of the spell.

Perhaps it will be better to render no detailed account of the few days which followed, days in which poor Arthur sounded all the depths of folly and degradation, impelled by the feverish need of distraction, of forgetting his past miseries and avoiding the thoughts of his future prospects. This was his period of Bohemianism, a phase of life from which few escape who are raised above the crowd by the fineness of their sensibilities, the warmth and strength of their imaginative powers. It lasted scarcely a week, by the end of which time every farthing was spent and every article on which money could be obtained sold or pledged. The last night was one of vulgar and brutal debauch. One does not practise economy with one's last sixpenny-piece, and there are few depths to which those will not descend whose motto has become, " Let us eat and drink, for to-morrow we die."

On the morning which followed, with hideously-swollen features, with clothing filthy and torn, shaking as if in a palsy, Arthur slunk along the back streets of Islington, seeking for some means of earning a mouthful of bread. He would not have dared to present himself at any printing-office, for his own figure reflected in the windows of the shops he passed made him shudder and shrink away in disgust. He

could now only hope for work of the meanest
kind, and that he accordingly sought. He
saw a paper in a public-house window making known the fact that a " potman " was
wanted there. He offered his services, but,
owing to his lack of experience, they were
refused. He entered one or two warehouses,
and, though at the cost of terrible struggles
with his pride, asked if they wanted a porter.
In each case he was contemptuously bidden
to go about his business. By this time it
was noon, and the odour of dinners steaming
out of the cook-shops he passed excited his
hunger past endurance. So famishing did he
at length become that, on noticing half an
apple which some child had thrown away in
the street, he waited till he thought himself
unobserved, pounced upon it, and, retreating
down a neighbouring alley, devoured it
eagerly.

Exhausted with these sufferings, he at
length sat down to rest on one of the seats
by the reservoir on the summit of Pentonville
Hill. As all who have had the misfortune
to endure semi-starvation know, the first terrible pangs of hunger are wont to be succeeded by a deadly sickness, and, when this
passes away, neither hunger nor sickness is
any longer felt, but the sufferer is for a brief
space at rest. This stage Arthur had now
reached, and for more than two hours he sat
watching the passers-by, wondering at the
ease he enjoyed. All the time his mind was

engaged in the peculiar process of unconscious reflection. Whilst he persuaded himself that he was only looking about him in a lazy manner, he was in reality engaged in accustoming himself to face the dread necessity of begging, whether of private persons or at the workhouse. What other resource was left to him? If he had shrunk from facing his friends when only deterred by shame on another's account, how utterly impossible was it now for him to request their aid when his very appearance bore unmistakable evidence to the degradation of his life. Rather than William Noble should see him now, he felt that he would die of hunger.

Evening approached, and once more the voracious wolf, hunger, began to gnaw angrily at his vitals. If he was not to die in the street, he must do something now. He rose, but at first could not walk, staggering back against the wall. Turning out of Pentonville Road he went by the quieter neighbourhood in the direction of Gray's Inn Road. Before long he arrived before a baker's shop. No one was inside but a young girl, and she seemed to Arthur to have a pleasant look. He felt that it would be but little degradation to beg of her, and, if she refused him, he was sure she would do so gently. So, after a moment's hesitation, he forced himself to enter the shop, and, with face burning and voice which did not seem to be his own, he begged for a penny roll. The young girl looked at him for a moment in surprise, perhaps alarm, but the next he saw her eyes lighting up with womanly compassion, and he knew that he had not begged in vain.

"Put it in your pocket, quick," she said, as she gave him a small loaf. "If father was to come in he wouldn't like me to give it you."

Arthur only replied by a look of the intensest gratitude, and instantly left the shop. Never had food tasted so sweet to him as this did, but, alas! how little there was of it. Nevertheless, it had stilled for the time the fiercest pangs of hunger, and, as he had not the courage to beg again, he began to make his way homewards, hoping to forget in sleep all the agonies of the past and the still gloomier prospect of the future.

He rose early next morning, weak and feverish, but resolved once more to set forth and endeavour to find employment. In a day or two he would have to pay his rent again ; failing that, he would most likely find himself homeless as well as starving. Yes, for this one day he would do his utmost to find work. If he should again fail he had no idea what he should do. Possibly the extremity of need might drive him to the humiliation of seeking either Mark Challenger or William Noble. With no other refreshment than a glass of water, he issued forth on his hopeless task. But he had over-rated his strength. With the utmost difficulty he toiled slowly along, past the Angel and as far as the reservoir; but here his powers altogether failed him, and he was obliged once more to make use of the seats. Every limb trembled with exhaustion, his forehead bathed in a cold sweat, at his heart a feeling as though a great flood of tears was there gathering in readiness to rush resistlessly to his eyes; he sank upon the bench. As he did so a deep sob broke involuntarily from between his lips.

On the same bench was sitting an elderly gentleman, engaged in reading the newspaper. Arthur had scarcely noticed him, but, when the sob of anguish made itself heard, the old gentleman looked up from his paper and regarded Arthur curiously. The latter's eyes were fixed upon the ground in a dull despairing gaze. After once or twice looking up from his paper, the old gentleman moved slightly nearer to his companion on the bench, and asked him if he was in trouble. Arthur stared at the speaker for a moment as if unable to collect his faculties, but then a ray of hope lit up his countenance, and he replied that he was indeed in trouble, for he had been looking for employment a long time without success. The old gentleman, still surveying him with the somewhat critical eye of one who did not lack experience in the world's impostures, proceeded to enquire as to the kind of employment he required, and, on receiving the information, turned back calmly

to his paper, and for some minutes appeared to peruse it in forgetfulness of Arthur. Such, however, was not really the case; for all at once he turned round, and handed the paper to the young man, pointing, as he did so, to an item in the advertising columns. Arthur saw that it was an advertisement for a compositor, the address being in Edgware Road.

"Do you think it worth your while to go after it?" asked the stranger, still eyeing Arthur keenly.

"Certainly I do, sir," he replied, with as cheerful a voice as he could command. "I shall go at once. Thank you very much for your kindness."

The old gentleman nodded pleasantly, and Arthur rose with a fresh impulse of hope. But the first few steps showed him how miserably weak he was. Edgware Road was at the very least three miles away. He felt that it would be impossible to walk the distance. He was on the point of falling from absolute exhaustion when he felt a hand on his shoulder, and, turning, saw again the old gentleman by his side.

"Bye-the-by," asked the latter, "have you had any breakfast this morning?"

Arthur replied in the negative, with a sickly smile.

"Or any dinner yesterday?"

Arthur shook his head.

"Then how are you likely to get work?"

asked the other. " Or what use would it be
when you'd got it ? "

Arthur made no reply, but he saw that his
unknown friend had in the meantime taken
out his purse.

" I have a mind to try an experiment,"
said the old gentleman. " There's half a
sovereign, and there's my card. If you get
work and feel disposed to consider this money
as a loan, you can come and pay it back to
me at that address. You understand ? "

" Perfectly well, thank you sir," replied
Arthur. " If I live to earn a week's wages
you will certainly see me."

" I hope to do so," returned the other.
" Now go and get something to eat, for you
look as if you wanted it."

Arthur stammered out his thanks as well
as he could, and the old gentleman, after
nodding pleasantly once more, departed on
his way.

Without further detail I will state that
Arthur succeeded in obtaining the employment he sought, though not without great
difficulty, owing to his lack of recommenda-
tions. It was a very small business, and the
master was not a particularly agreeable man ;
but he saw that Arthur would be a useful
man in his office, and took advantage of the
circumstances of the case to arrange with
him for the lowest possible wages. They
would be just enough to live on, however,
and at present this was all that Arthur cared

for. The same evening he gave up his garret
in Islington, exchanging it for a far less
agreeable abode in Chapel Street, distant
only some five minutes' walk from his employment.

With the following day began a period of
hopeless, grinding toil, of long days spent in
miserably-recompensed labour, followed by
nights which hunger often made hideous with
restlessness or terrifying dreams. For, spite
of terrible temptations, the strength of which
could only be realised by one who has been
in similar positions, Arthur persisted in his
resolution of saving every penny he possibly
could towards paying off his debt. It took
him a month, with the utmost economy, to
save the ten shillings. How often, as he
returned from his work at night, was he
tempted to spend some of his savings and
enjoy the luxury of a satisfying meal; what
ghastly fascination was there in the glaring
fronts of the public-houses, beckoning him to
enter and, in a few draughts of fiery liquor,
forget at once his hunger and that vain folly
which men call honour. Why should he suffer
so to pay this debt? The lender did not
know his name, and it was scarcely probable
that he should trouble to remember the address of the advertising printer. For all that
Arthur was determined to repay the debt:
common gratitude, if no finer feeling, demanded that he should do so. And, after
hours of fierce conflict with himself, after

weeks of the most utter misery which even these few shillings could greatly have relieved, Arthur did repay the debt. He would not venture to carry the money in his pocket as far as Islington, where the old gentleman lived; the temptation on the way might prove too strong, and any little accident, such as the gentleman's absence from home, might lead to a fatal hesitation. The difficulty was better got over by the agency of a post-office order. With a sigh of ineffable relief, Arthur addressed this from the card his benefactor had given him, and posted it.

This was on Saturday afternoon. The same evening Arthur sank into a terrible despondency, a sickness of the heart, exceeding in misery even that bodily suffering to which he was now becoming almost reconciled. With the repayment of the debt, it seemed as though an impulse to healthy exertion had been suddenly withdrawn; henceforth there was nothing to look forward to but an arid future spreading out into interminable tracts of hopeless toil. To obtain a better place was almost impossible, for he now knew his employer sufficiently well to be sure that he would not aid him the least to improve his position, but would rather do his utmost to retain him in this state of servitude. Arthur was rapidly losing all self-respect, all hope of better things, all thoughts above his every-day labour and every-day needs. He never opened a book to read a page, for he felt no longer any interest in the cultivation of his mind. To what end should he trouble? Even the recollection of the wealth of which little more than half a year would make him master brought with it no saving grace. For he had lost all faith in himself. How would he be better off when he possessed his five thousand pounds? Certainly he would not suffer from starvation, but, otherwise, how would he differ from what he was at present? Evidently fate had declared that his should be a useless, unproductive life, and it was vain to struggle against the decree. With a bitter smile he reflected upon the hopes and the aspirations of past years; already they were growing so dim, so unsubstantial to his memory, that he could with difficulty realise the power they had once exercised over his life. He thought of Helen Norman—indeed no single day passed on which he did not still think of her—and he was glad that her portrait was in the safe keeping of his friend Noble; if it had been in his own possession he could not have refrained from continually looking at it, and the indulgence could have had no consequence save perpetual self-torture. Of course, she who was still his wife in the dogged estimation of the law, he thought of less often, and always with a vague species of compassion which was not altogether without a mixture of resentment. If she was now suffering from the consequences of her folly, what else could she have expected? And was *he* not suffering ? Had he not suffered as much as, aye more than it was possible for her to suffer, and wholly in consequence of her conduct? On the other hand she might still be living in luxury, supported by the infatuation of some wealthy admirer; and in that case was she worthy of pity? Aye, even then worthy of infinite pity. For she had voluntarily exchanged the devotion of a faithful heart for the sensual caprice of a fop, an unprincipled rake, and her hour of utter wretchedness could not in any case be far off. In such passing moments Arthur felt that there was still a spot of tenderness in his heart for the poor, weak fool; but the love, the passion which had once inflamed him, that had gone never to return.

Monday came, and he went to his work as usual. When he came home at dinner-time he was surprised to find a letter for him, directed in a hand of which he had not the least knowledge. He opened it, and found it contained a short note from the old gentleman in Islington, acknowledging the receipt of the ten shillings, expressing his extreme gratification at finding Arthur's promise adhered to, and, finally, returning the money with the request that Arthur would accept it as a mark of his creditor's esteem.

It was a fatal present. With this unwonted wealth in his pocket, Arthur no longer felt compelled to deny himself so vigorously as hitherto every little indulgence that might make his life at least more tolerable. The same night he yielded unresistingly to the attraction of the public-house, and, after the first draught, he continued to drink with the sole object of inducing oblivion. In his present condition this was the utmost happiness he could hope for, and this he attained. Even whilst doing his best to enervate his faculties of thought, however, he remembered the narrowness of his resources and resolved to avoid wild debauch. Not to-night only would he need to deaden his self-consciousness, but for many and many a night to come, and he must carefully husband the means for purchasing forgetfulness. He knew that on the morrow he should pay the penalty in horrible suffering, but what was that compared with these few hours of blessed delight?

Soon every night saw him wandering from bar to bar, brutalising himself with whatever cheap poison came within his means, then staggering home to his garret to spend the few hours before daylight in heavy unconsciousness. The day grew to be nothing but a preparation for the night, a dreary waste of hours which must somehow be plodded through in order that the oasis of the night might be reached. Life such as this soon destroyed his appetite, and the diminished need for food left more money for drink. He was past reflection; in the few hours during which he was capable of

continued thought he bound his mind down
to the task before him, not daring to look
before or behind. He grew altogether negli-
gent of his personal appearance, and his very
features seemed to partake of the degeneration of his mind. Day by day the clouds of
misery seemed to envelope his life closer and
closer. It seemed as if either the hospital
or the gaol must ere long behold the close of
such a career.

At length he lost his place. Of late he
had been growing more and more irregular
in his time of appearance at the office, and
for some weeks his master had been on the
point of discharging him. At length, without
any warning, he was supplanted in the office,
and was told that his services were no longer
needed. The same evening he was under an
obligation to pay considerable arrears of rent,
or else to quit his lodgings. Taking the
money his master paid him, he discharged as
much of his debt as possible, and once more
found himself homeless and penniless in the
streets, just as night was falling.

In this moment of despair came a thought
which had several times of late passed through
his mind, but which he had never yet been
courageous enough firmly to face. Now with
the thought, the courage came also. He
dwelt upon it, looked at it in all its phases,
made up his mind to pursue it even to the
end. That thought led him along the
Marylebone Road, eastwards. As he passed

the workhouse, it was the time when the "casuals" were beginning to assemble in order to seek admittance for the night. They stood in a long row against the wall, wretches of all ages, and of every degree of misery, some emaciated with incurable disease, some hale and strong, their only ailment being laziness, all exhibiting in their persons the results of abject poverty. Ever since early morning it had rained unceasingly, and at this moment the rain streamed down pitilessly from the blackening sky upon the row of drenched and shivering creatures. The sight of them made Arthur pause for a moment, as if a doubt had crossed his mind, but the next moment he walked rapidly on muttering to himself, " Never, never ! "

The thought led him down Tottenham Court Road and then off to the left into Huntley Street. He stood still for a moment in the darkness before the house where he had lived with Carrie, and a thrill of horror at the recollection of all he had suffered there made his heart chiller than the body which contained it, though the wet and cold of this November night had numbed every limb. With a bitter curse upon his fate, he passed hurriedly on, again crossed Tottenham Court Road, and found himself in a few minutes in Charlotte Place. He knew that Mr. Tollady's shop had long since disappeared, being replaced by a larger one of a different nature, but still it was a pleasure to him to see the place where it had been, the narrow street in which the only happy time of his life had been passed. John Pether's shop was also transformed. He and Mr. Tollady were at rest. Mark Challenger, the third of those friends of his boyhood, no doubt still lived, but Arthur's business was no longer with the living.

The thought soon bore him away, once more eastwards. It was now black night, and the rain came down more pitilessly than ever. Twenty minutes' sharp walk brought him into the Strand, and here he hesitated. The object of his thought now lay at a very short distance below him. Which of these narrow streets should he take in his way to the river? What spot was likely to be the quietest? Where could one seek eternal rest with least danger of interference?

Unconsciously he had passed at a very short distance from Noble's abode, which was in one of the dark and narrow streets between which he was choosing. As he meditated, the recollection of this occurred to his mind. Why not choose that street as well as another? Possibly there might be a light in Noble's window, and the comparison between his friend's condition and his own would be a new means of strengthening his resolve. At once he crossed the Strand and entered the narrow street.

*   *   *   *   *

On the present evening William Noble was sitting alone in his lodgings, pursuing a train of thought, which, to judge from his countenance, was none of the most agreeable. His room was a very small one, on the third story, at once a bed and a sitting room. A cheerful fire burned in the grate, and its warm rays did their best to expel the recollection of the dreary waste of waters upon which the night had descended. Noble had drawn a little deal-topped table near to the fire, apparently with the intention of reading. At his elbow lay open a volume of Mill's "Political Economy," and on the table were also volumes exhibiting the names of Ricardo and Malthus. On one side of the room was a small book-case, containing some thirty or forty books of a very substantial appearance, a closer examination of which would have shown them nearly all to be works bearing on social problems. The library was an index to its owner's mind. By nature grave, earnest, enthusiastic, and, withal, intensely matter-of-fact, Noble found a thoroughly congenial study in the severe problem of social science. Though tender-hearted as few men are, he knew little of literature in its more humanising products; poetry and all the sweet and tender offshoots of the imagination he cared nothing for. Intensely convinced that he lived in an age of savage facts which required the most resolute facing, it was in the attempt

to face and master them that he found his
highest delight.

But even John Stuart Mill seemed to have
but little attraction for him this evening. He
sat over the fire with his forehead resting in
his hands, much troubled in countenance.
And in fact he had much to make him sad
and thoughtful. The club which he had
worked so hard to establish and to inspire
with some portion of his own lofty unselfishness had utterly collapsed a few months since,
collapsed beyond hope of reconstruction. The
history of this enterprise had done much to
disabuse Noble of his extreme confidence in
human sincerity and strength of purpose. He
saw that the problems before him were indeed
far more difficult than he had been wont to
represent them to his own mind. His confidence in his own powers of judging individual men, moreover, had lately received a
severe shock. A friend of whom he thought
very highly had recently obtained from him
a loan of a very large portion of his savings,
and had immediately disappeared, without
trace. The loss of the money weighed but
little with Noble in comparison with the loss
of trust in his friend.

But at present these matters, though supplying a gloomy background for his reflections, were not the principal object of his
thoughts. Just now he was thinking of Arthur
Golding. For months he had lost sight of
Arthur completely ; he knew not whether he

was living or dead. Shortly after the death
of John Pether, he had been visited by Mark
Challenger, who had told him all that he knew
concerning their common friend, but beyond
this he had been able to learn nothing whatever. The loss of Arthur's companionship
had been felt severely by Noble, more severely,
indeed, than he could have anticipated; for
now that he had had leisure to reflect long
upon the memory of his friend, he felt that
his had been the only one among his acquaintances upon whose genuine sympathy and
understanding he could truly rely. He saw
clearly the many points in which Arthur's
character differed from his own, but he understood also that it was on account of these
very differences that he had grown so to like
him. About Arthur there had always been
something of pleasing mystery, in reality the
halo of genius, to the impression of which
Noble had gladly submitted, though in no
wise comprehending its nature. Had he
known the real bent of his friend's genius it
is probable that he would not have sympathised with it at all; but as long as the
genius had merely found expression in the
glance of his eyes, the energy of his conversation, the unselfish nature of his aims, Noble
recognised in it a vague superiority to which
he had himself no claim, and grew to love
its possessor.

So ill at ease did he become by indulging
these thoughts, that before long he found it

intolerable to remain alone. He was quite unable to study, and, after one or two vain efforts at so distracting his mind, he closed his books, rose, and prepared to go out. He resolved that he would visit Mark Challenger and ask if he had any news of Arthur. No doubt the errand would be in vain, but a most unwonted restlessness rendered it absolutely necessary that he should be active. A sharp walk through such a night would surely restore him to his usual quietude, if anything would.

Noble put on his top-coat, took his umbrella, and descended the stairs. As he threw open the front door and was on the point of leaving the house, he suddenly started back confounded. The light from the hall lamp streaming out into the black street had illuminated a face and form bearing some kind of hideous resemblance to the object of the past hour's uneasy thoughts. Something like a startled look of recognition had also risen to the face before him, whose pallid ghastliness was for a moment shot over with a slight flush; but the same instant both face and form had vanished, swallowed up, as it seemed, in the darkness. At once Noble had re-collected his faculties, and darted out in pursuit. He caught a glimpse of a black shape fleeing beneath a street-lamp a few yards before him, and he chased it like a hunter in pursuit of his game. The black shape had just come into view beneath the next lamp, and Noble was on the point of springing upon it, when suddenly it fell prostrate, with a thud which sounded clearly through the quiet street. As the object of his pursuit fell, Noble sprang to his side.

" Golding ! Arthur Golding ! " he exclaimed, bending over the prostrate form. " Is it you ?"

But there was no answer. Turning the face up to the light, Noble saw that it was without doubt his friend whom he had encountered, but whether now living or dead it was more difficult to decide. Arthur was pallid and cold as marble, and his limbs seemed to have stiffened as he fell. No trace of breath escaped from between the thin lips. His hat had fallen off in the chase, and his matted thick hair was rapidly becoming soaked with the rain, as all his clothing already was. As he raised the prostrate head, Noble felt something warm upon his fingers, and, hastily examining them by the lamp, found that it was blood.

With the aid of a policeman, who fortunately happened to pass, Noble quickly removed the insensible man into the nearest public-house, where means were rapidly applied for his restoration. In half an hour Arthur was able to rise and accompany his preserver home. Since his recovery he had scarcely spoken, and his replies to Noble's questions were brief and incoherent. Fearing lest some serious illness should overtake him in the

night, Noble put him at once into his own
bed, and himself sat up till far into the night.
About two o'clock, seeing that Arthur slept
a sound and apparently healthy sleep, he
made a bed of the arm-chair and sought by
the fire-side a few hours' rest.

In the morning, Arthur woke with his
faculties undisturbed, though so weak in
body that he was quite unable to rise. Accordingly, Noble left him in bed, whilst he
went to his day's work. Arthur lay all day long
occupied with his own mingled reflections,
scarcely knowing whether to be glad or sorry
that fate had rescued him from the death he
had contemplated and brought him once
more in connection with his friend. He felt
no disposition to stir, or to find other occupation than that afforded by his thoughts.
He needed these hours of quietness to become
reconciled to the change in his prospects, to
call his mind once more back to the world
with which he had believed himself to have
done. As yet he was not able to regard himself as a responsible being. William Noble
had saved his life, and with him must lie the
disposal of his future. Probably this day of
perfect mental and bodily rest was the
happiest Arthur had experienced since his
marriage. He was, as it were, transformed
into a child. Who of us that has lived to do
earnest battle on our own account with the
stern forces of life would not be glad to return, even for a day, to the condition of a

child, to be devoid of cares for the future, of regret for the past, to think of nothing save the moment's joy, secure in a parent's omnipotent affection? Such was Arthur's state of mind throughout this day. With the desire of life he had cast aside all life's responsibilities. To Noble belonged the care for his future, and in Noble's friendship he had absolute confidence.

He could scarcely believe that a whole day had passed when his friend returned in the evening. Noble asked no questions, but evidently left it to Arthur himself either to relate or withhold his story. It was Arthur's first wish to make a confidant of his preserver, to impart to him without reserve the long course of troubles which had so nearly terminated in his death. And this he did the same evening, Noble sitting by his bed, listening with a sad interest as Arthur passed from point to point of his melancholy narrative. The narrator had no expressions strong enough to give utterance to the scorn, the hatred with which he regarded himself for his conduct during the past few months. He did not beg for sympathy, he spoke no word of self-justification. He had wittingly and of set purpose endeavoured to brutalise his own nature, and it might be he had so far succeeded that his old self had gone for ever. In his bodily weakness he even shed bitter tears of self-reproach. The emotion did him good, and the whole confession, by forcing him to behold himself in an objective light, imparted a healthiness to his mind which it was very long since he had enjoyed.

When Arthur ceased speaking, Noble reflected in silence for nearly ten minutes.

" And of your wife you know absolutely nothing?" he asked at length, regarding his friend with the sharp but kindly scrutiny of his clear grey eyes.

" Nothing," replied Arthur, who had sunk back enfeebled.

Again there was a long silence.

" I have thought over the course to be pursued during the whole day," began Noble again, " and in what you have told me there is nothing to make me alter my plans. Do you feel very weak?"

"At present, very. But it will soon go. I am not feverish, or otherwise ill. I shall be myself to-morrow."

" Let us rather say in a week. Now listen to what I propose. You remember the Vennings?"

Arthur nodded.

" They have a room to let in their house. Now I propose that you should take this room. I tell them that you have had an illness, and that gets over all difficulties. In the meantime I look out for a place for you, whilst you occupy yourself in getting strong. How do you like the scheme?"

" But, my dear Noble," said Arthur, turning his head, with a smile more resembling that of old than had yet risen to his face, "you forget that I am penniless."

"Certainly not. It is you that forget that I am your friend, and may claim a friend's rights. Sufficient to say that *I* am not penniless. Have you any other objection?"

Arthur's strength was already well-nigh exhausted by the long conversation, and, had he wished to object further, he had not the power. Taking Noble's hand, he pressed it firmly between both his own. Then he closed his eyes, and, still holding the hand of his staunch friend, dropped to sleep like a child.

CHAPTER V.

HEART-CRAVINGS.

THE reader—whom it is an author's happy privilege to suppose profoundly interested in the book before him—may possibly have felt some little inquisitiveness relative to Mr. Gilbert Gresham's movements since he took prudent flight before the dangerous attractions of his ward. Prior to the autumn of the present year, the artist had maintained desultory communication with the house in Portland Place, his brief letters being in each case addressed to Mrs. Cumberbatch. He always requested to be kindly remembered to Miss Norman, and desired that she would not fail to acquaint him with any service he could perform for her. Politeness required such sentences as these, and it was very rarely indeed that Mr. Gresham deviated from the laws of conventional courtesy. For the rest, he appeared to have perfectly recovered his health and spirits. He was somewhat unsettled, living principally in Italy, with an occasional visit to Switzerland or Germany; but lately he gravitated towards Paris, always his favourite city, but which he could not persuade himself to visit till quite assured that he should find there peace and quietude. His art was by no means neglected. During the present year, he had sent several pictures to England, three of which had found a place in the Academy exhibition.

But, early in August, Mrs. Cumberbatch had received a letter from her nephew, containing more momentous news than that with which his epistles were ordinarily freighted. In the first place, he acquainted his aunt with the fact that the end of the month would in all probability see him again in England. He was coming over with a party of friends from Paris, who were desirous of making a brief tour in the United Kingdom, some half-dozen of whom he would probably entertain for a few weeks at his house before they commenced, and as they returned from their expedition. The next and more important item of intelligence, was to the effect that the lease of the house in Portland Place terminated on Christmas Day of the present year, and that, all things considered, he did not think he should renew it. He was at present in negociation for the purchase of a house in Versailles. Should he effect this purchase, he should take up his abode indefinitely in France. Nothing was said of either Mrs. Cumberbatch or Helen Norman. The former might, of course, consider herself as very shortly to be *de trop*. The latter, when, made acquainted with the contents of this letter, could not help wondering somewhat anxiously what views her worthy guardian entertained with regard to her future.

The suspense of both was put to an end when, towards the middle of August, Mr. Gresham himself appeared, accompanied by the threatened Parisian friends. The meeting with her guardian was not so awkward as Helen had feared. Mr. Gresham had come forward to meet her with a pleasant smile, and, whilst shaking her hand, had spoken a few agreeable words in a manner as far from embarrassment as could well be imagined. He was evidently quite his old self, with the exception that his cynicism had become even a little more pronounced. Throughout his guests' stay, he spoke but little with Helen, limiting himself to gentlemanly solicitude on the score of her health, and exchanging a few words with regard to Maud and her husband, both of whom, bye-the-by, were present once or twice to meet the French visitors. Helen could not help marvelling where his paternal feelings had gone to when he spoke on the latter subject. He mentioned Maud very much as he would have mentioned any newly-married young lady with whom he had been acquainted, and appeared glad that she moved a good deal in the world. Maud rather wanted *ton* he said, and in this way she would acquire it.

Helen was rather surprised that her guardian made no mention to her of his proposed change of residence, and at length concluded that either he had altered his mind, or he would not speak on the subject till his return from the tour. But, on the last day, Mr. Gresham intimated to her that he would be glad of half-an-hour's private conversation in the library, and she went thither with pleasure in the prospect of having her doubts solved.

Mr. Gresham stood with his back to the fire when his ward entered, and, stepping forward with a motion of the utmost politeness, he begged her to be seated. He began to speak as if the conversation was to be no more than an ordinary one.

" I am glad to see, Miss Norman," he said, with a smile of polished cynicism, " that you have abandoned to ruder, and therefore more suitable, hands the task with which you were employed when I left England."

He had always addressed her as Miss Norman since his return, never as Helen.

" I fear I have obtained your good opinion by false pretences," replied Helen, also smiling, though in her own frank manner.

" What! You still play the part of an aggravated species of sister of mercy ? "

" I still do what little good I can," she replied.

" But I think you have never been absent for any great time since we have been here ? "

" It would have been scarcely respectful to these ladies and gentlemen to absent myself each day."

" And you continue to go to the unknown regions of the East ? "

" There is still no lack of employment there."

He paused for a few moments, still smiling, though with a subdued expression of surprise upon his countenance.

" Mrs. Cumberbatch probably acquainted you," he resumed, " with my intention to give up this house, and live near Paris ? "

" She did."

" Yes," he continued, looking up to the ceiling with a curious smile of self-ridicule. " I hesitated long and gravely between the Dorsetshire farm and a very passable little house in Versailles, and at length I arrived at the conclusion that my temperament lacked somewhat the bucolic side. It is just possible I might be *ennuyé* in Dorsetshire before many years had passed, just possible. So I decided ultimately for Versailles. Do you approve the choice, Miss Norman ? "

" I think you did wisely to follow your individual tastes."

" You do ? Then I am happy. Well, my lease here is out at Christmas. Do you think you can arrange with Mrs. Cumberbatch to be ready by then ? "

" You forget, Mr. Gresham, that you have not acquainted me with your plans regarding both of us."

" My plans ? " he returned, with an affectation of surprise. " *Mais certainement—*

pardon me, I should say, certainly I have. Of course my house is entirely at your service, Miss Norman, whether it be situated in London or Versailles."

Helen stood silent in extreme surprise.

"Have you any objection to living in France?" continued Mr. Gresham.

"No objection on the score of the country," she replied. "But at present I could not think of leaving London. I need not explain my reasons, Mr. Gresham. In your eyes they are foolish enough, no doubt, but with me they outweigh every consideration."

"*Mon Dieu! Ces Anglaises!*" exclaimed the artist, imitating with comical accuracy the tone and gesture of a Frenchman. "Well, to tell you the truth, Miss Norman, I was more than half prepared for this, and I had considered the contingency. Probably if I proposed it to you, you would only too gladly consent to take up your abode in one of those savoury courts or alleys which abound in the Oriental clime. But in such a course I fancy I see something scarcely becoming Miss Norman's position. Indeed there might be some people so evil-disposed as to censure Miss Norman's guardian under such circumstances."

"I think it probable," returned Helen, smiling.

"Just so. Then it remains for me to think of some suitable habitation for you. You would, of course, think it desirable that Mrs.

Cumberbatch should continue to live with you?"

Helen assented out of mere politeness, though it is needless to say she would gladly have dismissed Mrs. Cumberbatch from her sight for ever.

"Again, just so. Then, may I ask, Miss Norman, whether there is any quarter of London in which you would prefer me to look for a suitable house?"

"I have only one ground of choice," replied Helen. "It must be within easy access of the East End."

"So I imagined," replied her guardian, smiling sardonically. "Then you permit me to be your agent in this matter?"

"I shall feel grateful if you will undertake the trouble."

"No trouble whatever," replied Mr. Gresham, politely.

And so the conversation ended. When she reflected upon it, Helen could not but wonder at the easy manner in which Mr. Gresham relieved himself of the more tedious responsibilities of guardianship. It was evident that he had never seriously contemplated her accompanying him to France. There was something of refined selfishness in the whole arrangement; Helen perceived it, but it did not distress her. Indeed the prospect of living in a small house of her own was very delightful to her. Mrs. Cumberbatch was the only drawback, but she scarcely saw how it could be possible to relinquish that lady's chaperonage. With Mrs. Cumberbatch herself, meanwhile, Mr. Gresham had held a longer and more serious conversation. The aunt and nephew understood each other wonderfully well. Mr. Gresham knew that in Mrs. Cumberbatch he had someone on whom he could thoroughly rely, as long as he made it coincident with her own interest to be trustworthy. Among his instructions to her were strong injunctions that she should do her utmost to bring Helen more into society. The sooner the latter was comfortably married out of the way, the better for Mr. Gresham's ease, regard for which bade fair soon to monopolise the whole of that gentleman's attention.

The visit of her guardian and his guests had furnished a brief distraction from Helen's ordinary life ; certainly no highly agreeable distraction, but still sufficient to give a momentary new current to her thoughts. The exercise of French conversation, which she had so long disused from lack of opportunity, was in itself pleasant, awakening all manner of strange by-gone memories, wafting back to her, like a sweet perfume, the recollection of happier years. Then the anticipation of a pleasant change of abode at the year's end was useful in giving her fresh matter for reflection, and averting her mind from the perpetual brooding over sad thoughts which had long since begun to set its mark upon her face in

pallid cheeks and dark circles around the
eyes. But these sensations were not of an
enduring nature. Scarcely had the strangers
left the house, when her mind renewed the
thread of its every-day reflections, and continued to spin out the sorrowful web of its
existence as though the task had known no
interruption.

In addition to the sadness caused by the
gradual annihilation of too sanguine hopes
as regarded her toils among the poor, Helen
had begun to suffer from causes of a more
personal nature, from pain which had its
beginning and end in the circumstances of
her own individual being. Though she had
hitherto been rather wont to pride herself on
the possession of a philosophical mind which
was all in all to itself, finding in her studies,
her reveries, and the reflections to which her
every-day work gave rise, all sufficing
sources of occupation, of late a sad conviction had been working its way into her heart
that these were not enough, that her being
suffered a lack of nourishment, and yearned
for stronger food. Sad conviction indeed it
was, for to Helen's mind it implied some loss
of self-esteem, some perceptible falling away
from the ideal life to which she had trained
herself, some condescension to the weakness
of less noble natures. The uneasy longing,
which months ago had assumed no more definite shape than that of occasional depression
bred of disappointment in her aims, had now

grown to proportions far more formidable, and was every day assuming the character of a recognisable aspiration. She felt lonely. She knew not the sweet pleasure of possessing some true friend to whom she could impart the secret workings of her spirit, from whom she could look for quick, unfailing sympathy, and to whom in turn she could become the source of vivifying consolation. Mr. Heatherley, though in many things of great benefit to her, was not and could not be such a friend as this. Though standing on the common ground of universal charity, the impulse of each came from such entirely opposite quarters, the highest sympathies of each were so totally different in their natures, that the growth between them of anything resembling a perfect union of the spirit was never to be thought of. And yet Mr. Heatherley was the nearest friend that she possessed. All others were mere acquaintances. Living as she had always done in almost complete seclusion as far as the society of cultivated people was concerned, Helen had only once found herself in contact with a nature before which her own felt disposed to bow. Once and once only had a voice struck the chords of her heart and elicited what seemed to her like the barely perceptible prelude to a delicious harmony. It was possible she might have been mistaken; closer acquaintance might have dispelled this first illusion and rendered to her her freedom;

but the chance of thus proving it had never been afforded her, for the object of her first timid heart-stirrings had suddenly vanished, and, what was more, in anger with herself. Yes; Arthur Golding's long-cherished worship was not without its counterpart, though struggling and undeveloped, in Helen's breast. Nor was it altogether unsuspected by its object, for Helen never forgot the circumstance of her own portrait so carefully separated, as if from less precious things, among Arthur's drawings. And now in these days of increasing trouble, when the yearning for individual fellowship seemed to be consuming her physical powers, the noble-minded girl dwelt more frequently than ever on the recollections which Arthur's name awakened. If the secret portraying of her face had meant anything more than a mere artist's fancy, did the feeling which had prompted it still live in the young man's heart? Frequently when she sat down to think of other things she found herself drifting away to thoughts of Arthur, wondering where he now lived, whether he still pursued the study of painting, whether he had changed in appearance? There had been a certain mystery in his sudden break with her guardian, the cause of which she felt convinced could not merely lie in that capricious temper to which Mr. Gresham had referred it. The knowledge she had since gained of the latter's character induced her to believe that the fault had been more probably on his side than on that of his pupil, and the circumstance of Arthur's relinquishing the benefit of his legacy till he could legally claim it decidedly pointed to a loftiness of spirit which would be superior to petty irritations. She would very much have liked to ask her guardian whether he knew anything of Arthur, but delicacy forbade her doing so. She had half unconsciously begun to hope that, when the time came for the payment of the legacy, she could not but hear something more of the young artist; but with her knowledge of Mr. Gresham's plans came the certainty that this hope would be frustrated. Much better to expel these foolish fancies from her mind and strive to reconcile herself to her dread loneliness.

I said that Mr. Heatherley was Helen's only friend, but it will perhaps be remembered that I have previously, when speaking of Lucy Venning, intimated the growth between the latter and Miss Norman of an attachment very similar to real friendship. And indeed, though there was too little of mental equality in the case to furnish a basis for the highest reciprocal affection, the benefit derived from their strengthening relations to each other was not exclusively on the side of the least gifted. Lucy, it is true, looked up to Helen as to some superior being, listened with the attention of an admiring disciple to her lightest words, and doubtless profited much by her conversation. On the other hand, to talk with Lucy was a sweet refreshment to Helen's moral nature. The girl's heart was so frank, so joyous, so absolutely pure, the piety which ruled her every thought, word and action was so unaffected and genuine, that Helen was not unfrequently led to compare her own acquired refinement with Lucy's natural perfection and to feel that she was the loser by the comparison. In her examination of the depths of this limpid nature, Helen had long since arrived at its one and only secret, and in this secret, she had since fancied, lay the origin of much that was charming in Lucy. The reader already knows what this secret was. Wide as was the apparent distance between them, Mr. Heatherley had, without effort, and, indeed, unconsciously, obtained the complete conquest of the young girl's heart. He was all in all to her. Long ago she had regarded him with no other feeling than the deepest reverence, due at once to his personal character and to the office which he filled. But as the clergyman's intimacy with her father had grown, and she saw more of his abundant charity, his unfailing kindness and gentleness of disposition, his manly fortitude of character, she had insensibly cherished warmer feelings, and now she knew to her sorrow that she loved him. William Noble she respected and felt warmly for as a friend, but his entrance never caused her heart to leap and her face to blush as did that of Mr. Heatherley. She knew well the feeling with which William regarded her, and knew also that nothing would have pleased her father more than to see her his wife ; and the consciousness that her heart was devoted to a hopeless affection, refusing to turn where prudence and filial love seemed alike to point to, often made her sad when her sadness could not be observed.

Helen had divined all this almost as soon as she had become sufficiently intimate with Lucy to visit occasionally at her house, and make the acquaintance of Mr. Venning. Lucy's talk to her was so frequently of Mr. Heatherley that she could not but suspect how matters stood, and one or two questions so put that Lucy could not foresee their purpose, soon completed the discovery. It grieved Helen that she could see no trace in the clergyman's conduct of his being aware of the girl's passion, to say nothing of in any way reciprocating it. It appeared to her that Lucy would make her friend an admirable wife ; just such a wife, indeed, as a man in his position should desire. She knew that he placed more value on moral worth than on intellectual attainment, and also that he was enough of a Radical to altogether disregard Lucy's inferiority in social status. It seemed scarcely probable to her that Mr. Heatherley's affections were already engaged. What a pity it was that, perhaps owing to a mere lack of perception on his part, the possible happiness of two lives should be neglected.

One Saturday afternoon, very shortly after the departure of Mr. Gresham and his friends, Helen was oppressed by a fit of unusual despondency. At such times as these she felt her loneliness acutely, knowing how easily the looming clouds could have been dispersed by one word of earnest and affectionate sympathy. The causes of her melancholy were such as it was impossible to confess to any one with whom she was acquainted, if indeed she herself really knew them. As the afternoon drew on her sufferings grew intolerable. A horror of her solitude crept over her and became a physical pain. Company of some sort she felt she *must* seek. Mrs. Cumberbatch was out of the question, though doubtless she would have been ready enough to talk. Of only one person could she think with any degree of consolatory pleasure, and that was Lucy Venning. She would set off at once to Lucy's house, and pass there the few hours before the evening class.

Arrived at her destination, she knocked and was admitted by a maid-of-all-work occasionally employed in the house. On going into the parlour she found Mr. Venning and his daughter sitting side by side, the former with a somewhat grave expression of countenance, the latter's eyes showing unmistakable traces of recent tears.

Both, however, rose at once upon her entrance, and Mr. Venning greeted her in his ordinary kind and unrestrained manner.

"This is kind of you to come this afternoon, Miss Norman," he said. "You couldn't have come at a better moment. Lucy has a little headache, and is a trifle out of spirits. I'm sure your voice will do her good at once; won't it, Lucy?"

His daughter only replied by a sweet smile and a cordial pressure of Helen's hand, which sufficiently bespoke her contentment.

"I am afraid I shall be a poor comforter," said Helen. "My very reason for coming was that I did not feel very well myself, and knew that half an hour's talk with Lucy would restore my spirits. Well, I see we must prescribe for each other, Lucy. I dare say the amusement of doing so will dispense with the necessity of any disagreeable medicine."

Lucy laughed, helping Helen the while to remove her hat and cloak. But there was still a dimness in her eyes, and her lips trembled slightly in a way which made her fearful of trusting her voice.

"I know you will excuse me, Miss Norman," said Mr. Venning. "Though it is Saturday evening I have still business to attend to. Never mind," he added with a quiet laugh. "To-morrow is the day of rest. The thought of its enjoyment keeps me up all through the week. I often wonder what we working men should do without our Sunday."

As he spoke he withdrew from the parlour, and Helen took a seat by Lucy's side.

"Now let us open our budget of sorrows," she said. "I strongly suspect, Lucy, that yours will outweigh mine in dolefulness. You have been crying."

Lucy's frank nature was incapable of deceit even in trifles. She only paused for a moment before replying, then said, without raising her eyes—

"I have been low-spirited all day. I think it must be the heat, or—or I don't know what."

"I think you must take a holiday to-night," said Helen. "You know Mr. Heatherley almost always comes to the class on Saturday. I'm sure he will be glad to take your work if he knows you are unwell; or, if he should not come, I shall have very little difficulty in managing by myself."

"Oh, no," interposed Lucy, lifting up an eager face, " indeed I would not stay away on any account. The headache is going away; it—it has not been very much. I could not think of staying at home."

"Then you must promise me," said her friend, " to work a little less hard than usual. I'm sure I marvel at your patience sometimes when I see you working with those poor children as if your life depended on it."

"I do my best," replied the girl, "but I'm sure I don't know who wouldn't, with your example before them, Miss Norman. Mr. Heatherley often says that—"

"Well, what does Mr. Heatherley say?" asked Helen, smiling, as Lucy suddenly stopped short, and became a little red.

"He says he never knew a more excellent teacher than yourself, Miss Norman," hastily returned Lucy, averting her face.

"Oh, Mr. Heatherley is only too ready to speak well of everyone, isn't he, Lucy? No doubt he says just as pleasant things of you."

Lucy shook her head slightly, still blushing, but made no reply. Helen watched her a few moments curiously. At length Lucy suddenly turned her face towards her companion with such a look of simplicity, wherein were blended sorrow, bashfulness and trust, that the latter was moved to take her hand and bend forward to her with an answering look, as if inviting confidence.

"Miss Norman," faltered Lucy, the tears glistening in her eyes, "may I ask you a question—a—a rather strange question?"

"Anything you like, Lucy."

"Did you ever think that I spoke too much of Mr. Heatherley?" This last word broken momentarily in the middle by a sob. "That I—might—might make people think by the way I spoke of him—that I—"

"Who has put such a thought into your

mind, dear ? " asked Helen, willing to relieve the blushing girl of the difficulty of completing her sentence.

"Father has talked to me very seriously this afternoon, Miss Norman," replied Lucy; "not unkindly, you know; he never does that; only very seriously. And I'm sure that all he says is for my own good. He says that I had better try to think and speak less of Mr. Heatherley. But I didn't know that I spoke very often about him, Miss Norman, indeed I didn't. Do you—do you think I do?"

Helen did not reply immediately, but regarded her companion with a tender and compassionate smile.

"I see you think so, Miss Norman," said Lucy, speaking quickly, with downcast eyes. "Oh, how foolish I have been. But, indeed, father and you are mistaken. I—I never thought of him in that way. At least," she added hurriedly, "I *think* I never did. I'm sure I never meant to be so foolish. Don't think the worse of me, Miss Norman. I will be very careful in future."

"Think the worse of you, Lucy?" returned Helen, pressing Lucy's little hand between her own. "But you have been guilty of nothing improper. You are naturally so quiet that I am sure you have not spoken so freely to anyone but your father and myself."

"Indeed I have not," broke in Lucy, eagerly. "You and father are the only people who hear me speak without fear just what I think."

"Then you *do* think much of Mr. Heatherley?" asked Helen, with rather a sad smile.

"It would be foolish and wrong to try to hide the truth from you, Miss Norman; you who have always shown me such great kindness. I have often thought of Mr. Heatherley, but I'm sure only as a kind friend. I could never forgive myself if I led you to believe anything else. But father is quite right in what he said, and I know that I should be acting foolishly and wrongly if I don't try to turn my thoughts quite away from him—for a time, at least. I have already begun to do so, and I had no idea that it would be so much trouble. But it is my duty, and I shall have strength given me to perform it."

She ceased, and sat looking before her with the slightest shade of melancholy upon her features. Helen, who recognised in the simple girl's utterances kindred tones to those which for ever whispered in her own heart, felt herself drawn closer to Lucy by strong bonds of sympathy. There was consolation, too, in hearing her speak of her simple troubles, more than could have been found in any learned sermon and philosophical essay whatsoever. For a moment the thought arose that Lucy's untutored mind could not nourish such sufferings as those born in her own sophisticated imagination, and that therefore her pains were not so hard to

struggle with; but this Helen's better sense
at once rejected with scorn. The bitterness
of yearnings never to be satisfied could be no
less bitter to Lucy than to herself. If the
former showed less of what she suffered it
must be attributed to superior self-govern-
ment rather than to any lack of sensibility.

After a silence of several minutes Helen
spoke, using to her simple friend the same
reasoning she had often applied to herself.

"You are right, dear," she said. "Every
necessity in this world becomes a duty, and
we must struggle to submit to it as best we
may. And the best way to gain our own
peace is never to lose hope. Though the
path we have to tread may be painful enough
at first, we must never cease to hope, never
yield up the conviction that it will lead us to
some great happiness. What that happiness
may be we are often quite unable to foresee.
If we begin to struggle against a selfish
desire, never losing faith in the justice of our
efforts, we may some day find in renunciation
itself a greater happiness than the fulfilment
of the desire could have brought us. Depend
upon it, our happiness is seldom worked out
in the way we expect it to be. Why this
should be so, would puzzle much cleverer
people than you and I, Lucy, to explain; we
must just be content with knowing what
usually happens and apply this experience to
our own cases. Look back through your
own life and reflect how many longings you

have cherished, thinking their fulfilment at the time absolutely needful for your future happiness; and notice how many of them have resulted in disappointment which seemed at the time inexpressibly bitter, but which you can now smile and wonder at. They have all passed away, but not without leaving their effect upon you; no, not a word you speak, not a thought you think, is without some effect on your own nature. To be able to look back on these struggles and see their lessons is what we call wisdom, and those are the happiest who are able to apply this wisdom to their present guidance. You understand what I mean by this little sermon, Lucy?"

"Quite well," replied the girl, with a grateful look. "I believe I have been trying to think the same things myself, but they were not so clear to me as you have made them."

"Suffering is an excellent teacher," returned Helen, smiling sadly, "and to minds which face her honestly she teaches very much the same lessons."

Shortly after this, as the evening was drawing on, Lucy rose with a brighter face and prepared tea, at which her father joined them. And when at the chapel that night Mr. Heatherley shook hands with her in his ordinary kind way, Helen noticed that she replied to him with less embarrassment than of late; and sighed to think that her own counsels should have so much more weight with others than with herself.

CHAPTER VI.

THE months passed quickly on. Mr. Gresham and his friends had returned from a highly delightful tour, which had embraced the finest scenery of England, Scotland and Ireland, and, after spending about a week in Portland Place, had all once more set off for Paris. By means of an agent, Mr. Gresham had already succeeded in finding a house for his ward and her protectress, Mrs. Cumberbatch. It was in the district of Highbury, and, though rather dreary-looking in the November twilight, would doubtless be a pretty place in summer time. It was one of those neat little villas of which such numbers have recently sprung up in districts immediately surrounding London, with a bow window on each side of the door, and in front a pleasant little garden, concealed from the road by high holly bushes. Owing to the latter circumstance, the villa had been christened "Holly Cottage," which name was tastefully carved on the stone pillars at either side of the gate. It was decided that the ladies should take up their residence here about the middle of December. Mr. Gresham had graciously undertaken to come over from Paris to superintend their removal.

One Saturday evening towards the end of November, Helen Norman had again called to spend an hour with Lucy, previous to their setting out together for the chapel. She was paler and thinner than she had been even a few months before, and, owing to the persistency with which she pursued her work, even in the worst weather, had contracted a severe cold, which at times rendered her almost speechless. Mr. Heatherley had frequently pressed upon her of late the necessity of her paying more attention to her health, but as yet had succeeded in obtaining little more than promises. The truth was that Helen was bound to be active. She dreaded shutting herself up in the house alone with Mrs. Cumberbatch, or even alone with her own thoughts, for these had become the more insufferable companion of the two. To renounce her daily work would, she well knew, be equivalent to succumbing under an attack of illness. Such a prospect presented itself to her in the guise of unknown terror. To lie day after day, alone and suffering—no ; rather work till she fell down in the street from mere exhaustion. The horror of such a fate would be considerably less than that of gradually wasting away in a sick room, haunted by the demon of *ennui*. Death, and speedy death, she felt could alone terminate such suffering as this would imply.

She had a special object in seeking Lucy's society this afternoon. During the last few days a thought had ripened within her mind which had held out to her such a cheery gleam of consolation that she could lose no time in seeking to realise its promptings. When she and Lucy had taken their seats by the fire in the cheerful little parlour, she proceeded at once to communicate the main purpose of her visit.

"In a few weeks I am going to change my home, Lucy," she said.

Her companion looked up into her face with a startled expression.

"Indeed, Miss Norman!"

"Yes, I am going to have a little house of my own."

"You—you are going to be married, Miss Norman!" faltered Lucy, looking a little frightened at her own boldness in suggesting such a possibility. And when she saw a smile of amused astonishment rise to Helen's face, followed at length by one of her cheerful laughs, she reddened, and stammered excuses.

"Married!" exclaimed Helen. "What have I done, Lucy, that you should be so ready to attribute such enormities to me? There, you have done no harm, dear. Do you think I am so foolish as to be offended at any word that *your* lips could speak? Should you like to see me married?"

"Yes, I should," replied Lucy, with a

blush, after reflecting for a moment. " For I am sure you deserve as much happiness as it is possible for any one to have."

" And you think that marriage is the highest possible happiness ? "

" I think—perhaps—I scarcely know," stammered Lucy, in some confusion. " But I often think that no woman can be so happy as she who has a good husband to devote her life to, never thinking of anything but how to please him, and being able to ask his advice in every difficulty or trouble. How quiet one's life must be, when one feels there is always some one close at hand to trust in, some one who can never lead you astray, but whose advice is always for the best."

" I am afraid there are few such husbands, Lucy. But haven't you your father for a guide ? "

" Oh, yes, I love my father," replied Lucy, earnestly, "and have no greater pleasure than to obey him. But—but a husband must be so different—"

She broke off and sat in silence, her eyes drooping somewhat sadly. Helen suppressed a sigh, and returned to the subject she had most in her mind.

" But I was speaking of my new home," she said. " I am going to live in a very delightful little house in Highbury. I shall not be quite by myself, for a lady I have known some time, and who is much older than myself, has kindly promised to come and keep house for me. But still I fear I shall be a little lonely through the winter. I have scarcely any friends in London, and even those I have will be a long way from me. Now I wanted to ask you, Lucy, whether you thought you could manage to come and live with me, to be a companion for me when I am at home. You cannot think how glad I should be if you could do so."

She paused and observed Lucy's face, the expression of which had passed from surprise to delight, and then again to surprise mingled with doubt. Such was the confusion introduced into her thoughts by this most unexpected proposition, that she was quite unable to reply at once.

" You are thinking of your father," continued Helen. " I know I should be robbing him of his greatest comfort, but I cannot help being selfish in this matter, Lucy. You could always spend Sunday with him, and also an evening or two in the week."

" But the house-work ? " said Lucy, faltering between her delight at the proposal and the difficulties which stood in its way. " I am often afraid that father is not very comfortable as it is, for I have only the evenings and about an hour every morning to give to keeping our rooms in order. We have a girl in now and then to do rough work, but she couldn't get father's meals and keep his rooms neat."

"But suppose you found some better kind of servant to do that work?"

"I am afraid we are too poor for that," replied Lucy, simply.

"But if I took you away," replied Helen, "it would be only fair that I should provide some one in your place. So that we needn't trouble any more about that. Would you be willing to come to me, Lucy, if your father gave his consent?"

"It would make me very happy," replied the girl, sincerity speaking in her tone and look.

"Not more so than it would make me," said Helen, who really felt that with this single, child-hearted girl beside her she would be able to set at defiance the melancholy which so oppressed her. "You will see my library, then—more books than you ever saw in your life, Lucy. And we will read together; and I will teach you to like the things that I like, and will teach you foreign languages. Won't it be delightful?"

"Oh, it is too good to be true," said Lucy, covering her face with her hands. Helen, too, became silent, but in happy visions of the delight she would find in training this pure intelligence and seeing that sweet character expand in her presence. Another thought there was in her mind, a thought which had not been quite without its influence in determining her to this step. Bent, as always, on the good of others, Helen had reflected that, if Lucy lived with her, Mr. Heatherley would have his attention more attracted to the girl's virtues; she would be able to talk more to him about her, and so to assist in some measure to render the termination of Lucy's secret love happier than at present seemed possible.

As they sat thus in silence only two sounds were audible in the room; the one was the crackling of the fire, the other was the unceasing tread of a footstep pacing backwards and forwards in the room above their heads. To the latter sound Helen's attention had already been once or twice directed, but now that it became still more observable she could not help wondering who it was that paced thus perpetually. She broke silence by asking the question.

"Oh," replied Lucy, looking up from her happy reverie, "that is Mr. Golding, a lodger we have in our spare room. He nearly always spends his evenings in walking up and down his room."

"What did you say his name is?" asked Helen, with an interest in her tone which surprised Lucy.

"Mr. Golding," she replied. "He is a printer. He has only just recovered from a bad illness, and I am afraid he is not quite well yet."

"He is a printer, you say?" continued Helen. "Do you know what his Christian name is, Lucy?"

Lucy looked up in some surprise.

"I really forget," she said; "but I can—oh, I remember; his name in the rent book is A. Golding. I don't know what A. stands for."

"He is a young man?"

"Yes, quite young?"

"And—rather handsome, Lucy?"

"I think so," replied Lucy, smiling; "but his face is very pale, and he always looks sad. Whenever I see him I feel to pity him. I suppose it is his illness that makes him look so."

Helen's eyes had been fixed immutably on her companion's face since the latter had pronounced the lodger's name, and their expression had something in it of strange pleasure which added to Lucy's surprise. As she spoke of his illness, this expression changed to one of sympathy, and this continued now for several minutes, whilst neither spoke. Helen was gazing into the fire, and evidently listening to the footfall overhead.

"How long has he been here, Lucy?" she asked at length, speaking in a lower tone.

"About a fortnight," was the reply; and then she added, seeing Helen still much interested—"He was recommended to us by a friend of ours who comes to see father now and then, Mr. Noble. Once, a long time ago, Mr. Noble brought him here on a Sunday night, and he had tea with us. He's very pleasant whenever he does speak, but that's very seldom. Once or twice we have asked him to come down and sit with us in the evening, but he has only consented once. Hush! he is coming down stairs. I heard his door open."

"I must see him, Lucy," whispered Helen, rising from her seat. "How can I see him and not be noticed? Stop, if I hear his voice it will be enough. Could you go out and speak to him? About anything. He is coming down stairs."

In the utmost astonishment, but eager to do anything to oblige Miss Norman, Lucy quickly left the room, leaving the door slightly ajar behind her, and, standing just outside it, she addressed to the lodger some question concerning his meals, which, in the morning and evening, she always prepared for him. Helen had stolen up close to the door, and heard distinctly the questions and replies. As soon as the lodger spoke she recognised Arthur's voice.

He went on and out of the house, and Helen, trembling in every limb, sank into the nearest chair. At first she felt angry with herself for her weakness, but the next moment a warm glow of pleasure had rushed over her whole body, driving away every other feeling. Then Lucy re-entered the room, and Helen, with a low laugh of joy, folded her in her arms and kissed her on the forehead. Lucy's face flushed with delight, but her eyes still retained their expression of astonishment. She feared, however, to make any remark, and resumed her seat in silence by the fire-side.

"It is as I thought," said Helen, speaking still in a very low voice, and fixing her eyes, which glowed with unusual brightness, upon her companion's wondering face; "I once knew Mr. Golding. Lucy, you say he passes the evening with you and your father sometimes?"

She replied in the affirmative.

"Do you think my name has ever been mentioned in his presence?"

"Yes, it has," replied Lucy. "Mr. Heatherley came in last Wednesday night, when Mr. Golding was with us, and he asked me if I did not think you looked very poorly, Miss Norman. And then he spoke for some minutes about your untiring patience."

"And Mr. Golding?" asked Helen, bending forward and taking Lucy's hand. "He said nothing?"

"I—I think not," returned the other, fearful lest her answer should displease.

There was silence for some minutes, during which Helen still held Lucy's hand, playing with it now and then whilst varied emotions made themselves seen upon her features.

"What must you think of me, Lucy?" she asked at length. "No doubt you are quite at a loss to understand my strange behaviour. The truth is that Mr. Golding is an old acquaintance, in whom

I have much interest. I have not seen him for more than a year, and had no idea where he was, so you may imagine my surprise when I heard you call your lodger by his name. Would you do me a kindness, something very difficult for me to do for myself, but easy for you to do for me?"

"I will do anything in my power for you, Miss Norman."

"Then it is this. When next you have an opportunity of speaking to him alone will you say, as if by chance, that I had heard of him from you, that I had recognised him as an acquaintance, and had made friendly inquiries with regard to him—all this, you know, as if coming naturally from yourself? —I wish him to know, in short, that I am aware of his being here. And I should like to know how he hears this, Lucy, with what expression of face, or what reply he makes. Are you artful enough to practise all this deceit, dear?"

"I think it will be a very harmless deceit," replied Lucy, with her customary *naïveté*. "I can easily find an opportunity to do this. Very likely I shall be able to bring you word next Tuesday night at the class."

"And you—you will not say anything of this to your father, Lucy? It is only a foolish fancy. I can trust you, but others, who do not know me so well, might—you know what I mean."

"Indeed, I will tell no one," replied Lucy

earnestly, truth beaming from her wide blue eyes.

Helen smiled gratefully, and, drawing the girl towards her, pressed an affectionate kiss upon her lips.

On the following Tuesday night Helen was in the schoolroom rather earlier than usual. She had come in the hope of having a quarter of an hour's talk with Lucy before the lessons commenced, but in this she was disappointed, for Lucy, who usually made her appearance some time before eight o'clock, was late to-night. Helen's cold had increased in severity during the last few days, and to-night she was scarcely able to speak. Prudence had urged her throughout the day to send a note to Mr. Heatherley, begging him to take her place that evening, but the temptation of the news she hoped to hear from Lucy was too strong and she had braved the night air. The girls were collecting in the white-walled school-room, each one curtseying as she entered, whilst Helen was looking over a number of dictation exercises, when Mr. Heatherley suddenly appeared, his face flushed with rapid walking, and a dripping umbrella in his hand. A look of pain and vexation crossed his face as he saw Helen sitting at his desk.

"How extremely imprudent of you, Miss Norman!" he said, pointing to the wrapper in which Helen had encircled her throat. I certainly hoped you would have remained at home a day like this. In fact I made so sure you would, that I especially arranged to be able to take your class to-night. As I was on the way here I just stepped into Mrs. Hawley's, and imagine my horror when I heard that you had been walking about as usual all this morning. Poor Mrs. Hawley was in despair on your account. 'She's killing herself, Mr. Heatherley; she's killing herself!'—that's all I could get from her. And, upon my word, I believe she's quite right. Now, Miss Norman, I beg you will go home at once, and let me take your place to-night."

"It is very kind of you to be so concerned on my account," replied Helen, in a voice but little above a whisper. "Indeed, if you can spare the time, I shall be very glad to have you take my class. I fear I could not make myself heard. But you must not send me away. This room is very warm and comfortable, I am sure."

As she spoke the clock in the chapel struck eight.

"Where is Miss Venning?" asked the clergyman, looking round in a kind of despair. "I ought to have her to second my entreaties. I really believe she has been afraid to come out to-night."

"Oh no," replied Helen, quickly, "I am sure she will be here. She does not allow herself to be withheld from her work by a little rain."

The girls were all sitting in expectant silence at their desks, books open before them.

"We must not set an example of unpunctuality," said Mr. Heatherley, in a low voice. "I will begin the lesson, and leave further remonstrance till afterwards. In the meantime prepare yourself for severe things, Miss Norman."

Then he turned to the pupils, and spoke to them in that frank, friendly tone which made him liked wherever he went.

"Scholars," he said, "I shall have the pleasure of teaching you myself this evening. Miss Norman, I grieve to say, is suffering from such a severe cold that it is impossible for her to talk to you as usual. She has, however, too great an interest in you to stay away even under these circumstances. I trust you will appreciate the value of such a teacher and never fail to do your best to please her. I will take the first class to begin with. The second class will please to study quietly for the present."

When he ceased to speak of Helen, a murmur of approbation and sympathy had made itself heard in the room, and all eyes were turned with glances of pitying affection to the latter's face. At any other time Helen would have been profoundly moved by that manifestation of feeling, but at present she scarcely knew what was happening. Where was Lucy Venning? Why was she absent

for the first time just when Helen wished
especially to see her? In spite of herself,
Helen had become the prey of an intolerable
impatience to hear how the intelligence of
her interest in him had been received by
Arthur Golding. The impatience had been
increasing ever since Saturday night. Reason
was powerless against it. She endeavoured
to impress upon herself that in all likelihood Arthur would hear of her with some
surprise, and the next moment dismiss her
from his mind. And why should it be otherwise? What special interest could she expect him to take in her? Nay, what was
the explanation of this strange excitement
which had continued to trouble her ever
since she had listened for his voice and recognised it at the first tone? Two or three
months ago she had never thought of him;
why should she have all at once conceived
this violent desire to see him once more, this
eager longing to hear that her name was not
altogether indifferent to him?

She had become so absorbed in these reflections that the sound of voices in the room
had altogether died from her ears. But all
at once a fresh voice spoke at her side, making her start nervously, whilst a flush covered
her face. It was Lucy Venning, who had
entered unseen by her.

"Good evening, Miss Norman," Lucy
whispered. "I am so sorry I am late. Is
your cold worse?"

"A little," whispered Helen hurriedly in return; then asked, with an eagerness she could not subdue, "Any news?"

"Yes," replied Lucy, meeting the other's look with eyes full of affectionate sympathy. "That is what made me late. I must tell you afterwards."

Then she quickly took her usual place and commenced the lesson of the second class.

It seemed many hours to Helen before the lessons were at an end. But at length the last copy-book had been closed, the last question asked and answered, and the last girl had curtseyed and disappeared. Then Mr. Heatherley once more turned his attention to her.

"Miss Venning," he said, looking at Lucy, who sank her eyes, "I must ask for your assistance here. Do come and help me to persuade Miss Norman to take a few days' rest. Promise us, Miss Norman, that you will at least exercise the ordinary prudence of remaining in-doors till your cold is better. Indeed, in my position of your director in the work you have undertaken, I must insist on your doing this."

"If you speak so authoritatively," replied Helen, smiling, "I have no alternative but to obey. Yet it distresses me unspeakably to think that at the very time when the poor need most assistance I should keep away from them."

"Just so," replied Mr. Heatherley, "but

you appear to forget, Miss Norman, that it is better to lose a week now than to be laid up for several months during the winter. Your zeal blinds you to this self-evident truth. Pray, have you seen your physician ? "

" I have scarcely thought it worth while to do so."

" Then, once more, I speak authoritatively, Miss Norman, and request you to do so without delay. These colds are often more serious things than one imagines. Will you permit me to call upon you—say on Thursday morning, and inquire after your health ? "

" I shall be very glad to see you, Mr. Heatherley," replied Helen, speaking, as she had done in reply to each question, with mechanical effort. She was burning with eagerness to be alone with Lucy.

They all three left the chapel together. It was raining hard, and bitterly cold. They walked in silence towards the railway station, Helen all the time distressing herself with the fear lest Mr. Heatherley would accompany her all the way there, as he frequently did, in which case she would have no opportunity of speaking with Lucy. But the latter also foresaw this, and, with an artfulness of which her simple nature could only be capable under the inspiration of her tender regard for Helen, obviated the difficulty. They had to pass her house on the way to the station, and, on arriving at it, she appeared suddenly to recollect something.

"Oh, Miss Norman," she exclaimed, "please to come in for a moment whilst I fetch the book you lent me. I finished it yesterday, and, as I shall not see you for some days, I should be sorry to keep it longer. Please to step in, too, Mr. Heatherley. Father is alone and will be glad to see you."

The clergyman was about to make some remark as to the lateness of the hour, but Lucy had already opened the door, and Helen was following her into the passage, so he was obliged to enter also. Lucy quickly introduced him into the parlour, where her father was sitting, in his usual brown study, and then she beckoned to Helen, who followed her upstairs. At the top of the stairs were two doors, from between the chinks of one light was evident. The other was Lucy's bedroom, and into this she led the way.

"I could think of no other way," said Lucy, laughing quietly at her own address. "We must speak very quietly, Mr. Golding is in his room."

Helen listened, and again she heard the steady footfall going up and down the floor in the next chamber. She seized Lucy's hand, and looked into her face expectantly.

"I found an opportunity," began Lucy, in a whisper, "on Sunday night. At first he didn't seem to understand exactly what I meant. No doubt it was my awkwardness; so I repeated to him what you wished him to know, of course making him understand that it was my own thought to mention it. Then he looked at me rather curiously, and said, ' Please to tell Miss Norman that I have heard of her inquiries, and that I am much obliged to her.' I think these were his words, and they were said very coldly, quite in a different way from his usual manner of speaking to me."

Helen suddenly relinquished the speaker's hand, and turned away her head. " Come, let us go, Lucy," she said, quickly. " I am sorry I troubled you about such a foolish matter."

" But that is not all," hastily added the other. " That was only the first time I saw him. But just as I was leaving the house to-night to go to the chapel, Mr. Golding met me in the street and asked me if I would let him walk a short distance with me, as he wished to ask me one or two questions. He spoke in a rather confused way, and I couldn't think what he meant; but, as it was raining, I asked him to return and speak to me in the parlour, for father was not at home. When we were in the room, he didn't seem quite able to begin at first, but when I asked him what he wished to know he said that his questions were about Miss Norman; would I mind telling him whether you had ever said anything about him except what he had already heard? I was rather put about for an answer, but at last I said that you had not. Was I right, Miss Norman ? "

"Quite right," replied Helen, who was now listening eagerly again. "And then?"

"And then he asked me how you had spoken of him, whether you seemed sorry to hear that he had been ill, how you looked when you asked after him. Again I was troubled to know how to answer, but—I hope I wasn't wrong, Miss Norman? I said that —that you had spoken in a kind way, but you always did that of everyone, and that I felt sure you were very sorry to hear of his illness. I hope I didn't say more than was proper, Miss Norman?"

"And then?"

"Then he said he should very much like to see you."

"To see me?" broke in Helen, much surprised, and trembling slightly.

"Yes; but he spoke in a very respectful way. He wished to know whether I would tell you this, and ask if you would be willing to see him. There was something he very much wanted to speak to you about. He should consider it a great favour. And he spoke so earnestly that I'm sure he has some very good reason for asking it."

Helen became thoughtful, and, as she mused, a slight smile played fitfully about her lips. Still the footsteps in the next room paced backward and forwards unceasingly, and she even thought that she could hear something that resembled a deep sigh.

"Will you tell Mr. Golding," she said, all

at once, " that I will expect him between six
and seven to-morrow evening ? But stay, is
he free then ? "

" He is always home at six."

" Very well; between six and seven then,
in Portland Place. Will you tell him this,
Lucy ? And—and will you say that I shall
be quite alone ? "

" I will let him know to-night," was the
reply.

They passed down stairs again, and found
Mr. Heatherley growing impatient. He insisted upon accompanying Helen to the station.

" But not a word on the way, Miss Norman," he said. " Please to cover your mouth
up closely, and on no account to take off the
scarf."

Helen laughed as she obeyed him, and they
walked quickly the short distance which remained to the station. Neither spoke on the
way, but Mr. Heatherley frequently glanced
aside at his companion's face whenever the
light from the shops or the street-lamps
illumined it.

" On Thursday morning I shall take the
liberty of calling upon you," he said as he
shook hands at parting. " I beg you will see
your physician in the interval, and on no
account think of going out."

Helen had scarcely heard him, so much was
her mind disturbed by what Lucy had told
her. What could be Arthur's object in
wishing to see her ? This she was utterly

unable to divine. Her mind was distracted by doubts as to whether she had done rightly in granting an interview. What must be Lucy Venning's thoughts of the singular mystery in which she had been made to play a part. Lucy evidently saw nothing shocking in the course her friend pursued, and her pure mind was a far better judge of propriety than all the conventionalities of a prurient society. But what kind of man was she about to receive? A year may effect a great change in character, and could she be certain that Arthur was still the high-minded youth he had appeared to her formerly? Of his life in the interval she was totally ignorant, and it might be that he had altered much for the worse. Yet that was an idea to which she could not reconcile herself. In the conversation between him and Lucy, which the latter had repeated, there seemed so much of his old manner; it was so clear that the boldness of his request was forced upon him by some exceptional need; no, she could not believe that he had deteriorated. And then came the thought of his suffering, the recollection of the monotonous footfall going to and fro, at which her heart warmed with womanly tenderness and pity. It was clear he was not happy, that he was suffering in mind as well as in body, and if indeed she could do anything to relieve him how gladly would she venture much more than a mere unusual *tête-à-tête*.

On reaching home she at once sought her own chamber. The excitement of the evening had brought on a severe headache, and this, combined with her cold, made her feel so ill that she was glad to extinguish the light and seek rest at once. It was some time before her thoughts would allow her to become sufficiently composed to sleep, and when at last her eyes closed it was only in a troubled slumber, broken by shapeless dreams. These at length assumed the form of a terrible nightmare, in which she seemed to be struggling for her life with some fearful monster which had encircled her throat and was stifling her. Just as the agony was becoming intolerable it awoke her. She was coughing with dreadful violence, each gasp causing her excruciating pain. When the fit came to an end, she reached her hand to the table which stood beside her bed, and struck a match. The little flame shot up, illuminating the hand that held it, but surely with a strange light. The colour of her fingers was blood-red. For a moment she thought her eyes were deceiving her, but then she felt something warm upon her lips. She wiped them with her other hand, and that too became red. Then she knew that it was really blood which she saw. The same moment the match went out between her fingers, and she shuddered with horror in the darkness.

CHAPTER VII.

THE TRIUMPH OF ART.

ALL the next day Helen sat in her own room,
at times reading a little, but for the most
part sunk in reveries. Her cold appeared to
be a little better, but her face wore a sicklier
hue than on the previous day. The hands
which lay crossed upon her lap seemed almost
transparent in their pale delicacy, and only
the pink tints of the nails gave evidence of
warm life-blood. Had she made no promise
to Mr. Heatherley, her physical weakness
would have sufficed to hold her in-doors to-
day. To rise from her chair cost her a painful effort, and after crossing the room her
limbs became as feebly tremulous as though
she had but just risen from a long illness. As
she reclined in her great chair, her hands
folded before her, her eyes fixed with a gaze
expressive of calm inward joy upon the
glowing fire, which, in the shadowed room,
often cast a faint rosy radiance upon her
brow, and deepened into dark gold the richness of her brown hair, she much resembled
some sweet and placid-faced Madonna gazing
herself into beatific reverie before an infant
Christ.

For her thoughts, as the day progressed,

became calm and cheerful, engrossed in anticipation of the interview she was about to enjoy. Throughout the night and during the early hours of the day she had suffered much, and, instead of the present peace, an expression of trouble, at times even of anguish, had disturbed her countenance. After the dread waking from the nightmare she had scarcely closed her eyes, but had lain through the long silent hours struggling with a fearful spectre in her thoughts scarcely less terrible than that which had oppressed her dreams. The blood upon her hand and upon her lips she felt that she understood only too well; it brought back recollections of her father's last years, and re-awakened in her a dread to which she had long ago been subject, but which her active life had recently dispelled from her mind. Her mother had died very early, if not of consumption, at all events from some trifling illness operating upon a most feeble constitution. Her father, as the reader knows, had struggled through long years with his impending fate, only keeping himself alive by the exercise of the most scrupulous precautions. Helen reflected again on these things during long hours of wakefulness, and the flickering night-light became to her the symbol of a miserable destiny. What if her life was fated to burn only during a few years of dark striving, of toiling in the gloom of misapplied efforts and fallacious hopes, and then, when at length the dawn began to break upon her, when she could see her path more clearly, and the certainty of progress had grown strong within her, should flicker, and droop, and become extinguished even as this night-light? In the dim radiance which kept her company during this night of suffering she saw pass by her bed the terrible forms of Disease, Despair and Death, and it seemed as though another ghostly shadow which had taken its place by her side whispered their names to her as they passed, and the name of the shadow itself was Fear. For hours she lay in a cold sweat, her soul writhing within her, her body prostrated as though already under the crushing hand of sickness; and only towards the morning did she once again sink into troubled slumber, to be still haunted by the same ghostly shapes. No wonder that she at length arose shattered and feeble, desiring nothing but to sit quietly throughout the day by the fire-side. The cup of coffee which had been brought her at breakfast-time remained beside her at noon, still untouched; then it was exchanged for a cup of tea, after drinking which the calm into which she had gradually been sinking became more perfect, and by degrees she forgot her fears in happy reverie.

As the time for Arthur's visit drew nigh, Helen paid some attention to her toilet, and descended to the library, where she had ordered a fire to be lighted. Into this room she knew Mrs. Cumberbatch very seldom came, and here she gave instructions that Arthur should be shown as soon as he arrived. Taking up a favourite book, she sat down by the fire-side, not to read—for that was impossible—but to subside into a state of calm preparation.

Exactly at the hour of seven, she heard the visitor's bell ring, down in the lower regions of the house, and she knew that he had arrived. She sat and listened. A servant passed quickly through the hall, the front-door opened, there was a momentary silence, and almost immediately a tap at the library-door. The servant announced—

"Mr. Golding."

Helen rose from her seat and advanced to meet him. Now that he was in her presence she had recovered all her self-command, and could even comment to herself upon his appearance. Certainly he was much altered; whether for the better or not it was difficult to say at once. He looked much older. His face was thinner, and bore traces of anxiety, if not of keener suffering. But his eyes still wore the same expression, were still alive with the bright glow of talent and enthusiasm. For the excitement of the visit had also animated Arthur, and just now he felt more like his old self than he had for a long time.

On Helen's part there was no air of condescension, no restraint, no sense of being engaged in anything unusual. When

Arthur stood still and bent before her, she
advanced yet a step, and held out her hand
to him with the perfection of natural grace.
He took it, and held it for a moment, gazing
into her face with a look before which her
eyes fell. Then she pointed in silence to a
chair, and herself became seated.

Neither had given utterance to a word of
common-place greeting or politeness, for each
felt that the meeting was one which would
be fruitful in consequences to them both.
As soon as they were seated, Helen looked
towards Arthur with a smile of expectation.
But she saw the same moment that he was
under the influence of feelings which would
not allow him to speak at once, and she resolved to relieve his embarrassment.

"My friend, Miss Venning," she said,
"told me you had expressed a wish to see
me, Mr. Golding. I am sorry that you
should have hesitated so long before paying
me a visit."

"I was not quite certain, Miss Norman,"
he replied, reassured completely by her quiet,
friendly tone, "whether you would permit
me to speak to you if I came. I feared you
were offended at the abruptness with which
I quitted Mr. Gresham's studio a year ago."

"Had you any reason to think I was
offended?" asked Helen, after a moment's
reflection, her tone being one of simple inquiry.

Arthur hesitated for an instant, raised his

face as if to make a confession, but apparently altered his purpose, and spoke in his previous respectful tone.

"No reason," he replied, "except the consciousness that my behaviour must have appeared strange and even rude to you." Then, after slightly pausing, he added, in a lower voice, "I had no means of knowing how my absence was explained to you, or, indeed, whether it was explained at all. Possibly it is presumptuous in me to think you ever cared to ask the reason."

An expression of surprise rose to Helen's face as she listened, frank surprise which she did not in the least try to conceal. Arthur's eye caught the look, for a moment they gazed at each other without speaking.

"I am quite unable to understand what you have just said, Mr. Golding," said Helen at length, a touch of pain making itself evident in her tone. "Your memory must be strangely unretentive. Could I have given better evidence of my being concerned at your sudden departure than by coming to enquire for you?"

It was Arthur's turn to look surprised, and he appeared even more so than Helen had previously been. For some moments he struggled desperately with his memory in the endeavour to disclose any possible explanation for her words. Helen saw that his astonishment was sincere, and smiled as she again spoke.

" When you spoke of my being offended, I certainly thought you could only refer to one circumstance. Can you recall no occasion on which you behaved to me with what I will call severity? I do not use the word impoliteness, for I am sure you were labouring under some strange mistake, as well as suffering from affliction."

" If you refer," replied Arthur, " to something that happened after Mr. Tollady's death, I am quite unable to understand you, Miss Norman."

" You were not aware that I called at the shop immediately after Mr. Tollady's burial, and was informed that you declined to see me ? "

Arthur started to his feet.

" Who told you so? " he cried; but, at once recollecting himself, he resumed his seat, and added, " I beg your pardon, Miss Norman. I am so astonished at what you tell me that I forget myself. May I ask who behaved so rudely in my name? Do you remember—"

He ceased suddenly, for he remembered it could be but one person, and before Helen could reply, he had solved the mystery in his own mind.

" It was a tall, strange-looking man," he added, eagerly; " a man with a red stain on one of his cheeks, was it not, Miss Norman ? "

" It was," she replied. " I remember him

distinctly. Indeed, at the time I thought him mad."

"And such he doubtless was," returned the young man. "He has since died—a maniac."

He became silent, for the solution of the doubt which had so long weighed upon his mind, imparted to his thoughts an activity which wholly occupied him.

"And am I to understand," asked Helen, "that this man spoke without authority from you?"

"Entirely so," returned Arthur, suddenly looking up.

"But that is very extraordinary," said Helen, looking up keenly into her visitor's face. "What could be the reason of his putting such words into your mouth?"

"Upon my word, Miss Norman," exclaimed Arthur, returning her gaze with unflinching candour, "strange as it appears to you, it is true. Till this moment I knew nothing of your visit. You will think me presumptuous when I confess it, but for several days after Mr. Tollady's sudden death I hoped that you might—that your interest in him might induce you to—visit the shop, as you had frequently done, and make some inquiry with regard to him. I hoped you might do so, for I could not help thinking that all who knew Mr. Tollady must be as much afflicted by his death as I was myself. But when a whole week had gone by, and I still thought

you had not called, I was forced to conclude
that I had been foolish in attributing to you
feelings with which you had no concern. Or,
as I sometimes feared, Mr. Gresham had so
represented the reason of my quitting him,
that you did not think it consistent with—
with your dignity to visit the house in which
I lived."

"If you knew me better, Mr. Golding,"
replied Helen, smiling, "you would know
that I held in very little esteem that conventional *dignity* which you hesitate to express. I'm sure I don't know whether it
would have been dignified in me to keep away
when I heard of Mr. Tollady's death, but it
would certainly have been unfeeling. The
fact is, I came to visit Mr. Tollady himself,
so little did I know of what had happened,
and it was after I had learnt it from the
strange man in the shop that I asked to see
you, and received the answer you know.
Then, perhaps," she added, smiling, "some
question of dignity did act to prevent me repeating my visit, which I was naturally persuaded would be useless."

A silence ensued, during which both were
deeply occupied with their thoughts. Arthur
was the first to look up and speak.

"I am not as well acquainted as I should
like to be, Miss Norman, with the ways of
the society in which you live, and possibly
you may regard the question which I ask as
grossly rude. If it is so, I hope you will not

hesitate to tell me. Might I ask how Mr. Gresham explained to you my sudden departure from his studio?"

"It is your right to know," replied Helen. "Mr. Gresham spoke of your action as one which had more of folly in it that of any more serious fault. He said that your capricious temper rendered you incapable of receiving instruction, and that some slight reproof which he addressed to you on some occasion when you deserved it, led to your going off in anger, and writing him the rude letter which terminated the connection between you. Excuse the freedom of my expressions. I repeat, as nearly as I can remember, the words Mr. Gresham used."

Arthur was silent for some minutes from extreme indignation. When he looked up he saw that Helen continued to watch him.

"Will you permit me, Miss Norman," he asked, restraining himself to speak as calmly as possible, "to tell you *my* view of this matter, to tell you, in short, the truth?"

Helen lowered her eyes before the emphasis of the last word.

"That is also your right," she answered quietly. "I beg you will do so."

"Then, Miss Norman," resumed Arthur, with energy, "as I value your good opinion above anything in this world, but could not stoop to possess myself of it under false pretences any more than I could rob you of a sum of money. I declare that there is not one

word of truth in what you were told, and what,
no doubt, you have hitherto believed. I do
not think my temper is capricious, and I certainly never behaved to Mr. Gresham otherwise than with the utmost respect. As to receiving his instruction impatiently, I could not
value it highly enough, and listened with the
utmost attention to every word he spoke to
me. Notwithstanding this, Mr. Gresham all
at once began to treat me with the most unaccountable coldness, and then even with
harshness. I do not hesitate to affirm that
he was unpardonably rude in his manner towards me. I respectfully asked an explanation, but it was haughtily refused. That
same day, on returning home, I found Mr.
Tollady evidently ill, and suffering in mind
as much as in body. With great difficulty
I succeeded in persuading him to tell me the
cause of his depression, which I had observed
for a long time, and then I found that
necessity had compelled him to mortgage his
house under peculiar circumstances, that the
time had come for the repayment of the
money, and that, as he was quite unable to
meet the debt, he saw no alternative but
giving up the house. In my distress I
would have done anything to spare Mr.
Tollady this suffering. Without a thought I
came to Mr. Gresham and begged he would
advance me out of my legacy the sum necessary to pay off this debt. He replied that it
was impossible to do so, and almost taunted

me with the fact that he had already supplied me with money before he was legally
obliged to do so. I bore with this indignity,
and begged he would *lend* Mr. Tollady the
money on his own account, for pure pity's
sake. This he altogether refused to do, and
at once dismissed me with the utmost harshness. I returned home, and, even now I recall it with irrepressible horror—I found Mr.
Tollady dead in his chair. The very next
day I wrote a letter to Mr. Gresham, acquainting him with what had happened, and
saying, in words which I am sure had nothing
of impertinence, that, under the circumstances,
I could not continue to receive any kind of
favour from him. This is the true story,
Miss Norman, strange as it may seem. To
this day I cannot account for Mr. Gresham's
changed manner towards me, but I am perfectly sure that he wished to bring about the
end which actually arrived, and drive me
away from him."

As the narrative progressed, Helen sat with
her eyes fixed upon the carpet, and once or
twice a passing glow had manifested itself in
her pale cheeks. A veil seemed to be removed from her eyes by Arthur's story, and,
strange as Mr. Gresham's conduct might
appear to the latter, she had no longer any
doubt as to the interpretation of it. She
remembered her guardian forbidding her to
speak to Arthur Golding, and she completely
recalled his tone and manner on that occasion,

which at the time had puzzled her. She could no longer hesitate to recognise jealousy as the cause of his conduct towards Arthur, and, strange to say, she felt a hot glow of pleasure fill her veins as the certainty forced itself upon her. When Arthur ceased to speak, she did not at once reply, but the former could see in her face that she was convinced of the truth of his story, and that she was not displeased at hearing it.

"It was very unfortunate," she said, at length, without looking up. " Evidently there was some strange misunderstanding between yourself and Mr. Gresham. I cannot comprehend it at all. But," she added, as if to get rid of an unpleasant subject, " was this explanation the object of your visit, Mr. Golding ? "

"Not the main object," replied Arthur, his voice expressing doubt and hesitation, " though I certainly had hoped to be permitted this justification of my conduct. My desire to see you was caused by—by circumstances and feelings which I now scarcely know how to describe to you. Indeed it would take me long to do so, I should be obliged to go over almost the whole story of my life. But do not be afraid, Miss Norman," he added with a smile, misinterpreting a look which passed over Helen's face, " I feel deeply your goodness in giving me this opportunity of freeing myself from disagreeable suspicions ; I shall not inflict upon you any

more of my troublesome confessions. Once
more permit me to thank you earnestly for
your goodness."

He rose as he spoke. Helen rose also, but
not with the intention of saying farewell.

"You have said that you are not much
acquainted with social forms," she said, with
a smile whose sweetness thrilled through
Arthur's frame, "so you will not be offended
at my venturing to instruct you. It is certainly not in accordance with etiquette to
request an interview, and terminate it with a
polite evasion of the object for which the
interview was granted. Pray take your seat
again, Mr. Golding."

Arthur gazed at the speaker's pale loveliness till he felt his senses becoming confused
and his power of thought fading in a delicious
dream. He spoke at length with hardly more
consciousness of what he was saying than if
his words had been uttered under the influence of some powerful drug.

"Will it indeed interest you, Miss Norman,
to hear of my sufferings? Shall I not be
intruding on your leisure? May I venture
to speak freely before you? In your presence
all my courage has left me. I can scarcely
conceive it possible that you would deign to
listen patiently to my doubts, and to give me
the advice which I need."

"And I, for my part, Mr. Golding," replied
Helen, her face aglow with pleasure, "can
scarcely conceive that you should think it

worth while to consult me on any important point. It is you who do me honour. I beg you will not hesitate to speak with the utmost freedom. You can say nothing that will not interest me—deeply."

She added the last word after a pause for breath, occasioned by the inward excitement which she, no less than Arthur, was struggling with, and, as she said it, she sank again upon her chair. Arthur, too, again became seated, his eyes still fixed on Helen. In this moment he knew for the first time the real nature and extent of the feelings her image had created in him. No thought of violated faith came to disturb his inward rapture. He knew that he had never loved before now, and the voice of nature was louder in his heart than that of violated social laws.

"Then I will indeed speak freely," he said, "and for once in my life I will disclose the depths of my nature to one capable of understanding what they contain. It is nothing dreadful or shocking that I shall try to disclose to you, Miss Norman, but merely a conflict which has been going on in my own mind for many years, and which was perhaps never fiercer than at present. To you it will perhaps seem trivial, you may smile at the earnestness with which I speak of so slight a matter; but the peace of my life is at stake, and to me that is not unimportant."

And he forthwith proceeded to relate, in simple yet eloquent words, the story of his life from the day on which he had escaped from Bloomford Rectory, dwelling more, however, upon his inward experience than on external events. He spoke of his early struggles, aspirations, sufferings; and showed how, amid them all, there had grown up within his being that passion for art which had been his incentive in discouragement, his glory in calmer days. Then he passed to his connection with Mr. Tollady, and told how the latter had striven to make an artist of him, yet how, at the same time, the good man's daily teachings and example had awakened in him a burning spirit of philanthropy, which, exaggerated by subsequent circumstances, ended by crushing the artistic impulses and throwing scorn upon them, as an unworthy growth. He explained to his listener how he had suffered in the contest between these two passions, his doubts, his agonies, his vain desire to reconcile their co-existence. Of his connection with Carrie he spoke not a word, and did no more than hint at the period of suffering and deprivation which had ensued upon it. Yet the recollection of it all was ever present in his mind, and gave fire to his utterances. Before proceeding to detail the latest phase of his self-questionings, he paused as if to collect his thoughts, and in the pause Helen spoke.

"I wonder whether I am clairvoyant enough to divine what remains," she said. "Shall I try?"

" I have faith in your skill, Miss Norman," replied Arthur, with a sigh of relief, meeting her kind and sympathetic look.

" What you are going to tell me, then, amounts to this. Your democratic *furor* has in time burnt itself out, and you feel distressed at your lack of stability. Is it not so ? "

" Partly so."

" And moreover—I hope I may be right— the old love of art has once more grown strong within you, and you are in doubt whether you ought to harbour it."

" I am flattered at the accuracy with which you guess my thoughts."

" And can you doubt for a moment, Mr. Golding," asked Helen, earnestly, " what course you ought to pursue? Has not the struggle in your mind now received as decisive a termination as it is capable of? Is it not as clear to you as daylight that the artist's instinct has prevailed, that it would be a sin against your nature to seek once more to destroy it ? "

Arthur kept silence. His eyes were fixed sadly upon the fire, and a deep sigh escaped from his bosom. Helen watched him unceasingly, and her cheeks glowed with the emotions of her heart.

" Have you resumed your painting ? " she asked at length.

" I have not touched a pencil for more than a year."

" But you feel a passionate desire to recommence? You feel all your old aspirations stronger than ever? You feel that there can be no real happiness for you save in a life devoted to art?"

Arthur suddenly looked up, and Helen fancied that it was moisture which made his eye gleam so brightly.

"All this I feel," he exclaimed, "but I cannot convince myself that I do right in yielding. When I think of giving up my daily work and living a life of ease—study though I may call it—it seems as though I were committing a sin, as though I were scorning these thousands of poor wretches who cry ceaselessly for sympathy and aid. Remember, Miss Norman, that I have been one of them, and that I can realise this misery so well! I will confess that I did not expect you to counsel me for this selfish life, a life that can at the best only give pleasure to myself and a few rich people who care for art. I have a friend who has consecrated his life to labour in the cause of the poor. I have told him what I have to-night told you, and he has urged me strongly to strive against this fondness for art. He wishes me to use my money to establish a Radical paper, to join him in such efforts as men of our position can make to show the people their wrongs and the methods of righting them. He believes that we can do much, for he is enthusiastic, like myself, but far more stable."

He had risen in the excitement of speaking.

Helen likewise rose, and drew nearer to him when he ceased.

"What made you think of coming to ask my advice, Mr. Golding?" she enquired, regarding him with a seriousness which rendered her sweet face irresistible. "It is so long since we saw each other that I almost wonder you have remembered me. Could you think my advice worthy of consideration after that of your friend—the advice of one with whom you are so slightly acquainted, of whose character and thoughts you know so little?"

"You do well to reprove me, Miss Norman," replied Arthur, turning slightly away. "It was unpardonable boldness in me to request this interview at all. You do, indeed, know too little of me—"

"Mr. Golding," interrupted Helen, "you invert what I said, and distort my meaning. After what you have related to me to-night, I flatter myself that I have sufficient insight into your character to venture upon advice, if it is asked. But why have you such confidence in me? Why do you think it probable that my advice may be of use to you?"

"I think so, Miss Norman," exclaimed Arthur, "because from the first moment that I saw you I have regarded you with the deepest respect. At first I respected you in obedience to an instinct, but later I came to know you in some degree, and to find solid grounds for my feeling. I know that you are an exception to the class to which you belong, an exception even to mankind in general. You sacrifice willingly that ease and luxury which wealth might provide for you, and make it your chief work to aid and to instruct the poor. Since I have lived at Mr. Venning's your name has been constantly in my ears, and always associated with such praises as few can deserve. Is it not most natural that I should come to you to be confirmed in the path which you yourself choose to follow?"

There was silence for a few moments, during which Helen's eyes were fixed on the ground. At length she spoke, looking into Arthur's face with frank simplicity.

"Will you consent to do as I advise?" she asked. "May I consider my word as final?"

"You may!" exclaimed Arthur, every nerve thrilling to the almost tenderness of her tone. "Whatever you say I will do! Whatever you say *must* be right!"

"Then," replied Helen, whilst her cheeks flushed, and her whole noble form seemed magnified by her emotion, "I bid you give yourself henceforth solely to art, for you are born to be an artist. The feelings of infinite compassion for the poor which work so strongly in your mind are most natural, but you must not allow them to lead you astray. Every high-minded man feels the same, in a modified form; the circumstances of your life have brought them into special prominence and occasioned the inward struggle you speak of. The example of your enthusiastic friend and of myself can be no law to you. Your friend, from what you say of him, is doubtless as evidently born for active work as you are for art; and for myself, I am merely distinguished from the crowd by the possession of money, and if I did not follow this sole road of usefulness which is open to me I should indeed be a wretched creature. *You* are different from both of us, for from what you tell me, and from what I have myself seen of your work, I am convinced that nature has gifted you with genius. Such a gift carries with it grave responsibilities. That you should have been tempted to consider the artist's work as trivial and useless, I can understand; it was owing to peculiar circumstances acting upon a peculiar nature. But it is now time that you saw your error. We who toil on from day to day doing our little best to lessen the sum of the world's misery are doing good work, it cannot be denied; but what is this compared with the labour of men of genius, labour the result of which stands as mile-stones on the highway of civilisation, each one marking a great and appreciable advance? Do you think it is to the benevolent monks of the Christian church, to the army of unknown philanthropists toiling through ages, to the host of men who have struggled throughout history for justice and freedom, that the highest praise is due for our high state of civilisation? These have only followed the spirit of the age; that spirit itself was created by the great men whose works, howsoever performed, direct the history of the world. Without the works of a Raphael our civilisation could not have been what it now is. You say that a beautiful picture only pleases its painter and a few rich *dilettanti.* In appearance it may do no more, but in reality its spirit permeates every layer of society. Like the lump of leaven in the old parable, it ultimately leavens the whole mass. I often read in the papers speeches by men who ought to know better, insisting on the necessity of what they call the *useful,* from which term they generally exclude everything which cannot be of immediate use to their own narrow natures. But nothing in this world is more useful than the *beautiful,* nothing works so powerfully for the ultimate benefit of mankind. Think of Mr. Tollady, whom you justly admire so much. You say that he never checked you in your passion for art, but that rather he urged you on to the utmost. Certainly he was not deficient in sympathy with the poor and with those who endeavour to benefit them. I am sure he would have spoken much as I have done, and have said that in becoming a pure artist you would do far more to advance the ends he had in view than by wearing away your life in petty efforts to do immediate good. Genius has always had, and always will have, laws to itself, laws not applicable to the mass of mankind. If you disobey this natural inclination of yours, you will some day bitterly regret it, when it is too late."

A long silence ensued, during which Arthur reflected, and Helen kept her eyes fixed upon his face. She saw that she had moved him, that his countenance expressed joy as her eager words fell upon his ear, and now she waited till he should make known his resolve. At length he raised his eyes slowly to those which were regarding him, and the bright radiance of his look showed the feelings which had been excited in his breast.

"I promised to obey you," he said, "and you might have merely commanded. As it is, you have convinced instead. I shall not endeavour to thank you, Miss Norman; spoken thanks are only a fit return for slight benefits. I hope my life will prove my gratitude."

"You will begin to work at once?" asked Helen, joyfully.

"At once. For some months I must, of course, continue to support myself by my work during the day. But every spare hour shall be given to drawing."

He made a motion as though in preparation to depart. Helen's brow had contracted as he spoke, as though a sudden thought crossed her mind. For a moment she seemed about to speak, but hesitated; then made up her mind, and said—

"You have done me a kindness, Mr. Gold-

ing, in accepting my advice; it is only fair
that you should let me do something in
return. You know that I am rich. Indeed
I have so much money that I scarcely know
what to do with it; for, though I am still a
ward," she added, smiling, "my guardian
permits me to act as though I were already
my own mistress. Will you permit me to
lend you some of my superfluity, what you
think necessary to enable you to give yourself
entirely to study till you obtain possession of
your own? Indeed it would be a kindness
to me to let me do so," she continued, quietly,
noticing the expression of his face. "It
would be such a pleasure for me to know
that my money was being of real use! Some
day you will be rich, and then you shall repay
me."

As she stood looking up into Arthur's
smiling face, her own features suffused with
a warm glow, half resulting from the consciousness of doing rather a bold thing, half
from the eagerness with which she hoped
that her offer would be accepted, her beauty
was so maddening that the young man afterwards wondered in himself that he had not
fallen prostrate at her feet and given vent to
his anguish of emotion in a passionate declaration of love. As it was, he stood for
more than a minute in a state much resembling
the ecstasy of the old saints, feeding his soul
upon her loveliness. At length he saw her
eyes droop and her cheeks burn before his pas-

sionate gaze, and the change recalled him to himself. He spoke in a very low voice, which yet seemed to him to break too rudely the rapturous silence of the room.

"Miss Norman, you are goodness itself. How I have deserved all your kindness, I cannot tell; I can only be conscious of the happiness it causes me. But you have already laden me with benefits, for every one of your encouraging words has been worth more to me than gold. You have restored my peace of mind, and have given me an impulse to labour which will not fail as long as my life lasts. More than this I must not accept from you. I should be unjust to myself if I did so, for I should be depressed with the sense of obligations which I could never hope to discharge. It is far better that I should work under difficulties for a short time; too great prosperity might spoil me."

"I am disappointed," returned Helen, seeing in his face that it was useless to persist, "though I appreciate your energy. It is such a natural thing that money which is lying useless should be entrusted to those who can put it to a good purpose; I should not be conferring an obligation on you, but merely performing a duty."

"I have no thanks to express my gratitude," replied Arthur. "Though I cannot accept this kindness, may I beg you to grant me another in its stead? Will you permit me, Miss Norman, to show you now and then the results of my work? If I complete a drawing or a picture which I think worthy of being shown to you, will you allow me to ask for your judgment upon it? You have inspired me with more enthusiasm than I have ever yet felt, and I know of no better way than this in which to prove my enduring recollection of your goodness."

" You grant unasked what I was about to beg as a favour," replied Helen. " I suppose you will continue to live with the Vennings? I frequently call to spend an hour with Lucy, and so I shall have many opportunities of seeing your work."

Fearful of saying too much, Helen limited herself to this. She said nothing of her approaching change of residence, thinking it most likely that he would hear of it from the Vennings, when her own proposal with regard to Lucy was discussed. But in her heart she thought with delight of the future, which this one evening had made golden before her imagination. As Arthur took his leave she gave him her hand, and the light touch of his fingers, which she had not dared to press, thrilled through her with a sensation so acute that it resembled pain.

CHAPTER VIII.

A PRIESTESS OF VENUS.

ONE night, close upon the end of the year, a number of young men were standing at the bar in a restaurant of no great repute not far from Leicester Square, delighting their souls with congenial chat. One or two had before them glasses of suspicious-looking wines, others were content with more homely ale, and all soothed their spirits by luxuriant puffing at more or less evil-odoured cigars. Their talk was of the town, towny. One related to a couple of entranced listeners the story of a recent *tête-à-tête* enjoyed with some second-rate favourite of the ballet, his graphic rendering of certain passages—more entertaining than polite—being received with bursts of Homeric laughter by the youths who were drinking and smoking at his expense. Another group was listening to another *coute moral*, which had for its subject the exploits of a gentleman referred to as " Brandy Dick," the climax of whose practical witticisms seemed always to be reached in the Police Court. " Brandy Dick's " very latest piece of bravery proved to be of that nature usually referred to as " assault and battery," and, having been practised upon the person of a woman was, of course, worthy of more than ordinary applause. Deserting with regret the company of these humourists, we must pay more particular attention to a third group, consisting of four young men of somewhat more staid demeanour. They were also occupied in smoking and drinking, and their faces bore the unmistakable traces of lax lives; but they evidently belonged to a higher grade in society than the other joyous spirits. Their talk was more earnest and in lower tones. Evidently they were engaged in going to the devil by a more decorous route than that pursued by the eulogists of "Brandy Dick."

"Oh," exclaimed one, who wore a spruce chimney-pot and a white waistcoat, "in my opinion Fanny's played out. Drink plays the very devil with women; when once they begin they never know how to stop. She used to be something like a singer, but you should have heard her at the Alhambra last night. She was screwed to begin with, everybody could see that; and in the last act she was simply blazing drunk."

"Well, I'm sorry for Fan," drawled another of the quartette, turning round a diamond ring on his finger. "She's so devilish good-looking. I s'pose she'll have nothing else for it now but to take a turn at the *poses plastiques*. She'll always draw there."

"Now dash it, Jack," interposed the third, with frank directness of manner, "I always did say you were a mean devil! If I'd known Fan as well as you have, hang me if I wouldn't fork out a quid or two for her. I wonder she don't bother you more than she does; I would, in her place."

"Bother me more!" exclaimed Jack, with a curl of the lip. "Why it's a whole month since I had anything to do with her, and do you think it likely she remembers me? No, no; her acquaintances are too numerous for that."

The other three laughed quietly, with a refinement of cold-bloodedness which would have made a humane man shudder.

"Tell you what it is, you fellows," broke in the fourth, who had hitherto occupied himself in alternately sipping his wine and winking at the barmaids, "if Fan has a right to bother anyone, it's Whiffle. It's my belief," he added, lowering his voice, "that that girl has set Whiffle up in a good deal more tin than one 'ud like to mention. He's a rum devil, is Whiffle, and how he comes it over the girls as he does, beats me hollow! Why, there was Lily Parker, you know, the girl who did the cheeky business at the Strand! There was good stuff in Lily, let me tell you, and she was fast getting to be a favourite, but she got so spooney on Whiffle that she let him drain her of every penny she made. What's the result? She's kicking up her heels at one of the Music Halls for a shilling a night, and Whiffle 'ud see her hanged before he forked out a tanner for her."

"Aye," said the gentleman in the white waistcoat, after a moment's silence, " but I've a notion Whiffle has met his match." And he nodded his head, and winked one eye after the other, in an extremely knowing manner.

"Met his match?" asked the one called Jack. " What do you mean, Smales?"

Mr. Smales continued to smoke for a few moments, as if in disregard of the question, only removing his cigar from his lips to exclaim " How do, Polly?" to a woman who entered the restaurant by herself and sat down at one of the tables.

"I know well enough what he means," said the fourth gentleman, at length, also assuming a deep look. " Yes, I should decidedly say that Whiffle has found his match."

"What the deuce do you fellows mean?" cried Jack, waxing a trifle warm with impatience. " Why can't you tell it out at once without so much mystery?"

"Don't get excited, Jack," interposed Smales, with a smile. " Haven't you noticed that Whiffle has fought shy of the Argyle and the other places about here lately?"

"Why, yes. I wondered where the deuce he'd gone to."

"Well, he has a good reason," begun Smales, when the one who appeared to share the mystery with him broke in like Marcellus in the ghost scene.

"Look!" he whispered. "Here she comes."

All eyes were turned to the doorway, when there entered a tall girl, showily dressed, with features of considerable beauty, but spoiled by thick daubs of paint applied to conceal the pallor of the cheeks. Her face wore a devil-may-care expression very attractive to those who were not induced to reflect upon its probable significance. Her eyes had that bleared, indistinct appearance so common in girls of the town, and her features afforded numerous indications of the ruin she was bringing upon her constitution by excessive drinking. By her air and dress she appeared to belong to the aristocracy of the *demi-monde.* Her hair was of the colour of dark gold, a hue too rich to be natural, and hung in a long single plait down to her waist. As she entered she threw back a heavy paletôt, which the coldness of the night rendered necessary, and displayed a robe of dark blue silk, the front of which gave to view the curves of a magnificent throat and bosom. After one quick glance round the room, in which she appeared to recognise only one person, she walked straight to the table at which the woman, addressed as Polly, had seated herself, and, after exchanging a few whispers with her, also assumed a seat, demanding two glasses of sherry from a waiter who passed.

Our four friends followed her with glances expressing more or less open admiration.

"Damn me!" exclaimed Jack, in a whisper, "I've seen that girl everywhere lately, and I've often meant to ask some fellow who the devil she was. Now, Smales, out with this story of yours, and don't keep a chap so long waiting. Is that Whiffle's match?"

Mr. Smales replied by an affirmative wink.

"And what's more," he added, "I'll wager a thousand to one she's after him to-night."

"Ho, ho!" chuckled one of the others. "She sticks to his heels, does she? But, upon my word, she's a devilish fine girl!"

"Drinks like a fish!" put in Smales, with an expressive nod of the head. "Didn't you notice she lurched a little as she came in?"

"But who in the name of fate is she?" asked Jack.

"Don't know," replied Smales, "but I've a shrewd notion it was Whiffle who first got her into a scrape; and now I'll bet he'd give a little to be rid of her. She lived with him somewhere up Bayswater way for a month or two. Then, I've heard, she gave him the slip with some lord or other—the devil knows who; and now she's just on the streets again."

"What's her name?"

"Carrie—that's all I know. But just stop a minute, and I'll go and speak to Polly Hemp. If those two are up to something here, we may as well stop and see the fun."

So, trimming his hat, and pulling down his white waistcoat, Mr. Smales picked up his cane and sauntered towards the table at which the two girls were sitting. Leaning on the back of a chair he talked to them for some five minutes, during which his companions eyed him impatiently. Then he returned with a peculiar smile about his lips.

"Well?" exclaimed Jack.

"All right, old boy," returned the other. "It is as I thought. If we stay here a quarter of an hour longer we shall have a lark. You know Whiffle's strong at the cards; to tell you the truth, I think that's how he lives chiefly when he's no miserable devil of a girl to keep him. Well, Polly Hemp knows that, and she's promised to bring some deluded fool or other with lots of money to meet him here. But that's only a trick, do you see, to coax Whiffle out of his hole, so that Carrie may get hold of him. It seems Carrie's devilish hard up just now, and she's promised Polly so much out of every quid she gets from Whiffle. Good dodge, eh?"

The three laughed in a subdued chorus, then reflected for a moment upon the scene in preparation. All looked at their watches. It was eleven, and at a quarter past Mr. Augustus Whiffle was expected. It was necessary to find some new topic to pass away the intervening time, and this was introduced by the gentleman addressed as Jack.

"Been at the Eau de Vie, lately, Hawker?" he inquired of the most silent of the party; a consumptive-looking youth with a yellow tie and staring gloves to match.

"Was there the other night," replied Hawker, biting the end off a new cigar. "Tremendous row. Jackson—you know him, Smales; Billy Jackson, the big bully you used to meet in the city—he found himself cheated at some game or other by Waghorn, so he got up and shouted out so that all in the room could hear him: 'You're an infernal cheat, Waghorn, and that's all you come here for.' Waghorn was a little screwed, and jumped out and yelled: 'And you're an infernal liar, Jackson, and it's not the first time I've told you so.' Then there was a scuffle, and Jackson knocked Waghorn down; the cleanest hit from the shoulder I've seen for many a day. My stars! It did me good!"

The others laughed heartily.

"That Waghorn's a rum fellow," put in Smales. "I could tell you a tale or two about him, and one particularly that Maggie Twill told me the other night at Evans's. You know Waghorn has a big house somewhere up Regent's Park way, and plays the nob when he's at home. I believe he's devilish rich, or at least was, for I should think wine and women must have made a pretty big hole in his pocket. Well, Maggie Twill and two or three other girls had been

having supper with him at Evans's, and the
end of it was, as usual, that Waghorn got
pretty well screwed. So Maggie, who was
in for a lark, asked him whether he wasn't
going to take them all home with him; it
would be so much better than his going
home with one of them. And—sure enough!
—at last they talked old Waghorn over into
taking them all with him. So they squeezed
into a cab and went off, and when they got
to the old fool's house he showed them into
his drawing-room, and brought out his best
wine, and they all began to kick up an awful
shindy. This was between one and two
in the morning, mind. Well, just when the
row had got to its height, and when old
Waghorn, with his arm round two of the girls,
was dancing round the room, suddenly the
door opened, and Mrs. Waghorn made her
appearance in a dressing-gown and with a
wrapper round her. Maggie says her eyes
flashed fire and she looked like the very devil.
But she only waited for a minute, then
slammed the door terrifically and disappeared.
What a joke it must have been!"

The laughter which greeted this story was
uproarious, but it was suddenly interrupted
by the entrance of no less a person than Mr.
Augustus Whiffle. All eyes turned rapidly
from him to the table where the girls were
sitting. Polly had faced round and was
beckoning to the new-comer, but her companion was completely hidden behind a large

newspaper she affected to be reading. With
a nod to the assembled gentlemen, Augustus,
whose "get up" was the perfection of
dandyism, sauntered in the direction of the
beckoning girl. As soon as he had reached
the table, the newspaper which had concealed
the other, fell, and his face paled slightly as
he found himself before Carrie.

"Awfully sorry," said Polly, with a rather
malicious grin. "I couldn't persuade the
gentleman to come to-night, so I looked in
with a lady friend of yours. I thought you'd,
maybe, like to see her."

Whiffle leaned forward on the marble-
topped table, with his back to the bar, as if
conscious that so many eyes were watching
him, and spoke to Carrie with suppressed
anger.

"What do you want with me now?" he
asked. "You'll gain nothing, you know, by
making a scene here, so you might as well
talk quietly."

"You know very well what I want,"
replied Carrie, tossing her head slightly, and
avoiding his eye. "You owe me a five
pound note, and want to get out of paying
it."

"Owe it you? For what?"

"Didn't you promise me a five-pound note
when I left you and went to live with you
know who? And didn't I promise you in
return that I wouldn't ask you for any more
money as long as I lived?"

"Promise you five pounds!" repeated Whiffle, with quiet scorn. "I never promised you anything at all—except the lock-up if you come pestering me any more."

Those parts of Carrie's features which were not smeared with rouge turned deadly pale. Her eyes flashed terrible anger, and for a moment her fist clenched as though she would have struck him.

"You're a devil!" she hissed out, close to his face. "You've been a curse to me twice now. If it hadn't been for you I might have been a respectable girl still, and when I had a chance of going back to a quiet life you came and enticed me away again."

And she uttered curse after curse, in a tone clearly audible to the young men at the bar, who laughed aside with the utmost glee.

"Carrie, you're a —— fool," replied Whiffle, endeavouring to appear calm. "If you're short of money you know how to get it, well enough, without sponging on me for it. Go to your husband and get it from him!"

Carrie's face now flushed a deep red, and for a moment she could not speak. A reply was on her lips when Polly Hemp, who had listened hitherto with a cool smile, broke in with an exclamation of surprise.

"Her husband! Why, I never knew as you was married, Carrie?"

"No more I am!" replied the girl, hoarse

with passion. "No more I am! It's one of that devil's lies! He'll say anything to spite me, and to get out of paying what he owes me. I look much like a married woman, don't I, Polly?"

And she laughed, a bitter laugh at her own expense. Amid all the degradation of her broken life this terrible laugh was a proof that there still existed some fragments of a better nature. In reply to the laugh, Whiffle smiled, and winked at Polly.

"You may think you'll escape me," cried Carrie, seeing that the young man stood up as if to go, "and so you may do to-night. But I'll have the money out of you—if I steal it. You don't mind stealing all *I've* got, and why shouldn't I take what I can? So look out! You may laugh, but if I dash this wine-glass in your face you'll laugh in a different way."

Her excitement had risen so high that she spoke in a voice audible to everyone present. One or two waiters ran up to prevent an outbreak, and, whilst they were enjoining silence, Whiffle quietly turned and walked out of the restaurant. Carrie and her companion shortly followed, the former replying with a glance of the haughtiest scorn to one young man who was so daring as to invite her to drink with him.

"What did he mean when he spoke of your husband, Carrie?" asked Polly, as they issued together into the street.

"He meant a lie, I tell you!" replied Carrie, turning fiercely on her questioner. "Husband, indeed! What have I got to do with husbands! Perhaps you believe I'm a married woman with children, do you?"

"Well, well, don't look as though you'd eat me!" exclaimed the other, turning away her head with a laugh. "There's no harm in asking a question, I hope, is there?"

This Polly Hemp was as evil-looking a personage as one could encounter in the streets of London. Not that she was ugly in her features, for she had, indeed, what some would call a fine face. But it was the expression of this face which impressed the beholder more than its mere outlines, and that was wholly and absolutely evil. She had greenish eyes, out of which gleamed malice, and cunning, and lust, and every bad passion which could be imagined as lurking in a woman's heart. She had a habit of holding her lips slightly apart, so as to exhibit the remnants of a very fine set of teeth, which now had a fierce, resentful, tigerish air about them. In stature she was short, and rather stout. This woman could never have been other than evil-minded, but long years spent on the streets, and in all those nameless vicissitudes which, as a rule, render the prostitute's life mercifully brief, had reduced her to something far more akin to beast than man. Of iron constitution, she still, at the age of forty, showed no sign of yielding health, though she drank desperately, and had several times been almost killed in the fierce brawls which were her delight. Among Polly's numerous friends and acquaintances it was generally believed that she was saving money. Some said that she still looked forward to settling down to an old age of respectable comfort; and wits had been known to assert that she contemplated devoting her money to the erection of a church. In any case it is certain that, among Polly's endless passions, avarice was that which she most carefully nursed. To obtain money she would do anything, her unscrupulousness being only matched by her skill in avoiding discovery. Such a woman was a hopeful companion for Carrie.

The two sauntered along side by side through some of the back streets of Soho. Carrie was gloomy, and but little disposed for conversation; but her companion seemed especially talkative.

"And what's to be done now?" she asked, stopping by a public-house at a street-corner.

"What do you mean?" replied Carrie, carelessly.

"Where's tin to be got?"

"I don't care if I never get it," returned the other, humming a tune under her breath.

"Don't you? But I do, I can tell you. You seem to forget as you owe me three weeks board and lodging. Why don't you look out for money like the other girls do?"

"Never mind what I do and what I don't do," replied Carrie, impatiently. "You'll get your money some day, if I have to go and steal it, and that ought to be enough."

"Well, well; there's no call to have a row over a few pounds, is there?" rejoined Polly, looking askance at her companion. "Come, it's near closing time. What are you going to drink, Carrie?"

The girl appeared to hesitate for a moment, but her own pockets were empty and the temptation was irresistible. She followed her evil genius into the gin-palace and they mingled with a thick crowd which was clustering about the bar, all eagerly swallowing as much as they could before the place closed.

Polly had called out in a stentorian voice for "two brandies hot," and had turned to talk to an acquaintance who stood near, when Carrie, who heeded nothing that was going on around, was suddenly startled by having her arm grasped. A half-drunken woman was standing by her side, calling to her by name and asking her to drink.

"Don't you know me?" hiccoughed the woman. "You're too proud to come an' see me an' my daughters now-a-days, I reckon? Why don't you come an' drink a quiet glass like as you used to, eh?"

After some little difficulty Carrie recognised the speaker as her old landlady, Mrs. Pole. Seeing that the latter had no command over herself, and fearing lest some reference to her husband should catch Polly Hemp's ear, she took hold of the woman's arm and tried to draw her away to a different bar. But Mrs. Pole, who was at the obstinately merry stage in her cups, refused to budge, and talked on in a voice loud enough for everyone to hear. Carrie saw, moreover, that Polly had turned round and was listening.

"And 'ow's yer 'usband?" cried Mrs. Pole, with a jocose wink. "What's ee got to say to yer comin' to such-like places as these o' nights? He-he-he! I ain't got no 'usband, I ain't; ain't I lucky?"

Polly turned away her head to hide a particularly malicious grin as she heard these remarks. She had no wish to let Carrie see that she heard, so she at once began talking to some men who were near her. Nevertheless she kept an eye upon Mrs. Pole, and when, shortly after the lights were lowered, and the crowd of excited drinkers reeled and crushed out into the street, with hideous laughter, and screaming, and yells, Polly eluded her former companion and followed the other woman some distance along the street. At length she went up to her. The formation of an acquaintanceship between two such individuals is no difficult or ceremonious matter, and Polly Hemp speedily received and accepted an invitation to take a glass in Mrs. Pole's kitchen. The latter was at present living in Gerrard Street.

The result of this interview was seen on the following morning. Shortly before noon Polly Hemp issued forth from the dingy abode which, with playful reference to the character of its inmates, she was won't to term her "Convalescent Home," and, attired in the manner of a highly respectable matron, wended her way to Huntley Street. Here she speedily found the house in which Arthur's brief married life had been spent, and, in a conversation with worthy Mrs. Oaks, was deeply grieved that the latter could afford her no intelligence whatever as to the whereabouts of her dear nephew, Mr. Golding. On second thoughts, however, Mrs. Oaks recollected that she knew the address of an intimate friend of Mr. Golding, namely, Mark Challenger, and she suggested that in all probability the distressed lady might be able to derive from this latter gentleman the information she desired. Polly Hemp accordingly took her leave with a profusion of thanks, and later in the day waited upon Mr. Challenger, at his lodging in Gower Place.

Here she played a different *rôle*, namely, that of the aunt of Mrs. Golding. She had known the address in Huntley Street, she said, but, on calling there, had been bitterly disappointed to find her niece departed, no

one knew whither.   Simple-hearted Mark
Challenger was the last person to suspect
fraud in such a case.   By means of a few
carefully-framed questions he elicited, as he
thought, the fact that his visitor knew nothing
of Carrie's absconding, and then, unwilling
to be the conveyer of such disagreeable intelligence, he contented himself with giving
her Arthur's present address.   With a gleam
of joyful hope irradiating the melancholy of
her countenance, honest Polly Hemp took her
leave with many expressions of gratitude.

All this happened a few days after the interview between Helen and Arthur recorded
in the last chapter.   This afternoon Arthur
had hurried home as quickly as possible
from his work, and, without thinking of
refreshment, had sat down at once at
the table in his bedroom, inspired with the
utmost ardour for his work.   On the previous day he had purchased several plaster
casts, and from one of these—a head of a
Venus—he was engaged in making a drawing in crayon.   He had placed his lamp so as
to afford a striking effect of light and shade,
and, having roughly sketched in the outlines,
was commencing, with a hand which trembled with delight, to work at some of the
broad shadows, when he was suddenly interrupted by a tap at his door.   Unable to rise,
he called out " Come in ! " and Lucy Venning responded.

" There is a lady down stairs who wishes

to see you, Mr. Golding," she said, looking, as she spoke, with curiosity at Arthur's work.

At the word "lady" Arthur had involuntarily started to his feet, and his blood, which had just now been coursing so warmly through his veins, seemed suddenly chilled. Had Lucy been looking at his face she must have noticed that he had suddenly turned pale, but luckily her attention was fixed upon the cast and the drawing.

"A lady?" repeated Arthur, as soon as he could speak, doing his best to make his tone one of mere surprise. Whoever can it be? Is it an old lady, Miss Venning?"

"Yes; she looks rather old," replied Lucy.

Arthur sighed with relief; but the next moment a vague fear took possession of him. He stood reflecting.

"How very beautiful that is, Mr. Golding!" exclaimed Lucy, who seemed almost to have forgotten her errand in her admiration of the drawing. "Is this how you always employ yourself? I had no idea that you could draw."

"A little," he replied, doing his best to smile. "But I suppose the lady is waiting?"

"Oh yes; she is in the parlour. There is no one in, and I thought it best to take her there."

"Thank you," replied Arthur, speaking mechanically. "I will go down at once."

He turned and went down-stairs, leaving Lucy to close the room door. In the parlour he found the middle-aged, respectably-attired lady whom the reader is of course prepared to recognise as Polly Hemp.

"Mr. Golding, I think?" she began, with a slightly affected cough, as soon as Arthur had entered the room.

The young man bowed acquiescence, assuring himself the while that this visitor was an absolute stranger to him.

"Then," continued Polly, "I may as well say what I've got to say at once. My name's Mrs. Hemp, and I'm a quiet widow as keeps a lodging-house Piccadilly way. It's now about a month since a young lady, as called herself Miss Mitchell, came and took a room in my house, which the rent of it, together with two meals a day, was to be twenty-five shillings a week. I don't as a rule like taking single ladies, they're often fast-like, you know, sir, but this one seemed so very respectable-looking as I couldn't think of refusing her. Well, she come to me, and she paid the first week's rent in advance, as of course I always make it a rule. But, since that, she hasn't paid no rent at all. And that isn't the worst. I soon began to find out as she wasn't at all proper—had gentlemen to visit her at all hours, and such like things, you see, sir. Well, that of course would be the ruin of a respectable house like mine, so I just give her notice, and thought to myself I must just

be content to be at the loss of my money.
When she was going, the other day, I asked
her if she meant to pay me what was due,
and she said as she hadn't no means of paying, but that she was married—a thing I
never knew before—and if I liked she'd give
me a letter to take to her husband, asking
him, you see, to pay the rent as was due. She
couldn't tell me just where her husband
lived, but she told me to go to a Mr. Challenger, as lives near the Euston Road, and he
would give me your address, you see. So I
went, and Mr. Challenger give me your address, and I've come to see whether you'll be
so good as to pay me what your wife owes.
And here's the letter."

So saying, Polly produced a sheet of note-
paper, on which was written the following, in
a hand very admirably imitated from poor
Carrie's scrawl. This was not the first occasion on which Polly Hemp had found skill in
forgery, a very important feature of her stock-
in-trade:—

"DEAR ARTHUR,—

"Will you please pay Mrs. Hemp
three pound fifteen which is what I rightly
owe her. I am sorry to trouble you, but I
have no money and she says she can get it
from you in a cort if it isnt paid.

"Yours afectiontely,
"CARRIE."

Arthur held this scrawl in his hand for

some minutes after reading it, unable to speak, scarcely to think. Not for a moment did a doubt of its genuineness cross his mind. He recognised too well the old handwriting which he had striven so hard to improve, and even thought that he remembered some of poor Carrie's pet faults in spelling. The indelicacy of the act shocked him, and yet he felt that it was only too much in harmony with what he knew, or thought he knew, of Carrie's character. At this moment there was a strange warfare in heart. Convinced as he was that his old love was dead past reviving, he yet felt a deep pity excited in him by what he had heard. That which we have once intensely loved can never be wholly indifferent to us, and the thought of Carrie, she who was still his wife, fallen into hideous vice and wretchedness, pulled terribly at his heart-strings. And if pity was awakened, a sterner voice, that of conscience, also began to speak within him. He could not forget that he had made no serious effort to discover his wife and bring her back to live with him. In the months which had intervened since their parting he had frequently consoled himself with the reflection that this marriage, which was a mere name, a form, had in reality been rendered null and void by Carrie's own behaviour. For all that he could not help feeling at times that he had blinded himself by a sophism, and at the present moment he experienced a pang of actual remorse.

" And where is—is she now?" he asked at length, recalled to a sense of the business in hand by a cough from his visitor.

" I don't know no more than you do, sir," was the reply, with a shrug. " People as leaves houses without paying their rents ain't so ready to let one know where they go to."

Again there was a pause, during which Arthur struggled between his desire to question this woman further with regard to Carrie, and the feeling of disgust which her face and tone excited in him. Polly naturally thought he was reflecting whether he should pay or not, and did her best to assume the look of one patient under injury.

" Did she say anything else to you about me," asked Arthur, at length, " except that I might perhaps pay her debts?"

" Nothing else as I remember," replied Polly, after a moment of rapid reflection.

" Did—did she seem in good health when she was in your house?" was Arthur's next question.

" Moderate well, I think sir," replied Polly.

" And you know nothing whatever of her at present?"

" No more than you do yourself, sir."

Arthur sighed as his eye again fell upon the note.

" If you will excuse me for a minute," he then said, " I will fetch the money for you."

He went up to his room and returned in a

very few minutes, holding the money in his hand. He had of late resumed his habit of parsimonious living, and every penny he could save was put aside in fear of unexpected calls upon him.

"You will write me a receipt on the back of this note," he said, laying the letter upon the table. "Please to put your address at the top; it might someday be useful to me."

Polly wrote the desired form, adding, it is needless to say, a fictitious address, and, with a hand which trembled in spite of herself, took the money and dropped it into her purse.

"I hope, sir," she said, as she rose, in a tone of dignified humility, "I hope as you don't think I've done wrong in coming and troubling you about this little matter. Though I do my best to keep up a respectable appearance I'm only a poor woman, and I could ill afford to lose three weeks' rent. I hope you understand me, sir."

"I understand perfectly," replied Arthur, in an absent manner, without looking at her.

"Then I wish you good-night, with many thanks, sir," said Polly.

"Good-night," returned Arthur, leading the way mechanically to the door.

He returned to his room, and for an hour paced the floor in the old manner, grievously troubled in mind. But the absolute silence of the house, the genial warmth of the fire in his grate, the dim light in the room (for the rays of the lamp were concentrated, by means of a reflector, full upon the bust), these at length operated with calming effect upon him. His thoughts slipped from gloomy imaginations of Carrie's sufferings to the interview with Helen Norman. Here was an antidote for all ills. Opening a drawer, always kept carefully locked, he took out his portrait of Helen, which he had obtained again from Will Noble. Preferring this original drawing to any subsequent copy, he had carefully patched together the torn halves, and had enclosed the whole in a simple frame. He did not venture to hang it openly in his room, but at night, when the house was still, and he alone awake, he hung it up on the wall before him, that the calm, sweet look of the beautiful eyes might afford a never-failing source of courage and inspiration. This he did now, after imprinting a kiss upon the outlined lips, and at once he recovered his interrupted zeal, and so laboured far into the night.

In the meantime Polly Hemp had regained her abode, joy in her heart and money in her purse. Before letting herself in with the latch-key she obeyed her invariable habit and looked up at all the windows on the front of the house. There was no light save in one on the top floor, and Polly smiled to herself as she recognised Carrie's presence. But the smile was immediately followed by a frown. This was no time for her young lady lodgers to be taking their ease at home. To do so had, however, been frequently Carrie's custom of late. Polly entered with a determination to speak seriously.

The house was perfectly quiet, and perfectly dark. Polly, who always walked about with an ominously light and cat-like step, seemed also to have the eyes of a cat, for she guided herself without the slightest noise along the passage and down a short flight of steps. Then she stopped and called with a low voice down into the realms of darkness.

"Jo! Jo!"

A species of growl was the only reply. Probably it was a dog whom she thus addressed by his name. And yet that could hardly be so, for she went on to ask questions.

"Anyone been, Jo?"

"Not as I knows on," replied the voice, with a drunken hiccough.

"Anyone in?"

"Not as I knows on."

"Then you're a fool, Jo," rejoined Polly, still in the same quiet voice, "and you'll get the sack if you don't know your business better. Carrie's in?"

"Don't reckon her," replied the man, for such appeared to be the speaker. "She's always in. She come in above an hour sen'."

"Alone?"

"Of course."

"You're half drunk, Jo," said Polly, after

a moment's silence. "I shall have to find another bully, mind if I don't."

Another growl was the only response, and this terminated the conversation. Polly then retraced her steps with equal silence into the passage, and thence up to the top of the house. She tried the door of Carrie's room, and it opened.

It was a rather ill-furnished bedroom, with here and there traces of worn-out finery which had probably been removed from the better rooms below. As well as the bed, there was a sofa, and, hung against the wall, a long gilt-framed mirror, cracked across the middle. On the floor was a strip of carpet which had once been gaudy, and the chairs were seated with what had formerly been bright green cloth, now resembling a dingy yellow. In one corner was a spittoon, and a man's old hat was hanging on a peg behind the door. On the sofa lay the present occupant of this chamber. She had apparently thrown off her paletôt on entering, and she lay in her blue silk dress, which was open at the bosom. She was asleep, a heavy, drunken sleep, more resembling a state of insensibility than ordinary slumber. The cushion had slipped from under her head, which drooped almost to the floor, and her features were terribly distorted and discoloured by the position. One hand was clasped on the back of the sofa, the other lay on the floor. Lying thus, Carrie might have served for a personification of brutal drunkenness.

On the table was the lamp which illumined the room, and, close to it, a spirit bottle and a glass, the former empty, the latter still containing a few drops. But the table showed something more interesting to Polly than these everyday objects. There, glistening in the light of the lamp, lay three bright sovereigns. Polly no longer paid any attention to the sleeping girl, but at once seized on the coins and clasped them in her fist. Then, with a hideous grin upon her face, and still treading with the utmost quietness, she glided from the room, muttering to herself, " At last ! "

CHAPTER IX.

LOVES AND FRIENDSHIPS.

MR. GRESHAM, faithful to his promise, appeared once more in London early in December, and remained till he had seen his ward, together with her safeguard, Mrs. Cumberbatch, comfortably settled in the new house in Highbury. The intercourse between Helen and her guardian during the period of removal was extremely slight. The former left to Mrs. Cumberbatch, who gloried in the trust, the whole business of choosing the furniture, and Mr. Gresham was not displeased to have this means of avoiding communication with his ward, in whose presence he could never feel altogether at his ease. Only once did Helen consult him as to her future life, and that was with reference to Lucy Venning. The artist, with characteristic politeness, expressed his complete concurrence in Miss Norman's plans, saying that he esteemed it a most happy idea, and one which, had he been acquainted with a suitable person, he should certainly have himself suggested. But he showed no desire to make the acquaintance of Miss Venning, being quite content to repose all confidence in Helen's discrimination. As Mr. Gresham grew older he became

more and more convinced that the true
philosophy of life consisted in minimising
one's share in the troublesome details of the
world's business. On the very day succeeding that of Helen's ultimate settlement in
Holly Cottage, Mr. Gresham took his departure. Even now he felt that unnecessary delay in the neighbourhood of his fair
ward would be dangerous to his peace of
mind.

Mr. Heatherley lost no time in paying
Helen a visit in her new home. He came on
New Year's eve and found her sitting alone in
the pleasant little room which was especially
her own, and which she had arranged in the
manner of a study. Mrs. Cumberbatch was
enjoying herself at a festive gathering with
some of her numerous acquaintances, and
Lucy Venning, who now made her home with
Helen, was passing the evening with her
father. Helen met her visitor with a cheerful,
even a gay, reception.

"Doubtless I disturb you in some deep and
serious philosophical investigation," said the
clergyman, with that slight tone of good-
humoured banter with which he generally
spoke of Helen's studies.

"By no means," she replied, resuming her
seat by the fire. "I must actually confess
that I had descended to the frivolity of the
newspaper. To tell you the truth I feel a
little tired to-night and not quite fit for
serious work."

" I suppose you have been receiving a good many visitors since you became settled ? "

" Visitors ? " asked Helen, smiling.

" Yes," replied the clergyman. " I mean your friends and acquaintances."

" You are the first of such visitors, Mr. Heatherley," said Helen, " and in all probability will be the last. Besides yourself I have neither friends nor acquaintances upon whose visits I may depend."

" Your life must be a strangely solitary one, Miss Norman," said Mr. Heatherley, after regarding her for a moment with some appearance of surprise.

" I will confess that I have now and then felt it to be so," returned Helen, " and on that account I persuaded Lucy Venning to come and be a companion for me."

There was a brief silence, during which the clergyman knit his brows and appeared to be reflecting upon some rather disagreeable subject.

" I heard of that for the first time," he said at length, " about a week ago, from Mr. Venning."

" With pleasure or the opposite ? " asked Helen, adding immediately, " perhaps with indifference ? "

" Certainly not with indifference," he replied, coughing slightly and keeping his eyes fixed on the fire, whilst he rested his hands upon his knees in a manner customary with him when about to speak seriously. After

pausing for a moment, during which Helen
regarded him with a curious look, he again
coughed and proceeded.

"May I ask what kind of companionship
you look for from Miss Venning?"

"The companionship of a pleasant friend,"
replied Helen. "When I am merry she chats
with me; when I am in a more earnest mood
she saves me from the unpleasant habit of
soliloquy. We have taken up a course of
reading, too, together. I hope to be able to
teach Lucy much that she has hitherto had
no opportunity of learning."

"That I anticipated, Miss Norman," said
Mr. Heatherley, "and it was partly in consequence of this anticipation that I came to
see you to-night. If I speak to you with
some freedom on a matter of grave interest
to me, I am sure you will not take it amiss?"

"I trust you will not do me the wrong of
thinking otherwise, Mr. Heatherley."

"Then I will take the liberty of asking you
one more question. Does it enter into your
plans to impart to Miss Venning your views
on the subject of religion?"

"I have no such intention," replied Helen,
smiling. "Lucy believes me as orthodox in
all such matters as she is herself. Indeed, I
feel sure that her simple mind is incapable
of conceiving heterodoxy as grave as mine;
or, if it be, she certainly could not attribute
such depravity to the most abandoned of
criminals. So careful have I been lest I should

prove a rock of offence to her, that I have resolved to be guilty of habitual falsehood, in leading her to suppose that I visit a place of worship in the West End each Sunday. I think you will admit that it is a pious fraud, Mr. Heatherley?"

The clergyman made no immediate reply, but continued to sit with his hands upon his knees, gazing into the fire.

"What are you reading with her at present?" he asked.

"One or two of 'Macaulay's Essays,'" she replied, with a smile.

"Is Miss Venning an apt pupil?"

"Extremely so. Her intelligence is admirable, and the excellence of her heart is a guarantee for the soundness of her moral judgment."

"You have relieved my mind from a very disagreeable load, Miss Norman," said Mr. Heatherley, after a brief silence. "If you think I have been guilty of an injustice towards you in being for a moment fearful, I beg you will pardon me in consideration of the interests at stake. Since Miss Venning's joining you in the work of the evening classes, I have seen in her qualities which before I had never suspected, knowing her only as a good and quiet member of my Sunday School. I will confess, too, that your evident fondness of her society has increased my interest in her. It would have been impossible for me to stand by whilst the foundations of her faith were being attacked, and perhaps hopelessly destroyed. But, as I said, you have relieved my mind."

Finding Helen's eyes closely fixed upon him, his face coloured slightly as he finished speaking, and, almost immediately, he turned the conversation into a wholly different channel. At the end of about half-an-hour he rose to go.

"I have not made a formal enquiry after your health, Miss Norman," he said, as he was drawing on his great coat, "for I deemed it unnecessary. For the last few weeks I have been astonished at your improvement. The weather has been so extremely trying, and yet you appear to grow better in health and spirits every day."

"I certainly do feel much better than I did," replied Helen, with a slight laugh. "I am somewhat at a loss to account for it."

"Well, do not, for all that, presume upon your strength. You certainly ought not to walk about much in the snow. Pray take counsel from the past, and exercise prudence."

"Oh, Mr. Heatherley," exclaimed Helen, "how can you have the heart to advise me to think so much of my own comfort, when the poor are suffering so terribly! I think if I were ever so ill the thought of starvation in those terrible hovels in weather such as this would compel me to keep at work. Help is more than ever needed just now, and certainly there is more gratification in affording it than when the need is less obvious. I met this morning a wretched woman whom I scarcely ever see sober, and could not help buying her a warm gown and a cloak. I feel almost sure that before to-morrow they will both be pawned for drink, but I *could not* do otherwise."

"I often think I am becoming somewhat hard-hearted," replied the clergyman, as he held out his hand. "I refused charity this morning under very similar circumstances. I cannot afford to throw away what might be of real use."

The next two months passed quickly both for Helen Norman and for Arthur Golding. During that period they only saw each other once, and then without interchange of more than a bow, and yet there were not many minutes during the day in which the thoughts of each were not occupied with the other. Both were happy, for both were nourishing their hearts with the anticipation of a blissful future, though probably neither ventured to peer too closely into the golden mist which swam before their eyes.

During this time the constant presence of Lucy Venning was inexpressibly comforting to Helen. Without assumedly making her simple friend a *confidante* in the secret emotions of her heart, Helen did not hesitate to speak to her of Arthur as she would have spoken to no one else, reposing the most absolute trust in Lucy's discreet and affectionate nature. The latter soon understood that it gave Helen the utmost joy to see any specimen of Arthur's work, and her woman's nature taught her how to meet half way Arthur's wish that she should be the means of taking drawings to Holly Cottage. Every Sunday she spent at home with her father, and sometimes one or two evenings in the week also; and at such times Arthur was sure to find an opportunity of giving into her care a small parcel which she took away with her, and brought back on her next visit. Once or twice Lucy was entrusted to express to Arthur, in private, Miss Norman's special delight in some drawing she had seen; whereupon Arthur at once sent it back again, begging that Miss Norman would accept it from him. And these gifts Helen treasured up with unspeakable care.

At length, early in March, Lucy was once more entrusted with a message to the effect that Arthur would feel grateful if Miss Norman could accord him an interview on a matter of some importance. She brought back the answer that on the following Sunday morning, about eleven o'clock, Miss Norman would be at liberty. At this time Helen knew that Mrs. Cumberbatch would be attending her special place of worship in the Mile-end Road, exercising her eternal curiosity on the concerns of heaven instead of those of earth. She felt sure she knew the purpose of Arthur's visit, and she looked forward to it with an impatience even greater than that she had experienced three months ago.

She received him in the drawing-room, a handsomely-furnished apartment which looked out on to the little garden in front of the house, the view being strictly circumscribed within this small area by the high hedge of impenetrable holly-bushes which skirted the garden on all three sides. The privacy thus secured was delightful to Helen, who detested the sight of vulgar and pretentious people, such as she knew her neighbours on either side to be. She looked forward with delightful anticipation to the warm days of summer, when she would be able to sit on the lawn, and yet be as private as though in her own room.

They met with perfect freedom from embarrassment, and with a keen joy on both sides which neither affected to conceal. After a few introductory sentences exchanged, Arthur proceeded to state the object of his visit.

"A fortnight to-day, Miss Norman," he said, "will be my twenty-first birth-day. As Mr. Gresham has, of course, no knowledge of my address, I wish to apprise him of it; but before I can do that, I must know where to write to."

"I will give you the address," replied Helen, taking up a piece of paper and writing upon it. " Mr. Gresham lives in France now."

Arthur took the paper, and, after reading the address, put it in his purse. There was a minute's silence, during which his eyes wandered round the pictures on the walls. At length they fell upon one of his own drawings, hanging framed in a good light. He turned his head quickly towards Helen, and their eyes met. The latter blushed, bent for a moment over a book which lay open on the table, and then forced herself to speak.

" Are you a reader of poetry, Mr. Golding ? " she asked, rustling over the leaves before her, whilst Arthur stood enraptured with the unconscious grace of her attitude and the glowing beauty of her countenance.

" I have had neither time nor opportunity to read as much as I should like to," he replied. " Shakespere, and many of the older poets, I learned to love from Mr. Tollady. Of the modern writers, I think I know Shelley best. But perhaps I am more capable of appreciating his principles than his poetry. To enjoy the latter requires, I fear, more culture than I may pretend to."

" Oh, you underrate your own powers, Mr. Golding," replied Helen, earnestly. " The very fact that you like Shelley proves you are able to appreciate him. He is not a poet to attract vacant minds by mere empty jingle or easily-digested platitudes. I myself learnt

to love Shelley from my father when a mere child, and now I prize him as my surest safeguard against despair of the world. Those who, like myself, see too much of the evil and discouraging side of life, cannot afford to dispense with poetry."

" I have often thought the same with regard to my own art," replied Arthur. " I know scarcely anything of the life which is raised above sordid cares and miseries, except from what I have read in books and imagined in my too-frequent day-dreams; yet no sooner do I take up a pencil than I seem to taste all the delights of a higher and nobler existence, where the only food which is yearned after is that of the mind and the heart, and where the joys and sorrows are deeper and purer than those of the every-day world. How much I have to thank you for, Miss Norman !" he added, with a voice which trembled with emotion. " Had it not been for your encouraging words I might still have been suffering unspeakable wretchedness. At present I look back upon that time in which I had no thought of art as a period of something worse than death. I think it would be impossible for me to sink into such apathy again."

" I trust it would be," she replied. " And yet I am not sure you do right in speaking of it as apathy. Even then your mind was occupied with no ignoble thoughts. No, no; you must not call it apathy; for the thoughts and the plans which then engrossed your attention were the very same which will, I trust, form the occupation of my whole life. I have become convinced, Mr. Golding, that we should not regret any single event in our lives which was not absolutely the result of an evil purpose. Every such event has been necessary for our development; without it we should have lacked some useful experience which has contributed to the formation of our character. I am very optimistic in my philosophy," she added, smiling, "and it is happy for me I can be so. The difference between my own point of view and that of a pious Christian who says that everything is for the best, is not really so great as it might at first sight appear."

She watched the result of these words upon him carefully, and was pleased to see the smile of intelligence and sympathy which rose to his lips as she spoke. There was something of pain, too, in the expression of his face, which she attributed to the recollection of some by-gone unhappiness, and which affected her with compassion unspeakably tender. Again a brief silence ensued, during which she turned over the leaves of the book on the table.

"I was reading Tennyson when you came," she said. "There is a deep, glad ring of hope throughout his poems which chimes delightfully with my own best thoughts. You have read Tennyson?"

"With the exception of a few short poems," replied Arthur, "I do not know him."

"Oh, then you must lose no time in making his acquaintance!" replied Helen. "Please to let me lend you his works. Will you take all at once, or one volume at a time?"

"I shall be very grateful," replied Arthur, his face flushing with joy. "But only one volume at once. It is but very little time I can find for reading, for I almost grudge every moment which is not given to drawing."

"Then you shall take this volume," she resumed. "I think it likely you will find many suggestions for pictures here. One verse particularly struck me this morning, and made me think of—that an artist might make a wonderful painting from it. It is in 'The Palace of Art,'—a delightful poem. It is this," she added, opening the book and reading :—

> And one a full-fed river, winding slow
> By herds upon an endless plain,
> The rugged rims of thunder brooding low,
> With shadow-streaks of rain.

Or this, if you are in a wild, instead of a melancholy, mood—

> And one a foreground black with stones and slags,
> Beyond, a line of heights, and higher
> All barr'd with long white cloud the scornful crags,
> And highest, snow and fire.

Are they not grand?"

" Wonderful pictures, indeed," replied Arthur, upon whose ear the melody of her voice had fallen with intoxicating sweetness. " Is it a long poem, Miss Norman?"

" Oh no; comparatively short."

" How I should like to hear you read it all! Poetry never sounded so delightful to me as in those two verses from your lips."

He spoke thoughtlessly, allowing himself to be carried away by the current of his passion. Helen blushed, but with pleasure, and motioning him to a seat, at once began to read. Her voice was rich and full, and lent itself admirably to the expression of the varying moods of the poem. At first there was something of timidness in her tone, but this speedily faded, and, seeing her hearer sunk in the deepest enjoyment, she read her very best. When she had finished Arthur made no remark. Commonplace compliment would have been ridiculously out of place. Silence was the best way of showing the impression made upon him. Helen was the first to speak.

" This poem," she said, " contains an admirable moral, very applicable to myself. How often have I been tempted to build just such a Palace of Art, and to shut myself up in it with an infinitude of intellectual delights, heedless of the rest of the world. Happily I have hitherto been able to resist such temptations, as I trust I may always do."

Very shortly Arthur took his leave, and walked home with a heart brimming over with happiness which left no place for a single speck of gloom or doubt. During the afternoon he plunged into the delights of the volume Helen had lent him, the fact that the book he held in his hand was hers adding unspeakably to the genuine enthusiasm which the poetry aroused. He turned over the pages delicately, and held the book with an exquisite tenderness of touch, as though it were the hand of Helen herself. Many times did he read through to himself " The Palace of Art," for with the sight of the printed words came back upon his ear, with an almost startling distinctness, each gentle modulation of the reader's voice. Every peculiarity of emphasis or of punctuation reproduced itself as from a ghostly tongue in the silence of his room. He felt that if he were to lay the poem aside for fifty years and then once more read it, he should still have that voice in his ears, and once more thrill through every nerve to the sound of its exquisite melody.

As the evening deepened into night he sat by his fire brooding over the two verses which Helen had indicated to him, for already he had resolved to do his utmost to depict the scenes in visible form, in order to have the pleasure of offering them to his idol. The tender gloom of the hour and the kindled enthusiasm of his mind worked together to arouse his imagination, and when at length the silence was slightly broken by the sound of a solemn melody played in the room below, the inspiration of the air came upon him, and in the glowing embers he saw distinctly the outlines of the first scene. He fixed his attention so strongly upon it that it attained to absolute reality. Snatching up a piece of paper from the table he drew rapidly in broad dark lines the main features of the landscape, for all, even to the moulding of the low, black clouds, was plain before him. The whole thus secured, he exerted his eyes for a moment, and, as he did so, a piece of coal crumbled into ruin, veiling the vision. He reflected, listening to the solemn music half unconsciously the while, and by degrees his eyes once more wandered to the fire, where the heat had now built up new forms. Before long the subject of the second verse began to grow before him, and at length, from the black foreground to the glowing summits, he saw it all. Again he took paper and hastily outlined the bold mountain masses, fixing in his mind all the rich gradations of hue which burned before him, and which on the morrow he would exhaust his pallet to obtain. In this way he spent two hours in an artist's dreamland, issuing from it purified and exalted, as though he had drank of the water of an enchanted spring.

Soon after six o'clock he was disturbed by

the arrival of a visitor, William Noble. Of
late he had grown rather to fear Noble's
visits, both because he knew that the latter
looked with but little less than contempt
upon the choice he had made of his life's
work, and because Noble's inflexible moral
judgment so often found expression in sentiments which had a disagreeable application
to Arthur's present state of mind. Noble
constantly spoke of Carrie, taking it for
granted that Arthur would never cease to
exert himself to rediscover the unhappy girl.
Already once or twice Arthur had been compelled to tell a direct falsehood in answering
his friend's questions, and the awakening of
conscience subsequent upon such conversation had caused him several hours of acute
misery. Very much of the old cordiality
had already faded from their intercourse, and
the subjects upon which they could converse
seemed to grow fewer and less interesting at
each meeting. Arthur often thought that
Noble assumed a monitorial tone to him
which was scarcely warrantable, and, though
withheld by the gentleness of his disposition
from provoking an open outbreak, by degrees listened with less of good-humour to
the other's moral strictures.

Noble seemed in unusually high spirits
to-night, a circumstance explained by the
first words he uttered.

"Well, I have succeeded at last!" he exclaimed, on entering. "The club is to be

established once more, and, I believe, on a firmer foundation. During the last few days I have made the acquaintance of an admirable man, by trade a builder, who has risen from the extremest poverty to comparative wealth, and, on my asking him to join me in this work, he offered out of hand to pay the rent of a club-house, if I could only find half-a-dozen men willing to subscribe a shilling a week and to work with a heart. We have decided to begin upon a rather different plan, though. When I got together the old club I expected rather too much, I fear. It's difficult to find a number of working men who will give their money and their time for other people's advantage, and be content to derive nothing themselves except the sense of doing their duty. This time we shall go more on the lines of the ordinary benefit society. We shall have a certain minimum subscription, and shall try to collect our members from the poorest and most wretched classes. We shall have men, women and children—anyone in short who will join, and in return for the subscriptions we shall do our best to give assistance to any member who really wants it. The lectures and debates we shall continue as before, and no doubt before long we shall be able to have a reading-room, and perhaps a library. Having a building ready to our hands and free of expense, of course gives us a glorious start. Well, I have got four of the half dozen subscribers; men I know well myself and who can be depended upon. Now I have come to ask you to make up the total, Golding. I didn't come before, because I felt sure I could depend upon you, and I knew you would be glad to hear what progress I had made. Your help will be invaluable in keeping the thing well together and making the men enthusiastic. I haven't forgotten how you used to speak at the old club. When have you a free evening? When shall I take you to see Lawton?—that's the builder's name."

Arthur was silent for some moments before replying. To refuse to join in this scheme would, he knew, deeply grieve, if not offend, Noble, and yet he felt it impossible to give his assent. He spoke at length in a voice which betrayed his embarrassment.

"I am glad, heartily glad, Noble, that you have such an excellent prospect of carrying out your plans. No one could possibly feel their excellence more than I do, and no one could wish you success more heartily. But I fear it is impossible for me to join you in the work as I did before. What money I can possibly spare I will gladly devote to the club, but my time I must be so selfish as to withhold. I know you do not approve of the path I am following; it seems to you one of mere idle self-gratification. But it is my nature; I act under impulses which I feel compelled to obey. I could not be content with giving you only part of my time and

my thoughts; either you must have all, or
none. You have no need of half-workers,
and such I should be, even in spite of myself."

Noble listened to these excuses with a look
of surprise, passing into one of pain and
displeasure.

"I certainly couldn't have believed you
would refuse your help in such a matter as
this," he replied, whilst Arthur's eyes drooped
before his stern gaze. "Have you then lost
all interest in what you were once ready to
devote your life to?"

"You must do your best to understand
me," rejoined Arthur, gathering courage and
resolving to act independently. "Did I not
say that I still retained the utmost interest
in this work, and was willing to help it
with money as much as ever I could?"

"But you refuse any personal participation in my plans. To say that I must have
all your time or none is absurd. I should
not think of asking for more than you could
reasonably spare—an evening once or twice
in the week, or so. I should be quite
satisfied with that. It is your personal influence that I need far more than your
money. Surely you will not refuse so slight
a sacrifice?"

"It's extremely difficult to make you see
my reasons for refusing what seems so little,
for you have no sympathy with the work I
am wholly devoted to. I am working at art

under difficulties just now; having to give my whole day to bread-winning labour, and only having the nights and the early mornings for my real work. Under these circumstances I confess, Noble, I should grudge a single hour even for such a cause as yours. Very shortly I hope to be free from my daily labour, and you will perhaps think I might at least then be able to spare a few evenings. But if I hope to succeed as an artist, even the whole day and night is scarcely enough for me; I shall dread to lose a minute. And besides, in joining you there would be something even worse for me than the mere loss of precious time. It would be such a terrible distraction. When I ought to keep my thoughts constantly fixed upon one object, I should be occupied perpetually with a thousand, and each one of them sufficient to make me weary and wretched. I tell you plainly I should fear to recommence with you, for I know well what an irresistible fascination your scheme would soon exercise over me. Indeed, Noble, you must pardon me, and *try*, at least, to believe that I am not altogether actuated by an ignoble selfishness. There is something higher than that in this art work of mine, though I fear it would be useless for me to endeavour to make you see it. I see you are angry. Well, I am sorry for it, but what can I do? Surely you should be the last, Noble, to compel anyone to act in the teeth of his firmest convictions."

"Your convictions seem to have so little consistency in them," replied the other, with something of bitterness in his tone, "that I confess myself unable to respect their latest form. Can you seriously tell me that—after seeing as much as you have done of the evils of poverty, after being so strongly convinced that it is the duty of each honest man to do his utmost to lessen them, after seeing how much can be done even with the slightest means, if only there is real energy to back them up—can you seriously say that, after all this, now that there is a better opportunity than ever of being useful, you believe it your duty to turn aside from the work and spend your life in devotion to a mere unreasoning passion, in efforts directed towards a useless end? If you mean that, it is indeed useless to try to make me understand. I can only be sorry for the fate of all your good resolutions."

For a moment Arthur was on the point of replying angrily, but with a great effort he checked the rising irritation, and, after pacing the room once or twice, spoke calmly.

"Then you are resolved to be uncharitable in your views, Noble. Perhaps you even think me ungrateful in acting as I do since I owe you so much. In all probability you saved my life, and you think it only just that I should spend it henceforth according to your guidance. But believe me, I am making a better use of my life than you would have me do. I am so certain of this, that I even risk your worst misinterpretations. Perhaps you will some day see that I was right. Pursue your own path; it is a glorious one, and for you the only right one. But I know well that it would only lead me astray."

"Good-bye!" exclaimed Noble, holding out his hand, as he turned to go.

"Till when?" asked Arthur.

"What is the use in our continuing to meet?" returned the other, with sadness in his tone. "It would be a constant pain to me to see you. I should always be reproaching you, or, if I did not speak what I thought, you would be conscious of all I felt, and could not be at ease with me."

"But cannot we still be friends? Do you hold that all who are not with you are against you? Cannot we meet on the ground of mutual liking, and see whether that will not improve into mutual respect? I have not so many friends, Noble, that I can afford to quarrel with one of the best."

"For the present, Golding," returned Noble, "we had better part. My life is so bound up in this work that I have no leisure to devote to one who has no share in it. Don't think I speak harshly. You plead to me the constitution of your mind, and I must do the same to you. No, you are not against me, but you are indifferent. I have somewhat downright habits of thought and speech, I fear, and it would be impossible for

me to affect cordiality when I did not feel it.
Good-bye."

"Since it must be so then," replied Arthur,
"good-bye.   But I feel sure it is only for a
while, Noble.   Where shall I send my subscription to?"

"From you I could not accept it, Golding.
It would only make me think of the help you
might have given me.   You may alter your
purpose, still.   If you do you know how it
will delight me to see you."

They parted with a silent hand-grasp, and
Will Noble went on his way, convinced that
he had behaved as his principles required.
The hard work of the world he felt could not
be done by mere time-service, and lack of
firmness in little things seemed to him as bad
as in great.   Noble was not the only man
who obeys an exaggerated consistency, but
there are few who trace the principle to so
pure a source.

CHAPTER X.

BREAKING INTO BLOOM.

By dint of feigning a few days' sickness, a stratagem which under the circumstance he had no hesitation in employing, Arthur managed to obtain daylight for working at his two pictures, and on the Saturday preceding his birthday they were finished. In them he had given free rein to his luxuriant imagination, and had succeeded in producing an intensely weird effect, an admirable embodiment of the ideas which had inspired him. They were small water-colours, and doubtless gave evidence of a hand still lacking technical dexterity, but the soul which breathed in them could only have been imparted by true genius. Like all excellent pictures they suggested much more than they actually expressed, and in the heart-rending melancholy of the one, the stern, maddening grandeur of the other, there lurked a spell which, powerless over vulgar natures, at once seized captive sympathetic souls and bound them in a day-dream of glimmering fancies. Never had Arthur felt within his veins that throb of so intense a life as when, with pencil in hand, he added touch after touch, and saw the colours speak in answer to his thoughts, or, as was often the case, learnt from them some new mystery of beauty far excelling what he had designed to embody.

He continued to gaze at them, and to add slight touches first to one then to the other, until the early night closed in, and he could no longer see his work. The fit of enthusiasm, which ever comes as the reward on the completion of a work of art, was now upon him. He enjoyed with rapture that clear, calm consciousness of superiority to the everyday world, a feeling so distinct from vulgar vanity which it is granted to genius alone to experience. So excessive was his joy that he felt light-headed; he would have been glad to commit some folly, to plunge into a stream of thoughtless gaiety, to sing, to shout his enthusiasm. His room was soon quite dark, but at present he could not have borne to have it otherwise. In the faint flittings hither and thither of rays from the fire, and in the motion of the shadows they caused, his excited fancy could picture legions of spirits filling the air about him. Even the physical senses were affected. He seemed to breathe delicious perfumes, his forehead and cheeks were fanned with cool, scented airs, he felt the touch of fairy hands caressing his hair. His heart throbbed ecstatically painfully; his hands were hot as fire. Seizing the volume of poems which Miss Norman had lent him, he pressed it again and again to his lips, murmuring passionately, "Helen! Helen!"

The moment passed and he was calmer, but still unable to be at rest. The solitude of his room now oppressed him, and he dreaded lest Mr. Venning should come, as he often did on Saturday night, and request his company. He resolved to go out. The night was fine, though cold, with a cutting wind, and the firmament was thickly sown with stars. The first breath of the keen air, meeting him full in the face as he issued forth, quickened his pulse, and increased the yearning for excitement. It was long since he had visited a theatre, and the thought of an evening there came to him as an irresistible temptation. He purchased a newspaper and ran over the list of advertisements. At one of the large houses he found that "Romeo and Juliet" was being played, the heroine's part by an actress equally celebrated for loveliness and talent. The play was congenial to his mood, and he went.

Shaken and bruised with emotion in his inmost heart, he hastened home as soon as the play was over, eager now to be alone with his thoughts. A resolve, which had first made its presence known by a timid whisper whilst he was completing the pictures, had been fostered into life and strength by the warm passion of his soul as he listened to the hapless lovers of Verona, and now panted to find utterance in louder and more decisive tones than those of reverie. On entering Arthur found his room

cold, for the fire had long since gone out.
Already the house was wrapt in the silence of
sleep, but the morrow was a day of rest, and
there was something to be done before he
could close his eyes. Whilst the fire was
burning quickly up, he again left the house,
but only for a few minutes, bringing back a
most unwonted luxury, a bottle of wine. But
it was the eve of his twenty-first birthday,
and he had work to do which called for a stout
heart.

In a quarter of an hour the fire had reached
a clear, strong glow, and the room was again
warm and cheerful. Arthur established himself
in his arm-chair, and opened a small portfolio
upon his knees. It was writing-paper that
he took from it, for now he was about to use
the pen, not the pencil. He drank one or
two glasses of wine, and felt his faculties
freshened and made more acute. At length
when a neighbouring church-clock chimed
half-past twelve, he dipped his pen in the ink,
and began to write, at first slowly and
timidly, afterwards with a firmness of purpose and clearness of thought which allowed
him no pause till he had finished. It was a
letter he had written, and it ran thus:

" DEAR MISS NORMAN—
        " When you suggested to me the
two verses from Tennyson's 'Palace of Art'
as good subjects for pictures, though I said
nothing of my purpose, I at once resolved

to follow the suggestion and to do my utmost to render them worthily. Working in such intervals as my daily employment allows, I have to-day succeeded in finishing two small drawings. I need scarcely say that the execution of them is far inferior to what I could have wished ; perhaps that is the fault which practice will remedy. If there be any merit in the conception, it is wholly due to you, who in reading the verses gave such expression to the idea that no mind endowed with the slightest powers of fancy could have failed to picture to itself the scenes described.

" I have worked hard to finish these to-day, and for a special reason. To-morrow is my birthday, on which day I wished to offer them to you. Yet not only for their own sake would I offer them, but as a symbol. As it is you whom I have to thank for awakening in me the artist's impulse and enthusiasm, so do I likewise owe to you the consciousness of a yet more powerful instinct. In laying before you these poor pictures, I offer at the same time a devoted heart.

" I said that to-morrow was my birthday, but I should have said to-day, for I am writing in the silence of midnight. What I now write I feel that I could not have spoken, courage would have failed me. I have long wished to give utterance to this strongest feeling of my nature, but to-day I do so with, I will not say more confidence, but less of misgiving than I could have felt in expressing it earlier. To-day I am a man, and, in the eyes of the world, responsible for my actions. To myself, also, I owe duties, and the first of these is to terminate this constant agitation in which I live. I will do so, trusting to your infinite goodness if I appear guilty of presumption.

"Miss Norman, I love you. I cannot know whether that word carries to your ears the same sense which it has for mine, but, as I write it, I wish to express a passion omnipotent, unending, holy, the voice of which is, in its briefest utterance, a revelation of unknown worlds, an unveiling of the mystery of life. When first I saw you in the studio I was taken captive by your loveliness; since I have been permitted some insight into your mind what I have discovered there has filled me with unspeakable admiration, has led me to feel that happiness cannot exist except in your presence and in the sight of your smile. I should try vainly to express in words the emotions excited in me by the sound of your voice, by the touch of your hand, by the mere thought of your exquisite beauty. But, believe me, there is not one among these feelings which is not sanctified by the purity of its object. I can say with truth that my love for you has made me a better man, with higher aims, purer motives, richer thoughts. For this alone it would be my duty to thank you, as I do momently with the utmost fervour of my being.

"But it is the nature of love to seek for love in return, without that it must fall short of its highest power and lack some portion of its utmost beauty. And it is on this account that I have chosen to write rather than to speak. I could not—no, I *could* not bear to hear you repel me with a cold answer; the agony would be insupportable. To be told by you that I was guilty of unwarrantable boldness, that I had presumed upon your good-natured friendship to insult you by an offer of my love—that I do not think I could hear and live. But yet you would not reply to me in such words, your goodness would forbid it. You would feel for me, and would show me the madness of my conduct in kind, gentle words. And am I not right in supposing that it would give you pain to have to speak even so; you, who think of nothing but how to spare your fellow-creatures suffering? So it is better that I should write. Then if you scorn me you can tell me so in a few brief plainly-written words—and then an end.

"*If* you scorn me! It is well to be prepared for the worst, and so I have for a moment supposed that you will read my letter with pained surprise and, perhaps pity my folly. But it would be an imputation on the sincerity of my love if I had in reality no better hope than this. Hope cannot be separated from love, as neither can it from any one of the best impulses of our nature. Yes, I have the

boldness to hope! Sincere love is so precious
a thing that he who possesses it cannot reckon
himself altogether poor, altogether beneath
respect. I know but too well that in the eyes
of the world I am infinitely beneath you, for,
though my birth was not mean, my life has
been one of toil and poverty. But am I not
right in thinking that, in the clear mirror of
your mind, all these social conventionalities
assume their true proportions? I should do
you much wrong, I feel sure, if I did not believe you capable of distinguishing the nature
from the outward form, if I thought you
allowed yourself to be bound in the slightest
degree by those bonds of foolish prejudice to
which weak and vulgar minds so readily, even
joyfully, submit themselves. I might urge
that my father was a most intimate friend of
your father, and that thus we are in some
degree related; but I had rather you thought
of me as I am in myself, of my nature pure
and simple in so far as you know it or can
read it in these confessions. As such, then,
I once more declare that I love you, truly,
passionately, and I ask you whether it is
possible for you ever to respond to my affection? Perhaps you may not think so now,
but do not, I entreat you, do not reply to me
with a hasty negative! Could I think that
you felt but the least affection for me, my joy
would be almost too great to bear; but that
I dare not ask for. At some distance of time,
in a year, in two years, might I hope by un-

ceasing devotion to win you? I shall labour unwearyingly at art, and such efforts as I shall make, added to a natural disposition which I feel that I have, cannot but result in some success. If I made a name, if my pictures came to be acknowledged as worthy of attention—should I then be hopelessly below you? Yes, yes, I know too well that I shall always be unspeakably your inferior in the highest qualities of the heart and mind; but shall I be unworthy of your love? Oh, how I will labour to deserve you! As others strive after what they call their salvation, with just such a passionate striving, nay, with one unspeakably mightier and more unfaltering, shall I work upwards to the heights where you stand. For will you not indeed be my salvation, in a truer sense than that heaven in which I know neither of us put our trust? If I win you, I shall have won a joy which will alone render life worth living. Your love would give significance to an existence of which I am too often tempted to despair. With your hand in mine I could say that I had conquered the world in the attainment of perfect happiness.

"I can write no more. The passion with which I thus offer you my soul has made my hands tremble and my mind fail. I shall send this letter to you early in the morning by some messenger, together with the drawings. I shall soon know whether in thus addressing you I have for ever forfeited your friendship.

If so, I bid you farewell with a thousand blessings! I have fulfilled my fate.

"ARTHUR GOLDING."

This letter carefully folded in an envelope and directed to Miss Norman, Arthur lay down to rest. Though physically weary, his mind was still unusually active, which rendered it impossible for him to sleep. For some hours more he read in Helen's book, till at length, just as the last ember in the grate was extinguished, he felt drowsiness creep over him. His dreams were of Helen, whom he had transformed into Juliet, and whom, as Romeo, he addressed in impassioned verse. He felt the soft warm pressure of her hands clasping his, and thrilled as the delicious fragrance of her breath wandered over his hair and his cheeks. Then it seemed to him, still following the play, that he heard the Nurse's voice calling to Juliet, and it aroused in him a sense of the utmost impatience. Still the Nurse called, and, just as he was embracing Juliet ere she ran from him, he awoke.

The calling had not been entirely imaginary, for as he came to his senses he perceived that some one was knocking loudly at the door, and calling his name. He at once recognised Mr. Venning's voice, and replied.

" A large parcel has just been left here for you, Mr. Golding," said Mr. Venning. " I will put it down outside the door. Bye-the-by, do you know what the time is ? "

Arthur saw that there was bright sunshine outside ; evidently it was broad day.

" I have no idea," he replied.

" After ten o'clock. Haven't you had an unusually good night ? "

" I went to bed very late," replied Arthur.

Mr. Venning withdrew, and at once Arthur opened the door, burning with impatience to see what the packet could contain, and wondering extremely whence it had come. It was a large brown-paper parcel, and rather heavy. In a moment he tore it open, and at once his eyes were greeted with a wonderful sight. There was an extremely large box of oil-colours, together with all the appurtenances necessary for painting, including half-a-dozen small canvasses. It was a spectacle to make a young artist's mouth water. Inside the lid of the case was a folded sheet of note-paper, which bore these words :

" A faint acknowledgment of the many beautiful drawings I have received from Mr. Golding. " HELEN NORMAN."

Arthur's heart leaped almost to bursting as he read this at a glance ; then he pressed the paper madly to his lips, whilst the room swam before him. For a moment he was obliged to seat himself upon the bed, fearing lest his emotions should deprive him of consciousness. It was many minutes before he recovered calmness enough to thoroughly examine his present, and then, as he did so, he kept exclaiming to himself, "She did not forget—she did not forget."

Should he add any intimation of having received this to the letter he was now about to despatch? On deliberation he decided not to do so. Who could tell what kind of answer he should receive? This delightful present had excited hopes in his mind which he had hitherto scarcely dared to harbour. Possibly he might have to thank her with his own mouth; if not, it would not be too late to write.

He was in a slight difficulty as to the means of sending his little parcel, it being Sunday, and no available messenger at hand. But, as it was getting late, he soon determined upon the method to be pursued. Hastily completing his toilet, and making a cup of coffee suffice for his breakfast, he left the house, with the drawings and letter in his hand, and walked quickly in the direction of Highbury. When within sight of Helen's house he had no difficulty in securing the services of a decent-looking child who happened to be passing, and whom he watched as she entered the holly-hid garden. In a few minutes the messenger returned, gave a satisfactory report, and received the promised fee.

And now Arthur looked forward in a state of mind bordering on distraction to the hours, perhaps the days, which were to elapse before he could expect to receive an answer. Instead of returning home, where the quietness of the room would have been intolerable to him, he took advantage of the fine sharp morning to have a long walk. Where he went mattered little, but it was necessary for him to be active, to keep pace in bodily exertion with the hurrying current of his thoughts. These thoughts were infinitely varied in hue, at times black with the shadow of despair, at times glowing in the full radiance of passionate hope. Once or twice he was checked in the midst of a rapturous portrayal of the future by a cold breath of doubt and fear chilling his soul as he remembered that in sending that letter to Helen he had been guilty of a crime. There would arise within him comforters in the shape of hopes and calculations for harbouring which he detested himself. From self-loathing was born irritation, then passionate anger against the decrees of fate. Why should a moment's folly, long since seen and regretted, compel him to a life of wretchedness, to the renunciation of delights such as it is given to few of earth's inhabitants to enjoy? He was angry with himself for being so foolish as to find anything wrong in the step he had taken. Long since he had committed the one great error of his life, and was it not right that he should do his utmost to obliterate it from his memory, to strike himself free from its miserable consequences? Even if he should be so happy as to win some return for his

love, he could not hope to attain its object
for some indefinite time, say, till he had won
a name as an artist; and before then what
might not happen? And the hopes for which
he cursed himself came back in full strength
upon him. It was impossible for Carrie to
lead her present life long without sinking
into the depths of degradation; if her
favourite vice continued to grow upon her,
as doubtless it did, it would not be long
before she drank herself to death. He knew
well that, if she desired to do so, nothing
would be easier than for her to discover him,
and he looked forward with dread to a repetition of demands upon him such as that lately
made. On the day after he had seen Mrs.
Hemp he had received a letter from Mark
Challenger, stating that an *aunt* of Carrie's
had called upon Mark and had been directed
to Arthur's abode. Upon reading this, he
had conceived uneasy suspicions, which, however, for the sake of his own peace, he had
dismissed from his mind and refused to be
troubled by. In youth, and especially when
under the power of strong and delightful
emotions, we possess a wonderful power of
contenting ourselves with the bright face of
things, and putting off all gloomier considerations to some indefinite morrow. And this
was what Arthur did now, despite the serious
nature of his forebodings. He refused to be
cast down, he asserted his right to enjoy life,
to drink deep of the sweetest joys which the

world has to offer. Troubles might come, but they would be dealt with in their time. Sufficient for the day is the evil thereof.

Doubtless the clear sunshine and the sharp air of the March morning had much to do with sustaining this hopeful mood. Scarcely knowing what direction he took, he had walked continuously westward as far as Hampstead Road, and then, following the track which had grown familiar to him from walks with Mr. Tollady, he pressed on as far as Hampstead Heath. Thence he went round by Highgate. As he passed the cemetery, he did not even think of the friend who lay there. His thoughts were with the future to day, not with the past; life had more to teach him now than death. Already the afternoon was far advanced when he began once more to draw near to the city. It was his custom on Sunday to dine with the Vennings, but their dinner-hour was one o'clock, and he was glad to have missed it. But as the brisk walk had given him a keen appetite, he turned into a coffee-house, and there satisfied his hunger before going home.

As he had hoped to do, he gained his room without being met or questioned. Here he again began to gloat over his beautiful present, again pressed the note a thousand times to his lips, repeating Helen's name in every variety of low impassioned tone. Thus he whiled away the hour which remained before the approach of darkness. When at length

the shadows began to deepen in the room, and
the rays from the fire began to play upon the
ceiling with a warmer glow, he lit his lamp
and drew down his blind, and sat down
with the intention of forcing himself to read.

Scarcely had he done so when he heard
footsteps ascending the stairs. As if in obedience to a mysterious impulse he started to
his feet. The steps paused, and a gentle
knock came at his door. In a moment he
had opened it. Lucy Venning stood there
holding a letter in her hand.

" This has been left for you, Mr. Golding,"
she said.

Arthur looked hastily at the envelope. It
had no address.

" Was any message left with it ? " he asked,
playing with the letter, and affecting to speak
calmly.

" No. Some stranger left it."

He was left alone, and could read the letter
at his ease. Aye, but it must first be
opened, and to do so demanded a firmness of
resolution which he could not at once command. He never doubted from whom it
came, but the contents—what might they
be ? Was he to be exalted to a heaven of
delight, or plunged into a hell of anguish
and despair ? The conflict lasted two minutes,
and appeared to him to have endured almost
an hour. Then he tore the envelope violently
open, read at a glance all that it contained,
and threw up his arms with a cry of joy.

"Come to me at once. I am alone this evening."

That was all, but it said more than all the eloquence which tongue of orator ever poured forth. In a moment Arthur was ready. His was no dandy love. He could not pose for half-an-hour before a glass before venturing to present himself to his mistress. He flew rather than walked over the distance between his home and Helen's, and, on arriving before the house, was obliged to pause before he could approach the door and ring. For a moment he endured intolerable agony—a physical pain which scarcely left him strength to stand. The next he pressed both hands firmly against his heart, breathed less quickly, and rang the bell.

He was conscious of nothing till he found himself standing in the drawing-room, where the lustre of the modest chandelier seemed to dazzle him, and render him incapable of seeing. He heard the door closed behind him, and, as his senses undazzled, he at length saw Helen walking towards him, with her hand extended. He took it, pressed it slightly, and released it.

"I feel rather tired and not quite well this evening," she said, in a very low tone. "Take this chair by me and let us talk quietly."

For the first time he looked into her face, and saw that it was deadly pale. She trembled, too, and he could see her bosom heaving as though it cost her efforts to breathe.

"You are ill!" he exclaimed anxiously. "Miss Norman, why are you so disturbed? Am I the cause of this suffering?"

"No, no!" she panted, whilst her eyes suddenly filled with tears, and the colour came and went in her cheeks. "I am not ill—it is nothing—you have made me too happy!"

The last words broken by hysterical sobs. She took one step towards him, and faltered as if about to faint. He held out his arms to support her, and the next moment she was pressed to his heart.

"Is it true? Is it true?" he whispered passionately. "Can you love me?—Helen, dear Helen!"

"Yes, Arthur, it is true!" she whispered in reply, and, raising her head from his bosom with a motion of exquisite grace and simplicity which no words can describe, offered him her lips.

They sat down side by side upon the sofa, and for many minutes neither spoke. For Arthur there was no consciousness save of the pressure of her head upon his shoulder, save of the beating of her heart against his side. For him there was no outer world; they two in themselves formed a universe— two all-embracing souls melting into one. It was as though he had been smitten blind by looking too closely in a wondrous sun of joy, he could see nothing save a shapeless glow of warm light, not even the face of his beloved. It was her voice which first broke the silence, and his heart throbbed to the tones as if in echo to celestial music.

"You have made me too, too happy," she said, raising herself, and looking into his face with a ravishing smile. "And yet you have made me feel my weaknesses, feel that I have a woman's heart which naturally yearns for the support of one stronger than itself. I cannot understand it. Since I read your letter I have felt as I never did before. Till now I have lived a very lonely life, dependent upon no one but myself, since I had no one to whom I could appeal in troubles of the mind or heart. I had come to regard myself as destined to this perpetual loneliness, and had almost succeeded in strengthening myself to face the prospect; but how often have I passionately wished that my fate had been a different one, more like the lot of ordinary women, who from their earliest years regard themselves as dependent upon the protection and subject to the guidance of stronger natures. And when I read your, oh how welcome letter, it was as though I had renounced self-guidance for ever. I was weaker than water, in both mind and body. Scarcely had I strength to write you the reply. My whole being seemed at once concentrated in one desire—to fall before your

feet and call you my master. Can you understand this entire abnegation of self, this passion to annihilate one's own being in that of
another ?"

"Can I understand, dearest?" he replied.
"It is as though you asked me whether I
really love you. All that you express I have
myself felt. In future I would have no independent life. I would exist only in you."

"Arthur," she continued, after a pause,
"confess that you have read my love long
since; that you knew I was yours if you
asked me to be so; that the doubt in your
letter was only feigned. Since the morning
I have been distressed with all manner of
fears. I feared that you should think me too
open in my behaviour towards you; that I
took too little pains to conceal what I felt;
that I too boldly encouraged you. Have you
ever conceived such thoughts, Arthur?
Another would have stood more upon her
dignity, would have been more careful of
conventionalities than I. But I am not conscious of having done anything immodest. I
loved you, daily more and more loved you,
and feared—oh, how I feared!—lest you
should never return my love, lest you should
fail to see what I felt for you. Could I do
otherwise than I did? How could I gain my
end otherwise than by showing you what interest I took in your work, your hopes, your
doubts? Do you think even this confession
too unmaidenly? No, no; you cannot think

so, Arthur ! If a woman loves, why should she submit to have her heart rent by despair rather than permit herself to take one step towards the attainment of her end ? To such social codes I can owe no allegiance. In so much I have dared to think for myself, and why not in this ? "

" Oh, I know but too well," replied Arthur, " that you never overpassed the boundaries of friendship. For your friendship I was infinitely grateful ; but, believe me, I did not dare to hope that it could conceal a warmer feeling."

" Not even when you received my present this morning ? " asked Helen, smiling ; " for I suppose you did receive it ? "

" I did, and felt a joy only less than that your summons caused me. But no, upon that I did not dare to build hopes, for I knew that your goodness was inexhaustible, and that you would lose no opportunity of giving pleasure even to your humblest friend. But now I know that only a heart which beat as one with mine could have divined the gift which would give me the most delight."

Again their lips met, and again ensued a period of silent happiness.

" Helen," said Arthur, at length, " in one thing alone you displease me. Can you guess what that is ? "

She looked up at him with pained surprise.

" Oh," he resumed, " how I wish that you were poor ! Could I have taken you to my heart with all your perfections, but lacking this burden of wealth, how perfectly happy should I be! What would I give to know the joy of working for you, the delight, which every poor man can experience, of feeling his wife dependent upon him, of doing everything for her sake! But for you I can do nothing. Who can tell how long I must wait before I can ask you to be my wife, and at the same time offer you a worthy home?"

"You are unjust to me, Arthur!" she replied. "You wish to have all the pleasure to yourself. Do you think I regard this wealth of mine as any hindrance to our union? Surely, surely you see the world with clearer eyes than that. Because chance has given me wealth, whilst the same chance has made you poor, should that be a barrier between us? But for your unhappy lot you might at this moment have been sharing it all as my brother. I am three months younger than you, Arthur. In three months I shall be free from my guardian, and mistress of my own conduct. When that day comes, whether you are rich or poor is nothing to me; if you will take me for your wife, I am yours."

"I dare not look forward to it!" exclaimed Arthur. "I must grow accustomed to your love to believe that it is real. But shall I not often see you? No, no; it will be impossible. Though we may scorn the world's opinion, we must still fear its tongue.

I must guard you against all manner of foolish or malicious misconstruction."

"We must be prudent, dearest," she returned, "for both our sakes. If we cannot see each other as often as we wish, we can at least write. Yes, I will write you often, send you my whole heart in letters. It will be a new experience for me, a fresh, inexhaustible, life-giving delight! Oh, I shall tire you with my confidences!"

"Never, dearest!" he replied, whilst deep earnestness of love flashed out of his fair eyes as they met hers. "I, too, shall have an infinity of things to tell you. There is within me a whole world of thought and feeling which I had never suspected till love made me conscious of it. What exquisite joy will it be to share with you all my hopes and achievements! If anything can make me an artist, Helen, your love will do so."

A peculiar smile rose to her face as she heard these words.

"Shall I tell you," she asked, "of a discovery I made long ago, not so very long after we first saw each other in London, something which startled me not disagreeably at the time, and to which my thoughts have frequently recurred for consolation, though a slight one, when I have feared lest you regarded me in no other light than as a friend?"

He looked at her questioningly, wondering much what she could refer to.

"You would never guess," she continued, "so I must tell you. One day I paid a visit to Mr. Tollady, and he showed me a great number of your drawings. They astonished me, Arthur, for indeed many of them were extremely beautiful, and wonderful as the production of a self-trained artist. We must look over them all, both together, and you will tell me how they were suggested, and when they were done. But among them, though carefully put in a portfolio by itself, was a portrait. How and when the portrait was drawn I could have no idea, but I thought I knew the face, and Mr. Tollady, who seemed as surprised as myself, recognised it too."

"You saw it!" exclaimed Arthur, eagerly. "Oh, it was not worthy to be seen by you, so infinitely less beautiful than the original! I drew it from memory, because your image even then haunted me in my room as I sat drawing, and I could not rest till I had made a feeble copy. But such as it was I prized it more dearly than any other possession. Now I never sit down to work without having it hanging before me. As I look into its eyes I feel they speak encouragement to me. Oh, dearest, I should be ashamed to repeat to you all the fond, passionate, endearing words which I have addressed to your picture. Had I never had courage to tell you of my love I should yet have continued to worship before that idol to the end of my life."

"I am not worthy of such devotion, Arthur," replied Helen, blushing deeply, whilst delight mirrored itself in her moist eyes. "How shall I ever repay it?"

"One word of affection, one slight look of tenderness from you, love," whispered Arthur, passionately, "would repay the devotion of my life. Oh, I am too happy! I cannot believe it! Helen, Helen!"

He sank back pale and exhausted with emotion, and, in the excess of her happiness, Helen's tears fell fast upon his hand which she held pressed against her heart. After a long silence she looked round at the clock upon the mantel-piece, and a shadow passed over her face.

"You must leave me, Arthur," she said, rising. "Any moment now we may be disturbed. I must have time, too, to bring back the wonted common-place expression to my features, for I am sure my eyes betray my happiness. You will write to me, Arthur? Soon?"

"And you to me, dearest?" he replied, rising with a sigh. "It is dreadful to have to leave you so soon. But shall I never see you? I cannot live without seeing you, now that I have once tasted the sweetness of your love. I *must* see you sometimes!"

Helen stood with her eyes fixed upon the floor, and a slight blush rose to her cheek when she at length spoke.

"You know me better, Arthur," she said,

" than to misjudge my motives in wishing to preserve secrecy for the present? All my nearest connections are in reality strangers to me; I have no sympathy with them, nor they with me. In particular the lady who lives with me here, as a sort of guardian for me, is possessed of the greatest share of curiosity and meddlesomeness that is possible for human being to have. But there is one friend in whom I can place full confidence, and whose true and simple heart is the most natural repository for a secret such as ours. If I told Lucy Venning, she might enable us to see each other sometimes at her father's house."

"Yes," exclaimed Arthur, "no one could help us more than Lucy."

"I will tell her to-night when she returns," said Helen, blushing and smiling, "Confession is notoriously good for the soul, and it would be well if no one ever confessed to a less guileless being than Lucy."

Arthur took both her hands, and strove to find words in which to say adieu.

"I have forgotten to thank you for your pictures," said Helen; "that which accompanied them at once drove them from my mind. But they are admirable. I am proud of you, Arthur."

She raised her lips to his with an expression of the sweetest simplicity and devotion, and, as they met, she felt herself drawn towards him and pressed in a long, silent embrace.

CHAPTER XI.

It would not be easy to describe Arthur's state of mind as he returned homewards this Sunday night. Incapable of reflection, he reacted over and over again in his mind, with mechanical persistency, the scenes of the evening, and continued to intoxicate his senses by dwelling upon each fond word, each caress, each passionate look which he had given or received. The tumultuous character of his thoughts rendered him unconscious of all outward circumstances. Instinct alone guided him in the right direction homewards, and when he arrived before the house he could scarcely realise that he had walked all the way from Highbury.

He had drawn his latch-key from his pocket and was on the point of inserting it in the lock, when he became conscious of someone standing close behind him. Nervous from his excitement, he turned quickly round. He then saw that he was standing face to face with a girl whose shabby dress of worn-out finery was sufficient to indicate her character. At first the darkness prevented him from seeing her face, but there was something in her form and position to which his memory responded with the startling suddenness of a lightning-flash. His heart, a moment before so hot and bounding, seemed chilled to ice in his breast and checked his breathing as with a heavy load. A cold sweat broke out upon his forehead; he became deadly faint, and, had he not stretched out his hand to the wall, he would have fallen. It was as though some terrible supernatural shape had come before him in the darkness, and had pronounced his doom.

Though he opened his lips to speak no sound issued from them. He tried to move away from the door, but had not the strength to stir. The silence was first broken by the girl herself, who moved nearer to him, and said, " Arthur, don't you know me?"

He knew her but too well, and his eyes by degrees perceived all the lineaments of her face; he shuddered at the dreadful change wrought in her once beautiful features by so short a period of vice and misery. Her cheeks had become hollow, and looked all the more ghastly for the traces of artificial colour still evident upon them; her eyes were red and bleared, with livid circles round them; her hair, cut short across her forehead, gave her a wanton, abandoned look; and the way in which she constantly shivered showed that her thin dress of vulgar frippery was almost the only clothing she had to protect her against the keen night air. For all that he knew her only too well, and not the soul of

Belshazzar, when the finger wrote ruin upon the walls of his festive chamber, experienced a deeper revulsion of anguish than Arthur in this moment suffered.

Mechanically, he beckoned to her, and she followed him some distance into a by-street where there was no chance of his being observed by anyone that knew him. In the shadow of a lofty warehouse he stopped, and again faced her.

"Was it by chance you met me?" he asked, avoiding meeting her gaze.

"No," she replied, searching his face for a glimpse of the old kindness, but seeing nothing save pale resolution. "I found out where you lived from Mr. Challenger, for I wanted to speak to you very much."

"You had not asked for me at the house?"

"Yes, I had," she replied, after a moment's hesitation. "They told me you were out, and they did not know when you would be back. I was bound to see you to-night, so I waited near the door."

"Did you tell them who you were?" asked Arthur, forcing his tongue to utter the question, though it was in the most fearful suspense that he awaited the answer.

"No," said Carrie, "I only said as I wanted to see you—upon my oath, that was all! I was bound to see you to-night."

"And why? What do you want?"

In his momentary relief at her reply, he

had spoken these words with more of harsh sternness than he intended. She shrank back from him as though he had struck her, and burst into tears.

"Don't speak so hard to me, Arthur," she sobbed, leaning her head against the cold damp wall and covering her face with her hands. "Don't speak so hard to me. You wouldn't if you knew what I've gone through. I've been ill in bed for more than a week; and because I couldn't pay nothing they've taken all my clothes from me. I know as I oughtn't to be out at night now; I'm too weak still; it may be the death of me. And I came to see you and tell you this, and to ask you if you'd help me a little, just a little. You was kind to me once, Arthur, and you used to say as you loved me!"

Loved her! With mingled pity, remorse, and horror he heard her utter the words which that evening had been so sanctified to him, and was compelled to own that she spoke the truth. Yes; though he now shuddered in looking at her, though he drew back from her lest his hand, fresh from the clasp of Helen's, should be soiled by the mere touch of hers, though the intervening sorrows and joys had removed to what seemed a distance of centuries those nights when he had watched beneath her window and been agonised by the thought she might be unfaithful to him—for all that he could not forget that he had so watched, that her mere presence had once

brought him ineffable delight, that he had
kissed her lips and praised her beauty, in
short that he had loved her. Love! Love!
Could he use the same word to express the
excitement of the senses which Carrie
Mitchell's prettiness had once had power to
cause, and that holy passion which, ignited
by the hand of Helen Norman, burned like a
pure, unquenchable flame upon the altar of
his heart? How he scorned his past self;
surely he was another being now, with other
thoughts, other feelings. And yet she stood
there before him, sobbing with her head
against the wall, shivering at every keener
blast which swept along the dark street, and
told him that he had loved her. His heart
would indeed have been of iron had it failed
to soften to the appeal of such a crushed and
suffering creature. So keen was his compassion that he could have joined in her
tears, and yet it was nothing more than compassion. No faintest spark of any warmer
feeling lived within him. Save that she could
appeal to bitter memories common to both of
them, she was no more to him than any other
wretched outcast starving in the streets.

"We mustn't talk of that, Carrie," he
said, wondering as he spoke at the different
sound the name had now to his ears than
when first he learned to use it. "It is useless to remember it; let us talk as if it all
never happened. You say you wanted to ask
me for help. What do you mean by help?

Do you mean you want money from me to enable you to buy fresh dresses and to go back to the old life?"

"No, no!" she exclaimed, eagerly, raising her tear-stained face. "Upon my soul, I don't want it for that! I've done with that! I've done with it all for good! I've been thinking whilst I've been ill in bed that, if ever I lived to get up again, I'd never go back to that life. I hate it. It's killing me fast, I know; I often wish as you'd let me die in the snow—that night as you found me. It would have been much better, so much better."

"What do you intend to do, then?"

"If I had enough to buy a little better clothing, I'd go and get work. I'm not very strong now, but that doesn't matter; I'd rather work my fingers to the bone at some honest business than go back again to the streets. I know I haven't no right to ask you for anything, Arthur. When you was kind and good to me I didn't know the value of it, and all as you did for my good worried me and made me wish for a freer life, like. But I've seen enough since then to make me wish as I'd never left you, Arthur. I know as I gave you a great deal of pain, but you mustn't think of it. You must try and forgive me, for you shall never see me again; I promise you never shall. I shouldn't have come to you now if I hadn't been helpless and like to die in the streets for the want of something to eat. None of those people as I've been with knows as I was married. I wouldn't tell them, Arthur, for fear some one might hear it as knew you; I never would."

"And yet," returned Arthur, after a slight pause, "you sent a woman to me with a letter asking me to pay some rent for you. Do you forget that?"

Carrie stared at him in perfectly natural surprise.

"I don't know what you mean," she said.

"Didn't you recommend a landlady of yours to apply to me for money you couldn't pay her?"

"Never! Upon my soul, never, Arthur."

"Then I was deceived," he replied, searching her face keenly. "She brought a letter as if written by you. I felt sure it was your writing."

"What was her name?" asked Carrie, quickly.

"Mrs. Hemp," replied Arthur, after a moment's reflection.

"So help me God!" exclaimed the girl, "I never told Polly Hemp as I had a husband. Did she come and get money from you?"

"She did. I was foolish enough to believe her tale and to pay her."

"I never knew; upon my soul I never knew!" cried the wretched girl, again bursting into tears. "But you won't believe me, Arthur. It was my only comfort all through my wretchedness that I had never said a word of you. My God! How I wish I was dead!"

"If you tell me that I was deceived, Carrie," said Arthur, profoundly moved by her despair, "I of course believe you. I didn't like the woman's appearance, and I can easily believe what you say."

"You believe me?" she asked, checking her violent sobs. "That's all I want, Arthur. I can't bear you to think me altogether bad, and upon my soul I'm telling you the truth. I wasn't so bad once, but it's drink as has done for me. Oh, I'm so cold. Go away, Arthur; go home and don't think no more of me. I'll go and see if they'll take me in at the workhouse, and if they won't, I shall find some way of putting an end to my wretched life. Oh, my God! my God! how cold it is!"

She crossed her arms upon her breast and seemed to be endeavouring to warm herself, all the while muttering to herself and sobbing. Arthur was pierced with compassion, which he was, however, unable to express. Words of comfort seemed unmeaning before such wretchedness as this. There was only one way in which he could help her, and the sooner he put an end to this painful interview the better for both.

"If I gave you money to pay for a lodging," he asked, "would you know where to find one?"

"Oh yes," she replied, "I could easy do that."

" And you promise me that you would use
it in a proper way ? "

" Oh yes, yes ! So help me God, I would ! "

At the beginning of the interview, Arthur
had done his utmost to harden his heart
against her, and, in his own interests, to leave
her to her fate. But this had been only a
momentary purpose. Such cruelty was impossible to his nature, and then reflection told
him that to drive her to despair would most
likely be the very way to awaken all her worst
passions and to cause her to ceaselessly per-
secute him. He had not been at all prepared
for the self-reproachful mood which the girl
had shown, her suffering and repentance had
touched him inexpressibly. But to do more
for her than to give her the means of subsisting for a few days till she could find employment, if indeed it was her purpose to do so,
was impossible. It must not be thought
that he had not likewise his feelings of bitter
self-reproach. Had he been free, had not this
day been the commencement for him of an
era of hope and bliss unspeakable, against the
endurance of which Carrie's very existence
was a threat, then indeed he might have
acted very differently towards her. He had
to make his choice between her and Helen,
but he never for a moment wavered in his
determination. He suffered severely, he
could not bear to look into the miserable
girl's face, and his conscience never ceased
to whisper to him that he was committing a

cruel wrong. Who could tell whether, even at this eleventh hour, the influence of constant kindness, the prospect of a quiet and comfortable home, might not suffice to save her? But he was not hero enough to sacrifice his life in order to save hers. Had she come to him with a brazen face and made mercenary propositions without shame or disguise, he could have either acceded or refused as his discretion led him, and without remorse of conscience. But, as it was, to give her only what she begged, mere charity, cost him terrible pangs. Already the dark shadow of clouds had encroached upon the visioned heaven of his future; he knew as he stood face to face with this miserable outcast, who was yet his wife, that what he was now about to do would haunt him till his last day. He knew it, yet he *could* not relinquish at once so vast a treasure as Helen Norman's love. Better to die than to do so.

For about a minute they stood in silence, whilst these thoughts fermented within his brain. At length he spoke in the tone of one who had taken his part.

" I have no money with me," he said ; " will you wait here whilst I fetch some from the house ? "

She nodded in acquiescence, and he left her. Within five minutes he returned.

" I am not rich," he said, as he dropped some gold coins into her hand. " This is all I have, and I must borrow for my own neces-

sities till I am paid again. Will it be enough
for you?"

"Quite enough, quite enough," she replied.
"I shall be able to get into a new life with it.
I knew as you'd help me, Arthur."

"I hope you will do all you say with it,"
he continued, forcing himself to speak in unbroken tones. "But I give it to you on one
condition, Carrie. We must never see each
other again."

"No, no; never again," she sobbed. "I
know as we oughtn't never to have met, and
though I might once have lived happy with
you, that is all over now. I shouldn't have
come to you to-night, Arthur, if I hadn't been
forced to, indeed I never should. Never as
long as I live shall you see me again."

He endeavoured to say good-bye, but the
word stuck in his throat, he could not speak.
Neither could he give her his hand. She did
not seem to expect either, but, muttering a
few words of thanks, hurried away into the
darkness, leaving Arthur to his remorse.

Driven by supreme misery to one desperate
attempt to free herself from the slough of a
vicious life, Carrie had been perfectly sincere
in all she said to Arthur. Oppressed by
hunger, cold, and the results of a brief but
violent fever, she had experienced a fit of
bitter repentance such as had never before
visited her. No degree of self-humiliation
was too deep for her whilst in this mood,
and, remembering with unwonted vividness

all Arthur's past kindness to her, she felt
humbly grateful for the help he had rendered
her. She did not look for more. At this
moment the distance between herself and him
she had called her husband seemed infinite.
It is probable that few of her miserable class
are without better intervals in which they
realise with fearful pain the full extent of
their degradation; and such a reaction it was
from which poor Carrie was at present
suffering.

Leaving Arthur, she went straightway to
the only decent lodging-house in which she
felt sure she might be received. This was
that kept by the woman, Mrs. Pole, somewhere in Soho. Carrie knew nothing of the
acquaintance existing between Mrs. Pole and
Polly Hemp, and as in the circle of the social
hell to which this poor girl had fallen, virtue
is in a most emphatic sense merely comparative, she looked up to the former as to a
model of propriety. Mrs. Pole was a drunken,
low-minded, sensual creature, but yet she
managed to keep a moderately respectable
house, probably because experience had convinced her that it was most profitable in the
end to do so.

As Carrie hurried along the cold streets,
clasping the coins tight in her hand, numerous were the temptations which beset
her. It is not easy for ordinary people to
realise the agony of inward strife with which
a nature, which has accustomed itself to

limitless indulgence in any vice, struggles for the first time to throw off its allegiance to the tempter and follow the voice of reason. Every flaring gin-palace which she passed called to her with accents sweeter and more tempting than those of the sirens, and when, as often occurred, she found herself between two such places, one on either side of the street, it became a veritable struggle as between Scylla and Charybdis. She walked, when it was possible, along the middle of the streets, looking straight before her, that she might not see the inside of the bars, or scent the odour of drink which steams forth whenever a drunkard reels in or out of these temples of the Furies. She was so terribly cold; how one small glass of spirits would have warmed her. But by the exertion of marvellous resolution she escaped the danger. Arriving at Mrs. Pole's house, she found that she had not miscalculated the woman's temper. A trifle surly to begin with, when she thought that Carrie had come to beg for charity, she soon brightened up at the sight of the money. Carrie wanted a room? Of course; nothing could be easier. She happened to have a delightful little room empty. And Carrie rested that night with a more untroubled slumber than she had known for many wretched months.

Exactly a week after this, on the Sunday afternoon, Mrs. Pole's kitchen was the scene of a rather interesting conversation, the con-

versers being the landlady herself and her
occasional visitor, Polly Hemp. They sat,
one on each side of the fire, in large round-
backed chairs, for both were somewhat portly
in shape, and fond of sitting at their ease.
There was a blazing fire in the grate, which,
as evening was coming on, did more to diffuse
light through the room than the grated
window looking up through another grating
into the murky street. The kitchen was
stone-paved, the stones being only hidden
here and there by a rag of carpet, but one or
two large mahogany dressers, together with
an oaken press, a crockery-cupboard, and some
other articles of substantial appearance, gave
the room an air of moderate comfort. On
the table, close by the elbows of both women,
stood sundry jugs and bottles, as well as two
glasses more or less full of a steaming liquor,
from which they constantly took draughts to
clear their throats. The two faces were a
study for Hogarth : that of Polly Hemp,
round, fair, marked with an incomparably
vicious smile, the nose very thin and well-
shaped, the lips brutally sensual, the forehead
narrow and receding; that of Mrs. Pole
altogether coarser and more vulgar, the nose
swollen at the end and red, the mouth bestial
and sullen, the eyes watery and somewhat
inflamed, the chin marked by a slight growth
of reddish hair. At the present moment
both faces, different as were their outlines,
vied in giving expression to the meanest

phase of the meanest vice, that of avarice.
In Mrs. Pole's face the passion showed itself
in every lineament; in Polly Hemp's it
gleamed only from the eyes. The latter was
more skilled in concealing her designs than
the lodging-house keeper.

"And how d'ye know as she's here?" asked
Mrs. Pole, at the moment when we begin to
overhear their conversation. "That's what
I want to know. 'Ow d'ye know it, Mrs.
Hemp?"

"Well, if you must know," replied the
other, sipping her liquor, "'tain't so hard to
explain. One o' my girls see her comin'
out, and come and told me. Do you understand?"

Mrs. Pole was silent for a minute, apparently revolving something in her mind.

"Well, and what next, Mrs. Hemp?" she
asked at length. "I s'pose as I can 'ev what
lodgers I like in my 'ouse, eh?"

"Of course you can, Mrs. Pole," replied
Polly, with much good-humour. "You don't
understand me right. I only come as a old
friend of Carrie's to arst her how she gets on.
It's a sort of friendly interest, that's all."

"I hain't in the 'abit of hinquirin' much
into my lodgers' affairs," returned Mrs. Pole.
"She gets on well enough for all I know."

"May be she isn't in now, Mrs. Pole?"

"I don't think as 'ow she is, Mrs. Hemp."

"Do you think she'll stay long with you,
Mrs. Pole?"

W

" I don't know no cause why she shouldn't," replied the woman.

There was again a brief silence, during which both drank from their glasses, directing one eye on the liquor, one upon each other. And the expression in the eyes which performed the latter part was indescribable.

"You don't happen to know, Mrs. Pole," resumed Polly at length, "whether she's seen her 'usband lately, eh?"

Mrs. Pole shook her head.

" Well, I do," continued Polly, closing one eye and looking shrewdly with the other.

" You do, eh?" inquired Mrs. Pole, a little startled.

" And shall I tell you how, Mrs. Pole?" went on Polly, winking and smiling. " The girl as see Carrie comin' out of your house stopped her and had a talk, and Carrie told her as how she'd begun a different kind of life. And when the girl arst her where she got her tin from to pay her lodging—for she know'd as Carrie went away from me without a blessed farthing—Carrie out and said as she had a good friend who gave her the money. And if that warn't her husband, I'm a stupid fool!"

For a moment Mrs. Pole looked keenly with her blurred eyes into the other's face, then she pulled her chair a little forward, and bending her body still further forward towards Polly, rested her hands upon the latter's knees.

" Now look 'ere, Mrs. Hemp," she said, in a lower tone than that she had hitherto used. " It ain't easy to come it over you, I can see that. What's the good of us two a beatin' round about the bush in this blessed way? Let's out and say what we mean at wunst. Don't yer think as 'ow it 'ud be much better and straightfor'arder? Eh?"

"I don't know but how it would, Mrs. Pole," replied Polly, taking a sip at her glass, and smacking her lips after it with much satisfaction.

" Well then, look 'ere," pursued Mrs. Pole. " It's clear to me as 'ow we're both wantin' the same thing. I want to keep Carrie in my 'ouse and make money of her; you want to get her back to yourn and make money of her too. Now why can't we do this little business both together, eh? Maybe if we go on workin' agin' each hother we shan't get nothink at hall, either on us; but if we work together we can share. What d'yer think, Mrs. Hemp?"

" I'm agreeable," replied the latter, thinking as she spoke that present compliance might bring her information which she could afterwards apply to her exclusive profit. " I arst nothing better, Mrs. Pole."

" Then I've got a secret to tell yer," said the other woman, still bending forward. " When Carrie come 'ere to my 'ouse larst Sunday night, she 'ed several soverin's in her hand. I couldn't quite hunderstand at

the time 'ow she'd got 'em, but as she wanted
a room it was none o' my business, yer see,
to make myself hinquisitive. But Carrie and
me is old friends, and on Monday night she
come down into this kitchen to 'ave a bit 'o
talk. And then she told me as 'ow she was
tired of her old doin's—arsting yer pardon,
Mrs. Hemp—and as she wanted to find some
work to keep herself. She wasn't very open
like, at first, but I know'd as she liked her
drop to drink as well as either me or you,
Mrs. Hemp, so I sends out my Jenny for a
quartern of Old Tom, and I soon gets her
talkin' 'ard enough. An' then I draw'd it all
out of her, an' she said as 'ow she'd seen her
husband, an' he give her some money, an'
then she promised as she wouldn't never see
him again."

As she ceased speaking the two exchanged
significant smiles.

"And has she found work?" asked Polly
Hemp.

"No, she 'asn't been able to find no one
as 'll take her. An' worse 'n that. Last
night she come 'ome very late, and quite
screwed. She couldn't walk upstairs by herself, an' I ad to 'elp her up. An' when I'd
undressed her and put her i' bed, I took the
liberty like of lookin' in her pocket, an' I
found she 'edn't a blessed farthin' left. Well,
I see her this mornin', an' I arst her if it was
quite convenient to pay her rent; an' she
said as she 'adn't no money; but she'd go an'

get some. When I arst her where she'd get
it, she wouldn't say. An' now she's been
out all day, an' I 'even't seen nothink hof
her."

" Then she's gone to her husband again,
be sure o' that," said Polly. " I'll tell you
what, Mrs. Pole. It's my opinion as that
husband of hers is a fool, and anyone
can do what they like with him. And we
may be quite sure as Carrie knows that too.
All this story about getting work and so on,
it's all make-up, we may be sure of that.
Very like this husband of hern has promised
to give her so much a week to have her leave
him alone. Most like he's plenty of tin, and
doesn't miss it. If we keep our eyes open,
Mrs. Pole, this might be a good lay for us."

" I believe you," replied the other, grinning in such a way as to show all the hideous
stumps which served her for teeth. The
next moment she raised her finger, as if
listening to some noise. Polly also became
attentive, and heard the front door of the
house open and close. Then a voice was
heard in the passage above, singing a popular
song.

" It's her ! " exclaimed Mrs. Pole, rising.
" It's Carrie. Shall she come down ?"

" May as well," replied Polly. " She's
screwed, I know. She only sings when she's
screwed."

By this time the voice was sounding nearer,
and then steps were heard descending the

stone stairs. All at once the singing stopped, and Carrie called out, "Mrs. Pole!"

"Come in, come in!" responded the latter. "No one 'ere."

Carrie obeyed and entered the kitchen. She was dressed in plain but good clothing, the result of a purchase she had made early in the preceding week; but her face indicated only too clearly the wreck of all the good resolutions she had made in the period of her misery. It was flushed in the extreme, and her eyes gleamed with an unnatural light. Her hair had all escaped from its ribbon and hung in magnificent tresses down to her waist. Her hat was crushed and out of place, and she wore only one glove.

"Why, Polly!" she exclaimed, as she walked with an unsteady step into the room and her eyes first fell on her old acquaintance, "what are you doing here? I thought you said you was alone, Mrs. Pole?"

"Oh, I didn't count Mrs. Hemp," replied the woman; "she's an old friend."

"She may be a friend of yours," cried the girl, coming forward and striking with her fist upon the table, "but she's no friend of mine. I let you know it to your face, Polly Hemp; there!"

"What the devil's up now, Carrie?" asked Polly, with affected surprise.

"What's up?" echoed the girl, in a shrill key. "Why, I'd like to know what business you have to be keeping all my dresses and linen, and turning me out of your house without them. You're a thief, Polly, that's what you are; and I'm not the first as has told you so."

" Why, bless the wench," exclaimed Polly, " what's she talking about? Ain't the dresses waiting for her day after day in her own room, if only she'll come and take 'em. Don't you use no hard words to me, Carrie, because I haven't deserved it of you. If it comes to thieving, I'd like to know why you ran away from me before you'd paid the rent as was owing? Eh?"

" Now don't you two get 'avin' words together," interposed Mrs. Pole, whilst Carrie was beginning a shrill and angry reply. " Just sit down, Carrie, there's a good girl, an' 'ave a drop o' somethink 'ot. I know you like it. He, he, he!"

Carrie took up the offered glass in her trembling hand, and drank off its contents at a draught. Then she staggered back into a chair, and remained for some moments in a half-stupefied state, staring vacantly into the fire.

" And 'ave yer brought me my rent, as you promised, Carrie?" asked Mrs. Pole, presently.

" Course I have," replied the girl. " Here! Can—can you give me change?"

She threw a sovereign on to the table as she spoke.

" I dessay I can find it presently," replied

the landlady, taking up the coin and exchanging a meaning smile with Polly Hemp. " But you don't drink. Come, try this."

Carrie needed little temptation to induce her to drink. She had done little else since Saturday morning, and her moods alternated rapidly between semi-stupefaction and wild excitement. She took what was offered, spilling half of it on the front of her dress.

" You're flush of coin, Carrie," said Polly Hemp, following the sovereign with wistful eyes as it dropped in her ally's pocket. " Where did you pick it all up ?"

" Never you mind, Polly," she replied. " You want to know too much. That always was your fault. You don't sup—suppose but what I've plenty of ways of getting money when I want it ?"

" Pity you can't get enough to pay off your debts," retorted Polly, winking at Mrs. Pole to indicate that she was playing a part. " If *I* had a husband I'd see he did something to support me. What do *you* think, Mrs. Pole ; eh ?"

" Husband ?" repeated Carrie, staring strangely into the speaker's face. " Who's talking about husbands. It 'ud be a good thing if you'd learn to mind your own businesr, Polly Hemp ; so I tell you."

" I mind my own business right enough," returned Polly. " All I said was, as if I had a husband I'd see he did somethink for me, and didn't leave me to get my own living as best I could. There's no harm in that, I hope?"

"Yes, there is harm!" cried Carrie, the drink she had taken seemed to be rendering her momently more excited instead of stupefying her. "I know well enough what you mean Polly, and I say again, I'll thank you to mind your own business. What's it got to do with you whether I've a husband or not? We all know how sharp *you* look after your money, and we know you're not partic'lar how you get it either. Who writes letters and puts other people's names to 'em, eh, Polly Hemp? Who does that?"

The last words she screamed into Polly's face, her eyes glaring with anger which was almost madness. Her words confirmed Polly Hemp in her suspicion that Carrie had reinstituted relations with her husband, and she became all the more eager to play her part out to the end.

"I don't know what you mean by that," she retorted, "but I know as I wouldn't have a husband who didn't own me."

"No, more wouldn't I," put in Mrs. Pole.

"And no more I have," cried Carrie, growing every moment more passionate and excited. "If you know anything about my husband, Polly Hemp, or you either, Mrs. Pole, you don't neither of you know nothing bad of him; I'll take my oath to that!"

"I s'pose you'll pretend as he gave you this money to-day?" continued Polly.

" No I don't," cried Carrie, " and there you have it. I got this money as best I could, and you know very well how, Polly, without me telling you. So I didn't get it from my husband, if you want to know ! "

" Very good reason why," cried Polly, with a laugh. " He wouldn't have given you any if you'd gone and asked him. Ha, ha ! "

" Wouldn't he, Polly," retorted the maddened girl. " Then you're a confounded liar, that's what you are, and I tell you to your face ! If I wanted money and told my husband as I wanted it, I could get it any minute; so now you both know."

Both the women joined in a chorus of jeering laughter.

" Oh, ain't she talking large ! " sneered Polly. " If I'd such a good husband as all that, Carrie, I'd go and live with him, that I would. Poor man ! How he must miss you ! What a 'fectionate husband he must be, to be sure."

" Ho, ho, Carrie," put in Mrs. Pole. " I'm sorry for all the money as you get from your 'usband. I'll bet you a bob I could put it all in my eye, and see none the worser fur it. Ho, ho ! "

" You say as he won't give me any ? " cried Carrie, suddenly starting to her feet, and staggering forward, though in a moment she seemed to regain her balance and to be as firm on her feet as ever. " You say as he won't give me any ? Come along with me, then, both of you, and see whether he don't, when I ask him. Ah! you daren't come. You know it's all true as I've said, and that you're a pair of liars; you know it!"

"What's the good of our a comin'?" asked Polly, tauntingly. "We ain't going to be made April fools of. It's a month too early for that yet, Carrie."

"Come and see; come and see!" screamed the girl. "If I don't get money from my husband to-night for the asking for it, may God strike me dead before the house! Are you afraid to come? Ah! Are you afraid?"

"Yes, yes; we'll come, hard enough," said Mrs. Pole, who kept exchanging signs and words with Polly. "Put your hat on, Polly; we'll go."

"I'm ready!" cried Polly. "But your husband mustn't see us, you know, Carrie; or maybe he won't like it. We'll wait at the nearest corner, you see, and you'll bring us the bundle o' sovrings as he gives you. Maybe you'll want help to carry 'em 'ome."

"Ha, ha!" laughed Mrs. Pole, drinking off the remnants out of all three glasses with laudable impartiality. "Maybe she will. We'll 'elp her, Polly, eh? Don't fear, we'll 'elp!"

*　　*　　*　　*　　*

About eight o'clock the same evening Lucy Venning and her father were sitting together in their little parlour, enjoying that silence,

only very occasionally broken by a word,
which was Mr. Venning's delight. He
relished his daughter's society on Sunday
evenings more than ever now that she was
not always with him. They had sat for nearly
half-an-hour in perfect quietness, Lucy reading a favourite old devotional book, and her
father sunk in congenial meditation, when the
latter looked up and said—

"It's a long time since Miss Norman
called here, isn't it, Lucy?"

"Yes, more than a month, father," replied
Lucy, looking up from her book, but turning her eyes to the fire instead of to her
father's face.

Whenever the ingenuous girl was conscious
of a secret withheld from her father she felt
uncomfortable if their eyes met, and the
mention of Miss Norman's name was now
equivalent to reminding her of a secret.

Mr. Venning again became silent, but
Lucy seemed disposed to continue the conversation.

"But she constantly asks after you, father.
She said only a few days ago that she could
never forget the first Sunday evening she
spent with us here; that it would always form
one of her happiest recollections."

Mr. Venning laughed quietly, and sank
back into his brown study. But shortly he
again looked up, as if something had suddenly
occurred to his mind.

"Bye-the-by, Mr. Golding told me a very

strange piece of news last night. I wonder I didn't let you know of it, Lucy; but I seem somehow to have had other things to think of all day. Could you believe it, Mr. Golding has just become heir to five thousand pounds?"

Lucy raised her face with the best expression of surprise it was possible for her to assume.

"Never!" she exclaimed.

"Why, yes, it is very extraordinary, isn't it? And can you think what he intends doing? He has given up his place in the printing-office, and is going to study to become an artist."

"And—and will he continue to live with us?" asked Lucy, her heart reproaching her for the deceit she was practising.

"Yes, he says so. His money is invested so as to bring him just about enough to live comfortably upon. Very strange, isn't it? Some very distant relative, he tells me, has left him the money. Very strange."

The next moment Mr. Venning was off again into the land of reveries, perhaps meditating on Arthur's unexpected rise to wealth, but more likely wandering in fancy near the picturesque old castle of Conisboro' and the woody banks of the Don. Whatever his meditations were, they were suddenly disturbed by a sharp, loud knock at the house-door, which was repeated before Lucy had time to rise.

" Whoever can it be ? " exclaimed the latter. " It quite startled me."

" Take the little lamp in your hand, dear," said her father.

She took it, and went to open the door. For a minute she seemed to be exchanging words with some one; then all at once came running back into the parlour, with a pale and frightened face.

" Oh, father ! " she exclaimed. " Please, please come. There is a drunken woman asking to see Mr. Golding ! She is so violent—"

Before she had ceased to speak a staggering footstep was heard in the passage, the parlour door was thrown forcibly back, and Carrie reeled into the room.

" Arthur Golding ! " she cried, glaring round the room out of blood-shot eyes in a manner more like a maniac than one merely drunk. " I want Arthur Golding. I—I don't believe he's out. Why won't he see me ? "

" What do you want with Mr. Golding ? " asked Mr. Venning, stepping towards her.

" I want to see him, I tell you. Can't you understand ? Who are you ? I don't want you. I want Arthur Golding. I want my husband."

" Your husband ? " repeated Mr. Venning, whilst Lucy stood by trembling like a leaf, " you don't know what you're talking about. Leave this house at once, or I shall call a policeman ! "

"Leave the house!" she echoed. "Not till I've seen my husband, I tell you! I don't know why he hides from me just when I want him. Tell him his wife wants to see him, I say!"

"Mr. Golding is not at home," said Mr. Venning, exchanging a look of amazement with Lucy. "Come, you must go at once."

He took her gently by the arm and pushed her towards the door.

As soon as she felt his hand, she began to cry "Arthur! Arthur!" with loud shrieks which must have rung through the streets, at the same time struggling violently.

"Run to the door, Lucy," cried Mr. Venning, "and see if there is a policeman near, there's a good child. Don't be frightened, dear."

Lucy ran accordingly. Standing outside near the door she found two women, one of whom approached her as soon as she appeared.

"Is that her as is kicking up that shindy?" asked the woman. "Is it the one as knocked at the door?"

"Yes," replied Lucy, panting for breath. "We can't get her away. Are you with her? Is there a policeman near?"

"Never mind a p'liceman," replied the woman. "Isn't her husband in—Mr. Golding, I mean?"

"No, he is not in. Oh, please come and take her away if you can."

The woman, who was Polly Hemp, ran promptly into the house, where the cries and sounds of struggling still continued, and in a moment released Mr. Venning from his difficulty. She dragged Carrie by main force to the door and out into the street. Lucy followed, and closed the door quickly behind them. Then she returned into the parlour, where her father was standing, a picture of troubled astonishment.

"What ever can it all mean, Lucy?" he asked. "Did—did you ever hear that Mr. Golding was married?"

"No, no, never!" replied the girl, and, as she spoke, sank back upon a chair and burst into tears.

CHAPTER XII.

LOVE OR HONOUR?

MR. VENNING, though himself much troubled by this most unwonted disturbance of his Sunday evening's quietude, did his utmost to restore Lucy's calmness. Knowing her gentle and timid nature, he was scarcely surprised at the distress she manifested. After the first outbreak, she quickly subsided into suppressed sobbing, but it was some time before this could be completely checked. In truth, as the reader knows, it was far more from acute grief that she was suffering than from the mere results of the momentary alarm; and this grief was all the more poignant since it was felt on behalf of a person very dear to her, and not on her own account. Lucy was one of those tender, loving natures which seem to have no independent existence, but always live in the life of others —a being whose mission it is to lighten the suffering of those about her by the sweet exertions of sympathy, or to increase the total of happiness by reflecting the joys of those she loves.

So pale and low-spirited did she appear during the rest of the evening, that Mr. Venning strongly urged her to remain at

home that night, and to return to Highbury
in the morning. He even offered to walk to
Holly Cottage himself, in order to explain
to Miss Norman the cause of her absence.
But Lucy resisted these propositions with
an eagerness which showed her father that it
would but make her unhappy to insist upon
her staying. He proposed that they should
sing together as they were accustomed to do
on Sunday evening; but Lucy, the tears
rising afresh to her eyes, begged that he
would allow her to refuse; she did not feel
well enough to sing. So they sat together in
scarcely-broken silence, both occupied with
strange and unpleasant thoughts, till the
clock struck ten. Then Lucy rose as usual,
and was on the point of going upstairs to
dress for her walk, when the outer door
opened, and a step which they knew was
Golding's followed in the passage. Both
dreaded lest Arthur should knock at the
parlour door, as he not unfrequently did;
but happily he passed without doing so, and
went directly up to his room. As soon as
they had heard his door close, Lucy ran
softly up, and in a few minutes was ready to
start.

Her father insisted upon accompanying
her, and would not be refused. So they
walked side by side, scarcely exchanging a
word, as far as the gate of Holly Cottage.
Here Mr. Venning kissed his child quietly,
and, after exacting from her a promise that

she would let him know if she were not better
in the morning, turned back homewards.

Lucy passed through the gate into the
holly-circled garden, but did not ascend the
steps to the door. There was but one light
in the front of the house, that from Mrs.
Cumberbatch's bedroom. The two front
rooms were dark. Helen, most probably,
was in her study, the window of which
looked out upon the back. Under these circumstances the little lawn was perfectly
dark, for it was a moonless night, and no
glimmer from the road could pierce the
hedges of holly. For nearly half-an-hour
Lucy paced up and down here, engaged in an
internal struggle which caused her to cry and
sob, and sometimes to wring her hands in the
extremity of distress. Should she tell Helen
what had happened to-night? That was the
question which tortured her, driving her
mind, so unused to grave doubts and apprehensions, almost to the verge of distraction.
If she told Helen what she had heard, she
would be the means of causing her dear
friend such suffering that a bitter foe could
not wish to inflict deeper. On the other hand,
if she did not tell her, she knew too well
that she would fail in her duty towards
Helen, to say nothing of destroying from
that day forward all trace of her own peace
of mind. Yes, yes, clearly it was her duty
to tell all she knew. It might be a falsehood
the drunken woman had told; if so, and if

Helen proved it to be so, no harm would have
been done, but great good in the quieting
of her own conscience and the confirmation
of Helen's confidence in her lover. But if it
were true—Lucy covered her face with her
hands as if to shut out some terrible sight,
when she had thought for a moment upon the
consequences of its being true. And so she
had her period of bitter inward strife out in
the cold dark garden—strife such as all of us
have to go through one day or another;
and, because she possessed a good, true and
affectionate heart, the result of it was that
she conquered, and chose the right path.
Doing her best to dry her eyes and calm her
nerves, she ascended the steps and entered
the house, resolved to tell Helen before she
slept.

The door of Helen's study was ajar, and
the gleam of light issuing from within alone
illuminated the hall. As soon as Lucy had
entered and closed the front door behind her,
she heard Helen's voice calling to her in a
clear, pleasant tone from out of the study.

" Is that you, Lucy ?"

" Yes, Miss Norman."

" Don't trouble to go upstairs, dear," she
continued. " Come here; I have something
to show you."

Lucy's heart beat so fiercely as to cause
her pain. She walked slowly along the hall,
feeling as if she were about to commit a
crime. She knew only too well that she

bore a message which would turn the glad tones of her dear friend's voice into those of suffering and woe. She entered the study. Helen was sitting near the fire, with a large book open upon her knees. She did not turn round as Lucy approached her, but, without looking round, held out her hand, and, when Lucy clasped it, drew the latter's arm over her shoulder.

"Look at this, Lucy," she said. "I happened, quite by chance, to open this old book about half-an-hour ago. It used to stand in my father's library at Bloomford, and, when I was quite a child, was rather a favourite of mine; you see, there are such a lot of pictures in it. I think it cannot have been opened for more than ten or twelve years. Well, I was turning over the pages quietly, recalling all manner of strange old recollections, when all at once I came upon this piece of paper, in between two pages. Look! Can you guess what it is."

Lucy looked and saw an old yellowish scrap of writing paper, on which were written, between ruled pencil lines, several words in a large, tremulous child's hand. Looking closer, she saw that they were names. First came "Arthur Golding," then "Helen Norman." Lucy did her best to make some suitable remark or inquiry, but she could not speak. Her mind was distracted with thoughts as to how she should break her painful news.

" Isn't it strange ? " pursued Helen, in a voice of almost childish delight. " It is Arthur's own writing, when he was being taught at Bloomford by Mr. Whiffle—you remember, I told you of Mr. Whiffle, our curate. And it has lain there all these years unnoticed, as it would seem merely for the purpose of giving me delight, now that I am becoming aged. No doubt it was Arthur himself who put it there. You know he was always fond of looking at pictures, and he must have been looking at these one day and left the paper there by chance. And both our names ! Oh, how I shall prize that piece of paper ! "

Lucy maintained absolute silence. Her face had become pale as death. Her hand was chilled in Helen's warm grasp. Her breath came in pants. She felt as though about to faint. Suddenly Helen turned her head round and looked into her face.

" Whatever is the matter, Lucy ? " she asked. " Are you not well, dear ? What is it ? "

Instead of replying, Lucy covered her face with her hands, and once more burst into bitter tears. For a moment Helen stood in speechless astonishment, then she drew the suffering girl close to her, passing one arm round her, and with the other fondling her as she would have fondled a distressed child.

" What does it all mean, dear ? " she asked, in a caressing voice. " Won't you tell me ?

Won't you let me share your trouble? Your grief shocks me, Lucy. What can have occasioned it?"

"It is not on my own account, Miss Norman," sobbed the poor girl; "not on my own account, but yours."

"On mine, Lucy?" asked Helen, in astonishment. "You are crying for me? And when I never was so happy in my life? What strange fancy has taken possession of you?"

"Oh, something has happened to-night which I *must* tell you of, though it will almost kill me to do so! Say you will forgive me, Miss Norman, for the pain I shall cause you? Oh, how I wish some one else could have told you! I cannot bear to make you suffer!"

Consternation had taken the place of mere surprise on Helen's countenance. With a lover's instinct her heart foreboded some evil connected with Arthur. She grew almost as pale as Lucy, and pressed her hand against her heart.

"Lucy," she said, doing her utmost to speak composedly, "whatever it is, you must tell me at once. Now, indeed, you are causing me unnecessary pain, though you do not mean to do so. At once, at once! What have you to tell me?"

Forcing back her tears, Lucy clasped Helen's hands tightly in her own, and forthwith told her, in few and simple words, all that had happened. She neither softened nor exaggerated a single feature of the event, nor did she draw any conclusion from it. She could not attempt consolation, since it was impossible for her to know what faith was to be reposed in the strange woman's assertions. Much as she yearned to lighten the effect of her story, she could do nothing but wait and see how Helen would receive it.

The latter listened with forced calm to the end of the relation, but Lucy felt the hands she held clasp convulsively and become moist. A single twinge of acutest agony found expression upon Helen's features, then they became pale as death, but otherwise undisturbed. The story done, she turned from the reciter, and walked once or twice up and down the room. When she faced Lucy again she was smiling, a strange, weird smile, more trouble to Lucy than a burst of agonised tears.

"The woman lied!" she exclaimed, with a violence of tone and expression most strange to her lips. "Of course she lied! Surely *you* don't believe her, Lucy!"

The other kept silence, not knowing how to reply.

"You foolish child!" pursued Helen, with a forced, unnatural laugh. "Who can tell what miserable notion the wretched creature has for saying such a thing? She was drunk, you say—so drunk she could scarcely stand?"

"Oh, yes, I am sure she was," replied

Lucy. " Yet she did not speak much like—
like that."

" What was her face like? "

" I can't remember ; I scarcely dared to
look at her. I can only remember that her
eyes glared fearfully."

Again Helen paced the room, smiling in
this same strange way.

" We mustn't think any more of this
Lucy," she said at length. " I feel sure it
can be explained. Arthur will explain it to
me. No, no ; we mustn't think of it. Poor
girl ! you were frightened almost to death by
the woman's violence, dear. You may even
have misunderstood what she said. Come,
you are tired out, and your eyes are quite
red with crying. Give me a kiss, Lucy, and
get off to bed. Upon my word, it is half-
past eleven. Off with you ! "

Lucy drew near to kiss her, but having
done so, instead of at once departing, she
clasped Helen to her arms, and sobbed
against her bosom. The sight of the poor
child's suffering was too much for Helen, and
for some minutes they mingled their tears, only
the sound of sobs breaking the silence.
Then Helen gently freed herself from her
friend's embrace, and, kissing her on the
forehead, whispered a good-night.

Lucy soon slept, worn out by her unwonted
emotions, but for Helen there was no rest
that night. Though the nobility of her
nature bade her keep up a good heart and

refuse to believe anything that could taint
the honour of him at whose feet she had laid
the priceless treasure of her love; nay, though
forcibly withheld from believing by a vague
and terrible fear which, like a shapeless
shadow from the realms of darkness, stood
menacing her with ghastly vengeance if she
dared to approach, in this long night of
anguish there were moments when her soul
knew for the first time all the bitterness of
despair. When midnight was long past, and
the fierce beating of a hail-storm against
the window was the only sound which could
be heard, in one such moment she flung herself upon her knees by the bedside and, with
hands clasped above her head, gave vent to
the anguish of her soul in a wild prayer. She
had not prayed since those old days of religious fervour when she had almost become a
Roman Catholic, and this act was now no offspring of her reason, merely the result of
passionate yearnings for comfort in suffering
so terrible that human aid seemed vain. Thus
she passed one of those nights which work
upon the human body and mind with the
effect of years.

She made her appearance at breakfast outwardly calm; only Lucy could distinguish
upon her features traces of the suffering she
had endured. It was Mrs. Cumberbatch's
habit to maintain throughout this early meal
an almost absolute silence, smiling to herself
unceasingly the while. In all probability she

was discussing in her own mind the probable events of the day, dwelling now and then, by way of diversion, upon some incident of yesterday. Mrs. Cumberbatch had still the delight of reigning as supreme mistress in the house, for, well knowing her powers in that direction, Helen had given into her hands the whole direction of household affairs. This silent habit of hers at breakfast was always grateful to Helen, this morning especially so. The poor girl's mind was in no humour for trivial conversation.

Before any one else in the house had risen, Helen had been out and posted a letter, the contents of which were urgent. During the morning she passed an hour or two in reading as usual with Lucy, but did not speak a word of last night's matter. Her companion was surprised at this calmness; it distressed her because it seemed so unnatural. About twelve o'clock, when they had partaken together of lunch, Helen entrusted Lucy with several little commissions, some of which would take her to a considerable distance. As soon as she was once more alone, she repaired to the front sitting-room and sat down by the fire. She had no book in her hands, no occupation of any kind; only she kept glancing impatiently at the clock upon the mantle-piece, as if in expectation of some arrival.

At one o'clock exactly, she heard the door bell ring. At once she became rigid upon her seat, and her features, in their endeavour to be composed, assumed a sternness of expression very little in accordance with the emotions struggling within her heart. Then there was a knock at the door, and the servant made an announcement. She endeavoured to rise upon her feet, but her strength seemed utterly to have failed her. A few quick steps across the carpet, and Arthur Golding was bending over her.

Then she arose, and gave him her hand, but with so little of her usual fervour that Arthur was amazed, and fell back a step or two. He did not speak, for her face forewarned him of some evil, and alarmed him into silence. He stood still, interrogating her with his countenance.

" You were surprised at my urgent note?" asked Helen, breaking the silence with a voice which was low, uncertain, and somewhat sad. " When a difficulty occurs to me, Arthur, it is my habit to go at once to the root of it, as it were, to dig it up out of my path, if my strength suffice to the task. I am face to face with such a difficulty at present, but I cannot remove it without your help. And so I have sent for you."

A load seemed lifted from Arthur's breast. Surely she could not speak thus calmly of anything serious affecting the relations between them. Ever since he had received her brief note summoning him immediately, he had been haunted by all manner of horrible fears and suspicions. He felt now that he had been mistaken.

"Whatever the task be," he replied, smiling, "you know you can depend upon my best efforts."

"Yes, Arthur," she continued, "I have absolute confidence in you ; but at present I have no difficult achievements to impose upon you. I have sent for you to ask a question, and because I absolutely trust you. I shall require nothing beyond a mere negative or affirmative for my answer."

His face paled, sure token that the pressure had resumed its place within his heart. Her eyes were fixed unwaveringly upon his, and he forced himself to return the gaze with equal steadiness.

"You know," she pursued, "that it is Lucy Venning's custom to spend Sunday evening with her father. When she returned to me last night, she was in sad distress, the result of something that had happened at home. What this was she told me, thinking, and rightly thinking, it her duty to do so. It seems that she and her father were sitting quietly together, when a loud knock came at the door, and Lucy went to answer it, and was alarmed by finding it to be a drunken woman, who asked to see Mr. Golding. Lucy replied that you were not at home, but the woman would not be satisfied, disbelieving the reply. She said that her name was Carrie, and that you would see her if you knew she was there. Then she forced her way into the house, she behaved violently, crying that she would see Arthur, that she was—*his wife*, and insisted upon seeing him. With difficulty she was removed from the house, and did not return. Well, this is the whole story, as Lucy told it to me; and I ask you, Arthur, to tell me whether you can explain this assertion which the woman made, that she was your wife."

Arthur's eyes, whilst she spoke, had wandered from her face to the pictures upon the walls, and, resting on one in particular, had endeavoured, for the space of a minute, to discern some object in it which the light rendered obscure. Failing in this, he had looked towards the window, out upon the holly-bushes, which were glistening in the sunshine which had followed upon a sharp shower of rain. Thence his eyes returned for a moment to Helen's face, and, as he looked at her, she trembled slightly, and resumed the seat from which she had risen at his entrance. Then his face fell, and for more than a minute, he stood in silence, his brows bent, gazing down at the floor. Helen no longer looked at him. She, too, was now looking through the window at the holly-bushes, and thinking how beautiful they were in the sunshine. Words at length broke the silence, uttered in a low, but firm, voice.

"I can explain it perfectly. The woman spoke the truth. She *is* my wife."

Had his life depended upon it he could not have lied to her. Indeed, at this moment, the renunciation of her love, of all the endless joy which that love guaranteed to him in the future, was far more bitter to him than mere loss of life could have been; but still the truth was forced from him by her presence, by the sound of her voice which still seemed in his ears, by the expression of her marble-pale face, illuminated by a beam of sunshine, and, as it was turned upwards, resembling that of a grief-shaken Niobe. When he had ceased speaking, she rose, and for a moment seemed to hesitate. Then she addressed him, and her voice had no trace of feebleness.

"In many respects," she said, "I think I am not like ordinary women. My life has been one of quiet study, and practical work which few hear of, and perhaps I have learned to weigh my own actions and those of others more in the scale of reason, and less in that of mere emotion, than those of my sex usually do. You need not fear passionate reproaches from me, Arthur. They would be unavailing, and only cause both of us needless suffering. I think I can still be just to you, though you have failed in the full measure of confidence towards me. I have experienced enough of life to divine what misery lies hidden beneath this confession of yours, and my own heart tells me well enough the strength of the temptation to which you

have yielded. Let us be glad that the discovery has come so soon; how infinitely
better than that we should have been allowed
to become indispensable to each other, and
then be forced to undergo the death-agony of
parting. Good-bye."

She held her hand to him; he took it,
held it a moment, and dropped it. His
tongue had not the power to utter a word,
only his eyes followed her, fixed in an unin-
telligent stare, as she walked towards the door.
She turned the handle, and was on the point
of passing out, when suddenly she staggered,
reeled, and fell heavily to the ground.

In a moment Arthur had encircled her in
his arms, and, as easily as though she were a
child, had lifted her on to the couch. He
would not call help, the joy of having her
alone with him, wholly dependent upon his
assistance, was too great to be relinquished,
especially when his brain kept repeating to
itself with fierce persistency the words, " For
the last time. For the last time." There was
water in a decanter upon the side-board, and
with this he sprinkled her forehead. One long,
passionate kiss he had pressed upon her lips,
when consciousness returned, and her eyes
opened.

She seemed at once to realise all that had
happened, and lay quite still, her eyes straying round the walls, and at length becoming
fixed upon the ceiling. As Arthur stood
bending over her, anguish rendering him

mute, he saw great tears start from beneath her eyelids, fill her eye, and fall slowly on to her cheeks. The sight of her tears seemed to loosen his tongue. Clasping her hand he fell upon his knees beside her and broke into passionate exclamations—

"Helen!—My own love!—Dear, dear Helen!—Let me hear you speak one word— one word of forgiveness, one last word of affection. I cannot, I *will* not leave you without one word! Oh, if you knew all that I have suffered; if you knew my motives; if you knew my heart!—Before you, Helen, I am a monster of imperfection; who is not? But I cannot bear that you should think ill of me, that you should confound my act with the coarse brutalities of vulgar natures. No, no, for my insincerity to yourself I have no excuse to offer; no judgment upon it can be too severe. But if I might explain how it arose, if I could lay before you the dark places through which the current of my life has flowed, Oh, you would not send me away unforgiven, you would not think me unworthy of a last kind look, of one last affectionate word, to assure me that you will sometimes think of me. Speak to me, dearest!—One word!"

With a sigh she raised herself to a sitting position, and looked at him with wide, sad eyes.

"I thought you would understand from what I said," she replied, "that I had forgiven you ; or rather, that I did not presume to judge you, and so could scarcely presume to offer forgiveness. I am no bigoted upholder of conventional forms, Arthur ; no worshipper of the gods of society. But still how can I act otherwise than I do? You confess to me that you are married, that you have undertaken to devote yourself to one woman for the rest of your life ; and how is it possible that you can offer me such devotion ? Your conduct towards me may have been dictated by the purest and highest feelings, but necessarily it was mistaken conduct. You should have reflected how easily it might bring both of us into the extremity of wretchedness. It was terribly unwise."

"I was not responsible for my actions, Helen," he returned. "Love for you had maddened me, and I could not behave otherwise than I did. But perhaps I was not so culpable as I may appear, in leading you to believe that I was free. You must not think me cowardly to justify myself at the expense of another. Let me lay before you the plain truth ; let me show you how my error was brought on. You *must* hear me, Helen ; justice requires it. Noble, high-minded, good as you are beyond any living creature, you yet cannot help feeling some bitterness against me in your heart."

"You attribute high qualities to me," she said, smiling faintly ; "but I feel only too well that I am a weak woman, very, very far from a heroic one. I have suffered terribly since I heard of this from Lucy last night; and I feel that my nature will not bear much more. Why should you enter upon a naration which can only be excessively painful to both of us?"

"I will spare you all details," he urged. "You shall hear nothing but what is necessary to understand the circumstances. But so much I *must* beg you to hear! You will not refuse, Helen? It is perhaps my last prayer."

She sighed, but bent her head in assent. Then Arthur forthwith related to her, in few and simple words, the circumstances which had led to his first connection with Carrie, showed how the influences which at that time ruled his life had irresistibly bidden him exert himself on the sufferer's behalf, and how excess of compassion had by degrees developed into a feeling which he had mistaken for love. Very briefly he described his married life, the efforts he had made to raise Carrie from her degraded state, the terrible struggles he had carried on with her besetting vice. Then he passed quickly to her sudden disappearance, and to the life of intolerable misery which had succeeded for him.

"During all this time," he continued, "I never saw my wife. I had no idea where to seek for her, even had I desired to renew the old life; and can you blame me, Helen,

when I say I could not desire to do so?
Only on returning home from here a week
ago did I for the first time see her again. She
was in a state of wretched poverty and in
great mental suffering ; she protested her
desire to return to a better life, and begged
me to give her a little help. I gave her
all the money I had. Less than that I
could not do ; and, with your confession of
love still ringing within my soul—how
could I do more? Nay, I dare to say it—
it would not have been right to do more !
What had I to do with her, any more than
with any beggar whose story might touch
me and make me pity her? It would have been
blasphemy against true love to have spoken
to her one word of affection ; it would have
been unjust to you, Helen ; for to you my
heart belongs, not to her.—My wife? My
wife?—What does it mean, this word—*wife?*
Does it signify a relationship which can be
made or sundered by laws and idle ceremonies? Never! She was never my wife,
for I never truly loved her. What right has
she to come and put forward such a claim,
when even the slight validity which her de-
pendence upon me might have given it had
been long ago annulled by her own deliberate
act.—My wife?—This degraded, horrible,
brutalised creature to call herself my wife !
If the word means anything at all, it is you,
Helen, to whom it should apply. Yes, you
are indeed my wife, have been my wife from

the moment when our lips first met, when we breathed to each other the first utterance of love, the first vow of constancy. The law may recognise that other one as wife ; but I, never—never ! "

As he spoke he had gradually become more and more passionate, overcome by the violence of his love, which seemed to increase in strength at the moment of its bidding farewell to hope. As he ceased, he flung himself on his knees by Helen's side, grasping her hand, and pressed it wildly to his lips. Almost immediately it was withdrawn with an effort which his strength could indeed have rendered useless, but which respect would not allow him to resist.

"I cannot have you speak so wildly, Arthur," she replied, becoming calmer in proportion as he lost self-control. "I pity you profoundly, but my conscience will not permit me to grant the truth of what you say. Such theories would result in the destruction of society, and we, who pretend to have the welfare of society in a more than ordinary degree at heart, should be the last to allow passion to blind our reason in a matter such as this. But your confession has relieved me ; the fact that your wife had left you voluntarily, and had remained so long out of your sight, renders your conduct as concerns myself less morally culpable. Your graver faults began when she appeared before you and begged your assistance. Then you should have recognised the course which duty clearly pointed out to you. Her behaviour then showed that you might perhaps still have exerted some influence upon her, and it was a grave error to neglect the opportunity. I was no good angel to you when my image induced you to shut your ears to the voice of conscience and let your wife once more go her way."

"But what do you bid me do?" he exclaimed, in a choking voice. "Must I renounce you? After enjoying the greatest, the only bliss of existence for a few poor days, must I relinquish it for ever? Better bid me end my life at once, for what use will there be in living?"

"You do not mean—you do not know what you say," returned Helen, looking down at him with infinite compassion as he still knelt by her side. "You must leave me, Arthur, and think over all this in solitude, when your mind has become calm. Then you will be compelled to acknowledge the justice of what I have said; you will see that we *must* forget each other."

"Then you do not love me," he cried, starting to his feet. "You have never loved me, Helen! Why did you feign passion and lead me to think myself happy in your priceless affection? What cruel jest was it? No, no, you have never loved me, or you could not speak so calmly of our forgetting each other!"

"Arthur, you are cruelly unjust!" she replied, the tears starting to her eyes. "You are cruelly unjust, and you will see it when you become calmer."

"Then you *do* love me?" he asked, again approaching. "You *do* love me, Helen? Ah! But it cannot be such love as mine. Your love is but little more than mere friendship, a cool, calculating feeling, looking to means and results, and capable of denying its object when the possession of it might prove dangerous to self-interest. My love is not of that nature. It reigns supreme in me, subduing *all* considerations, rendering *all* objections futile. To deny its omnipotence would be blasphemy. It is a sacred passion, and all its promptings must be lawful!"

"But how am I to understand you?" exclaimed Helen, with sudden animation. "If you deny my love with such violence, it can only be that you wish me to prove it. How would you have me do so? Do you wish me to be your mistress? Nay, don't start at the word and look terrified; my modesty is not of such trivial nature that it shames to be put face to face with truths. What else can you mean by this talk of the supremacy of love, of the lawfulness of all its promptings? You know that marriage between us is impossible as long as she who is already your wife can come forward at any moment and prove her claims upon you. Am I not a human being? Have I not passions like your own, the

thwarting of which causes me pangs as keen
as those you suffer from ?   What, then, am I
to understand ? "

He stood absorbed before her, unable to
reply a word.

"I repeat, Arthur," she resumed, more
calmly, "you do me cruel wrong when you
deny that I do love, or have ever loved you.
Your own passion cannot be greater than
mine, but my sight is the clearer.   I know
perfectly well you would never make a degrading proposition to me, that you would
suffer your whole life through rather than
inflict on me a moment's pain.   I know that,
because it is how I also feel towards you.
Shall I not suffer in parting from you ?   Will
it not be a life-long regret that I gave my soul
to you for so short a time, only to lose you for
ever ?   And in acting as I do, I spare you pain ;
if you suffer for the moment you will quickly
see how preferable this was to unending
remorse.   For such could not but be your
fate if you neglected the commands of your
conscience.   Understand me, I am not speaking of your duty towards myself, but towards her who is your wife.   Degraded and
miserable as she is, she has still claims upon
you ; nay, all the greater claims in proportion as she *is* degraded and miserable. How
can you, who have been so strongly impressed with the sufferings inflicted by
society upon the poor and outcast, permit
yourself to altogether forget this wretched

woman, careless of what becomes of her?
How can you think that I, who make it
the work of my life to relieve all the misery
1 can, could be happy in the perpetual consciousness that I was robbing her of the
care you might otherwise extend to her?
Even if you would, Arthur, I know that
you cannot be altogether indifferent to her
fate.   Those whose fates cross our own
with any great influence, either for good or
for evil, we can never altogether forget.
Nor is it right we should.   What other
bonds are there so effective in the progress
of the world as those knit by Fate, which
we are often tempted to call chance, between those who have nothing else in common
save their humanity?   Upon the conduct of
the individual in cases such as these, upon
his greater or less degree of honour ; upon
his more or less clear perception of the principles of duty, depend issues which, if we
look upon the world as of any consequence at
all, it is impossible to over-rate. Oh, Arthur,
you place me in a false position ; you force
me to become your counsellor and strengthener,
when I am so sorely in need of such a comforter myself.   Spare me, I beg you to spare
me, further pain."

Whilst she spoke Arthur continued to
stand with his eyes fixed upon the ground,
when she ceased he turned away and walked
to the window.   For some minutes he stood
here, engaged in a fierce conflict with himself.

At length he turned, and again advanced towards her, his face pale, but less disturbed.

"Helen," he said, "you are indeed my good angel. Now for the second time you decide an all-important point in my life. If I am by nature passionate and too little disposed to reflect, I am also capable of recognising the good and the true when they are set before me. You have spoken no word but what is the essence of truth and honour, and I promise you solemnly to act upon what you have said. It only remains for you to forget me as quickly as possible."

"When I used that word, Arthur," replied Helen, "I scarcely knew what I said. I can never forget you; your memory will be a part of my nature, and will last till I die. But I shall endeavour to think of you as a dear friend, as the brother you might perhaps have been to me if Fate had permitted it. Try to think of me, too, as a sister."

"Do not mock me, Helen. My love is not capable of such transformations, I fear, however much I may resolve to make it so. I cannot promise to forget you; that would be beyond my power. You shall lie in my heart as the good-genius of my life; and your voice, the tone of which will never quit my ear, shall be an inward monitor to me, a conscience louder than my own. Neither can I promise you to relinquish all hope. If ever—"

Helen held up her hands warningly. He bent his head, and was silent.

"If you grant to me such a high place as the guiding spirit in your thoughts," she said, solemnly, "let my voice be always exerted in the name of duty. Duty must rule in every act of your life, not only in the one circumstance to which you will first apply yourself. If you neglect that highest gift of nature, that genius which should have power to raise you above so many every-day troubles, you will be grievously neglecting that duty. For some time we must not see each other, perhaps only after years ought we to permit ourselves to meet again; but in the meantime I shall not lose sight of you. I shall see your name becoming famous, I shall hear it spoken with praise, I shall see your pictures and rejoice at the thought that no one can understand them so well as myself. Promise me that it shall be so, Arthur; that you will strain every nerve to fulfil your part in the world's work, that this brief passion of ours shall have for its result only a higher degree of activity, the striving after higher ends. With me, it will be so. Let me cherish the hope that it will also be with you."

"I shall always remember this as your last wish," replied Arthur. "It shall be inviolable to me."

She stepped towards him, and gave him her hand, smiling with a content such as only noble natures are capable of experiencing. To Arthur's eyes, dimmed as they were with moisture, her countenance appeared radiant, a halo seemed to play around her head and glorify her. It was in vain he tried to say farewell. Neither did Helen pronounce the word, but, murmuring, "For your sister, Arthur," she offered him her lips. Then he relinquished her hand, and first the room-door, then the house-door, closed behind him. Before he had stepped off the holly-circled lawn out into the road, Helen had sunk upon the couch, once more in unconsciousness.

CHAPTER XIII.

DOMESTIC.

On the same morning which saw the last sorrowful interview between Helen Norman and Arthur Golding, a conversation, not very striking in itself, considering the interlocutors, but of some importance when viewed in the light of succeeding events, was being held in Mrs. Waghorn's *boudoir* between that lady and her husband.

Maud had risen, in accordance with her usual habits, at the reasonable hour of eleven, and towards noon was lying on an extremely comfortable couch, close to a cheerful fire, with a tempting breakfast arranged upon a low table within easy reach of her hand. Now and then she ate a mouthful of toast or sipped her coffee, then she would seem to forget everything in a fit of deep reverie; another moment she would take up the book which lay open upon the chair beside her and read a page or so with apparent interest. The book was "Madame Bovary," and to all appearances, Maud was reading it for the first time; at all events she was only about the middle of it. Time was of little consequence to Mrs. Waghorn, and the announcement of the hour of twelve by a little silver-voiced clock upon the mantel-piece did not even cause her to raise her head.

Another sound, however, making itself heard upon the stairs a few minutes after, seemed to have more effect upon her. It was a quick, heavy step, which she knew perfectly well and which appeared somewhat to surprise her. The step was unmistakably approaching her door. She had scarcely time to resume her attitude of careless ease before her door was thrown violently open, and Mr. John Waghorn made his appearance. She did not raise her head as he entered, and only a slight fluttering of the pages of her book indicated that his entrance made any impression upon her.

"What the devil does that mean?" he cried, advancing close to her and holding a piece of paper so as almost to touch her face.

"Thank you," she replied, calmly; "but I am not at all short-sighted. If you will have the kindness to let me hold it at a proper distance I may be able to answer your question."

He threw it upon her lap, and stood regarding her with a fierce, malevolent scowl. Mr. John Waghorn's personal appearance had not improved with time. Though still eminently respectable, when not seen at the domestic hearth, it was assuming something of haggardness, which the kindly disposed would impute to business cares, the more

knowing and the less friendly to troubles of
a somewhat different nature. At all events,
the woman who could with impunity be made
the subject of a regard such as the present
one was scarcely to be envied.

Maud placed the piece of paper on the
open pages of " Madame Bovary " and contemplated it for a moment. Then she replied,
with much calmness, and without raising her
eyes—

" It strongly resembles a milliner's bill. It
is a somewhat strange time though for bills
to be sent."

" It was sent because I wrote for it," replied Mr. Waghorn. " But what the devil
does it mean, I ask you? £110 odd, since
Christmas. How do you explain it?"

" By the simple fact that it is customary
for ladies to wear dresses," she replied, sar-
castically, "and that I do not pretend to sufficient moral courage to make an appearance
in public without one."

" Damn your fine airs ! " cried the gentleman, seizing the bill rudely from her hands.
" Answer plainly. Is this a correct account,
or isn't it ?"

" I see no reason to doubt its correctness!"
replied Maud. " I really cannot be expected
to remember every article which is sent to me,
together with its price."

" Very well ! " he exclaimed, folding up
the bill and thrusting it into his waistcoat
pocket. " Then I shan't pay it, that's all ! "

" Indeed ? " she asked.

" No, I shan't ! " he repeated. " They may take an action, if they like ; most likely they will. But they can't get money out of empty pockets, that's one satisfaction. What's more, I shall send a notice to all your trades-people that they're not to supply you in future, and, if that's not enough, I'm hanged if I don't advertise you in the papers. See if I don't ! "

" You are of course at liberty to behave with just as much rudeness and brutality as accords with your nature," remarked Maud, taking up her book as if to resume her reading.

Mr. Waghorn stood with his hands thrust into his trouser-pockets, biting his lower lip. Perhaps is was his position which suggested Maud's next remark.

" You made some allusion to empty pockets," she said. " Did you mean anything by it, or was it one of those pieces of gentle irony in which you are wont to find pleasure?"

Mr. Waghorn turned slightly away, but almost immediately faced round again.

" You will know sooner or later," he said, kicking over a handsome little buffet which stood before the couch, " so I may as well tell you plainly at once. If I said empty pockets, I meant it. You needn't be surprised any morning if you have to leave this house. I shall have to sell it, and the sooner the better."

"Or, in plain words," suggested Maud, laying down her book, and, for the first time, looking her husband in the face, "you are about to become a bankrupt?"

"It isn't unlikely. It's well I have your money to fall back upon, or things might go devilish hard with us."

As he ceased speaking he began to whistle to himself, and walked to the window. Maud's eyes followed him with an expression half of surprise, half of gratified hatred.

"I didn't quite understand your last remark," she said, after a moment's silence.

"I said," he replied, turning only half towards her, and still pretending to look at something down in the street, "that if I hadn't your money to fall back upon, things might go devilish hard."

"My money?"

"Yes, your money," he repeated, with irritation. "I suppose it isn't all spent, is it?"

"If you mean what was settled upon me at my marriage, I am happy to be able to inform you that neither principal nor interest has been touched. As to your having it to fall back upon, I am at a loss to understand the expression."

She rose as she spoke, and stood in front of the fire, drawing a light shawl about her shoulders. Over the mantel-piece was a large mirror, in which she regarded herself. The mirror reflected a peculiar smile.

"It isn't hard to understand plain English," exclaimed her husband, suddenly facing her. "If my money's all done I suppose we must make yours go as far as it will, mustn't we?"

"Mr. Waghorn," was the calm reply, "we had better understand each other at once. The money which is mine, I mean to keep to myself. If necessary I must live on it; but I should wish immediately to relieve your mind from any expectation of sharing it with me. Perhaps you will understand me better if I say that I would not draw a cheque for one guinea to save your life to-morrow."

She gave expression to this amiable sentiment with a quiet clearness of tone and a firmness of countenance which showed very plainly she meant what she said. For a moment Mr. Waghorn regarded her with lowering eyebrows, evidently at a loss how to reply to this declaration of opinion.

"In other words," he remarked at length, in a lower voice than ordinary, "if you find the ship sinking you'll just do your best to get clear of it."

"Precisely," replied Maud.

At this reply, extinguishing the last ray of hope which had served to sustain the impudent courage of his base nature, Waghorn suddenly gave reins to the passion which was boiling within him. His eyes flashed and his face became red with anger.

"I dare you to say so!" he cried. "By

God! I dare you to say so! Who is it that has done most to ruin me, if not yourself, with bills like this? And now you think to get out of all the consequences and run away to live on your own money. But you shan't do so, don't think so. Do you know who it is you are trying to bully? Damn you, you she-devil! Who's master here, you or I?"

"It appears by your own confession," replied Maud, stepping back a little before his violence, but speaking with undiminished firmness and calmness of tone, "that you won't be master here long. If you flatter yourself that you have ever been master of *me*, I assure you, you are strangely mistaken. I, indeed, am to have the charge of ruining you made against me, am I? I suppose your own temperance and frugality are so eminent that you are at a loss to account for expenditure otherwise. If you ever gambled, if you ever drank, if you had ever kept mistresses, it would have been a different thing. But then your abstinence from all those vices has been so wonderful. If you had been in the habit of betting on horse-races or losing money at cards, your friends would certainly have talked of it, and I should have heard their amiable comments, which, as it is, I have never done. If you had been in the habit of drinking too much I should certainly have noticed it, I might even have seen you intoxicated at times; it is even possible you might have been so unlucky as to figure in the police-court for drunken assaults ; but as I never knew you anything but strictly sober and gentlemanly in your demeanour that suggestion is of course impossible. Then, if you had had a weakness for the society of second-rate actresses and ballet-girls, one might have explained a great deal of expenditure, but such a hypothesis is of course out of the question. Otherwise I should certainly have seen ill-spelt letters to you occasionally, lying about your bedroom; I might have noticed you driving about in hansoms at night with young ladies of dubious appearance; or even such a thing might have happened to me as to go down into my own drawing-room after midnight and to find you revelling there with some half-dozen common prostitutes. But how shocking such things would have been; how happy I should esteem myself that I have a husband so absolutely faithful to his wife! Yes, certainly I must be the cause of your ruin. I can see no other explanation of it!"

She had scarcely pronounced the last word of this speech, burning throughout with the fiercest sacasm, when passion overmastered the hearer's last remnant of self-restraint. Uttering a frenzied oath, he sprang forward, and, with his open hand, struck her a fierce blow upon the head. With a shriek, half of alarm, half of pain, she fell back upon the couch; but in a moment started up from it again. Whilst Waghorn stood, quivering with passion, and blind to her movements, she had sprung to a drawer, wrenched it open, and grasped something which glistened in her hand.   There was an instant flash, a loud report, and the mirror over the fireplace shattered into a thousand pieces.   Whilst the sound of the pistol-shot was still echoing loudly through the room, Waghorn once more leaped like a tiger upon the maddened woman, wrenched the pistol from her hand, threw it aside ; then, grasping each of her arms, dashed her violently upon the floor.   Twice he raised her by her arms, and twice dashed her down again, she shrieking loudly.   At the last blow she became insensible.   Then he took up the pistol, and, thrusting it into his pocket, left the room in time to meet the servants who were rushing up-stairs, and give them a satisfactory explanation of the alarm.

*   *   *   *   *

After Arthur's departure, Helen Norman passed the rest of the day in strict seclusion; not even Lucy Venning was summoned to keep her company.   The fits of violent grief, almost of despair, which alternated with her hours of silent suffering, were such as no one might be witness of.   She knew well that this agony would be but transitory, that the morrow would find her once more calm and resolved to struggle with her fate ; but in the meantime the storm of passion must have its way, must wreak its full fury upon her frame, must make her weak in body in order that she might become strong in soul.

In the course of the afternoon she was disturbed by a knock at her door. She did not open, but asked what was wanted. A servant informed her that Mrs. Waghorn had called and wished very much to see her. Helen shuddered at the thought of an interview with Maud, in her present state of mind; she knew that it would be impossible for her to endure the stream of small talk, flavoured with cynical comments upon the speaker's self and the world in general, which Maud had of late only appeared capable of. She sent her compliments to Mrs. Waghorn, begging she might be excused on consideration of somewhat severe indisposition. Apparently this message sufficed, for the servant did not return.

During the night she woke up in a fit of coughing, such as had once before broken a sleep of anguish, and with the same results. There was blood in her mouth. Again the hours of nameless terror had to be endured, again she seemed to see ghostly figures sitting beside her bed. Again she felt acutely her painful loneliness, more now, after the brief taste of such delightful companionship than ever before. Lucy was sleeping in the next room, but what was to be gained by waking her? Lucy was a dear, affectionate child, a sweet associate of calm hours, but for midnight scenes such as this all unfitted.

Peace came with the following day, partly as a consequence of almost complete physical prostration. Helen was so entirely worn out that her mind gladly took refuge in any trifle to escape the painful and ever-renewed struggle with grief. Through the morning Lucy was a welcome companion at her side, as she lay upon the sofa. Lucy, with a woman's tact, readily divined what had passed, and understood, moreover, Helen's reason for keeping silence thereon. She saw that her friend could not as yet bear to speak of her sorrows. The time would come when to speak of them would be a relief, and Lucy knew well that Helen would then choose no other than herself for a *confidante*. When in the afternoon Mrs. Cumberbatch made her appearance Helen did not view her approach with as much annoyance as usual. Friendly faces of whatever kind were welcome to her at present. Mrs. Cumberbatch made a few inquiries in a low tone with regard to Helen's health, then took a seat, and, in her ordinary manner, became absorbed in needle-work. We have mentioned that it was her habit to smile much to herself when thus occupied; but to-day she smiled to a quite extraordinary extent; so much so that Helen, who, perhaps for the first time, found some amusement in watching her, and speculating upon the character of her thoughts, felt sure that there was something more than ordinary upon her mind.

"Have you any news to-day, Mrs. Cumberbatch?" she asked, at length, almost surprised at the curious frame of mind which urged her to provoke the dialogue she generally so much dreaded.

"I presume you have yourself heard none, my dear—h'm?" asked Mrs. Cumberbatch, in her quiet tone, looking at Helen out of the corners of her eyes, without raising her head from her work.

"None whatever," replied Helen, smiling slightly. "I see but little of what is known as 'the world'"

"Then you know nothing of the strange occurrences at the Waghorns'—h'm?"

"Nothing," replied Helen. "What occurrences do you allude to?"

She smiled as she asked, knowing well the kind of incident to which Mrs. Cumberbatch was wont to attach importance.

"Very strange occurrences indeed," said Mrs. Cumberbatch, slightly raising her eyebrows. "As yet they are only whispered among the intimate friends of the family. I should scarcely be justified in repeating them to anyone but yourself."

Helen continued to wear upon her face a ook of interrogation.

"You will scarcely credit what I say, my dear," pursued Mrs. Cumberbatch, who evidently had the utmost delight in detailing her intelligence. "It is whispered—only whispered—that a dreadful scene took place in the house yesterday; in short, a terrible quarrel between Mr. and Mrs. Waghorn; the end of which was that Mr. Waghorn suddenly took a pistol out of his pocket and fired it at Mrs. Waghorn. Fortunately he missed his aim."

Helen looked at the speaker for some moments in the utmost astonishment.

"Surely, Mrs. Cumberbatch," she said, " this is some strange exaggeration."

"I should myself have thought so," replied the other, "had not I learned it from one who was all but a spectator of the incident, Mrs. Waghorn's own maid."

This she said with an air of great confidence, and with many motions of the eyebrows. Helen remained mute for a while, then suddenly asked—

" Do you know the hour at which this extraordinary event took place?"

" I think very shortly after noon."

Helen remembered that it had been nearly four o'clock when Maud's visit was announced to her. She sank into troubled reflections.

" But that is only part of the news," pursued Mrs. Cumberbatch. " Shortly after this occurrence, Mrs. Waghorn appears to have left the house on foot, and at noon to-day she had neither returned nor been heard of."

For Helen this was distressing news, not merely because she still retained a friendly interest in Maud and could not have heard

of any misfortune happening to her without
pain, but also for reasons which were extremely characteristic of her exquisitely
sensitive mind, reasons which to ordinary
persons would appear visionary, but which
were sufficiently serious with Helen to cause
her acute suffering at a moment when she
had believed that her capacities for suffering
were exhausted. She deceived herself in
thinking that pain of her own could ever be
so engrossing as to deprive her of sympathy
with the pains of others, and the sympathy
now excited in her on Maud's account found
its own reward in the diversion of her
thoughts from their previous rugged channel.
At once she imagined to herself, with a vividness entirely new, all the wretchedness of a
marriage which could result in events such
as these; she realised for the first time the
supreme unhappiness which must have
formed the under-current of Maud's life for
so long a time. And, as she did so, she reproached herself bitterly for that cold indifference on her own part which had led her
to turn away from the playmate of her childhood as from one with whom she had nothing
in common. More than ever did her conscience smite her when she reflected that
only yesterday afternoon Maud had called to
see her, and had been refused admission,
when in all likelihood she came to make a
last appeal for Helen's support, to beg for advice in the midst of all manner of troubles.

and temptation. Certainly there had been
no sufficient ground for refusing to see her.
Helen blushed as she reflected that this had
been one of the most flagrant cases of selfishness which memory could bring to her
charge. Her conscience, moreover, took a
wider range. One of the principal reasons
for her constant neglect of Maud had been
her own absorption in her daily work among
the poor and the suffering. But, after all,
did not charity begin at home? Was it
right of her to neglect the opportunity of
saving from wreck a life which had long been
in such close connection with her own, because, forsooth, she was preoccupied with
plans for the feeding and clothing of those
who were complete strangers to her? Helen
felt that there was something wrong in this.
Perhaps her own sufferings of the last few
days had taught her to appreciate more
keenly than hitherto the fact that there are
other pains in the world besides those involved in want of clothes or food, and that
people who never knew what it was to lack
these necessaries may yet be subject to perhaps acute torments. Helen feared that her
method of thought had somewhat lacked
breadth, that she would have been none the
worse for nourishing a more universal charity.

These thoughts crowded upon her in the
interval of the present conversation, but it
was not till after she had revolved them for
some days that they began to assume dis-

tinct shapes in her mind. In the meantime she made many attempts to discover the place of Maud's retreat, but altogether without success. In these attempts she made Mrs. Cumberbatch her ally, forcing herself at the same time to study that lady's character more closely than she had hitherto done and to discover what good elements it contained. She found that with the exception of a monstrous curiosity in all things, and a perverted bigotry in matters of religion, there was nothing especially objectionable in Mrs. Cumberbatch. Among her, at any rate more useful, qualities was a degree of worldly wisdom which surprised Helen, and which appeared likely to be of considerable use in the present undertaking. She appeared to have no doubt of the circumstances under which Maud had disappeared, stating plainly, though with that *entourage* of nods and frowns and interrogatory particles which always marked her communications, that Maud had gone off somewhere or other with Augustus Whiffle. In the course of confidential talk she incidentally owned to Helen that she had for some time been in the habit of receiving special intelligence from Mrs. Waghorn's *fille de chambre*, probably under the instigation of no other motive than unadulterated curiosity, and from this young woman she had learned secrets of a somewhat peculiar nature. One of these was that Maud had of late frequently lent considerable sums to young Whiffle to aid him in his enterprise on the turf, and had received back most of them with interest to boot. To Helen's horror, Mrs. Cumberbatch saw nothing at all unlikely in the supposition that Maud was at present living somewhere with Whiffle, who was doing his best for them both in those special kind of speculations to which his genius was adapted.

Mrs. Cumberbatch's sagacity and knowledge of circumstances had led her to a fairly just opinion of the state of affairs. A month or so after Maud's disappearance from London, a lady and gentleman of genteel appearance established themselves for a brief period in one of the finest hotels at Scarborough and made a great figure among the visitors whom the early spring found amusing or doctoring themselves at that fashionable sea-port. The pair were written down in the visitor's book as Mr. and Mrs. Baldwin. What title they had to this name will appear from a brief conversation between them as they strolled together one evening along the esplanade.

" I tell you," said the gentleman, who appeared slightly out of temper, " that it was nothing but a piece of devilish bad luck. The horse stumbled over a stone, or some other cursed thing that stood in the way, and so the race was lost and your five hundred at the same time. It couldn't be helped. We must just submit to it."

" If we have to submit to many more such little accidents," replied the lady, with an ill-pleased shrug, " I fancy we shall be obliged to dissolve partnership in consequence."

" Pooh, pooh, Maud," replied the young man, in whom the reader of course recognises Mr. Augustus Whiffle. " I thought you were too cool a hand to fret yourself on a matter such as this. Now look, I'll tell you something to revive your spirits. I've got the very best tip for the second spring New-market that ever fellow had. Sure to clear a gold mine. So cheer up, old girl."

The evening air soon becoming unpleasantly keen, Mr. and Mrs. Baldwin shortly returned to their hotel. On their way they passed the post-office. Augustus took the opportunity to enter and inquire for letters. He came out with two in his hands, one directed to himself, and one to Maud.

" Ho, ho ! " exclaimed Augustus, as soon as he skimmed through his letter. " Here's a little news for you, Maud. Thompson writes me that Waghorn has gone past redemption, and that the house is for sale. He doesn't seem to know exactly what brought on the big smash. At all events everything is to be sold up—advertised in yesterday's papers. Don't you feel disposed to go and bid for one or two of your own things ? "

In the meantime Maud had glanced over her own communication, which was from a female acquaintance in London.

"Oh, don't flatter yourself you have the monopoly of news," she exclaimed, as she folded the letter up and replaced it in the envelope. "It may interest you to hear that Mr. John Waghorn has just filed a petition for divorce from his wife on the ground of her—&c., &c. You can imagine the rest."

"The devil!" cried Augustus, suddenly standing still. "Are you serious?"

"Perfectly, and I have no doubt whatever the news is true. I am delighted to hear it. I'm off to town by the first train to-morrow morning!"

"But, I say, Maud—damnation! Think of the infernal scandal. Why, I shall appear in the newspapers as co-respondent."

"Of course you will," returned Maud, with the utmost *nonchalance,* "and in consequence I shall get my freedom. Thank your stars you have the power to confer a benefit on someone. I assure you, I'm perfectly delighted!"

In consequence of this intelligence the two returned to town the following day. Maud took a couple of modest rooms for the present in Gower Street, and Mr. Whiffle returned to his ordinary abode and his customary avocations, very much disgusted at the prospect of having his name ere long associated with proceedings in the Divorce Court. His apprehensions were completely fulfilled. One morning early in May, Mrs. Cumberbatch had the pleasure of pointing out to Helen the following passage in a daily paper :—

" WAGHORN v. WAGHORN AND WHIFFLE.

" Mr. —— appeared for the petitioner.

" The petitioner married the respondent in August, 1871, and they lived together at the former's residence in London until early in March of the present year, when the respondent left her husband, subsequently accompanying the co-respondent to several parts of England as his wife. The petitioner now prayed for a divorce on the ground of his wife's adultery. There was no defence, and the Court granted a decree *nisi.*"

As we shall not again have the pleasure of meeting personally with Mr. Augustus Whiffle, I may as well state that, despite the above little incident, his father's influence in time obtained for him a " cure of souls," to which was attached emoluments of a highly satisfactory nature. There is every reason to suppose that to the present day the reverend gentleman fulfils his ecclesiastical functions with, to say the least, all that ardour of disposition by which we have seen him so distinguished.

CHAPTER XIV.

THE BEGINNING OF THE END.

AFTER the first shock of passionate grief had been lived through, and when Arthur was capable of calmly reviewing his position, he found that he could look forward to the future with something more than resignation. Nor will the reader be at a loss to account for this apparently strange condition. In constitution of mind eminently an idealist, he was yet, as we have had frequent opportunities of seeing, singularly dependent upon external influences for the shape which his idealism should for the time assume. The secret of his life lay in the fact that his was an ill-balanced nature, lacking that element of a firm and independent will which might at any moment exert its preponderance in situations of doubt. Hence it resulted that he was one of those men whose lives seem to have little result for the world save as useful illustrations of the force of circumstances—one of those who, had Fortune directed his path amid congenial scenes, might have developed a rich individuality. As it was, though noble impulse unmistakably constituted the soil of his mind, adverse circumstances forbade his giving to the implanted seeds that care which might have nourished them into flower and fruit. All the more sensible was he to the influence of those who, assuming the position of his own will, exerted themselves to direct the cultivation of his nature. Once he had possessed such a guide in William Noble; at present he was as clay in the hands of Helen Norman. In both of these friends he felt the presence of that which he himself lacked —a strong will; and in both cases he clung to the leadership of this will with a presentiment that it was his best resource. William Noble he had formerly followed from respect for his sterling character and admiration of his lofty aims. But both these feelings had yielded before the influence of Helen Norman, who established immutably, with the seal of passion, the power which her ideal character might only have exerted for a while. Thus it was that Arthur looked forward with a strange kind of pleasure to the strict pursual of the course which Helen had enjoined upon him. The fact that the injunction carried with it the infliction of fearful torture rather attracted than terrified him; he was about to suffer for *her* sake, in the pursuit of a noble ideal which *she* had set before him, and this consideration was to Arthur Golding an impulse stronger than that which any prospect of mere worldly ease could have afforded. Indeed, it was only in the pursuit of such ideals that he could ever hope to find ease. It was nothing to him that the way led through unheard-of suffering. Already he had suffered much more than falls to the lot of ordinary men, and he might reasonably hope that, by constant endurance, his torture would become his element.

To say that it was pure idealism which drove him onward to his dread task would not be the whole truth; there was also hope. To say that he hoped for an ultimate termination of his strife, that he hoped some day to be able to claim his reward, is but to say that he was a man. The hope was not one upon which he could permit himself to dwell, which, indeed, he could venture to contemplate as existing at all; but for all that it was there, no inconsiderable element of his determined courage. Instinctively he knew that Helen also was nursing the same hope. They were both young; both could wait, untroubled by the faintest distrust of each other's purposes. What power could forbid them to hope?

Arthur's first task was to re-discover Carrie. He could not tell whether she would again come to his lodgings, but it was possible, and he must not miss her in case she did. Accordingly, he took the resolution of telling Mr. Venning the facts concerning his marriage, and also his future intentions. This step taken, he began an active search. He knew that there was little chance of discovering Carrie in the day time, so through the day he applied himself steadfastly to his

work, and at night went forth and wandered
for hours about those districts where, as his
former experience told him, women of
Carrie's class were most wont to congregate.
Save such vague guidance as this, he had
absolutely no clue to her whereabouts. He
frequently inserted advertisements in the
newspapers, but they remained without
answer. Many a time when walking late at
night along the Strand, or in the Haymarket,
or about Regent Street or Oxford Street, he
caught a distant glimpse of a form resembling that which he sought; then he would
hurry in pursuit, and only when the approach
of his quick step had caused the girl to look
round would find that he had been deceived.
At such times he was absolutely proof
against all seductive arts; the sensual part
of his nature seemed for the present subdued
before the seriousness of his task. Night
after night he frequented scenes of gaiety, of
debauch of the most depraved licentious-
ness, but always with the same sad, fixed
face, the same impatient eagerness of glance,
which denoted something very different from
the pursuit of pleasure. He had somewhat
the air of a gambler, wandering about in
feverish search of an opportunity to retrieve
his ruined fortunes. He never spoke to any
one, and, as he lived in unbroken silence
during the day time, his manner showed that
nervous shyness peculiar to those who live
much in solitude. Possibly the nature of

his search may also have contributed to make him timid and shrinking, for he dreaded to meet with Carrie at least as much as he desired to do so. His feverish imagination exhausted itself in the picturing of horrible circumstances amid which he might find her. Every crowd in the street caused him a vague dread. He became by degrees nervously sensitive to unusual noises; sometimes an unexpected touch when he was passing along the street would cause him to start violently. Doubtless much of this was due to ill-health, caused by want of sleep and the constant mental trouble he endured. Soon he had not even the resource of wholesome work, for alas! art was becoming once more distasteful to him. He missed the cheerful energy which had lately urged him on whenever he took up the pencil, the ever-active imagination revealing to him worlds of glorious possibilities, the rapid heart-beat which was his reward when he had achieved a success. Now he was obliged to force himself to his easel, and the labour of an hour wearied him inexpressibly in body and mind.

Already he had begun to ask himself whether this search could endure for ever, and what course he should pursue if unable to attain his object, when, one night towards the end of April, his wanderings came to an end. It had been a severe night, bitter with alternating snow, hail and rain, and with a piercing wind which never ceased to rush along the muddy streets, setting at defiance every protection. Despite the weather, Arthur had wandered about as usual, partly from mere habit, partly because his own room was intolerable to him. Though he had scarcely any hope of recognising the face he sought, he never ceased to scan the features of every woman that passed him, feeding the melancholy in his heart upon the endless variety of woe which was thus exhibited to him. But about eleven the storm became so fierce that it was hardly possible to stand against it. At this moment he found himself near a lighted entrance into which several people were hastening, and hither he too repaired, in the intention of seeking shelter till the violent hail was over. It was a narrow doorway, situated in a very shabby back street, and, as he entered, he found himself in front of a second door, on which was a large placard, exhibiting the words, " Tableaux Vivants." Hearing the sound of music within, he pushed the door open, and entered a moderate-sized room, lighted only by a jet of glass suspended from the low ceiling. Standing and sitting about the room were some thirty or forty men, engaged in watching the entertainment. Their eyes were directed to a small elevated platform, of circular shape, which was placed imme-diately under the gas-jet, the rays from which were concentrated upon it by means of a large shade. On the platform, which kept slowly revolving to the sound of a melancholy hand-organ, stood two women, at first sight apparently naked, but in reality clothed in tight-fitting tissue of flesh-colour. The fact that one was in the act of offering an apple for the other's acceptance rendered it probable that the group was meant to represent Adam and Eve. As the platform revolved, the two engaged in a slow pantomime indicative of conversation. Such was the entertainment, watched in silence, only broken now and then by a coarse laugh or a whispered comment. Of course it was meant to be vicious, and certainly was indecent in character; but surely not the severest moralist could have devised a means of showing more clearly the hideousness of vice. The cold, bare room, swept through by a gust from the street whenever the door opened, the wailing hand-organ playing a waltz in the time of a psalm-tune, and with scarcely a correct note, the assemblage of gross and brutal-featured men, whose few remarks were the foulest indecencies, the reek of bad tobacco which was everywhere present, the dim light, save on the revolving platform where the shivering wretches went through their appointed parts,—surely only in England, where popular amusement is but known in theory, could so ghastly an *ensemble* attract a single spectator.

But to Arthur it was no opportunity for moralising. Scarcely had he taken half-a-

dozen steps towards the end of the room
where the platform was, before he suddenly
stopped. As he entered, the backs of the
women had been towards him, but now the
revolution had brought their faces under the
light, and that moment he knew that he had
found Carrie. The one holding up the apple
could be no other than she. Her features
were paler and thinner than they had been
even on the night when he last saw her.
Her hair, which had always been wonderfully long and thick, now fell quite loosely
upon her shoulders, and to below her waist.
Her face was distorted with the semblance
of a smile; but so intensely was she suffering from the cold that her parted teeth
frequently chattered, and her hand trembled
visibly.

On either side of the platform, green curtains shut off a portion of the room, and
behind these the two performers disappeared
as soon as their pantomime was at an end.
Inquiry of the door-keeper informed Arthur
that the payment of a shilling entitled the
spectators to go behind the scenes, or, in
other words, behind the green curtains.
Almost throwing the money at the man, he
hastened to avail himself of the privilege.
Besides the two performers, who had cast
over themselves a little extra clothing for
the sake of warmth, he found two or three
other women, evidently preparing to go upon
the platform, and chatting the while with

half-a-dozen low-looking men, who stood there with their hands in their pockets, smoking. At Arthur's entrance, Carrie raised her hands, with an artificial smile of welcome; but, recognising him the same moment, she involuntarily gave utterance to a low scream, and rose to her feet, as if with some thought of escaping. Arthur made no sign in reply, but simply drew near to the wretched girl and addressed her in a low voice, inaudible to the others present.

"I have been seeking you for many weeks, Carrie," he said, "and had almost given up in despair. Quick; dress, and come out of this horrible place."

"Come?" she repeated, as if not understanding, while every limb trembled. "Where to?"

"With me, with me," said Arthur. "I cannot explain. Only be quick."

"But I can't go," she replied. "I'm engaged for an hour yet. He won't let me go," she added, nodding towards the other side of the curtains.

"Who? The man at the door?"

"Yes."

"How much has he paid you?"

"He hasn't paid me yet; but he'll pay me five shillings at the end of the week."

"Dress at once, then. I will go and speak to him."

Half-a-crown to the man at the door removed all difficulties, and in a very few minutes the two issued together into the street.

The violence of the storm had by this time spent itself, but the rain still fell heavily. They hurried on together, side by side, in silence, till at length Arthur stopped before a small coffee-house.

"Are you hungry, Carrie?" he asked, turning and looking into her face.

She shook her head.

Beckoning her to follow, he pushed open the door and entered. In a few moments he had paid for a night's lodging, and, accompanied by Carrie, was shown upstairs into a small and not too clean-looking bedroom. The waiter gave him a candle and retired. Arthur turned the key in the door, and then faced Carrie, whose eyes had followed his motions with wonder.

"Last time I saw you, Carrie," he said, speaking in a low voice, lest he should be heard through the thin walls, "I behaved cruelly to you. You told me how anxious you were to return to a better life, and how you repented of the past, and yet I let you go away without a word of kindness or an offer of forgiveness. For a long time I have tried to find you, wishing to make amends for my unkindness. Now let us forget the past. Come and live with me again as my wife. Will you, Carrie?"

As he regarded the girl's suffering face, a deep feeling of compassion had by degrees awakened within his heart, and he nourished it eagerly, trusting that it might render his task easier to him.

"How can I be your wife, Arthur?" returned Carrie, sobbing. "You don't know what I have gone through; you don't know what a miserable wretch I am. I am not fit to be your wife."

"Yes," replied Arthur, "you are more fit than when we first met. You have suffered severely; you are better able to understand the pleasures of a quiet, virtuous life. You will no longer think me foolish when I urge you to improve yourself; you will feel that I was always anxious for your happiness, and could see more clearly than you how it was to be attained. I assure you I shall never think of the past, and you will soon forget it in the happiness of a better life. Have you still any love for me, Carrie?"

"I have always loved you," she said, weeping bitterly. "It isn't you as has been cruel to me, Arthur; it's me as has behaved as if I hated you, though all the while I loved you better than I ever loved any one else. It was all the drink; it drove me to do things and to say things as I shouldn't never have thought on, and as I didn't mean —no, upon my word, I didn't. If I can only keep from drink, Arthur, I could be a faithful and hard-working wife, indeed I could. I'll do my best, I will. But I feel I'm not fit to live with you. I never was fit."

"We won't talk any more about it, Carrie," said the young man, pressing her hand kindly. "It is possible to begin again and correct all our mistakes; for I have made mistakes as well as you. Only promise me that you will do your very best, for, you know, it cannot be done without an effort."

"Yes, yes, I will promise," said Carrie. "I'll do my very best, indeed I will. If I can only keep from drink you shan't have nothing to complain of. Kiss me, Arthur! Oh, it's so long since you kissed me, and I've always loved you, all the while."

He bent his head, and she clung to him with a fervour resembling that of the early days of their love. There was no feigning in this outbreak of passion, it was a genuine gleam of womanly nature making itself visible amid the foul gloom of a desecrated humanity. When she said that she had always loved him, she spoke the simple truth, strange and incredible as it may seem. This feeling it had been which had alone preserved her from sinking into absolute brutality, as the majority of such women do; upon its development depended her only chance of rising to a purer life. And Arthur, though he could not persuade himself into a belief of reviving passion, yet experienced so intensely the emotion of pity, felt so keenly the full pathos of her broken words, was so profoundly touched by the sense of her helplessness, that the thought of once more being a providence to the poor suffering outcast melted his heart, and for the moment made him forget to compare her with Helen.

Already, in anticipation of this event, Arthur had realised in cash one hundred pounds out of his Three Per Cents., and with this he was enabled to take and furnish two rooms for himself and Carrie. In order to remove her as far as possible from the temptations of the town, he chose his lodgings in a quiet little street in Hampstead, at this time of year a delightful neighbourhood, where he hoped that the calmness of the surroundings, the fresh, healthful air, and the constant presence of nature, would likewise act beneficially upon his own mood and renew his artistic impulses. It was with strange sensations that he sat down to pass the first evening in his new home with Carrie at his side. For more than a week the latter had been engaged in purchasing articles of clothing for herself. Arthur had not attended her on these shopping excursions, being unwilling to arouse the suspicion of distrust, and he had been astonished at the moderation which Carrie had exhibited in the quality and number of her purchases. It seemed as though she had made up her mind to destroy at a blow all the extravagant propensities of her nature, and to demonstrate by the severe simplicity of her external appearance the change which had come over her mind. To-night she sat in a dress of her own making,

an extremely plain print gown with no trace
of adornment; her hair done up into a single
plait behind her head, and fixed with merely
a piece of black ribbon. Attired thus, she
still retained much of her old beauty, though
her eyes were dark and heavy and there was
a woeful hollowness in her cheeks. In her
behaviour she was extremely quiet, not often
speaking, sitting most of her time with an
absent, melancholy look, and often sighing
deeply. Her health was utterly shattered;
even the performance of the lightest household work taxed her strength almost beyond
its endurance. Yet as he sat gazing at her
in the evening twilight, pretending to be
engaged with a book, Arthur felt his heart
warm with a glow of delight, which was no
other than the glad sense of having performed
a just action. He had once more raised
Carrie from the depths of wretchedness to
comfort and respectability. His mind was
almost at ease this evening. There was
something like hope pictured before him in
the warm hues of the western sky, a calm,
sober hope, which should have its source in
nothing but the steadfast performance of
duty. When at length his look met Carrie's
by chance, he smiled upon her, with a kindliness which was scarcely distinguishable from
affection.

In this way Arthur conscientiously did his
best to adapt himself to his circumstances and
render his life tolerable. His was a nature

which ever found its amplest joy in the gratification of others, and during the first few
weeks of his new life, he was even happy in
watching Carrie's delight at every fresh instance of his thoughtfulness and care for her.
He had recommenced his work, too, and was
constantly engaged in making studies for what
he meant should be a great picture, the subject to be the Pleading of Portia. As was
always the case when a new and strong idea
suddenly possessed itself of his mind, Arthur
worked with the utmost enthusiasm for
several weeks. Carrie he used for his model
of the female form, for male figures he
secured the services of a good-for-nothing,
but finely-built and handsome young fellow
who was perpetually lounging about the door
of a public-house hard by, and who was only
too glad to earn a few shillings by means so
admirably adapted to his constitutional indo-
lence. Having made his first rough cartoon,
he purchased at some expense a fine work on
costumes, by means of which he was enabled
to clothe his figures in appropriate raiment.
The scene which he was illustrating had been
a favourite one with Mr. Tollady, who had
many a time made Arthur read it aloud to
him, insisting on the utmost nicety of tone
and expression; so that the eager artist had
his zeal redoubled by the dear recollections
amidst which he worked.

Another incitement, too, he had, perhaps
of a somewhat perilous character, but which

he had persuaded himself was innocent.
Ever since his love for Helen had unmistakably declared itself in his heart, her image
had become for him the ideal of female excellence. So, whatever book he read, whatever
fancies he meditated upon, as often as the
figure of a noble woman was called up before
his mind's eye, it inevitably appeared in
Helen's shape, looked forth from Helen's eyes,
and spoke in Helen's tones. Thus, in depicting Portia, it was Helen who sat for the
likeness. An exquisitely graceful, yet tall
and commanding, form; a firm, lithe neck,
connecting head and trunk with ideal apti-
tude; features of classic purity, wherein
every line spoke character, mobile, expressive of the finest shades of subtle thought
and feeling, ravishing when lighted with a
gleam of tenderness and joy, awe-inspiring
when moulded to the utterance of rebuke,
at all times the incarnation of lofty purity;
such was the idea which Arthur had conceived of Portia, and which his heart held
embodied in the shape of Helen Norman.
Unable to wait for the completion of the
subsidiary details of the picture, as soon as
he had designed the main groups he threw
himself upon the canvas with a desperate
ardour, and scarcely laid down his pallet
till, as it were, the ghost of Portia looked out
upon him from the midst of still more ghost-
like shapes. For the arrangement of the
drapery Carrie stood as his model.

"Is it the Queen, Arthur?" she asked, one morning, when her eyes was able to discern something of the commanding shape.

"Yes," replied Arthur, in a low voice, adding to himself—"My queen."

"But you must put the crown on her head," urged Carrie, with an overwhelming sense of the importance of the symbol.

"Perhaps I may do; but I am not sure."

"Oh, but how can it be the Queen without a crown?" asked Carrie. "Nobody will know who it's meant for, Arthur."

"Perhaps not, Carrie, I must think of it."

With all sincerity, Arthur believed himself innocent in thus dwelling upon the memory of Helen's loveliness. He convinced himself that she was no longer a woman to him. She was now a mere personification of a principle, the bodily presentment of the high spirit she had breathed into his life, of unshakable consistency and aspiring effort. He felt that it was good for him that he should have her image ever present in his mind; it constantly reminded him of his promise to her, urged him not to falter for a moment in the path of self-sacrifice upon which she had bidden him enter. She was his patron saint, his divinity; he would scarcely have esteemed it folly to pray before her effigy.

When his hand sunk in weariness from its perpetual task, and his mind irresistibly craved relaxation from its intense toil, it was the occupation of hours to sit and dream of the

time when his picture would be completed.
He would send it to the Academy ; it would
be received, he felt sure it would be received ;
and there Helen would see it. Perhaps it
would make him famous—who could tell?
Perhaps she would read glowing eulogies of
him and his work. Oh, it was Heaven to
wander through long summer evenings about
the country lanes, feeding the fire of his
imagination from the warm, rich sunsets,
chastening the conceptions of his passionate
heart in the calm, cool light of the rising
moon.

At first he had always taken Carrie with
him when he went on these evening walks,
but by degrees her commonplace chatter,
her vulgarisms of thought and language, her
utter insensibility to the impressions of the
season and the hour, rendered her company
at such times intolerable to him. He could
not bear that the deepest joys of which his
nature was capable should be vexed and
sullied by these wretched admixtures of
vulgar inappreciativeness. Carrie had not
the faintest conception of the beauties of
nature ; when amid delightful country scenes
she yearned for the lights of the shops and
the coarse tumult of the pavement. Though
country-born and bred, the fresh air of the
fields, the glad light of a cloudless heaven,
the odour of flowers, the verdure of tree and
meadow, awoke not a single tender reminiscence within her heart. She was emphati-

cally a child of the town, dreaming of nothing but its gross delights, seeing in everything pure and lovely but a sapless image of some town-made joy. One evening Arthur endeavoured to make her appreciate the grandeur of a sunset scene from the Heath. After looking at it for some moments, she exclaimed, " It's almost as pretty as the theaytre, isn't it ? "

Comfort had a demoralising effect upon Carrie. In the midst of physical suffering she seemed to become somewhat finer natured, manifesting sensibilities worthy of respect, and, thanks to her personal beauty, exciting deep compassion and sympathy. But as the recollection of her pain began to lose its edge, she became perceptibly coarser; her language, her very features seemed to bear witness to the reviving animal within. Arthur observed this only too well; it made him shudder for the future. Scarcely had this genial life endured two months, before occasional words and actions on Carrie's part began to remind him of that hideous period in his life which preceded her desertion of him. Once more she showed signs of becoming headstrong and wilful; her temper was being aggravated by her constant ill-health. At first Arthur turned aside her impatience by the softest of answers, resolved to endure anything rather than be unfaithful to his task. He reflected that she had at least successfully struggled with her main vice for his sake; and it would be ungrateful to forget that. Everything was tolerable, compared with this ghostly phantom, which, though inactive, still seemed to sit by his fireside, brooding over horrors fatal to his peace.

But the phantom could not for ever remain inactive. One evening it began to stir—very slightly, but very perceptibly. Carrie's health had rendered it necessary that she should be seen by a physician, and for several weeks she obtained from the latter bottles of medicine, which she kept on the top shelf of a cupboard in the bedroom. One evening when Carrie was out making purchases, Arthur had occasion to look for something on this top shelf. In front of the bottles of medicine, of which there were some half dozen, stood the wine-glass which served as a measure. This appeared to have been recently used, and in the bottom of it a little liquid still remained. Out of idle curiosity, Arthur took up the glass and smelt it. The smell seemed to inflict a sudden shock on his frame; he started and almost dropped the glass. He smelt again, then tasted the drop which the glass contained, and he could not doubt that it was pure brandy. With a trembling hand he took out each of the medicine bottles from the dark recess, and the last he took, which was also the largest, he found to be half full of spirits.

It was, of course, possible that the physician

had ordered the use of brandy, but, in that case, why had not Carrie informed him of it? How slight a chance there was of such a supposition being true, when put face to face with that dark dread which ever sat by his hearth, which seemed to whisper a fearful contradiction in the silence of the room. At first he decided that he would affect an unrestrained manner, and ask Carrie plainly whether the spirits had been prescribed; but his very soul shrank from the possibility of hearing a shameless lie, which subsequent enquiry could at once expose. No, he could not speak to her about it; but he would adopt a plan just as sure. He would take the bottle, throw away the contents, and then replace it, empty, amongst the others; then await the result, if any.

This was on a Saturday. On Saturday evenings Carrie was always out a long time, owing to the number of purchases she had to make for the week. As a rule, Arthur welcomed this absence, enjoying the quietness it secured, and working at his easel as long as it remained light. But this evening he was once more a prey to that terrible mind-canker which robs of all delight in existence. For the first time he turned away from his picture in distaste, and paced the room in wretchedness of spirit. Was he, then, about to undergo once more those fearful tortures which had already once ended in all but his total ruin? He regarded his daily life with a bitterness which he had long succeeded in keeping aloof, and his heart nourished the seeds of anger against her who once more threatened to be his curse. " It is vain ! It is vain ! " he cried to himself, with the voice of his thoughts. " All my efforts are vain ! I cannot raise her to my level ; but I feel only too well that she has the power to drag me down to hers. It is my fate to suffer, to conceive plans and hopes which time only shatters, like a child its playthings."

Carrie had left the house at five o'clock, and it was nine before she returned. Arthur received her on her entrance with an angry face.

" How is it you are so late ? " he asked impatiently.

" Late ! " she repeated, with a careless tone. " I don't know as I'm late. I've been far enough to find something for your dinner, anyhow."

And, as she spoke, she flung her basket on to the floor. She had not gone out in the best of tempers, and apparently had returned not at all improved.

" You have been out about four hours," said Arthur, doing his best to speak calmly. " It is impossible for you to spend all that time in shopping."

" Is it ? " she retorted. " Then do your own shopping next time, and see, that's all ! "

And she straightway walked into the bed-room, banging the door behind her.

Arthur was left in that distressing state of body and mind which he knew only too well. His throat, tongue and lips parched and burning, his heart pressed down by a terrible weight, a sickness of the soul crushing his whole being. For the first time he tasted the full bitterness of the task he had taken upon him, and looked forward to the future as if into the very jaws of despair. Utterly unable to fix himself to any work, he took up a volume of poetry and tried to lose himself thus, but not a word impressed itself on his mind, and, after staring for an hour at a blank page, he turned out the light and went into the bedroom. Carrie was in bed, but not asleep. He addressed a few words to her, but, receiving no answer, he lay down in silence by her side, and tried to sleep. Hour after hour went by, finding him still wakeful, his forehead burning, his whole frame oppressed by the first onset of a fever. Carrie had soon fallen asleep, but into a sleep which was perpetually broken by tossings, mutterings, and occasionally cries. Already the earliest morning light had penetrated through the blind when Arthur forgot his sufferings in a dreamless slumber.

Carrie awoke about ten o'clock, complaining bitterly of a severe headache. She evidently remembered nothing of what had occurred the evening before, but she was sullen, and, for the most part, silent. The morning was gloomy, threatening rain, but about noon it began to clear, and by two o'clock the sun was shining brightly. Carrie had declared herself too ill to rise, and had refused breakfast, which Arthur was obliged to prepare for himself as well as he could. As soon as the sunshine gave promise of endurance, he gladly seized on the chance of breathing fresh air, and prepared to go out. When he was ready, he went, after a moment's hesitation, to the bedroom door, and asked Carrie if she cared to accompany him. He received no reply, though he could see she heard him, and at once left the house alone.

For two or three hours he drank deep of the healthful summer air, refreshing body and mind in a wander over the Heath and out into the country beyond, thanking Heaven for the blessing of solitude. As was always the case when the fit of irritation had passed away, he thought of Carrie with pitying tenderness, accusing himself as the cause of all their misunderstandings, reproaching himself for lack of consideration towards her, in short, longing to return and ask her forgiveness for wrong he had never committed. In this mood he hastened homewards, arriving towards six o'clock. He hoped to find Carrie waiting for him, with a comfortable tea. Instead of that, he found her still in bed, her face disfigured with signs of long weeping, her eyes red with meaningless passion. Mastering his disappointment, he approached the bed and said calmly—

"Don't you feel better, Carrie?"

"A great deal you care!" was the reply, in a fiercely passionate tone. "Better indeed! Ain't you sorry as you haven't found me dead? It 'ud a' been a good riddance, wouldn't it?"

"How can you say such things, Carrie?" asked Arthur, studiously maintaining a mild tone. "What has made you so angry with me?"

"Angry, indeed!" she pursued, her voice rising, though she still lay with her head motionless upon the disordered pillow. "What do you mean by going out and leaving me alone here for five or six hours? A deal you care what I suffer. Leaving me, too, without a mouthful to eat all day."

"Now, Carrie, don't talk foolishly," returned Arthur. "You know very well you indignantly refused to take any breakfast, and would not answer me when I asked you afterwards to have something to eat. And as to my going out, didn't I ask you before I went whether you cared to go with me? If you are not disposed for a walk, must I also remain moping at home?"

"You know very well," broke in the girl, "that I've not had a mouthful to eat all day. What do you mean by neglecting me as you do? What right have you to go out and leave me alone here, hour after hour?"

Arthur paused for a moment before speaking. It was only by a fierce internal struggle that he suppressed an angry reply to such inconsequent reproaches. At last he said—

"You are out of temper, Carrie, and don't know what you are saying. In a short time you will see how unjust you have been to me. Don't let us talk any more of it. Shall I make you a cup of tea?"

"Make tea for me, indeed!" she retorted. "It 'ud be something new for you to do anything for *me!*"

"You really think what you say?"

"Yes, I do, so there you have it straight. I've seen it day after day, how you neglect me more and more. Do anything for *me,* indeed! Not you! You only wish I was dead."

Stung to madness by the cruel injustice of these taunts, Arthur bit his tongue to keep down an angry reply, and at once left the room. But the air of the house stifled him; he could not remain indoors. In a few minutes he was once more pacing quickly along the quiet street, heedless where he went, only driven perpetually onward by a devouring fire within his breast. Oh, he knew the meaning of the scene just enacted only too well. Despite his precautions, Carrie had once more fallen beneath the power of her old vice; most likely she had been drinking all the time of his absence. Certainly it was foolish to be made angry by the senseless clamour of a drunken woman, but human nature contains a far greater portion of passion than of philosophy, and only after an hour's violent bodily exercise did Arthur regain something of calmness. Till the moon and stars were bright above him, he wandered about the fields and lanes, pondering with a dogged persistency, the result of hopelessness, on the means of rendering his life at least tolerable. It was clear to him that he must have more society, that he must create for himself some more definite and immediate aim than that which his higher purposes in art afforded. If he could not conquer the terrible evils of his domestic life, the only course left for him was to flee from them. When at length he returned home, he had conceived a plan which he resolved the following day should be enacted.

Carrie slept soundly throughout the night, and in the morning awoke vastly improved. With true womanly logic she refused to acknowledge that she had been wrong, but yet asked Arthur to forgive her. With a smile and a sigh Arthur accorded the desired forgiveness. He did not venture to hint at the true cause of what had happened, for, indeed, at the moment he dreaded more a repetition of Carrie's violence than the results of leaving her vice unreproved. The same morning he wrote a letter to the editor of a well-known popular weekly journal, stating that he was an artist, and very much wanted to find employment in the illustration of works of fiction and the like. He requested that the editor would grant him an interview, for the purpose of exhibiting specimens of his workmanship. In a day or two he received a brief reply, merely stating that the editor had no vacancy at his disposal, and that therefore the desired interview would be useless. Not discouraged, Arthur addressed himself by turns to several other papers, and, after some three weeks, was fortunate enough to find occasional employment in beautifying the pages of a weekly paper, the character of which was, however, far below what he had aimed at. But his main object was gained, for he was thus enabled to form a few acquaintanceships, and so break, in some degree, the intolerable monotony of his life.

For, in the meantime, things had become steadily worse. Shortly after the outbreak just described, Carrie one day threw aside all concealment, and was found by Arthur, on his return from a sketching excursion, mad with drink. For several hours during the night, he had to restrain her by force from making her way out of the house, and her yells and shrieks were plainly audible by passengers out in the street. On the day after, they received notice to quit from their landlady, and within a week removed to a lodging in Highgate. But change of locality made no alteration in Carrie's habits. Having once more surrendered herself, body and soul, to the passion for drink, it seemed as if no earthly power could check her course to utter ruin.

Entreaties, arguments, adjurations, menaces, all were tried by the wretched man whose wife she called herself, sometimes with momentary effect, never with enduring benefit. Her character underwent a sensible and rapid change for the worse. She seemed to have lost all sense of shame, and, in the brief moments when she could converse peaceably with Arthur, took endless delight in describing to him the horrors of her life in the interval of her separation from him, relating details which a woman of the least sensibility would have shrunk from ever recalling to mind. More and more did Arthur absent himself from her, passing his time either in the company of such acquaintances as his connection with the paper had secured him, and who were, on the whole, miserable creatures, or else in wandering about the town alone, nursing his despair, and brooding over all manner of desperate thoughts. Sometimes a revival of the old enthusiasm would lead him to spend a whole day in the National Gallery, or among the antiques of the British Museum, but very rarely now did he conceive an impulse sufficiently strong to call him back to his easel. He visited the theatres frequently, and at one time suddenly conceived the idea of turning his thoughts to literature and writing a play. But even in his imagination this work never got beyond the first act, and not a word was ever written. By degrees he came to exhibit very much the appearance of a listless, idle man about town. He even paid more attention to his external appearance than of old, a sure sign that his mind was ceasing to furnish him with occupation. Yet, amid all this rapid degeneration, he never sank into absolute vice. From that he was withheld by the ever present aspect and voice of that pure being whose effigy still graced the undefiled sanctuary of his soul. Helen's parting words were as loud in his ears to-day as they had been when spoken, months ago. These alone could supply him with courage to live, these alone forbade him to utterly relinquish the task they had imposed.

But, in truth, it was an utterly hopeless task, one which, if persevered in, could only lead to death, first of the soul, then of the body. Though there occurred lucid moments in which Carrie gave way to passionate weeping and wailing over her misdoings, entreating forgiveness with an almost fierce persistency, and vowing reformation in the name of all conceivable sanctities, yet these were but moments, and were followed, as they had been preceded, by whole days, sometimes weeks of disgusting debauch. Owing to her disreputable conduct, Arthur was compelled to change his abode repeatedly, coming at each time nearer to the town, for the sake of the increased privacy which—paradoxical as the assertion seems—a crowded neighbourhood secured for them. At each of these removals Arthur made a fresh desperate endeavour to check her madness, but always with a result so utterly disheartening, that he was obliged to content himself with being as much away from home as possible. All the terrible scenes which had been so familiar to him during the old life in Huntley Street were now re-enacted, though with more terrible earnestness, and against a background of the deepest gloom. All the old tricks to obtain money were once more resorted to, and, since the furniture of the room was now Arthur's own, it now was easier to find the means of procuring drink than it had been before. Arthur noticed day by day that articles disappeared, but remonstrance, angry or gentle, was utterly vain; he was obliged to submit to the inevitable.

Early in December an event occurred which was destined to bring about the end of this terrible conflict. One evening Carrie had strayed out of Camden Town, where the two were then living, as far as Tottenham Court Road. Though the wretched girl had been powerless to resist the temptations of her master-vice, she had hitherto continued to preserve sufficient regard for Arthur's feelings to keep her from renewing her associations with the old companions of her abandoned life, though the inducements to do so had often been strong and the opportunities manifold. To-night she was in a despondent mood, resulting from a long period of debauch, and was beset with an overpowering desire to find some kind of companionship. She well knew where this companionship was to be had ; she well knew that a quarter-of-an-hour's walk would place her in the old sphere of licentious gaiety ; and she asked herself what it was that withheld her from satisfying her longing. Carrie never reasoned about anything ; to apply that term to her mental processes would be a hopeless error of nomenclature ; but even now, as the temptation rose in her mind, a vague species of emotion rose to oppose it, a flickering shadow of that feeling which, in a purer being, would have been gratitude to a benefactor. Brought to a pause in this faint involuntary reaction, she stood and gazed into a shop window, a jeweller's, such a window as had always exercised a baneful influence over her. Already she had begun to reflect how easily she could procure the means and the opportunity of decking herself in some of the gaudiest trinkets exposed for sale, when a voice sounded in her ear, a voice which she knew well, and which made her start. Turning, she met the look of no less a person than Mistress Polly Hemp.

"Well, I'm blest!" exclaimed Polly, who had not perceptibly changed in appearance since Carrie last parted from her. "And is it really you ! Why, I never thought to see you again."

"And I don't know as ever I thought to see you, Polly," replied the other, after a hesitation of a second or two. "How do you do?"

"Pretty middlin'. And what are you up to here, eh? But come, talking's thirsty sort o' work. I don't like to be shabby when I meet a old friend. Come and liquor."

Again a hesitation, this time perceptible.

"What!" pursued Polly, "You've growed proud, have you, Carrie. Above drinkin' with me, eh?"

It was decided. Carrie turned and accompanied her tempter, following the voice of Fate.

*　　*　　*　　*　　*

About a week after this meeting, Carrie took advantage of a day when she knew Arthur would be absent till late in the evening to invite Polly Hemp to visit her in her own lodging in Camden Town. There was something of vanity in this invitation, as well as a desire for companionship, for she was not sorry to show to one who had known her in her most miserable days the comparative luxury amid which she now lived. Fortified by the inevitable bottle of spirits, the two discussed each article of furniture, went over Carrie's wardrobe, and even ransacked the drawers containing Arthur's apparel, Polly Hemp all the time exhausting herself in eulogies.

" All I can say is," she exclaimed at length, " you may think yourself deuced lucky, Carrie, to have dropped into such a crib. And your 'usband a hartist, is he? I'll go bail he makes a bloomin' sight of tin out of it, too. Now don't he, eh?"

Carrie shrugged her shoulders.

" I don't know as he does," she replied. " At all events *I* don't get much out of it."

" Then it's a cursed shame, that's all I've got to say!" affirmed Polly, after tossing off some half-quartern of raw whiskey at a gulp. " And you say he even grumbles at your having a drop o' something comfortable now and then? I'm blest if it isn't a shame!"

" Yes, and him with so much money, too, he don't hardly know what to do with it," put in Carrie, with a wink.

" Has he, though?" asked the other, sharply, the old evil light gleaming in her little pig-eyes. " Has he, though?"

" Never you mind," returned the other. " He don't know as I know of it. But I know if the money was mine, I wouldn't be so mean with it."

Carrie's voice stammered somewhat as she spoke. At present she was in that maudlin condition which with her always preceded a period of hopeless intoxication.

" But how much has he got, eh, Carrie?" asked Mrs. Hemp, in an insinuating voice. " No secrets 'tween friends, you know."

" No more there shouldn't be, Polly," returned the girl. "You look here, and hold your eyes tight for fear they drop out of your head—ha, ha!"

As she spoke she staggered up from her chair, and leading the way into the bedroom, with some difficulty unlocked one of the top drawers in a chest. At first sight this appeared to be filled with drawings of all kinds, but Carrie, lifting up these, drew from underneath a large leather pocket-book. Out of this she took a folded piece of paper, and, holding it still in her hands, allowed Polly to glance at it. The paper was a printed form, headed "Consolidated £3 per Cent. Annuities," after which, on the same line, were written the figures £5,000.

"Do you know what that means, eh, Polly?" asked Carrie, her face distorted in a grin of foolish glee.

"No fear," returned the other. "'Tain't the first time as I've seen that kind o' thing. My God! What a heap o' tin! And he don't know as you're up to this, eh?"

"Trust him," said Carrie, winking. "And he's got more than this. He has a bankbook, too. I see it wunst, but I don't know where it is now. Ain't I in for a good spree some day?"

"I believe you," agreed the other, leering hideously.

Shortly after this, the two went out together, and, after visiting sundry favourite haunts, ultimately bent their steps to Polly

Hemp's own abode. Throughout the day
Polly had continued to urge her companion
to drink, and now that they took their seats
one on each side of the fireplace, in the
kitchen with which the reader is already
familiar, they had still glasses on their laps,
from which they solaced themselves unstint-
ingly.

"I believe you, Carrie," said Polly, resuming a subject she had constantly harped on
through the day. "You are a lucky wench,
if ever there was one. I s'pose your 'usband's
made his will?"

"I don't know," replied Carrie, giggling.

"You take my advice, and find out," remarked Polly, bending forward, with one eye
closed. "If he was to go and kick the bucket,
and hadn't made no will, I s'pose you know
as you wouldn't have all that tin?"

"Who says I shouldn't?" asked Carrie, de-
fiantly, making a motion with her hand
which spilled half the liquor from her glass.

"Why, I say so," pursued Polly, "and what's
more, the law says so. I say, Carrie, what
a kick up we would have if you was to come
in for that tin, eh?"

Carrie made an expressive gesture.

"My God! Wouldn't we!" continued
Polly; then added, in a lower and impressive
voice, "But, I say, if your 'usband was to go
and make his will and leave it all to somebody else? How then, Carrie?"

Carrie's countenance fell for a moment.

" I don't believe as how he'd do that," she replied, with a shake of the head.

There was a silence of some minutes, during which the fire crackled loudly in its efforts to seize firm hold of an obstinate piece of coal, and at length, achieving the victory with a miniature explosion, which scattered pieces of glowing slate upon the hearth, flared up and illumined vividly the faces and figures of the two women. There was an unusually wicked expression in Polly Hemp's eyes as they looked alternately at the glass on her lap and the face of her companion. Apparently she was meditating.

" Now tell the truth, Carrie," she said at length, with a low laugh, " you wouldn't cry your eyes out if your 'usband was to kick the bucket to-morrow."

" Ha, ha, ha!" laughed the girl, raising the glass to her lips, " I don't know as I should—quite."

" Well," pursued the other, consolingly, " there's worse things than that happens *every* day. And more unlikely things, too. My God! What a lark we would have. Nobody to put a stop on your drink then, Carrie. Nobody to say as you shouldn't go here, or shouldn't go there. Eh?"

She had drawn her chair a little nearer to her companion's, and was looking significantly into her face.

" Yes, yes; we'd have a lark, if it was the

last!" muttered Carrie, who appeared to be thinking.

"Do you know what I should think, Carrie," pursued Polly Hemp, with devilish insinuation, "if I was in your shoes?"

"What's that?"

"Well—I don't say as I should, you know—but I *might* p'raps think as how there was other helps to widow's caps besides the fever, and the small-pox, and sich like."

"Eh?" said the girl, looking into the speaker's face as if she had not understood her meaning.

"Why, I might p'raps think as there's other deaths besides nat'ral deaths, Carrie; d'ye see? And I shouldn't be the first as had thought that either—no, nor the first as has done *more* than *think* it, too, and lived happy ever after, as they say."

Polly's face had approached very near to Carrie's as she spoke, and a gleam of something like pleasure had risen to it as she noticed that at length her hint was understood. But her pleasure was only short-lived. For a moment Carrie turned her head away, as if to think over what had been said, then, with a movement as sudden as unexpected, she dashed the contents of her glass full in the eyes of her tempter, exclaiming as she did so—

"Not so bad as that neither. Take that, Polly Hemp, and good-night to you!"

CHAPTER XV.

However lightly others might skim over or altogether cast aside the tasks of the stern schoolmaster, Life, their strict and conscientious performance was to Helen Norman a duty which she durst not neglect under any circumstances. Despite the fact that she was sadly conscious of the poor results which had in the aggregate attended her long months of labour among the destitute, despite the weary burden of unabated suffering which ceaselessly weighed upon her heart, despite the fact that her health was unmistakably giving way, that the dread signs of hereditary disease daily became more pronounced—no argument could as yet induce her to cease from her daily work. But this work had by degrees undergone a modification, partly owing to her failing strength, partly in consequence of reflection and much discussion with Mr. Heatherley. Instead of toiling day after day through the wearisome miseries of a whole large district, she had resolved to confine her attention to one fixed locality of small extent. By so doing she was enabled to acquire a completer knowledge of the needs of the poor to whom she ministered,

and also had the power of affording more
substantial assistance where it was really deserved.   But it was to her evening school
that she now devoted herself with the utmost
ardour, looking to her work therein for
higher and more wide-spreading results than
her mere charitable exertions could be expected to produce.   Here her efforts received
each week their unmistakable reward.   Those
girls who at their first coming to her she had
found rude in manner and speech, grew by
degrees gentler and more refined, the deplorably ignorant gradually struggled out of
their slough and began to show that they
were creatures possessed of mind as well as
body, the few who had already begun to yield
to the fascination of vulgar vice became
ashamed of their conduct when in their
teacher's presence and from the mere sound
of her voice, the radiance of her beauty,
conceived ideas of a purer life.   From two
evenings in the week, Helen, during the
summer, increased the attendance to three,
with appreciably good result, and was already
contemplating a yet wider extension of her
work in the sphere where she felt herself
especially adapted for usefulness.

But her noble nature was not destined to
attain to that perfection of active benevolence which she more ardently yearned after
in proportion as her physical powers grew
less and less capable of performing their
part in the grand work.   Towards the middle

of the summer, notwithstanding the prevalence of genial weather, Helen contracted a severe cold, followed by a cough which would yield to no degree of careful treatment. She herself surmised only too clearly the significance of this cough, and the physician she was ultimately persuaded to consult confirmed her in her fear. He had at first appeared timid and inclined to ease his patient's mind by euphemistic expressions and consolatory predictions; but Helen at once told him that she had for some time suspected the truth, and begged that he would not think her so weak-minded as to be unable to face the future with all its consequences. The physician made close inquiry into her habits of life, and at once urged that she should cease at all events the severest parts of her work, in particular the work of the school. But to this Helen could on no account be brought to consent. She said that if her life was to be held on but brief tenure, so much the more need that she should labour to the utmost while it lasted. Seldom chargeable with weaknesses distinctly feminine, in this matter Helen showed herself a true woman. She would listen to no argument. Her work, her work, that was her only thought.

Mr. Heatherley was a constant visitor at Holly Cottage, but Helen did her utmost to conceal from him the failure of her health. The increasing paleness of her cheek, the constant cough, these she could not prevent

his observing, but any reference which he
made to these signs of weakness was at once
put aside and made light of. Moreover,
Helen fancied she observed that the frequent
visits of Mr. Heatherley were not entirely for
her own sake, and it pleased her to think
they were not. Able to sympathise as few
could with poor Lucy's quiet, self-restraining
unexpectant devotion, she lost no opportunity of directing the clergyman's attention
to her companion's many virtues, and it
afforded her keen pleasure when she thought
she could observe Mr. Heatherley's eyes more
frequently resting upon the sweet face of the
timid girl. Once or twice she had purposely
allowed Mr. Heatherley to remain alone in
the room with Lucy for half an hour; and
after each such conversation she made herself happy in the belief that the clergyman's
face wore a happier look than usual. Yes,
it was a true pleasure which her pure nature
derived from the prospect of poor Lucy being
requited for her long and patient love; but
she would have been more than human had
not the thought of so much happiness at
times smitten as with the breath of a cold
and deadly wind upon her heart, and forced
into her eyes tears of bitterest anguish.

Poor Helen! It seemed as though Fate
had decreed she should pass through the
deepest and darkest waters of suffering without the consolation of any hand clasped
within her own. From the depths of her

own heart could come her only comfort, and alas! how often did it seem to her as though too constant draughts from the spring had at length exhausted its resources. It would be vain to endeavour to depict in mere words the suffering she endured even on her days of least depression. The unconquerable dread of being left alone with her thoughts, the fearful anticipation of what her life would become if she yielded to her feebleness or relinquished her work, this feeling had perhaps equal strength with pure devotion to principle in determining her to work on at all costs. Could she but have heard of or from Arthur from time to time, could she but have known that he was working on stoutly at his art—nay, could she have received news of his death, anything would have been preferable to this losing sight of him entirely.

Often in the early summer dawns she awoke from a brief and troubled slumber, crying "Arthur! Arthur!" In her dreams she was for ever seeking him, seeking him over wild, trackless deserts, amidst ghastly shapes and horrors unutterable. Often she saw his form afar off, always far off, beyond the sound of her voice which called upon him in tones of heart-rending anguish; and, bitterest suffering of all, he generally appeared to her not alone, but with a vague shape by his side, the shape of a woman. Yes, that was Arthur's wife. O God! To think that

a wretched being, so unworthy of the least
of Arthur's smiles, so incapable of appreciating a word he uttered, of entering into
the very humblest of his aspirations, to think
that *such* a one could boast herself his wife!
Oh, it was unjust, cruelly unjust. In her
bitterest moments she said in her heart that
injustice was the beginning and the end of
all things human.

Towards the end of August she was sitting
one evening quietly in Lucy's company,
when the last post brought two letters, one
addressed to herself, one to her companion.

" A letter for you, Lucy ? " she said, smiling. " That is indeed an unusual thing."

" Whoever can it be from ? " exclaimed the
other, scanning the direction closely. As
she did so, a blush rose to her cheek. She
looked timidly up at Helen, who was however already engaged in reading her own
letter, then she broke open the envelope.
Her first glance was at the last page, then,
slightly averting her face, she began to read
with an almost frightened countenance, the
paper rustling tremulously in her hand.

The contents of Helen's letter appeared
to be interesting. We will transcribe them—

" Versailles,
" Aug. 18th, 1872.
" MY DEAR HELEN,—
       " How well I can imagine your
grave surprise on opening this letter and see-

ing the signature of a shameless runaway.
I cannot tell how much or how little you
know of my story, which really I may some
day be tempted to present to you in the
familiar three volumes. I think it might go
down excellently with the patrons of Mudie's,
especially if the character of the heroine
were a trifle idealised; *that*, I am sure you
will agree with me, would be absolutely
necessary. But whether you know much or
little, you have in all probability heard
enough to convince you that I have suffered
all sorts of horrors, and that I may fairly
lay claim to your congratulations on the
occasion of my once more becoming a free
denizen of this tolerable world of ours.

"Yes, Helen; I made a mistake. In
marrying Waghorn I knew that I was marrying a wealthy fool, if not something worse,
but I had convinced myself that, beyond my
change of name, I should be able to keep
myself as distinct and separate from ' my
husband ' as though I had still been single.
I married, in fact, for the sake of a *position.*
Now-a-days an unmarried woman of more
than one-and-twenty stands in an anomalous
situation. Her maidenhood brings with it
absolutely nothing but disadvantages. You
will say that I might have made a better
match. Well, I suppose I might; but, to
tell you the truth, there was something of
perversity in my act. I had always a strange
pleasure in doing and thinking differently

from other people, in forcing circumstances
to suit my own whims rather than in bending
myself to circumstances. In this case I had
resolved to have the delight of leading an
agreeable life amid surroundings which would
have driven any other woman crazy. Of
course I had miscalculated my own powers.
I found that I had to deal with quite an exceptional brute, and at length I bitterly repented my folly.

"Now this letter is meant to be a little
reproachful. Among all my acquaintances
in London there was one, and one alone, who
ever had any power over those tenderer impulses of my nature which it is customary to
call the better part of one. One acquaintance I had who, by continuing what she had
once been to me, a frank friend, might often
have lightened my suffering and guided me
in the paths of *prudence*—that is the word I
prefer to substitute for such high-flown
terms as ' virtue,' ' honour,' or even ' wisdom.'
But that acquaintance was too much disgusted with my lack of seriousness to long
retain her interest in my doing or suffering.
Even at the eleventh hour, when I had determined to leave ' my husband's ' house, but
was as yet uncertain where to go, I called
upon this acquaintance of mine; but, alas!
she was too unwell to see me; and so—
Never mind what followed. Can you guess
who the acquaintance was?

"No, no, Helen; I am not, after all, writing to reproach you, but merely to let you know that I am once more comfortable, and probably in a fair way to be so for the rest of my life. What interest was it likely you could take in me and my affairs? We were pursuing such wholly different paths; both of us philosophers, but belonging to what different schools. You were a species of Stoic, given up to the pursuit of intensely serious aims, which aims presupposed the sacrifice of your own pleasures. You could see nothing good in a life which was not wholly devoted to the benefit of others. You were pre-eminently *sage*, in the French sense of the word. Who could imagine Helen Norman in love, to say nothing of being married? But I, for my part, was a sort of Epicurean; and yet I think not exactly an Epicurean, but that term is the closest my philosophical knowledge will supply. I looked upon the world with contempt, and made gratified egotism the sole end of my existence. How was it likely you could continue to be my friend?

"You will say that I must have seen that my philosophy is delusive, and that consequently I have given it up. *Pas du tout, ma chère.* I still pursue with intense avidity what I have ever considered the main object of this frivolous life. And shall I tell you to what it has brought me? I am on the point of being affianced to—to a Russian prince! Yes; believe it or not, as you please. Poor fellow! He has been desperately in love with me for—can you believe it?—more than a month. Though I am not yet technically divorced, he persists in considering me so, and threatens to make me his property as soon as possible. Papa looks upon the undertaking with a quiet smile of —I know not what. All the reply I can get from him on this matter is, ' *Mais, cela ne me regarde pas ; c'est une affaire à toi, ma fille.*'

"Think of me occasionally, Helen; and, when you do so, picture me amid the horrors of a Russian winter, over the ears in bear skins. Are you happy, yourself? I will hope so, but I have my doubts. Depend upon it your philosophy is horribly unpractical. Think it over, there's a good girl. Your Russian prince may even now be waiting for you, if only you knew it.

"Yours affectionately, dear Helen,

"MAUD."

Helen laid aside the letter with a deep sigh, and for a few moments was sunk in her own reflections. When she at length looked up, she saw that Lucy's eyes were fixed upon her, with a curiously mingled expression of pleasure and pain.

"Will—will you please to read this, Miss Norman?" asked Lucy, holding out the open letter, her face suffused with a deep blush.

Wondering much what the contents could be, Helen took it and read. It was a proposal from Mr. Heatherley, a manly letter, very characteristic of the writer. There was no rapturous declamation, no exaggerated passion; merely the offer of a deep and unwavering affection, of a share in all his future joys and sorrows, of active participation in his life's work. Far from drawing imaginative pictures of a lover's paradise, he clearly intimated that the duties of a clergyman's wife were often laborious, often distasteful, and she who would fulfil them duly must be distinguished by piety, good sense, and infinite patience. Of all these he believed Lucy was possessed, for he had long watched her closely and every new discovery he had made had served to strengthen his affection by convincing him that it was based on reason. He urged her not to be hasty in her reply, but to write to him after several days' consideration.

"And your answer, Lucy?" asked Helen, smiling, though with something of sadness.

The girl at once left her chair and seated herself on a low stool at Helen's feet. As she spoke she looked up into the latter's face, and her eyes were suffused with tears.

"I cannot leave you!" she whispered, whilst the tears slowly gathered and overflowed. "I could never leave you!"

"Dear, affectionate child!" exclaimed Helen, passing her arm round Lucy, and looking down upon her with a calm tenderness which seemed to invest her pale

Madonna-like face with a halo of sanctity. "Do you really mean that your love for me would overpower that you have so long felt for Mr. Heatherley?"

"Indeed—indeed I feel it does," sobbed Lucy. "Now you have more need than ever of me, now that you are so weak and suffer so much. How could I leave you alone, or, still worse, bear to think that some one else was filling my place in your regard? I am sure Mr. Heatherley does not know how ill you are, or he could not wish to persuade me to leave you."

"But it is hardly fair, dear," replied Helen, "to make Mr. Heatherley's chance of a wife depend upon the state of my health. Mr. Heatherley I am sure wishes me well, but to expect him to remain a bachelor for an indefinite period on my account would be rather too much."

There was silence, during which Lucy sat with her face resting upon her hands.

"Do you love him well enough," pursued Helen, still with the same calm smile upon her lips, "to take him as your husband? Are you undaunted by this formidable array of wifely duties?"

"No work could be too severe if he set it me," replied Lucy, without uncovering her face.

"Then," continued Helen, "much as you regret leaving me, Lucy, you must not let that influence your answer. Who am I that

I should hold you back before such a prospect of happiness? We need not part for ever, dear."

"Not yet, not yet!" exclaimed the other, her sobs breaking out afresh. "The winter is coming on, the time when you will need more care than ever. I could not leave you till the warm weather returns and you are quite strong and well again."

"I am not sure that I shall be here through the winter, Lucy," replied Helen, with a slight sigh. "The doctor has been warning me very seriously of late that it might be absolutely necessary to seek some warmer climate before the winter begins. I think he is too anxious, but still I must not endanger my possibilities of future work by neglecting a few precautions. And it would never do for me to take you into foreign countries. You might come back a Russian Catholic, and what would Mr. Heatherley say then? Promise me that you will answer this letter in the affirmative, and at once. I earnestly desire it. You will not refuse to please me?"

"I am so young," urged Lucy. "I have so much to learn. In a year you would teach me so much. Let me wait one more year."

"Mr. Heatherley will make a better instructor than I, Lucy," said Helen.

There was something of yielding, of reluctance in her friend's tone which strengthened Lucy's purpose. Helen had often said to her that without her she would indeed feel lonely, and the affectionate girl could not bear that a reason she thought selfish should be the cause of her leaving Helen now that the latter was ill in health. Knowing, too, all that Helen had suffered from the destruction of her life's hope she could not bear to set before her a picture of happiness which could only render her desolation more bitter. Armed with the strength of a pure unselfishness she spoke in a tone of decision which surprised her friend.

"Miss Norman, I must beg you to let me have my own way in this. I could not be happy if I left you at once and married Mr. Heatherley. And indeed I am too young; I have too little experience. It will be much better for him to wait another year."

"With what terrible calmness you speak of a year, Lucy," said Helen, half jestingly, half sadly. "Is it not presumption in you to look forward so far into time, and say: At the end of a year I will do such and such a thing? Especially in so grave a matter as this, delay may mean the sacrifice of a life's happiness. You must not think that our parting will be so absolute, Lucy. Mr. Heatherley will not monopolise you. As soon as I get rid of this weakness and can go out again and attend to my work I shall often call at your house in the afternoon and ask you to let me sit in your parlour for half an hour.

Then you will make me a cup of tea in your daintiest manner, and perhaps you will cut me thin slices of bread and butter, like you do now when you wish to coax me to eat. Oh, what chats we will have! Doesn't the picture tempt you?"

Lucy shook her head.

"When you are quite well again, Miss Norman," she said; "but not till then. I will tell Mr. Heatherley that if he will wait for me till next midsummer I will be his wife. But not till then."

"And you will keep the promise, Lucy, whatever should happen to me—I mean," she added quickly, "you will not let my state of health influence you then. In any case it shall be next midsummer? Promise me that solemnly, Lucy. It will be a great comfort to me."

"I promise," said Lucy, with a sigh.

"That's right! Kiss me, dearest. Why, next midsummer will be here in no time. The secret of making time pass quickly, Lucy, is to have something to look forward to. Time has gone rather slowly with me of late; it may now be so good as to mend its pace."

It will be seen from this conversation that Helen had at length been induced to reflect upon her condition and to allow some weight to prudent counsels. Her physician, an eminent practitioner, who took the utmost personal interest in her case, had exerted all his powers of argument to induce her to cease her work, ultimately addressing her in a tone of kindly authoritativeness which it was impossible to resist. He had, moreover, given her to understand that it would be quite impossible for her to remain throughout the winter in England; under such circumstances he could not promise that she would live to see the spring. With a sad sigh and many a gloomy anticipation, Helen had at length yielded. Very hard had she begged to the last moment to be permitted to continue her school. The most that the physician would allow her to do was to receive some three or four of her most promising pupils at her own home during the evening.

A sad task remained before her, that of bidding farewell to her class. This now consisted of some five-and-twenty girls, at least half of whom had been receiving her lessons for more than a year. It was Saturday night that she chose to visit the school-room for the last time, for on that evening the attendance was always much fuller than on the other two. Mr. Heatherley was apprised of her intention, and promised to be present.

The knowledge of what was about to occur had somehow circulated among the girls, and it was with more than ordinary solemnity that they resumed their places on the evening in question, and, without opening their books, sat in expectation of Miss Nor-

man's rising.   Mastering with difficulty a
sob which rose in her throat, Helen stood
up, and, after glancing for a moment over all
the expectant faces, began to speak in a low
and unequal voice—

"It is with the deepest sorrow that I have
to tell my pupils to-night that I am compelled
to bid them good-bye.   I hope you feel sure
that it is not a slight cause which would make
me give up my position as your teacher, a
position which I value beyond expression,
which has been the means of affording me a
long series of very, very happy hours.   But
I am warned by those whose sincerity I cannot doubt, that I could not with safety continue to give these lessons ; my health would
not allow it.   I have consented to cease—but,
I firmly hope and trust, only for a few months.
That has been my principal inducement to
relinquish the pleasure, the hope that I may
in the meantime obtain a fresh supply of
strength, and at length come back to you
better able to exert myself for your advantage.

"For, believe me, my dear girls, I have
your good sincerely at heart; I have no
stronger wish than that you may have so far
benefited by my teaching as to lead henceforth a happier, a higher, a more useful life.
Will you forgive me if I ask your attention
for a few minutes to a last short lesson, one
which I hope will not be too hard for you to
understand, which I hope you will endeavour
to take to heart and think over long after I

have ceased to speak to you. Though, as I have said, it is my firm hope that I may before long come back again and once more give lessons here, yet I fear it would be too much to hope that I should still have all of you for my pupils. In the interval, short as it may be, many of you will have left your old homes, changed your employments, be scattered in many different directions upon the stern work of life. For many of you are already no strangers to the sternest work, young as you are; and I should like to give you a little advice which may perhaps render your hardships lighter to bear, and encourage you to endure all suffering with stronger and more hopeful hearts.

" Wherever you may be, then, whatever your work, however mean or ill-paid it may appear to you, never forget two things : first, to do the work as well as it lies in your power to do it; then, to aim at preparing yourself for something better. By the first, you all know very well what I mean ; the second is not as difficult to carry out as you may think. An honest, brave-hearted girl has always the means of improving herself, if she will. Those of you who have only just made a beginning in learning to read and write, continue to persevere in what leisure moments you can find. If you cannot get on by your own exertions alone, you will always, I am convinced, find somebody able and willing to give you a little assistance. You that are

more advanced will find it still easier to continue your work of self-improvement. But
under no circumstance allow yourselves to
lose courage. Some of you may say to yourselves, 'Oh, what is the good of my trying
to better myself? I shall never have a chance
of showing what I know, and where will be
the good?' I earnestly beg of you never to
admit such a thought! In the first place it
will not be a true thought; believe me that
very few people set themselves to the task of
seriously bettering their minds without in
consequence, sooner or later, greatly benefiting their condition in the world. And in
the second place, even supposing that you
should be so unhappy as to be utterly neglected, and still have to toil in a mean position,
when you feel capable of better things, even
under such unhappy circumstances there is
a thought which, if you can try to get it
firmly into your minds, will never cease to
afford you consolation. It is this. No one
can work hard for her own improvement
without at the same time doing good to every
one with whom she comes in contact, and to
the whole world in general. I tell you with
very great seriousness that every one of you
who now listen to me has the power, if she
choose to exert it, to make this world of ours
better for her striving. There is hardly an
evil from which we daily suffer which has not
ignorance for its cause. If you strive to rise
out of your ignorance, you will see every day

more and more clearly how wise it is to be
honest, and virtuous, and good; how dreadfully foolish it is to be otherwise. You will
see that your own happiness lies within your
reach, if you are willing to take the trouble
to climb to it. If I have succeeded in making one of you more thoughtful by my lessons,
I shall myself be the happier for it all my life;
and my parting request, nay, my prayer, to
you is, that you will never forget these last
words from your teacher, that for her sake,
for your own sake, for the sake of the whole
suffering world, you will endeavour to lead
pure, patient, hopeful lives!"

Several of the girls sobbed as Helen ceased,
and, herself very much overcome, resumed
her seat. All showed signs of having been
strongly impressed. After a brief pause Mr.
Heatherley stood up and, in a few well-chosen
words, addressed the pupils. After speaking
in the highest terms of Helen's exertions, and
thanking her earnestly for all the work she
had done, he went on to say that he should
do his utmost to find some lady who would
be willing to continue the classes. Then he
dismissed them all with a few kind wishes
and exhortations to them to remember what
had been said. Each one of the girls as she
went out passed by the teacher's desk and
curtseyed, and Helen gave her hand to all.
She said no more than a single good-bye, lest
she should appear to favour some above the
others, but the expression of her eyes indi-

cated those with whom she had been especially pleased.

For a little more than a month Helen continued to live at Holly Cottage, but towards the end of September her physician one day definitely declared that he could not allow her to pass October in England, so the sooner she thought of making her arrangements for departure the better. Helen assented, though with grievous regrets. She could not hesitate as to the choice of her destination; the many tender and sad associations from her early years pointed at once to Mentone. Indeed the grief with which she resolved to relinquish her tasks and leave England was, in the end, somewhat mitigated by the prospect of once more seeing her dearly-remembered southern home. It was ultimately decided that Lucy Venning should accompany her. Lucy's gentle companionship had become indispensable to her.

It was a fine autumn evening, the last which she spent in England. Helen had had no definite premonition of a visitor to-night, but she knew well that one would arrive. And about seven o'clock the door-bell rang, a well-known voice was heard enquiring for Miss Norman, and then Mr. Heatherley entered the room.

"I expected you," said Helen, with a quiet smile, as they took seats. They were alone, for Mrs. Cumberbatch and Lucy were both out.

" This evening?   Didn't you rather expect me in the morning?"

"No.   I knew you liked to say all you have to say without having the effect of it injured by undue hurry."

There was silence for a moment.

" Are all your arrangements made?" then asked the clergyman.

"All.   Mr. Gresham meets us at Dieppe, and accompanies us straight to our journey's end."

" Would it not have been more agreeable if Mr. Gresham had come as far as London?"

" Perhaps it would have spared us a little trouble; but Lucy and I must pluck up our courage.   You know I am an old traveller."

She laughed slightly, and there was a short silence, broken at length by a succession of short, tight coughs from Helen.   The clergyman looked at her with a pained countenance.

" No better?" he asked, in a low voice.

She shook her head.   Mr. Heatherley bent forward and took her hand in his own.

" We are about to say farewell to each other, Miss Norman," he began, in a rather solemn tone, " and which of us can foresee what the next few months may bring about? You will forgive me if I speak seriously to you for a few minutes?   You will consider that I speak in my character of clergyman, a privileged one?"

Helen drooped her eyes, and uttered a low " Yes."

" During the whole time of our acquaintanceship," continued the other, "I have studiously complied with your request, and have never spoken to you earnestly on those matters nearest my heart. I am not sure that I have acted rightly; my conscience reproaches me somewhat. Tell me, Miss Norman, in the spirit in which I ask—do you still hold the same opinions with regard to religious matters as formerly?"

"The same, Mr. Heatherley."

"In reflecting upon your position, amid such thoughts as I well know your state of health must often have brought into your mind, can you sincerely assure me that no longing for the comforts of Christ and His gospel has ever occupied your heart? Have you never even felt in your weakness the ardent longing to repose upon the succour of an almighty and all-merciful God?"

"It would be untrue," returned Helen, "to say that I have never been so extremely impressed by the sense of my weakness as to long for the support of some stronger being. But to the consolations which religion offer I cannot say that I have ever been induced to turn my thoughts. My reason has always forbidden it."

"You have no hopes of a future life; no hopes of anything beyond this world of misery?"

"None. I do not deny that there may be such; but my reason is unable to conceive of it."

There was a long silence, broken by a low exclamation from Mr. Heatherley.

"I pity you; from my soul I pity you!"

"But not condemn?" asked Helen, regarding the other with a serious smile.

"No, not condemn," returned the clergyman. "Did I not know your perfect truthfulness and loftiness of mind, Miss Norman, I should boldly say that I did not believe you; for hitherto I have scarcely believed in the possibility of such a noble life devoid of the knowledge of God. All I can do is to bow my head in humility, and say that the Almighty has ways which are not our ways, thoughts not our thoughts."

"Yet do not cease to pity me, Mr. Heatherley," returned Helen, "for I am greatly worthy of your pity. Just as I am outgrowing the weakness of youth—just as my mind is becoming maturer, my experience widening, my power of usefulness expanding, just as I raise the cup to drink deeply of the sweet wine of life—the dark, shadowy hand is preparing to dash it from my lips. Do not think that I deceive myself as to my fate; I read it but too well. Let your thought of me be always one of pity. Oh, how much would I have done if I had had time! But the day proves too short, the sunlight fades, and the night cometh wherein no man can work."

CHAPTER XVI.

THE END.

In a few days it will be Christmas, the Christmas of the year 1872. The time is about mid-day, and the scene—not the streets of London, but the banks of the River Mersey, amid all the bustle and confusion of the Liverpool docks. The clocks, at all events, tell us that it is mid-day, but, judging from surrounding appearances, it might rather be supposed to be midnight. For everything is wrapped in the densest of fogs, a thick, rolling, dark-brown mass of stifling vapour, scarcely allowing one to see as far as the hand will stretch, and making the ear the only possible guide to a knowledge of what is going on around one. And the ear is not left without occupation. Every imaginable cry of the human voice, incessant shrill whistles from steamboats near and far, the dull roar of vehicles landwards, the steady, endless tramping of feet upon the wooden landing-place, the occasional crash or thud of heavy baggage from the shoulders of porters, all these and a hundred other indescribable and unrecognisable noises combine to make, as it were, a muffled Babel. And hark! a new sound, close at hand, suddenly rises above all the others, forcing attention to itself alone. It is the loud and long clanging of a bell, a clanging impatient and almost fierce. It sounds from the deck of the boat which is waiting to carry passengers out to the good ship " Parthia," Cunard steamer, of one knows not how many thousand tons burden, now lying two or three miles down the stream in the midst of the dense fog, whence it will in a few hours be working its way into the purer air of the Atlantic.

The bell is now ringing for the second time, and will give but one more warning before the boat starts. Despite the fearful day, a considerable number of passengers have already collected in the little saloon, where they sit in the midst of piles of miscellaneous luggage, most of them very silent and a few looking already somewhat pale and dismayed. There are women among them, and one or two children, driven across the ocean at this time of the year by Heaven knows what strange whim or necessity; but the passengers for the most part have the air of men of business, individuals who sit reading their letters or their newspapers with the most unconcerned air by the light of the swinging oil-lamps. One baby there is amid the company, which lifts up its shrill little voice in emulation of the clanging bell, and at moments decidedly succeeds in making the more noise of the two, at all events to the ears of those in the saloon.

As the bell at length became silent a new comer stepped on board, a tall young man, wrapped up in a great overcoat, carrying in one hand a small portmanteau, in the other a carpet-bag. On entering the saloon he looked round in the semi-darkness with a somewhat shy air, and, after a moment's hesitation, seated himself in a vacant corner; then, when he had surveyed once or twice the faces of those who were to be his fellow passengers, by degrees sank into abstractedness. Those who had the curiosity to inspect his face closely could see that it was rather handsome in outline, but severely pale and careworn in expression. He appeared nervous, too, for at every unexpected sound he started slightly and for a moment his face wore a pained expression. He had put the portmanteau and carpet bag at his feet. The former alone bore a direction, in handwriting, which ran thus:—"*A. Golding, Passenger to New York.*"

After a delay which appeared to be endless to those waiting in the saloon, the loud bell clanged for the last time, and the boat moved off into the darkness. Half-an-hour's careful voyaging brought it beneath the shadow of an immense hull, in the side of which appeared a large square of reddish light, through which the passengers forthwith made their way on to the body of the "Parthia." Arthur Golding—for the young man described is no other than our old acquaintance—was one of the last to go on board. After a long straying about pitch-dark and narrow passages, after ascending and descending innumerable almost perpendicular stairs, after endless collisions with wanderers like himself, after repeated questionings, to which unintelligible answers were returned, he at length found himself at the door of his own state-room where he was glad enough to throw down his burdens and rest for a few minutes. The state room had berths for two, one on the top of the other, and Arthur saw that the top one was already occupied, at all events some-one had deposited his luggage there in sign of taking possession. Having reconnoitred the locality as well as he was able, he once more made his way through the labyrinth of passages and staircases up on to the deck. In half an hour the great ship suddenly vibrated to the motion of her machinery, the sluggish river at the stern was all at once lashed into angry wave and foam by the revolution of the screw, and the "Parthia" had begun her voyage.

As the inclemency of the weather rendered it impossible to remain on deck, and the company in the saloon offering few if any attractions, Arthur very early retired to his berth. He had no desire to sleep, but a great desire to be once more alone in order to reflect upon the past and speculate as to the future. Let us see what subject for thought the past afforded him.

On the evening when the last conversation between Carrie and her temptress took place, Arthur returned home about nine o'clock. All day he had suffered from depression even greater than usual, and for hours after it had become dark he wandered aimlessly about the streets, sunk in miserable reflections upon his wasted life. Several times he crossed the river, and on each occasion paused for many minutes to look down into the black depths, made blacker by the reflection here and there of the lights upon the banks. He remembered how near he had once been to plunging himself and his sufferings for ever beneath that gloomy surface, and he even now did his best to re-summon the state of mind in which he had been capable of such a resolution. How gladly would he long since have sought the rest which the river always offers to the despairing, had it not been for that ever-present image whose smile forbade more strongly than the sternest words such an abandonment of duty. Moreover, it seemed as if out of the very extremity of his misery was arising an increased love of existence, a passionate desire for active exertion in an entirely new sphere, a keener appreciation of the joys which life *could* afford to those in happier circumstances. Oh, how weary, weary, intolerably weary did he feel of the life he had led for so many months, this life in which no day passed without bringing the acutest agonies, which opened up no vistas of the future where the

light of Hope burned ever so dimly or ever so
remote, but was closely hemmed around by a
blackness of woe into which the eye dared
not endeavour to penetrate! Before, when
desperation had driven him to the fixed idea
of suicide, it had been in consequence of self-
degradation, because he had felt that every
spark of noble aspiration had been extinguished in his soul, because it was to himself
that he owed his wretchedness, the utter
destruction of hope and energy. But now it
was different. He had set before himself a
lofty ideal, and had conscientiously done his
best to live up to it. That he had failed in
attaining the hoped for end was not, could
not be considered, his own fault. His worst
crime had been to submit to almost irresistible
despondency; he had not now soiled the
purity of his purpose by yielding to any
ignoble passion. To live thus amid the circumstances Fate had gathered round him he
considered, and rightly, as a self-conquest, a
step upwards in the scale of being. Why
could he not be free to expand his nature to
the uttermost, to develope all his faculties to
that rich fulness of which he felt they were
capable? As he thought of this, his depression threw off its passive character and became
active anger. By what law, human or divine,
was he compelled to sacrifice his life thus,
without even the recompense of conferring a
benefit upon a fellow creature? He knew
that his efforts to reform Carrie were utterly

useless, would for ever remain so. Was it incumbent upon him, knowing this, to add his own ruin to the inevitable ruin of her whom the world called his wife? Could even Helen Norman, when made to understand the circumstances, still bid him persevere in his desperate course? And, if she could, would it not be mere narrow-minded worship of conventionality in her, would it not satisfactorily prove that her advice had never been worthy of acceptance? A thrill of self-reproach ran through him as his bitter indignation thus forced him to canvass unworthy suspicions regarding her who was his good angel; but still the hard facts of the case remained, and reason would not refrain from drawing her conclusions. In this moment Arthur loved Helen as sincerely as he had ever done, but there was an ideal which unfortunately urged its claims to even greater devotion, and that ideal was Liberty. He was so young, he had means at his disposal so all-sufficing, he shuddered so at the thought of death, and yearned with such an unutterable yearning for the pleasures of existence. Leaning over the parapets of London Bridge and communing thus with himself, of a sudden he smote the damp stone violently with his clenched fist, and then turned homewards.

As I have said, he reached home about nine o'clock. It did not at all surprise him to find the rooms in disorder and Carrie out; these were circumstances to which he had grown only too well accustomed. As it was severely cold, his first employment was to light a fire. This done, he walked about the room ceaselessly for more than an hour, at times covering his face with his hands, now making wild gestures as if in the acutest agony, now even uttering low cries. With the exception of the fire he had kindled no light, and as the flame in the grate by degrees sank, giving way to a red glow, he was in almost total darkness.

About midnight a staggering footstep on the stairs told him of his wife's approach. In haste he lit a candle, and waited for her appearance. Carrie was in a mood of maudlin affection to-night, and, as she reeled into the room, threw her arms round Arthur's neck. With a gesture of disgust and loathing he forced her away from him. He did not speak a word, knowing that at such times it was useless; but his action had changed the current of the girl's humour, and she at once broke out into the coarsest reviling and abuse. For more than an hour he had to submit to this torture, which ceased only when exhaustion obtained the ascendancy over passion, and Carrie sank into beast-like stupor, it could not be called sleep, upon the nearest chair. With difficulty Arthur removed her into the other room and laid her upon the bed, she all the while struggling feebly in half consciousness. There she once more became silent and still.

He knew from experience that her unconsciousness would last probably for many
hours, and for once he welcomed the prospect;
for this latest trial had suddenly ripened in
him the resolution around which his mind
had been all day wavering. Away all hopes
and fears in which this degraded creature had
a part! Away all hesitation! Away even
every thought of that other one whose power
had always been great! Away everything
before the might of the animal instinct of self-
preservation!

In feverish haste he drew his largest trunk
into the middle of the room, and commenced
to pack it with all that he most valued. No
need to do it so silently; if the house had fallen
above her head Carrie would have perished
in her unconsciousness. By half-past one
the packing was completed. Most of his
clothing he had left; he only cared to take
articles such as books and drawings which
had an intrinsic value for him. Next he took
down his half-finished picture of Portia's
Pleading from the easel where it had stood
so long untouched, and carefully enveloped
it in sheets of brown paper, tying up the
whole into a portable parcel. Then he sat
down and wrote several letters, most of them
of a business nature. The one he wrote last
he did not, however, put in an envelope like
the rest, but, stepping lightly into the bedroom, pinned it in a prominent position upon

the blind, immediately above the looking-glass. This letter was brief, and ran thus:

" DEAR CARRIE,

" I can bear this life no longer and think it better for both that we should part. I am taking with me everything that I care to keep. The rest I leave for you. That you may not want for money to go where you think fit, I have put two sovereigns in your purse on the dressing-table; and, lest you should come to want in the future I shall make arrangements that you may receive one pound a week—as long as I am able to pay it. This you will have each week, by calling upon Mr. Venning, whose address is ———. He will not pay the money to anyone but yourself. I trust you may yet see the miserable folly of your life and carry out some of those good resolves you have so often made in vain. Good-bye.

" ARTHUR."

When he had completed these tasks it was nearly half-past two. He then made some slight alterations in his toilet, put in his pocket all the loose cash he had in the house, together with his valuable papers, and forthwith softly descended the stairs and left the house. He was only absent some five minutes, returning in a cab. He entered the house with the cabman, led the way up to his room, and both together carried down the packed trunk and picture, doing all with the utmost quietness. It was not, however, done so quietly but the landlady, who slept on the ground floor, overheard what was going on. On hearing her door open, Arthur went and exchanged a few words with her, informing her that he had suddenly been called away on a journey; and, as he was irreproachable in the payment of his rent, the good woman made no further comment. By three o'clock Arthur was driving away in the cab. He had not even returned upstairs to take a last glance at Carrie.

He drove as far as Charing Cross, and here stopped at a hotel which kept open its hospitable doors all night. Obtaining a bedroom, he did his best to snatch a few hours sleep, but with poor success. He succeeded however, in killing the hours up to half-past seven o'clock, when he partook of a slight breakfast, and immediately set forth on foot. His aim was Mr. Venning's house, which he reached just as that worthy man was sitting down to his breakfast. Without the least circumlocution Arthur told him all that had happened, laid before him frankly and honestly the reasons for his conduct, then went on to show the plans he had formed for Carrie's welfare and to ask him whether he would be willing to act as trustee in the matter. Mr. Venning, as we have seen, was a sincerely religious, but by no means a narrow-minded man. He had always entertained great personal friendship for Arthur, and had sadly deplored the misery of the latter's fate when first it was made known to him. Now, when so startling a drama was suddenly unrolled before his eyes, and he was called upon to take an active part in it, for a time he hesitated. But it was only for a time. Arthur's words, his looks, carried absolute conviction. There was no doubting the truth of all he said, and at length Mr. Venning confessed that his action, though grievous, might still be necessary, even wise.

"But you are placing great confidence in me," he said, when somewhat reluctantly yielding. "How can you be sure that the trust will always be properly carried out?"

"I know quite well, Mr. Venning," replied Arthur, "that you are a man of principle. Moreover, you are a religious man, and religion with you is more than a mere profession. It operates within your heart before it finds utterance upon your lips."

"And yet, Mr. Golding," pursued the old man, "I think you hold my religion in but light esteem."

"Only when it is a meaningless babble in the mouth of fools," replied Arthur. "Every real life-guide, whatever it calls itself, my conscience compels me to respect. How I wish that I had had the strength to conceive and act up to a religion of my own!"

"But what are your plans? Where are you going?"

"I am sorry to say that I can answer neither question. I think it likely that I shall leave England, but in any case you shall always have my address."

The old man sighed as he looked into Arthur's fine face, which bore such fearful marks of suffering.

"Well, Mr. Golding," he said, "you are in the hands of God, whether you acknowledge His guidance or not. I hope—I trust —I am doing nothing wrong in giving my consent to these plans. But I fear you would not heed me whatever advice I gave."

"Forgive me," replied Arthur; "I could not act otherwise than I am doing. A thousand thanks for your great kindness. But there is yet one more task. I have a picture of my own painting which I desire to be given to Miss Norman. I suppose she still lives at the old address?"

"No, no," returned Mr. Venning, shaking his head sadly.

"No? Where has she gone?"

"She left England for the south more than a month ago. Lucy is with her."

"But why?" asked Arthur, holding in his breath.

"Her failing health made it impossible for her to stay in England through the winter. I saw her just before she went, and she had worn away to a mere shadow. She told me, in the quietest tone imaginable, that her father had been consumptive, and that she felt there was no chance for her."

The old man spoke in a tone of the deepest sadness, sighing as he ended.

"But you hear from them—from Miss Venning?" asked Arthur, when able to speak.

"Frequently, and there is very little encouragement in the letters, I am sorry to say."

Arthur turned away and walked once up and down the room.

"Then I must send the picture to her myself," he said, at length, the pallor of his face showing what a blow the intelligence had been to him. "Mr. Venning, will you promise me that you will always preserve absolute silence with regard to myself? Promise that you will never give anyone the least information with regard to me, except, perhaps, that I called and obtained from you Miss Norman's address? I am sure you will promise that."

"I will," said Mr. Venning, in his quiet but resolved tone, which always meant much. He then gave Arthur the desired address, and they took leave of each other. A few hours after, Arthur had despatched his picture on its journey to Helen—his last offering. He sent no word with it, but let it speak for itself. Who knows, he thought, whether she will ever see it?

For three days he continued to reside at

the hotel, during which time he transacted all business matters connected with the disposition of his money. Five hundred pounds he realised at once for his own necessities. That in future he should be obliged to live upon his capital did not trouble him. He desired nothing better henceforth than to earn his own living once more by strenuous exertions. The interval between this and the day on which we have seen him embarking at Liverpool—a space of about a fortnight—was spent in the consideration and rejection of endless plans. He had not continued to live in London, for to remain still was torture to him. It was in Manchester that he at length decided upon the course to pursue. He would go to the New World, not to its civilised parts, but out into the extreme West, where in arduous struggles with the powers of Nature he might forget all his past existence and— he could conceive it possible—in time lead a happy life. His money would purchase land for him and secure him the services of labourers. His heart throbbed at the prospect. At once he wrote and secured his passage in the next Cunarder that left Liverpool. Upon his precise destination he did not endeavour to decide. There would be better opportunity of doing that when he reached America.

The voyage proved long and stormy, yet from the first morning of his going up on deck to look out on to the Atlantic to the coming to anchor in the docks at New York,

Arthur's body and soul were pervaded with exuberance of health such as he had never enjoyed. When he lay in his berth at night, listening to the lash and thunder of the waves against the sides of the vessel; to the cracking and straining of the masts and cordage, to the shrill whistle upon deck, now and then making itself heard above the duller noises, his heart was filled with a wild wish that the winds might sweep yet more fiercely upon the heaving water, that the ocean might swell up to mountainous waves, such deep delight did he experience in the midst of the grand new scene. Throughout the day, no stress of weather could suffice to keep him below. It was his chief pleasure to sit in the stern, in the shelter of the wheel-house, from whence he could overlook the whole length of the ship as it plunged down the sides of the huge water-gulfs. How little she looked, for all her thousands of tons burden, and what a mere mite she would have made in the gullet of the insatiable deep! Then, to turn and look down into the frothy hell beneath the stern; to watch for minutes the fierce whirlpool where the untiring screw was struggling amid a thousand conflicting currents, and then to feel the vessel rising upwards, upwards, till at length a mountain of deep green water surged from beneath her, showing a surface smooth and solid-looking as ice, threatening the very sky in its upward striving. Day after day the same spectacle

l ay before his eye from morning to night, and
yet he never wearied of watching it. Though
towards evening the wave-splashed deck became too slippery to stand upon, though the
ropes were stiff with ice, though the wind cut
through the darkening air with the swift
keenness of steel, yet not till he was obliged
would Arthur descend to the saloon, the
picture was too engrossing in its majesty.
He almost believed that the mind expanded
in the mere act of watching; he felt capable
of greater thoughts than formerly; the
thought of his security in the midst of such
terrors gave him a loftier and truer conception of human powers than he had yet attained
to.

*   *   *   *   *

A year passes, and once more we are within a few days of Christmas. Arthur Golding
is sitting to-night in a little room which he
has inhabited for more than a month, a
longer period than he has rested in any place
hitherto since he arrived in America. Though
there is no cheerful English fire to impart
comfort to the room, yet there is no
absence of warmth, for an abundant supply of
hot air issues from the "register" in one
corner. Outside everything is covered with
deep snow, and the night is wonderfully clear
and still, the deep blue sky sprinkled with
stars of a brilliancy never beheld in our misty

clime. Not a breath of wind is stirring, and occasional crunching of feet on the hard snow beneath the window would be the only sound, were it not for a heavy, deep-noted, unceasing roar which, though perfectly audible, forces itself so little upon the ear that it can be easily forgotten amid the else perfect silence of the night. Arthur does not notice it at all, for it has been in his ears ever since he took up his abode here, sometimes much more distinct, sometimes scarcely perceptible. If you asked him for an explanation of it, he would tell you that not quite ten minutes' walk from his door would bring you to the edge of the cataract of Niagara.

Arthur's face is that of a middle-aged man whose life has been one of constant care, for all that he is some months yet from the completion of his twenty-third year. Since his arrival in the New World his life has been that of a wanderer. At first he travelled for pleasure, passing in hot haste from end to end of the Continent, now wandering over the endless prairies, now exploring with ceaseless delight the marvels of California, at one time basking amid the plantations of Carolina, and shortly after revelling in the delicious sunshine of New England. But during the last three months he has been the prey of ever-growing wretchedness, beginning in mere weariness at this unsettled life, and passing at length into strong disgust at his own inactivity, coupled with moments of bitter regret at having ever quitted England. For a year he had not known what it was to hear the voice of a friend. Naturally retiring in his disposition, he seldom, if ever, addressed a stranger. Such of the Americans as he had had the opportunity of seeing more closely he could not persuade himself to like. He had nothing in common with them; their taste seemed to him hopelessly vulgar. With society which would have been in harmony with his nature he had no means of mixing. The agricultural schemes which had been so ardently conceived before he left England, he had never even attempted to carry out; in his travelling he had seen quite enough to show him that he could not endure the life. That perpetual indecision, that lack of a firm and independent energy which had been the great evil of his life, now came back upon him more strongly than ever, nourished by his unsettled state. A thousand times he said to himself that it was necessary he should seek some fixed position, that he should endeavour to assume a place in the world's work, if for no other reason, at least for the sake of his future prospects. But it was this future which he could not bear to contemplate. To art alone had he ever devoted any steady application, but for art he had just now lost his taste, without acquiring a taste for any other work. His was a wrecked and ruined nature, hopelessly drifting about on the currents of circumstance, blown hither and thither by

fitful blasts of passion and remorse. How
often did he curse himself for being so reckless, for removing himself so far from all who
knew him, when a hundred wiser and more
hopeful courses might have revealed themselves to his mind. He had imagined that he
wanted freedom ; choked beneath the nightmare of his intolerable life he had thought
that free air and unrestricted liberty to wander
about the world was all that he needed. For
the moment he had forgotten the sincerest
yearnings of his heart, those depths of
genuine and life-long feeling which, like the
depths of the ocean, would remain calm and
undisturbed, however the surface might be
troubled. Satiated with the freedom he had
cried for, he now saw that it had been gained
at the loss of that honour which he had
pledged to her who truly loved him. He saw
that in casting himself loose from all worldly
bonds, as he had done, he had been guilty of
a heedlessness of others which had wrought
its inevitable vengeance upon his own life.
He had acted as though he was his own
master ; whereas, even if his wife had forfeited all claims upon him, there remained
another who had an indefeasible right to con-
trol his recklessness, the right of pure affection guided by a lofty mind. Living amid
the rigour of winter, friendless, companion-
less, objectless, he seemed to hear night and
day in the roar of the great cataract a ceaseless assertion that man is for ever dependent

upon his fellows, that it is at his peril he breaks all the bonds of a lifetime, in the presumptuous belief that they are a mere hindrance to his future existence. The never-ending roar of waters bade him look back upon his life and see how every purpose had been frustrated; or, if he yet ventured to raise an eye towards the future, murmured sternly, "Too late! Too late!"

Only once or twice during the year had he heard from Mr. Venning, his constant movements having doubtless caused many letters to go astray. The last he had received at Chicago, now nearly three months ago; and it informed him that Carrie still came to take her money, though at very irregular intervals. Arthur had been bitterly disappointed that it contained no mention of Helen Norman. In his few and brief communications, he had always wished, though never dared, to ask news of her. He felt sure that in the event of anything decided occurring, Mr. Venning would not fail to acquaint him with it. Immediately upon his arrival at Niagara, he had written to London, this time begging distinctly for news concerning Helen, saying that he would remain where he was for at least six weeks, in order to receive a reply before deciding upon his future course.

He was sitting alone this evening, sunk in the vague abstractedness which had for some time supplied the place of rational thought with him, when he was disturbed by the en-

trance of a servant, who held in her hand a
letter and a newspaper, both showing English stamps.   Arthur took them, and first of
all tore open the letter in eager haste.   It
was from Mr. Venning, written immediately
on receipt of Arthur's last.   It stated that
Carrie had, for more than a month, ceased to
apply for her money, when the writer, driven
by anxiety to make enquiries, had discovered
that she had been for several weeks in a
hospital, suffering from a malady which was
the consequence of her dissipated life, and
which left her but the faintest hope of recovery.   He desired to know what Arthur's
wishes were under these circumstances, and
begged that a reply might be sent as quickly
as possible.   This was the only matter which
the letter contained.

Arthur's first thought was one of compassion for the miserable girl, but this was
almost immediately expelled from his mind
by the reflection that, in all probability,
Carrie was already dead.   If so—was he not
free ?   Could he not return from his exile,
and—— ?   He dared not think out the
thought to the end.   Was it possible that
Fate, with sweet irony, was now bringing
about such a termination of his sorrows ?
Arthur opened the letter once more and ran
quickly through it.   Certainly Mr. Venning
wrote as if assured of the result—but then
there was no mention in his letter of Helen,
and had he not been explicitly desired to

send news of her? Suffering a moment of
the cruellest indecision, Arthur suddenly remembered that the newspaper still remained
unopened. Pooh! what did he care for a
newspaper? What was the world's intelligence to him, whose world was contained in
the compass of a woman's heart? Yet why
should his friend send it him? He had never
done so before. Arthur reflected, and suddenly the cold sweat broke out upon his forehead as a horrible dread possessed itself of
his mind. Certainly this paper *must* contain
an answer to the most pressing part of his
letter; Mr. Venning could never have neglected that. He tore off the wrapper, and,
clenching his teeth firmly together, as if to
keep down his emotions, slowly opened the
paper upon the table, and cut the pages with
a knife. It was the *Times*, and bore a
date early in December. Forcing his eyes
to do their office, which they would feign have
refused to, he glanced rapidly up and down
the columns for some mark which should
have been put to guide him. *One* column he
steadfastly refused to look at, though his good
sense told him that only there could he hope
to see any mention of Helen. Yet to this
column he was obliged to come at last. He
looked through the list of marriages—no, she
was not there. He looked at the list of
deaths, and at length read this :—" On the
20th of November, at Mentone, Helen,
daughter of the Rev. Edward Norman

(deceased), in her twenty-second year." That was all.

Some hours after, when it was close upon midnight, Arthur issued from the house, bearing in his hand a letter, which he seemed to have come out to post. This done, however, he did not return, but, though he wore only his light in-door clothing, very little adapted for a night-walk in the temperature which now prevailed, he set off at a sharp pace over the crunching snow. The deep roar of the falls was in his ears, and it guided his footsteps. Within ten minutes he had come to the river-side, and the whole glorious panorama lay unrolled before him.

A full moon reigned in the heavens, making it almost as light as day, though tinging everything with her own peculiar silvery hue. Just on the edge of the precipice, where the gathered waters took their fearful plunge, hung a second full orb, a perfect reflection of that above, the clear, luminous circle seeming scarcely disturbed by a wrinkle on the surface, the hue of which was a pale emerald. From the abyss into which the torrent disappeared, rose vast columns of spray, transparent, glistening with a marvellous brilliancy, fading at length into the air like breath. Along either shore of the river, and on the dark barrier which Goat Island interposes between the American and Horse-shoe Falls, frost had built all manner of fantastic shapes, seizing upon the feebler jets of water which part from the main mass, and holding them suspended half way down the precipice as gigantic icicles; freezing the spray as it fell, layer upon layer, till huge blocks had been formed; daring even to encroach upon the very edge of the majestic cataract, and skim it with weird bridges, firm as adamant. And over all this was spread a thick coat of snow, itself frozen into a thousand strange forms, making the eye ache to behold its dazzling purity. In contrast to the white banks, the river, as it issued from the spray-hidden depths at the foot of the falls, and once more went on its accustomed way, seemed a wonderful, deep green, flecked here and there with patches and long streaks of slowly-moving foam, not less white than the snow itself. How marvellously still was the deep-green water, all but motionless, as though it were resting after its wild leap. Only by intently watching one of the foam-streaks could the direction of its flow be ascertained. And from the midst of all this dread magnificence spoke the solemn voice, not harshly loud, not so overpowering as to render other noises mute, but in subdued, melodious thunder, as though proclaiming with calm, passionless decision, the immutable power of destiny.

With hands clasped behind him, Arthur stood for a long time gazing at the glorious scene. Moonlight is always saddening, and the gleam of the cold silvery beams reflected

from the vast watery mirror filled his soul
with an infinite passion of woe. In
thought he reviewed his whole life. He
strove with memory to gain back the full
taste of his childish sufferings from those dim,
far-off days when his father still lived—those
sufferings, how light they now seemed, viewed
amid the consciousness of present despair—
nay, he felt that those days must in reality have
been days of happiness, could he but have
known it. All the dim forms of those he had
known and loved best passed before his eyes,
all, all gone for ever. Mr. Tollady, the
guardian of his youth, the model of heroic
constancy set up before him for his guidance
in life—long since dead. How clearly he
now saw that the old man's death had been
the beginning of his misery, though at the
time he had believed it to be the commencement of his true life. And she who, through
good and evil, had never in reality ceased to
be his ideal—she who had been noble and
worthy effort personified, whom he had
always worshipped in the innermost of his
heart, however with his lips he had declared
his allegiance to false gods, she whose
lofty counsel might even at the last have
saved him, had he possessed the energy to
obey her—Helen Norman was gone. And
she being gone, what remained? In her
person the ideal of his life had perished, all
that he had ever lived for had ceased to exist;
he found himself straying amid the billows of

life like a wrecked and manless ship upon an ebbing sea. Why should he live? Why had he ever lived? In vain he surveyed his life for the traces of any positive result, of any real good accomplished, any real end gained—he could find none. Failure was written upon it, written irrevocably. Why should he live?

Moving as though mechanically, whilst his countenance still showed him to be sunk in thought, he drew nearer to the edge of the cliffs, and began to descend them by the path which leads to the foot of the Falls. His eyes were fixed upon the cataract, and never wandered from it. In the bright moonlight he could even watch individual masses of foam as they appeared on the summit of the Fall, and, slowly, slowly, curved over and were lost for ever. How slowly they seemed to pass, as though being reluctantly dragged downwards and out of sight. He watched these, and, as he watched, still descended the path and drew nearer to the vast columns of spray, till at length he felt his face moistened by their breath. So long and so fixedly had he gazed, that the plunging water had begun to exercise a terrible fascination over him; involuntarily he drew nearer and nearer. The deep, musical voice from out the hidden depths seemed to call to him irresistably, and he followed. A wild and mad longing to probe the dread mysteries veiled beneath that curtain of ever-rising spray took despotic hold upon him; with a delicious joy he contemplated a struggle with the roaring whirl-pools, with a fierce longing yearned to experience their unimaginable horrors. Now he was at the lowest end of the path. He stood upon a vast mass of mingled ice and snow, and his garments were drenched with the rising vapour. Yet one step, and he gained the elevation of a huge shapeless block which seemed to promise him a view straight down into the depths. But still the mists gathered thick beneath him, and from out of it called to him the voice of the whirl-pool, now so loud within his ears that at length it silenced thought. For a moment his blood boiled, his pulses leaped, his brain was on fire with the fierce joy of madness; in the next he shrieked in a voice which overcame that of the Falls, " Helen! Helen!" and plunged into the abyss.

THE END.

Printed by REMINGTON & Co., 5, Arundel Street, Strand, W.C.